The Tireless Advocate

An Epic Journey of One Autistic Who Refused to Surrender

By Matthew Kenslow

The Tireless Advocate

This is a work of fiction drawn from real events and experiences. While some real historical events, public figures, and cultural references may be included for context, all characters and narrative elements are fictionalized. Certain characters are composites or have been significantly altered. Names, places, and certain details have been changed. Any resemblance to actual persons, living or dead, or actual places, is coincidental.

ISBN 979-8-234-06841-5 (print)

ISBN 979-8-234-06842-2 (e-book)

For Worldwide Distribution

Connect with the author:
Matthew Kenslow on Instagram, YouTube, TikTok, X, LinkedIn, and Facebook

Table of Contents

Preface

Sometimes I think about designing a shirt, the back of which clearly states, "I'm autistic, deal with it!"

My name is Matthew Kenslow, and I was diagnosed with autism circa 2001. I was about six years old when I received the diagnosis, but I wasn't formally told until ninth grade. Within two years of finding out I was autistic, I became an advocate.

Revisiting my lifelong passion for writing, I began working on a fictional trilogy about an autistic person soon after entering Orange Coast College in August 2013. Long story short, I instead published an anthology, *Juggling the Issues*, in 2019, describing firsthand what being autistic is like and what has helped me in the journey. I assumed life would be easier from there on out, being a voice for the voiceless, helping the entire world accept disabled people, spreading awareness and inclusion, and motivating everyone to keep going in life.

Nothing could've been further from that assumption.

Trying to navigate life as an author, I was deeply troubled by the persistent ableism and bullying I still witnessed, not just directed at me, but at other disabled people too. Those experiences soon transformed me into the tireless advocate I am today, speaking on various news stations, radio programs, and podcasts worldwide. Concurrently, I posted on my own social media channels: "Matthew Kenslow" on YouTube, Instagram, TikTok, Facebook, X, and LinkedIn.

In addition to news and social media, I endeavored to lead volunteer assemblies at all the schools in Orange County, California, but my efforts met with mixed success. From 2022 through 2026, I had spoken to over 13,000 students in a couple of dozen schools without asking for a dime. And that was it—in a county with over half a million students and hundreds of schools, public and private. This was despite years of communication with school boards, PTAs, and the Orange County Department of Education, involving not just my own efforts but also the voices of many people speaking on my behalf.

With eternal gratitude, I have received several dozen testimonials from students, parents, and faculty about my assemblies. Parents commented that my assemblies were the first thing their child mentioned after school that day. I've been told that I "changed lives," seen many people moved to tears of hope, and received a myriad of letters from students thanking me for what I taught them and how I made it stick.

Meanwhile, I kept reading stories about bullying related to disabilities elsewhere, which only strengthened my unwavering determination to keep up the good fight—in person, in news media, and on social media.

While I was striving to be an advocate, facing so much opposition, I continued to pursue my education. I've earned an Associate's in Chemistry in 2019, a Bachelor's in Biochemistry in 2021, a teaching credential in mathematics from California in January 2023, and a Master's in Education in 2024. In addition to being an advocate, I chose a career as a math teacher in secondary education. I completed my student teaching at Ensign Intermediate School in 2022 and, early on, also became a substitute teacher in the same district, Newport-Mesa Unified.

As of publishing this book, I am a substitute teacher and an independent private math tutor, endeavoring to lead assemblies in as many schools as possible before settling into a full-time career as a math teacher.

Both student teaching and substitute teaching changed my life. I've been called the "best sub" by hundreds of students across several schools, with many begging for me to return. It helped me find purpose in life and gave me hope for the future. The acceptance I've received from most students, administrators, and parents helped prove that we can be limitless, despite a disability, even if some of us need to work through extra challenges. I tell the full story about it in my second book, *Unstoppable* (2023).

However, at the same time, I still perceived ableism in my own area and online. Although I knew I could never eradicate ableism and other forms of bullying from the face of the earth, I nevertheless wanted to try my best, going to such drastic lengths that I nearly risked my livelihood several times over. Again, I fought through opposition, but in the end, I defied many odds that were stacked against me.

The gripping story of what I've gone through is told through a fictional lens in this book. Being a work of fiction this time around, I took the liberty of consolidating multiple stories, adding to others for the purpose of clarity, and rearranging the chronology, but overall, nearly every story of Zachary Corwin was drawn from my real-life experiences.

1

The Difference a Friend Makes

"Go away, Zachary! You're *not* playing with us!" shouted Madeline and Max on the swing set at Washington Elementary School.

It was a sunny day in spring 2001, with not a cloud in the sky. 5-year-old Zachary Corwin, in his new pair of blue overalls, had gone up to two of his classmates, simply wanting to spend time with them.

"W-why?" Zachary stammered. "Our teacher said, 'We're *all* friends.'"

"You're *not* our friend, shaggy hair!" Max retorted.

As he continued to reason with them, Madeline ignored him, staring down at the sand and softly singing the pre-chorus to Britney Spears' recent hit "Lucky" to drown him out.

Zachary felt dejected. It took him enough courage just to go up to them in the first place. The other seven students from his special day class were playing soccer in the field, a sport he didn't care for. Feeling the pangs of hurt and loneliness billowing up inside his chest once again, he turned around and walked away.

He only had one good friend at that school, Thomas, who usually spent time with him during lunch, but on this day, he was on a field trip. Thomas, a third-grader, helped him take his mind off his social anxiety. The following day, he came up to him during recess and sat beside him at the lunch tables, shaded by the tall pine trees surrounding the area.

"Hey, champ! How are you today?" Thomas asked.

Zachary returned the greeting with a subtle smile.

"Anything wrong?"

"Mmm, no." He shook his head.

"Zach, I can tell," Thomas said compassionately, placing a hand on his shoulder. "Your classmates were mean to you again, weren't they?"

After a deep sigh, Zachary admitted, "Yeah. And, uh, Max keeps calling me 'Shaggy hair.'"

"So what? I always wear my hair shaggy too. This is Max from your class? That kid thinks he's Nick Carter. Call him 'Curtain hair.' Ha-ha! Give him a taste of his own medicine."

"Mmm, I don't feel comfortable name-calling back. I don't hate anyone."

"Well, you're a very kind person. Then just ignore them. Hey, so how about we play handball?"

"Sure."

"Bet I'll get there first!" Thomas sprinted to the courts.

Zachary immediately jumped up and raced him over there.

"Ah, man! You beat me again!" Thomas said, catching his breath.

Zachary was, after all, the fastest runner in his class.

"Wait, I don't even have a handball, dude," he said with a laugh. "Wait a sec."

Catching his breath as well, Zachary happened to glance at the swing set to his right about thirty yards away. Shuddering, he saw Madeline and Max swinging beside each other again. He could hear Madeline singing Jennifer Lopez's new "Love Don't Cost a Thing," minding her own business. Her golden-blonde pigtails trailed freely as she glided back and forth. Max swung beside her, trying to spot animals in the cumulus clouds above.

After school that day, Zachary stood outside Washington Elementary, waiting for his bus. A gentle breeze brushed past him and the scent of nearby pine trees filled the air.

"Any plans for the weekend, champ?" Thomas asked as he skateboarded up behind him, fastening his helmet's chin strap.

"Um, I have, uh, Royal Rangers tonight," Zachary stuttered.

"What's that?"

"It's something I started last September. It meets at a church and, um ... It's like Boy Scouts."

"That's cool! I'm in Cub Scouts. How are you liking it? You never told me about that before."

"It's fun. We're in groups of four or five and, uh, each group meets in red teepees. We collect beads, pins, and colored feathers. Um, and our commander reads us a story around the fire pit outside. Sometimes, we make s'mores. We learn how to tie knots and other things too."

"Learned the square knot yet?"

"Yeah," he replied, nodding. "That was the first knot I ever learned."

"Make sure you do it right. Don't tie the granny knot. That would be very *knot*-y." Thomas giggled.

Zachary also laughed as he turned around, seeing his school bus pull into the parking lot. Lou Bega's "1+1=2" was heard playing on the bus's radio.

"Catch you later, champ!" Thomas patted Zachary on the back.

"See you later, Thomas," he responded, beginning to feel joyous again.

2

The Moment of Diagnosis

"Mrs. Corwin, your son is autistic."

"What?" Mrs. Corwin choked, wondering if she heard Dr. Gallagher correctly. "I beg your pardon. Are you talking about *autism*?"

The small doctor's office grew even quieter, contrasting the jazz music playing softly on the Sony stereo system back in the waiting room. Static seemed to hum from the office's white walls. Mounted neatly above Dr. Gallagher's head hung his three degrees, stacked vertically in the order in which they were conferred, the latest one on top.

"After all our tests and observations, we concluded that it's definitely autism, but he's remarkably intelligent for his age. He can continue schooling and activities like anyone else—"

"Wait, Doctor. Give me a second to get my thoughts straight. Autism? It can't be. Aren't those the people who live in mental asylums for the rest of their lives? Or people who can't talk at all, except gibberish? Or people who spin and jump all around, screaming? That can't be Zachary."

"Ma'am, based on—"

"And Doctor, sorry, I don't mean to belittle those people. I have a beloved uncle who is autistic and has been living in an institution in Boise. But Zachary?"

"Ma'am, listen. Based on our current definitions, understanding, and diagnostic criteria, autism encompasses a *broad range* of characteristics and needs. Yes, it includes people who need lifelong support, like your uncle, but it could also include people who only need mild or moderate support, like Zachary does."

Mrs. Corwin's vision blurred, her entire worldview shifting, yet she refused to reach into her purse for a tissue.

"It's going to be all right, Mrs. Corwin," Dr. Gallagher said sympathetically, leaning forward.

"Doctor, I'm going to get through this with a stiff upper lip. Continue, please."

"Autism is a neurodevelopmental disability that affects social communication and development. Common characteristics may include, but are not limited to, difficulty reading social cues like eye contact or body language, intense or focused interests, challenges with learning or attention, social limitations, and sometimes co-occurring anxiety or depression. As it stands currently, autism is a spectrum often categorized by severity, but between you and me, every individual is different and has their own strengths and weaknesses. Diagnostic criteria may change in the coming years, but that's what our manuals say for now. Anyway, you said he had a diagnosis of a speech delay, right?"

"Yes. Two years ago. It was February 1999."

"That's common as well. And what did that doctor tell you to do?"

"Um ... Well, we enrolled him in an intervention program. Technically, it was preschool. And there, he began speech therapy."

"Is he still in speech therapy? I've noticed him having trouble with some of the phonemes."

"The what?"

"Phonemes, or units of sound. For instance, his G's sound like D's and his Th's sound like F's."

"Yeah, I've tried working with him on those."

"I suggest you continue speech therapy at his school."

"Okay, Doctor."

"How was he in preschool, socially?"

"I don't know. Zachary rarely talks to me about school. I just ask him how his day went, and he always says, 'Fine.' I figured he's tired after school."

"Don't you talk during dinnertime?"

"No." Mrs. Corwin thought for a second and continued, "I mean, sometimes we eat at the table, but he usually doesn't eat much. It's difficult for him to sit still at the table or in restaurants, so I simply began bringing food to his room. He eats more when he draws, makes his flipbooks, watches television, or puts a puzzle together. He's currently drawing all the U.S. presidents."

"I see." Dr. Gallagher nodded. "Any extracurricular activities or anything like that?"

"He's involved in Royal Rangers. It's the highlight of his week, every Friday evening. He tried karate a month ago, but they kicked him out. He wasn't cooperating well, and they told me to try again when he's older. He's still in swimming lessons, which he seems to enjoy."

"I'd advise you to have him continue these activities and any others that might come up in his childhood. Continue giving him those opportunities to enjoy. Do you know if he has friends in school?"

"Only one. Thomas. He's three years older. He's the son of my coworker."

"That's a good start. Encourage him to make more friends as he gets older and to spend time with them. As you probably know, he's very shy. When I, personally, talked with Zachary, he often looked down or got distracted by his surroundings, but I was able to ascertain from our conversation that he was still listening. And once he got started, he talked my ear off!"

"That's Zachary!" Mrs. Corwin laughed, followed by a deep breath of optimism.

The conversation lasted for the next twenty minutes, answering all of Mrs. Corwin's questions and concerns.

"There's nothing to fear, ma'am, for Zachary," Dr. Gallagher reassured her. "Catching autism early enough is much more beneficial to him (and *anyone* for that matter) than detecting it later on in life. His early intervention, I could tell, is helping. We encouraged him as best we could. His teacher, I'm sure, is doing the best she can. But you're going to be the main influence in his life as his mother. Correct me if I'm wrong, but your father lives across the street?"

"Yes, he moved there since my husband left me," Mrs. Corwin spoke softly and looked down. "That was right before Zachary was born. My father has been an incredible help, taking care of Zachary while I'm at work, going with us on family outings, and stuff like that. Anyway, thank you, Dr. Gallagher. I'll definitely be advocating for him, now that I feel better equipped and know more about his needs. I'll try to motivate him to work on social skills, and I'll continue giving him opportunities in life."

"Yes, and here's one last thing I'd encourage you and your father to do: keep reminding him that he can talk to you at any time about anything. He might need time alone to process his thoughts and feelings, but encourage him to talk things out."

3

Teacher's Apprentice

"Larry."

"Here."

"Pete."

"Here."

"Madison … Madison? Absent."

"Barney."

"Here."

"Okay, class. We just said our pledge, sang 'You're a Grand Old Flag,' and took attendance. Now, please take out your notebooks. Today, we're learning about subtraction and borrowing."

Zachary opened a little notepad for Larry, one for Pete, and one for Barney, taking them from the one bookshelf in the room. He then gave them each a star for their sticker chart.

"Name and date on top, please. Let's make sure we show our work. As I write on this whiteboard, I want you to copy down everything I write, okay? 293 minus 177."

A few seconds ticked by.

"What'd you say, Pete? Huh? That's a warning. Next time you speak, I'll pull your card from green to yellow. Okay, who can walk us through the answer?"

Zachary stepped over and lifted up Barney's right purple arm.

"Yes, Barney. Tell us."

"Well, you can't take seven from three, so you have to borrow from the nine, and—"

"Zachary," Mrs. Corwin interrupted, knocking and opening the door. "Dinner is almost ready. Be down within two minutes."

"Ah, Mom, I just began my lesson!"

"Sorry, Zachary, but it's a special occasion. It's your grandfather's birthday, and we can't keep him or the guests waiting. They'll all be here within five minutes. You must remember our etiquette when we have guests in our home."

"Mom, um, do you have another check register for the attendance sheet?"

"That was the last extra one I had, and—"

"You've got mail!" called a deep unfamiliar voice from outside the door.

"Who was that?" whispered Zachary, frozen and wide-eyed with fear.

"Oh, that's from our new computer. I must've gotten this email or whatchamacallit."

"And those strange noises from earlier?"

Shaking her head, clearly annoyed, she explained, "The AOL dial-up. Something about the modem or whatever. Yeah, I thought it was broken or something, and I started panicking."

"You whippersnappers!" Grandpa Corwin said, appearing out of nowhere, sporting his old homburg hat.

Mrs. Corwin and Zachary screamed.

"Sorry for spooking you guys," he said with a laugh, tidying his recently trimmed white beard and adjusting his red suspenders with his left hand. The hue of his suspenders perfectly matched his bow tie and handkerchief. His medium-brown suit jacket lay folded over his right forearm.

"It's okay, Dad," she said, exhaling and placing her hand over her heart. "I didn't hear you coming up the steps."

"Happy birthday, Grandpa!"

"Much obliged, sonny. Now, as I was saying, don't you be getting my dander up. Back in *my* day, we used typewriters. If we made a mistake, we had either white-out or correction tape. Then we had to send it in the mail and wait. And wait. And wait. Nothing wrong with learning patience, is there? I still assert that *The Lone Ranger* is incomparable, and don't even get me started talking about the days of phonograph records. I proudly listen to some Tex Beneke, Glenn Miller, and Guy Lombardo every week, or my name isn't Eustace Corwin."

"And then *my* generation saw the rise of 8-tracks," added Mrs. Corwin. "Well, I'm sure we'll hear some 'In the Mood' tonight as tradition."

"Mm-hmm." Grandpa Corwin gave a warm smile, tipping his hat, beneath which his dark-gray hair was slicked back with a dab of Brylcreem. Turning around and heading downstairs in the shoes he had just polished, he said, "Can't wait to find out what you whipped up for supper, sweetie."

"I know you're going to like it. Oh, and for dessert, vanilla ice cream drizzled with butterscotch, your favorite. We'll both be down in a second."

"Mom, can I please finish my math lesson first?"

"It's '*may* I,' and my answer is no. Do you still want to watch *Stuart Little 2* in the theaters next week for *your* birthday?"

Zachary's face paled as he nodded his head, daring not to speak a word.

"I thought so. Look, you play school with your stuffed animals almost every day, so missing two hours won't hurt anything."

* * *

One hot Sunday afternoon not long after, beneath a breathtaking display of cirrocumulus clouds, Zachary kept himself busy watering the lawn and the waxleaf privets lining their property, which was part of his weekly routine. He also enjoyed sweeping, mopping, dusting, vacuuming, raking, and washing dishes too, each done in his own meticulous order. The sweet, honeylike fragrance emanating from the white panicles of the waxleaf privets still filled the air, though not as strongly as in spring and early summer.

"Why don't you water the mailbox so *it* will grow, like *you* grow after polishing off all your vegetables?" Grandpa Corwin called out from across the street. He was carrying a small box of vintage books he retrieved from his 1928 Ford Model A, his father's first vehicle. Frankie Lymon's doo-wop song, "Why do Fools Fall in Love," was heard coming from the gramophone behind his living room window.

"Okay!" Zachary giggled, old enough to know his grandfather was trying to be funny, but he played along anyway.

After Grandpa Corwin's hearty laugh, Zachary teased, "And let's water the bench here so *it* will grow."

Slapping his knees, Grandpa Corwin laughed at the sight, nearly dropping the box he held in his other arm.

"And let's water Grandpa so *he* will grow!" Without thinking, Zachary aimed the hose at him and, using his thumb, increased the water pressure enough to reach across the street.

Grandpa Corwin's face instantly dropped from cheer to alarm. Three seconds later came a shriek Zachary had never heard before … and hoped *never* to hear again.

4

The Confrontation

"Raise your hand if you want Zachary to leave," said Abe Lindsay one Saturday morning.

The fog's ominous presence loomed over the entire street. One would be lucky to make out more than two houses in all the haze. Abe and the three other boys with him, all sitting in a circle on the grass, raised their hands.

"Scram, Zach," Abe growled with a sinister smile, peering through the thick strands of his mop top hair.

"Bye, bye, bye," a couple of the other boys sang, mimicking the *NSYNC hit.

"No, I'm going to stay right here," Zachary, now a fourth-grader, stood his ground for the first time, standing five feet away from them. "You, um, almost always tell me to leave. Uh, we only spend time with each other during our birthdays."

All four boys, Abe, Sam, James, and Christopher, jeered at him.

"Because our parents *force* us!" Abe snapped. "And we all pretend to be your friend, Zach. Now scram!"

"Aww, Zachy thought he was one of us," Christopher laughed, sporting his mullet. "Go home and watch *Caillou* or *Franklin* or *Little Bear* or something, you baby!"

"Mmm, come on," Zachary insisted on staying, not knowing what else to say. He was now standing ten feet away as a precaution.

"You're weird!" shouted James with a smirk that made Zachary shudder.

He took another step back, but forced himself to stop, composing himself. In his mind, he began hearing all the string instruments performing a foreboding minor scale in spiccato.

Four seconds passed.

It was like a standoff.

All eyes were on Zachary, and Zachary's eyes were on them.

"You ret—" James started before being cut off.

"*Hey!*" Abe slapped James on the back of his head lightly. Mimicking a strict grown-up, he pointed at him with a bossy finger and continued, "One more remark like that, son, and I'll throw you into the principal's office."

After the four of them erupted in raucous laughter, Christopher added, "I'm sure Zachy gets called that a hundred times a day while he's at school, but let's give the toddler a break on the weekends. All right, gang?"

"Yeah," Sam chimed in. "Remember last month when that third-grader chucked a handball at Zach's face, and he ran away sobbing like a baby?"

"Yo! You should've been there in class last week when he screamed over a little-bitty cricket," said Abe. "Scared us all half to *death.* He would've gotten the *chair* if someone *died.* I don't know why they took him out of *special* education and threw him in classes with us *normal* kids, even though half the time he goes to a special class, probably to take a nap."

"They call it '*mainstreaming,*'" chuckled James. "The stupidest thing ever."

The boys began to laugh and ridicule. Zachary's heart, filled with pain and weakness, felt like it was going to beat out of his chest. He continued to stand there, tight-lipped, embarrassed over his past (even though he couldn't help it). His legs were about to fail him, exacerbated by the fog's cold mist. The social anxiety. The name-calling. The rejection.

Five more tensed seconds ticked by, but to Zachary, it seemed like five minutes.

"Geez! Let's teach him a lesson, fellas." Abe jumped up with the rest of the boys, some of them cracking their knuckles.

Zachary's heart sank to his stomach. His eyes widened.

Sam and Christopher stood on either side of Zachary. Their half-open hands were inches from his arms, ready to grab him within a fraction of a second. James stood behind him, hovering his hands above his shoulders. Abe slowly walked up with a smirk and came face-to-face with Zachary. "I'm gonna give you five seconds to run away … or else!"

"O-or else, w-what?" Zachary could not suppress the shakiness in his voice, wondering if he was about to lose his breakfast. He was now caged in the center of them.

"One!"

"Two!"

"Three!"

Zachary endeavored to contemplate, but his mind completely shut down under the intense pressure, like a computer that had just crashed. All he wanted was true friendship with peers instead of being cooped up inside the house every day (besides school and church), playing school with his stuffed animals, drawing alone, watching television alone, putting puzzles together alone.

"*Four*!" Abe said, stretching out the word.

The hands of the other three boys now hovered millimeters from his body.

Zachary began panting.

"Five!"

A nanosecond later, all four of them grabbed ahold of Zachary.

I'm dead, Zachary thought to himself as all the boys began taunting and laughing at him.

"Take him to my garage!" Abe shouted, yanking at him with the rest of the boys.

Hearing "garage" made Zachary visualize all the dangerous tools usually found in such a place: hammer and nails, a drill, a machete, a chainsaw. Assuming these boys had no mature understanding that everyone only has one life, he mustered all the strength he had, fueled in part by a surge of adrenaline.

"How would you like a haircut, Zachy?" taunted Christopher in his evil voice.

"You've lost your chance. Now, you'll *never* escape us," sneered Abe. "We're gonna keep you in there *forever*! You'll *never* see your family again."

"Help!" Zachary managed to holler before James muffled him with his hand. He exerted more force than he ever did in his lifetime, planting his feet firmly on the grass.

"C'mon," Sam said in disbelief. "How's this scrawny kid so strong?"

Doom shrouded Zachary like the dark cloak of the Grim Reaper. He knew no one could possibly see them through all that fog. Moreover, anyone hearing the commotion would assume it was just boys being boys. He then began thinking about the last time he saw his mother, just fifteen minutes prior. He thought about the smile she gave when he said he was going to spend time with his friends. He then assumed it would be the last time he would see her.

"Grab his darn legs!" Christopher suggested.

Sam and Abe tugged sharply at his legs. Zachary's adrenaline was depleted. After a laborious ten seconds, they managed to completely lift him off the ground. Zachary was no longer in contact with the planet.

This is it! This is how it's going to end, Zachary lamented, regretting that he had gotten up that morning. He berated himself for thinking that friendship with peers would bring him peace and joy in life. Feeling queasy and suffocated, he resigned to his fate, but he continued crying out for help the best he could through James' fingers. "God! He-Help! He—" he barely got out.

They were a few feet away from the garage's entrance.

"Ha! This is so easy now," Christopher said, laughing.

"*Hey!*" cried a loud voice that shook the four bullies to their core, dropping Zachary onto the cemented driveway.

"Ow!" Zachary squeezed his eyes shut and clutched his upper left arm, afraid it was broken or dislocated.

The four bullies fell silent. Trembling, they glimpsed a dark silhouetted figure through the misty haze, like some eerie apparition.

"You losers, leave Zachary *alone*!" thundered the voice.

Zachary slowly opened his eyes, partly out of fear, partly out of pain, and partly out of hope.

Coming out of the fog was a young teenager charging at them with clenched fists, wearing his skateboard helmet with the buckle unfastened.

"*Thomas!*" Zachary cried before gasping for air.

Seconds passed by. "It's four against one," Sam managed to say.

The three other boys stood still, speechless.

"W-W-We beat a middle s-schooler a couple weeks a-ago," stuttered Sam.

Thomas folded his arms. *Are these punks serious?* he thought, shaking his head.

"That's right!" Abe joined in and took a step forward toward Thomas, followed by Sam.

Christopher and James stood frozen, mouths hanging open.

"You babies!" Abe chided. "Come on! Together we'll drag both of them in there, alive … maybe."

The four bullies took a few steps closer to Thomas. Abe and Sam radiated the most sinister confidence, smirks spreading all across their faces.

You losers are relentless, Thomas laughed inside, though still looking tough on the outside.

Zachary wailed in pain as another wave of soreness shot through his left arm. "God, *help* me!"

The four boys fiercely approached Thomas, who remained still with his arms folded. Their faces twisted into lionlike grimaces. "Listen, fella. It's four against one," Sam taunted, hitting Thomas in the chest, trying to shove him off balance. "We'll easily overpower you and throw you *both* into the garage."

"Are you jerks sure about that?" Thomas smirked.

The four boys quickly grabbed ahold of Thomas and began yanking on him.

Zachary wailed.

Thomas maintained his stance, his arms still folded tightly across his chest.

Abe laughed. "You think you're so tough?"

"Hey! Pudding-for-brains," boomed a voice.

The four boys froze in their tracks, still forcefully gripping Thomas' polo shirt and arms. A second silhouette emerged from the fog, resolving into another middle school boy, Jake, holding his bike helmet by the chin straps with his left hand. "That's four against *two*."

The bullies became as still as statues.

"B-Big deal," Sam blurted out, gripping tighter on Thomas' shirt. "Y-You guys are s-still outnumbered."

"Airhead! That's four against *three*." Andrew, a third middle schooler, skateboarded out of the fog. He kicked up his skateboard and, holding it at his side, marched toward them with pursed lips.

Thomas' smirk got wider.

Quickly, the boys loosened their grips.

"Ha!" A fourth boy manifested. "You little punks were celebrating, thinking that *we're* outnumbered?"

"Well, Mike, they were clearly wrong," declared a fifth, stepping forward, as Zachary's tears of trepidation became tears of hope and comfort. "Looks like *you* were outnumbered all along! Let's see … even though I'm the only girl here, I *will* be getting my black belt next month. It's funny, because I didn't know how I was going to practice for it … until *now*."

A tremendous, unearthly terror coursed through the four bullies from head to toe. In one millisecond, they let go of Thomas, and in the next, they sprinted inside Abe's house, double-locking the door behind them.

Thomas and his four friends wasted no time and rushed to Zachary's side.

"Zachary, champ, where are you hurt?" Thomas asked, gently helping him sit up.

Zachary was too overcome with emotion to speak, trying hard to hide his distress, but he foundered.

"Just relax, bud," Andrew said, placing his hand on Zachary's right shoulder. "We're here for you. We'll make sure no one ever hurts you again."

"Are you able to gently move your arm, like this?" Thomas was putting his First Aid training from the Boy Scouts into action.

Zachary copied what Thomas did with minor soreness, then nodded his head.

"Can you stand up?" asked Olivia, the girl who was training for her black belt.

Thomas, Andrew, and Mike helped him up.

"I'm fine," Zachary tearfully said, looking down at the ground.

"You sure, champ?"

"Yeah."

"Well, let us at least walk you home," Jake insisted. "We'll get you there safely. Where do you live?"

"Next door," Thomas answered for him.

"Oh goodness. Those creeps are your neighbors?" Jake stood dumbfounded.

Zachary nodded, but clarified, "Um, one of them is. Another lives down the street. The other two, I don't know."

"They're just cowards pretending to be tough," said Mike. "Did you see how fast they ran into the house? You even heard them locking the deadbolt."

"It's a miracle we were out," Thomas said aloud on the way to Zachary's front door, marveling. "It was too foggy to be outside, so we decided to rent a movie at Blockbuster and come back. Then, we almost didn't turn down this street."

"Next time they try to do that again, let me know, and I'll take care of them," Olivia vowed. "They'll wish they never messed with you."

"Thanks," Zachary said before entering his house and shutting the door behind him.

The five middle schoolers walked onto the street, getting ready to ride off on their skateboards and bicycles. All but Thomas placed their headphones over their ears from their Sony Walkman cassette players. As Mike was clipping his to his belt, he told Thomas, "You know? It's crazy your Walkman ran out of batteries after leaving Blockbuster."

"Totally!" Olivia said after overhearing Mike, just before she started playing "I Want It That Way" by the Backstreet Boys, her favorite song. "You would never have heard them and stopped the rest of us."

"No kidding," Thomas said. "I was really bummed about not getting to listen to 'All Star,' but now I care less."

Walking head down, Zachary climbed up the stairs and passed by his mother's room.

"Oh, Zachary! How was it?" called out Mrs. Corwin, dipping her novel slightly and sipping some coffee.

Slowly, Zachary walked a few steps backward so his mother could see him from her open door. By then, the redness all over his face had faded. "Fine, Mom," he lied, which made him feel worse.

After closing his bedroom door, he walked past his lone ottoman, kicked off his only pair of shoes, and slumped onto his one bed.

I just don't get it, he thought. *Sure, half of them aren't in my class, but still. Now I know how Charlie Brown feels all the time.*

He hardly ate for the next several days, but he always felt comforted by what Thomas and his friends did for him. He kept replaying the scene over and over again. He kept rehearing their words, spoken in his defense. He kept feeling their hands of protection on him. He began to sense that there were, in fact, truly supportive people out there in his neighborhood besides Thomas, albeit a few years older than he was.

In spite of this, the idea that many people simply wouldn't accept him plagued his mind. Even though he might scream at bugs, be slow to process what others tell him, have a speech impediment, or get upset when he loses at games, he could still be a good friend to spend time with. He never wanted to hurt anyone, physically or emotionally. He was still a human being with a heart, longing to spend time with his peers.

5

You Just Be Yourself

"Zachary, smile!" someone shouted.

"What?" The spontaneous yell caught him off guard as he had just set foot on the veranda. Seeing his friend Thomas, he grinned.

"Ha-ha! That was great, dude. You're always the photogenic one. Ready for school?"

"Yes." Zachary walked up to him. He felt ready for the day, invigorated by the bright, immaculate morning, not a cloud in the sky. The air carried the fragrance of the front yard's waxleaf privets. It was neither scorching nor freezing, neither humid nor dry. Edvard Grieg's "Morning Mood," which had been stuck in his head for a while, reverberated in his ears.

"Thanks again, Thomas!" yelled out Mrs. Corwin from the front door with a smile, holding a mug of hot coffee.

"No problem, Mrs. Corwin!" A moment later, both he and Zachary began walking toward Washington Elementary.

"Thomas, is that what I think it is?" Zachary inquired.

"*Yeah, buddy!* A flip phone with a camera in it. Just got it for my birthday last week, along with a new pogo stick. Incredible technology these days. What could they possibly think of next?"

"I'm amazed to see one in person, just like when I saw the new colorized twenty-dollar bill for the first time, or the new Jefferson nickels these past few years. Um, how was Manhattan?"

"Just beautiful. Spent my birthday walking through Central Park, went up to the Empire State Building's observation deck, saw a musical at the Broadway Theatre, and took a ferry to the Statue of Liberty."

"Mmm ... *Cool!* Um, New York City's on my, uh, bucket list."

Thomas looked over at him with a tight-lipped smile.

"I-I didn't say it right, did I?" Zachary questioned, feeling embarrassed.

"It's not that, dude!" Thomas explained, laughing. "You said it correctly. I just never heard you say 'Cool' before."

Zachary, his face neutral, turned to look straight ahead as he continued walking down the street, passing by the ubiquitous star jasmine that was planted in nearly every front yard.

"Don't sweat it, champ," Thomas said sympathetically.

"I just feel awkward when I use expressions that you all say," he complained. "I appreciate you calling me, uh, 'dude,' and, um, 'champ,' but *me* saying it? I don't know. Same with certain songs, like "We Will Rock You." It's catchy, but I don't want to sing, clap, and stomp in front of others. That's sort of why I was thrown out of karate too because of all those yells."

"Ah, I know what you're saying. The kiai."

"Yes. Also, last year, I spilled ketchup on my brand-new white shirt during lunch, and, um, I told my classmates, uh, 'My mom is gonna kill me.' You know what they said? 'Call the police.' Seriously, they weren't joking or being mean to me or anything. I thought it would make me, um, one of them, you know? I thought that was a common expression. I heard others say it. I heard it on my favorite shows on Nickelodeon and Disney."

"And how did it make you feel after you said that, *before* they told you to call the police? And how did you feel just now after saying 'Cool' to me?"

Zachary exhaled. "I felt funny. Um, I didn't feel like myself."

Thomas stopped, knelt down, and looked him in the eye. He placed a hand on Zachary's shoulder and said encouragingly, each word deliberately sincere, "Zachary, you don't ever have to pretend to be someone you're not. You don't ever have to change your vocabulary just to 'fit in' with others. If people treat you poorly, that's on them. It does *not* reflect who you are as a unique, one-of-a-kind individual. *You* just be yourself."

As they neared the gates of Washington Elementary, Thomas slowed down and pulled something out of his jeans' pocket.

"Got something for you, champ. Actually, two things. Consider these as belated birthday gifts, since we were both born in the summer. I found this old penny in New York. Thought you might like it."

"It's a 1945 Wheat cent. Thanks, I'll add this to my collection. I've been collecting these and all the new Statehood Quarters. I earned the Coin Collecting Merit at Royal Rangers last year."

"Yeah, no problem. Also, I was cleaning out my room and throwing away lots of stuff, but I thought you might like this, knowing that you love playing on your Game Boy Advance. It's a game cartridge, and I don't need it anymore."

"Wow, *Donkey Kong Country 2*. I always wanted to play this, ever since beating the first part with a 101% a dozen times."

"I know. You kept talking about it. Just make sure you take breaks this time instead of spending hours on your Game Boy, or Minesweeper, or 3D Pinball: Space Cadet. Same with Cartoon Network and now Millsberry. Your mom and I don't have to remind you what happened last spring, right?"

"Absolutely. It was just, um, back then, I didn't want to stop until I beat everything."

"Always take breaks."

"Of course. Uh … this past summer, I would spend an hour playing my Game Boy, an hour putting a puzzle together, an hour working on merits for Royal Rangers on my own, an hour writing books or movie scripts on our computer, an hour playing school, and an hour making animated movies. That way, I'm not spending four or five hours on my Game Boy anymore, which made me literally see bananas everywhere, even when I stopped playing."

"Whoa! That's all okay … I guess? Did you spend *any* time with friends, other than on your birthday? You said you started making some more this past year."

"Oh, uh, well … not exactly," Zachary stuttered. "I, uh, wanted to. It's rare, though. I mean, a couple of times, friends came over to drop off a little gift, but they didn't stay too long. I meant, um … I mean, they enjoyed seeing me. I-I know they weren't faking it. Their gifts were real, uh, from their heart." He spared the details of how truly isolated he felt. Some days, he waited for the friendly mailman just to have someone else to say hi to before sinking into an afternoon of loneliness in his room.

"Did you get out of the house much at all?"

"I watched *Cars* in the theaters at the outdoor mall down the boulevard, but just went with my mom. I saw two friends from school there, though."

"That's good, but try to tag along with those friends next time."

"*Oh!* I almost forgot. Earlier in May, I watched *Hoot* in the theaters with some of my neighbors. Their families invited me to join them. Then we ate at a local El Torito. I suppose that's a start."

"Well, champ, today's the first day of your last year of elementary school. Make it a good one. Be brave. Get out there. Find your friends who care about you, and ignore those who don't. Talk to your teacher or principal if you don't understand something. Don't be shy to go up to your friends and say, 'Hey! Can I tag along?' *And speak in a way you're comfortable with.* Okay?"

Zachary drew in a deep breath of the fresh air, which carried with it the aroma of pine and a trace of freshly cut grass. "Okay, Thomas. And you, uh, enjoy your first day of high school too. I want to hear all about what it's really like."

6

The Truth Comes Out

"You must be Mrs. Corwin!" said Mr. Martinez, Zachary's sixth-grade teacher.

"It's a pleasure to make your acquaintance." Mrs. Corwin shook his hand. It was the last day of September, and it was their Back-to-School Night. "How do you do?"

"I'm well, thank you. Mrs. Corwin, your son is an exceptional student. His work is phenomenal. His disposition and mannerism are unparalleled. *Very* unpretentious. You should be highly proud of Zachary."

Exhaling with joy, she replied, "Mr. Martinez, it makes me so happy to hear that. All of his teachers—and I mean *every* one since preschool—say the same thing about him."

"I'm not surprised. He's polite to me and my colleagues, not part of the troublemakers, and gets, well, *most* of his work done. He struggles with reading the most, but he excels in math and history, especially the presidents."

"Yep, he loves math. He has drawn all the presidents by hand twice. One Saturday, he watched an entire special on the History Channel where they discussed each one in detail."

"How'd he come to like the presidents?"

"I bought him a book after he was born. That way, once he learned how to read, he could get an appreciation for American history. He also loved the animated series *Liberty Kids* which focused on the Revolutionary War."

"Excuse me, but are you Zachary's mom?" interrupted a parent.

"Yes, I am."

"Aw, I got to meet him while picking up my son, Timothy, last week."

"He's talked about Timothy quite a bit."

"Yes, they're best friends, and Zachary, your son, is the sweetest."

"I'm so glad to hear you say that. I'm grateful that Zachary is hanging out with friends more."

"Thought I should let you know," the parent said, smiling. "So sorry I interrupted. Have a good night."

"That's quite all right. Good night."

"Good night, Mrs. Thompson," said Mr. Martinez.

"Goodness, I'm glad I brought my umbrella," Mrs. Thompson said as she walked out the classroom door.

"Um, Mr. Martinez, I first wanted to ask you how Zachary was doing academically, socially, and all that, from your perspective as his teacher."

"Well, other than his kind disposition and his struggle with reading, I have noticed that he's easily distracted. Although he unequivocally has a sense of humor, I had to tell him that some jokes came at inappropriate times, like when I'm lecturing or while everyone's working quietly."

"Yes, he's always the jokester. And about him being distracted, yes. One thing I wanted to tell you this evening are the triggers: helicopter noises, loud plane sounds, and sirens. Those are the top three."

"Yep, those are usually the culprits when I see him distracted. I could tell he has the urge to leap out of his seat and run outside to see the aircraft."

"*Did* he do that?"

"No."

"Thank goodness. I worked with him on that a couple of years ago. Usually, it's out of curiosity or the desire to see it (the plane or the fire engine, for example), but other times, he says it's out of compulsion. He worries that something bad will happen if he doesn't see it. I told him it's just superstition and to take a deep breath. By fifth grade, he was almost a completely different boy."

The classroom lights began to flicker ever so slightly as the rain outside began to pick up.

"I'm glad he's starting to free himself from those things. I've noticed that he exhibits more anxiety than most of my other students. As we discussed the five-year anniversary of the 9/11 terrorist attacks back on September 11, he seemed restless. Last week, when we read about Adolf Hitler and the Auschwitz concentration camp, he came up to me whispering something, but I couldn't make out what he was saying, and I asked him to tell me afterward. I didn't understand until I spoke with him during recess. He was asking if we could stop talking about all that stuff. I felt so bad. I should've sent him to his special ed room to do worksheets or play an academic game on the computer there, like *Oregon Trail* or *Carmen Sandiego*."

Mrs. Corwin exhaled deeply. "Yes, I knew that. Last week, he hardly ate anything at all. Some nights, he hardly slept."

"That explains his sudden change in mood in the middle of last week. He almost fell asleep after lunch and his breathing seemed labored too. I wanted to send him to the nurse, but he seemed to have a panic attack when I suggested it. He told me he was fine, just tired."

"Well, on one of those nights, he knocked on my door and told me it was because of the horrors of how Jews were murdered in those camps during the Holocaust. He wondered what it would've been like if it had been us living at that time. Just that image upset him."

"Oh, I apologize, Mrs. Corwin. The curriculum that we teachers follow *is* a bit too graphic. I don't know what to say."

"It's not your fault, Mr. Martinez. He seems to be doing better now. Anyway, it's a quarter to eight. The last thing I really want to know is, how is he doing with his peers?"

"Socially, he's on the shy side."

Mrs. Corwin nodded knowingly.

"I know that he's been bullied harshly in his past and—"

Mrs. Corwin cleared her throat, trying to hide her emotions, but Mr. Martinez discerned that something was wrong.

"Didn't you know that, Mrs. Corwin?"

"I knew he got teased every now and then back in kindergarten, but … is he still getting bullied today? He never told me."

"U-Uh … yes, Mrs. Corwin. A couple of weeks ago, after school, he came up to me with two other students. One of those students bullied him a lot toward the end of fifth grade; the other one witnessed it."

Mrs. Corwin gripped her purse strap tighter.

"Zachary said he was greatly nervous to admit it, but he couldn't hold it in anymore."

Just then, lightning flashed outside, followed by the sounds of pouring rain.

"But I let that student know exactly what he had caused Zachary—that Zachary had held in those painful feelings for three months before telling anyone. Not only that, but he had to endure it all summer long. 'Imagine how that'd make *you* feel,' I told the student."

The sound of thunder rumbled in the distance.

Mr. Martinez continued, "We all talked for about five minutes, and it ended in a truce. Apparently, this boy would tease Zachary over his speech impediment and for getting upset after losing a round of handball or basketball. I'm sorry, I assumed he would've told you by now."

"No, he *didn't*." Mrs. Corwin sounded upset as her face flickered, due to another flash of lightning. "I *always* remind him that he could talk to me about anything, any time. Who's this bully? Do I know him? What's his name?"

"Abe. Abe Lindsay."

"Craaash!" roared a thunderclap in the mist of the worsening rainstorm.

Mrs. Corwin couldn't speak for a few seconds but then regained her composure. "Abe? But Abe's our neighbor. Abe's his friend … or so I thought." After saying her goodbyes, she rushed home, walked past her father who was fast asleep on the couch, and stormed upstairs to Zachary's room.

"Um, come in, Grandpa," Zachary said upon hearing the knocks on his one wooden bedroom door.

Mrs. Corwin swung the door open with pursed lips as thunder continued to growl in the distance.

"Oh! Mom!" Zachary exclaimed, wide-eyed, spilling the colored pencils he'd been using for his hand-drawn animated movie on the floor.

"*Sit down*, Zachary Corwin!" she ordered, walking past Zachary's one ottoman and taking a seat on his one chair. Zachary sat down at the foot of his one bed.

For the next three hours, Zachary unloaded everything he had held in over the past half-dozen years. There were tears and there were occasional laughs. In the middle of the interrogation, Mrs. Corwin asked Zachary if he could recount another recent story.

"Well, um, in the beginning of fifth grade, when I would volunteer with those severely disabled students during recess and lunch, there would be a few fourth-graders also there, uh, and they were helping out, but they always picked on me, calling me weird, laughed at me when I was, um, crying in the dugout—"

"Why were you crying in the dugout?"

"Because I thought I had no *real* friends."

Mrs. Corwin got up to get a tissue at that point. "Go on, Zachary," she said, blowing her nose.

"Sometimes, mmm, I just, uh, ran away during P.E. and hid toward the back of the school, wondering if anyone would notice my absence. They didn't. They probably thought, um, I went to the restroom or classroom, or that I was just acting up. I felt so alone. I mean, I have a lot of friends in my class and in the after-school program for keyboard lessons. Sometimes we'd play together, but other times, we didn't. I'm too shy to go up to them myself. I always wait for them to come to me."

Mrs. Corwin threw away her used tissue and grabbed a few more, just in case.

"Back in third grade," Zachary continued, "uh, students would tell me to 'Take a hike.' I pretended to take it literally, thinking that humor would win me friends."

"And be accepted by others." Mrs. Corwin nodded, knowing where he was getting with this.

"Right, so, uh, I thought, hiking meant climbing, like climbing up a mountain, so, um, I pretended to climb up one of those big storage containers that they kept the P.E. equipment in. It didn't work. There were other things I tried to take literally, but they also didn't work. I tried doing card tricks like my classmates. A couple of them taught me, but when *I* tried them, either I messed up or they knew how I did it. Either way, they laughed at me. I mean, Mom, uh, to tell you the truth—"

"Zachary, *always* be truthful. Never hold in these feelings … ever again!"

Starting out slow, but gradually speaking faster, Zachary continued, "Some nights I lie awake, um, imaging myself being the world's best musician at my age, or making all the basketball shots, or never getting out in handball, or hitting home runs in softball, or being the strongest person, or flying a helicopter and landing at my school to get the attention of others, or, um, having superhuman powers like the shows I watch on Nickelodeon and Disney, such as flying. I would imagine flying in front of the entire school, or doing all the neat stuff that Darkwing Duck does, a-and, uh—" Tears welled up in his eyes.

"Just slow down, Zachary. Had you ever pretended to do anything like that, or lied to your schoolmates?"

Zachary gulped. "My fifth-grade teacher picked out popsicle sticks. Each one had our class number on it. He would pick one whenever he wanted someone to answer a question. Um, one day, during a math lesson, he picked one early, and I saw the number. I had all the students' numbers memorized, just like the presidents. The number was eighteen, and I was twenty, so he was a couple of desks down from me. I whispered to him, out of courtesy, 'Caleb, you're next.' 'What?' he asked. 'You're next,' I repeated. At that instant, the teacher called out the number, and it was eighteen. At least five classmates nearby jerked their heads at me."

"Oh, God." Mrs. Corwin closed her eyes.

"Mom, I didn't mean to pretend that I was a psychic, but when I saw my classmates' eyes light up, um, uh … I felt valued. I felt accepted. They actually seemed amazed by me. *They* were the ones calling me 'psychic.' I just nodded. I didn't say I was."

"We shouldn't be entertaining the notion, Zachary, much less dabble in that sort of stuff."

"I *didn't*. I just pretended."

"Well, how did your snake oil sell? Um, meaning, tell me what happen. Surely, you got exposed."

"It was hard to keep it up. My, uh, friends kept asking me who was next, or what was the math topic for the next day. I would privately ask my teacher, and he would tell me. I also told him that it might be easier to pull out the popsicle sticks a few seconds early, um, to be ready. He thought it was a good idea, but really, I just wanted to get a glimpse at the number. It lasted about two months. Sometimes I had to squint and sit up a little more. Um, and one day, the teacher called me out on it."

"And that's how it all ended."

"Yes. The teacher said, in front of *everyone*, 'Zach, please stop doing that! I know you're trying to see the numbers I picked, but it's distracting and frankly annoying.' And that's all he said. Immediately, all eyes turned my way. The person next to me whispered, '*Oh*, so *that's* how you knew.' I felt utterly humiliated."

"Well, you learned your lesson, right?"

"Absolutely," Zachary said, still embarrassed over the debacle. "Mom, very, very deep down in my mind, I still wish I could've gotten away with it."

"What?! Why?!"

"Because I still don't feel totally accepted. Yeah, I, uh, have about thirty or so friends now, but I don't spend time with them outside of school. Again, it's because I'm rarely asked by them. Plus, some of those 'friends' tease me half the time—"

"Well, *those* students aren't truly friends, Zachary," Mrs. Corwin pointed out. "You need to come to terms with that. They may invite you somewhere, but you'll end up in a knock-down-drag-out fight. For the other thing, you need to just go up to them and ask, 'Hey, can I hang out with you? Want to get a burger or pizza somewhere?'"

"I'm too nervous, and I, um, don't know who to fully trust. Also, my friends talk about inappropriate things, or stuff I'm not interested in, like, um, rock music and sports and skateboarding and violent video games on their PS2s, or the latest Xbox 360 whatever. And after that scary incident with Abe and his gang, I just question whom I could trust."

Mrs. Corwin shuddered and felt queasy again, since she had just found out about it an hour before this part of the conversation.

"In fifth grade, I overheard my friends talking with each other. One was mad at one of my best friends for ruining his computer game. I heard him say, 'I'm gonna take Tim after school and beat his head against the bricks until it breaks!'"

Mrs. Corwin gasped.

"I'm sure he wasn't serious, but he and his two friends started laughing. I felt sick and uncomfortable. Um, I *had* to let the teacher know about it, and the teacher talked to him after school. Even though he was talked to by the teacher, oh, and the principal too, I still wouldn't trust him, *or* those other guys."

"Yeah, people who talk like that aren't people you want to hang out with. If they get in trouble with law enforcement and you're with them, you'll probably be punished equally."

Zachary shuddered.

"And you have the right mindset," she continued. "You shouldn't fill your mind with violence or inappropriateness. Moreover, they first need to prove you can trust them before spending time together."

Zachary tearfully added, "I just don't know if, uh, people at my school fully realize that life isn't a game with multiple lives. You can't just start over. Once you're dead, you're dead. No do-overs. I've honestly been disturbed by a lot of different shows I've watched on Nickelodeon and Disney. I still love the shows, but, uh, for some darn reason, once in a while, they had to show things that would ordinarily kill a person in real life, or would be considered cruel punishment or torture. And some people laugh at that. I overheard my classmates laughing while retelling these familiar scenes. Um, there was one scene on television where a character was choking in school, and everyone around was cheering. It never showed anyone rescuing him. He appeared in other episodes afterward, so it must've been implied. Also, some commercials these days are disturbing, like being trapped in a school locker, for instance; even the night janitor wouldn't rescue him after crying for his mother."

"Well, that's just television. It's unfortunate that many kids these days would laugh at another person's expense. I can't control what *they* watch, but I *can* control what you watch, Zachary. I think it's wise to stop watching some of those shows. Unfortunately, I can't help what they show in commercials, but I also watched that one, and it's definitely a cliffhanger."

The night wore on. The storm clouds dissipated. The first quarter moon was almost set.

Toward the end of the candid conversation, Mrs. Corwin said, "I have one remaining thing to ask you about, Zachary Corwin. Why the heck are you *now* telling me all this? Why the heck didn't you tell me, your grandpa, or your teachers *right* away? Why did you not say anything about Abe Lindsay? Do you realize that you unnecessarily held in stress and pain *all* summer long for that alone, not to mention what he and those other boys did to you a couple of years ago? That was a *burden* to you! I mean, Zachary, I love you. I'm just upset, and I wouldn't be like this if I didn't care about you."

Zachary wiped the tears from his eyes, took a deep breath, and softly replied, "I just didn't want you guys or my teachers to worry about me."

7

New Horizons

Zachary slowly walked down the hallway toward the cafeteria one sunny Tuesday. The line was already long enough that it snaked out the cafeteria door. Shouts and laughter from dozens of students reverberated all throughout the hallway, flooding his ears. Aaron Carter's rendition of "I Want Candy" played on the radio in the cafeteria, and some students were nodding to the beat.

Zachary took his place at the end of the line before more students lined up behind him. He instantly started having second thoughts and was about to leave. Just then, the student in front of him turned around. Zachary shook to his core as if the living daylights had been scared out of him.

"Hey!" the boy greeted him, smiling. "I'm so happy to see you again."

Zachary couldn't speak, but had to say something. "Oh, um … Hey!"

"How's the first day of middle school going?"

"*Uh* … It's going okay?" Zachary lied.

"Anything the matter?"

"Uh, no, Abe. Just, um … good to see you again too."

"Isn't middle school great, man? No more being cooped up inside one classroom all day, and so many different choices for lunch."

"I guess."

"How's your summer been?"

"My summer? Well, nothing much. I was doing another animated movie about aircraft, but I didn't finish in time, which stressed me out. I must've used over 300 pieces of paper so far, with, um, each picture being a hair different than the previous one to create the illusion of motion."

"Dang, man."

"Yeah, and I've been collecting those new presidential dollars, um, and more Wheat cents. I've practiced more juggling and piano skills; I can juggle four now and arpeggiate chords."

"That's sick, man!"

Zachary was taken off guard. He tried to say a filler word, but nothing came out. *Did I hear right?* he thought. *I knew this was too good to be real.*

"Oh." Abe perceived that Zachary was uninformed. "'Sick' these days is another word for 'Cool.'"

"Oh, phew," Zachary exhaled. "Sorry."

"Don't sweat it. I know you don't speak our lingo much. I can't wait to hear you play piano again."

"Really?"

"Yeah! And you gotta show me some juggling. It was si-, uh, *cool*, when you juggled in the talent show last year at Washington."

"Thank you!" Zachary beamed. "How was your summer?"

"No worries, man. My summer was amazing. Surfed the gnarly waves at beaches near Los Angeles, mountain biked in Moab, Utah, saw Mount Rushmore while visiting my grandparents—"

"You saw Mount Rushmore?" Zachary was envious of that alone.

"Yeah, and then I hung out with my friends almost every other day. We would have sleepovers at my treehouse almost every weekend … You should tag along with us next time."

Zachary was taken back once again, but this time blurted out, "Oh, sure. Yeah."

Abe smiled and nodded.

Zachary was still feeling queasy from the jitters of being in a bigger school with five times as many people in it. "Oh, Abe, I forgot something in my last class. I need to go get it," he said, employing his acting skills.

"Okay."

Zachary turned around and started walking away, perplexed.

"I'll save your spot!" Abe called out, hammering Zachary further with mixed emotions.

He rushed into his special ed room and slumped onto the couch. His teacher, Mrs. Johansen, allowed him to be there any time he needed to.

"Anything wrong, Zachary?" asked Mr. Andrews, the Instructional Aide for all the special ed students.

"No, no. I just need to think."

I cannot believe that just happened, Zachary thought. *Did Abe remember who I was? Did he remember how he used to harass me? How is he talking to me like his lifelong friend? Is this a pretense? I'm grateful, don't get me wrong, but still. Even saying, 'I'll save your spot'? Can I trust him? If I ever have a sleepover with him and his friends, would I come out alive the next morning?*

The last period of the day was Physical Education.

"So, tell us something about yourself, Corwin," said Coach Whittaker.

Zachary was standing before his classmates at the basketball courts.

"Well, mmm, I like to juggle," he said semi-confidently, which drew murmurs from his now-impressed classmates. "I, uh, like to play piano, and I also know a lot about the presidents." There were tons of things Zachary could've said, but he knew he couldn't speak for an hour.

"No way! Like *all* the presidents?" marveled Coach Whittaker.

"Yeah."

"Well, team, what should we say? How should we test your knowledge, Corwin, to make sure you're not lying to us?"

Zachary was old enough to know that Coach Whittaker was speaking playfully and wasn't doubting him. However, seeing the coach's smile helped validate that in his mind. "Have someone pick a number between one and forty-three," he said.

"You heard him," hollered the coach.

"Twenty-Seven," called out a girl.

"Our twenty-seventh president was William Howard Taft. He was born in 1857, died in 1930, and served from March 4, 1909 to March 4, 1913."

The entire basketball court fell silent for a few seconds. Classmates' mouths were dropped in awe. A few laughed, utterly impressed by his memorization skills.

"U-Uh, thirty-four," the coach said to continue testing him.

"Our thirty-fourth president was Dwight David Eisenhower. He was born in, uh, 1890, died in, uhh—" Zachary was on the spot, but he quickly recovered, "He died in 1969, and served from January 20, 1953 to January 20, 1961."

"Whoa, so if any of you need help in your history class, you know who to go to." Coach Whittaker patted Zachary on the back. "Great job, Corwin. You can stand back at your spot."

Just before the bell rang, students were hanging out with each other. Ten of them surrounded Zachary, testing him on presidential trivia. A couple of classmates asked him what else he liked to do.

He told his mother all about it during the drive home. "Mom, I was queasy all day being surrounded by hundreds of students I never met before, but then, at the end, I got to meet new friends. They came to me, wanting to talk with me. Nobody teased me or laughed at me, and in P.E., I wasn't called "brainiac," "smarty-pants," "know-it-all," or other things I heard on TV. I felt accepted. As God is my witness, I felt accepted. I didn't have to lie about doing incredible things that I can't do, because, um, I *knew* the presidents. I knew that making such a claim would demand evidence, which I provided. Um, I told them that I could juggle and play piano, which I know I can prove when put to the test. Overall, my first day at Canyon Mountain Middle School turned out amazing."

Zachary waited for a response. "Um … Mom?"

Mrs. Corwin sniffled. "That's so wonderful to hear. It's my answer to prayer."

Half a mile further down the road, Mrs. Corwin remembered to say, "Oh, Zachary, I have a surprise for you."

"What it is?! I *love* surprises." Zachary perked up with excitement.

"I was talking to one of my friends on the phone today. I've known her since before you were born, since the eighties. You've met her and her husband as a toddler (the Montgomerys), but I doubt you remember."

"Mom, according to you, um, my earliest memory was when I was one or two years old, according to what I described."

"Well, you might just remember the Montgomerys then. Anyway, she and her family invited us to spend time with them for Thanksgiving and Christmas, but just to let you know, they live fifty miles away. We'd be staying with them for a few days. I told her I'd have to ask you first."

"Are you kidding?! Absolutely!"

"Great. I'll call her back as soon as we get inside." Mrs. Corwin smiled and parked her Toyota Corolla.

* * *

Over the next few weeks, Zachary continued to make friends, partly due to his knowledge of the presidents and other skills, and partly due to his kind heart. Some students had him juggle tennis balls of theirs, sometimes drawing crowds. At one point, the campus safety officer had to break it up because the cheering became restless. Zachary felt contrite about it, but the safety officer told him that he needn't worry.

Academically, he excelled in most subjects, but, as always, he struggled in reading. Some group projects went over his head, and he was thankful that his teammates took the lead. Then he would feel guilty over getting a good grade for work he did little on.

Socially, he never got rid of his shyness. He only talked with people who came up to him first. Rarely was it the other way around. During nutrition (a five-minute break between second and third period) and lunch (which came after fourth period), he would walk around the campus until someone stopped him for a conversation.

"Hey, Zach! Your joke was so funny yesterday," one of the students commented while Zachary walked by, sitting on a bench with her friends. "I repeated it to my cousins after school, and they cracked up laughing."

"Thank you."

"Do you have more?" a second student in the group asked.

"Uh, no, not at the moment."

"Are you writing these jokes yourself?"

"Um … no."

"*Oh*," the first student exclaimed. "I thought you wrote those yourself. I was going to say I was impressed."

Zachary didn't know what to say and stood there, awkwardly.

"But they were still funny, though. Thanks for telling them to us," she said with a reassuring smile.

"You're welcome." Zachary gave a little smile and walked away. He felt crushed. Unlike his supposed-psychic-powers fiasco in fifth grade, he wasn't trying to pretend he was creative enough to write his own jokes. From then until the end of his middle school days, he began writing his own jokes, even though some were embarrassingly corny. His friends still got a kick out of them, nonetheless … most of them did, that is.

In October of that first year of middle school, Zachary got back into playing basketball. He'd play traditional basketball, but he'd also play a variant of the game that his peers made up. However, the variant game was tied to painful emotions from Washington Elementary. (It was the first day of fourth grade, and he was already feeling lonesome because Thomas had just started middle school at that point. During recess and lunch that day, he thought he saw Thomas a couple of times, but they were just lookalikes. After attempting to play the variant basketball game, he got out immediately. He tried explaining to his peers that they hadn't been clear about the rules, but they weren't listening. As he tearfully walked away after begging for a second chance, his peers laughed and pointed at him, one cruelly calling him the R-word.)

On this cool day, as Halloween approached, the sky was overcast by altostratus clouds. The area around the sun looked as if a small piece of the cloudy sheet had been punched out, opening a portal. A silhouette of a high-altitude Airbus A340 elegantly glided across the cloudy curtain. Zachary was in charge of the basketball. Like in elementary school, anyone could come and join. He decided on playing the variant game, since a lot of his peers were asking to play it. As the game continued, one student got out in the same way Zachary did the first time, three years prior.

"Sorry, uh, I didn't know the rules," said the student. "This is my first time playing."

"Can he have a second chance, Zachary?" the student's friend requested.

"Uh, well, I wasn't given a second chance when I didn't know the rules … but I'll give you a second chance."

"Thanks so much, pal."

Zachary knew to treat people the same way he would want to be treated, a principle drilled into him at Royal Rangers. At this point in the ministry, he was in the third age group, called Adventure Rangers. He was advancing up the ranks toward the second of three medals in this particular age group. He had already earned all three medals in the previous age group after hundreds of hours of work—most of it on his own—including community service hours.

8

Ethereal Glimpses of Inclusion

As Thanksgiving 2007 drew near, Zachary and his mother stayed a few days with the Montgomerys. Their home was picturesque and spacious. The scent of eucalyptus welcomed them upon entering the threshold. Behind the houses on their side of the street lay a small wheat field, beyond which ran a small river, and behind that stood a forest of conifer trees.

The family greeted them with hugs and smiles. They had two children, Marshall and Clara, both a couple of years younger than Zachary. Sporting a faux hawk, Marshall regularly wore a plaid flannel shirt, while Clara, in a wispy ponytail, wore overalls with a simple cotton shirt underneath. Mrs. Corwin and Mrs. Montgomery caught up with each other after ten years.

Marshall and Clara asked Zachary a million questions to get to know him before playing board games, watching a movie together, and jumping on the trampoline outside. The first movie they chose to watch together was *Because of Winn-Dixie*. Zachary had just finished reading the book in his Language Arts class and completed his final essay on it.

Each evening after dinner, both families would clear the dining table and pick one board game to play together, keeping warm by the glowing fireplace. This was when Zachary was introduced to Clue. (He loved it so much that when he came back home, he made his own out of paper, just to keep playing it.) His other favorite board game was Monopoly, but hardly anyone wanted to play it with him … until he visited the Montgomerys. Marshall and Clara were equally enthusiastic, happy to spend hours to play a single game of Monopoly.

After playing a board game, a traditional folk music session followed. Marshall was on his junior drum set, Clara strummed the acoustic guitar, Mr. Montgomery plucked the banjo, and Mrs. Montgomery played the fiddle. One problem: their keyboard sat untouched, since none of them learned how to play it yet.

"May I?" Zachary asked, exuberantly.

"You play the keyboard?" Mr. Montgomery, with his grizzled beard and homespun shirt, looked astonished. "Well, I'll be. You're in our band now! Here's the chord chart."

"Thanks." Taking the chart, he made his way to the keyboard and sat down. "'King Kong Kitchie Kitchie Ki-Me-O' by Chubby Parker? Hey, I know this one! It's quite catchy and upbeat."

"Sing along with us too, Zachary," Mrs. Montgomery encouraged.

"Oh, if you don't mind, I'll just play the keys and hear you guys sing. Um, I don't want to be held responsible for busting eardrums with my singing," he joked.

Playing with the family filled him with a sense of serenity, especially since the song was one he knew well. He had always wanted to jam with others, and they gave him that experience. The next night, it was "Little Liza Jane," a folk song he and his classmates sang all the time in second grade, followed by "Rocky Top" on the final night.

After nightfall, Zachary, Marshall, and Clara would spend time outside, play games with their flashlights, run through the wheat field, and look up at the thousands of stars glistening overhead.

Zachary had a blast each time he visited the Montgomerys throughout middle school. He had a sense of peace and friendship like never before. When he would think about seeing his friends again after the break, his heart would sink. It was *odd.* It was as if he were going back to a boring job. School didn't compare with the pure sense of joy and inclusion that spending time with Marshall and Clara brought him.

Many times in his life, he got asked, "Do you have any siblings?" His reply would be, "No, but I always wanted one or two, though." (The typical response was that it was both a blessing and a curse in countless ways.)

Perhaps this was because, at home all his life, he had mostly stayed indoors—drawing, writing, watching TV, you name it.

Sometimes he'd ride his bike around the block … alone.

Sometimes he'd play at the park … alone.

Sometimes he'd practice the piano or his juggling for hours on end … *alone.*

He did spend time with neighbors and family friends who were older, and he wouldn't trade those memories for anything. However, by the time Zachary was in middle school, a couple of them tried to encourage him by saying, "It's great that we spend time with each other, and I'm not saying I'm annoyed, but try to use some of your time hanging out with people your age. Likewise, once you get to high school, go to *all* the events: football games, dances, *everything.* Once you graduate, that's it forever. You'll never get those days back, so make the most of it."

Despite that, he still spent several hundred hours a year by himself in his one room.

Spending time with Marshall and Clara, who treated him like a best friend, was what he had been seeking all of his life. When it was almost time to see them again, Zachary would start counting the weeks, then the days, then the hours until he could go to their place again.

Besides Marshall and Clara, Thomas was Zachary's best friend, but as he got older, Thomas didn't always have time to spend with him, especially being in high school and having different interests, such as career research, romantic relationships, and which vehicle to choose.

After watching *The Straight Story* on the final night of their first visit with the Montgomerys, it took half an hour for them just to say goodbye. Neither family wanted the other to leave. Marshall literally pulled Zachary back into the house, wishing he could stay.

Alas, they had to depart. School was starting back up the next morning.

9

Forlorn

It was May 2009, just weeks before his final day at Canyon Mountain Middle School. (Zachary had already been asked to sign the Pledge of Allegiance at the graduation, something that Mr. Martinez taught him in sixth grade.) He, his special education teacher, and counselor were preparing for his final IEP meeting of middle school.

"You can sit over there toward the end of the table and make yourself comfortable, Zachary," said Mr. Dubois, the counselor, in the conference room. He was in the middle of pouring himself a cup of coffee and adding hazelnut creamer. "Your mother should be here momentarily."

"Okay, thank you," replied Zachary, walking to the chair.

"Need water or anything?" the counselor added.

"U-Uh, sure."

"Did you have a good Memorial Day off on Monday, Zach?" asked Mrs. Johansen, his special education teacher.

Zachary paused a few seconds. "I guess."

"Anything wrong, Zachary?" Mr. Dubois came and sat down in the seat across from him, stirring his coffee.

"I had to say goodbye to my best friends, Marshall and Clara. The family is moving to Kansas, um, over a thousand miles away. We were there from Saturday to Monday. Saturday was the moving sale; Sunday was the going-away party."

"It's always rough saying goodbye to friends, especially best friends," said Mrs. Johansen sympathetically. "What did you do on Monday with them? Surely, you made the most of it, didn't you?"

Zachary moped, trying to be soothed by the birds singing outside the window. "I wished I had enjoyed every millisecond of it."

"What happened?" asked Mr. Dubois.

"At the party, somebody gave them both, um, one of those new, uh, Apple iPods? I think? And someone else gave them the brand-new, uh, *Plants vs. Zombies* computer game. Well, they were utterly glued to those things and spent over half of our final day together playing with them. Even while jumping on the trampoline, they were searching for songs to listen to on their iPods. No offense, but the songs "Kids" by MGMT and Beyonce's

"Single Ladies" have been stuck in my head ever since. I tried talking to them, but their headphones were on, blasting music."

"Oh, I'm so sorry, Zach," said Mrs. Johansen.

"At least we watched a movie together each night. They let me choose first. Being a history buff, I picked *National Treasure 2: Book of Secrets*."

"Ah, your favorite," Mrs. Johansen said, smiling. "I remember you wouldn't stop talking about it after seeing it in the theaters a couple of years ago."

"Yes. The next night, the children picked *Nim's Island*, and the following afternoon, the parents chose *Kit Kittredge*, both of which came out last year."

"Those are enjoyable movies," said Mrs. Johansen. "I took my family to see those in the theaters."

Zachary maintained his composure and revealed, "I'm ashamed to admit this, but I teared up right after we left, saying, 'I'm going to miss them so much.'"

"Never be ashamed," the counselor said, consoling him. "Always talk it out. You have your mother. You have your teachers. You have me."

"Well—" Zachary could not believe he was entertaining the notion of divulging everything. He looked up at the clock and figured he had enough time, since the IEP didn't start for another ten minutes. "Remember, um, last year, when you two told me to go on outings more with my friends? And we set up goals for me to ask at least one friend two or three times a week?"

"Mm-hmm." His teacher and counselor nodded.

"Well, I completely failed. Just … failed. Last year, um, in seventh grade, I asked one of the Miller twins if he and his brother would like to go to the movies. 'Sure,' he said and gave me their number. I called Saturday morning. The father answers. Never heard of me. That was that. I called other friends many times, but I usually got answering machines, or they were busy practicing an instrument, or celebrating a family birthday. It never worked."

"I'm so sorry," both said apologetically.

"Thanks, um—" Zachary didn't know how to properly respond to their sympathy in a way that showed gratitude. "I just couldn't muster up the courage, um, to ask anyone if I could tag along, even though dozens of them would say hi to me, in or out of school. Friends would even stop and have a little conversation with me when they saw me in the neighborhood, but that was it. Often, they cheered me on as I practiced juggling by myself at the park; then they'd race off on their bikes. Once I was home, I was … usually home. One day, I was walking home after school. Uh, I started walking more as it's one of my favorite hobbies. Anyway, a student on his bike said with a smile, 'Hey, Zach! You know, if I could, I would be you for one day!' and then he rode off."

"Aww." Mrs. Johansen smiled.

"But honestly, those were the only types of interactions I ever got from my peers, despite making tons of friends here at Canyon Mountain and at Royal Rangers. Sure, there were some mean boys at Rangers, but, um, there were a couple who really made me feel alive and appreciated. Spending a few days with Marshall and Clara made me realize something. There is a difference between hanging out with peers all day *outside* school and spending time with them *inside* school. I know you said *I* was the one who needed to ask. My mom has been telling me the same thing for years, but that's easier said than done. And, embarrassed to admit it, the minuscule number of times I *was* asked, um, I made up an excuse. Then I kicked myself for 'chickening out.'"

Mr. Dubois and Mrs. Johansen both listened patiently and intently to Zachary, allowing him to speak everything that was in his heart and mind before responding.

"Um … uh … Now, I'll admit to you something I, um, never told anyone," Zachary announced, stumbling over his words. "In the past two years, I would watch a movie on Friday night, alone in the living room. Afterward, I would go upstairs to bed as usual, but when I would wake up the next morning, I'd get this sudden, forlorn sensation. It was *weird*! It was *bewildering*! It was *depressing*! I felt like I didn't have a friend in the world. I felt abandoned! I felt an unsettling presence of loneliness. I can't explain it any other way. I woke up replaying the scenes I watched the night before—how the characters watched out for each other, went on adventures together, stood up for each other in the face of bullying, and comforted each other when they were sad—"

Zachary banged the table with his fist, tears welling up in his eyes.

"And I've hardly experienced *any* of that!"

10

Zachary's Big Speech

"To my fellow classmates, hello. My name is Zachary Corwin."

The lecture hall, currently housing ninety students and three English teachers, fell silent. If a pin dropped outside the building during Zachary's pauses, everyone would surely hear it. The obnoxious buzzing of the room's fluorescent lights, however, bounced off the walls, but only Zachary seemed to notice it. Notwithstanding, he—in his three-piece suit accented by his favorite American flag necktie—was not going to let the sensory overload destroy the speech that he had rehearsed ten times over … each day … for a week. A few English classes at a time had to meet together for a few weeks until everyone gave a speech. It was part of a major project required for graduation.

"These last four years at Ironwood Peak High School taught me the biggest lessons in life, and not just academically. In the personality test that we all took for this, my results showed that I am more extraverted than introverted. That shocked me, since I am very shy.

"Ever since elementary school, I knew I was in special education, taking speech therapy, needing extra time on my exams, and struggling with reading and social skills. I know it must be surprising to hear this, but I found out that I'm autistic only a few years ago. As a freshman, I asked my mother if I had anything, and that's when she revealed to me that I got diagnosed with Autism Spectrum Disorder when I was six, in 2001.

"Astounded by such revelation, I began making sense of my entire life. I was like, *So* that's *why I had special education classes and speech therapy. So* that's *why people made fun of me. So* that's *why it was hard to comprehend everything I was told right away.* It was just the norm, if you will.

"By junior year, I was an advocate. First, I was a self-advocate. Then I started speaking on behalf of all autistic individuals. This year and last, I was a speaker, slash juggler, slash pianist, at a huge, annual benefit for Autism Awareness and Acceptance. I was telling my story about being autistic and how we're not different than anyone else. It's just how our minds operate. It made me feel valued to have those opportunities to help others, while entertaining them at the same time.

"So what else makes me feel like a human being with purpose? As a sophomore, I went back to my third-grade teacher, Mr. Collingsworth, at Washington Elementary, who is the only teacher I had who still works there to this day. He allowed me to visit about six times a year to juggle for his class. Toward the end of junior year, I got to juggle for the entire third grade, followed by the entire sixth grade at the last moment. The principal told me that I could do an all-school juggling assembly in September, sharing my story of what juggling has done in my life. Thus, I was going to do that this year. I was all excited and everything, but over summer break, the principal got promoted and started working in the district office. After meeting the new principal, I asked her if I could lead an assembly, but she ended up forgetting about me.

"All I ever wanted to do in life is bring joy in people and put smiles on their faces. That's partially what I got while juggling at Washington Elementary these past few years. Now, many of those students say hi to me around the neighborhood, and it makes me believe that there is a reason I'm alive.

"What was my biggest achievement during my high school years? Earlier this year, just under the wire, I submitted all of my paperwork, and I was formally awarded the Gold Medal of Achievement at Royal Rangers. This is equivalent in rank to the Eagle Scout Award, which my lifelong friend, Thomas, got a few years ago in the Boy Scouts. Procuring this prestigious honor looks great on résumés and applications, and it will give you an extra stripe on your arm in the United States military. I spent over ten years working for it, and it taught me leadership and survival skills—and not just surviving in the wilderness, but in life as well. I went on quite a few campouts and other adventures with my outpost, earning some merits, but most of them, I earned on my own, working on merit requirements after school or during my summer vacations.

"What was my biggest challenge in high school? It's impossible to choose between my social anxiety and science.

"To address science, I had grown up hating it with a passion, especially those science projects in elementary school. In middle school, I chose to take the arts (art, music, drama, and foreign languages) instead of the sciences. As high schoolers, we are required to take two years of science. I was optimistic as a freshman taking Earth Science, telling myself to focus, to study, and to ask Dr. Zhao, my teacher, all the questions I had.

"After getting an A in that class, I was enrolled in Honors Biology as a sophomore. By April or May that year, I was depressed. Ashamed to admit it, I felt envious of my classmates who seemed to understand everything, like cellular respiration, DNA replication, photosynthesis, et cetera. I felt ignorant and therefore, it was hard to enjoy life. I felt incomplete. However, I'm grateful for my mother, who found books for me at the local library. It was a series written for teachers, spanning from the kindergarten standards to the sixth-grade standards. This included English, math, science, and social studies.

"That's when everything seemed to change by junior year. Previously, I had dealt face-to-face with a ton of career choices: firefighting, musician, professional juggler, movie and television actor, animator, comedian, author, you name it. Since I have a big coin collection now, I thought about becoming a banker or somebody in finances. Since I memorized all the presidents (now their birthdays and death dates), *and no, I don't have a photographic memory*, I thought I'd get into politics … and maybe become president of the United States once I'm just past thirty-five. However, many of my older friends told me, 'Whatever you do, stay out of politics.'

"Then, to earn the Gold Medal of Achievement, I had to be First Aid and CPR certified. Taking EMT nearly set me on the path toward the medical field. Suddenly, I felt filled with a sense of purpose again, helping others medically, taking vital signs, communicating with patients, consoling their families, and working with a team of fellow medics. That motivated me to take Human Anatomy in eleventh grade, which taught me so much. Understanding science now somehow gave me a sense of worth … as strange as that might sound.

"However, remember those aforementioned books from the library? I spent dozens of hours not just teaching myself out of those books, but pretending to teach a class. I hardly told anyone this detail about me, but I would play school all the time since I was a boy, teaching my stuffed animals. Rest assured, by the time I reached the fourth grade, those stuffed animals just morphed into 'invisible people.' As some people in this lecture hall remembers, I had the surreal privilege of being 'Teacher for a Day' in sixth grade, after years of entering tickets and not getting chosen.

"Upon deep reflection, later in junior year, I solidified my career choice: becoming a middle school or high school teacher. The subject, you may ask? I returned to my first joy. *Mathematics*. At least I have some medical training to help people, just in case, and the building blocks of science, but I truly believe that teaching math is my passion. In fact, once I locked in my career choice, I was so excited that I told everyone … and I mean *everyone*. One of my former teachers asked if I knew what those feelings were called. 'No,' I replied. Smiling from ear to ear, he told me, 'That's passion!'

"Right then and there, I knew that being a math teacher is who I'm destined to be.

"However, I now want to reopen some of my previous points: I'm autistic. I'm shy. I assumed I was introverted. I felt like I lacked proper social skills. But recall what I just said within this entire speech. I desired to help people, teach people, encourage and motivate people, work with people, and entertain people, bringing them joy in life. In return, I'd get the feelings of worth, value, respect, and belonging, knowing that I'm being a big help while spending time with people. That's all I ever wanted in this entire life.

"Does that sound like an introvert to you? Does that sound like a person who's scared to death at other people?

"So when my personality test came back saying that I'm extraverted, I realized that that's who I am ... Okay, maybe 'ambiverted,' which *is* a word someone told me exists, blending both personalities, which seems perfect in my case.

"*All* that said, I'm *not* antisocial! I can't speak for every autistic, but in my observation, it seems that many of us desire to socialize. I decided to attend the youth group at the church down the street in ninth grade, where many of us go. After a year, I was sick and tired of standing against the wall—my eyes darting back and forth, my head spinning—and seeing all of my peers, some of whom are in this lecture hall, inviting themselves in conversations. I mean, you all were going up to a table of fellow high schoolers and entering their conversations like it was no big deal.

"As an aside, I'm not saying that there's anything wrong with that, but I was just standing there, feeling isolated, thinking, 'How do you do that?' For me to do that is like being that pastor who has to ask everyone for their tithes and offerings, fearing that people would assume he's a charlatan.

"I currently describe it as a 'Block of Nervousness,' which I define as an invisible force magnetically repelling me from another person.

"I feared that if I went up to people, even friends of mine, then the one time I do that, I'd get yelled at to go away. I'd get questioned about why I'm intruding on them. That happened a couple of times at this school within the past four years, just to say. Someone told me a few months ago that if people act like that toward me, then *they're* the ones with the problem. Not me.

"So here's what I resorted to do: I would arrive at the youth group early enough where I was the first person there. I pulled the chairs from four or five tables and set them around the couch area. Then I just sat there in the middle, waiting for people to show up and find a place to take a seat. And guess what? Since most of the chairs were around the couch, they came over and started having a conversation with me. It seemed to work.

"You see? Again, we're not necessarily antisocial, and we usually love conversations, but it really helps when other people start the conversation with us first. Alternatively, when I'm placed in a team by the leaders, that also helps. Every other month, the youth group had a big game night. Most of them were always a blast and gave me a sense of belonging and peace. I'm serious! That's because I worked with teammates who accepted me as a human being. We collaborated to try to win challenges, and when we lost, we just laughed about it. No competitiveness at all … well, mostly. The same thing occurred more often at Royal Rangers, since there were a ton of games to build teamwork and practice leadership.

"But once you strip all that away, I feel more than alone. I feel like I'm invisible. A nobody who ceased to exist, floating somewhere in the cosmos. It's *odd*! One time, I lost an FDR campaign button at Royal Rangers. I have a small collection of campaign buttons and would wear them everywhere to share one of my special interests: United States history. My mother drove me back to the church. By then, it was 2100 hours, and the only person there was the janitor. As I walked through the dark, empty corridors and rooms in search of the campaign button, I felt totally isolated. A forlorn sensation. Inside and outside that building was dark, and it felt lonely. It had been full of life just an hour earlier. I felt as though my nearest friend was a thousand miles away. I could still hear everyone and visualize what we did that evening.

"I felt like the sole survivor.

"Now please don't think I just stood there and didn't allow myself to practice social skills. In March 2012, as a junior, I confessed everything to one of my friends whom I met in third grade. I told him, 'I fear that I'd be invasively intrusive if I go up and talk to a person, just wanting to socialize with them.' 'No, don't think that at all,' he reassured me. He then invited me to hang out with him and his friend after school a few times. I felt very happy. I started to breathe again. He showed me the place on campus where a lot of the juniors would hang out during the break between periods.

"While at that spot, my peers would regularly come to me and ask me how my day was, how the test was like, if I did anything over the past weekend, or if I had plans for the upcoming weekend. Although I'm grateful for those conversations, they never left with us. In other words, once the bell rang, the conversation was over. After school, I never spent time with them. I would shyly ask my friends to consider hanging out with me over the weekend. They were either too busy or they never reached out afterward.

"Consequently, I had to force myself to jump out of my comfort zone. During our last spring break in April, I got out the directory.

"I rehearsed what I was going to ask.

"I pressed all ten numbers.

"My palms were sweating.

"I rehearsed once or twice more.

"I pressed the dial button on my phone.

"I felt more and more queasy after each rang. Once the ringing paused, my heart stopped! I knew the next sound I would hear would either be a human or an answering machine.

"And I either got parents or answering machines.

"What I just told you took anywhere from ten to thirty minutes … each. That day, I started calling around eleven in the morning and was still trying to reach friends by three in the afternoon. Admittingly, I gave up.

"One Sunday afternoon last month, I was about to hang out with a friend and play basketball, but at the last minute, he messaged me on Facebook, saying he had forgotten it was his sister's birthday and would have to postpone. To this day, he never got back to me. I was getting desperate, since high school graduation was just around the corner, after which it would be all over, and most of my friends would move away for college. Then they'd get busy with academics, work, and raising families.

"One of my friends on Facebook once posted, 'Ah, man! I don't have anyone to hang out with this weekend.' I thought, *If only you knew what it was like as a daily reality.* It had gotten to the point where the bitter pain of loneliness infiltrated my dreams. For years, I had recurring dreams in which I finally—*finally*—had plans to hang out with one of my friends from this school, but something always went wrong. They never showed up. A thunderstorm precluded their arrival. Or, sadly, I would simply awaken from the dream.

"As I returned to that hangout spot on campus toward the latter half of this school year, I honestly hid my emotions. As you all know, there's that dogwood tree right next to where we'd meet. I would look at that tree while waiting for someone to come over and talk with me, estimating that it must be a bit older than I am. That tree was there and alive all those years I was growing up. That means, all those years in elementary school being bullied and all these years in middle and high school, it was planted there. As I grew, it grew. I reflected back on those years of being frustrated and self-loathing.

"I never admitted this before, but there were days when I leaned against that tree and, even with my hands, started pushing against it. I knew I couldn't possibly make it snap, but I imagined that if it did, it would symbolize the end of my misery and loneliness.

"Fellow members of the Class of 2013, it is imperative for me to turn this around and acknowledge that I *did* make wonderful friends and unforgettable memories at this school. One of the proudest things I did was getting myself involved with the movie that this school produced in freshman year. Personally, I felt very proud of myself. *I* was the one who decided to try out for a part. *I* chose to meet one evening a week rehearsing for it. It gave me a sense of purpose, and I got to work with my friends outside of a school day.

"If I could go back in time and fix things, I'd do so in a heartbeat. I've never stopped dreaming about that for years, even back in my days at Washington Elementary. I've come to realize that I've wasted *thousands* of hours since elementary school dwelling on this very thing, and my autistic brain cannot help it sometimes. I need to come to terms with reality and move forward. This is what I'm currently working on.

"In the end, I believe I came out stronger and can now help younger people in life, so they don't make similar mistakes I did.

"What will my life be like after graduating high school next week? I will always be an advocate. A voice for the voiceless. I will always promote Autism and Disability Awareness, Acceptance, and Inclusion. I plan to attend the local junior college to get the core requirements completed and transfer to Tributary University thereafter. My major is mathematics with a minor in chemistry (long story short). After getting a Bachelor of Science in Mathematics, I plan to get a teaching certificate to teach math.

"I will never forget all my friends here, all my teachers, and everyone else who worked at this school. I will always remember the fun opportunities I got and the life lessons I learned, such as being a self-advocate. Also, I am grateful to know that there are friends who truly support me for who I am.

"From my heart, thank you."

Everyone in the lecture hall gave Zachary a standing ovation as he gave the deepest exhale of relief in his life.

11

Chronically Overlooked

College life wasn't exactly a hop, skip, and a jump for Zachary Corwin.

For starters, he later discovered that he was placed in courses below his level, essentially wasting his first semester. Furthermore, during his first couple of years in college, he was a part-time student, not because of a job, but because his high school special education teacher told him, "I recommend that you take two or three courses at a time so you won't be overwhelmed."

Nevertheless, attending college two days a week gave Zachary ample time for his volunteer work and projects. This included his biggest project to date: writing a novel about a boy who is autistic.

"Listen," he told himself after he opened a brand-new Word document, "I wrote a hundred books and movie scripts from elementary school to high school, which wasted my time because I never pursued any of them. If I'm going to take the time to start yet another writing project, I'm going to *finish* it this time and get it published!"

He never stopped typing. Day and night. He was completely immersed in it, pouring out stories and feelings like a deluge, interjecting what he would say to encourage his character, who lived vicariously through him. He hoped and believed that it could encourage and motivate millions of neurodivergent people worldwide, as well as educate neurotypical people who are ignorant.

After one month, he had completed his first draft. He printed out four copies and gave a few of them to close friends to critique.

As for his volunteerism, it came with assertiveness and stress.

"Hey, Pastor Joseph." Zachary went up to the senior youth leader, feeling more confident in life than he had a couple of years prior. It was the Sunday before his first day of college and two weeks before the school year began in his district. "Um, is there, by any chance, a need for a volunteer leader in the youth group?"

Zachary always loved it when he gave devotions over the years at the youth group, at Royal Rangers, and at FCA (Fellowship of Christian Athletes) at his school. He had read over half of the Bible so far and believed he was well equipped.

"Um … thank you, Zachary," Pastor Joseph, a youth leader only in his late twenties, said, trying to break it gently. "I think we're good for now, but if I need someone, I'll reach out, okay? Thanks, I gotta run."

Zachary smiled as the pastor rushed past him, but his heart sank right afterward. He saw the truth behind the pastor's smile. Perhaps they wanted qualified people with schooling. He wasn't sure.

"Hi," Zachary said, approaching his former children's pastor.

"Hi, Zachary. My, have you grown. You're like, what? Six-four?"

"And a half."

"Hey, like Lincoln, your favorite president," the children's pastor remarked, smiling. "How may I help you?"

"Uh, I know that a year ago, um, when I believed I was called to be a school teacher—"

"Excuse me, what? Please slow down," the children's pastor asked nicely, though not everyone was as nice.

"Sorry." Zachary took a deep breath, always annoyed with himself for constantly being asked to repeat what he said. However, this significantly helped him throughout his college years and beyond to slow down and enunciate better. "I was going to say I asked you a few times if I could volunteer in the children's ministry every other Sunday. Well, I haven't yet heard back after that time I observed you guys." Zachary was nervous, not wanting to give the impression that he was confronting someone.

"Oh yes! I'm so sorry, but I got busy," the children's pastor apologized, speaking at a hundred words per minute. "Let me get back to you on that sometime this week."

"Okay, thanks so much." Zachary beamed and walked away, quickly letting his smile fade. He refused to cling to false hopes like his past. This time, he guessed correctly. He never heard back from the children's pastor. He gave up, not willing to approach her for the fifth time about this.

A couple of Sundays later, he walked up to the church's worship leader who sometimes led worship in the youth group.

"Um, hey, Antonio," Zachary said, hating to interrupt the worship leader as he packed up his music equipment in the chancel of the sanctuary. The sanctuary was palatial, complete with a large ornate pipe organ and balcony seating.

"Hey, Zach. What's up?" Antonio, sporting a mid fade, only glanced at him for a fraction of a second before resuming putting his guitar away in his case.

"Uh … Oh, I'm doing good."

"No. I asked you, 'What's up?'" Antonio stared at him, wrapping up his guitar strap.

"Huh?" Zachary couldn't speak for three seconds, now fearing that he was looking like an incompetent human being, despite being friends with Antonio. "Mmm, the ceiling! That's what's up, ha-ha!"

Antonio laughed heartily. "That's a good one, Zach. You always know how to tell good jokes."

Zachary gave an awkward chuckle and, under the time pressure, started to ask him his question. "First, I want to thank you again for all the tips you and the pianist gave me the past few years, since I'm mostly self-taught on piano: the arpeggios you guys taught me and using the sustain pedal properly."

"Yeah, no problem, bud." Antonio continued packing up his equipment, never glancing once at him.

He wondered if Antonio was really listening. He kept hearing him whisper, "Okay, that XLR cable is there" and "Just one more direct box."

Seconds ticked by.

"I'm listening!" Antonio snapped, startling Zachary.

"Oh, uh, I know we've discussed me playing keys in the band … and I'd love to *volunteer* on Sundays and on Monday evenings for youth. Um, I rarely heard back from you. Can I please ask again if I could serve in this way?"

"Hmm, sure, but first, I want to hear you play more at youth."

"I know, but they only allowed me to play a couple of preludes three or four times in the past four years, and you were only there for one of those occasions," Zachary explained, just starting to become more assertive at this juncture in his life, though he didn't want to be misconstrued as combative.

"*Yes*, Zachary," Antonio said, his tone growing stern, "but I need to hear you play a few more times at youth. That must happen before I can trust that you're ready to handle a congregation of fifteen hundred."

"I understand." Zachary disappointingly nodded his head. He wasn't about to remind him that he had been asking for *three years* … and to *volunteer* too. He doesn't have to be paid to be included and feel accepted in life! He doesn't have to be paid to bless others and spread joy!

"Hey, ask Pastor Joseph about it," Antonio suggested, brainstorming an idea that might work. "When he gives you the dates to play for the youth again, let me know, and I'll be there."

Zachary stormed home and opened Facebook on his one laptop resting atop his one desk made of cherry wood. After messaging Pastor Joesph, he went down to warm up some lunch. Upon returning upstairs with his meal and taking a bite, he saw that he had a notification. His heart sank. He regretted having committed to a bite.

The notification was from Pastor Joseph which read:

"Greetings, Zachary. I appreciate you taking the time to write this message. I read every single word and understand how stuck you feel when you're not given opportunities to help others. You're awesome, and I admire how committed you are to serve our Lord. We need more young men like you with that fire in their hearts. However—"

Zachary's worst suspicion ended up being real.

"I always wanted to create an all-youth band. If one of the kids in the band can't make it, we'll offer the spot to another kid by asking, 'Who can play this instrument for us?' If no one raises their hand, then we'll offer it to one of the leaders. Only if none of the leaders can play, and no other kid shows up who can play, then I'll reach out to you. Keep trusting God as you go through roadblocks and detours. He has a plan for you. Best of luck, and enjoy your first semester of college! I'll be praying for you."

Zachary slammed his one laptop closed and was about to lose his lunch. Queasy, he threw his lunch in the refrigerator and went back upstairs. The room felt suffocating. He opened his window wider to let in fresh air. He turned on his lone fan to the most powerful setting and opened his mouth right in front of it, desperately trying to get a breath in. This wasn't the first time he had to do this. Not working, he went outside the house, pacing back and forth, still nauseous and breathless. (Similar experiences occurred when he listened to certain music that reminded him of his past, making it dawn on him how lonely he felt, even though some songs were upbeat and cheerful-sounding. One of many examples would be "The Triple R Song" from *The Adventures of Spin and Marty*.)

After forty-five long minutes of physical misery and questioning why he existed, he hobbled back upstairs and went to bed, slowly climbing in as his stomach was still hurting.

12

Finding His Home

"Well ... might there be time for me to come and juggle again soon?" Zachary shyly asked Mr. Collingsworth at Washington Elementary. Even though he asked the same thing multiple times per year, Zachary still found himself being nervous.

"Why, sure!" Mr. Collingsworth spoke boisterously as he opened up his planner. With his trademark cordial smile, he suggested, "Why don't you come next Friday at 2 o'clock?"

"Perfect!"

"I wrote it down in ink, so it's a done deal! So, how's life? How's college?"

"I just started my, uh, tenth semester at the community college."

"*Tenth*?!"

"Yeah, um, I've been taking two or three courses each semester. I've just completed all my core requirements last spring, and now I can focus on just math and chemistry."

"Dang! Are you working part-time? Is that why you can't take too many courses?"

"Um, no. My special ed teacher recommended it. She thought I'd get too overwhelmed if I were there full time."

"But Zachary, you're like, what? Twenty-one now? After nine previous semesters, did you ever consider that you might be ready to take on a full load, especially if you're not working? And first, how are you paying if you're not working?"

"Uh, I get financial aid. I did consider taking a fourth class. A year ago, during the Fall 2015 semester, I took fourteen units: Biology 100 and the lab, the first course in General Chemistry and the lab, and Precalculus. It was a doozy. I thought I'd die at the end ... I mean, *not literally*."

"Yeah, I know what you mean. Well, then, I do declare, you're wise to take your time."

"Yes, I concluded that it's more advantageous to take your time and focus on the material rather than rush through it and retain nothing, especially with my autistic brain."

"Have you ever considered working somewhere? Or are you using all your free time studying?"

"I volunteer at many other places, not just here. I'm still an usher at the church I grew up going to and had youth group at. I'm an Usher Captain now. I started when I was a freshman, and within two years, they promoted me. I've gained so much leadership experience as an usher captain, such as assigning ushers to rows for passing out bulletins and the offering plates. There are more duties as an usher captain, but suffice it to say, it has been giving me purpose for over six years. Plus, it's a camaraderie, being with fellow ushers, especially since I went to high school with most of them."

"I bet."

"Yeah, but it's interesting you ask now, because, um, I'm currently battling my heart over whether I should switch churches."

"Hmm, would you want to talk to me about that?"

"Sure. Um, it just feels good to get it off my chest. I was a master at holding things in, growing up."

"I'm all ears, Zachary."

"A few years ago, after graduating high school, I asked if I could volunteer for the youth ministry on Monday nights, or the children's ministries on Sunday mornings, because I believe I'm called to be a teacher. They either turned me down or got too busy for me. I also tried volunteering for the worship ministry." Zachary exhaled deeply as he knew he was about to replay hurtful thoughts. He proceeded to tell him all about what happened and how it was still not reconciled.

"Oh, my goodness. That was *horrible*," Mr. Collingsworth responded afterward.

"I felt so unwanted. So mistrusted or abused or whatever. Not taken seriously. Thought of as some joke. For crying out loud, I am equivalent to an Eagle Scout! This young youth pastor knew me for only two years, but he should've known me enough to trust me, right?"

Mr. Collingsworth nodded in sympathy and support.

"On top of that, I asked for *three* years (before he even came) if I could volunteer playing piano. Heck, I attended and even contributed to that youth group for *four years*. Everyone, including the leaders, appreciated me. How can he deny me from volunteering? He talks about 'roadblocks' and 'detours.' Doesn't he realize that *he's* the one setting them up against me?"

Mr. Collingsworth shook his head, trying to reason how this story could be true. He believed him, of course, but it sounded too dystopian.

"And being an usher captain even came with its pains. My favorite services to usher at are the church's concerts throughout the year. It's assigned seating, so I take people's tickets and lead them to their seat. I don't know about you and the majority of humanity, but I always loved it. There are fifteen-hundred seats, but I know where each one is, based on the alphanumeric code. I get praised each time by fellow ushers and superiors for having it memorized so well. However, I'm autistic. I'm slow at processing. I just need two or three seconds to look at the code, then visualize it in my mind. Well, one Sunday afternoon, I must've taken too long. One impatient gentleman yelled at me, saying, 'Are you sure you're a captain?!' and just walked off … He said that because we all wore name badges, and mine had 'Usher Captain' under my name."

"*Geez!* Just for waiting a few seconds? How crass. That grump must've woken up on the wrong side of the bed. 'Sorry, I didn't mean to ruffle your feathers,' I would've told him, sarcastically. I'm sure you were just trying your best."

"Um, I try to think about what good I've done for all the *other* people. I try to remember the hundreds of times people thanked me for my services as an usher. This was only *one* gentleman, and I've never seen him before or since."

"*That's* the right attitude, Zachary! Don't let one person ruin your mood; remember the thousands of people whose days you've brightened by now."

"I try so hard, but in the moment, I ashamedly forget all my friends, family, and the compliments. Then I feel guilty over not remember you guys."

"Well, *you* just need to work on that," Mr. Collingsworth said firmly, but with care in his voice.

"I intend to … Anyway, I *have* endeavored to get a part-time job. According to the church's website, there was an opening for an assistant teacher during the week for elementary school students."

"Right up your alley. Hey, you're always welcome to list me as a reference."

"Thank you. Yeah, so I filled out and submitted the application, waited, went to the church offices, and, *surprise*! They didn't receive it. I had to resubmit online all over again. I waited, called, and emailed. Finally, I got an email after two months saying that the position had already been filled."

Mr. Collingsworth's countenance of hope slowly faded into one of melancholy.

"And I was really starting to get assertive during the process, which is out of my comfort zone."

"Yeah, I know it is, but sometimes it's necessary, and it'll show employers that you really want the job. And if one door closes, another will open elsewhere."

"I've tried so hard to hang onto that hope, and I'm still hanging onto it, but it's as if I'm hanging onto a thread now."

"Look, Zachary, asking as a person who cares for you, is there anything you're doing now that's bringing you joy, besides volunteering in my classroom or ushering?"

"Yes! First, it brings me incredible joy to volunteer here. It not only evokes memories from when I was a student here, but it also allows me to be the person who brings joy and puts smiles on people's faces. I get to witness that when I juggle for your students every year. Last time I juggled for your class in early June, one of your students saw me as I walked toward the classroom door, and his entire face lit up in excitement. Once, I was signing in at the front office before coming in here, and one of your students asked me if I was going to juggle and do card tricks. When I said, 'Yes, I am," she started jumping and cheering. Whenever I walk into your classroom, all the students call out my name, happy to see me again. When I'm walking in my neighborhood, at the local park, or at a store or restaurant, a few of your students or former students would run up to me just to tell me hi or ask, 'How's your day?' This all makes me know that I'm alive and worth something."

"And let me tell you something, Zachary: whenever a student says hi to you, it means you've made a difference in their life. I've been a teacher for over thirty years. It's the most rewarding part of the job, knowing you've made a difference in the life of a student."

Zachary was very appreciative for Mr. Collingsworth's comment, but being autistic, he didn't know how to acknowledge it other than thanking him for it. Continuing, he said, "And you've given me some opportunity to actually teach students, like when I taught about George Washington or Abraham Lincoln, or taught different knots that I learned in Royal Rangers, or how a compass works. That's equally my joy, since I want to be a teacher too. Thank you very much."

"No problem. I'm sure you'll be an outstanding teacher one day. What grade?"

"Middle school, or maybe high school."

"Uh—" Mr. Collingsworth paused, scrambling to find the right words. "Mmm, maybe think about eleventh or twelfth grade. Middle schoolers? Most of them are kind at heart, but still."

Zachary nodded in acknowledgement, though in his mind, he was nearly set on teaching middle school. "So, um, you've asked me if there's anything that's bringing me joy during my college days. As I just told you, I've been rejected from every ministry I desired to serve in at my church, except the ushering ministry, *not* out of hatred or discrimination against me … Well, at least for the most part."

Mr. Collingsworth listened eagerly.

"But in September 2013, I actually went up to the senior commander at my Royal Rangers outpost. I asked him if I could volunteer as a commander, which is something I always wanted to do after getting the Gold Medal of Achievement."

"*And?!*" Mr. Collingsworth's voice got louder as he leaned forward.

"*He said yes!*" Zachary grinned with sheer thankfulness.

Mr. Collingsworth raised his arms high in the air and began to clap his hands loudly, so much so that the echo bounced around the classroom.

"So all this time within the past three years, I've been a commander on Friday evenings at my outpost."

"My, that's *outstanding*!" Mr. Collingsworth laughed in gratitude.

"Yeah, and I've kept myself very busy. I typically volunteer on most Saturdays and Sundays too. Whenever events happen outside a typical Friday evening, I'm usually there. For instance, I enjoy helping out on trips, teaching during all-day merit camps, or manning a booth after church to represent Rangers and answer questions. I've also participated in commander trainings to further my knowledge, skills, and preparedness. Thus far, I've taught the Astronomy, Rope Craft, and First Aid Skills merits on my own, leading instruction and various fun activities."

"Wow, you go! You're quite a busy beaver."

"My commanders call me tireless and sometimes, I wear them out."

"Has it always been positive."

"Well … um, mostly. On the very first day as a commander, I was wearing my awards vest. I'm decorated with seven medals, almost a hundred merit badges, and other pins and patches of achievement. Right before I entered the door, one of the ten-year-olds disparagingly called out, 'Overachiever.'"

"Geez!"

"The first comment I ever got as a commander … Forever cemented in the archives, I guess."

"You mustn't take it to heart."

"I tried not to. When I walked inside the big room, all the other boys marveled. One of the commanders said the boys treated me like a celebrity all night. Afterward, however, in my mind, I couldn't stop hearing that boy saying 'overachiever.'

"Back when I was in high school, I'd go overboard on my art projects. Teachers and students would think that a computer did them, but no, I drew them by hand. Well, one person called me an 'overachiever' then too. That's what happens: one word evokes another harsh memory and so on.

"That same boy later questioned why I'm so skinny. I-I just didn't know how to answer that. It's just who I am. Genetics, I guess.

"Moreover, in my second year as commander, I spent hours meticulously designing the outpost's dollar bills. Boys earn them for the store that we have twice a year. The night they entered circulation, one of the boys made a face and said, 'These are the new dollars? They look *horrible!*'"

Mr. Collingsworth's eyes widen out of pure shock as if he were the one who received the negative criticism.

"I stood speechless for a couple of seconds. Then I said, 'Well, *I* was the one who designed them.' He got very remorseful, and I could tell. He quickly said, 'Oh, I meant to say they look great.' Although I appreciated his attempt, I still knew his true opinions. Later that night, during my astronomy lesson, I was teaching about the lunar phrases. On the board, I accidentally drew the same one on both sides. Um, in other words, I drew the Waxing Crescent phase twice, instead of drawing a Waning Crescent. It was the first time a boy corrected me. I'm definitely not mad, and I want to be corrected, but he started to laugh, bragging that he 'corrected the teacher.'"

"It happens to *all* of us, Zachary, especially as we start out in teaching," Mr. Collingsworth said, sighing. "When you do your student teaching experience, I'm sure it'll happen to you again. That boy will probably forget it and only remember the *astronomical* things you taught him."

"Hmm, I think the only reason I used to get perturbed about mistakes is because I assumed everyone would remember it. I realized that not everyone has the memory I do. I remember back when I was one or two years old, and I retain hundreds of memories in vivid detail from preschool and kindergarten alone. Most people tell me that they can't remember what they ate for breakfast yesterday."

"Ha, I can't either."

"I mean, he might remember and tease me about it later, but I know I shouldn't worry that every mistake of mine will be remembered by every single person. I used to irrationally worry that one mistake would make the school newspaper in high school."

"Yeah, that probably *is* irrational as you said."

"However, later, the senior commander told me that one of those boys hated coming to Rangers, but when he was learning about astronomy from me, he was the most captivated and enjoyed coming."

"And I bet that just made you feel so good about yourself, didn't it?"

"Yes, it sure did. So, um, one Sunday morning, after a campout, we returned to the church. We were early enough, so we just stayed for the service. There, I ran into many people who volunteered at Royal Rangers, even if they only volunteered a couple of times a year. I ran into parents whom I've gotten to know over the past few years too. All the greeters were eager to meet me. I felt like I was at, well, *home*. They said they might need a piano player, but no guarantees. However, they said I could help with the cameras, direct, and work the sound board. That's what I've done at yet another church for a few years on Sunday afternoons, back in high school."

"I do declare, Zachary, you're a man of many talents. You certainly have an aptitude for math, history, survival, juggling, piano … and tech too?"

"Surprise. It was another thing that brought me joy, though I'm not too tech-savvy, ironically. The church said I could volunteer for their children's or youth ministries too. Since I volunteer at Royal Rangers, they already know I'm competent to serve and have passed my background check every year. And remember that I'm an EMT?"

"No!" Mr. Collingsworth laughed, completely amazed.

"Well, I never applied for a job as an EMT, and I'd have to get retrained anyway, but they said I could be a part of their medic team too."

Mr. Collingsworth was beaming from ear to ear, slowly shaking his head.

"And the whole time I'm there, I'll be wearing a name badge with a red cross on it. It just makes me feel so great and fulfilled knowing that I can jump in to help people and possibly save a life at a moment's notice."

"Well, it seems like you already made your decision."

"Yeah … Ha-ha, I guess so."

After saying goodbye, Zachary began to walk home. The day was pristine, without a cloud in the sky. A cool late-summer breeze wrapped around him perfectly along the journey.

Just then, outside the school gate, a spontaneous thought struck him like a brick. Typical. He quickly took out a folded piece of printer paper and a pen that he always carried with him. He jotted down a couple of ideas to add to the novel he was writing.

Within the past couple of years working on it, he carried scrap pieces of paper wherever he went—college, neighborhood walks, errands—and scribbled ideas for his storylines. Some days he went to college with a blank sheet of paper and came home with every square inch covered in handwriting. It became common to go over entire storylines during his cathartic walks or even brushing his teeth. He'd then rush to his laptop and type as fast as he could before forgetting the details.

After going to bed for the night, he'd keep getting ideas, but was too tired to get up and turn on his one laptop. Fearing he'd forget them by morning, he would tape a sheet of paper to the wall beside his one bed each night. He'd groggily reach over, grab a pen from his one nightstand, and blindly write down his ideas.

Continuing his walk home, he decided to take an amble through the park he had grown up going to, ever since he was a baby. Entering the park, he noticed two teenagers sitting on the bench in the middle of the path, roughly fifty yards away.

"Oh, *perfect!*," Zachary sarcastically told himself.

Ten yards closer, the two teenagers glanced over at Zachary, stared for a second, and then fixed their gazes elsewhere, continuing their colloquy.

Zachary continued walking as normal as he possibly could through all the sensory overload and social anxiety that spontaneously came upon him.

He was fifteen yards away when the teens looked over at him a second time, this time for three seconds before looking away again.

How am I supposed to look? Zachary questioned, now five yards away.

Both teenagers looked up at him for the third time and stared.

Just, *stared.*

Zachary walked past them, looking straight at the ground. He then couldn't remember if he maintained his neutral face or if his mouth was hanging open. Before he could process it, he heard the insolent, obnoxious laughter coming from those two teenagers. He kept walking, intimidated as if he were being followed, even though he knew he wasn't.

As the pathway curved in a quarter circle, Zachary took a quick, subtle glance at the bench, careful not to seem as if he were looking at them. Sure enough, both teens were still staring at him. He exited the park and continued down the street, accelerating slightly and looking over his shoulder every half a block.

13

Soliloquies

"What's that?!" Zachary called out, swinging around.

Pause.

"What're you laughing about?"

Pause.

"I heard you laughing. Is that the only pleasure you seek: laughing at a person just for walking by awkwardly, which is because I'm autistic, by the way? That doesn't mean I'm an alien, for crying out loud. I just don't know how to act when passing by people."

Pause.

"That's what I wanted to tell them, but I'm such a darn coward! I just don't know how to pass by people. If I say hi, they might get offended or laugh, but if I don't or look away, they might assume that I'm a callous person. If I look over at them, they might think I'm staring at them or mocking them in my mind."

"Has this happened a lot to you?"

"Well, sort of. I rarely told this to anyone, but when I was in kindergarten, a couple of my classmates yelled at me by the swing set one sunny day. I still remember it as if it happened last month. They were like, 'Go away Zachary! You're not playing with us! You're not our friend!' A few years later, some boy chucked a handball at my face. A few other students would call me the R-word over and over and over again. One student lied about me, and the teacher took his word over my truthful word. On top of all that, I had neighbors my age who would vote me out of their presence half the time. One day, I genuinely believed they were going to kill me, and my best friend saved my life."

"Had you ever tried to do anything about this?"

"Yeah, I suppose. I didn't always tell a teacher, and usually that didn't help. A lot of students began calling me a 'snitch' or 'tattletale' anyway. I was like, 'Why bother?' In fifth grade, during recess and lunch, I would volunteer my time helping the special education class for students who are severely disabled. I would try to talk with them, teach them the alphabet, and assist the teachers. I would push their wheelchairs when they went to the playground or to their bus after school."

"That was very kind of you."

"However, three fourth-graders would later come and help out. For whatever stupid reason, they always picked on me, laughed at me when I cried, and said, 'Hi, Zachy! You're weird!' I didn't get it. After two months of this abuse, I had a thought. One afternoon, when we weren't helping the class, I splashed water in my eyes and walked all the way over to them at the far baseball field. By then, my fake tears had dried.

"As soon as they saw me coming, they made stances like Roman centurions. As I got closer, two of them dropped to their knees, rushed at me on all fours, howled like wild animals, and clawed at my legs. I forced myself to twist this scene into a sadder one. I forced myself to think of the saddest thoughts on the planet. Finally, a real tear trickled from my eye, and at that point, the waterfall formed. I had no clue what I was expecting. Even in retrospect, if they laughed at me when I cried in the past, what on earth was I assuming then?

"But then a miracle happened. Unexpectedly, these three fourth-graders totally changed their demeanor. 'Oh, Zachary, what's wrong?' one asked. 'Are you okay?' asked another. Here they were, bullies for two months, and *now* they changed? I told them that I didn't have many friends and that they made me feel sad. From then on, they truly understood me and instantly became my best friends. They always said hi to me thereafter and enjoyed talking with me."

"Wow, what a story. Did bullying stay with you or did things change?"

"Uh … well, you know … bullying went down drastically as soon as I entered middle school. I still experienced difficult encounters from seventh to twelfth grade, not to mention loneliness from being shy. Overall, however, I made lots of friends and was known as 'the nicest' by everyone. One night after youth group, a friend I had known since middle school came up to me. Without saying a word, he gave me a quick hug and said, 'Zach, you're one of the nicest, friendliest people I know.' In fact, that evokes a memory from eighth grade, when another friend came up to me and said, 'Hey, I was having a bad day, but I saw you smiling just now, and it made me feel better, so keep smiling!'"

"That must've made you feel good."

"It sure did. It made me realize that in this world, my life has meaning and that I have a reason to live. However, upon graduating high school, that's when all you-know-what began to break loose. Before this recent incident at the park with those two teenagers, I had already been perturbed by people staring at me for no 'apparent' reason. I understand it's human nature to stare at others, but five or ten seconds? I try to tell myself, 'Maybe they're recognizing me from somewhere," or 'Are they mistaking me for someone they know?' But as soon as I see smirks or hear laughter, I can't arrive at any other conclusion; they must be assuming I'm an alien, weirdo, someone who doesn't know anything, or worse.

"Heck, I have a high school diploma, I'm an Eagle-Scout equivalent, part of the NREMT, a pianist, a juggler, and I'm going to college for mathematics and chemistry! And *all* of that gets overlooked within the first ten seconds someone sees me. I know I'm very tall and thin, and I may appear disoriented due to being autistic, even though I try to walk as normal as possible. One day, I was walking down the street when some passenger in a vehicle, half a block away, shouted to me, 'Hey, tall!' but disparagingly, judging by the tone of his voice."

"Well, Zachary, when was the first time you noticed people staring at you all the time?"

"Um, the first time I recall this phenomenon was when I was fourteen. We were driving home and pulled up to a red light. I was riding shotgun, and we were first at the intersection. It was a wide boulevard too. Two teenagers, about my age, were walking down the crosswalk. Something inside me told me that one of them would glance over at me at any second. As if ESP is real, that's *exactly* what happened. Uh, I'm *not* saying I have ESP; it just blurted out."

"I understand. Keep going."

"But this teenager, looking down as he walked, just shot his gaze up at me, eye-to-eye. *Not* at my mother, who had been driving. *Not* at anyone in any other car (by that time, a half dozen cars were already waiting at the red light). Just at me. It lasted a second or two. That was it. It probably wasn't the first time, and unequivocally not the last. And yes, *believe me*, I'm *positive* it was just a coincidence, but still.

"There were times since my graduation, three years ago, where people *do* stare me down. And after each time, seemingly out of compulsion, I just talk everything out like I'm talking here, dwelling over many past misadventures. I call them 'Soliloquies.'"

"Solilo-what?"

"Soliloquies."

"Soliloquies?"

"Yes."

"What the heck are soliloquies? I've never heard of that word."

"A soliloquy comes from Shakespeare. I learned it in twelfth-grade English when we read Hamlet. It's when the character gives a monologue. In the play, no one is hearing him, but the audience does. The character is releasing all of his innermost thoughts and emotions that are in his mind.

In turn, the audience gets deeper insight into the character than any of the other characters in the play.

"Hence, what I do is similar to that. It's so convoluted. I talk, sometimes for three or four hours at a time. And usually, it occurs in the dead of night too. It's perhaps an ode to discrimination, hurt, or loneliness, if you will."

"How do you conduct your soliloquies?"

"I usually pretend I'm talking to the people who discriminated against me, or to friends who still don't understand me enough and hurt me unwillingly, or to people who allow me to vent everything just to get it out. I usually retell many stories in my soliloquies, including those stories from elementary school. The only problem is, *nobody* else is around, and if I were to repeat it to anyone, it would take equal time to speak it. And usually, in real life, I forget the right order of events or the right words I want to say."

"Geez. Would you like to share with me some of your recent misadventures that you haven't gotten out yet?"

"I bet I only have time for a couple. I'll make them quick, and I thank you for listening and helping me out. You should probably consider becoming a therapist or counselor someday. One evening in March 2014, I was walking to my pastor's house for an ushers-appreciation party. On the way, I passed by a few children running around, probably four or five years old. They paused to stare at me walking by. I didn't mind that, since they were young, but across the street, there were over a dozen adults sitting on chairs in the driveway. My assumption was that everyone was there for a party. Anyway, in my peripheral vision, I noticed that one woman had twisted completely around in her chair, just giving me the death stare. Like, what did she think I'd do? I'm going to kidnap one of those children? That night, I couldn't help but have a soliloquy.

"A month later, my family was driving home from church. In the middle of the road were seven or eight middle schoolers on their bikes and skateboards, holding up traffic on both sides like it was no big deal. We came to a stop as they lazily moved out of the way for us and the other cars. Again, I was riding shotgun. I noticed one of the teenage boys glancing over at me, and then he wouldn't stop staring. I was wearing sunglasses facing straight ahead, but my eyes were actually on him, wondering why he was staring at *me*. It was ten seconds before we were past them, and he never stopped staring. At the same time, those teenagers were hollering and laughing at each other, but in the middle of it, I heard a cuss word and the R-word. Coincidence? I don't know. That fear of not knowing got to me. As soon as my mother parked the Toyota Corolla, I rushed inside the house, slammed my one bedroom door, and just processed everything, instigating a soliloquy for the next hour.

"Later that year, I took two children to the park. They were the son and daughter of a member at my old church. We were there for Thanksgiving, and I was asked to walk the children to the park and supervise them. They quickly met a new friend at the jungle gym. After playing tag, that friend came over and sat beside me on the bench, catching her breath. Being the neighborly person I am, always hoping to bring cheer and hope to humanity, I smiled and asked her, 'So, how has your Thanksgiving been?' Her face lit up as she burst out laughing at me and sprinted off. (I've since seen one or two other children sprinting like that when they saw me walking a half block away, and I still can't ascertain why. I was just out on a walk.)

"As I was walking the two children back, one of them said, 'That girl back there was very mean. She was calling you a weirdo.' In my mind, I was like, 'Thank you very much, I did *not* need to hear that.' It reminded me of a time, eleven months prior, when I was asked to serenade on the piano at a big Christmas party. As I was playing carols, a girl came over to watch me play, completely intrigued. I turned and smiled, but when she saw that, her countenance twisted in horror, and she ran away. *The heck?!* I jerked my head over to the music before I missed a beat and successfully recovered, but I felt hurt.

"I'm sure you guessed right: I had a few soliloquies for *days* after both those holiday events.

"I hated 2014 with a passion, to be honest, for these reasons. Heck, sometimes I almost lost my dinner. 'Why am I alive?' I'd question myself, nauseated.

"Moreover, I can't tell you how many people at the college—students, professors, and staff—stared at me with peculiar looks. All I did was walk from point A to point B. I'm certain that many of those incidents were complete overthinking on my part, especially after so many *real* occurrences of discrimination and bullying. They may have recognized me from somewhere, or maybe they mistook me for someone else. Or maybe they were looking at something past me. I don't know. I *do* know, though, beyond a shadow of a doubt, that there were nuanced occasions when people at the college *did* think I was clueless, but I won't talk about them now.

"Suffice it to say, I acknowledge that this blurred the line between genuine ableism and mere misunderstandings … and I *hate* it. Uh, ableism is the discrimination against disabled people, just to clarify. Um, anyway, thanks for listening."

Zachary began heading over to his one light switch. Two knocks thumped on the door, like a doctor arriving at the examination room, throwing him into a cold sweat.

The door creaked opened.

"Who on earth were you talking to?" Mrs. Corwin asked, groggily, her eyes half open.

"*What?* Did you hear me, um, or something?" Zachary's heart was pounding as if he'd just been caught shoplifting by the police.

"Well, I *thought* I heard you. Maybe I'm still dreaming."

"Mmm, maybe?" Zachary hated withholding the truth, but he would die if his mother ever heard him reveal those stories, fearing she'd get alarmed again like that night in sixth grade. Notwithstanding, he knew that keeping them to himself was unhealthy. In fact, he wondered why he withheld these stories from most people, not just his family.

"All right, but what're you doing up so late? It's 2 o'clock in the morning, and we're leaving for Thomas' wedding at 9 a.m. sharp."

"Um, I guess I couldn't rest."

"Just get some sleep, Zachary! That'll help clear your mind." Mrs. Corwin, almost asleep again, turned off his light and hobbled out the door.

Zachary sighed, saying under his breath, "Okay, good night."

With his head down, he traipsed the path to his lone bed, illuminated by the moon's pale light streaming through the window.

He glanced at the time on his one grandfather clock, which he had proudly bought for himself in 2012, unable to believe that yet another soliloquy had struck. He felt terrible about how long this one lasted. As soon as he pulled the covers over himself, his mind laughed at him, reminding him that he had wasted so much time—*again*—thereby preventing him from making much progress on his novel. He felt stressed, knowing he would inevitably be like a zombie during the wedding due to sleep deprivation.

Once again, he felt completely alone and broken.

14

Chasing Acceptance

"Hey, what's with the uniform, brother?" asked a stranger at a bookstore.

"Oh, uh, Royal Rangers?"

"What'd you say? Something rangers?"

"*Royal Rangers*," Zachary enunciated.

"Ah, neat. Never heard of it. Is it British?"

"No, sir. It started in Missouri."

"Oh. So, is it like the Boy Scouts?"

"Yes. It's like a faith-based version of it."

"I'll be darned! Are you going for Eagle, or whatever the equivalent is?"

"I already earned it, and it's the Gold Medal of Achievement." Zachary pointed it out on his awards vest.

"Well, congratulations, young man!"

"Thank you."

"Hey, Zachary, I'm ready to check out." Mrs. Corwin walked up to them.

"Okay, Mom."

"Is this your son," asked the man whom Zachary was speaking with.

"Yes," replied Mrs. Corwin.

"Well, you have an awesome son. Well-mannered and highly accomplished."

"Thank you, sir," Zachary and his mother said, smiling.

"No worries. Take it easy," said the man as he left.

"That was nice," Mrs. Corwin whispered.

Zachary, maintaining a smile, felt very alive. In his right hand was a basket filled with notebooks, pencils, and other stationery. In his left, he carried a couple of textbooks for his upcoming Spring 2017 semester.

"That reminds me of a time when you were in high school, Zachary. After you checked out your groceries at our Albertsons, the clerk complimented you, calling you a 'very polite gentleman.'"

Suddenly, as they were in line to check out, Zachary was hammered with guilt. Right before going to the bookstore, he had stopped by the local coin shop he frequented most Saturdays. He was in the midst of filling his nickel, dime, and quarter collections. He had already completed the Wheat cents (barring the 1909-S VDB, '14-D, and '22 plain) and the PDSS Statehood Quarter collection. Upon entering the doors of the shop, another regular customer looked at Zachary in his awards vest. "Where'd you win that?!" he questioned, giving him a peculiar look.

"I didn't win it. I *earned* it." Zachary, feeling offended, tried to answer nicely and calmly.

The older gentleman closed his mouth and looked away, not saying a word. To Zachary, that suggested the gentleman might not have believed him, much less all the knowledge and skills he had. For a year at this point, that man hadn't seemed too fond of Zachary as a person anyway.

He continuously dwelled on it for the next hour and a half until that kind stranger walked up to him in the bookstore. He ran through hypothetical conversations (which had overall grown more frequent since he began high school) about what he'd say if he confronted him, asking why he seemed to view him as a clown.

Zachary volunteered at Royal Rangers on Saturday mornings, but it wasn't every Saturday that they had something. This was one of those Saturdays, but Zachary wore his uniform anyway. "Hey," he told himself, reasoning in his mind, "I want every boy to benefit from the program which I most benefitted from, and I'm technically promoting it, right?"

From his heart, he genuinely wanted every outpost to overflow with members. At the same time, wearing his awards vest was his way of showing society that he wasn't an incompetent freak. Of course, Zachary knew that 80-90% of everyone he came across didn't view him as such. It was just the 10-20% of people who discriminated against him or seemed uncaring of his achievements.

That's what messed with his mind.

As he wrote parallel stories from his life in his novel, he wondered how his true friends would feel, particularly events where his character was bullied. In his frequent neighborhood walks, he would occasionally run into friends, young and old. The conversations, despite how long or short they lasted, always brightened his day.

Then guilt hits!

"You didn't trust me?" a friend might tell Zachary. "I'm your friend! Did you forget about me? Why the double hockey-sticks did you get all depressed because one person teased you?"

He always worried about that.

Of course, he appreciated every friendship. He just wished that everyone would understand that he needed to *talk things out.* Soliloquies helped a little, but they're short-lived. He could have a soliloquy about the same event a hundred times over.

Wearing his awards vest in public without an apparent reason was daunting, however. He didn't really have an excuse other than promoting Royal Rangers, which was true per se, but he was also seeking acceptance in society.

He tried a similar tactic back in 2014, when he'd wear the stethoscope he got from his EMT course around his neck everywhere (college, restaurants, stores, or just on neighborhood walks). He figured that being a medic, albeit just an EMT, required a ton of knowledge and skill—something an alien life form wouldn't have (or whatever these ableists thought Zachary was, staring and laughing at him at first sight). Otherwise, he assumed that no one would believe his qualifications if he ever encountered a real-life medical situation out in public, even if he showed them the NREMT card he always carried in his wallet.

The caveat of wearing a stethoscope is that people might assume he was someone with a higher scope of practice than an EMT, like a nurse or a doctor. Grandpa Corwin put an end to that by making him realize how strange he must appear to the average person. "Most people would surely think you're crazy, especially since you're not wearing scrubs or a white doctor's coat," he explained. At first, Zachary was disappointed, but he eventually realized it was probably best.

For the Rangers uniform, people might mistake him for being in the military, especially when he wasn't wearing the awards vest, but just the utility uniform that held military-like ribbons above his left pocket. When that happened, he quickly explained the difference and refused to accept their praise. The last thing he wanted was to inadvertently overstep his own purview. Through it all, honesty was his number-one priority.

Overall, he felt that wearing his Rangers uniform was better, especially since he usually received positive reactions and was rarely mistaken for someone he wasn't. Sometimes he could tell people he was heading to a meeting or coming from one; other times he had to admit he was simply promoting it. But surely, he wasn't going to reveal the other reason: he simply wanted everyone's acceptance.

15

Burnout and Grief

Zachary began his first day of Calculus 3 on January 30, 2017, and on February 2, he dropped it immediately after the class adjourned. The professor, Dr. Davidson, was not making any sense to his brain, though many other students seemed to understand his teaching style. Worn out at this part of his life, Zachary had just entered his eleventh semester at a junior college. This marked the beginning of a series of 2017 heartaches.

"Did you drop? I haven't seen you there the past couple of classes," one of Zachary's good friends, Hassan, asked. He was a physics major who ran into Zachary in many of his math and chemistry courses over the years.

"Uh … mmm—" Zachary never wanted to admit it, but he had no choice. "I knew I had to tell you eventually, but I got lost with Dr. Davidson. Tutors didn't help. I instantly fell behind."

"Two days?"

"Four lecture hours. A lot of new imperative material was covered within that time. Taking physics concurrently (and studying for *that*) took away my ability to prioritize Calc 3. I knew Dr. Davidson was too busy after class. I couldn't just ask him to go over four or five topics. Plus, his only office hours conflicted with my availability. Again, I tried getting tutored. *Two* tutors, in fact."

"Didn't you say you ordered and pre-read your textbooks ahead of time?"

Zachary stared at him, nodding his head a little but unable to find the right words to explain. Often, he pre-reads two or three chapters of his math or science textbooks, but then falls behind one month in, oddly enough. Part of it was his math courses, as he'd spend five or six hours doing homework, not because it was always hard, but because he immersed himself in it. He loved math insofar as taking his time and doing extra problems. Another part of it was because he wanted to understand every nook and cranny of science. He'd watch five or ten YouTube videos on the same concept until it solidified in his brain. Then, he'd talk it out, pretending to teach it to someone.

Preparing for this semester, however, he couldn't motivate himself to begin pre-studying until one week before school began. He only got half of a chapter read from his physics textbook by day one of class.

"Well, okay," Hassan responded, sounding a little disappointed. "If the class started out that hard for you, it may have been a good thing you dropped. That way, you could focus on your other courses. What else are you taking now?"

Feeling under pressure, he replied, "Um, Calculus-Based Physics: the first course, which is mechanics. And, uh, you know, I have to look at my schedule for the exact course titles. Um, so, how *is* Dr. Davidson out of curiosity? I only survived two of his lectures."

"He's really good," Hassan started.

Phew. Zachary subtly exhaled. He also didn't want to admit that he started with only two classes that semester, now having one. *What would he have thought of me, or anyone else for that matter?*

"Dr. Davidson actually makes you understand it, which is why, at first, his manner of teaching seemed so foreign."

"Well, I'm thankful he's helping everyone else, but to me, I couldn't make sense of his teaching strategies."

"That's understandable. Hey, I've been meaning to ask you for over a year now, but when we had the same classes, you weren't there during exams. Obviously, you took them because you passed the courses, but, where?"

"Oh yes, um, I'm part of the Disability Services on campus. I receive test-taking accommodations, including extra time and a quieter place."

"*Huh.*" Hassan shook his head with a peculiar look. "For some reason, I can't see you as disabled."

"Oh, i-it's because I'm autistic." Zachary was worried that he was stuttering.

"Hmm, I wouldn't have known unless you told me."

"I've actually gotten that a few times since high school."

"That explains how you got 100% on all four algebra exams *and* the final a couple of years back. Is your brain photographic or like Rain Man?"

"Uh, no. That's a common misconception. Not all of us are prodigies. We all struggle, some more than others. Some autistics experience more significant challenges. I have a granduncle, Elmer, who can't speak and lives in an institution in Boise."

"Sorry to hear that."

"Um, well, it's nothing to say sorry for, necessarily. It's not a disease. Although my granduncle is nonverbal, he is a remarkable artist. His works had been published in magazines across the country over the years. Just remember, once you've met one autistic person, it doesn't mean that you've met *all* autistic people; you've only met that one."

"Well, thanks so much for the education. I know a bit more about autism now. I'll plan to ask you questions if I get any in the future." Hassan looked at his watch. "Hey, I gotta get to class. Catch you later."

Zachary said goodbye and walked into his physics classroom.

"What's with the getup?" one of his classmates asked.

"Oh, it's Royal Rangers. It's every Friday, so I have a meeting tonight."

The professor, Dr. Friedman, entered through the side door, walking past the front row. Every day, he wore a different yarmulke.

Since middle school, Zachary had always chosen to sit up front to wordlessly show everyone that he enjoyed school and took it seriously, hoping to subliminally motivate others to adopt such a mindset (if they hadn't already).

Passing him, Dr. Friedman turned around and met Zachary's eyes for a couple of seconds. Zachary noticed the professor's big, goofy smirk etched on his face, as if forcing himself not to laugh. He had seen that look before. From then on, he questioned whether the professor thought he was a joke. He seemed to already view him as a lazy student seeking special help on his exams, even though he was simply asking for details to prepare properly.

Earlier, in the previous semester, Zachary stood in the hallway during a break. Reading one of the displayed science posters, he noticed a figure in his peripheral vision. He turned briefly and caught a glimpse of Dr. Friedman for a second and a half. As the professor walked into his office, he stared at Zachary, his smirk widening. The professor's eccentric gaze lingered on him, almost as if asking, "Who let this mental patient escape and saunter onto my campus?"

Since Zachary was twenty-one years old at the time, he knew better than to conclude that as irrefutable fact. He tried giving Dr. Friedman the benefit of the doubt.

It was the seventh day of physics class, but the first time Zachary had worn his Royal Rangers uniform all semester. He felt like he had to, as the continuous stares across campus for no apparent reason were still daunting. Being a Friday, he felt he had a genuine excuse, though it still felt weird wearing it in front of people like Hassan, who accepted him for who he was. He also had a bizarre feeling of imposter syndrome, even though he genuinely knew various survival skills.

A couple of Sundays after this, Zachary was scrolling through Facebook. His black paisley tie, which he wore at church that morning, hung casually loose underneath the unbuttoned top of his purple dress shirt.

Lately, many of his friends were posting about their latest achievements: a bachelor's here, a huge job promotion there.

On top of that, he couldn't help but notice that all of his friends would post a picture and get over a hundred likes each time. Half of the people who liked and commented were mutual friends, but 98% of his own posts hardly got any reaction. It's important to note that he was not one of those young people who believed their value came from a social media following or that he deserved more likes than anyone else. He simply felt ignored and consequently hurt, especially when sharing noteworthy updates about his life, acts of service he did for other people, or words of encouragement meant to motivate others.

Facebook seemed to be the litmus test of true friendships and personality. Over the years, he sent friend requests to people he knew from school and church, but they never accepted them. However, he noticed that they kept posting or commenting, so they weren't inactive accounts. If people were to unfriend him, that would potentially say something about them. Unfortunately, that happened several times too, making him question what he had done wrong.

Knock, knock.

Just as Zachary finished checking his minimal notifications and finally opened his physics textbook to study, someone came to the house. He heard his mother approaching their front door and opening it.

"What … *What?!*" Mrs. Corwin wailed.

Zachary wasted no time. He sprinted out of his room and down the stairs, skipping steps along the way. He rushed through the threshold to find his mother and grandfather standing on the veranda.

"I'm just beside myself." Grandpa Corwin collapsed onto the outdoor bench, took off his homburg hat and squeezed it tightly, pressing it to his chest. Mrs. Corwin sat down next to him with an arm around his shoulder, visibly holding back tears. It was one of the few times in Zachary's life that he saw his strong, Navy-veteran grandfather break down in tears.

"Come sit down here," Mrs. Corwin softly told Zachary.

Shakily, Zachary did so, wondering if this was a nightmare.

"You can tell him," said Grandpa Corwin, rubbing his eyes.

"Zachary, your grandfather's brother, Elmer, just passed away."

"Oh." Zachary, imbued with sympathy, didn't know what to say. He slowly stood up, watching his grandfather sob and wiping away his tears with his handkerchief. Mrs. Corwin embraced him, barely holding back tears herself, for she loved her uncle too.

"Mom … U-u-uh, I have to go to the church real quick," Zachary whispered.

"You go ahead."

Zachary walked off the veranda, down the front walkway, and onto the sidewalk. Once he was out of sight from his family, he picked up the pace, eventually sprinting for a couple of blocks. He arrived at the church where he currently attends and meets for Royal Rangers. There were still congregants talking with each other and custodians cleaning up the premises.

"Are you okay, Zachary?" one of the children's pastors called out, noticing him speedwalking and limping.

He turned to her, who stood a few yards away, but he couldn't speak. Catching his breath, he tried to convey to her that something wasn't right. Wiping the sweat from his forehead and looking lost, Zachary hobbled into the sanctuary.

"Wait! Tell me what's going on," the children's pastor said, following him inside.

Zachary sank to the floor in front of the altar, unknowing what he was doing, how to react, or how to impart what happened.

"Zachary, what's wrong?" Pastor Nguyen, the senior pastor, quickly came over, knelt beside him, and placed his hand on his shoulder.

"Let us help you." The children's pastor arrived a second later, along with a few other worried friends of Zachary.

At that point, tears began to rain down Zachary's cheeks as he not only felt mournful but embarrassed too. He didn't know how to address it, but he eventually conveyed that his granduncle passed away.

"Just seeing my mother, and especially my grandfather, break down the way they did got to me. I'm twenty-one, and witnessing my grandfather's generation dying off nowadays makes me anxious. I have numerous friends and family who are his age, and there will come a day when most of them aren't living anymore. And I'm scared to death that that day is getting sooner and sooner. All of us aren't getting any younger.

"Additionally, I met my granduncle once before. He seemed to be full of joy, even though he hardly spoke at all. I'll never forget how much he loved listening to the classic song, "By the Light of the Silvery Moon." I think of him every time I hear it … Um, sometimes, he had hurt himself by accident. He gave me a deeper understanding about those who are severely autistic. It helped me know how to approach and communicate with them. For years, I was plagued by sad thoughts about him and people like him. I worried that he would get himself killed, like somehow walking out of the institution, unaware of the dangers, and falling off a ladder or getting hit by a car.

"Their final phone conversation took place during dinner last week. The institution called. Elmer had just been placed under hospice care. I'll never forget my grandpa telling him, 'There's never a day that goes by where I don't think about you, brother.'"

After being consoled by pastors and friends and praying together, Zachary walked back home. He tried to eat a little that evening but was too sad to.

There was another, less significant reason for his sadness that he withheld from his friends at church that day. Zachary grew up old school with a traditional American heritage. He grew up with shows like *I Love Lucy*, *Leave it to Beaver*, *The Adventures of Spin and Marty*, and *The Andy Griffith Show*. He tried speaking in the vernacular and mannerisms of people from the nineteenth and mid-twentieth centuries. He was enamored with classic music, such as those from the Big Band era, often listening to Glenn Miller's "In the Mood" or Tex Beneke's "Chattanooga Choo Choo." He was raised with hymns and classic patriotic songs, like "Holy, Holy, Holy" and "This Land Is Your Land." Additionally, in high school, he bought himself a collection of fountain pens and a typewriter, using them to write letters or complete parts of his schoolwork. However, he never managed to find a rotary or candlestick telephone to add to his vintage menagerie.

Most of his friends loved all the contemporary stuff. During his time as an usher, transitioning from the traditional service to the contemporary one felt like culture shock. He was the only one dressed in a suit. Thus, as more and more people from the generation he felt he belonged to died, he felt that a part of him was dying too.

On top of this, he couldn't concentrate on studying whatsoever. He began to get stressed out. Already, he had fallen behind in his studies for the physics class. He assumed he wouldn't be able to concentrate when he got back to class on Wednesday due to his granduncle's passing. He already felt socially intimidated by the professor and other people on campus.

For the next two days, he tried his hardest to catch up. It took him a while to organize everything around him, which he felt was required to fully concentrate on his studies. Once he started, his mind would freeze, causing him to work slowly. Again, he would read a section, watch a few YouTube videos to solidify the understanding, read through it again, and move on.

By Wednesday morning, he had finished studying chapter one. Even though he had barely accomplished that, Dr. Friedman was going to begin chapter two that day. Ideally, Zachary wanted to have the entire chapter read before starting a new one.

He knew he couldn't entertain the self-deception any longer. He knew he was too far behind and needed to review prerequisite knowledge. He knew that his intruding thoughts would further cause delay. His mind was a palatial palace for stress and anxiety.

Periodically, he kept getting hammered with discrimination by people in the neighborhood or at stores: condescending stares, mocking laughter, and degrading comments.

"*Don't* ask him questions," a young-looking father once whispered loudly to his seven-year-old daughter.

Zachary, pushing his Target shopping cart, looked up to see the crossed-armed father and his wide-eyed daughter staring at him from a hundred feet away. Feeling despondent over it, he was reminded of a time during middle school at the public library. He had sat down at one of the computers next to a boy. After opening up Internet Explorer, he heard loud footsteps coming from behind. Swinging over, he saw a man charging at him. Pointing to the computer on the other side of the table (without ceasing to walk), the man commanded him in a thunderous voice, "Can you please move to that computer over there?"

Without defending his rightful place, since no one else was using that computer to begin with, Zachary said, "Okay, um, I'll just, uh, use the one on the other side of the boy."

"*No!* I told you to move over there," the man yelled, pointing, his face red with anger. If cartoons were real, steam would be coming out of his ears.

Intimidated and shaking, Zachary complied with a "Yes, sir," quickly moving to the far computer. The room was otherwise empty—just the boy, the man, and a librarian putting away books according to the Dewey Decimal System, indifferent to what was going on.

The irate man, who turned out to be the boy's father, sat down and began browsing the web.

Still shaking and regretting that he ate his lunch beforehand, Zachary overheard that boy defending him in a whisper, saying that there was nothing wrong with him being there, but his father quieted him down.

Upon that flashback, Zachary got reminded of a community event in October 2015, where he passed by a family and heard a small boy chatter about something. "Yeah, he's a weirdo," said a gentleman. Zachary swung around to see the man smirking at him, eye-to-eye.

He then remembered a recent Saturday when he decided to stop by a yard sale. The elderly gentleman hosting the sale did not seem to care about his prospective customers. "Thank God that woman left," Zachary overheard him say to someone else. The man was selling hundreds of vintage items, large and small, but his asking prices were too high for Zachary. Whenever he asked about an item, the man seemed either listless or annoyed as he explained. While suffering decision paralysis a half dozen times, Zachary felt uncomfortable; the irritated man kept urging him to buy something. Pretty soon, the man grew more belligerent, causing Zachary to leave. Since then, he had wondered if the man gossiped about him like he had about that woman.

One memory led to another, which led to another. By the time he finished up his last memory, it was 11 o'clock in the morning. His physics class started at noon, and he had not even begun chapter two.

"Oh, *darn* it!!" Zachary screamed at himself, realizing that he wasted two hours with another soliloquy. *I can't do this! I can't! I also need to get my book published and* now*!*

He made up his mind. He hurried to the college and stood outside Dr. Friedman's office, hearing music from the radio playing behind the professor's closed door. He had his fist up, about to knock, but he froze. He scripted what he wanted to say for the fifth time but remained an iceberg.

The seconds ticked by. The lack of air conditioning in the building weighed heavily on Zachary, combined with his stress which had already made his breathing labored enough.

"Need to talk to me, Zach?" Dr. Friedman, looking busy and carrying a stack of packets, walked around the corner, breaking the relative silence of the second floor, barring the radio. He was just returning from the copy center.

Startled out of his mind, Zachary maintained his composure on the outside. "Uh, yes, Dr. Friedman."

"All right. Let's sit down in my office," the professor said, unlocking his door. "We have twenty minutes before needing to be in class."

Zachary took a seat in the cramped, windowless office while Katy Perry sang "Roar" on the radio. He marveled at all the math and physics textbooks on the professor's tall bookshelf.

"How can I help you today, Zach?" the professor asked as he dropped the packets on his desk, turned off the radio, and sat down, adjusting his yarmulke.

"Dr. Friedman, um, I've done a lot of thinking, debating the pros and cons. As hard as it may be to hear, especially for me, because it feels like I failed, I just can't keep up. I can't concentrate. It's been exacerbated by my grandfather's brother's demise this past Sunday."

"Oh, I'm sorry to hear that."

"Thanks, um … I feel like I'm in some type of burnout, like an *academic* burnout, or whatever. Although I started attending this two-year college a few years ago with a declared major and a solidified career choice, I'm, uh, just taking an unusually long time here. I felt like I needed to be under full time so that I wouldn't get overwhelmed. When I was here full time in the Fall 2015 semester, I thought I'd die, barely passing my courses; I retained far less than I would have if I had taken fewer classes. I spent all winter break recuperating instead of studying what I missed or getting ahead for the upcoming semester. Plus, I have, um, a special writing project I'm doing."

"And what do you want to do with your life, Zach?"

"Become a math teacher. I placed more focus and time on my math courses because I loved them so much: algebra, trigonometry, precalculus, and calculus. However, I *do* have an interest in science. I'm minoring in chemistry, so I'd like to know everything about chemistry and physics too. I just get behind. It feels like … *paralysis*. I still need to transfer to a university for a bachelor's degree and *that's* going to take at least two years. I thought I might as well go for my associate's in mathematics here, on top of the IGETC certification."

Zachary looked drained after unloading all of that.

Dr. Friedman took a deep breath. "Okay, look, Zach. I can tell that you really want to be a teacher and have a strong propensity for education. That's very admirable of you. We need teachers, but let me impart some wisdom to you as I've been teaching here for over four decades. *We* don't know everything, even us with doctorate degrees. I'm an expert in my field, but that doesn't mean I know everything. *I* still learn new things every day. Also, I can't retain everything. Each semester, I still have to give myself a crash course on some of the more challenging subtopics before teaching each chapter."

Zachary nodded with his eyes glued to his professor. He always held scientists and mathematicians in high esteem, typically envying their knowledge and experience.

"Now, I like you as a student. I think you're doing well; you're very polite. And I've noticed you're very conscientious. Plus, not everyone has an academic or career plan figured out this soon."

Zachary couldn't believe what he was hearing.

"But, to have the best chance for success as a student, your mind must be alert. You need to be confident in your understanding of the prerequisite knowledge. It sounds like you have a lot to review for my class alone. If that's the case, you'll have to buckle down. Chapter two is covered today and Friday. One- and two-dimensional kinematics will make up the bulk of it. Next week, we're moving on to chapters three and four, which will cover Newtonian forces and the dynamics of uniform circular motion, respectively. As you may have noticed, those chapters are quite dense." Dr.

Friedman gave a sympathetic, tight-lipped smile. "That's being honest. The decision is yours, but if I were you … hmmm, if I were you, I-I would take the semester off to recuperate. Then, after a couple of months, make a plan, divide your time, and hit those books."

Zachary exhaled deeply. After a few seconds of pondering, he said, "Dr. Friedman, thank you. I appreciate your advice. Um, I think that's the best thing for my mind and my future. I'd rather learn things and remember them than barely get by just for a degree. As far as what you said about learning in the process, my eleventh-grade U.S. History teacher allowed me to teach his son about Theodore Roosevelt because he knew I had a passion to teach. While preparing for it, I learned in the process. He told me that I learned one of the most valuable lessons about teaching."

"Absolutely." Dr. Friedman smiled. "We're always learning in the process. That was imperative advice from your teacher. Sounds like he's a great one."

"Yeah, um, he *was* a great one. He passed away of cancer a couple of years ago. I'm still sad over it."

"I'm sorry to hear that too. He sounded like an extraordinary teacher who had a lot of passion for his students' success and investment in his career."

"He was indeed. Hmm, right now, I *so* want to proceed with this semester. Some of my friends from high school are already enjoying their careers, including some who became teachers and—"

"Don't compare yourself with others, even if they're your friends. That's another piece of advice I'd give you."

"*I'm not* … or, um, I'm hoping I'm not. I know we're all unique, but it's hard to have patience. I'm so passionate about teaching others and am rarely given opportunities, other than Royal Rangers—"

"Oh, is *that* what you were wearing the other week? I thought I saw 'Rangers' on there. I wasn't sure if you were a park ranger or what."

"Yeah, I've been in it since I was five. It's a faith-based mentoring program."

"Oh, nice. Like, through a church?"

"Yes. We do everything the Boy Scouts do, but a bit more, including Christian service and Bible lessons."

"Hmm, I may have heard about it before."

"Had you ever, um, by any chance, attended the church off of Thornwick Boulevard, down the street from the water tower … or any other church that might have had Rangers?"

"Uh, no. I'm culturally Jewish, but I've lived as an agnostic since high school. I hardly know anything about religions anymore. I know it's confusing to hear that and then see me wear my yarmulkes. It's convoluted, but suffice it to say, I take pride in my heritage and my identity. Besides, most of my family still practices Judaism. If people want to follow a religion or pray to a certain deity (something that gives them a sense of purpose, hope, peace, and a set of morals), then that's fine with me," he explained with a warm smile.

"I completely understand what you're getting at, Dr. Friedman, and I respect your opinion. Um, if you ever want to ask questions about *my* faith, and why I personally choose to believe it, I'd be willing to try and give an answer." Zachary smiled.

"Aw, how kind of you. Sometime, but not now. I'll let you know, though."

"Fair enough." Zachary nodded as he didn't believe in shoving Christianity down the throats of people who weren't yet receptive to it. "Anyway, I've got to stop agonizing over this decision. I'm … um … going to drop and come back for the summer semester. I have to take Health, so I'll probably knock it out this summer. I apologize."

"Never apologize," Dr. Friedman said, standing up. "I sincerely hope that the next few months are restorative for you, and if you retake physics, I'd be obliged to have you as my student. Keep up the good work at your Royal Rangers program too."

"Thank you so much." Zachary got up and walked out. Two steps into the hallway, he was hammered with the guilt for assuming the worst about Dr. Friedman the other week.

He proceeded to the Disability Services center on campus and withdrew from the semester.

16

Volunteering in the Shadows

Songbirds alighted on the telephone wires rather early the following Monday morning. Zachary got dressed and prepared for the day, soothed by the warblers' chirps from the trees outside his window. He poured some French Vanilla creamer and a little bit of sugar into a cup of coffee he had made with the Keurig in the kitchen. A quarter to seven in the morning, he walked outside with his only laptop and settled on the veranda, periodically warming his hands on his single cup of coffee against the cool morning air.

Just then, he heard a high-altitude plane soaring overhead. After turning on his laptop and going online, he opened FlightAware to see the details about that plane. It was a United Airlines Boeing 777, heading toward Chicago O'Hare International Airport. According to the website, a Lufthansa Airbus A380 from Frankfurt was trailing behind it. Zachary rushed onto the walkway and pulled out his pocket-sized Canon camera, ready to snap pictures of it.

Planespotting was a new special interest of his, which he started to love as much as coin collecting. He began familiarizing himself with the different models from Boeing, Airbus, Embraer, and Bombardier, training his eye to distinguish between them. Already having photography as a hobby, he was able to combine the two interests seamlessly. Although he never earned the Aviation Merit, he did earn the Photography one.

Not only did he take pictures of the jets flying overhead, but he also recorded videos, especially when airplanes began departing his local airport at seven in the morning. The airport was small, mostly handling 737s and A320s, though he might occasionally spot a FedEx Airbus A300 or a few 757s. Sometimes he'd take the bus there to film the planes taking off and landing.

He walked back up to the veranda and opened a tab for his local radio station for background music, which was currently playing Adele's "Send my Love."

Once he was comfortable, catching the scent of the aromatic waxleaf privets, he began proofreading his entire novel for the sixth time, hoping it would be his last. It took him days to resume the task, a consequence of his lifelong struggle with decision paralysis. Because he was out of school until the Summer 2017 semester, his priority was finishing his novel and publishing it. Once that was out of the way, he could concentrate on studying and restudying everything needed for his physics and Calc 3 courses in the fall.

Meanwhile, he wanted to see if he could work as a math tutor somewhere, get ready for future merits that he might teach at Royal Rangers, categorize all the books on his one bookshelf, work on his coin collection, and organize all of his albums on Facebook. (Unlike most users, he was fixated on arranging every picture chronologically and categorically in albums.) Contrary to the past few years, he began prioritizing his decisions after writing a to-do list, something that took a hundred pounds of weight off his shoulders.

After a couple of hours of planespotting and proofreading each morning, he would take everything back to his room and go for a cathartic walk. As before, his mind would go over storylines and sometimes spin off new side stories.

In the afternoons, he'd find himself working on his novel or sometimes putting coins in his Dansco albums. He couldn't resist buying and selling coins on eBay or at the local coin shop. By that autumn, after collecting for over fifteen years, he had nearly completed the entire uncirculated sets of Lincoln Memorial and Shield Cents, Jefferson Nickels, Roosevelt Dimes, Washington Quarters, Kennedy Halves, and the various dollar collections, starting with the Eisenhower dollars.

("Good heavens! That's going to be his retirement," Grandpa Corwin said aloud, nibbling on butterscotch pecan cookies, as Zachary shared his collection that Christmas. Frank Sinatra's "The Christmas Waltz" was serenading the household on Grandpa's gramophone near the wooden coat rack at the time. Zachary felt a sense of pride for building it.)

By April 2017, he had finished his novel and was certain it was ready. His next dilemma was figuring out how to publish it. He called a couple of self-publishers, but he couldn't afford their packages. Besides, he wanted a traditional release: a novel that would sell strongly and successfully, attract media attention, potentially inspire a theatrical adaptation, and be translated into multiple languages.

For a couple of weeks, he researched and contacted a couple of literary agents. One came back and offered a consultation call in early May for a small fee. Upon finishing the call, Zachary and the agent agreed to work together. The next step was to print out the novel at his local Staples and ship it to the agent in West Virginia, which he did so by the middle of May.

Meanwhile, he never stopped desiring to help and teach people in mathematics, science, history, music theory, and survival skills. Thrice in the past six months, he reminded some of the pastors at his church about his proposal to start a free tutoring evening once or twice a week, but it never got anywhere.

In his walks all spring and summer—heck, for several years—Zachary often went over various topics in his mind as if he were teaching them to someone. It wasn't limited to walks, but also occurred during his studies in his room. That's partially what made him fall behind every semester because he wanted to ensure that he comprehended and retained the material. He had always wanted at least one person with him to teach. His hundreds of walks each year felt more and more and more lonesome, not to mention painful at times when discrimination struck.

What's the point of learning if I can't help others? he would lament. *I'm not working hard and learning* for myself. *I did not procure the Gold Medal of Achievement* for myself. *I'm not breaking my brain's back with mental gymnastics* for myself*!*

The only organization that was giving him a chance to teach and share his knowledge was Royal Rangers. At the beginning of his commander days in 2013, he would tell people that he was overwhelmed with joy, which was in stark contrast to the other church that kept crumpling his heart like a hydraulic shredder. For years since, whenever he came home from Rangers, he would feel a sense of exhaustion, not out of weariness, but out of loneliness—saddened that it was over and that he'd have to wait a whole week to return.

For this reason, he always sought additional opportunities to serve on weekends, whether it was an outpost event or an event for the whole section. Eventually, he asked to lead his own merit camps with the commanders to teach boys various skills: using a compass, handling tools properly, tying knots and lashing poles together, building a fire, setting up a campsite properly, and various tricks of survival.

Pretty much nothing could make him miss a Friday evening.

One Friday in 2014, he had an endoscopy.

He was at Rangers that night.

One Wednesday in 2016, he had his wisdom teeth extracted.

He was at Rangers two days later.

The youth ministry at his church wasn't as promising. He alternated between that and the multimedia. The music ministry still didn't need his gift of piano playing.

"Zachary! Can you come up here for a second?" asked Robby, the youth leader, in front of everyone; his hair was styled in a pompadour. The youth ministry averaged fifty students each Sunday, sixth to twelfth grade.

After opening together with a game, a corny joke or video, worship, and devotion, they split into smaller classes.

Me? Really? Zachary was surprised. *Are you finally going to let me give a devotion or, at the least, finally introduce myself after all these months and months?* He walked between the rows of students, optimistic. Some of the students were in Royal Rangers, but they were the ones who rarely cared to say hi to him. One of them, Oscar, vehemently turned his back every time he saw him coming for no apparent reason.

"Hey, please take this stack of books and place it on the table back there," ordered the youth leader.

"U-Uh—" Zachary's hopeful smile morphed into a strained one. "Sure, Pastor Robby." He turned around and walked through the center aisle again. On the way back, he glanced at various students, some of whom were just staring at him, probably wondering, *Who is that guy?*

In the past five years, he had seen many people who earned the trust and confidence of children and teenagers. They always seemed happy to see their leader and do what they were told. Even though most Rangers respected Zachary, many didn't say hi to him like they did to other leaders, much less ask, "How has your week been?" or "Can you remind me how to tie the bowline?"—whether on a Friday evening or Sunday morning.

Zachary placed the stack of books where Pastor Robby had told him to and thought, *Man, at least he didn't say—*

"And Zachary! Please turn off the lights as we enter our time of worship," Pastor Robby interrupted.

Zachary smirked and nodded, whispering to himself, "Yes, Pastor, as I do every week."

Am I reduced to nothing, sir? Zachary couldn't help but scream in his mind, dreaming he was telling this to him. *I don't mind helping out like that, but the only reason I signed the contract with you to volunteer here was to teach, give devotions, and get involved. I'm* not *volunteering my time to be some nobody whom these students ignore or wonder whether he's mentally coherent. You refuse to let me teach all these months? Even to juggle? Recite a president's bio? Introduce myself? Something to prove that I'm a person they could trust? Someone who can teach them many things in life? Anything? You're almost no different from Pastor Joseph at my old church; you're just one year younger! Once my book comes out, you and everyone else will finally understand and give me purpose in life! I did* not *come here to be—*

Zachary stopped himself, quickly feeling a mix of guilt, anger, and frustration. Pastor Robby was an incredibly nice person otherwise. He often inadvertently made Zachary feel guilty for the things he said to him in his thoughts. Still, like once a month, at least, he'd assertively remind Robby about his willingness to teach. Robby seemed to brush it off, lying to Zachary that he'd get around to it someday, but he never did.

It was starting to be no different than his old church. He was quickly reminded about a time when Antonio, the worship leader, called him up to the chancel before the service started one Sunday in 2015. The other musicians surrounded Antonio, warming up their fingers or voices. Zachary walked between the pews with high hopes.

"I need a favor from you, Mr. Usher Captain," Antonio said, grinning.

Finally going to ask me to play the piano? I always bring my music wherever I go, just in case.

Antonio picked up a small vase of pink flowers that had been carefully placed on the lectern. "Would you kindly take this into the ushers' room for me? Thank you, buddy."

Dispirited and embarrassed, Zachary took the walk of shame, carrying the flowers to the ushers' room.

Now, at his new church, he was stuck. There wasn't a need in the children's ministry. He began to enjoy volunteering in multimedia more, even though his main calling was teaching others and playing the piano. He remained hopeful of teaching the children and youth someday, as well as starting to build trust with others. He wasn't some stranger in the back of the room, turning on and off the lights (not that there was anything inherently wrong with that). He was a human being with a kind, gentle heart who cared about the lives of everyone on earth, including them.

Consequently, he asked Pastor Nguyen if he could volunteer for 2017's Vacation Bible School that summer, since his health class was an asynchronous online course. Perhaps that could be a start.

"We'd love to have you, Zachary. We need a leader for the sixth-graders," said Pastor Nguyen with a beaming, reassuring smile.

A couple of weeks later, at the end of the meeting with all the VBS volunteers, the director came up to the pulpit to give her final comments and suggestions. At the end, she added, "I encourage all the leaders and assistant leaders to call their eight students. Get them excited for VBS, and tell them that we can't wait for them to show up."

Perfect, Zachary thought, sarcastically. *I'm* not *good at this, especially on the phone.*

Notwithstanding the pressure, he reminded himself that being a teacher meant speaking with students and parents on the phone.

Phone in hand, he tapped the numbers for the eighth student.

Hmm. Zachary sighed with a trace of hope. *Maybe it'll be another answering machine like the other seven fam—*

"Hello?" a woman answered, interrupting his thoughts.

"Oh, hey!" Zachary perked up, his heart beating fast. "My name is Zachary Corwin, and I'll be Maya's leader at VBS this upcoming week."

"Zachary, of course. I'm glad you'll be Maya's leader. Want me to put her on the phone for you?"

"Yes, please."

"Maya! You have a phone call!"

A moment later, Zachary overheard Maya say excitedly, "For me? Who?"

"Mr. Zachary, from church," the mother replied, happily.

"Oh," Maya instantly said, moping, her voice giving her feelings away.

The mother whispered something unintelligible to her.

"Hello," Maya said, drained of vivaciousness.

"Uh, hi, Maya. This is Mr. Zachary, and I'll be your leader this week at VBS … Um, we're excited to have you, and we know you'll have the best week ever!"

"Thanks," she replied in a monotone voice.

"Well, um, that's all I called to say. Have a great day."

"Bye." She hung up the phone.

Zachary exhaled deeply, not because he had rehearsed what he would say four times over before *each* of the eight phone calls, but because he just couldn't understand why life treated him this way.

Why can't I get everyone to accept me and trust me for who I am? Most of these students at the church know that I serve at Royal Rangers and earned the Gold Medal of Achievement, which took me ten years *to earn, yet they rarely say hi to me. How* can't *I be trusted? How come they don't come up and ask me about some of the merits on my awards vest, like the Compass Merit? Then, I could teach them the powerful skills of using a compass, or why a compass works, or astronavigation, or topography. That's why I* always *carry a compass in my cargo pants. At least* some *Royal Rangers appreciate me for who I am and my willingness to help them.*

Getting a sudden twinge of depression again, losing his appetite, and feeling debilitated in a rut, he found his light at the end of the tunnel in the publication of his novel. He assumed it would show his community, *and the world*, that he was a human being deserving of a chance in life: a chance to teach, encourage, entertain, and motivate others.

He quickly opened his emails and asked his literary agent for an update.

17

Finding Impact Amidst Chaos

"Fellas, stop!" Zachary exclaimed. "Come over here!"

The three sixth-graders from his VBS group returned the command with smirks, laughing at him.

"I said, *come over here*," Zachary sternly repeated. "And *you* guys, get back in line, please."

Two other boys kept dancing in circles together, ignoring what he said. "I like turtles!" one of them said, distorting his voice.

"Ha-ha," one of the original three sixth-graders laughed. "We don't have to listen to *you*, Mr. Zachy. Today's going to be lit since the other leader isn't here to stop us from having some fun!"

"And why are you wearing that kiddy's outfit?" teased another. "Are those just participation medals or something?"

"I-I-I must've not known I was wearing it," Zachary panted apprehensively. "I-It's Royal Rangers, and it took me years to earn all of this. I-It's equivalent to being an Eagle Scout and great for the military and—" Zachary's ability to speak ceased, unable to believe what he was being reduced to in the eyes of the boys and girls in his group, despite everything he had ever accomplished.

"Aw, you're making him upset," retorted Maya, "and I don't care. We're *never* impressed with you!"

"I'm not seeking fame! I-I just want God to give me purpose in life by teaching all you guys."

After hearing his response, all the sixth-graders laughed at him, a few resuming their conversations.

Zachary's breathing got more and more labored as if breathing through a straw. Unexpectedly, something attached to the ceiling above his head fell right on top of him, causing him to collapse in pain, nearly knocking him out.

The sixth-graders began cheering, did the dab like quarterback Cam Newton, and ran down the hallway, completely abandoning him.

Zachary lay there helplessly with a headache, struggling to breathe. Tense, suffocating seconds ticked by as he tried to get up, but couldn't.

Suddenly, he shot up out of bed, gasping for air. Dizzy and peculiarly debilitated with a headache, he caught his breath. As he sat there on the side of his bed, getting his bearings, the idiosyncratic, forlorn feelings he'd experienced in middle school crawled over him like cockroaches. He walked over to sit at his one desk and dissected his nightmare, telling himself what was true and what was untrue, attempting to console himself.

It is true that people have treated him that way within the past few years. He was never seriously injured like that, much less laughed at for nearly being knocked unconscious. Even though those sixth-graders in his dream were the same students in his VBS group, they all obeyed his directions in real life.

Yet there was another element in his nightmare that was accurate: no matter how much he accomplished, he had never seemed to earn everyone's confidence.

Would I even be the teacher I want to be, or would most students treat me like garbage just for being autistic, not listening to my lessons—despite attaining the Gold Medal of Achievement and a few degrees, despite taking up the practices of juggling and piano playing, and despite being a nice person who actually cares about their future? Heck, what if I served in the military, earned the Purple Heart, became a medical doctor, found a cure for a few fatal diseases, got a doctorate degree in education, or, um, whatever? Would they still *not listen to me?*

The Gold Medal is equivalent to the Eagle Scout ... and that should mean something!

Zachary got up and walked to his lone desk. It was Saturday, the day after VBS week ended. He decided to reflect on his experience as a leader. He actually had a wonderful time serving. The week started with most of those sixth-graders not knowing who he was and ending with them saying hi to him whenever they saw him. That always made him feel happy and accepted, something he only experienced at Royal Rangers and Washington Elementary for the most part. (Some boys would arrive at Rangers saying hello, but most of them walked past him, greeting him only if he said hi first.)

The following day, the church held a massive event to commemorate the fun week. The sanctuary was packed with the children and their families. Outside were bounce houses, inflatable water slides, various lawn games, and food catered by Smashburgers. The bright blue sky juxtaposed the few towers of cumulonimbus clouds hovering over the distant hills. The church invited the local police and fire departments to offer tours around their emergency vehicles.

Giant speakers blasted some of the recent hits. The premises echoed with children laughing, parents talking, and Justin Timberlake's "Can't Stop the Feeling!"

"How was your first summer helping out at VBS, Zach?" asked the director, walking up to him with the outpost's senior commander.

"*Very* fun," he replied, smiling.

"A *burger*!" teased the senior commander. "Yeah, get some meat on those bones. Glad to finally see you eating."

Zachary laughed. "Well, I eat a lot, but rarely in public. Um, so anyway, VBS was a blast."

"I heard so many wonderful things about you, Zach," announced the director. "The sixth-graders and parents all said you made an impact on them."

Zachary's eyes suddenly began to hurt as if he were straining them to stay open.

"I'm not surprised," said the senior commander. "He's the best commander of our outpost."

"I know," the director agreed, nodding.

"Y-You have?" Zachary's heart skipped a beat. He squeezed his lips a bit tighter, trying to cover up his emotions.

"Yes, and it wasn't just those sixth-graders, but many others. The kids and parents kept talking about the friendly leader who showed them card tricks. They said you were the first one to give them a smile, someone they looked forward to seeing, someone who made them laugh, someone who knew first aid and patched one of them up, and someone who prayed for them."

Zachary squeezed his paper Smashburgers tray with his right hand, his left curled into a fist. He was thankful to be wearing sunglasses, hiding the trickle of tears from his eyes. Somehow gaining enough composure to mask his emotional voice, he softly said, "It's so validating for me to hear that, especially for such a time as this."

"Of course, Zach!"

"Wasn't Oscar there all week?" the senior commander asked aloud.

"Oh, yes, but not in Zach's group. The other sixth-grade group."

"So, um, I wanted to ask." Zachary spoke up, a bit nervous. "On Monday, before we started, you were talking about, uh, how some of the children were coming from unchurched families or a background of being bullied?"

"Mm-hmm."

"And you said that one is currently a bully because he had been bullied in his past?"

"Mm-hmm."

"I bet, um, that was Oscar, wasn't it?"

"Yes."

"I knew it. I didn't want to assume, but I wanted to keep it in the back of my mind regardless. It makes sense that he was bullied in his past, judging by how he treats us commanders and the rest of the boys. I had to talk to him a few times after he hurt people's feelings … or even *physically* hurt someone."

"It's a sad situation."

"I had discerned that he always hid pain; I could tell by his eyes. I try my best to remind him he's valued, along with all the other children and teenagers I help. When we were at the arts-and-crafts station last Tuesday, I noticed him drawing *incredible* sketches of eagles, like a professional artist. I complimented him for that, but he didn't seem to care."

"Well, you continue to do the best you can, and give the rest to God. We can't change people; they have to make the decisions themselves. Just continue to pray for him and encourage him without overdoing it."

Zachary nodded just as one of the sixth-graders ran up to greet him.

"Hi, Mr. Zachary!" he said, eyes lighting up.

"Hey, Chris."

"Let's go see the fire truck. Come on!"

Zachary turned to the director and senior commander. "Well, I guess I have to run."

"Looks like you do," the director said, grinning. "Talk to you later."

"Are you done with your burger?" asked the senior commander. "I can throw it away for you."

Zachary looked down at his half-eaten hamburger and said, "Yeah, I had enough of it. Thank you."

As the speakers played "Believer" by American Authors, Zachary and Chris walked over to the parking lot, where the pristine, bright-red Ladder 138 stood. The tiller's aerial ladder extended 100 feet into the air. Next to it was Truck 17. Families lined up around both fire apparatuses, eager to climb inside.

Chris walked briskly ahead, causing Zachary to catch up. He was autistic himself and therefore got along well with Zachary. He felt like he was a great leader who understood him the most. "I'll get in this line, and you get in that line, so we can both be in the fire truck together," he said.

"Okay." Zachary nodded.

Just like that, Chris ran around to the other side. Zachary, third in line, was now by himself. He only decided to get in the fire truck for Chris. Other families got in line behind him.

After the girl in front of him hopped out of the driver's seat of Ladder 138, Zachary asked the fireman if he could get in next.

"Uh … sure," said the fireman, patiently.

"Come on, Mr. Zachary!" Chris was heard calling from the other side as he climbed into the captain's seat.

"Thanks," Zachary courteously told the fireman as he climbed into the engineer's seat. "My friend wanted both of us to be in here at the same time." There he was, seated before the steering wheel … unknowing what to do next. He sat there awkwardly as Chris sat there silently. One thing he did know: a noisy line of people was outside, waiting.

"Uh—" Zachary was about to suggest to Chris that they exit the fire truck.

"I would like the flashing emergency lights to be on," he interrupted.

Zachary sat there, hesitating and wide-eyed.

"Ask the fireman," Chris said eagerly.

Slowly, Zachary turned his gaze toward the fireman, who stared up at him with a neutral expression. "U-Uh, my friend wants the emergency lights on. Um, I'm not sure if—"

"Why don't you come on out and let others have a turn?" the fireman said, obviously faking a smile.

Immediately, Zachary hopped out, and the fireman helped the next boy climb in.

"Thank you for your service, sir," Zachary told the fireman, as he usually said in deference to all firefighters, police officers, and military personnel, past and present. The fireman, crass and pretentious as he was, didn't care to acknowledge his gratitude. He animatedly talked to the boy, just as any public servant would speak to a child, similar to the firemen Zachary visited back in fourth grade at his local fire station. Back then, he dreamed of becoming a fireman when he grew up and visited the station often.

"Mr. Zachary, want to go up to the tiller seat at the back?" Chris asked, running around from the other side.

"Uh, no. I'm good, Chris," he said, trying to break it gently. Already, he saw Chris' smile start to fade. "But *you* can if you want to." Still shaking about the fireman's assumption against him, Zachary added, "Um, I need to talk to someone over there, okay? I hope to see you at Rangers one of these weeks."

"Okay. Bye, Mr. Zachary."

He smiled, waved, and turned to walk away. A moment later, he collapsed at the tables and buried his head in his hands, nearly ripping out his hair. His heart felt like it was quivering as if it might beat out of his chest. He forced himself not to shed a tear, this time out of feeling worthless and thought of as a buffoon. It didn't matter how many compliments he got. As soon as one person didn't take him seriously, he forgot everyone and felt utterly alone. He tried to concentrate on his thoughts, but Imagine Dragons' "Whatever It Takes" was playing loudly through the speakers.

It's conclusive. That fireman must think I'm some toddler in a grown man's body who listens to imaginary friends. I'm sure he didn't notice Chris' voice talking to me from the other side. Good thing I didn't eat the rest of that hamburger; I would have lost it by now.

Heck, is there something with firefighters these days? A few months ago, I walked by a fire engine in a parking lot with firemen inside, about ten yards away. I started waving at them just to be nice and spread cheer to humanity, but the engineer just grimaced at me, as if I was some evil guy about to run up and ... shoot them or whatever! Gosh, my soliloquies can start anywhere, *can't they? Oh, swell, I'm going to get hammered with guilt the next time someone compliments me.*

Just then, he heard loud screaming from the children as if a celebrity had appeared out of nowhere. He quickly lifted his head from his hands. Ladder 138 was coasting around the parking lot with its lights flashing. Out of sheer, unexplainable instinct, Zachary pulled his small Canon camera from his pocket and began filming the scene. Three seconds later, Ladder 138 turned onto Thornwick Boulevard, sirens blaring.

Hmm, that was exciting, Zachary thought, marveling at the whole spectacle.

He supposed he had spontaneously decided to film it, just in case it somehow made history. Being a history buff, he liked the idea of documenting events. If he captured a moment in history, he could one day tell his grandchildren that he had pictures or footage of it, but he questioned its likelihood.

The following morning, he awoke from another nightmare that, once again, left him with a literal headache. He had great respect for firefighters, but couldn't help noticing a hint of arrogance in some of them, including those who seemed ignorant of what autistics look like. Before shaking about it all over again, he got up and opened his one laptop on his one desk. He prayed for a reply from his literary agent as he opened his emails.

Still nothing.

Disappointed, he opened Facebook, forcing himself to tightly hold on to the glimmer of hope that the day would come. It was getting harder, nonetheless. He remembered ushering at the Christmas Eve service at his old church back in 2015. As clear as if it were last night, he remembered being stationed at the far aisle with a stack of bulletins. He was enjoying the orchestra playing "What a Glorious Night," a song by Sidewalk Prophets. Seated in one of the overflow chairs was a man who wouldn't stop staring at him, holding a tight-lipped expression with a hint of disapproval.

Five seconds.

Ten seconds.

It was peculiar. "I'm *going* to be an author someday. I'm *going* to be an author someday," Zachary said to himself, trying to boost his optimism. "Then everyone will stop treating me and other disabled people this way."

Only five notifications? Zachary thought once Facebook loaded. *Sigh, nothing even significant. I pray to God that that will change once my book is published and that anything I post will be worth something to everyone.*

Next, he opened Facebook's "On This Day" feature and began scrolling through all his memories from that day.

Suddenly, he paused at a post from one year prior. It was him playing the classic patriotic song, "This is my Country," on the piano. He was about to continue scrolling when a thought that would change his life grabbed ahold of him.

He listened to the video again.

He contemplated.

He thought about all the rejection that he received for years and years.

He thought about all the times he wasn't given opportunities when he believed he could've handled them.

He thought about all the insolence and malice some people had thrown at him, from kindergarten to the present day.

He made up his mind.

He searched and found the original video file from his external hard drive and uploaded his first YouTube video. He drew in a trembling breath as if he had just invested in the stock market for the first time. Facebook was his own private corner of social media, only sharing posts with his friends. He avoided posting publicly as much as possible.

He endeavored not to look at the number of views or likes right away. He refused to get his hopes up, trying to avoid another debilitating blow, figuring that this gambit at gaining acceptance—*and* spreading a much-needed message of disability awareness, inclusion, and motivation—would most likely fail … sort of like everything else in his life. It was just something to tide him over until his novel was published.

Meanwhile, there was something that kept him going, proving to him that he *could* gain the confidence and respect of students. He walked to his closet and pulled out the VBS shirt he had worn all week. Turning the hanger around to see the back, he reread one of the comments a sixth-grader had signed: "You're the best teacher ever!"

18

Contemplation

Knock, knock!

"Come in."

"Um, Mom? Uh … I finally heard back from my agent."

"That's so wonderful! What'd he say?"

Zachary breathed out stressfully. "Well, he and his family were on a road trip for summer vacation, and he told me he's planning to start reading my manuscript next Monday."

"Oh, that's exciting! I knew you've been anxious over it."

Zachary sulked back to his bedroom. Slumping onto his one desk chair, he brooded over the additional wait.

Mrs. Corwin quickly followed behind. "What's wrong, Zachary?"

"He hasn't even started it yet," he said, gloomily, as bleak as the foggy ambience outside.

"Oh, come on, Zachary," Mrs. Corwin slowly said as she took a seat on the one ottoman. "Give the man time."

"I'm trying to have patience!"

"Well, you need to *learn* patience," she remarked, pointing. "I raised you better than this."

"As much as it's hard for my autistic brain to hear, I know that's wise. Um, I think I'll go for a walk," he said as he stood up.

"I think that's an excellent idea. It'll help clear your mind."

"It always does, Mom." Zachary walked out, adding in a whisper, "Mostly."

Zachary began his normal itinerary. He woke up that day stressed out, hurt, lonely, and queasy, and he *still* felt stressed out and queasy. The lack of social acceptance was what stressed him out the most, not so much his upcoming semester, which would begin in a couple of weeks.

He was already enrolled to retake Calculus 3 and Calculus-Based Physics: Mechanics. To prepare, he was teaching himself from his textbooks and dozens of YouTube videos. This time, he wasn't going to fall behind. The cost, however, was staying up all night working through countless equations and formulas, then sleeping most of the day … much like when he wrote his novel.

By the time he arrived at his local park, most of the fog had lifted. Having slept all day, he was now walking at dusk. He saw two people sitting on the infamous bench, which unsettled him every time. Honestly, he wasn't irrational about the bench and wasn't quitting life over those insensitive teenagers from long ago ... but still.

He could forgive, but never forget.

As he approached the bench along the windy path illuminated by the park's lampposts, he noticed that the two people were a father and his daughter. The father was pointing out the constellations to her. Arms folded, he turned to see Zachary walking by. A haunting gust of cold air splashed across Zachary's face as the low fog began to reappear, creeping down the pathway toward him.

Wait, what? Seriously, sir? Zachary caught the father's gaze on him from a few yards away. Upon passing them, a sense of foreboding settled over him as he saw the father at the edge of his periphery, still staring him down as if he were a criminal.

Unexpectedly, a voice broke the dark silence of the moonless night as the country prepared for a solar eclipse in a few days. "Hey, I remember you!"

Zachary swung around to see the daughter, now standing on the pathway, pointing at him with a wide smile.

"Mr. Collingsworth's—"

"No!" the father interrupted in a dark, thunderous, uncaring, monotone voice before Zachary could finish.

"No, sir, I was asking, I mean, um, I now recognize her from Mr. Collingsworth's class," Zachary stammered, legs subtly shaking. "I'm a juggler, so I've juggled and did card tricks in her class many times last year."

The father sat there with his arms crossed and a stone-faced expression like Buster Keaton, staring at him as if he didn't believe him or even his own daughter.

"Well, nice to see you again," Zachary said to the daughter, smiling in an attempt to cheer the man who must've woken up on the wrong side of the bed that morning. "Good night."

"*Good night!*" the father unneighborly boomed out.

Zachary swung around, continued walking, and disappeared into the fog like an apparition. He told himself, "It's okay! It's okay! It's okay! It's okay! It's okay! It's *okay*! It's *okay! It's okay*—"

BOOM!

Zachary lost his battle to hold it together by the time he crossed the little street adjacent to the park. He physically felt like a wild beast clawed at him, slashing his abdomen to shreds. His legs almost gave way, nearly sending him to the ground. His heart felt like it would stop any second.

Once he got back upstairs in his quiet, lonesome room, he immediately resorted to a two-hour soliloquy. Afterward, being almost midnight, he forced himself to stay motivated and taught himself more calculus and physics.

It was six o'clock the next day … in the evening. Zachary woke up and spent an hour checking his emails and notifications. He began receiving positive comments on YouTube, but each video was getting under a hundred views. At this point, he had three subscribers.

At least that's a start, he thought, feeling somewhat optimistic but still rational. All he wanted was to spread cheer and happiness, awareness and acceptance, equity and inclusion. Until he sat down to figure out *exactly* what he wanted for his channel, he gathered all his past videos and stored them in a folder on his computer. Then, every day, he'd pick one or two of them to upload. He had a couple of dozen videos of commercial, private, and military aircraft; a few dozen of him playing piano and juggling; some digitized home videos recorded on antiquated VHS-C tapes; and a couple of nature video about birds. Eventually, he planned to start producing Autism Awareness videos, as well as math and science tutorials. Since he had a passion for teaching, he thought that making such tutorials would help him retain everything better.

I might as well make videos about Royal Rangers and teaching merit requirements too, he thought.

Having everything organized in what he believed to be a solid plan, he took a deep, unlabored breath and decided to go out for an evening walk. He hoped it would make up for the previous day's evil encounter, replacing it with better memories so he could continue his studies effortlessly.

The atmosphere felt less ominous than the previous night. The cloudless skies of sunset hues warmed the evening's cool air.

Feeling insecure about what happened the night before and in recent times, Zachary went out in his Royal Rangers uniform again. He wanted to prove to everyone in his neighborhood that he was a human being who has an immense amount of knowledge, skill, and care for humanity.

Subliminally, this should also prove to everyone that I am *capable, and willing, of teaching many skills,* he reasoned. *Who in their right mind would ever go out in such a uniform like mine, pretending to be a Gold Medal recipient or an Eagle Scout, and not be able to prove it? If and when people test my knowledge, I* can *prove it. Give me a compass, and I'll point you in a direction at a bearing of 146 degrees while accounting for magnetic declination. Give me a piece of rope, and I'll tie the sheepshank, or the sheet bend behind my back, or the one-handed bowline. Give me four sticks, and I'll calculate the distance across a river for you. Ask me a question on a clear, starry night, and I'll teach you all about astronomy and astronavigation, based on what season it is.*

Unfortunately, over the past few years, several people have still treated Zachary as a joke, regardless of whether they believed him.

As he strolled along his usual route, carrying his sweater in case it got cold, cars began to drive past him. One car drove by and slowed down as it came to a stop sign. Zachary noticed a boy, probably eleven or twelve, looking out the window at him. A second later, the boy gave a warm smile and saluted him. Relieved and thankful, Zachary saluted him back. The boy's closed-lipped smile got wider before turning back and looking ahead.

You see? Something so subtle can totally change my entire day for the better, Zachary thought, feeling great about himself again. *Now if only I'd be able to teach him the skills I learned, so that I'm not keeping them to myself, or tutor him in mathematics or science.*

A few blocks later, he heard laughter. It was the loudest laughter he heard from a passenger in a moving vehicle that was more than fifty feet away. The laughter grew louder as the van approached him. Once it was close enough, Zachary made out the face of a middle-aged man in the passenger seat, laughing his head off … at him. Just like that, it was over, and the van was gone in a flash.

Zachary attempted to brush it off and kept walking, since there was now no way to prove anything, one way or the other. Hoping he was misinterpreting it, he couldn't find a reason why the laughing man's face kept pointing at him, even at the moment they passed by. He may have been laughing at a joke from the driver or some guy on the radio … and happened to naturally stare at people walking on sidewalks.

Turning the corner, while walking past an aromatic rose-covered trellis, he looked up to see a Boeing 747 jet gracefully soaring overhead. He took out his camera and, using 40x combined zoom, began recording video of it. Afterward, he looked up the details on his FlightAware app for the video's description.

At last, he arrived at the park, but coming from the other direction this time. He wanted his alternate route to symbolize a new and better chapter in his life. By this point, he had put on his jacket and zipped it up, since it had gotten too chilly for him, even though most people wouldn't yet.

Zachary walked down the pathway, about to pass by the playground. Just then, a girl told him with a wide smile, "Hey, I remember you!"

"Hi, nice to see you … a-again?"

Just a yard beyond the same daughter from the previous night stood the father, turned to say goodbye to one of his friends. Everything happened quickly and all at once. Zachary was frozen like a deer caught in headlights. He felt as if he were a burglar, one second from being caught red-handed by a watchful police officer, with absolutely no place to run or hide.

The father turned to walk to his daughter a second later. The millisecond he laid eyes on Zachary, his cheerful countenance completely vanished and was replaced with a grumpy, tight-lip frown. He instantly recognized him as "the creature" from the night before, a degrading sobriquet the father had privately used for Zachary when describing him to his friends earlier that day.

Zachary was not going to let up. He continued to hold the father's gaze until he said something.

The father continued walking in his direction, glaring at him with an antagonistic stare. He decided to say in a low, monotone voice, "Hey, how are you?"

Zachary smiled, hopeful that the man was a decent, unhateful person after all. He was more than willing to suffer the guilt of having been upset with him for no reason, both the previous night and throughout the day. "I'm doing good, sir. How are you?"

"*Don't Worry About It!!*" the father ferociously yelled, mercurially shifting his mean, glum expression into one straight out of a cartoon. He continued walking past Zachary and headed toward his pickup truck with his daughter.

"Dad?!" The daughter nervously laughed.

Zachary heard the father muttering something to her, but couldn't make out what he was spewing forth against him. He walked out of there quickly and decided to take the long way around back home, fearful of running into him again somewhere in the neighborhood. If he did, the father might assume he was following them. In the worst-case scenario, if that were to happen, the father would murder him.

He could not fathom how the same park he grew up going to (and where he started to hear students from Mr. Collingsworth's class saying hi) had turned into a park where he got rebukes and laughter for being who he was.

After he returned home and slammed his bedroom door, he began pounding on the comforter of his one bed with his clenched fist. His mother was already asleep for the night. He swerved around, collapsed to his knees, and began banging on the top of his one ottoman, followed by the one chair in his room. He took his one stack of organized math papers from his one cherry-wooden desk and flung it like a Frisbee. He stopped to catch his breath when he realized something for the first time in over twenty years.

The one.

One. One. One! One! *One!*

Just like having one of almost everything, he was the only one in that room. The only thing he heard and felt was his heart pounding fast. Feeling utterly alone—completely devoid of people, hurt by the pain ableists had caused him, and haunted by the nonstop replays in his mind—he began to quiver with anger. His jaw started to ache from all the facial strain he was causing himself.

Slowly, he turned around and focused his eyes on his emails, having to blink several times. Seeing there was no update from his agent, he slammed the lid of his one laptop shut, grabbed hold of it, and walked backward, causing the power cord to be yanked from its charging port.

A splitting headache set in as he looked around the room.

He saw one of his two windows.

His hands squeezed hard on his laptop.

He contemplated.

"Come on, Zachary," urged his rational brain, trying to stop him. "That's a four-hundred-dollar laptop."

"Shut up!" rejoined the brain's devil. "Zachary's a nobody anyway."

"Don't give up, buddy," consoled the rational brain.

"Why! Why! *Why* am I pushing myself this hard in school?" Zachary complained. "Why am I teaching myself calculus and physics at the moment? Why am I even in college? What's the point if no one's going to accept me in life, respect me for who *I am*, acknowledge what hell I've been through just to get where I am today? Why did I push hard for ten years for that Gold Medal if most people laugh at me and give me weird looks while wearing it?"

Tense seconds passed without hearing the voice of anyone.

Zachary's panting slowed down, softly adding, "Why am I alive?"

The devil beamed from ear to ear, hideously stretching far beyond a human's capability. Elated, he croaked, "*That's* the spirit, you ret—"

"*You* shut the—you know what—up, devil!" yelled the rational brain, silencing him. "Zachary, you've worked so hard for nearly twenty years. You wrote your book. Give it time. Give yourself patience. The agent *will* eventually get back to you. He *will* get you a publisher. They *will* publish your novel, and you *will* help billions of people around the world. Meanwhile, keep posting on YouTube, and you *will* build a huge following and help many, far beyond what you can count. You *will* spark incalculable communities of kindness, acceptance, and inclusion worldwide. You *will* be a highly respected math teacher for the rest of your life. Just be *patient*!"

The atmosphere stood still for fifteen seconds, which seemed like fifteen hours.

His rational brain and the devil both held their breaths.

Spiccato strings from an ominous orchestral score began to trickle in Zachary's mind, keeping him in paralyzing suspense. Tightly holding his laptop, he stared at his window, which was big enough to throw it through.

He then noticed the photo strip tacked to the wall next to his window. It showed four consecutive pictures of him inside a photobooth from his high school's grad night. It was one of two that he owned. How'd he get two? Because there wasn't a second person in that booth with him to give the other photo strip to. He had awkwardly sat there alone, unsure how to smile four different ways, all while fellow graduates watched and waited in line.

He recalled that four-year-old memory just for seeing the two-inch-by-six-inch photo strip on his wall. As a result, he no longer had to throw his laptop out the closed window, shattering the glass in the process. He was mere Newtons away from snapping his laptop in two like a wafer, the force of his grip on the verge of breaking it.

The dark, high-pitched violins in his head grew louder, now playing in sautillé, as another wave of lifeless pain and loneliness crashed upon him.

He turned his eyes toward the second window on the adjacent wall. Taped next to it was a certificate. In 2011, he was king of the prom … from the church's youth group. The current cinematic music blended with the sounds of applause from that night. He felt very thankful for the recognition. He could still hear some of the songs that were played that evening, such as Taio Cruz's "Dynamite," Owl City's "Fireflies," and Miley Cyrus' "Party in the U.S.A." He remembered all those fellow students and leaders who made an effort to make him feel special.

His grip on the laptop loosened as he was about to turn toward his cherry-wooden desk.

"Don't you do it!" demanded the devil. "Remember how much you felt hurt by that church. Remember how they *refused* to give you chances to use God's gifts. Remember that time when fellow seniors in small group grew impatient as you shared about your week. Remember how they teased and laughed at you when you described that spiritual experience you had. Remember the tears you shed that night, begging God to—"

"Shut the blazes up!" Zachary yelled aloud, completely silencing the orchestra in his mind.

Thirty seconds of deliberating passed.

"You know, I may have one laptop … one desk … one chair, one ottoman, one bed, one pillow, one nightstand, one lamp, one bookshelf, one keyboard, one closet, one pair of shoes, and one hat … but I have *two* windows! And although the one next to that wretched photo strip looks out to darkness, the other one looks out to light!"

"I'll see to it that those neighborhood kids start throwing rocks at those lampposts first thing in the morning," the devil grumbled in bitter rage.

"Ha-ha! Good look with that." The rational brain laughed sarcastically. "Never worked before, and it won't work this time. Better pack your suitcase, you million-time failure."

"I *will* pack my freaking suitcase because Zachary is so darn strong! But just a few blocks away lives a lonely, middle-age autistic man. Five minutes with him, and I know I could get *him* to commit suicide."

19

Slowly but Surely

"You must be Zachary Corwin," said Pastor Rick, offering to shake his hand. "Welcome to our little chapel!"

"Nice to meet you."

"Good morning, Zachary." Pastor Nguyen smiled. "Thank you for volunteering."

"No problem. Thank you for tagging me in that Facebook post."

"I know it's only a dozen seniors and that it may not be exactly what you were looking for, but I trust this will be a springboard to your music calling," said Pastor Nguyen.

"I understand. I'm thankful for this opportunity to bless the seniors at this retirement home on Sundays."

"Well, I got to head back to the church to preach the sermon, but I want to hear about it afterward."

"Take care, Pastor Nguyen," said Pastor Rick. "Zachary, again, thank you. It'll be quite special for you to play hymns on the piano for us for the time being. Hey, do you need some coffee? You look a bit tired."

"Oh, yeah." He nervously smiled. "I was, uh … I was just talking a lot last night. You know, just going over stuff in my mind."

"Well, there's coffee in the percolator over there. The cream and sugar are right next to it."

An hour later, Zachary played four hymns at the service's opening, with the small congregation singing along. He felt blessed for the opportunity. He loved playing the songs he enjoyed while others sang in the background. For the same reason, he started a Christmas choir with the boys at Royal Rangers, but it was only once a year, which made him sad.

At present, he was signed up to volunteer at this chapel every Sunday morning for an unspecified amount of time. It was a big decision because that meant foregoing all the ministries he had been part of at his main church on Sunday mornings. At least he still had Royal Rangers on Friday nights and certain Saturdays.

As he sat there during the sermon next to his mother, who offered to film his piano pieces to capture each week's memories, he felt riddled with heat and queasiness. Breathless with a loss of appetite, he couldn't help but think about that father at the park the day before. In fact, for one reason or another, the same sensation imbued him every time he sat there for the next few Sundays.

The day after that first Sunday playing piano, he went over to his community college for the Great American Solar Eclipse. At his location, it was just a partial one. Being part of the Astronomy Club, he volunteered to help with one of the solar telescopes. His joy came from teaching a bit about astronomy to the families that came up to him, making him feel trusted and resourceful.

Afterward, he got the bright idea to do a little grocery shopping at a local Trader Joe's. He usually went to Albertsons, but he thought he'd get "a change of scenery," if you will. The store was playing "Some Nights" by Fun over the ceiling speakers as he walked inside and grabbed a basket.

While suffering decision paralysis over what cereal to get, two young teenage boys stepped into the aisle and stood next to him, browsing the different cereals too. Suddenly, Zachary heard soft snickering coming from them. He subtly glanced over and saw one of the boys looking over at him with his eyes, even though the boy was still facing forward. After the boys gave him a smirk, they briskly walked out of the aisle, not taking any of the cereals.

Zachary forced himself not to assume the worst, but the trembling started to come on. Departing from the aisle, he recalled the revelation he got the other night. Focusing on the light at the end of the tunnel, he assumed that once his novel was published, everyone would treat each other as human beings, including those two teenagers.

He got in the back of a checkout lane with his three items. At that moment, he turned to his right and noticed the same two teenagers standing afar off. They were looking at him with weird smiles, laughing with each other. Zachary faced forward and endeavored to ignore it. A few seconds later, he noticed the older teenager walking toward him with a bag of chips in his hand.

"Oh, God." Zachary looked behind him to see nobody there.

The teenager got closer.

Zachary, with his heart pounding and stomach turning, noticed a husband-and-wife couple slowly pushing their cart toward the checkout lane, but from the other direction.

"God, please!" Zachary begged.

Suddenly the wife stopped the husband to review their shopping list before getting in the line. The teenager took his position in line behind Zachary.

"Hallelujah!" Zachary turned around to face the teenager. Smiling, he said, "Hey, you can go first."

"What?"

"You can go first?"

"A-Are you sure?"

"Look, I have three items, but you only have one. Sure, I'm sure."

"Um, thank you," the teenager said as he walked in front of Zachary.

A couple of moments later, the second teenager walked up to meet his friend, but he stopped dead in his tracks once he noticed him in front of Zachary. "Huh?" he said, giving a peculiar look.

"He let us go in front of him," informed the first teenager, sheepishly.

The second teenager looked at Zachary. "Oh, uh, thank you, man," he contritely said.

"You're welcome." Zachary smiled, seeing the genuine remorse painted all over their countenances. He forever felt thankful for what he did, repaying good for evil. He knew that to foster acceptance, one must sometimes offer unmerited kindness.

Walking home, he heard, "Zachary? How are you? How's your summer?"

Zachary looked over to see a boy with his eyes lighting up.

"Hey! Mr. Collingsworth's class, right? I remember you. My summer is … going okay. How is yours?"

"A blast!"

"I bet. You must be getting into sixth grade by now, right?"

"Yes."

"I remember sixth grade. I spent a whole good year of my life in sixth grade," he said, chuckling, causing the boy to laugh too. "Well, I gotta run, but enjoy the rest of your summer, okay?"

Moments like those reminded him how truly alive he was—that despite being hated and ridiculed by people at first sight, he still made some impact on others if they cared enough to say hi to him.

Upon walking back inside the house, he felt better than he had the past few days. Life was simply moving along, slowly but surely.

20

The Fire Pan and The Fire

The first few weeks of Zachary's fall semester were outstanding. He felt more prepared and equipped to take on Calculus 3 and Calculus-Based Physics. His professors were nice and broke concepts down that helped Zachary's mind. Reading ahead in the textbook and pre-studying the material aided to his success.

As his semester started, so did the local schools in his district. He still felt drastically underused as far as teaching or tutoring was concerned. Thus, he decided to do something about it. One Wednesday in September, he walked over to a local tutoring center and stepped in.

"Hi, how may I help you?" asked the center director.

"Hi. I was wondering, do you have an application?"

"Uh, yes, we do." The director pulled one from the front desk and handed it to him. "But, just to let you know, we only hire those who have a bachelor's degree or higher."

Zachary stared at the director for a second and said, "Oh, okay. I'm close to an associate's degree at the moment. Thank you." Disappointed, he walked out of there and onto the thoroughfare. He then noticed students from his former middle school, Canyon Mountain, walking inside a local Wendy's. *You're kidding,* he thought. *When I was in middle school, a lot of students went there for lunch on Wednesdays. Some things haven't changed.*

He decided to walk inside and order a chicken sandwich for lunch, with a refreshing Frosty for dessert. The restaurant was packed with a few dozen middle schoolers talking, joking, and laughing. Their ceiling speakers were playing Alessia Cara's "Scars To Your Beautiful." The loudness began to trigger sensory overload for Zachary. While he waited in line, three girls were heading out.

"Oh! Where's my animal!" one of them forcefully hollered.

Instinctively, Zachary turned to her, but what he saw was unexpected. He assumed that the girl was talking to her friends and got a bit too loud, but startlingly, she was looking at him eye-to-eye. Confused, he stared back at her and her vicious face. Two seconds later, she and her friends were gone, laughing as they went.

That was quite random, Zachary thought as he found himself in a quandary. *I'm thankful I decided to include those stories in my novel that's* going *to be published.*

The noise bouncing around the restaurant seemed to have gotten louder. Together with that girl's degrading insinuation, he was no longer hungry. Walking out the door, he ran into an older couple from Pastor Nguyen's church.

"Hey, Zachary! I haven't seen you in a while," said the wife.

"Hi. It's great to see you again. I've been attending the chapel at a local retirement home."

"I know," the husband said, nodding his head. "We enjoy hearing the music that you've been posting on Facebook. I was playing it the other week, and my wife goes, 'Who's playing the beautiful music?'"

The wife smiled and nodded. "Your music really blesses us whenever we listen to it."

"Thank you very much." Zachary smiled and proceeded to have a five-minute conversation to catch up on everything. On the way home, he could not stop feeling guilty. He kept replaying the entire conversation with that couple, realizing how meaningful he was to them and a lot of other people. He felt guilty for writing stories in his novel, paralleling them to real events of bullying in his life. He felt guilty that he kept forgetting all of his friends whenever a total stranger verbally attacked him, such as that father, two days in a row, or like that middle school girl, moments earlier.

Unexpectedly, an idea sparked in his mind. He thought about all the middle schoolers who came to the Wendy's. After mulling over it, he thought, *You know, since that tutoring place won't work, and since the church didn't take my offer of free tutoring too seriously, and since the other church wouldn't hire me as an assistant teacher, this just might work!*

The next Wednesday, he took his conspicuously large physics textbook and walked over to the Wendy's. After ordering a Sprite, he sat down at one of the tables and began studying the material. Ten minutes later was when middle schoolers started pouring in.

Month by month, he kept sitting at that same spot. Students took notice of him as the college student who always studied at Wendy's on Wednesday afternoons. Some would start waving or saying hi to him every week. A couple would ask him what he was reading. However, no one ever took him up on his subliminal offer: *he would be more than happy to help them with math or science for free.*

Some adults would periodically come over and have a quick conversation with him. "What are you studying?" an older woman asked, intrigued by the huge textbook. It was a cool afternoon in March 2018.

"Oh, um, part two of physics, which is electricity and magnetism, based on calculus."

"Wow. So, what do you want to do in life? Be a physicist or an engineer or someone like that?"

"I want to be a middle school, or high school, math teacher."

"God bless you!" the woman immediately said, closing her eyes and shaking her head. "We definitely need good teachers, especially for middle schoolers."

"Yeah, that's what I heard."

"But be warned, middle schoolers are tough," she said, her tone far from promising.

"I know, believe me."

"Oh? Had you worked with them or tutored them before."

"Um, not really. Just at Royal Rangers, but that's like Boy Scouts. I've had some run-ins with them before, though. I understand that one thing I'd need to establish is trust, that they can trust me. A month ago, I was walking by a Starbucks and saw a few middle schoolers saying goodbye to each other. One of them saw me and immediately called out to her friend (who was walking to the parking lot), 'And don't get abducted!'"

"Oh, how cruel. Had you ever considered teaching at the university level instead?"

"Um, sort of? I don't know. My heart is for children and the youth. They're the next generation. If they're not encouraged, they might not go to college to begin with."

"That's a very noble thing to say. I assume all your classmates at the college are better students, right?"

"Well, most of them, yes."

"Have there been cruel college students?"

"Honestly, yes. I was in lab for General Chemistry one day. The TA, who was then an Organic Chemistry student, started a nonrelevant conversation about presidents with a few students. Presidential history is my specialty on the side. I'm sort of a buff, you might say, so I couldn't help but listen in while doing my titration. And then one part, I couldn't help but chime in, but as soon as I did, the TA looked at me and said, 'What does that have to do with lab?'"

The woman shook her head out of disgust at the TA's remark.

"I know. I replied back, 'Nothing,' but I couldn't speak anymore. It was almost heart-wrenching all afternoon, but I was able to maintain my composure. I was like, hey, *you* are the one talking to the students about it while they're busy titrating, and I thought I'd give some fascinating trivia, based on what you were talking about. From then on, he didn't seem to have any regard for me. He laughed at me for accidentally misspeaking about solids and evaporation. He told me to put everything on the floor for one of the quizzes, but not for any other student."

Zachary continued the conversation for another couple of minutes before departing.

Hearing a recently departed jet overhead, he looked up and snapped a picture with his ever-ready, pocket-sized Canon camera. Looking ahead, a few middle schoolers rode slowly on their bicycles, conversing with themselves. As always, he longed for an excuse to say, "That plane is a Bombardier CRJ-700, operated by Delta Connection." He always had thousands of random facts ready to share with people, but he rarely got the chance, making him feel sad and isolated.

Once he got home and checked his emails, he cried out with excitement.

"Congratulations, Zachary!" read the email from his literary agent. "One of the publishing houses replied back with a contract, willing to publish your novel. I am attaching it below for you to review and sign."

Zachary, overwhelmed with emotion, printed out the 8-page contract and began reading it through. Everything had read perfectly until the very end, when he almost died.

21

Futile Efforts

"Um, Pastor Rick? By any chance, do you need greeting cards or holiday cards?"

"Hmm, I don't really send any out these days, Zachary, but what do you have?"

"Well, uh, back in high school, I would make and sell hand-drawn greeting cards," he explained, showing some samples.

"You drew these? By hand? They're magnificent! Yeah, I'll buy a couple. How much are they?"

"The normal cards are three dollars, and the pop-ups are four dollars."

"Listen, I'll buy five of them and give you five dollars each. Does that sound good?"

"Uh, sure," he replied, smiling with a hint of guilt for asking. He didn't want to appear like some money-crazed salesman, especially at what was technically a chapel.

"I'll let our seniors know about these. Let's go ahead and display them right over here."

Zachary was tremendously thankful. He started reselling his cards for the first time in a few years, but he had only gotten a few sales so far.

"Hey, Brian. Do you still need tutoring in Calculus?" Zachary nervously asked one of his friends at the college. "I remember you saying that you'd pay me, and I said I'd be willing to tutor for free."

"Oh, yeah. I'm good now. I found a free math tutoring resource here at the college, but thanks for asking."

Over the next couple of months, he took his old textbooks that he never wanted to get rid of to a place that buys used textbooks, but they couldn't take ninety-five percent of them because the textbooks were already outdated.

A philatelic shop wouldn't buy his old stamps because they were too common.

A bookstore wouldn't buy his books because they were either vintage or they weren't in ideal condition.

He applied for grants at a few places, which all rejected him.

He had posted on YouTube almost every single day—piano playing at his church, some math and science tutorials, planespotting videos, vintage home videos, and now Autism Awareness videos—but still only had fifty subscribers. He never wanted to appear like a YouTuber who was obsessed with a following or whatnot. He never told viewers to like, comment, share, and subscribe, as he was never comfortable telling people what to do. He simply wanted to share and encourage … and that's it. However, he started asking all his friends on Facebook to subscribe, adding, "only if you want to because I hate asking people to." He figured that the more subscribers he gets, the closer he'd be to monetization.

In his room, he looked at his shelf, filled with Dansco coin albums. Since all else seemed to be failing before his very eyes, he reluctantly decided to part with some of his older coins: an extensive collection of Flying Eagle and Indian Head Cents, Liberty Head "V" and Buffalo Nickels, Mercury Dimes, and Standing Liberty Quarters. He also threw in the Susan B. Anthony, Sacagawea, and Presidential Dollars. (Half eventually sold and half didn't.)

Well, I can always collect these again. At least I still have the Lincolns, Jeffersons, Roosevelts, Washingtons, and Kennedys, he reasoned, consoling himself. He proceeded to take pictures of his coin albums, individual coins, stamps, books, knickknacks (you name it) and listed them on his new eBay account.

Afterward, he went to Pastor Nguyen's church.

"Good afternoon, Zachary. Have a seat," said Pastor Nguyen.

"Thank you for seeing me on such short notice, and in person."

"You're welcome. I figured it must be urgent if you prefer face-to-face in lieu of calling or emailing."

"Well, Pastor, um, I'll preface this by saying how nervous I am to ask this. Whatever the answer is, I'll be okay with it. By any chance, is the church able to provide financial help or even a loan?"

"Hmm. We usually give financial help to our missionaries as well as to ministries that need supplies for soup kitchens, the homeless, children, and things like that. Why? What do you need?"

Already burdened by guilt for meeting him, he said, "Well, not too many people know this, but I wrote a novel."

"Wow, congrats! What's it about?"

"It's about a boy who's autistic like me. I already got a contract from a reputable publisher, but, um, I had no idea how much it cost to get a book publish. All I've seen growing up is that you go to a publisher, they publish your work, and you receive a royalty check as a result. No one told me it *costs* anything! I recently tried selling greeting cards and now coins that I've spent years collecting. I tried selling books and textbooks to no avail too."

"How much?"

"Um—" Zachary froze. Feeling ill at ease, his heart skipped a beat. "Uh, well, mmm, thirty-six hundred dollars."

Pastor Nguyen exhaled deeply. "Hmm. Well, Zachary, if the church does bless you, it could only be five hundred dollars, and that's only if this qualifies. Honestly, I don't think it would. We don't really give out any loans either. However, do not fear, Zachary. God's timing is perfect timing, and I'll pray with you for this. In fact, I'll have the elders pray specifically for it too."

"Thank you so much anyway, Pastor."

22

Triple Crown

In late May 2018, Zachary had dinner at Grandpa Corwin's place. In the middle of enjoying their Dinty Moore Beef Stew, Zachary shyly said, "Um, Mom, Grandpa, I have an announcement: I applied to be a carnival ticket seller at the county fair this summer."

"That's wonderful," they said, congratulating him.

"I remembered a career fair at the college a month ago, and people from the county fair were there. I think this would help pay for my book."

"Don't take any wooden nickels," Grandpa Corwin joked, adjusting his green suspenders which kept slipping. "What's your wage going to be?"

"Somewhere between eleven and twelve dollars an hour."

"*What?!*" Grandpa Corwin screamed, nearly falling out of the chair and dropping a forkful of his stew. "You gotta be kidding."

"No, I'm not. That's just above minimum wage."

Eyes wide open, Grandpa Corwin readjusted his homburg hat. Turning to Mrs. Corwin, he said, "Is he going places or what? My first job, back in the fifties, was being a shoeshine boy at a barbershop. I was fourteen years old and made fifty cents an hour. When I was fifteen, I worked down the street at a hamburger stand and made seventy-five cents an hour. With twenty-five extra cents an hour, I honestly thought I was a millionaire. Gas prices were also thirty cents a gallon back in my day."

"Didn't you say you were a part of the barbershop quartet?" asked Zachary.

"Who, *me*? No. I was asked to volunteer in the church choir when I was in my twenties. I got up there one Sunday, opened the folder, and, *surprise!* All the pages were blank."

Mrs. Corwin laughed, having heard this story a hundred times over.

"I couldn't sing anyway, and they knew that. They only wanted me up there for my *looks*!" Grandpa Corwin lightheartedly complained. "Had I ever told you about the time I got arrested for singing once?"

Zachary shook his head as Mrs. Corwin laughed.

"I did!" he continued, looking serious. "You know how I got them to let me out of jail? … I started singing again."

* * *

After the interview in mid-June, Zachary was immediately offered the position. It was his first employed job in his life, and for the first one, he knocked it out of the park. All of his fellow carnival ticket sellers and supervisors were thankful for what he contributed. When families came to his ticket booth, he would show simple coin tricks to the children. During his breaks, he would juggle around the fair for everyone.

"Za-cha-*ry*! Za-cha-*ry*!" a family chanted as they came over to watch him juggle. He had entertained them from inside his ticket booth half an hour prior.

"You're very fun!" a parent said with a smile after buying tickets at his booth. She had noticed him turning a quarter into a happy-face button for her son.

"Those buttons were for you guys," said the supervisor a week later.

"Oh, sorry. I thought they were for us to hand out. That's why I always took a handful."

"But it's fine."

For the most part, Zachary felt alive and appreciated.

After working all summer, combined with his efforts selling cards, books, and coins, he finally had just enough to pay for the publishing of his book. He promptly mailed the check and the signed contract to the publishing house. Upon receiving the payment, the estimated publication time was five or six months. Zachary didn't think he could wait any longer, but he trusted in the process.

Over the next four months, he took his final semester at the junior college with more hope in his future, tolerating all the strange stares the people gave him.

* * *

"Rangers, fall in!" Zachary commanded.

The sixteen present boys at Discovery Rangers (the third- to fifth-grade age division at Royal Rangers) quickly lined up in their three patrols.

"Attention!"

The boys stood tall, facing straight ahead, arms down at their sides, knees slightly bent, heels together, and feet at a forty-five-degree angle.

"Dress right, *dress*!"

"Ready, *front*!"

"Count *off*!"

After each command, the boys acted accordingly.

"May the Soaring Eagles lead us in the pledges."

All the boys in the Soaring Eagles patrol made a right face and marched around to the front, where they led the pledges for the American, Christian, and Royal Rangers flags.

"Excellent! All you new guys remembered the drill commands and flag salutes from last week. Great job."

One of the local churches had partnered with Pastor Nguyen's church, bringing in sixty percent more boys at Royal Rangers.

"So tonight, we'll be starting the Weather Merit, which is a very fun one. For the next five weeks, I'll be showing you science demos and teaching you how to build different weather instruments. Additionally … uh, *attention*?!"

One of the boys, sporting his signature faux hawk, immediately snapped back to the position of attention.

"Uh, what was that dance or whatchamacallit anyway, out of curiosity?"

"It's Fortnite," said the boy, beaming.

"Fort … what? Where?"

"It's a new game, Commander Zachary," another boy informed. "Everyone at my school is driving all the teachers crazy with these dances."

"Oh, so like the dab or whatever back in 2016?"

"Yeah!" A quarter of the boys did the dab, chuckling and whispering to one another.

"Guys! Don't talk over Commander Zachary," one of the fifth-graders said, causing the room to fall silent.

"Thank you, senior patrol leader. Well, are *these* things still trendy?" Zachary asked, pulling out a fidget spinner. "Because I was about to address it."

"Ha-ha," said one of the boys, laughing. "That's so 2017!"

"But that was only one year ago. Oh, who cares. Well, the reason I'm bringing this up is to explain the rules with these things, just for those who still might have them. In 2017, we commanders didn't know what they were. We thought it was distracting, and we confiscated them. However, I realized that these things can especially help kinesthetic learners concentrate. For that, I will allow it under one condition: they must stay below the table to avoid distracting others, *okay*?"

"Yes, Commander Zachary!" all the boys said in unison.

After a pause, Zachary laughed. "When I was your age, *everyone* except me had fingerboards and treated them just like you guys treat fidget spinners. I just didn't understand the fun of it. Besides, I could never ride an actual skateboard anyway."

"Aw, never say never, Commander Zachary. You can do it," a boy said with a warm smile.

Smirking, he nodded, realizing what he had nonchalantly implied. "Yes, if everyone works hard and perseveres, they can achieve great things. Anyway, one last thing: I forgot to say this last week, but if any of you need help with your homework, especially in math or science, please feel free to bring your worksheets and ask me before or after the meeting. All right, fall out!"

As the boys walked over to sit at their patrols, one of the fifth-graders lightly sang, "Once I was seven years old."

"*Silently*," Zachary whispered to remind him. "But hey, I like that song. Lukas Graham, right? I played that on the piano at a benefit once."

A couple of the new third-graders, Jason and Phil, smiled and saluted Zachary. He saluted them back, grateful for their respect.

* * *

Zachary stepped into the house in mid-December. He was greeted by his mother and grandfather clapping for him. The television was tuned to a channel that played Christmas music around the clock; it had just started "Sleigh Ride" by The Ronettes, one of his favorites to listen to.

"Congratulations, Zachary, for completing your associate's degree!" Mrs. Corwin smiled, about to pull out her homemade blueberry pie from the oven.

Letting out the biggest sigh of relief, he responded, "Thank you so much. *Phew!* I feel very confident on those finals."

"I bet," said Grandpa Corwin, darning his socks. "Mercy me! You studied till four in the morning, I heard."

"I wanted to be extra confident. It meant a lot to me. Anyway, the commencement is in May."

"We'll be there!" Mrs. Corwin assured.

"Now, I can relax for Christmas. I'm excited for this year's Royal Rangers' Christmas Choir and playing all those carols on piano, including 'Ding Dong Merrily on High,' one of my favorites to play, especially with a choir singing to my accompaniment. We've been practicing for months as we do every year."

"I can't wait," said Mrs. Corwin. "So, what's next for you as far as your education?"

"Well, I decided to take next spring off and start Tributary University in the fall."

"Tributary University is great and conveniently close, even closer than the junior college. It's a university of flow, connection, and growth. I had friends who attended Tributary."

"I believe it's perfect too. Um, I've decided to take next spring and summer off so I can tour with my novel. I should hear back from the publisher any day now."

"That'll be perfect," said Grandpa Corwin. "You need a break, regardless, even if that means cutting back on some of your volunteer work. Look, you serve in various ministries at a few churches *and* you're a college student simultaneously. You seem tireless, but I could tell when you're getting worn out. Have you ever had the pleasure of relaxing and actually being served by others instead of doing the serving?"

"Yes," Zachary replied. "And I *cannot* sit still when that happens. It's my nature. I've *got* to be moving. I've *got* to be performing. I've *got* to be helping people."

23

Navigating Patience

"Well, um, seriously? Sorry for, um, putting it that way?" Zachary was in a quandary, talking over the phone.

"It's just taking a longer time for us," the publisher explained. "I know you were expecting January or February. Then I said it would be mid-February, the latest—"

"And now, it's mid-March."

"Yeah, well, I'll give you an update as soon as I can, okay?"

Zachary exhaled in disappointment. "Okay."

"All right. Have a good day, sir. Goodbye."

Zachary hung up the phone and slowly walked over to his window, peering outside at the stagnant neighborhood through the open blinds. *That's just great!* he thought sarcastically. *I took this semester off just to tour around with the book.*

A light breeze came through the screen, causing the vertical blinds to flutter slightly. His heart ached, his stomach churning, as he envisioned the blinds' slats as prison bars. Looking out, he felt trapped, his breathing labored by the heat of the midday sun. His mind exacerbated it by reflecting on the bruising discrimination he received and the loneliness he felt. On days when he had nothing to do, he wasn't hungry much. Listening to certain songs (even cheerful ones) was still suffocating, literally, unless he listened to them on days he was fulfilling part of his purpose, like during his rare juggling or piano performances.

He figured that once his novel was published, he'd have a hundred times more opportunities to serve, speak at many events, be interviewed on news and radio, and perform at various occasions.

The following night at Royal Rangers, after setting up for his Fingerprinting Merit lesson, he walked out to the church's courtyard, where the other commanders brought the boys for recreation. The waxing gibbous moon was just about to cross the celestial meridian. The boys were playing a spirited game of Capture the Flag. When Jason and Phil saw Zachary from the field, they stopped and smiled, saluting him. Zachary smiled and saluted them back. Noticing two of the third-graders making noise with a water bottle, he walked over to ask them what they were doing.

"It's called bottle flipping," one replied.

"It's been a trend for a couple of years now," said the other. "It's so lit!"

"Huh, I've never heard of it until now. Looks quite challenging. Try to get ten in a row."

"My record's fifty."

At the end of the night's meeting, Jason ran up to him. "Commander Zachary!" he said. "I need help on a school project. Can you help me?"

"Sure, I'd be happy to. Let's sit over here." For the next ten minutes, he helped Jason on his science project about weather. "Well, that was fun," he said with a smile. "It's so interesting that you got a project about weather, since we just did the Weather Merit a few months ago."

"Uh, I actually *chose* weather as my topic."

Zachary looked surprised.

Beaming from ear-to-ear, Jason revealed, "It was because of that merit you taught. You inspired me!"

That moment, then and there, left an everlasting impact on Zachary. It was one of the first times a child said anything like that to him. Even though there had been weeks when he went home feeling like a failure, he acknowledged that he still made some kind of difference to others. This boosted his motivation to continue teaching and to keep getting better at it.

He knew he was on the right track.

* * *

"Zachary, I'm so sorry that I couldn't talk to you earlier," said the publisher, apologetically. "I got your emails and phone messages. I know how stressful it is to wait and wait for something so exciting."

"I understand, and I'm sorry too. I didn't mean to assertively spam you, but this means the world to me. I took the spring off in my studies to tour around with the novel, but it's already early May."

"I know, but … tell your friends and family that we're looking at May 30 as the publication date."

Zachary's countenance lit up, and he felt his mood soar. "Okay, wow, thank you so much! Also, thanks again for the cover design. It looks wonderful."

"You're welcome, sir."

A couple of weeks thereafter was his commencement, where he was conferred his IGETC certification and his Associate's Degree in Mathematics. (He had already been accepted to Tributary University.)

When he woke up that morning, he received emails from his publisher and agent. His agent congratulated him and gave him PDFs with tips on promoting and marketing his book. His publisher gave him the first proof of his manuscript to look over.

For the next three days, he read through his novel and sent back a few remaining corrections. After they were made, Zachary approved the final manuscript.

24

Total Serenity

"Hey, Commander Zachary. My twin sons are having a birthday party at a park on Saturday," said one of the Royal Rangers' fathers. "They told me that they'd love to have you there. Maybe you could do a little bit of your juggling and magic."

"I'd be more than happy to come. It'd be an honor to attend, juggle, and do, well, *sleight-of-hand* tricks."

He arrived at the park by noon that Saturday. It was the first time he recalled being at this park, which was a couple of cities away. It was spacious with a couple of playgrounds and a nature trail. He went up to say hi to the father, who was preparing hot dogs at the picnic shelter.

"Hey, commander! Glad you made it." The father greeted him with a cordial smile. Pointing, he said, "Phil's over there. I'm not sure where the other one is. You can go and say hi to him." His Bluetooth speaker was currently playing "On Top of the World" by Imagine Dragons.

"Hi, Phil." Zachary smiled and waved as he approached.

"Commander Zachary! You're here!" Phil exclaimed. "This is gonna be lit! Brandon! Commander Zachary's here!"

Brandon hopped down from a tree he climbed and ran up to Zachary to say hi.

Just then, two of their friends from school joined.

"This is Commander Zachary," Phil said, introducing him. "He's very nice."

"Hello." Zachary waved.

The two children gave only a friendly wave and eye contact. No smile or anything. They were either shy or just needed to get to know him.

"Hey, fellas!" the father called out. "Why don't you all play badminton over there?"

"Badminton?" Zachary marveled. "I hadn't played that since high school P.E. I used to love it."

The father handed Zachary the rackets and a birdie. As he and the four children walked over to the badminton court, he caught the cool breeze of the warm spring day, which carried with it a faint scent of pine trees.

Suddenly, he was jolted. He felt total serenity as if there were no worries or obligations in the world. For a moment, the weight of all the pain he had carried with him for almost twenty years vanished. He felt unequivocally accepted, spending time with families who treated him like a human being, without any negative judgment of his voice, height, thinness, or autistic traits.

Alas, it only lasted up to five seconds, but at least he felt it, and it kept him rejuvenated for the next few months.

25

A Published Author

Knock, knock, knock.

"Zachary." Mrs. Corwin opened his bedroom door. "There's a big package at the front door, waiting for you."

Zachary rushed down the stairs on this mid-June morning. "Can you please call Grandpa? Ask him to come in for a minute?"

Moments later, Grandpa Corwin arrived, and both he and Mrs. Corwin witnessed the victorious event.

With a ton of emotions, Zachary opened up the UPS package and pulled out his complementary copies of his novel. He stood there, speechless, flipping through its pages. *Oh, my gosh*, he thought, marveling. *And I wrote this.*

Afterward, he went upstairs to sign a half dozen books with personalized notes, thanking family and friends.

That night, before he brushed his teeth, he looked at himself in the mirror, proud to say that he *is* a published author.

The first major announcement he made was at Royal Rangers. He began by sharing his story as an autistic, along with the pros and cons. Then he revealed the surprise: his novel had been published, a secret he had kept from almost everyone for years. The boys, commanders, and their families marveled at this triumph. Some of the boys were proud of him and asked to buy an autographed copy.

"Douglas, the tenth-grader, came up to me afterward," Zachary told a fellow commander that night. "He told me he's now motivated to continue writing *his* books."

"Wow, you inspired him!"

"That's what it's all about: helping everyone find their calling and pursue it. I know Douglas is autistic too, so I could imagine how prone he might be to giving up, but if I had quit every time *I* got discouraged, a thousand of my own accomplishments wouldn't have happened."

By mid-July, he had revealed his authorship to everyone he wanted to surprise in person. Once everything was officially on Amazon, Barnes & Noble, and elsewhere, it was time to post about it on Facebook, YouTube, Twitter, and Instagram. (He had gotten Twitter and Instagram a year prior, hoping it would help boost his story about autism, kindness, and inclusion to the world. So far, nothing.)

His Facebook post went viral, garnering hundreds of likes and comments by wonderstruck friends and family members.

He tagged all the major news networks on his Facebook, Twitter, and Instagram posts. He shared his novel with various autism organizations on several social media platforms. He went to a couple of local autism organizations in his county to spread the word too. And *most* of it was to no avail.

26

Silence Enigma

"One news anchor shared it on her Facebook page. One autism organization eventually wrote a blog about my novel. One Royal Ranger friend from Panama talked about it on his podcast. But that was it. My YouTube video, where I made the huge announcement, got tens of thousands of views … but only because I took out a Google ad for it. Some people commented, saying "Congrats," that they're glad they didn't skip my ad, that it was inspirational, and that they'd check out my book. I went to the website where I can see how many books I've sold, and I've only sold forty … *to date.*"

"You've advertised? How much, Zachary?" Grandpa Corwin asked sternly, putting down his bowl of butterscotch ice cream. They were meeting in the living room of his house across the street.

Whenever Zachary heard his name in that tone, he knew he was in trouble. The fact that he didn't want to divulge the amount was bad enough. Now, he had no choice.

"Um … Well … $800."

"*Eight-hundred dollars!?*" Grandpa Corwin nearly fell out of his chair. "*What in Sam Hill?!*"

"And hey," he said in his defense, "that was *not* my fault. Google made a glitch, and I emailed them with screenshots proving what my budget was. It was only $200. They didn't seem to understand anything I said, so I ended up wasting most of it."

"My *goodness*, Zachary! Where did you get all that money to pay for it?" he asked, doffing his homburg hat and scratching his head.

"Well, as you know, I worked at the county fair again, selling carnival tickets."

"I *knew* that, Zachary, but, my word! What's $800 compared to what you made? More? Less? Same? What?"

Zachary never does well when pressed like this, especially in a losing battle, since he had made a grave mistake. Feeling ill at ease, he continued, "$800 was about half of what I made this past summer."

"Half your income?! … *Half* your income?! Haven't we taught you about budgeting and finances?"

"I am *desperate*, Grandpa!" he yelled out uncharacteristically. After taking a few seconds to regain his composure, lest he become emotional, he resumed, "I just don't get it! I stressed to death writing this novel for roughly four years, waited months for the agent, sold coins that I spent years collecting, worked all summer to raise the funds, spent almost everything I had on the publisher, and finally got it published a year after receiving the contract. Heck, I started the novel over six years ago at this time.

"Then, I posted about it all over social media every chance I got. I kept tagging news organizations and contacted many news personnel. Only a small percentage got back with me, but they were like, 'Congratulations, but we can't help you,' or, 'Congrats, but I'm just a reporter," or even, 'It's been pushed to the assignment desk.' One said I could mail in a copy with a note explaining why it'd be newsworthy. I did so, but it's been a couple of months; I still haven't heard anything.

"Moreover, a couple of news anchors gave me the emails to their producers or health reporters. The only one that got back was our local CBS affiliate channel. He was like, 'Congratulations, Zachary, but we're only interested in celebrities.' *The heck?* The entirety of CBS News? You got to be kidding.

"Oh, and my community college's newspaper? The student journalist interviewed me for forty-five minutes on the telephone. She spent the next day writing the article about me and my novel. I later went over to the college to pick up the newspaper, but the professor said, 'Sorry, that student dropped a month ago. We'll get you reassigned.' But I never was!"

"Mama told me there'd be days like this," Grandpa Corwin lamented, shaking his head, staring off at the damask wall in his living room beyond his dilapidated floral sofa.

"This past summer, at the fair, I noticed a vendor booth from a local newspaper—the one that did a featured story about me back in 2015. I thought I'd go up to the man during my break to let him know about my novel, but he never looked at me when we were talking with each other. He was scrolling on his cellphone and his face looked like he hated his job. I just turned around and walked away. Then I saw a vendor booth from the county newspaper. *Those* two people were the complete opposite. They were amazed that I published a book and gave me the number to their supervisor. I called it, but their department was in sales, not editorial, he told me. So, I'm stuck."

Grandpa Corwin absently ran his fingers through his long, white beard as he listened.

"Finally, I turned to my last resort. From September until today, January 2020, whenever I was done with my homework and studies at Tributary University, I looked up the emails for every single affiliate and owned-and-operated station for ABC across the country, then NBC. I was going to do that for every news network. I must've sent a hundred emails and news tips all across America so far. And you know what? Ninety-nine percent did not get back with me, and ninety-nine percent of the one percent who did wrote, 'Congratulations, but we can't do anything.'

"And then one percent of the one percent was either mean or false hope. One news director up in Idaho said I could be a part of an anti-bullying story, but then he stopped emailing me updates and eventually blocked me after I emailed him back. And another one just wrote, 'Hey, Zachy. This is Green Bay, nowhere near you.' And that was it!" Zachary banged the upholstered armrest of the sofa. "I mean, the freaking audacity. This is going to get me to start cussing … and I don't even cuss." He hoped a little levity would lighten the ambiance, but it didn't work.

"Well, I'll never! *Get a grip*, Zachary. I completely understand what hell you must've gone through, but trust God and give it time. It'll come in His perfect timing under His perfect will."

"But, Grandpa … I mean, first, I make myself believe that, a-and I do, but I just refuse to believe that now's not the time. There's so much bullying and ableism and discrimination in this world. I'm freaking sick and tired every time I have to open up Facebook, see a great picture of a smiling child, sometimes in a suit, and then read the caption that says, 'This precious boy (or precious girl) just committed suicide for being bullied at school.'

"*That's* why I'm on this quest, Grandpa. *That's* why I've sold many things I own and spent nearly all the money I had, many times over. I spent nearly a hundred dollars on Vistaprint for those little business cards for my book, and by now, I've left *hundreds* of them everywhere. I'm on a freaking rescue mission. I've been bullied and mistreated a lot, including the past few months. If it's happening to me, then it's happening to millions of other people. And I'm trying to do my part in eradicating it. Don't get me wrong, however. I know that we humans alone can't establish world peace, but still, why not relative world peace? I'm not giving up.

"And while I had tried desperately to get on the news and radio, I tried desperately to share on social media. Unfortunately, after posting every single day on YouTube for over two years, I only have 315 subscribers and hardly much feedback. I'm averaging, what? 10 likes and 5 comments … on a *good* video? Pinterest seems to be a joke; no one ever engages with me on there. I rarely get likes or comments on Twitter, except the occasional 'troll.' One random person, somewhere on earth, said that he called 911 on me. Two others told me not to have kids because I'm crazy. I mean, I put 'troll' in quotes because they're real human beings who have purpose and just need to be shown kindness, and I try my best. I point out how they're wrong and that we autistics aren't aliens or lost causes, but I do so in the kindest way possible.

"Oh, and speaking about Twitter, I was advised to look at the trending column. If I see a relevant hashtag or keyword in there, I can use it and potentially go viral that way. It usually doesn't work, but when it did, I would just get trolled. One user, who claimed to be a Satan worshipper with a creepy profile picture, said, 'We get it, Zachary. You published your book at age 23.' The heck? That was only one little detail in the entire tweet. What's this person so upset about? To this day, I keep looking at the trending column, but the only thing trending the past few days is about a doctor in China with a mysterious flu.

"So, since news media and social media aren't working right now, the other thing I've always dreamed of doing is leading all-school assemblies, talking about autism and my novel, as well as juggling. A year and a half ago, I came up with a juggling analogy: if anything drops in life, pick it back up and keep going."

Grandpa Corwin's eyes lit up. "Well, you know what, Zachary? That might be an *excellent* start for you. Just give it time. Perhaps the more assemblies you do, the more word of mouth. And the more word of mouth, the more chances a news station might pick up your story. And when that happens, other stations or newspapers might feature your story too. Then, after a while, you might get on national news, but it starts with baby steps. I'm in my seventies and am lucky enough to operate a flip phone, not all these smartphones that you whippersnappers have. Call me a fuddy-duddy, but I stay away from those things. I hardly know anything about YouTube, Face-something, Insta-whatever, or the modern-day Tweety Bird, but from what I know, they're powerful, so keep on posting and maybe one day or one month, something will happen … Hmm, in *my* grandfather's day, the latest amusements were Penny Arcades and Nickelodeons. None of that social media stuff. Anyway, had you begun asking around schools?"

"Yes, I already spoke to the new principal at Washington Elementary. She seemed to be in a hurry, but she congratulated me. I never heard from her again.

"I showed my novel to the new principal at Canyon Mountain Middle School. He said he would send an email about my book to every teacher; I have no clue if he actually did that.

"But then I spoke to the new principal at my former high school in November. Grandpa, he looked at me in the eyes and asked me, 'Do you want to speak?'"

"Well, I'll be." Grandpa Corwin smiled.

"I said, 'Absolutely, it'd be my honor to *volunteer* and speak. As always, everywhere I go, I keep stressing the word 'volunteer.' I'm just waiting to hear back, praying to God that it's not another fluke. Furthermore, I emailed the school district. Many still remember me from my advocacy days in high school and how I juggled every year at their special education banquet. They got me in contact with another high school, and I'm speaking in late March for ten minutes."

"Praise God. That's wonderful."

"And yet another high school in the district is having a vendor fair in April, and I'm going to be one of the vendors."

"You see? It's all going to work out. I'm so happy for you. Now, I want to talk to you about some of the startling things you just said."

Oh no. Zachary's smile faded.

"You described all those times being bullied and, what? Trolled?"

"Uh … yeah?"

"And lately? Was it here in this neighborhood?"

Zachary exhaled, closed his eyes, and shook his head. "I was just passionate moments ago. I said things I didn't want to reveal. I didn't want you or Mom or many other people to worry."

"Oh, Zachary," Grandpa Corwin said, disappointed. "Never hold in things. I recall the day your mother brought you back from the doctor after your autism diagnosis. One of the last things Dr. Gallagher said was to make sure you knew that we are all ears. Never hold in things again, all right?"

"Believe me, I know that nowadays, and that will be part of my message *when* I finally do school assemblies and get on the news. I have a science demo analogy where I make a cloud in a bottle. It's something I learned back in General Chemistry at the college. It's to represent not bottling things up inside, or else this might happen. And I release the pressure, creating the cloud. I will teach them how to release the cloud, which comes by talking things out to someone you can trust. That's one of the things I'm going to emphasize in March. I rehearsed it a dozen times so far, and I'm endeavoring to cut down. I only get ten minutes, and I really need to leave an impact, so that I'd get invited to lead assemblies."

"Well, don't worry about that."

Zachary shuddered inside.

"I know you'll do a great job. Once you start, it'll be just like when you rehearsed."

Zachary quickly regained his composure, but when his grandfather nonchalantly told him not to worry about it, he was instantly taken back to that ableist father in the park. "Uh, yeah. Um, I'm sure too. I guess I'm just overdramatizing."

"But tell me more about your recent experiences with bullying."

"Oh, uh—" Zachary felt nervous again. "Well, this isn't really bullying, necessarily, but on August 11, the last day of the county fair, I was eating a hot dog during my break. I walked inside the fair's indoor art exhibit. Immediately, a worker stands up, utterly sleepy or annoyed, and says, 'Sir, no food!' I replied, 'Oh, sorry, I didn't know.' I quickly turned around and headed toward the door. I heard him say something. To this day, I'm not positive, but it sounded like, 'Come on, man!' And even if he didn't, I did receive such remarks in my life, like 'Grow up.' With my autistic brain, one little thing, even if it's a misinterpretation, can evoke a dozen horrible memories that really happened."

"Well, don't let those nitwits get to you."

"Another took place at the church I go to for Royal Rangers. I'm still playing for the seniors at the chapel, but I've also been going to the church on Sunday afternoons to help the youth prepare for a big fine-arts expo. Again, I felt so down that my books weren't getting any attention. My senior commander spoke with the director of the Fine Arts Festival, who said that I could come and speak about the process of writing a book as well as sharing my testimony."

"That sounds fantastic. That'll leave a great impression for future authors. Had it happened yet?"

"Yes, it has, but the reason I brought it up is because of something that started on that first Sunday. I walked inside the room and there was only one person there: a young woman in her late-twenties, named Kaitlin McMahon, who volunteered with Andrés Enríquez, her fiancé, the high school pastor. I asked her if I was in the right spot, and all she said was, 'Yeah.' Now, I know when people are shy. Takes one to know one. And yeah, I'm sure she's shy too, but it was the way she acted around me.

"I gave the benefit of the doubt for months. Every time I saw her, I would say hi as I do with everyone. If I said hi within the first second of seeing her, she'd give a little smile and say hi back. If it was two or more seconds, she'd quickly look away from me. *That* is unmistakable. I'm not crazy or misinterpreting it. Every time I'm near, she looks down and refuses to look at me. And I'm offended because I have a book published that describes autism and is meant to spread universal awareness *and acceptance*. Thus, bullying and ignoring people, just for being autistic, should be eradicated. And *she knows* about my book. She knows about me being autistic and bullied all my life because she was there when I told it to the entire youth.

"One Sunday, I was standing outside the church, waiting for one of my fellow commanders, and I saw her walk in my direction. I faced a different direction, but through my sunglasses, I was looking at her, trying to disprove my assumptions. I noticed that she picked up the pace, veered off in a different direction, took out her cellphone, started to giggle into it, and … essentially made an unsuccessful attempt at pretending to talk on the phone.

"Look, Grandpa, with most people, I'm not seeking to be *best* friends. I'm not wanting to hang out with most people out there, including Kaitlin, Pastor Andrés, and others. A simple wave or chat would do. I'm autistic and am therefore socially shy. Plus, I'm too busy. There is a difference. All I want is acceptance from everyone. I'm neither after money nor fame. I just want people to treat me as a human instead of ignoring me.

"But there's more. Being on Instagram, I follow tons of people from that church. One day, I ran into Kaitlin's account. I started following it. Again, I was hoping I was wrong about her. Whenever she posted, I'd give a like and a short comment of encouragement, usually with a Scripture verse to prove that I'm a Christian and have a heart for people. Heck, that's what I do for many people I follow. I know I should never judge like this, but Grandpa, between you, me, and the fence post, I question whether she's a Christian in name only. I just can't imagine a person who works (not volunteers) at a church for people under eighteen and has utter contempt for people who are autistic, which is something the Bible would frown upon.

"I apologize for saying that, but I've held it in for months and had to get it off my chest. Anyway, the ultimate proof of her bigotry against autistics is this: she'd never like any of my comments on her Instagram, but she'd like everyone else's, unless she got a spam comment about being a brand ambassador or whatever. Is that what I'm reduced to in her eyes? And then one night, she just blocked me, categorically. No questions asked. Pastor Andrés sent me a direct message saying that she wasn't appreciating my comments. But again, my comments were of encouragement, like, 'Great job,' 'Congratulations on completing the semester,' or 'God has great things in store for you,' and no, I wasn't just writing clichés, but something to that effect."

"What in tarnation? That's terrible. Totally unjustified. I'm sorry about that. That nitwit should never be allowed to work with anyone under eighteen until she gets counseling. However, Zachary, after hearing everything, I need to impart to you some valuable pieces of wisdom.

Number one, thank you for finally getting this off your chest. Two, even though these experiences happen, there's nothing you can do about what was said or done. You can't change people; only God can change their heart. If they don't accept you right away, move on and remember the friends and family you have.

"*You*, Zachary, are in charge of your own happiness. It doesn't matter what people say to you or do to you. If you want to waste part of your life dwelling on it, then that's up to you. Believe me, more of this is going to happen, but you can choose to be happy and joyous, or you can allow the darkness to debilitate you for the rest of your life. I can't make the choice for you. You have to make it."

"Hmm. Thank you, Grandpa." Zachary struggled to find the right words of acknowledgement, but failed. "Um, thanks so much. I'll remember that. Perhaps I can use that when encouraging others."

"No matter how successful you might become, just know, you'll never ever get everyone in the world to like you."

"Yeah … I know."

"Don't even try. You'll burn yourself out."

Knock, knock.

Zachary lethargically hobbled over to the door and opened it. "Mom, you're back from work. I'm glad."

"Your son and I were having a big conversation," Grandpa Corwin said, smiling.

"Was it about what you needed to tell me?" asked Mrs. Corwin, setting her purse and car keys on top of the pony wall next to the front door.

"Um, no. Mom, Grandpa, I have some terrible news," he said, slowly sitting back down on the sofa as his body was sore. "I won't beat around the bush. I went on Amazon, and it said that there were only ten of my books left. It sounded like it was going out of stock. I tried contacting my publisher for days. Finally, I contacted my literary agent, and he emailed me back this morning. He said that the publisher went bankrupt, went out of business, and didn't tell anyone."

"*No!*" hollered Mrs. Corwin.

"I felt so down. I felt so depressed. I sat there in my room alone for a couple of hours. All my organs—bones, heart, muscles, you name it—felt pulled to the floor, due to gravity. I literally felt like my spirit was going to escape my body. That's how lifeless I felt. That's when I called you at work and came over here to talk to Grandpa as I waited for you."

Mrs. Corwin was in tears.

"Did your agent tell you what you could do?" Grandpa Corwin asked as he went to put an arm around his daughter. "Sounds like they pulled the wool over your eyes." Whispering to Mrs. Corwin, he said, "Everything will be fine, sweetie."

"Well, I'm not saying they deceived me, but it's totally unprofessional that they wouldn't notify us. The agent told me to contact a friend of his who's a publisher. Maybe I could get republished. It'll be a different publisher, but it'll eventually be sorted out on Amazon, so I can keep all the thirty reviews I got. He also said that it's impossible for such a book as mine to go out of stock, so I don't need to worry about that. As of now, I'm waiting to hear back from this new publisher."

"Oh, that gives me so much hope." Mrs. Corwin smiled with optimism.

"Let's pray it'll work," said Grandpa Corwin.

"Thanks … Um … Mom? Grandpa? If it's okay, I'd like to go back to the house. I'm enervated and need to rest."

"Sure, you go ahead," they said.

Tired, Zachary walked out the door and limped across the street. After climbing the stairs which felt like Mt. Everest, he changed into his pajamas, leaving his clothes on the floor. He collapsed on his bed and was asleep within one minute, something that was very rare for him.

At three in the morning, he woke up his mother, and they drove to the hospital.

"So, what brings you in on this early morning?" asked the nurse.

Zachary, nearly panting, said, "I don't feel well. I went to bed exhausted and with a headache. I woke up around three. The headache was still there, and I just felt, well, drained, I surmise. Fatigued, sweaty, aches all up and down my body."

"Hmm. Well, I'm pretty sure, judging by everything you're describing, this is the flu."

Zachary closed his eyes and sank his head into his pillow. "I can't believe this is happening," he muttered. "Are you sure?"

The nurse continued, "We do have a test where we stick a swab up your nose, but it's so uncomfortable. I don't want to do that to you just to prove something that I'm sure you have."

"And let me guess the prognosis. This will last 1-2 weeks?"

"I'm afraid so."

"Darn it! I'm taking sixteen units at my university, including two science classes and two labs. Missing at least one week will destroy me."

"Well, make sure you contact your professors and work something out. For now, don't overexert yourself. Rest at home. Drink plenty of fluids (water, orange juice, broth), and eat light meals like chicken noodle soup if you feel up to it. Keep an eye on your symptoms, and if anything gets worse, let a doctor know."

Zachary resigned to his fate, housebound for one week. His professors agreed to help him catch up once he felt better, including reteaching their lessons privately in their offices. Meanwhile, when he had strength, he would study the material and complete some assignments.

His brain was spinning. The situation with his publisher had depressed him, which probably lowered his immunity, causing him to contract the flu to begin with. The fact that his book and message was hardly getting out on social media or news media stressed him out. Being discriminated in his neighborhood and rarely receiving opportunities to tutor, teach, or entertain people in his community also made him question his worth and purpose once again.

On top of that, he was taking more than a full load this semester to keep his financial aid. His academic counselor advised him to stay on the two-year track. He figured that, since he was older and had years of practice and experience in education, he would be able to handle it. He felt more equipped entering this university than he did when he entered junior college, and even more than he did when he entered high school.

27

Ethereal Conversion

Snickering broke the quietude.

From the veranda, Zachary looked around but saw no one.

Giggling continued, along with periodic thuds and a noise like cement being sawed.

Zachary turned off the music on his laptop, which had been playing "Sleepytown" by Kid Runner, and stepped out onto the lawn to look around some more. Surprised, he saw two young teenagers who seemed to have appeared out of nowhere, walking toward him from down the street. Both of them were in their Little League uniforms. One tossed a baseball up and down, while the other dragged his bat along the street.

He soon realized that they weren't laughing at random jokes they were telling each other. As the teens walked past his front lawn, they couldn't stop glancing at him with weird smirks, off and on.

He pretended to be occupied with something but kept an eye on them through his sunglasses. *Seriously?* he thought. *It's 2020.*

Before passing by the house completely, one of the boys turned around one final time to smirk at him, as if to say, "Hey, look! An alien exhibit. This'll be lit!"

That does it! Zachary began marching to them, forcing himself forward even as his breathing grew labored. "Hey! What's the problem?"

The teens stopped and swung around, laughing at him some more. "What?" one of them asked. "*I* don't see a problem. Do you see a tree falling, Ricky?"

"No." Ricky tried to hide his smirk. "Are you mentally okay, dude?"

"*I am autistic!*" Zachary hollered, nearly gasping for air. "What is wrong with being autistic, which is something I *never* asked for?"

Both teens' disparaging expressions changed instantly, and they looked at him wide-eyed.

"We're one score into the twenty-first century. Don't you think bullying, discrimination, and ableism should have been *eradicated* by now?"

The teens began to look remorseful as though on the verge of tears, but Zachary assumed it was sarcasm. Continuing, he informed them saying,

"There's nothing wrong with being autistic, and hey, I published a huge novel about it, if you'd like to read it."

"Oh." The teens shook as if just realizing they had insulted a celebrity unbeknownst to them.

"I have quite a few YouTube videos talking about autism through my firsthand perspective too, if you care to educate yourselves."

"We're sorry!" one of them cried.

"What's your channel name?" the other said, dropping his bat and pulling out his phone.

"W-w-wait, seriously?" Zachary was confused. "You mean, just like that?"

"Sir, we're so sorry. You didn't deserve that. How do we find you on YouTube, and where can we buy your book?"

"Uh—" Zachary was purely shocked yet simultaneously blissful.

Suddenly, at the most inopportune moment in history, they disappeared. In fact, everything disappeared. Silence and darkness wrapped around Zachary like death itself. He opened his eyes. Instantly, death released its grip, but forlornness quickly took hold. However, with it came a touch of peace and optimism. He was staring straight up at his ceiling.

After making his morning coffee, he decided to post about his dream on social media including a YouTube video. He explained how he had another dream where people bullied him, but this time was different: he *finally* got through to the bullies, helping them understand people who are different. Alas, it was only a dream. After uploading the video to YouTube, sharing it in posts, and tweeting it out, his eyes drifted to Twitter's trending column.

"Oh, dear," Zachary said mournfully as he read about the death of the ophthalmologist in Wuhan. Just a couple of weeks before this, the first case of this particular flu in the United States was trending. He began recalling all the stories about the 2014 Ebola outbreak, especially the first case in the U.S., which was in Texas. He likened this new flu to that one and assumed it would be contained quickly, especially with further advancements in medicine.

28

The Pandemic

"Heavens to Betsy!" Grandpa Corwin exclaimed, dropping the grocery bags onto the living room floor and collapsing into Mrs. Corwin's new accent chair.

"You can't make that stuff up." Mrs. Corwin heaved her grocery bags onto the kitchen counter with a sigh of exhaustion. "And it's a Wednesday too."

"What's happening?" Zachary said, rushing down the stairs. "I heard hollering and many thuds."

"Do you have enough energy left to tell him, sweetie?" Grandpa Corwin asked, resting his eyes.

"Zachary," Mrs. Corwin informed lethargically, "between Disneyland parking and any of the grocery stores these days, I'd take Disneyland in a heartbeat, no question about it. Our Albertsons was like the streets of Manhattan: people pàssing by each other and knocking into one another. Shelves were literally empty throughout the store."

"You're kidding."

"No, I'm not kidding!"

Zachary walked into the living room to see quite a spectacle. "Um … Grandpa?"

"Hmm?" Grandpa Corwin was nearly asleep.

"Uh, like the adage, I guess a fella can't be too careful when it comes to stocking up … but, what's with all the packages of toilet paper?"

Grandpa Corwin opened his eyes wide and snapped upright. "Don't you be getting my dander up, sonny!" he crankily growled, pointing at him.

"Oh, *don't ask!*" Mrs. Corwin called from inside the kitchen.

"All right. I won't, then," he said, startled. He walked back into the kitchen to help his mother put away the groceries. "Mom?"

"Hmm?"

"I read reports that colleges and universities were switching to remote classes. Well, I got an email from the president of Tributary University, Dr. Jordan. This week will be the last week of attending school in person. After spring break, we'll be meeting on some website platform called Zoom. I'm not too tech-savvy."

Mrs. Corwin shook her head. "Well, it's just out of precaution, and we need to deal with it. My friends just began meeting on Zoom for their business. It's super easy."

"The president's talking!" Grandpa Corwin called out from the living room.

Mrs. Corwin and Zachary quickly took a seat on the living room couch as Grandpa Corwin turned up the volume. They watched live as President Trump addressed the nation from the Oval Office, announcing that the WHO had officially declared COVID-19 a global pandemic.

"Man alive!" Grandpa Corwin was stunned. "Last time I heard a president mention a quarantine was back during the Cuban Missile Crisis, when I watched President Kennedy's address live in October 1962."

"And those travel restrictions. This is huge," Mrs. Corwin said, her face contorted with grief and shock.

Suddenly, Zachary felt sicker, his face turning pale, and asked to be excused.

Two days later, at Tributary University, he had a spontaneous thought to make a YouTube video, showing how the coronavirus pandemic was impacting his town. Since he was ten minutes early to one of his chemistry labs, he walked around the campus to film. It was like a ghost town. He explained how local schools and churches were no longer holding in-person gatherings, and how it felt like he was being quarantined in his house. Once the lab started, only forty percent of the students showed up.

Afterward, Mrs. Corwin and Zachary drove to their local Albertsons to pick up some last-minute groceries. It was the first time Zachary had gone inside and witnessed the overcrowded pandemonium. As he walked in, he saw one of the managers screaming into his radio, calling for additional resources.

It was as crowded as an amusement park, but in spite of all the people, one could still hear "If Everyone Cared" by Nickelback being played over the ceiling speakers. Shelves were practically empty.

Beholding history, his brain absentmindedly decided to continue filming, adding to the video he had already started, hoping to document the event like an amateur reporter. He figured it would fit in with the miscellanea of his channel. He got on the camera, spoke for a few seconds, and proceeded to walk, pointing the camera at himself. He was not out to film people right up to their faces.

Halfway across the store, he saw the same manager from earlier. He was working crowd control by the checkout lanes, sporting his high fade. As he walked past the manager, he gave him a subtle smile, which the manager returned. The entire exchange took no more than one second.

After seeing him jumpy earlier and yelling at people in his radio, Zachary thought that if he had to walk by him, he would at least encourage him with a smile.

About ten steps later, he heard from behind him, "Hey! Hey!"

He immediately turned around and saw the manager running toward him, hopping and weaving between patrons along the way.

"Why are you filming?!" he shouted at him.

"What?" Zachary was in pure oblivion, immediately putting away his camera.

"What's *wrong* with you?!" he yelled, his face looking absolutely menacing. His eyes looked like those of an unearthly, snarling beast.

"Huh?" Right then and there, Zachary was traumatized. He couldn't speak and was shaken in fear. Another employee of the store rushed over to the manager's side.

I'm going to die! Zachary figured.

"You don't be filming in my store!" the manager yelled. "Don't let me take that camera away from you!" he added as he literally stormed off.

Zachary and the employee who just arrived looked at each other in confusion.

"I do apologize to him, the store, and the entire Albertsons chain, but, um, I didn't know you weren't allowed to film. I was just documenting how the coronavirus is affecting this town. That's all," Zachary elucidated, giving his defense. He smiled, still bewildered.

The employee smiled back and left.

At least we both left with a smile, but mine was faked, Zachary thought as he began grumbling in his mind and meandering aimlessly around the store. His legs felt like they were going to fail him. His abdomen was sore as if being locked in a confined space and no one knew he was stuck. He was so thankful he decided against a Starbucks Frappuccino, for he wouldn't have been able to keep it down after such an exchange.

"I'm sorry," he said, after running into a shopper, distracted by the depressing thoughts of what life is becoming, not just for him, but for everyone else. He put on a smile; the shopper smiled back. After leaving, Zachary instantly dropped his countenance again. Sometimes, even in the lowest parts of his life, he still tried his best to brighten other people's days. He still believed that that was why he was on Earth.

I completely own up to it, of course. I was ignorant and rightfully corrected, but it was in a wrongful, audacious manner, Zachary thought, still shaking. *He shouldn't have yelled at me like that, with the assumption that I had a problem. He probably assumed I was one of those teenagers (since that's how young I look) who pointlessly films random people as a joke. I just feel terrible, as I would never film at the expense of someone else. He obviously didn't know that I'm an author of a book about autism, which would prove that I have a heart and intelligence.*

Upon realizing there was no chance in proving it to him, his breathing became labored, exacerbated by the Disneyland-like rush of people around him.

"Hey, Zachary! I'm finished with my shopping. Are *you* ready?" Mrs. Corwin said with a wide smile.

"Mom, not now!"

"Huh?"

"Sorry, Mom. Y-You go check out. I need to walk home."

Unhesitatingly, he hurried out of the store. Walking through his local park, he filmed a video expounding on what had happened. This was his new coping mechanism; it was one that kept him from bottling up his feelings. Still, he made sure to act responsibly. He wasn't seeking revenge. He didn't want the manager fired. He wouldn't blast his picture on social media and shame him for it. He would be satisfied with a chance to apologize and to hear the manager acknowledge the full story.

As soon as he got home, no longer shaking as much, the first thing he did was go on YouTube, where he found countless videos of people filming inside Albertsons and other grocery stores, as well as department stores, filming things he would *never* bother to film.

Alas, over the next few months, this one incident caused him to lose sleep, instigating as many soliloquies as that father in the park had in 2017. It became so intense that he began shaking all over again, even months later. What depressed him was that he knew he wasn't a troublemaker, something the manager didn't care to consider. Moreover, when an autistic is yelled at like that, they easily misconstrue it as pure hatred. Additionally, when an autistic is corrected, it is already like a knife in the heart because the feelings of being a failure begin to seep in.

"I don't get it," Zachary told himself alone in his room. "One thing this did was give me a whole new perspective of the world. It's life-changing. It's like I'm getting the fear of YouTubing. How did that not happen to me before? What if it did? What if it had gotten worse inside Albertsons? How do other YouTubers do it and not get in trouble?"

He recalled a few fun memories at Tributary University, where students and staff recognized him from his YouTube videos. Each semester, he'd make a couple of videos documenting how his education was going at the university. This is where he discovered his passion for videomaking, piecing together A-roll and B-roll clips, accentuated with background music.

"And no one said anything to me then," Zachary said aloud in a quandary. "On the contrary, one employee told me, 'I love your videos. Keep YouTubing!' Therefore, what is the boundary line?!"

During the evening of the incident, he opened up his emails. The first one was from the senior commander at his outpost, saying that Royal Rangers was cancelled until further notice.

Respecting the decision, he still felt sick and lonely. Royal Rangers was the number-one part of his life that gave him the most purpose, joy, and satisfaction.

The second email was from Pastor Rick, explaining that the chapel was probably going to shut down indefinitely.

The next two said that the vendor fair and the long-awaited speaking engagement at those high schools were both postponed.

The fifth email was from his university. He was going to speak about his novel and his life being autistic to the student body in April, but it was also postponed.

He had *finally* gotten the chances to speak and had rehearsed many times, only for all of them to be cancelled at the same time.

The world was on lockdown. People were dying from COVID-19.

This is it.

He was confined to his house.

He was later required to wear a mask whenever he went out, but only for essentials.

No seniors to play piano for.

No children at Washington Elementary to put smiles on through his juggling.

No boys at Royal Rangers to teach imperative survival skills to.

Depressed to death, debilitated with lifelessness and isolation, haunted by dozens of memories of being yelled at, he crawled into bed. He felt numb and purposeless, queasy and demotivated, yet he looked out his window to see the warm glow of the lamppost out on the sidewalk, reminding him of the hope he had.

* * *

A few days later, Grandpa Corwin and Mrs. Corwin were resting (or more like recuperating) in the living room. Grandpa Corwin collapsed into the accent chair once again, and Mrs. Corwin sank onto the couch. Hardly had they settled for two seconds when shouts came from upstairs.

"*No!*"

Grandpa Corwin and Mrs. Corwin both perked up, startled.

"No!" Zachary repeatedly yelled as he thundered down the stairs.

"Where's the fire?!" Grandpa Corwin exclaimed.

"Mom! Grandpa! I just saw it trending on Twitter that this might last until 'July or August!'"

"Oh, no!" Mrs. Corwin lamented, rubbing her forehead and looking distressed.

"Well, sweetie," Grandpa Corwin said, reaching over to rub his daughter's shoulder to comfort her. "This is something we all need to live with, but it's temporary. I fought in the Vietnam War. It'll eventually be over." Turning toward Zachary, he added, "You won't believe *our* expedition this morning."

"Please tell me about it, but first, wait. You guys are back. You don't need to keep your face masks on anymore."

"Gosh, I keep forgetting I have it on these days," Mrs. Corwin said.

Grandpa Corwin yanked his off and threw it in the wastepaper basket next to the accent chair. "Ah, these cockamamie masks! They definitely ruffle my feathers. Anyway, for starters, Albertsons only let a few people in at a time. The line to get groceries stretched out the door, through the parking lot, and extended a half a block down the street."

"Wow, couldn't you go to another store?"

"Six of one, half a dozen of the other. The same phenomenon occurred at Trader Joe's, Walmart, Target, and everywhere else."

"You're kidding!"

"Does it sound like he's kidding?" Mrs. Corwin chimed in. "I can't believe how jumpy people get. All *I* did was sneeze, and *everyone* jerked their head at me as if I'm a disease."

Grandpa Corwin patted Mrs. Corwin's shoulder. "Anyway, Zachary, remember that manager?"

"Uh, yes." He shuddered, a chill running through his veins.

"Well, that little petulant sourpuss probably has a chip on his shoulder. I overheard him complaining about his own employees over his radio in the adjacent aisle, shouting, 'What's wrong with them?'"

"I'm sure he treats everyone that way," Mrs. Corwin added. "He just has an ornery disposition."

"Perhaps." Zachary sighed and nodded. "I actually went over to talk to the assistant manager. She happened to be the employee who ran up beside the manager that day and witnessed half the spectacle. Anyway, she was busy telling the stock clerk where to put some items, so I was already nervous about interrupting. Plus, just as you'd imagine, it was like a sardine can. I asked her if she or someone got my email. She asked what it was about. All I said was, 'Just a complaint.' The stock clerk then looked at me for one second. Ashamed to admit it, still being uptight about the whole situation with the manager, I was like, 'Don't *you* be looking at me like that!' I didn't say that out loud, of course. Anyway, the assistant manager said she didn't recall such an email, since she gets over a hundred emails every single day. At least she seemed sympathetic after we talked it through, but with my autistic brain, I couldn't get the stock clerk's cold eyes out of my mind."

"Well, I definitely have a bone to pick with that manager," said Grandpa Corwin. "I got a moniker for him that I learned from fellow sailors in the Navy, but I won't say it aloud in this house. I just wanted to encourage you: don't take what he said to heart."

Zachary nodded in acknowledgement. It was easier said than done.

29

The YouTube Comments

At a quarter to eight the next morning, Zachary awoke to a comment on one of his videos he did about Royal Rangers. Focusing his eyes, he read, "You're just a lonely weirdo! Just look at yourself! Even your planespotting videos are as disgusting as your face!" This was followed by a few laughing emojis.

Nearly falling out of bed and dropping his smartphone, Zachary shot straight up and read it again a couple of times. Then he checked out who this person was. Apparently, he was a fellow planespotter in Oman. He took a deep breath and reminded himself to keep calm when responding to such a person. He didn't hate the discriminator; he hated the discrimination. He didn't want him to feel hurt, assuming he's capable of feeling hurt. He hoped that this man—and everyone else on the planet—would go far with his purpose in life, but first, he needed to turn from his malevolent ways.

"Well, I've been called other things in the past too," he typed. "And I'm prone to it because autistics like me are often singled out. Heck, I've been treated like trash since kindergarten. That is why I became a traditionally-published author of a novel about it. In it, I tell the truth about the good and the bad of living with such an incurable condition. I sincerely hope it could help you be more tolerable toward us."

Zachary pasted the Amazon link before continuing, "And you gave me the title 'lonely weirdo.' If that defines a person as someone who loves to learn, works hard, gets good grades, and volunteers for children and teenagers to tell them they have a reason to live on this planet, then sure, I must fit that definition."

He then flipped it around to address the Omani: "But *you* are smart too. Perhaps smarter! I don't know you, but I trust that. Just don't give up, and if you are honest with yourself, you will go far in life! I don't know everything, just to say. I failed to get A's on everything, but at the same time, I did the best I could in this life. I'm sure you are doing the same! And for that, I'm happy for you. Congratulations! I really am! I just want to help and encourage people like you, so that they can go far in their life and not commit suicide. *You* might be the next best planespotter, writer, historian, or whoever, but you won't pursue it if you feel down and depressed all the time, questioning your existence on earth. Know that many people, like me, are here rooting you on! You do have purpose. We just don't root for you to discriminate, though. Many people are there for you if you give them the chance. Have a wonderful day."

Before hitting reply, he decided to translate it into Arabic to ensure he'd get the message, leaving the English underneath.

Reply.

After half an hour of chaos, he let out a sigh of relief. He went back to the man's channel and watched his four videos, which is how he knew he was from Oman and spoke Arabic. Wanting to simply spread the meaning of kindness and what it should mean to be human, he commented on a couple of his videos, praising him for his decent quality. He then became the man's fourth subscriber.

Since people were still permitted to go out for walks in March 2020, he decided to take a cathartic neighborhood walk to process everything and to clear his mind.

He honestly didn't know what to expect. Twelve months prior, a user called him a nerd on one of his Autism Awareness videos. After replying in the same way he had for this Omani, the user said, "Oh, I feel bad now. I'm sorry. I subbed." Zachary replied, "Don't feel bad. Sorry if I made you feel bad. I'm just glad you realized that we're human too." They continued commenting back and forth, getting to know one another. The "troll" realized that Zachary was kindhearted and that he jumped to conclusions too quickly, judging from his preconceived notions.

Even though changing the perspectives of others had happened a couple of times, other occasions were met with incessant crickets. One user on Twitter commented, "Wow, that's dumb. Did you ever go to school, bro? Stop being such a troll!"

He replied, "As a matter of fact, I have a degree in mathematics and a book published." To this day, he never heard back.

He figured it would likely be one of those two outcomes. After all, who in their right mind could be confronted with the truth, mixed with kindness, and *still* hold onto their former, misguided position?

By ten o'clock that night, he had forgotten about it, preoccupied with making a video about how he got into planespotting. He had the idea to make such a video for a while and finally took the time to record it while out walking in the neighborhood. However, bearing the Omani's insults in mind, he humbly said, "I may not be the best planespotter in the world, but this is one of my hobbies that brings me joy in life. I encourage you to find your joys and passions too, and no matter what people say, never quit."

He entered his third hour piecing this video together, as he always put his entire heart into these video projects, yet he felt disheartened that he only averaged twenty to thirty views per video and one or two comments. He still kept up the faith. After all, his subscribers slowly grew and were currently at 450. Notwithstanding, he had publicly stated, "Whether a video of mine gets one view or a million, I will never stop posting, and I pray that it will encourage someone on this planet."

As he was finishing up, he suddenly got a pop-up notification.

"Weirdos like you are costing taxpayers billions of dollars!" it said.

Nearly choking on a gulp of water that he had just taken at the most inopportune time, he clicked on it, opening up the entire diatribe from the Omani who replied to his heartfelt response.

"And what do we normal folks get in return? Nothing! If you were hurt and bullied in school, that's your fault! You could've chosen home schooling, but obviously you loved getting bullied. Or maybe you were too stupid to comprehend what bullying was. And you know, I'm not wasting $15 on a book written by a weirdo for other weirdos! I don't even believe you have the smarts enough to write a book. There's no way you wrote it.

"And another thing, weirdo, if you think that acting kind or pretending to be my friend will change my mind about weird, lonely autistics, then you are wrong!! Don't worry, I won't punch you in the face because you are too skinny. You wouldn't be able to even take it. And did I read in your bio that you want to be a school teacher? Are you that stupid? Are you too weird to deal with real adults? Who are you trying to fool? Wouldn't those school kids notice that you are weird and different? Look at yourself. You're too skinny and weak. You wouldn't be able to stop a school bully.

"Last thing, don't even think about starting a family! We real people don't need any more weirdos running around this planet. I'm actually not worried. I'm positive you never kissed a woman (or a man) in your life, loser!"

Zachary sat there, violently shaking, his heart beating out of his chest. He felt isolated and all alone. In that moment, he forgot about everyone who cared about his existence.

It's like he's telling us autistic individuals not to breathe, he thought as he spent forty-five minutes writing a lengthy reply addressing all of the man's half-dozen points, one by one.

He then considered all the ableism hell he had endured—from that manager at Albertsons a few days before, to Kaitlin at the church, to the father at the park in 2017, to the lady who thought he was a kidnapper in 2014, to Madeline and Max during kindergarten. Lo and behold, another isolating soliloquy began, lasting for four hours this time around.

He tried to console himself by remembering that he had gone through this before on social media, just not as drastically, and not necessarily about autism. In 2019, on Facebook, he read a comment from a butcher in the East South Central United States: "Don't tag me with Zachary Corwin again. I'm not wasting any more time with him." One of his friends had tagged him in a couple of viral posts about Order of Operations. Zachary was simply pointing out the correct order, being a math major, but the butcher replied in disagreement. After a back-and-forth, the butcher typed out the adage, "I'm giving up on you! You can lead a horse to water, but you can't make it drink."

That bothered Zachary for weeks, but if he got through it then, he can get through it now, especially with his new coping mechanism.

The next morning, he walked to a nearby public nature preserve. Piece by piece, he read through and broke down the Omani's diatribe on video, giving a defense for everything. He had his book with him, as he always carried it, to show the viewers his picture on the back, inviting viewers to compare his face with his headshot, proving that he was, indeed, the author. Toward the end of the video, he shared a couple of stories revealing how boys *and* adults at Royal Rangers and Washington Elementary appreciated him for who he was. *They* didn't think he was weird. At the very end, he prayed for the man to demonstrate what he believed all people should do for their enemies.

The only thing keeping him alive was *hope*! He posted the video hoping that people would watch it. Within twenty-four hours, that video garnered over 300 views, with a hundred percent supportive comments praising him for handling it like a pro while standing up for his principles. A couple said they felt quite blessed, and that made Zachary feel wonderful. It was the first time since before the shutdowns that he felt better.

You see? This is my purpose, Zachary thought, smiling, joy seeping into his innermost heart. *And I pray that that gentleman will get the message too and change. None of us autistics did anything wrong to deserve discrimination for being autistic.*

Despite an increase of twelve subscribers, his subsequent videos didn't get anywhere much. He never heard back from the Omani again until mid-May, when he commented on his video about autism and social interactions.

"Do you autistics even have real friends or an active social life? You are socially rejected! You're too weird to fit in. You see? Nobody, and I mean nobody, cares about autistics. By the way, did you get all the attention you wanted last time? Ha-ha-ha!" A few laughing emojis trailed the message.

Once again, Zachary froze for several seconds. *I thought I got through to him*, he lamented. *Who, with a brain, could* still *not understand, despite all the proof? And what's this remark about seeking attention? What?*

Zachary stayed up *all* night long going through his tens of thousands of pictures on Facebook, picking out a few dozen of them, and annotating them, irrefutably proving that he has had true friendships within the past twenty years and that autistic individuals *can* have a social life.

At the crack of dawn, with eyes stinging, he pressed the Publish button and shared the YouTube link all over social media. He subsequently collapsed in bed to sleep for the day. It was not unusual, especially in 2020, for Zachary to stay up late, tirelessly filming and editing Autism Awareness YouTube videos. It was hard to sleep anyway unless he put them together. On top of these, he still uploaded his typical math tutorials, piano music, planespotting videos, and other miscellaneous content.

Getting up that afternoon, he felt a mixture of hopefulness and nervousness.

Will I wake up to hundreds of views and supportive comments, or will my video be ignored like most of the other ones? Will I, in lieu of supportive comments, get another keyboard tirade from this gentleman again, or anyone for that matter?

All is calm. Not one word from that Omani. However, his video only got thirty views and two comments.

The first comment came from a Royal Rangers commander from across the country who was subscribed to his channel. "God bless you, brother," he started, "but you're giving this guy too much of your valuable time. You're a very smart man. Don't worry about what other people say. I enjoy all your videos."

The second comment read, "This is odd. To me, you're completely normal. I don't see you as different in the slightest, other than your apparent shyness and remarkable intelligence, but I'm proud of your honesty. I hope you could develop thick skin one day and laugh at your bullies instead of giving them a single iota."

This was not the first time he received such comments, nor was it the last. He always hearted them, replying, "Thank you so much. I appreciate your support."

However, although he meant what he said, he still had to speak it out and process it. At the same time, this spread awareness and eventual acceptance. Everyone needs to speak things out, but he chose to do so publicly. It did not mean that he didn't believe those who *do* support him, or that he was ungrateful toward them. He later chose to make a video specifically for that and referenced it whenever he had to make a similar video exposing the ableism he endured.

Publicly speaking about these experiences made Zachary feel better than private soliloquies, which by themselves brought him little relief, but it was better than nothing. There was more relief in posting about it on social media or writing in a book. Writing his novel, for instance, gave him a sense of purpose, though he was motivated primarily by the hope of helping millions of people through life (not just writing it for zero readers).

The greater relief would come with more book sales, social media views, and supportive comments. It would prove to him that there were, in fact, more people who cared about him than he had realized. The maximum relief would come with a formal apology from ableists.

Of course, he'd do everything for even one person, but it would help his strength and motivation if it were ten billion instead. Why not, since the technology of the twenty-first century is enough to make it possible?

30

The Lifesaver

As 2020 wore on, the world grew scarier. Curfews began to be enforced, locking the Corwins indoors from 8 p.m. to 6 a.m. Extended family members and best friends of theirs contracted COVID, some barely surviving.

Zachary's fall semester started out remote, barring a couple of in-person chemistry labs. As he worked through problems for Analytical Chemistry, a sudden knock on the door interrupted the silence. Opening it, he found his mother in tears on the other side.

"What happened?" Zachary's anxiety immediately hit the roof. "Is it Grandpa?"

"No," Mrs. Corwin barely choked out, shaking her head. "Zachary, I just got off the phone."

"And?"

"Thomas. His wife just passed away from COVID."

"W-what? Did I hear that correctly?"

"She had been immunocompromised her entire life. She went to Heaven at 2:30 this afternoon … Are you okay?"

"I-I just can't speak."

"Well, I wanted to let you know. If you think about it, call Thomas up. Let him know that you're thinking about him."

After, Zachary slowly walked to his ottoman and sat there, perplexed. He never knew anyone who died from COVID before. He went on Facebook and saw the last picture he had with Thomas and his wife. It was Christmas 2019. Everything felt like a bad dream.

The phone started dialing an hour later. Zachary took a deep breath as he wasn't good at this. A phone call, in place of an in-person visit, made it worse.

How do I make my intonations reflect the empathy in my heart?

"Hello?" said a tired, melancholy Thomas.

"Hey, Thomas."

"Zach? Champ, how are you?" He perked up a smidgen.

"I heard about Trudy. I-I'm so sorry. I-I couldn't believe it when I heard it. My condolences to you and the family," Zachary said, faltering.

"Thanks, Zach. It's been rough all afternoon, but not unexpected. She was in the hospital for the last two months."

After talking for another minute, Thomas changed the subject to catch up with him. "So, are you still in Royal Rangers, even though we're in a pandemic?"

"It's a coincidence you asked because we started back up last Friday, but on Zoom."

"That'll be something. I wonder how something like that would work, though. You wouldn't be able to build a fire or lash poles together."

"I know, but I've been brainstorming a lot and exchanging ideas with fellow commanders. I chose a dozen merits that I'd be able to teach remotely via PowerPoint. Some requirements will be given as homework and emailed back to me."

"Ah, that all sounds doable. PowerPoint? Didn't you used to go crazy with PowerPoints in high school?"

"Ha-ha! Yes, I have. It was one of the reasons I was called 'overachiever' a couple of times back in the day."

"I remember you saying that, and how one of your presentations was fifty slides long, with ten of them being the bibliography alone. Anyway, was it your idea to meet via Zoom?"

"Actually, no. I couldn't wait to meet back in person, and—"

"I bet! I know how much being a commander and teaching young men brings you joy."

"Yeah, but it looks like it still won't be in person for a while, and the boys at Rangers are falling behind on their tracks. When President Trump said 'July or August' back in March, I was like, 'No! It better not last that long!' But now, since it's September, with a dismal future ahead, I would've tolerated it if it *had* ended in July or August."

"Same."

"Anyway, I got emailed a video from one of the commanders. Jason, one of the boys, said, 'Commander Zachary, I miss you!' and his father, Commander Curtis, then said, 'Hey, Commander Zachary! Can you help us commanders figure out how to do Zoom so that our boys can stay on track?'"

"Aw."

"That's how it got started, but only fourteen boys and three commanders (out of an outpost of fifty) were able to handle Zoom. With minimal commanders, the outpost is divided into two meeting times: the younger two age groups are meeting at 5 p.m. and the older two at 6:30 p.m."

"Oh. Say, have you asked to volunteer for both?"

"Are you forgetting who you're talking to?"

"Ha-ha! I shouldn't have asked."

"They asked me if I'm willing to teach the older half. I gladly accepted the challenge, so now, I'm preparing two lessons a week. I'm teaching the Safety Merit to the third, fourth, and fifth-graders, and the Forestry Merit to the older boys. There's only one high schooler, so he'll be staying with the Adventure Rangers, who are sixth- through eighth-graders."

"That, with all your courses, should keep you busy."

"Uh, yeah."

"Are you still YouTubing? I haven't had time for any social media the past couple of years, but I used to watch your videos all the time, as well as all the hunting channels, since I'm a hunter."

"Yes, I am. Posting about every single day."

"Whoa, really, dude? I remember you posting those vintage home videos from the 1990s and early 2000s, and seeing myself in some of them."

"Yes. I always enjoyed taking our old VHS-Cs, digitizing them, and sharing the memories to the world. I especially love uploading them on the anniversary dates. For instance, I just posted our family trip to Big Bear, in California, earlier this month, twenty years later. I'll never forget being there."

"And reliving those memories."

"For sure."

"And how's your following these days."

"Um, somewhat … slow, but improving! I currently have 585 subscribers, the last I checked. I would've had 630, if people hadn't unsubscribed."

"Their loss, dude. Don't sweat it."

"There are a few people who regularly comment on every video. Some just comment on my planespotting videos. Others just comment on my Autism Awareness videos. And others just comment on my Royal Rangers videos. I, in turn, show my support too. I'm subscribed to dozens of fellow autism advocates, planespotters, Royal Rangers, jugglers, pianists, and even railfanners—"

"Railfanners?"

"Uh, yeah, or trainspotters. In other words, they film trains. Not being near a railroad leaves me out of the party, but I still support them nonetheless. And guess what, all these guys support me too. Some planespotters and railfanners stick around to watch my Autism Awareness videos, saying that they're autistic themselves, or that they have a family member or friend who is and wants to learn more."

"You see, Zachary? You always find a way to still make a difference."

"I'm personally grateful. There were a few videos I made answering questions people had about autism. One is a ninth-grader in Arizona and simply wanted to understand his friend better. Then, some of my YouTube friends said they live with other challenges for which they were bullied, like Tourette's, ADHD, OCD, a peanut allergy, et cetera."

"And this is a testament to patience and perseverance, Zach. I've got to hand it to you. You never gave up YouTubing for three years, and look at how far you've come. I'm proud of you."

"Thank you. I also owe a lot to a couple of firebuffers as well, and—" Zachary paused as he heard Thomas sigh.

"Um … firebuffers?"

"Ha." Zachary nervously laughed. "I got to remember. Firebuffers are people who film emergency vehicles, usually responding Code 3, and … what?"

Thomas couldn't stop laughing. "Helicopter noises, military jets, fire engines, I'm not surprised. You used to get distracted by these all the time at Washington Elementary."

"I know." Zachary chuckled. "I just never knew until recently that it's a sport around the world, like planespotting. Anyway, it all started back in August 2017 when I filmed Ladder 138 responding to an emergency from the church. I uploaded that to YouTube later in 2018, just to have something to post when I ran out of videos. Well, this past June, a couple of firebuffers along the West Coast found that one video out of a thousand. They left a comment, and I decided to follow their channel. They kept commenting on my planespotting and Autism Awareness videos, supporting them. I thought, 'The next time I see a Code 3 response, I'm going to film it for them and upload it.' And, um, that's how I became a firebuffer myself."

Thomas was heard giving a hearty belly laugh on the other end.

"And because I started posting more of those videos, other firebuffers found me, just like planespotters found me."

"Wow, that's too much, champ. Social media totally changed our world. I remember when we both got frustrated all the time with those rabbit ear antennas for the television set. Remember?"

"Yeah, and that was before most of us had DVRs."

"We had to tape everything on a VCR if we wanted to watch it again."

"Sometimes, the tracking was a pain to deal with, and if we weren't careful, the VHS tapes would get stuck or come apart like spaghetti."

"Ha! Just like those cassette tapes."

Zachary and Thomas laughed as they took a nostalgic stroll down memory lane.

"Kids these days will never know." Thomas chuckled. "And those game shows. I remember how much you loved those shows on Nickelodeon Games and Sports."

"Oh yes, especially *Legends of the Hidden Temple.* I always wished I had the opportunity to be on it."

"You might as well have been. I remember you saying in fourth grade that you converted the entire jungle gym area into an obstacle course, based on that show, and had your friends run through it with those Pendants of Life you hand-drew, while dodging Temple Guards."

"I'll never forget."

"*Figure It Out* was *my* favorite back in the nineties. Hey, champ, it's late. I want to thank you for calling me. Talking to you really lifted my spirits, and I believe it was the best thing for me."

"No problem." Zachary smiled, thankful and feeling good about himself for mustering enough courage to call. He was always unsure of how to talk to a friend who had just lost a close family member. Zachary could tell throughout the conversation that Thomas was smiling, but he could also hear the bereavement in his voice at the same time.

"Hey, Zach. I hope to see you and your family again soon. I'm completely alone now. Wife died today. Mother died of cancer a few years back. Never caught up with my dad after the divorce back when I was seventeen. Confined to my house due to the COVID restrictions. And the nearest friend or family member is sixty-five miles away."

"I'm so sorry to hear about everything you're going through. We'd love for you to visit again. It's been since last Christmas."

"Yeah, I know. Hopefully *this* Christmas, we'll meet again. That is, if this freaking pandemic ends before then. We always tried making every Christmas and Thanksgiving gathering that you guys hosted. Oh, and I heard you're close to a Bachelor's in Math?"

"Yep. Next May, 2021!"

"Well, congrats, dude. I'll plan to be there like all your other graduations."

"Thanks. Until then, I'll plan to call you now and again."

"Please do. Thank you for calling me tonight, Zachary. You're truly a lifesaver."

31

Life or Death Struggles

Over the next twelve months, as the COVID restrictions eased, Zachary was able to organize a few local in-person merit camps and activities. With permission from the senior commander, he took on more responsibility, including contacting prospective venues to schedule days to use their facilities, keeping track of every boy's requirements for merits and medals, and emailing parents about their progress, which all made him feel stronger and empowered.

* * *

One chilly late morning toward the end of January 2021, Zachary walked around the neighborhood to clear his mind. Heading toward his local park again, he noticed a ten-year-old boy holding a clipboard, with his college-aged sister standing beside him.

At this stage of the game, Zachary felt neutral out in public, so to speak. He wasn't always fearing the worse, but he did brace for it, just in case. As he walked closer, he glanced down and saw that his hidden body camera was still on.

Good, he thought, letting out a sigh of relief.

Ever since that earthshaking encounter with the furious man at the Albertsons, he chose to always wear a body camera, just in case he ever needed evidence to corroborate his story, if it ever came to that. He could also upload the footage to social media to prove that ableism still occurred.

Walking past the two people, unknowing what to expect, he heard the boy say, "You look cool!"

"What's that?" Zachary asked, seeing the boy and his sister smiling at him.

"You look cool," he repeated.

"Well … thank you," he said, smiling and feeling much obliged for the compliment. "Have a great day."

"You too!" they said.

As he walked down the park's pathway, about to pass by the notorious bench, he couldn't help but replay and dissect his conversation. He was simply dressed in regular clothes, nothing that distinguished him from anyone else. He took it as a random act of kindness and started to feel good about it, although his mind, as always, started to wonder if they were being sarcastic.

More typical are his post-conversation analyses. Even with his best friends, he stressed over every spontaneous conversation, wondering if he had said enough or if he had said things correctly. Sure, everyone may go through that, but every single conversation? Including the insignificant ones? With loads of stress? And sometimes years after you said goodbye?

In this analysis, he remembered the clipboard and paper the boy was holding.

Darn it! Was he doing a science project for school? Could I have possibly helped in some way? Duh, why didn't I put 'pi' and 'e' together? I could've turned around and asked them. Oh, brother, too late! Hey, what's this?

Toward the end of the pathway, next to the road, were bushes, on which was a piece of paper sitting next to an envelope. They looked like they were about to fly away, but they resisted the light breeze.

Zachary crept closer. Reading the front of the envelope sent chills throughout his entire body.

On the envelope read "SUICIDE LETTER."

Shaking slightly with sadness, sympathetic to those depressed, he began to read the piece of paper next to it. In no uncertain terms, the writer bashed the community and school district for not teaching morals, kindness, and respect. The writer complained about the bullying toward people who are different, bringing up "autism" in the list of examples. The letter urged schools and the district to bring people who are actually disabled to lead assemblies, speaking to students and parents. The writer concluded by saying that he or she will not take their own life if they see a positive change within the next twelve months.

Upon reading an authentic suicide letter, penned by someone who was honestly depressed, made Zachary's blood boil to the core.

Have I not been pleading with schools and the school district to let me speak?!?! he yelled inside himself. He paused, remembering that COVID stressed out the entire world, closing the schools down to begin with. Although his own plans for an assembly included juggling, he thought he could at least start by doing virtual assemblies. *Swell,* he lamented. *I was going to speak at a school in New Jersey virtually last April, and they forgot about me. And hey, speaking about April, what about the news media?*

At this stage of the game, he was still infuriated that the news media wasn't letting him speak about his story and promote his book. He only got two minutes on the radio in April 2020, and that was only because he emailed fifty producers. Pitifully, only one took him seriously. Could more opportunities have prevented this potential suicide?

And what about social media? he questioned. Although he was growing little by little, he rarely passed fifty views per video on YouTube. Getting a comment on Twitter was three or four times a month. Facebook and Instagram weren't as promising either. In the previous November, he ran a little experiment, making a couple of posts and asking his friends if they saw it. Some said they didn't see his posts, and he screenshotted their replies as evidence for his case. As before, his friends' posts on Facebook or Instagram would get hundreds of likes each, while he was lucky whenever he passed thirty … and that was when the blue moon arose. In this stage of his life, he firmly put "censorship" and "shadow banning" on the table. There seemed to be no other alternative.

A friend emailed him a couple of articles on how to grow on social media and market his book. He thanked his friend, but explained that he had already tried every single little point: posting consistently, using germane hashtags and keywords, connecting with pages and organizations in the same sector, sharing his posts and videos across multiple platforms, relying on word of mouth, distributing business cards, visiting local outreach programs, and running advertisements. All of these he had endeavored, even spending a couple thousand dollars more on Google and Meta advertisements with hardly any success. Whenever a relevant hashtag or keyword was trending, he'd make posts. He'd find every reasonable excuse to reshare one of his YouTube videos or his novel. Rarely did it work.

He took a picture of the letter to share across social media, wondering if anyone would even see it. In this case, many did. Some people living in his city expressed sympathy, saying that they will be more mindful of how they treat people, even nonverbally.

"I've seen these in my neighborhood too," a dozen people surprisingly commented.

"They were found all around the local schools. The principals and police department already know about them," informed another.

"Meh, they're probably written by one of those e-bike-riding middle schoolers, trying to make a joke," a couple of people retorted in a callous tone, obviously not having read the letter itself.

After spreading the word and encouraging people to be kinder toward one another, Zachary emailed a couple of people he knew personally at the school district, reopening his heartfelt offer to give volunteer assemblies, even if it starts out remotely.

They replied:

> *Thank you for your email, Zachary. We are certainly considering having you visit our schools once things open up. That way, you can juggle too. At the moment, we are managing the challenges of the pandemic and online learning, which requires our full attention as you can imagine. We need to address these priorities before scheduling any remote assemblies for you or anyone else. We hope you are doing well in these days. Take care.*

Not giving up, he messaged a couple of the local news anchors to reconsider interviewing him. They all said that their primary focus was COVID.

What else can I do? Zachary slumped onto his desk chair.

He continued making and uploading videos to YouTube. Once a week, he posted an Autism Awareness video. By the middle of the year, his views and engagement started to pick up, especially on his special interest videos, like planespotting and firebuffing. This was because channels were shouting out each other. People around the country and the world would shout out Zachary's channel, and Zachary would shout out theirs. Soon, he was asked to shout out YouTubers with other special interests, such as cubers (those who are good at solving various twisty puzzles, including Rubik's cubes) and artists.

Many of these fellow YouTubers, young and old, fully supported Zachary for being autistic. They were proud of him for what he was doing and were willing to stand up for him if or when necessary. Over the next couple of years, some of them posted a special video reviewing his novel. Others privately messaged him on Instagram, showing him a picture of his novel that arrived at their house.

One user commented: It always brings happiness to my day when you say, "Hello, this is Zachary Corwin …" because I know it's going to be an epic video. Thanks for making my day.

In a flash, Zachary's sadness and loneliness began to vanish. Life felt easier as he continued to fight, seeking to spread his message on the news eventually, as well as in schools and in churches. Producing his videos also became easier as the growing number of views and comments motivated him to continue.

32

Running for his Life!

In the middle of March, Zachary stood on the veranda as the cool breeze greeted him, one hour before sunset. The skies complemented his optimism, but the wispy cirrus clouds foreshadowed an ominous presence.

Is it real or is it just in my mind?

He looked down to turn on his body camera and clipped it on. Traversing down the walkway, he smelled the sweet aroma of the waxleaf privets.

Walking the first few blocks, he pieced together the components of his mission and prioritized his tasks to meet his goals. News media wasn't getting back to him; social media was like AOL dial-up. Nevertheless, he continued to show support to others, just as he wanted both the media and the community to support him. This meant giving shout outs on YouTube and sharing posts from fellow disability advocates.

The reason he had optimism was that, before he began walking that evening, he made and shared a YouTube video promoting a new book that featured drawings from a young mute teenager. It was one of the times he saw a major accomplishment and chose to share it, even though many organizations wouldn't share *his* novel. While feeling thankful for the opportunity to help a fellow author and advocate without being asked, a bicyclist abruptly surged up from behind him. Glancing over, he saw that the bicyclist slowed down right beside him to match his walking speed, looking at him.

"Hey," Zachary greeted the bicyclist in a neighborly manner, who seemed to be around fourteen; he was unsure what was going on.

The bicyclist didn't say a word. He kept staring into Zachary's eyes with a cross between a neutral expression and a smirk, paying no attention to the road ahead. After five or six feet, Zachary began to feel uneasy when, precipitously, another bicyclist came hurtling up from behind them, his tires emitting brief screeching cries. Startled, Zachary swung around and froze. The teenager turned as well, meeting the bearded bicyclist eye to eye, before the two of them raced down the street.

Just like that, the strange encounter with a father and his son on bikes was over.

What could that *have been the harbinger of?* Zachary dreaded.

An hour later, he was on the other side of town, walking down another suburban street. Unexpectedly, an SUV passed him and parked in the driveway a few houses down. At this point, he was regressing back to his younger self, over five years prior, when his brain would flood him with many potential interpretations over little things that happened in public. Walking a few houses past where the SUV parked, he noticed that the driver didn't get out.

Oh, great! Is this driver waiting for me to reach the next block before feeling safe to get out of the vehicle?

Just then, he heard the car door open. Not caring what the driver might think, Zachary looked back while still moving forward. The driver's gaze was already fixed on him and remained so for the next two seconds.

A few yards later, Zachary turned the corner, only to be greeted by a young couple taking an evening brisk walk. Without skipping a step, the husband slipped his arm around his wife's lower back and pulled her closer, reminding Zachary of tangential incidents back in his high school years. (Some mornings, as he walked to school, he noticed parents pulling their small children closer as soon as they saw him down the street.) The couple shot him death stares and refused to relent until they passed. As usual, especially when met with such strange looks, Zachary said hi as they got closer, but they ignored him and quickened their pace.

Looking up at the fiery orange skies, five minutes before civil twilight, he screamed out in his heart, *Why?!! Just, why?! What have I done?! If I'd speak in schools and churches, if my novel was well known, and if I wasn't censored on social media for trying to establish universal acceptance and kindness ... and* trust ... *then this would* not *be happening—to me or anyone else ever again!*

Not conceding to a horrific, lonely night filled with soliloquies, he pushed himself to walk several more blocks. Hopefully, a miracle from God would occur, and he'd run into a person who would say hi to him, which would dissipate most of the heartache he was feeling.

Turning down another suburban block about fifteen minutes later, he saw a lawn sign bearing a heart and the words "Be Kind" mounted above a small hedge of star jasmine. Believing this was the harbinger of answered prayer, he took a picture of it to spread the kindness on social media. He had already begun noticing similar messages throughout his neighborhood, in chalk drawings or children's artwork taped to mailboxes.

Hmm, come to think about it, he recalled, *a couple of the nearby schools, according to their social media, were actively promoting mental health awareness and anti-bullying. I wonder if those suicide letters had anything to do with it. I never noticed such an abundance of awareness and kindness campaigns before those letters. At least it seems to be working, and some people are getting the message … Why not everyone?*

After he snapped the photo, the sound of giggling unexpectedly pierced the stillness. Liquid fire flowed in the vessels that surrounded his heart. Goose bumps of fright chilled his extremities, exacerbated by the chilly atmosphere of nautical twilight. Looking beyond the camera, he met eye to eye with the father and son from earlier that evening. He quickly pocketed his camera and walked diagonally across the street, hoping they weren't thinking he was taking a picture of them.

As soon as he passed by them, he heard additional snickering.

He looked back while still walking forward.

The teenager was smirking at him, and the father was smiling with arms crossed, standing next to their bicycles.

Zachary turned and continued.

More laughter.

Zachary turned again and, walking backward, saw them still staring at him. Without warning, a gut-level instinct cloaked him like a phantom, and he booked it.

Maybe their smirks got wider.

Maybe they gestured toward their bike's handlebars.

Something.

Something beyond his conscious mind told him he would be in trouble if he didn't run. Having walked for nearly two hours, his sprint quickly downgraded to a jog, which quickly downgraded to a brisk walk. He was on a long, narrow street with nowhere to hide. He knew he could never outrun two bicyclists. He kept looking over his shoulder, fearing that they'd pull up from behind him at any second.

Could I hide behind parked cars? Could I knock on a person's door if I needed help within five seconds? Fifty-fifty chance someone would be home, with a ninety-percent chance they'd assume I'm some 'autistic lunatic.' That's just great! he thought sarcastically. *Hey, I always carry my pocketknife. Oh, good going, Zachary. I probably wouldn't win and would end up getting stabbed to death.*

These thoughts of impending doom kept slapping Zachary like a school bully all the way down the street, where he arrived at the entrance to his local park. He stopped to catch his breath.

Out of nowhere, the high-pitched whine of a motorized bike echoed through the atmosphere as cacophonous as a wet saw on ceramic tile. Crows began to caw, bursting from the trees in startled flurries. He quickly glanced behind him but didn't see anyone. However, with astronomical twilight almost settling in, a headlight beam shone from the street he had turned from. Instinct told him to take the long way around instead of cutting through the park. If that bicyclist turned onto the street, his headlight would surely catch him running down the park's pathway.

Minutes later, as Zachary jogged down his street, the motorized bike grew louder and louder. His house was only a couple of homes away, but just ahead of it lay the cross street that the bike was traveling on. If the rider looked down his way as he passed, he would definitely see him.

Is this how my life is going to end?! he dreaded. *Right when I'm yards away from my house.*

Zachary picked up the pace.

I'll take a chance!

The intersection ahead brightened as the bike's headlight approached.

The bicyclist slowed down, rolling to a stop.

Zachary leapt behind a bush. Peeking out ever so slightly, he saw the bicyclist appear a heartbeat later and come to a complete stop. After looking both ways, the rider sped off at a hundred miles per hour, disappearing down the street.

Zachary nearly collapsed, even though he was already on his knees.

I'm safe, he panted. *I'm home.*

After rushing inside, he splashed water on his face and collapsed onto his desk chair. He knew he had to expose this. While on camera, he stressed over every word, struggling to speak clearly, redoing takes again and again, each one worsening his queasiness. Fighting the nausea brought on by the way life kept treating him, he forced himself to piece the video together, uploading it within two agonizing hours.

After sharing it across social media, he pushed himself to study for his three upcoming standardized math exams, which were required to become a math teacher. He planned to knock them out later in the week, taking one exam per day for three consecutive days. He already passed the most basic exam for teachers three months prior, which tested on reading, writing, and arithmetic.

Problem was, *he couldn't study.*

He kept replaying the first and second encounters with those two bicyclists automatically and unconsciously. After getting over it, he started a practice problem, but five seconds later, they would return. Then a miniature soliloquy initiated, where he thought, what if he would've confronted them? What if he would've explained to them that he's autistic? What if he had his book on hand and gave them a copy? Some soliloquies caused him to pace back and forth in his room, talking them out.

This cyclically repeated on autopilot for the next hour until he gave up.

Man! No wonder why this city was littered with suicide letters recently! he thought, not surprised. *Come to think about it, last summer, I came to a cross street, looked both ways, and continued walking, only to see a middle schooler, basketball in hand, giving me a strange look. Why? For stopping and looking both ways? Because I'm tall and thin? Why? I noticed he was wearing his P.E. uniform, which told me he attended my former middle school. The least I could've said was, 'Hey, I went there.'*

Oh, great! Now I'm reminded of August 2017, when I turned around the corner of a residential street and saw a boy jumping on his trampoline. As soon as he saw me, he instantly dropped flat on the jumping mat, pretending to blend in like a chameleon, keeping his eye on me, still as a statue. For what? Did it look like I was walking directly to him? However, to be fair, he did get up and start doing impressive front flips and back flips before I passed by. Maybe he realized I wasn't a bad guy after all. The least I could've said was, 'Amazing job,' since I've always wanted to be a positive source of encouragement to everyone, especially younger people who need motivation the most. Obviously, this boy must not have had Mr. Collingsworth.

Heck, on that *day (and the days surrounding it), I was already intimidated with fear of running into that father at the park again (the one who hollered, 'Don't worry about it!') from the week before, and … shut up, Zachary!*

Before allowing his mind to recall more random, insignificant stories, he turned off the lights and got into bed, just past midnight. Darkness crept around his room, sparing only the light from the lamppost outside, which kept his hope aglow.

Boom! Those bicyclists were back in his thoughts.

Nauseated.

After a miserable ninety minutes, tossing and turning in bed, replaying the scenes a dozen times over, fighting his stomach, stressing over the math exams, and reciting different soliloquies of how he would have talked to them in a civilized manner, he drifted to sleep.

* * *

The cacophony of a large garbage truck woke Zachary at one in the afternoon. Sluggishly, he hobbled over to his laptop, his appetite nonexistent as he continued to be haunted by the previous evening's relentless rounds of ableism.

In a flash, things started to turn … for the better. His YouTube video that he uploaded the night before garnered five hundred views and a dozen comments. His Instagram and Facebook inboxes overflowed with messages. Twitter surprised him with a few additional comments too. From across the country and around the world, spanning multiple continents, Zachary received an outpouring of love and support. Each message, whether a single sentence or a whole paragraph, articulated sympathy and encouragement for him.

He certainly was not expecting that much support. He felt forever changed and appreciated. Ninety-five percent of his pain, loneliness, and depression completely vanished. If this hadn't happened, you could bet a million dollars he would have given up in life that week. If he had never started YouTubing—which was a result of feeling worthless and bullied to begin with—he would have given up in the previous year. As a result, he created a touching thank-you video featuring all the comments and messages he received.

He continued to study, but now and again, those bicyclists crept in his mind, but not as painful as before. All three standardized exams had strict procedures—ID verification, photo capture, and lockers for personal items. Every square inch of the lobby and test rooms was covered by several cameras. Each computer's webcam continuously recorded the test taker during their exam.

Zachary did his best to shift his attention from being scrutinized to focusing on his test, though he did understand the purpose for such surveillance. For all three exams, he gave an answer to every question, but didn't have time to thoroughly go over every single one. Test takers have a maximum of three hours unless accommodations are granted, which would require proper documentation. He did not want to go through all of that, considering how it was hard enough just to set up the appointments for each exam. Moreover, his tests were much harder than he thought, unlike anything he had studied, despite practicing with a couple of study guides that came from their own website.

Now, the dreaded wait.

He began feeling depressed and queasy. He felt that if he didn't pass, there would be no way for him to enter his dream career: a math teacher. Consequently, he decided to call the company, which was out of his comfort zone to begin with.

"How may I help you?" the man said, sounding like he hated his job.

Goodness, did I just wake you up out of a dead sleep, sir? Zachary thought. "Uh, hi. I just took three math tests this week, and, um, I was wondering if you offer a way, even if there's a fee, for you guys to grade earlier than—"

"No!"

After a pause, he said, "Excuse me, what?"

"No! We will *not* expedite the grading process for anybody!"

"Uh … okay? Have a great evening then."

"You too. Bye-Bye," he quickly said as he hung up the phone.

Zachary sighed, feeling his body sinking to the ground, but a few seconds later he quickly perked up, not wanting another flu like the time he felt lifeless in early 2020 due to his book situation. Looking at the time, he logged onto Zoom.

"Rangers, attention!" Commander Zachary started the first meeting of the evening. "Pledge to the American Flag. Those in uniform, hand salute; those without, heart salute. Ready, begin."

After leading all the boys and other commanders in the pledges, and after going through the announcements and handing out "virtual awards," they moved into their breakout rooms. Toward the end of the Bible lesson, one of the reflection questions evoked its theme: tribulations and praying for your enemies.

Zachary questioned if there would ever be a need to share his testimony from the other night. He was nervous about it, but he knew that it would complement that night's lesson, perfectly illustrating the theme in real life. In the middle of recounting the harrowing ordeal, when he got to the part about running for his life, he noticed the countenances of all the boys instantly change.

"Commander Zachary! No!" Jason interrupted, very concerned.

"Are you okay?" a couple of the other boys asked, sounding quite worried.

"Yes, I am," he said before finishing the story, concluding with, "I always choose to forgive instantly and to pray for them. They might just be having a bad day or going through a difficult part of their lives. As the Bible teaches, I don't believe in repaying evil with evil, nor in wishing death or destruction on my enemies. I don't hate those ableists. The difference is that, although I always choose to forgive, it's difficult to rid myself of the pain others have inflicted on me, especially being autistic.

"Anyway, I hope all of you will take on that mindset too. I acknowledge that there are Christians who have not adopted the same heart, whereas some non-Christians have. My final advice to all of you is to *always* speak up if something like that happens to you. Don't keep it inside you. You have your parents, pastors, and us commanders. Just talk it out to someone you trust."

Following the Bible lesson was a game. Zachary thought of many games that could be done on Zoom as part of their brain break, sometimes creating them himself. This followed twenty-five minutes of teaching a merit. He was currently teaching them the Railroading Merit, and the older boys the Chemistry Merit.

After concluding, a few boys (Jason, Brandon, and Phil) stayed behind to talk more about Zachary's horrific, close-call experience. They knew he was an author, talking about autism. They accepted him for who he was as an autistic individual. However, they never realized all the bullying he had gone through and still goes through.

"To us, you just seem normal, like everyone else," Brandon said.

"Well, what about those people who can't speak or can't walk?" Zachary turned it around. "Would you say that's *ab*normal? Or what about people with ADHD? Tourette's Syndrome? Spina Bifida? Muscular Dystrophy? Et cetera. Who are you comparing me with, in terms of 'normal'?"

"Uh, I don't know."

"I was just trying to get the wheels turning. In the future, consider, what even is 'normal'? I believe it shouldn't matter as far as our purpose is concerned. I believe everyone still has a purpose, no matter what."

"Even people who can't speak?" asked Phil. "Like those students in special education at my school?"

"Yes," he responded in a heartbeat. "My late granduncle, Elmer, who lived in an institution in Boise, had his artwork published. Recently, a mute teenager published a book featuring his drawings. I just promoted it on my YouTube channel, right before going out on that notorious hike, coincidentally."

"Wow!" The three boys marveled.

"Well, it was very mean for those guys to do that to you, Commander Zachary," Jason commented. "You never deserved that."

"And what I don't get is … *why*," Brandon added. "You're honestly the nicest, friendliest, and smartest person I know."

Zachary held back his emotions and said, "Well, I truly appreciate your guy's acceptance and support for me."

"Hey, speaking about your YouTube, those merit videos are very helpful. I enjoy them," Phil said.

"Thanks. As I was making the PowerPoints and teaching you guys, I figured I could record my narration whenever I'm not busy and make YouTube videos to help others."

"They really helped us stay caught up when we took our trip in February and missed a couple of meetings," said Brandon.

"I'm thankful. So far, I've uploaded a few dozen of them, and I've received nationwide appreciation. One commander emailed me, saying that I was helping boys at their outpost in Chicago who couldn't meet on Zoom. Another, from Texas, sent me pictures of all their boys watching one of the videos at a camp and taking notes for their merit."

"Oh, wow, that's so amazing, Commander Zachary." Jason smiled. "Must be so rewarding, huh?"

"It is, indeed. It definitely makes me feel like I have purpose. Anyway, I got to get ready for the older boys."

The three boys, of their own volition, saluted Zachary. He returned a full salute. Then the boys brought their arms down and logged off.

Zachary felt accepted and almost as tranquil as he did at the birthday party of Phil and Brandon. Such acceptance kept him going as he waited to begin his other callings, but he wasn't yet given the opportunities. However, the next morning, he saw that part of his wait was finally over.

One email came from Pastor Nguyen, inviting him to appear on the church's new podcast.

A second came from a commander who hosted a podcast for the entire ministry nationwide, asking to interview him about being autistic, an author, and a Royal Ranger at the same time.

A third came from a fellow YouTuber and autism advocate up north, asking him to join her livestream.

All three interviews were scheduled to be recorded and released the following month for Autism Awareness and Acceptance Month.

Just then, as soon as he replied to the third email, a fourth email arrived from a representative of the school district adjacent to his, Willowbend Unified School District. She had heard a lot about Zachary from members of his own school district, as well as his novel and willingness to lead volunteer assemblies.

It read:

> *As things fully open up within the next year or two, we'd love to have you speak at some of our schools. Meanwhile, please fill out our form, explaining what your assemblies are about, and I'll put it in our catalog for all the schools and their PTAs. They'll reach out to you if they're interested.*

Zachary wondered if he had been dreaming as similar miracles have only appeared in dreams … just to bring heartache upon waking.

Fortunately, this time was as real as the sunlight streaming through his window, the weight of a pen in his hand, and the scent of his morning coffee.

33

When One Instant Changes Everything … Forever

"Well, dude, it was great seeing you again!" Andrew smiled broadly at Thomas. "But are you sure you want to leave the party early? We'll be here for at least three more hours, till sunrise."

"Yeah, Andy, I'm sure," Thomas responded, giving a weak smile.

"Tom, you okay?"

Nodding, he explained, "I just have a … life-changing decision I'm making."

"Oh, is it another job application? Another woman?"

Thomas jerked his head up to lock eyes with Andrew.

"I'm sorry, Tom. I shouldn't have asked that. I know how difficult it's been since Trudy died. No one can replace her."

Placing his hand on Andrew's shoulder, Thomas said, "Andy, you've been one of my best friends since middle school. You've always been supportive of my future. You were the best man at my wedding. Don't worry about me right now. I just need time to think through a lot of things … as it pertains not just to my future but to everyone's future."

"Okay, Tom. Sounds like you need to get some sleep and clear your mind. Get a good night's rest, and you should be able to figure it all out in the morning. Take care."

Thomas nodded and walked away. He hopped inside his Chevrolet Camaro and began driving home.

* * *

Over twelve hours later, Zachary concluded his Royal Rangers meeting with the younger boys. It happened to end twenty minutes earlier than expected as he was struggling to find new material to teach virtually. Additionally, his final finals for the bachelor's degree were scheduled for the following week, some of which he had been stressing over.

He kept looking on the bright side, knowing that in seven days, he would be graduating from Tributary University. He still held onto that confidence.

The moment he ended the meeting and logged off, he heard a car swerve outside his house. Rushing to the window to see what happened, he saw his mother get out of her Toyota Corolla in great distress. She didn't even bother to close her car door. Zachary saw her run over and pound on Grandpa Corwin's door. He looked intently, wondering what could've happened. He started feeling sick to his stomach as he never saw his mother act this way before. Seconds later, Grandpa Corwin swung the door open, shaken and visibly concerned.

Zachary heard his mother sobbing, but couldn't make out her words. He quickly opened his window some more, pressed his ear against the screen, stopped breathing for a few seconds, and became as still as a statue.

"Dad … Thomas … Thought I heard … maybe an accident."

Zachary only made out bits and pieces, but he got scared, assuming Thomas was in a bad accident.

"Thomas?" Grandpa Corwin repeated before wailing out loud.

In that instant, Zachary sprinted from his bedroom, jumped down the flight of stairs, bolted out the front door, and dashed across the street. When he arrived at his mother and grandfather, they were crying over each other's shoulders. *This is more serious than I thought*, he dreaded.

When Mrs. Corwin opened her eyes and saw Zachary, she immediately pulled him into the hug. "Thomas is gone," she tearfully revealed to him.

"Gone? My best friend?"

Mrs. Corwin burst into more tears as her father gave her a handkerchief. Once she caught her breath, she continued, "I got a phone call at the office today from the police. They reached out to me because I was an immediate contact since his mother, my former coworker, passed away. They said he went to a late-night party last night, left early, and came home. Then the police were called by a neighbor saying that they heard a gunshot."

Hearing the word "gunshot" hit Zachary's heart like a hammer. "Accident?" Zachary asked weakly, confused since he knew Thomas was a skilled hunter and marksman.

Mrs. Corwin's tears and emotions precluded her from speaking. All she could do was shake her head.

"Murder?" His voice trembled.

"No," Mrs. Corwin said, sobbing.

Zachary stood still and waited.

"Police ruled it a suicide … He shot himself."

Zachary's world suddenly became still and distorted. He started panting as thoughts raced in his mind, nearly falling to his knees. Hearing "suicide" hit his heart like a bat studded with long spikes. He saw his mother beginning to cry again on her father's shoulder. Hearing his grandfather weeping like the time he lost his brother further broke his heart. It was an instant he knew would change his life … forever.

"U-u-uh, I need to go to my room." Zachary turned around and left. He slowly walked back to the street, looking both ways, even though the entire block was currently devoid of people. No one was out but them. As he crossed the street, he glanced at his neighbor's property where Abe used to live. He clearly remembered the day when Thomas and his friends saved his life. Walking toward the veranda, he remembered the times when Thomas would walk him to school, which evoked the times Thomas would kneel down, put his hand on his shoulder, and give him life's wisdom and encouragement.

Falling into his chair up in his room, he reclined, still hearing Thomas' voice calling him "Champ." He didn't know what to do. He was too distraught to shed a tear. Thomas was someone he always looked up to, ever since he was a young boy.

Part of him was in denial.

Part of him felt like the only person in the universe.

Part of him felt suffocated because he needed to talk it out to someone, but who?

Part of him felt like no one but his family would care.

Part of him felt angry that Thomas would do this, but felt sadder that he lived the end of his life in depression, probably hiding it.

He remembered the last thing he said to him, that he was a lifesaver. He started putting two and two together.

Life saver.

Life *saver.*

Life Saver.

That phone call may have prolonged his life. Would he have committed suicide that day had he not called? He did say that he was all alone and miles from friends. He did express eagerness to visit them soon.

Zachary contemplated. He thought. He rested, resting his eyes.

Silence.

"Hello!" a couple of voices came from his computer. In the midst of contemplating, he got the Zoom meeting for the older boys started and then turned off his camera. He opened up a Word document and wrote "Please say hello once you join." Then he shared screens so that when the boys started to come on, they would say hello.

"Hey. Um, how are you guys?" Zachary weakly said, putting on a smile. He conducted the entire meeting, asking if it was okay to conclude a bit early. After he got off Zoom, he called Commander Curtis to tell him the news, followed by the senior commander. That evening, he called Pastor Nguyen who consoled him for half an hour.

That night, Zachary tossed and turned with a splitting headache. Not being able to fall asleep, he walked out of his bedroom, unsure where he was going. His mother opened her door and started motioning toward the restroom.

"Zachary, it's one in the morning. What are you doing standing out in the hall?"

"This night is never going to end … and I have a headache. I'm going back to bed."

Not only did he go to sleep with a headache, but he also woke up six hours later with one. Once he got up for the day, he checked his voicemail. The senior commander called asking him how he was doing. Another commander called, saying that he heard the news; he sounded like he was about to cry as he offered his condolences.

Zachary was still too stunned to cry himself.

Nevertheless, he was determined to tolerate and push through his finals the following week. Sure, his academic counselor said he could have an extension due to the tragic circumstances, but he didn't want to attend graduation stressed that he still had finals to take, not to mention the fact that he'd be holding a degree in front of everyone that he had not yet earned.

The graduation went well, but Thomas' funeral took place the following Thursday. Attending the funeral was nightmarish. He saw a couple of people whom he hadn't seen in years, but instead of a happy occasion, everyone was mourning, dressed in black, and trying to hold back tears. He hadn't met most of the other attendees, yet. It was an all-day outdoor funeral at Thomas' favorite campground from Boy Scouts, forty miles from where the Corwins lived.

At high noon, Zachary sat on a stump from a 200-year-old oak tree. Alone, he gazed across the vast majestic panorama—the giant lake, the towering trees on the far shore, and the hills beyond. He just stared, and stared, and stared, watching time pass by him, unbelieving that his life was real … that this was really happening. Along the ridgeline of the distant hills, he saw a couple of wild horses, their manes whipping in the breeze as they roamed. He felt terribly isolated as he sat there, completely still, with more anger than sadness.

After sitting there for three hours, bereaved, he traipsed over to the funeral and sat down. He immediately had a flashback from the last time he attended a funeral, which was for a friend he made in middle school. Dead at twenty-two. A heart attack. Just that sudden. As that funeral

The third comment was the straw that broke the camel's back. Zachary was just re-mourning the death of Thomas and was shaken up just visualizing him, his best friend, taking his own gun and shooting himself. Then the notification for that comment came through.

It was astronomical twilight outside. Nighttime often felt suffocating for Zachary, especially when memories of past attacks resurfaced in his own thoughts.

He wasn't going to take any more egregiousness. He decided to make a video addressing all three gratuitous comments, but in the *epic* way: he wouldn't fight back. He responded with kindness, explaining how their stereotypes were wrong. He ended with a special message for the three ableists, encouraging them to start believing in themselves and in others, and reminding them that everyone, including disabled people, has a purpose in life.

Fellow autism advocates, planespotters, firebuffers, and other supporters flooded his new video with reassuring comments to cheer him up. He went back to the malicious comments and found each one receiving a half dozen replies, calling them out for writing such unwarranted remarks. As always, reading all the support brought him rest.

Nevertheless, the autistic brain is very powerful when it comes to mood.

On the last day of May, he was scrolling through his memories on Facebook. One year prior, he posted an original prayer that slipped from his lips: "God, help me to help the helpless when I feel helpless to help them." Frustrated that he was still praying that, 365 days later—despite all the heartache and work he had done, endeavoring to reach millions of people—he stormed out of his chair and began pacing around in his room, thinking.

Unexpectedly, a brand-new spontaneous thought hit him like a freight train. He grabbed his camera and recorded a brutally honest video, becoming completely transparent about his innermost struggles and frustration.

The hook for his video was the phrase he had just come up with: "I care -1% about myself and 101% about other people. Put together, -1 + 101 = 100%." Explaining further, he said, "I stopped caring about myself years ago. What I *do* care about now is the eight billion other people on this planet and the next generations. I want everyone to find purpose, success, and joy in life."

His subscribers already knew about the suicide of his lifelong friend and offered him comfort. They already knew about his past trauma from being bullied and misunderstood for twenty years. Now, through his drained voice, they were hearing about everything he'd done to get on the news and grow on social media (but failed).

The video wasn't just him being vulnerable; the latter half was filled with his message of hope, strength, encouragement, and motivation. At the end, he explained that he was stepping out of his comfort zone, humbly asking people to subscribe or at least share his content if they want to, emphasizing that they didn't have to if they didn't want to. Again, the last thing he wanted was to be misconstrued as a self-centered, arrogant YouTuber who only cared about himself or was just hungry for followers. All he wanted to be was a help. That's why he wrote the novel in the first place, assuming he'd be called off the hook everywhere on the planet as soon as it was published.

Soon after he shared the video publicly, he began getting comments and messages from his followers. Some let him know that they cared for him. Others expressed how he was already doing an incredible job so far. Many thanked him for his overall message and transparency.

The next morning, Zachary opened up YouTube Studio to scroll through his comments. One of his subscribers wrote, "Zachary, may God bless you. Thank you for this video. I shared it with my grandfather, and we watched it together. It gave me feelings of optimism. You see, at my middle school, I only have one friend, but because he became friends with me earlier this year, I'm starting to feel joy in my life. If you're ever in the South, I hope you get to do one of your assemblies at my school. They sound amazing! All of us students will benefit from it."

Zachary stood up as fast as lightning, exhaling sharply a few times. He ran his hands through his hair, nearly yanking some of it with a tenacious grip. In his heart, he was praying and had optimism. In his mind, he was worried to death that he'd never get the chance to help more people like the few he had helped thus far.

You see? Zachary thought. *If I could change a few people, especially that middle schooler who understands it, imagine what this world would be like once social media boosts my content to more people, once news media finally interviews me, and once schools, churches, and other public venues invite me to speak voluntarily! I am therefore, here and now, determined to do my volunteer assemblies in every single school in my entire county—public and private!*

He felt thankful to have reached some people, yet he was also overwhelmed by the sense that he'd been screaming through a vacuum or from behind thick glass. Overcome with a mix of emotions, he resolved that he would no longer take no for an answer. He tried everything with the news stations and social media. As he had been for almost four years at this point, he was still going to continue posting every day with hope in his heart, but in the interim, *he was not going to sit still anymore.*

"It's the first day of June," he said aloud. "I'll walk today, and I'll walk tomorrow, and I'll walk as many days as I darn well have to. As peculiar as it seems, I will embark on this mission and never stop until the day it happens!"

Thus began the agony of mid-2021—the most hellish summer of his life.

35

The Never-Ending Agony of Summer 2021

Perhaps somewhere in his city, or in his county, someone … just someone … could be the catalyst for him to carry out the mission he was always meant to do. He didn't know who or what it would be, but he knew it was out there. Not knowing what form it would take, Zachary Corwin was determined to search for it and find it.

And *nobody* was going to talk him out of it.

Every day, beginning on June 1, he took a neighborhood hike. At first, he offered a simple prayer, asking to be led to whatever he was meant to find, trusting that, somehow, it was out there waiting for him. Soon, however, those prayers became more fervent. He would lie prostrate on the ground for five or ten minutes, praying the Scriptures, offering praise to God, and laying out the reasoning why he, and everyone on earth, needed a yes answer.

Day 9: On a morning shrouded with June gloom, Zachary began to go the extra mile … literally. For one decade, taking these solo walks within a mile-and-a-half radius of his home had been his usual practice, but on this day, he crossed the thoroughfare and walked down Thornwick Boulevard, exploring other neighborhoods.

Day 12: After coming home at 8:30 p.m. from a three-hour walk, he took to Facebook, pleading with friends and family to pray with him, sparing most of the details. (Every three or four days over the next month, upon returning home from another uneventful wastage of a multi-hour walk, he would storm to his room and plead again on Facebook, growing more detailed about how stressed out and lifeless he felt.)

Day 17: He determined that walking through the denser, more active parts of the city greatly increased his chances of running into someone compared to quieter neighborhoods. He henceforth focused on walking up and down busy thoroughfares and past storefronts.

Day 20: Finding a small vial of anointing oil, he had an idea to help reinforce the sincerity of his heart and the depth of his devotion. He would anoint himself before his daily Bible reading to serve as a visible testament to the earnestness of his never-ending prayers. For years, the time of day that he would read the Bible fluctuated, but throughout that summer, it would be the first thing he'd do when he got up. Additionally, he would anoint himself with oil before lying prostrate in prayer, and again just before heading out for his walks ten minutes thereafter.

Day 28: Walking through a nearby plaza underneath the midday sun, a man caught his attention in his peripheral vision. Glancing over, Zachary noticed the man's grimacing face fixed on him like a laser, standing next to his car. He kept walking, but glanced back two seconds later to make sure he had seen correctly.

Seriously? he thought as the man's face still pointed at him.

Zachary was the only person walking down the path. He looked around to see if there was anything conspicuous. *Perhaps he's looking at something next to me?*

Looking back a third time, he stopped and turned toward the man. Sure enough, he was still glowering at him for no apparent reason.

That does it! Zachary thought and began marching toward the gentleman. Two steps in, the man angrily scoffed and quickly strode diagonally toward the grocery market on the other side of the parking lot. He followed him to the front door and lingered outside for the five minutes the man spent shopping. Zachary walked toward the side door, arriving there as soon as the man was heading out. Carrying his two bags of groceries and about to run into Zachary, he spun around and hurried the long way around, audibly grumbling to himself as he went.

Zachary, shaking a bit, could not ascertain why the man exhibited such animosity, especially since they never met each other in their lives. That night, he had a dream where he ran into that man. The man was about to walk through a door, but he stopped, pointed at Zachary, and yelled, "I just called the police!" storming off thereafter. Moments later, he witnessed that man morph into the father from the park in August 2017.

Upon awakening from that dream, physically sickened by it, he took out his camera and recorded a YouTube video, explaining that his autistic mind needed to process it aloud before it got worse. Some of his YouTube friends expressed how sorry they were to hear about his encounter with such an impudent man.

It wasn't the first time that month Zachary had noticed odd looks, which significantly troubled him. A week before, he strolled through the outdoor mall. Half the pathway was crowded due to the outdoor seating of nearby restaurants, as regulations and precautions from the pandemic were still ongoing. Thirty yards away, he spotted a young couple in line. The lady's back was toward him, but the gentleman hugging her fixed his gaze on him. All Zachary could see were his mercilessly cold eyes giving him the death stare, almost out of ridicule or defensiveness, poking above the woman's head. Zachary kept facing forward. Intimidated and with tunnel vision, he continued past them, yet he could perceive that the gentleman never wavered in his stare.

A few days before that, he was walking through a new park. One of its pathways was bordered with waxleaf privets, their white panicles sweetening the air as people strolled by. However, a swarm of bees hummed around them. Abruptly speeding forward, Zachary thought to himself, *I've never been stung by a bee before, and it's not going to be today.*

Further down the pathway, he approached a slightly older couple, briskly walking in the opposite direction. They moved out of the way for him since the pathway was slightly narrow. He gave a little nod and smile, but noticed they returned neutral expressions. After passing them, Zachary glanced back, seeing the wife turn and whisper to her husband, deliberately framing it as a private exchange.

What the freaking heck were you whispering about? Zachary thought, feeling agitated. *Do I really look like an alien? A murderer? A person belonging in an insane asylum? I mean, I'm not saying anything wrong about those who need psychiatric help, but still!*

These things had always bruised his heart, tied to the fact that he was a novelist and YouTuber whom no one seemed to recognize, having advocated for autism and for the idea that autistic people aren't weirdos, but deserve a chance in life. Neurodivergent individuals deserve to breathe the same air in the same neighborhood as neurotypicals. The anguish had propelled him to fight harder.

Day 35: Zachary decided to go inside Albertsons for a small bottle of water. Twenty feet from the automatic sliding doors, he noticed a lady in her sixties walking up from the parking lot. Seeing him, the lady stopped dead in her tracks as if a car was about to pass before she could cross the lot. However, no vehicles were currently driving nearby. Not even other people for that matter. Instead, she kept her eyes on Zachary and waited for him to pass and enter the store first. Only then did she feel safe enough to go in herself.

The heck? Zachary thought.

Day 36: Zachary saw a man go inside a frozen yogurt shop at the outdoor mall, and it almost shook him to the bone. Horror-struck, he noticed that the gentleman's face, hair, and build looked just like Thomas—so much so that the gentleman could have been his doppelgänger. This was not the first time, nor would it be the last in 2021, that Zachary saw someone who looked similar to Thomas, plunging him into a world of distress, like diving off a pier into freezing waters. It was like reliving the day Thomas committed suicide all over again.

(From time to time, he had to put away food, even after he had just prepared it. He was not only sickened by the fact that his best friend was no longer alive, but by the manner in which his life ended. One little sound, word, movement, or other insignificant detail could remind him of Thomas.)

Day 42: Zachary picked up his cellphone, which felt as heavy as a boulder. His strength was failing and his motivation dwindling.

"Hello, Mrs. Paxton," he said, endeavoring to sound as awake as possible, since he had only gotten three hours of sleep. Some nights, he stayed up working until daybreak—praying fervently and making YouTube videos—consumed with frustration. Then, he'd sleep for half the day, which was daily life for the first two weeks of his walking mission. Some mornings, he would go out and get his arduous hike over with, having pulled an all-nighter.

"Hi, Zachary. I'm calling from the Education Department of Tributary University."

"I've been eager to have this phone call for months now."

"I know you have. All right, the results of the standardized math tests you took in March came back. The first one (arithmetic, algebra, and statistics), you passed with flying colors. The second one (geometry and trigonometry), you barely passed, but at least you passed. The third one, (calculus), you didn't pass."

"Well, it's a relief knowing I passed two-thirds of them. I'm not surprised about the third one. They asked me questions I'd never prepared for or seen in my life. Their own study guides didn't include any of them, but I studied intensively for days."

"Let me tell you something: don't feel bad about it. This was just a standardized exam, an older model used to assess specific knowledge. However, it doesn't capture everything about you, like your full understanding of the material, your strengths, or who you are as a person. Several students have expressed similar sentiments about these exams."

Zachary sighed with relief, glad that he wasn't the only one, but frustrated over what this meant.

"Now, you have to pass all three if you want a *complete* math teaching certificate."

"I know. I've been dreading retaking test three."

"Well, you have nothing to fear. I've done the research, and I found a way to waive the exam since you now have a bachelor's degree in math."

Zachary felt like he was about to collapse, even though he was sitting at his desk.

"I bet you're so relieved."

"Oh yes. Unequivocally! Thank you, God. Thank you, Mrs. Paxton. Now, I have one less major thing to worry about, um, this summer."

"So, we look forward to you starting our teacher certification program in late August. To recap from the virtual orientation you attended via Zoom, during your first semester, you will be taught the foundations of education, education technology, lesson planning, and instructional strategies. Over the two semesters following your first, you will put everything into action at your placement site. I know you've been hoping to do your student teaching at Canyon Mountain, your former middle school, and I'm working to coordinate that. However, I can't make any guarantees at this time. I hope to let you know by December where exactly you'll be placed at."

"Thank you so much."

"Certainly! How's your summer going? Are you having a good break before hitting the books again?"

"Uh … um—" Zachary stuttered like an antiquated vinyl record that had been scratched up by a cat. "Uh … yeah, summer's okay." He had no intention of divulging a single detail about his mission. After hanging up the phone, he got ready, anointed himself with oil, said a prayer prostrate on his bedroom floor, and hiked for the next four hours … to no avail.

Day 49: Traipsing under the heat of the sun, Zachary pushed himself to start his third two-mile loop around the entire city, praying with each step, believing in miracles. In the end, after walking for over six miles, he resigned to his fate, crossed the thoroughfare, and headed toward his house. He felt utterly drained, dragging his legs as he walked.

Day 51: Walking by a house hedged with star jasmine and enveloped by the savory aroma of barbecue, he was perturbed by being on his second hike of the day, but he wasn't about to relent anytime soon. Orange clouds leisurely floated through the yellow skies above.

"Hey, you, young man!" shouted a man out of nowhere.

Zachary turned around to see an elderly gentleman walking toward him with a grin. "Yes?" he said, smiling in return.

"I recognize you. You used to be an usher at my church several years ago."

"Oh yes. I have." Zachary's mood changed, feeling like he was talking to a friend he hadn't seen in a while.

"Well, you were a doggone good one! My family always enjoyed walking in the service and seeing your smile as you handed us the bulletins or passed around the offering plates."

The short colloquy that followed was delightful. Zachary left feeling great, reminded of how much he had contributed in people's lives. He was then hit with pangs of guilt for having felt depressed about feeling underused and angry for taking all the ableism personally.

Nearing his house just past sunset, he decided that he wasn't ready to concede. He took a left turn instead of a right and decided to walk around a couple of blocks.

Half a circuit later, he walked past a group of three muscular men. As they were passing him, he couldn't help but glance at their faces. If they were looking at him in a neighborly way, he would say hi to avoid seeming callous or indifferent to others. However, two of them were eyeing him with a neutral or peculiar expression. A few yards later, one of the men, wearing his baseball cap backward, turned his head to speak to his friend but caught Zachary standing motionless in his peripheral vision, staring at them. The man jerked his head and began walking backward, catching the attention of the other two guys who quickly turned to see Zachary. They continued walking forward and turned the corner.

As Zachary walked down the sidewalk of his street, enervated, he heard a vehicle approaching from behind. They both neared a stop sign, the last street to cross before Zachary reached home.

How strange, Zachary thought. *We're still about forty feet from the stop sign. They don't have to slow down like that just yet. Why aren't they passing me?*

With the hairs on the back of his neck standing up, he realized that the vehicle matched his cadence and purposely trailed behind him. Once he arrived at the stop sign, the vehicle stopped. He felt too intimidated to look left for oncoming traffic, but he shakily glanced anyway, glimpsing the silver Ford F-150 for a second.

As he crossed the street, the vehicle was heard running, but it just sat there. Thoughts raced through Zachary's mind. Liquid fire circulated around his heart. He was unsure if, at any nanosecond, a bullet would be in his back. A few steps later, the vehicle surged forward and turned the corner. Consumed with curiosity, Zachary swung around just in time to meet eye to eye with the three muscular guys from earlier. The man who wore his baseball cap backward sat in the driver's seat. All of them wore disapproving countenances as they sped off.

Zachary froze, shaking his head, half in fear and half in disbelief. Upon storming upstairs, he had an unyielding urge to slam the door, just like every other time he came home since June 1, but he didn't want to alarm his mother. In his frequent Facebook posts, he had expressed how frustrated he became over unanswered prayers during his walks, so much so that he felt a compulsion to punch every streetlight pole as he walked past them.

After settling down, he made a YouTube video and shared it widely, warning people to beware of the silver pickup truck in his city that had followed him down the street. This followed an additional hour of fervent prayers, reciting the same things.

Day 58: "Today's the day. Today's the day. Today's the day," Zachary prayed with each step, something he had started doing every day by that point. Walking through the park across town, a man and his big white dog came from out of nowhere and nearly bumped into Zachary.

"Oh, pardon me," the man, who looked like a golfer, said with a smile.

"Sorry, sir. I—" Zachary froze in fear. "Uh, have a good day, sir."

"You too." The man waved, keeping his smile, and walked past him.

Nearly collapsing due to his shaky legs, he looked back to see if the gentleman realized who he was. It was the same man from the parking lot who scowled at him thirty days earlier. He briskly walked away.

Day 59: Living dangerously those days, Zachary decided to walk through the same park at the same hour of the day. Sure enough, he saw that same gentleman and his big white dog.

"Hi, um, excuse me, but you look familiar. Have we met before?" Zachary asked, deploying reverse psychology.

"Hmm, have you grown up around here? I lived in this city for over forty years."

"Yes, I have. Maybe that's it."

"I come to this park every day to walk my dog."

"Oh, okay. Well, have a good day, sir."

Zachary walked away, thinking, *I cannot believe this. Now I've seen everything.*

Day 71: It was a quarter past eight in the morning, and Zachary was finally about to go to bed when his cellphone rang.

"Hey, Zach. What's happening?"

"Hey, Pastor Nguyen." Zachary tried to sound like he didn't have a worry in the world. "Just the adventures of life, you know?"

"No, I don't know. Want to talk to me about this? I got a few calls, texts, and emails from your Facebook friends this morning. They're deeply concerned about your alarming posts this summer and the words you chose."

Zachary regretted taking the call, but he figured he had to give an answer eventually. "Pastor, I'm not going to lie to you, but life has been *hard*!"

"Join the club."

"Look, I know life will never be one-hundred percent easy. I know we'll all have trials and tribulations, especially for us believers. I acknowledge that, but now, I feel like I'm physically, mentally, emotionally, socially, and spiritually lost and exhausted. Physically, I'm weak, but I force myself to walk three, four, or five hours a day (usually without sitting, drinking, or eating anything). Mentally, there are days when I don't know what the derivative of x-squared is. It's 2x. Like, who doesn't know that? …"

"I didn't, but I know what you mean."

"Socially, I feel like most people *hate* me at first sight. Spiritually, I'm strong in my faith for salvation, but I *cannot* understand why I keep getting a not-right-now answer, especially since I don't have anything else to do. *Daily* and *nightly*, I'm begging God for Him to use me. All these years, I've spent hundreds of hours YouTubing, pouring my entire heart into videos meant to encourage people, and I'd be lucky if I get a hundred views on *any* of them. Meanwhile, videos that rot your brain and waste your time are getting billions and trillions of views. I mean, I'm not saying that occasional music videos, brain teasers, random trivia, um, or things like that are bad, per se, but still. Emotionally, I feel miserable and depressed over all of this … feeling purposeless, especially during the pandemic. And sure, things are opening up, yet I'm still not called upon to serve, to be interviewed by others, or to be a speaker somewhere."

"Whoa—"

"And real quick, um, sorry, Pastor, but I must add, I'm still tremendously thankful for our interview in April. Don't get me wrong. I hope you didn't feel offended or mad just now as if I had forgotten your kindness."

"Wow, Zachary. That was *a lot* you just unpacked. Thank you for trusting me with all that. I don't know where to begin. First, I'm not mad or offended, but one thing bothered me: you said people hate you. What did you mean by that, because 'hate' is a strong word?"

"I meant that, over the years, people have given me strange looks. Many have stared at me longer than four or five seconds. Real quick, would you agree that that's a bit too long to stare at someone?"

"Sure … I suppose."

"You might ask yourself, 'Do they recognize me from somewhere? Are they simply trying to determine that?' Sure, I absolutely force myself to remember that. However, some stares carried ridicule. I could discern it. I literally saw people smirking at me. I heard them snickering. This makes me positive that they're mocking me. No question about it. And what did *I* do? … Look like a tall, thin creep to them? Just yesterday, I had to walk past a middle-aged man along the boulevard; he *totally* looked like a mean, unhappy man. The silence added to the awkwardness. I don't know how to act when walking past … *anyone*. I was worried that saying hi might irritate him. I just walked forward, glanced at the buildings to my right, and looked at the traffic to my left. Right before we passed each other, I noticed through my sunglasses that he grimaced more, giving me some sarcastic hand salute like the military. And that was that."

"Wow, so random."

"Tell me about it. Last week, I hiked all the way over to the city's outdoor mall, um, *again*. I walked past a restaurant with outdoor seating. A couple was eating at a small table, and beside them was their dog, resting on the cobblestones. I smiled at the dog as I walked by, but then my eyes noticed the man's gaze. He looked at me menacingly. I kept walking, wondering, *Did I really see that?* I turned around to look back. A second later, the lady began to look freaked out, just because I was looking back at them. Her jaw dropped, and she became still as a statue. As soon as I refocused on the man, his head was completely turned toward me like an owl. Pastor Nguyen, I kid you not, as God is my witness, he was staring at me with threatening eyes just like a demonic spirit. His look still haunts me to this day. I just walked away."

"Man, I'm sorry to hear that, but remember: who you're called to be is what God wants you to do, not what man wants you to do. It's important to realize that it doesn't matter what the world thinks about you, but rather rest knowing that God sees you as His redeemed child."

"I believe that, but it's easier said than done. I mean, I can't stand it when people don't trust me, especially since I'm a friendly person. I'm not trying to boast about it. I'm certainly not saying I'm the best person in the world. However, I want everyone to trust me and all other disabled people. Heck, I want to be a teacher. I must earn the respect and trust of students, parents, and colleagues."

"And you will try your best. I'm sure of that. Same with pastors. Just because you go to seminary and get 'Reverend' in front of your name doesn't mean you're entitled to universal trust and acceptance just like that."

"Right, I acknowledge we must earn people's trust, but it's easier when they give me a chance in lieu of assuming the worst about me! Heck, last month, the day before my birthday—"

"Yeah, that's right, happy belated birthday. I saw that on Facebook."

"Thanks."

"Tell me quickly, you didn't spend your birthday laboring over a hike, did you?"

"Um—" he said, hesitating. "Well, uh, I spent a small birthday with family, opening cards and presents … but then I took a quick walk around for half an hour. Hey, I told God I'll do this every single day until I find what I'm searching for … what I'm praying for."

"Mind going in more detail?"

"Well … suffice it to say, I'm just praying that God will lead me to a person or group that, let's just say, will finally get me all around the world. In turn, I will be asked off the hook to speak in every school, church, library, you name it, in this county. I know it's crazy, but I've tried contacting the news media, and I keep getting ignored."

"Yep, they usually don't accept unsolicited requests."

"And I think that's stupid! Sorry, but I have an important message that may very well change the world. And they don't take the time to read and understand my emails? Anyway, maybe something will happen in one of my hikes. Like, say I'm interviewed by someone, amateur or professional, and it introduces me to the world, or at least the county or nation. That way, I could do my part in helping everyone, along with all the other advocates and world changers. One person on Facebook commented on one of my hundreds of recent posts, suggesting that I juggle at a park. Perhaps a news reporter might notice, walking their dog. I thought that was an excellent idea, although that's what I was doing hundreds of times as a child and teenager. Nothing happened then."

"Well, what happened the day before your birthday?"

"I was walking past a large family along Thornwick Boulevard—parents, grandparents, and three small children. As we passed, I noticed a couple of the adults giving me a peculiar look. I turned around and waited to see if they'd turn back. If they did, the only reason would be to look back at me. Why else, unless they were making sure I wasn't a threat? And I wasn't. To prove it, I didn't take a single step toward them; I merely looked back, standing still. There was no one else along the boulevard at that time, either. Sure enough, one of them turned back. Then he caught the attention of the other gentleman, who turned around and started walking backward. Both gentlemen were looking very concern and protective of their family as if I was a ten-foot beast ready to charge and attack. I saw the first gentleman speaking, but he was too far away for me to ascertain what he was saying. The next thing I knew, the women began to walk faster, practically dragging the children. One child looked back at me, wondering what was happening.

"And hey, the day before *that*, I was walking down that same boulevard, but from the other direction. I heard someone yell out loud. I turned and saw a passenger in a red SUV staring right into my eyes. His face looked incredibly infuriated … at me. For what? Just walking? You know I wear a body camera, so I posted it on YouTube with my commentary, just to prove that these sorts of things are still happening and must end. Why the heck scream, cuss, or run away from a person *solely* because of their looks, walk, voice, or other traits? And *yes*, I know the difference between *that* and other people screaming just to spook pedestrians. I could tell by this man's eyes."

"I'm so sorry those things happened, Zachary, but remember this too: your worth and value—who you are as a human being—is never predicated on what others say or do, or how *they* want you to look or behave."

"I understand that. I just can't be patient anymore. I refuse! I've tried being patient for a decade. Every freaking hour, I beg God, 'Let it be soon—*today* soon,' and when it doesn't happen, I pray the same thing, go to bed depressed, and hope that my life will finally change the next day, getting where it's supposed to be instead of remaining the worthless wretch I had become.

"In the past, I wasn't given as many opportunities, despite asking multiple times. The pastor from my old church is extremely nice and supportive, but, understandably, he wouldn't allow me to speak about my book to the congregation once it got published. 'Do you realize how many authors ask me to promote their book?' Well, I wasn't asking to sell it. I just wanted to tell the story God gave me. He said I could speak and juggle for the children's ministry, but then COVID happened before I could speak with the new director of children's ministries. Also, I couldn't tutor without a bachelor's degree, and my couple of years going to Wendy's, trying to see if I could tutor students for free, didn't go well either."

"And I'm still sorry that your proposal to set up a free tutoring club here at the church didn't work out. We simply didn't have enough resources that would be required, but we did try earnestly."

"I do appreciate the time you all put into considering it, though. Now we're in a pandemic. What am I supposed to do? I had my studies from Tributary University, Royal Rangers on Zoom, and made dozens of

YouTube videos, but that's it! I now have *all* this extra free time, especially since my graduation this past May, to speak somewhere, juggle somewhere, brighten people's day, encourage others, be interviewed by the news about what it's like to be autistic, see that I'm getting thousands of views and comments on each video. Oh, and please believe me, Pastor: I'm not one of those young people these days who are obsessed with superficialness. I'm *not* chasing views and subscribers *as my identity*. I've always seen the number as a measure of how many people I'm potentially *helping* with my videos. That's all. As I told God in my prayers, I'd rather use this one life to make a difference than spend an eternity in Heaven having done nothing on earth."

"Believe me, Zachary. That kind of futile, self-serving lifestyle, like those arrogant YouTubers or TikTokers, is the farthest from you. I know that. I'd put money on it if I were a betting man. Your loving heart is indeed rare in this world. You genuinely want to help people. You want to write books and post content that strengthens, edifies, and motivates them, instead of wasting their life away. That's very admirable. By the way, have libraries or bookstores stocked your book yet?"

Zachary let out a stressful sigh. "I emailed my two local library foundations back in 2019, one in my city and one in the adjacent city. They both rejected it because my novel isn't big or worthy enough … yet."

"Yet!"

"One told me that it must be found under some company called Brodart. This year, I finally found my novel in it. I sent them a screenshot, asking them to stock my book now, and all they said was, 'Zachary, we will not be stocking your novel.' I mean, they wished me the best of luck, but they literally said they weren't adding it to their collection. They must not trust it, despite my novel appearing in multiple countries."

"That's egregious! That's just stupid. Pardon my French. I'll pray for them."

"I was shaking for minutes after. I felt so hated, um, even though that's a harsh assumption, but what else could I assume? My novel could help people understand themselves and each other if or when given the chance. It will spread not just awareness, but *acceptance*."

"I believe it. I read it, and I personally think it should be in the curriculum at every school."

"Thanks so much. That's partly why I wrote the novel to begin with: to be read and studied in schools, like all the books we thoroughly annotated and wrote essays on. Heck, I stuffed it with so many literary motifs and symbols too, similar to the novels we read and discussed. One of my former commanders in Royal Rangers is a college professor for sociology. He recommended it to his class and said that my book is in their library. And one of my former sociology professors at the junior college put my book on her syllabus as optional reading for one of her big assignments. At the end of the semester, she sent me a couple of videos of her students giving PowerPoint presentations about me and my book."

"Zachary, that's absolutely incredible!"

"I felt so grateful, and it made me feel rewarded inside. Anyway, earlier this month, I went into a bookstore at the outdoor mall. I pretended to be a random person and asked if they had the novel I wrote."

"Oh, boy."

"Well, they eventually asked me if I was the author, and I couldn't lie. However, they were impressed. They asked for my email, saying that they would follow up, but so far, I never heard from them."

"Well, just give it time. It sounds like your novel will eventually be carried by libraries and stores everywhere. It'll happen one day; just give it time. Meanwhile, how is your YouTubing journey coming along?"

"It's fine. I just made my 767th subscriber special yesterday."

"Um, a '767' special? Isn't that a random number?"

"Not for planespotters. When I hit 717 subscribers, I took all my photos and videos that I took of the Boeing 717 and made a montage. I did likewise for the 737, 747, 757, and now, the 767."

"Very inventive. And you'll do that for the next ones, I presume?"

"Yep, once I hit 777 and 787. My planespotting subscribers get excited for them. I enjoy making them. Also, since I've been walking to farther places around the city, I've been getting so many catches of emergency vehicles responding code 3, as well as low-flying airplanes and helicopters. I'm not going on these walks looking for such content for my channel, but hey, I guess I'm sort of getting two birds with one stone, wouldn't you say?"

"Well, your YouTube channel has to pick up someday. I just believe it!"

Zachary and Pastor Nguyen continued to talk for the next ten minutes. Guiding him Scripturally, the pastor implored him to be patient and to trust God.

"Thank you, Pastor," Zachary said as he hung up. *But I'm just not taking no for an answer*, he thought to himself, although he felt a cloud of peace overshadow him. He fell to his knees and said his prayer before going to bed, since he had stayed up all night again. He got up at five in the afternoon. Within half an hour, he was outside walking in his weathered shoes, bearing in mind every word that Pastor Nguyen had encouraged him with.

A few blocks away, he approached a middle-aged man next to his pickup, struggling to hoist a sofa on top of the flatbed.

"Hey, amigo," the man said. "¿Ayúdame, por favor?"

"Sure." Zachary smiled and took one end of the sofa. The man took the other end, and together they lifted it onto his truck.

The man beamed with gratefulness and shook his hand. "¡Gracias, amigo!"

"De nada," he replied, thankful to have remembered some of his high school Spanish. He walked away feeling rejuvenated that he got to help someone like that. A simple act of kindness will go a long way.

Day 84: Deciding to go all the way to the outdoor mall, he met hostility the moment he stepped onto the crosswalk. Three teenagers on their e-bikes began to harass him, saying, "What's up, bro? What's up?!" and "Hey, man!" They continued to speed past him, the tone of their voices dripping with sarcasm.

Haunted by it, he nonetheless reciprocated it with a "Hey," hoping to spread a little cheer to the teenagers who were probably hiding the hurt feelings that led to their bullying behavior to begin with. Alas, the teenagers didn't bother to hear him.

Troubled, Zachary continued on his walk without respite, sauntering along the outdoor mall's perimeter. Making his way past the nearby HomeTown Buffet, he suddenly heard a man's loud voice, saying, "I watched your YouTube video." He looked up and saw a man a few yards away, cruising toward him with his hands in his pockets.

"Oh, you have?"

"Yes. I see you walking all the time, so when you popped up on YouTube, I said, 'Hey, I know that guy.' I gotta say, you expressed yourself very well. I wouldn't have known you were autistic, but then again, I never came up to introduce myself. I'm William, but you could call me Bill."

"Well, nice to meet you, Bill. You literally made my day."

"Anytime! Keep it up," he replied, smiling as he walked away.

Zachary continued his itinerary, which was uneventful the rest of the way. He felt amazed to be recognized from YouTube, especially since he only had under a thousand subscribers in a world of eight billion people. As always, unfortunately, he felt guilty for getting upset over the few ableists in his community and online.

Nevertheless, by midnight, he started feeling hurt again over those teenagers. Blurring the bodycam footage, he posted it on YouTube to expose that uncalled-for bullying still exists and must be stopped.

Were they trying to be mean to me, or were they showing friendliness with the oddest tone of voice? He endeavored reasoning through it, which was not his first rodeo. A few weeks prior, he was walking past a burger joint at the outdoor mall. A teenager wearing a bike helmet began smiling and waving at him through the window. Suddenly, about seven or eight other middle schoolers looked up at him and began to do the same thing. Zachary just gave an awkward smile and waved. Reminiscing about the peculiar spectacle, he thought, *I'm certain that was innocent teen humor; they probably did that to everyone. For that, I'm neither weirded out nor offended. There's no way in Heaven or on earth they recognized me, a small YouTuber.*

Day 92: Zachary trudged down one of his neighborhood streets. Firewood smoke slowly glided away from a nearby chimney, filling the block with its warm fragrance. Despite the inviting aroma he always loved, he was in the middle of praying fervently to God, begging Him to answer his prayer request and make him useful in the world, for the sake of others. Looking ahead, he saw three middle school boys on their bicycles heading in his direction.

Oh, great! Zachary lamented. His desire was to help, encourage, and teach young people, but all his life, most of them never seemed to trust him at first sight.

(Earlier that day, he ran into an old friend from the church where he used to usher. She introduced him to her seven-year-old granddaughter. When Zachary said hi, the granddaughter pressed her back against the park bench, widened her eyes in fear, and sealed her mouth shut. Zachary's friend didn't notice it and kept talking for the next minute.)

It pained him when children and teenagers went by, assuming Zachary to be an alien, incompetent for being autistic, or even some adult who was apathetic toward them. All couldn't be further from the truth. Why else would he devote his life to teach and mentor them? Why else was he volunteering as a Royal Rangers commander for all these years, asserting that he would rip up a paycheck if the church ever offered him one?

But now, however, he had to face whatever was approaching him. He looked down and continued walking as the three bicyclists rode by.

Unexpectedly, he heard, "Hello!"

Huh? Zachary looked up. "Oh, hello!" he replied, smiling at one of the teenage boys who greeted him, still pedaling his bike with his two friends.

"How was your day?" the boy called out.

"What?" Zachary questioned, honestly wondering if he heard correctly.

"How was your day?" the boy repeated.

"Oh, excellent! Have a good evening!"

"You too!" the boy hollered back, already past Zachary.

In a flash, his prayers of apprehension turned into prayers of thanksgiving as this random act of kindness momentarily washed away his pain and stress, which tided him over for the next few days.

Day 101: Crawling out of bed, he dragged himself to his desk and climbed up the chair. For the next month, every morning (or afternoon, depending), he decided to fast from coffee and breakfast. He anointed himself with oil and said his ten-minute prayer, before studying the Bible for one to two hours.

He was furious that his simple prayers still hadn't been answered after one hundred days, despite only seeking to change humanity for the better. He had gone so far to look up "Sackcloth and Ashes" on Amazon and eBay to seal his intention with a tangible sign of faith before God, but he decided against it. He did purchase another vial of anointing oil, since he used up every last drop of the other one.

On top of that everlasting stress, he just began his teacher certification program at Tributary University a couple of weeks prior. Furthermore, in-person Royal Rangers started back up that week. He had been praying so hard for his life to be set before re-entering school and Royal Rangers, so that he could focus on his coursework and the mentoring of young men. Since it hadn't arrived on time, he was still determined to walk every day until something finally happened, whilst simultaneously attending classes, staying on top of his assignments, keeping track of all the boys' progress along their advancement trails, and planning instruction for the Bible lessons, recreation activities, and merits.

Surely, it was a neverending summer of hell.

36

Kaitlin McMahon-Enríquez

The Royal Rangers hosted a barbecue for the church in celebration of the first in-person service in over a year and a half. Zachary helped supervise the boys and manned the utensils side at one end of the table. Suddenly, his heart began racing and his appetite dropped. Getting their plates on the other side of the serving table were Kaitlin and Andrés, who were now husband and wife and still led the high schoolers.

My, would Kaitlin still remember me and all the hatred she had for me? Zachary thought as they both got closer to him.

"Sure, I would love some corn," Kaitlin said nicely, smiling at the Royal Rangers boy who offered to serve her.

Zachary's stomach dropped further as she was halfway down the table.

"Yes, I'll take a hot dog." Kaitlin smiled, still looking down.

I can tell she's still a bashful person, which is okay. I'm not saying otherwise. I, of all people, understand. However, that does not make it okay for her to ignore me, pretend to have a phone call as she sped past me, and block me on Instagram just for commenting like everyone else! *Would she, right now, remember blocking me?*

Kaitlin was now three-quarters down the table with her plate almost full.

I don't think she once looked at me within this past minute. I have no choice but to be the one who hands her the utensils. I can't just run away, but why would I be such a coward? I am determined to know whether or not she grew up since COVID.

The utensils were next. Zachary's heart felt like it would beat out of his chest. All he wanted was for eight billion people to be *kind* to one another, especially the disabled, physical or neurodevelopmental, and there he was, being hated by someone who claims to be a Christian and *works* for the church, earning wages. He never said there was anything wrong with earning wages from a church, but he was just a volunteer and proud of it, for it showed a genuine heart in lieu of a questionable one.

"Um, two packs of ketchup and two packs of mustard, please," Kaitlin replied to the boy. After receiving the condiments, she sloppily grabbed a couple of napkins that were stacked in front of the utensils and stormed the heck out of there.

Uh, what? … What?! Zachary stood there aghast. *How stupidly pathetic! I'll continue praying for your soul, Kaitlin!*

"Hey, Zachy boy," the charismatic Pastor Andrés Enríquez said, beaming with an ear-to-ear grin. "How are you?"

"Oh, uh—" He was suddenly feeling depressed as if he were the most hated person in the world, when a voice of kindness changed that. Now, he was in disequilibrium. "Um, *hey*, Pastor Andrés! It's so great to see you again. And you're growing a mustache and a little beard, I notice." He could tell that his voice was weak and crackly, consumed with emotion, trying hard to pretend that he was energetic. The stressful situation was akin to running in a nightmare, unable to get more than a few centimeters forward.

After a small chat, Zachary thought, *Phew, Andrés didn't seem to detect that something was wrong with me.* His legs were on the verge of giving out as he decided not to eat that afternoon. He propped himself up by pressing down on the table's end. *But still, how? Kaitlin must've sensed me because she never looked up. Besides, how the* heck *does she think she's going to eat all that without utensils, especially her creamed corn? It's like she deliberately forewent the utensils as if she wants to eat messily … purely to avoid me. This is the first time we had seen each other in almost two years, when she blocked me on Instagram for supporting her and spreading encouraging comments like* every single other person at this church *who follows her. Why me? Why* just *me?*

37

The Tide Turning

"Your first mock lesson plan was phenomenal, Zachary," said Dr. Cornelius, his professor for Foundations of Education. "Also, your research paper for Gifted and Talent Education was a pleasure to read. Bravo! You're a great student, and I can tell that you were meant to be a teacher."

"Thank you so much, Dr. Cornelius. I got to be a teacher for a day in elementary school once after winning a fundraising drawing. I knew I wanted to teach ever since early elementary school, when I would play school at home and pretend to teach lessons."

"Really? That's amazing." Dr. Cornelius marveled with wide-open eyes.

"And when I was a senior in high school, my last class on odd days (uh, we had block scheduling), was special education. My teacher allowed me to stay afterward and get homework done or study. She would often leave to go to the main office as long as I didn't let anyone into the classroom. I'd use that time to study by pretending to teach a lesson, writing things down on the whiteboard."

"Well, I certainly look forward to seeing your lessons in action next semester. Each of you teacher candidates will have the opportunity to both practice and receive feedback on a few of the lessons you plan to teach during your student teaching."

After concluding his conversation with his professor, he decided to take a detour during his walk home. He headed toward the outdoor mall in spite of feeling enervated from his three-hour class. It was October 5, 2021, and he had just entered the fifth month of laboring over these daily walks, yet most of his walks had been reduced to twenty or thirty minutes as opposed to the four or five hours he used to take.

He didn't know what to expect anymore. He had already been cussed at down that boulevard by some angry passenger in a car a week earlier. But just the night before, October 4, his faith was restored in humanity. The credit card reader at a 7-Eleven wouldn't work. Not having cash to purchase his cappuccino, he was stuck. Unexpectedly, the lady who stood in line behind him offered to pay it for him. She said she'd buy him a hot dog too, but he wasn't hungry for one. Still, he was grateful for the unmerited kindness.

Walking home from Tributary University, he decided to stop at Circle K, a convenience store that came just before the mall, attached to a gas station. (Throughout summer, he started trying new things at various coffee houses, convenience shops, restaurants, and bakeries.) Approaching Circle K, a lady walked around the corner and stared at him, picking up the pace a tad. A few seconds later, as they passed by each other, Zachary said hi to the woman to be neighborly, but her stare widened, fearful and on guard. Her eyes wouldn't leave him until the instant they passed.

Wow! Less than twenty-four hours after my faith in humanity was restored, Zachary complained in his thoughts, shaking his head as he opened the door and stepped in.

"Hello, my friend," said the short man who managed Circle K.

"Hi. Just getting my new favorite cinnamon coffee."

"Ah, I love our cinnamon coffee."

Zachary felt thankful whenever he saw this manager. The employee who manned the counter on the other days didn't seem to care about people, or at least lacked patience for autistics. "W-why are you getting these newspapers?" asked the employee a few weeks prior, making a strange face at him. "Do you read them or something?"

"Uh, um, because it's the freaking twentieth anniversary for the September 11 Terrorist Attacks, a freaking horrific event I actually remember, unlike *you*, probably. Besides, I'm a collector of newspapers. Anything freaking wrong with that?" Zachary felt his irritation rising. He didn't actually say that … out loud … as he was uncourageous to do so, but part of him wished he had. He simply said, "Well, you guys are selling newspapers. People read them every day, and I like collecting historical ones."

The employee shook his head and ringed up the newspapers from the two different publications that they sold, which included *The New York Times*.

The indifference by this employee seemed to start when Zachary went up to buy a cappuccino a couple of weeks before that.

"Coffee?" asked the employee.

"Mmm, uh, um, cappuccino." Zachary, being a man raised with integrity, didn't know whether cappuccinos and coffee cost the same since there were no signs that made it clear to him. He assumed cappuccinos might cost more than ordinary coffee. Despite being considerate, the employee began bouncing with laughter, snickering contemptuously as he rang up the order.

"What could I do?" Zachary moped as he walked out.

After leaving Circle K on the evening of October 5, he walked across the street to the outdoor mall, holding his medium cinnamon coffee.

"Hey, I enjoy your YouTube videos," called out a random driver, stopped at a red light.

"Oh, thank you!" Zachary replied with a wide smile, astonished that he was recognized once again.

Walking with his head down, he noticed the mall playing Prince's "1999" over their sound system. As he ambled past the HomeTown Buffet, a man approached him by surprise. "Excuse me, sir," the gentleman said. "Who was our twenty-eighth president, and what is 5,052 squared?"

Zachary instantly looked up. Laughing with joy at seeing a familiar face, he rattled off, "Woodrow Wilson and 25,522,704."

"I do declare, Zachary, you're still pretty sharp," Mr. Collingsworth said, beaming. Pointing downward, he added, "I can't say the same about your weather-beaten shoes, though!"

Zachary looked down and gave an annoyed chuckle, though he concealed his emotions. "Yeah, they're quite dilapidated. I've been … doing a lot of walking lately."

"Hey, I want you to meet my wife and three children. Guys, this is Zachary Corwin. He's a world-famous juggler."

"Really?" the three children asked, eyes lighting up.

"Well, maybe not the 'famous' part."

"Sure, you are," he told Zachary. Turning to his family, he added, "He's an author of a novel and is on YouTube."

"Wow, what's your channel name?" Jerome, the nine-year-old son, asked.

"Just 'Zachary Corwin,'" he answered as he shrugged.

"How many subscribers?" asked Sheila, the eight-year-old daughter.

"Around 850 now," he replied as unpretentious as he could, feeling strange to speak as if he were a following-crazed maniac, though he was sure that was the furthest from their minds.

"Dude, you're so close to a thousand," said Justin, the eleven-year-old son, in amazement. "Are you gonna celebrate once that happens?"

"Yes, absolutely. It'll be one of my biggest accomplishments."

"So, what's your novel called, Zachary?" asked Mrs. Collingsworth.

Zachary went on to explain. After a cordial five-minute conversation with the family, he told his former teacher, "You know, a month ago, I was walking around this mall, and a couple of teenagers asked me, 'Wait, don't you juggle and do magic tricks?' Apparently, they were former students of yours and they remembered me from, like, seven years ago."

"See, Zachary, you *are* famous around here." Mr. Collingsworth smiled. "Hey, that reminds me, the school hasn't opened up to visitors just yet, due to the COVID regulations, but one of the PTA moms was actually asking me about you. She was wondering if you'd be willing to juggle at the school's Trunk or Treat later this month. If you'd be up to it, would I have your permission to send her your contact info?"

Zachary's countenance shone as bright as the sun. "Absolutely, yes. I'd love to."

Before departing, Sheila said, "You can have this. It's a little colored pebble."

"Thank you," Zachary said with a smile, taking it from her hand. "I appreciate it."

"Aw, that was very nice, Sheila," Mrs. Collingsworth complimented.

"Bye!" all three children called, turning back to wave as the family headed toward the parking lot.

Zachary decided to walk straight home afterward, trying to fight off the guilt he felt after such a pleasant encounter. Unfortunately, from 9 p.m. to 3 a.m., while struggling to get work done, he couldn't stop thinking about that lady by Circle K, which ushered in a slew of painful memories from 2021 alone. He thought about those suicide letters that popped up earlier in the year. His multiple soliloquies that night detracted time from a big essay he was writing for class. After a couple of hours of talking it out on camera and uploading it on YouTube, he got back to work with a less-distracted mind, just before the sun rose up beyond the hills.

A couple of weeks thereafter, his mind was totally cleared from the unfriendly experience. On Tuesday, October 26, Zachary was a juggler at Washington Elementary's Trunk or Treat. As a miracle, Pastor Nguyen called him the next day, asking if he'd like to juggle for all the children at their pumpkin carving party that evening. Furthermore, that Friday night, he was invited by his old church to juggle for a couple of hours at their annual Fall Fest.

"All right, God," Zachary prayed afterward. "I'm now going to pause those walks, indefinitely … as long as this isn't a fluke … Time will tell."

38

His First Days

"Hey, are you Zachary?" the lady asked, smiling behind her face mask.

"Yes, I am." He smiled behind his.

"Come on in!"

Zachary entered Room Twenty-Two at his former middle school, Canyon Mountain.

"You can sit over there and observe me as I teach the next few periods."

"Thank you, Mrs. Porter."

"Wait, come over here a sec. This is the workbook that we use. You can take notes in it if you want," Mrs. Porter said, handing him the workbook. "Just pay attention to classroom management for now. Then, my instructional strategies."

"Okay, thanks."

The bell rang seconds later. Zachary took his seat at the side table, and Mrs. Porter opened the door. Greeting the students, she said, "Happy new year, guys! It's good to see you. Come on in."

Seventh-graders poured into the classroom and found their seats, finishing up their loud conversations along the way. Those who sat near the side table looked surprised to see Zachary sitting there. He waved at a couple of them who met him eye to eye, and the students reciprocated it with waves and nods before settling into their seats.

"Do we have a guest?" one student at the front asked once the bell rang and class began.

"Uh, yes," said Mrs. Porter. "That was the first thing I was going to say. This is Mr. Corwin from Tributary University. He's going to be our student teacher for the next few months. His goal is to teach math."

"Hi, Mr. Corwin!" a student seated in the middle row called out.

Zachary waved, able to tell that the student greeted him with a smile, even though everyone wore face masks.

As Mrs. Porter began her lesson about operations with signed numbers, Zachary opened up the workbook to put his name on top of the inside front cover. Below that, he wrote, "Monday, January 3, 2022," underneath which he started a bullet-point list for classroom strategies and observations. He thought it was crazy that he was being called "Mr. Corwin," a new title he had to get used to.

Mrs. Porter's first period was a prep period, followed by seventh-grade math, eighth-grade math, her first accelerated math class for eighth-graders, lunch, sustained silent reading (SSR), her second accelerated math class, and basic skills for seventh and eighth-graders. The first day was reserved for observations. Zachary was scheduled to come twice a week, a routine that continued throughout January.

When the first day was over, he visited a couple of his former teachers from half his life earlier. They were all proud of Zachary and all his accomplishments in the past thirteen-to-fourteen years.

"By the way," he told Mrs. Johansen, his former special ed teacher, after saying his goodbyes, almost forgetting, "Does Mr. Andrews, the Instructional Aide, still work here? I haven't seen him since graduating, and I always wanted to say hi to him again."

"Oh, no," Mrs. Johansen whispered, turning back around to him with a completely changed mood and tone. "Mr. Andrews just died over the holiday break."

"What?"

"It was unexpected. Heart attack."

"I'm sorry to hear that." Zachary slowly walked away in melancholy, processing the loss, knowing that Mr. Andrews was still relatively young. They stayed in communication on Facebook, enjoying following each other's journeys. It was difficult for him to fathom, especially since he was too late to say hi to him in person one last time.

After his third day, two seventh-grade boys stopped him after leaving the front office. "Commander Zachary?" they questioned.

"Oh, my gosh!" Zachary exclaimed, marveling. "I haven't seen you guys since before COVID. You come here to Canyon Mountain now?"

"Yes. It's so great to see you again," they said, smiling.

"Likewise. Well, I attended this middle school too, when I was your age. I just discovered that all the students here were born in the same two years *I* attended here."

"That's wild."

"Tell me about it."

(Over the next few months, he had similar encounters, running into students from his Royal Rangers outpost and others who remembered him from juggling at Washington Elementary. He overheard a couple of them whisper, "Hey, it's the juggler," as he walked across the campus.)

After a brief catch-up with the former Royal Rangers, Zachary looped around the school and headed toward his house.

"Hey! Help!" a few students called.

Zachary swung around and saw a dozen students inside the school's fence, hollering at him. They were playing soccer after school when the ball was accidentally kicked over the fence and rolled across the narrow parking lot. He picked it up and prepared to kick it over. *Oh boy! If I miss this easy kick, I'll be a darn laughingstock to every middle schooler in this city*, Zachary told himself, nervous.

(It reminded him of a harsh memory back in ninth grade P.E. class. He missed an easy kick while playing soccer. Turning around, embarrassed, one of his teammates laughed at him. Hearing him use the R-word instantly brought back hurtful feelings from elementary school.)

Thankfully, he successfully kicked it over the fence.

* * *

"How were your first two weeks of student teaching, Zachary?" Pastor Nguyen asked after church.

"It was phenomenal, Pastor! Already, I got to help students in math, particularly in her basic skills class," Zachary informed, draping the church's keyboard with a black dust cover. "I'm tutoring the seventh-graders with integers and signed operations, the eighth-graders with systems of linear equations, and the accelerated math students with interest rates and exponential functions."

Pastor Nguyen shook his head in circles, closing his eyes. "You know, I was just standing here asking a question—"

Zachary chuckled.

"And then my brain checked out halfway through when you started spewing that mumbo-jumbo math jargon! That went over my head."

After laughing about it, Pastor Nguyen said, "Oh, I'm so happy for you, especially since you wanted to teach at your former middle school. That must feel so surreal. You're finally working with students, tutoring them in mathematics, which is what you always wanted to do."

"Yes, sir! One hundred percent."

"And speaking about getting the opportunities you've prayed for, how was your first month playing keys for us every Sunday?"

"Incredible. Playing for those seniors for a couple of years at Pastor Rick's chapel, until it closed down due to COVID, really helped me discover new ways to play piano. Now, I feel like I'm refining the skill even more, especially playing in a worship band with fellow musicians. The drummer gave me essential tips on tapping to the beat and hitting the chords at the right time. My internal rhythm is definitely improving. I especially loved soloing during parts of 'Build my Life' today, the song by Pat Barrett and the other co-writers."

"It sounded great!"

Zachary couldn't help but beam ear-to-ear, thankful that it sounded great, thereby blessing the congregation.

"I'm so happy for you. The old keyboardist gave us a thirty-day notice before moving to Wisconsin. You were the first person I suggested as her replacement, since you've been asking to play for, what? Five years or so?"

"Well, I truly appreciate it. Thank you."

* * *

One chilly February morning, Zachary stood outside in front of Room Twenty-Two, going over quadratic equations in his head. Out of nowhere, an eighth-grader walked by and said with a wide smile, "I subscribed!"

"Oh, you did?"

"Yes! My brother, who's in seventh grade, found you on YouTube. You popped up for him, and he recognized you from Mrs. Porter's class. Dude, you have over two-thousand subscribers!"

"Yeah, well, that came after four years of nonstop posting almost every single day, I surpassed a thousand subscribers late last year. It was one of the most rewarding accomplishments in my entire life. Suddenly, once I passed one thousand, I began growing at a faster rate."

"That's amazing! By the way, my name is Thomas, and it's nice to meet you in person." He stuck out his hand for a handshake.

Zachary froze, a chill running down his spine, but recovered after a split second and shook his hand.

"Is everything okay, Mr. Corwin? You just looked like you saw a ghost."

"Oh, uh, yeah. I was just taken off guard," Zachary revealed, putting on a smile as fast as he could. "You reminded me of a friend, also named Thomas."

"Nice, it's a great name. Well, I think you're very cool, Mr. Corwin. I look forward to more update videos about your experiences here. Later," he said, walking away.

"Thank you for your support." Zachary was overcome with gratitude. He felt accepted as a person, honored to have gotten this type of reception, not just from this eighth-grader, who wasn't even in any of Mrs. Porter's classes, but dozens of other students.

And if I hadn't started making videos about my education journey in 2019, when I entered Tributary University, Zachary pondered, *then I probably wouldn't have this new series on YouTube about student teaching.*

Consequently, he noticed growth on his channel, which led to increased engagement across its various topics, including his special interests. He still uploaded aviation, music, and firebuffing videos, among others, but some viewers subscribed only for certain topics while others gravitated toward different ones.

"Great job, bud!" Mrs. Porter said at the end of seventh period, her second accelerated math class. "I really have no other critiques, other than speaking a little louder and calling on students a bit more. Your pacing was great. You didn't rush through it. You worked the iPad well, even though you just started practicing with it yesterday at lunch. How did *you* think your first lesson went?"

"Mrs. Porter, I thought it was absolutely incredible. I loved every minute of it. It felt great to hear some of the students cheer a little when you told them I'd be teaching the lesson today. I'm quite appreciative of the patience they showed me. They stayed silent all the way through, raising their hands to respond to the questions I posed. I couldn't have asked for a better experience."

"And that classic experiment showing that two falling objects accelerate at the same rate in free fall worked well. Also, they loved the juggling at the end of the lesson."

"I'm thankful that my former P.E. teacher, Coach Whittaker, let me borrow a basketball and a baseball to demonstrate that. It brought the lesson on introducing quadratics to life."

"And you had actually heard the lightbulbs go off because most students assumed that the heavier object would fall first. Great job for asking them to make a prediction beforehand. I loved seeing a couple of the students asking you to drop the eraser and the basketball, and the pencil and the basketball, showing that it doesn't matter; they'd hit the floor at the same time."

"Except for lighter objects, which would be affected by air resistance." Zachary smirked, unable to help being technical. "That's why I didn't use Connor's piece of paper."

"Well, you got their wheels turning. Have you had experience teaching already?"

"For seven years, I've been a commander at Royal Rangers. I've taught hundreds of times. It's like Boy Scouts, so I've taught survival skills, like knot tying, using a compass, camping, hiking, you name it. It surely helped me implement pedagogy … even though I never heard that word until last semester."

"Ah, the art and science of teaching."

"Um, I was at a winter camp a couple of weeks ago, a big district one. A thousand boys, dads, and commanders were there. I actually got recognized a handful of times by boys and commanders who benefited from my merit videos on YouTube that I produced during the pandemic. One commander gave me a patch from his section just to say thank you."

"That's very nice to hear."

"Well, I just can't wait for the second lesson now?"

"How many do you have to teach?"

"Four required lessons. They recommend at least one that's direct teaching, like this one, one that's indirect, or student-centered, and one that's inquiry based."

"Well, that's like one lesson a month. You already determined last week that you can come every day if you want, even though the minimum is two days a week. That's totally fine with me. You're already a great help to all those students in my basic skills period. So, if you want, you can teach one lesson a week."

"I'd love to."

"And we can alternate between classes each week. For instance, one week, you can teach the seventh-graders, and then the second week, the eighth-graders—"

"Or perhaps one lesson per class per week?" Zachary was getting his foot further in the door.

"Or that, if you want to be thrown in the deep end. But I don't want you to get overwhelmed."

"Uh, I don't think I'll get overwhelmed. I love math, I love teaching, and I love helping students, sometimes getting to witness the lightbulbs go off in their heads. But I'll let you know if I need to cut down on the number of lessons I teach."

Walking down the thoroughfare on the way home, he noticed a middle school boy on his e-bike up ahead, crossing multiple lanes during a break in the traffic. As before, he wondered what the chances were that this student knew him. Was this person going to tease him like those teenagers on the boulevard? Was he going to do a random act of kindness and say hi like those three boys on their bikes? Or was he going to ignore him, which was more likely?

Out of nowhere, while Zachary's thoughts spun wildly as he considered all the options, he was interrupted by a loud, "*Mr. Corwin!*"

"Hey!" Zachary smiled and waved, now recognizing the teen from Mrs. Porter's class.

Continuing his walk a second later, he saw an older couple outside a pizzeria looking around, confused at the abrupt holler.

"Oh, I'm a student teacher at the middle school. He was one of the students I teach."

"That's what we figured," said the wife, laughing. A short chat about Zachary's life goals followed.

39

Navigating Student Teaching

"Okay, who wants to work with Mr. Corwin?" asked Mrs. Sanchez, Zachary's former seventh-grade math teacher during her SSR period. Taylor Swift's "Wildest Dreams" softly played through the teacher's Bluetooth speaker as the students took out their schoolwork.

A few students raised their hands.

"All right. All you guys can go sit outside the door on the grass. Just a reminder, you don't have to wear your face masks since you're outside if you don't want to. Zachary, like always, the whiteboard, marker, and erasers are on the back table. Thanks so much again. Students say how much you've helped them."

"No problem. My pleasure," Zachary replied, before volunteering again to tutor students in math during his break. It reminded him of the times he worked at the county fair, juggling around the grounds during his breaks to entertain the fairgoers. Likewise, he would tutor his former teacher's students for the next couple of months. Some of them complimented him, saying they were learning better from him than from their teacher.

Following Mrs. Porter's advice, Zachary had been observing various teachers to gain multiple perspectives on teaching. She also advised him to observe teachers from other subjects, like English, history, and science. Over the next couple of months, he would sit in the back and take notes on their instructional strategies, classroom management, and how they set up their learning environment. Half the time, Zachary stayed behind to ask a few questions, eager to learn new things and eventually become the best teacher he could. Once, he observed the same math lesson taught by four different teachers in a single day, noting what was taught similarly and differently.

There were a couple of teachers who benefited from his help and said that he could stop by to help on specific days if he wished. One seventh-grade math teacher, Mr. Suzuki, would devote Wednesdays for math practice, while an eighth-grade math teacher, Mrs. Jones, used Thursdays. Pretty soon, students were excited to see Zachary standing in the back of the classroom as they entered, some giving him a high-five or a fist bump.

He truly appreciated the sense of belonging, but it wasn't always accepting, however.

"Two teachers are in this room to help you, so raise your hand if you get stuck," Mr. Suzuki announced after telling his students that they were going to work on a small geometry packet. Usually, when he said that, a few students looked around, realizing that Zachary was the second teacher.

It was the middle of February, and students were learning about the radius, diameter, area, and circumference of circles. As Zachary began to walk around the classroom, he overheard a couple of girls whispering that they didn't understand how to do it. They were seated on the far right of the classroom, near the window. He overheard one of them proposing a solution, but he recognized her solution as a common error. "Can I help you both with that problem?" Zachary humbly offered, startling one of them.

"No thanks!" the startled girl said with an obviously snarky tone, "I get it."

Five seconds later, while standing in the middle of the back, he perceived Mr. Suzuki rushing over to the side of the room where he was just at. Turning around, he saw the girl ask Mr. Suzuki the question that she just claimed to understand. Feeling mistrusted, he continued walking around the classroom.

That was worse than the first negative experience I had in this room last week, he said, dwelling over it. (Standing by the window, ready to help students at a moment's notice, he overheard a boy in the middle of the classroom whispering something to Mr. Suzuki, sounding a bit unsettled. He could not ascertain what he was asking, but he did hear the teacher respond, "Oh, it's okay. He's just a student teacher. He's helping out for a few months.")

Following that period was SSR for the seventh-graders and lunch for the eighth-graders. As students were pouring out of the classroom, one boy waved goodbye to Zachary; he waved back. On the first day that he observed the class, in late January, this boy would periodically look back at him during the lecture. Zachary didn't understand what was happening until the boy introduced himself afterward with a pencil sketch of him.

"You drew this? It's incredible!" Zachary complimented.

"Thank you," the boy said, smiling from behind his face mask.

"This is the first gift I got from a student. Thank you."

"You're welcome."

While he walked over to Mrs. Sanchez's class on the other side of campus, Thomas, the eighth-grader, ran up to him. (Almost every day, Thomas would wave enthusiastically at him as soon as he saw him.) "Sorry about your granduncle," he said sympathetically.

"Oh, you must've watched my recent YouTube video."

"Yes, I did."

"Yeah, um, I can't believe it's been a half a decade now."

"Well, that was a heartfelt tribute you made for him. I'm sure he would've been proud of everything you're doing these days."

Walking away, Zachary felt very appreciative that someone, especially a student, had the heart to offer their condolences. It was better hearing it in person than reading all the comments he got on that video, although he was equally appreciative of them too.

Inopportunely, as he walked further ahead, the student standing next to Thomas called out sinisterly, "*Hey*, creepy teacher! … *Hey*, mob boss! … *Hey*, drug addict!"

Zachary forced himself to keep walking, yet he always imagined swinging around to respond to the student's petulant vitriol. He was grateful he didn't act on impulse and say something he'd regret. He went over ways to calmly educate the student about autism. That encounter pushed him to ask about leading assemblies soon, since obviously this student didn't get it … *yet.*

* * *

Some days, tutoring math in those classrooms was stagnant and boring, whereas other days, more students raised their hands. On one of those days, in early March, while endlessly waiting for a hand to go up, Zachary looked out the window and got distracted with his thoughts, reflecting on his progress in student teaching and reviewing different strategies he could use to guide students through a math problem. Meanwhile, students were working in groups of four on their practice test.

Out of nowhere, he began hearing audible voices floating through his thoughts. Growing louder and louder, he began to make them out: "Help! Help! Help! We need help! Help!" Suddenly, his foreground came into focus, and he saw four students a few feet away, turned back in their seats, all raising their hands and looking at him. Snapping back into reality, he rushed over to help. Since then, he ensured that that would never happen again.

Afterward, he walked over to Mrs. Porter's classroom to teach his fifth lesson to one of the accelerated math classes. Standing outside Room Twenty-Two to welcome the students as they entered, he saw three of the students approaching with smiles.

"Zachary Corwin: 3,965 subscribers!" the boy in the middle said, turning his phone to show him that he was on his YouTube channel.

"Make it 4K soon!" the boy on the right said, beaming as the three of them walked inside the classroom.

One moment later, another student walked in, asking Zachary, "Oh, are you teaching today?"

"Yes, I am," he said, smiling.

"Let's *go!*"

Zachary proceeded to deliver his lesson about factored form of quadratic equations and the zero-product property. Peculiarly enough, all the students clapped for Zachary after he concluded his lesson; this was the third lesson in a row that this particular class had done so.

"Oh, thanks. Maybe I should go on tour or something," he joked, prompting laughter from the students.

"Great lesson, once again," Mrs. Porter complimented. "I only have one thing to critique. Did you notice Henry and Xavier whispering to each other in the middle of the lesson?"

"Yeah." He nodded.

"Well, you let them drag on for about ten seconds."

"I apologize, Mrs. Porter. I had a lot on my mind—a lot of points I needed to say without rushing through it."

"Yes, but that could distract everyone around them."

"I know, and I was hoping they'd stop—"

"And they did, seconds later, but you want to cut it off immediately. It shouldn't bother all the other students if you take two seconds to say, 'Hey! Stop talking until the lesson is over. If you have a question about it, raise your hand.'"

"I'll definitely keep that in mind next time."

"Other than that, you're better at cold calling."

"Thanks. I finally have all their names down. Names aren't my specialty. Ironically, I forget them all the time. I'm better with dates. Many students gave me their birthdays over the past couple of months, and I still remember about eighty percent of them."

"That is amazing."

"And for several of them, I could tell them where I was on, or around, the day they were born. Again, they were born when I was a student here. For a couple of them, I actually have home video from that date posted on YouTube."

Eight times on the way home from the middle school that day, small groups of students walking or riding their e-bikes said hi to him.

Once he got home, he opened one of his new emails in utter disappointment. It said that he wasn't chosen for a documentary about autism that would be distributed worldwide. In early December, he emailed the producers to express interest and later made a YouTube video asking his subscribers to email them on his behalf, which a few of them did.

By then, he had already determined that he "spoke too soon" in October. After those three juggling events, he was never asked to serve in that way again. He decided to continue focusing on his schoolwork and post on social media.

Although he enjoyed compliments, it meant more to him to hear how much his videos spoke to them.

A woman in Scotland said that he was helping her better understand her son.

A college student in New York said that his girlfriend feels more confident in life and appreciates how kindhearted he is in his videos.

A high school junior in central California privately reached out to him on Instagram, saying that one of his videos had really spoken to him, motivating him to pursue a career in the fire department. The video was based on a spontaneous thought that Zachary had in November 2021, known as the Be-Number-One Encouragement, encouraging people to be themselves and never give up, despite a disability. "This video really makes a difference to everyone who watches this, including me," the high schooler wrote, followed by a smiling-face-with-tear emoji. He continued, "I always wanted to pursue a career in the fire department, and I now believe I have what it takes if I just be myself and not try to be someone else."

Comments like those greatly motivated Zachary to continue in life. "The only reason I'm living is to teach math, establish universal acceptance and inclusion for disabled people, and encourage billions of people worldwide," he said to himself with determination.

After getting over the bitter disappointment of being rejected from being featured in the documentary, a notification popped up on YouTube. "Thank you for teaching me the zero-product property, Mr. Corwin," one of the students commented, completely brightening the rest of his day.

A couple of weeks went by, and Zachary found his place in the world, teaching and tutoring students, which is what he always wanted to do. Suddenly, he didn't feel so lonely and useless five or six days a week anymore. Before, he would have to wait half a week or a full week before teaching at Royal Rangers again.

Additionally, the vast majority of middle schoolers were accepting him as a human being, listening to him when he taught or tutored, and giving him this chance to succeed in student teaching.

Delivering something to the school library, he walked by a half dozen middle schoolers and their substitute teacher. They were seated on benches outside one of the campus buildings because having to wear face masks was quite burdensome. They claimed to be able to work better outside. As Zachary was walking by, the middle schoolers began to call out in his direction, but he didn't turn to them, assuming they were just hollering among themselves, and proceeded to enter the library.

"Thank you for delivering this," said Mrs. Schlessinger, the librarian.

"You're welcome."

"Hey, aren't you Mr. Corwin?" an eighth-grader asked, coming up to him as he was turning toward the door.

"Yes, I am," he said, smiling.

"Wow, nice to meet you. I'm Abby. Hey, Mrs. Schlessinger." She turned to the librarian. "This is the author I was telling you about, who attended this school years ago."

"Oh, are you an alumnus of this school?" asked Mrs. Schlessinger to Zachary.

"Yes, I'm class of 2009 here."

"And now you're here student teaching. Full circle."

"Yeah, and I actually remember you. I was the student who turned in that watch I found in one of the bookshelves, back in April 2008."

"My gosh! I remember now."

"Well, Mrs. Schlessinger," said Abby, "as president of the book club, I propose that we get Mr. Corwin's novel."

Zachary was astounded, feeling like he was about to be featured in *The New York Times*.

"Sure! I'd love to read it, and I bet all the students would to. What's it about?"

"It's a novel about a boy diagnosed with Autism Spectrum Disorder, like me," informed Zachary. "You know, I do have a few copies left at home. It'd be an honor to donate an autographed copy to this library."

"That's very kind of you. We'd love that."

Zachary felt very grateful as he left the library. As he walked by the benches, the half dozen middle schoolers began calling out again. This time, he turned toward them.

"Hey, can we get a picture with you?" a couple of them requested.

Zachary was surprised that they were talking to *him* all this time. Walking over, he said, "Um, sure, if you really think 4,000 subscribers is notable."

"It is!" The middle schoolers began taking their phones out and taking selfies.

Zachary didn't know what to say to the substitute teacher. "Uh, sorry?"

"Don't worry about it," he said. "They're finished with all their assignments and were just chatting with each other these last few minutes of class."

"Look, Mr. Corwin." One boy showed him his phone. "I'm subscribed to you."

"Thank you for your support," Zachary said with a grateful smile.

"Yeah," one girl chimed in, "I watched your latest teaching update. It was so cool seeing our school on YouTube."

"Thanks. I hope those videos aren't getting boring, though."

"Oh, trust me, they're not," a couple said, reassuring him.

He proceeded to walk to the front office. Down the outside hallway, he made out the faint voice of one of those middle schoolers, shouting, "Fam, you just missed Zachary Corwin. He's a YouTuber and an author."

"Are you serious?" asked the student who just joined them.

At that point, Zachary was entering the doors of the office.

"Hey, Zach, how's student teaching going?" asked the office lady, who remembered him from being a student.

"It's incredibly amazing!"

"Hopefully, one day, you'll get a full-time job *here*."

"That's one of my goals. Anyway, I have an appointment with the principal at 11:45."

"Sure. She's just down the hallway, second door … Oh, *you* know!"

"Hi, Zachary." The principal smiled, wearing a dress sporting the school colors. This was her first year, since the principal whom Zachary spoke with in 2019 had been promoted somewhere in the district office.

"Hi, Dr. Peterson. Thank you for taking the time to meet with me. I won't be long. Uh, I just wanted to let you know that I'm an author of a novel about a person who's autistic, like me. I never gave up because I'm autistic, and I believe my story will be encouraging to people. That said, um, I firmly believe without a doubt that my message can motivate everyone at this school. I also bring in juggling, sleight-of-hand, and science for analogies, making my message very memorable. Dr. Peterson, I'm more than willing to lead an assembly at this school—completely volunteer, at my expense—probably in the next school year."

"Hmm … Well, congratulations on your book. That's outstanding. I think that with schools opening back up now, we'd be able to put something like that on, but it won't be this year due to the regulations. I'll definitely keep you in mind for next year."

"Thank you so much, Dr. Peterson." Zachary beamed, feeling reassured that someone like her wouldn't lie.

The next morning, on the way to Room Twenty-Two, he ran into Mrs. Sanchez, who happened to step out of her room as Zachary walked by. "Cool Kids" by Echosmith, her song of the day for when students entered each period, was heard playing in the background through her Bluetooth speaker. "Uh, Zachary?" she asked nervously. "Do you think you could teach my class today?"

Wondering if he was dreaming, he instantly replied, "Sure, I can. What's the topic?"

"Solving two-step equations. I have to pick up my sons from science camp. My husband texted me saying that there's a delay at the airport, so he won't be back in time from his business trip. I have to be the one to pick them up, but my students need to practice this for tomorrow's quiz."

"I understand. I'd be happy to."

"Thank you. I'll request a substitute so you can legally be in the classroom with students. He or she will just stay in the back while you teach, okay? I can stay for two periods. Perhaps you can observe me teach them, so you'd know exactly what I'm expecting from students for this lesson. Then I have two periods after that, which you can teach."

"Sounds perfect," he said, noting that he'd need to ask Mrs. Porter first to see if it would be all right with her, which it was.

In the middle of Mrs. Sanchez's second class, she gasped. All students and Zachary looked at her in suspense. "Oh no!" she whispered, before swiveling around in her chair and grabbing the phone. "Robin," she frantically told the office manager, "I need a sub *ASAP*! My boys got out of camp a couple of hours earlier than expected."

Moments later, an admin walked in to cover for her until the sub arrived. Purse in hand, Mrs. Sanchez told her students, "Mathematicians, Mr. Corwin is going to take over now."

A couple of them gave a silent cheer.

"If Mr. Corwin writes down any names or mentions any problems, that's an automatic detention and a phone call home. I'll be back tomorrow. Take care."

Zachary took his seat in the teacher's chair, a surreal mix of excitement and responsibility permeating him. He looked out at the class, seeing students quietly working on their practice worksheets. Hands would go up, and he would walk over to help them. Before teaching the next two periods, he put a piece of rope under the document camera. "Your incentive," he announced, "is this rope trick. How many small pieces of rope do I have tied together?"

"Three," some students said.

"Yeah, because there are three ends up here and three ends down there. I can show you the trick at the end of the class if we're all working and well-behaved, okay?"

Students nodded and Zachary proceeded to teach the lesson about two-step equations, followed by independent practice time.

One student asked for a calculator. After Zachary got one for him, he turned around and pretended to toss it from the other side of the classroom. The boy jumped halfway out of his seat, wide-eyed. He chuckled when he realized that Zachary was joking. (Throughout student teaching, he employed his sense of humor at appropriate times.)

"Wow!" all the students exclaimed, marveling after Zachary converted the three pieces of rope into one long piece of rope with two ends as opposed to six.

40

The Temporary Job that Changed Zachary's Life

"All the students enjoyed you, they told me," Mrs. Sanchez said a couple of days after Zachary taught her classes. "I wanted to let you know, I asked the students what they thought about you, specifically as a teacher. They all said you taught well and loved your rope trick, but a couple suggested speaking a bit louder."

"I definitely appreciate that feedback, and I'll always keep that in mind," he responded. "It was quite a wonderful experience. Thank you."

"No worries. By the way, are you planning to be a substitute teacher one day?"

"You know what? A few weeks ago, Mrs. Porter told me, 'I recommend that you become a sub. That way, if something happens, and I can't be here, you could sub for me.'"

"And?"

"Well, I thought about it. I overheard my classmates in the teacher certification program sharing stories about being a substitute. And, after considering it, I think it'd be a wonderful experience. I went back to Mrs. Porter, telling her that I'm willing to be a sub. The next thing I knew, a woman from the district office came over with a stack of papers as high as the ceiling: tax documents, background check and fingerprinting, doctor appointments I'd need, and dozens of forms to sign."

"So, are you a sub *now*, or close to it?"

"The last thing I need is to attend the orientation at the district office next Friday and turn in all those forms."

"Well, I'm so happy for you, Zachary. The reason I was asking is because I need a sub for a couple of days in April."

Zachary's eyes lit up.

"And knowing that you greatly surpassed your one-hundred-hour requirement for this semester, perhaps you can spare a couple of days?"

"I'd love to."

"Terrific! I'll let Robin, our office manager, know, and as it gets closer to the day, I'll review with you what you'll be teaching."

* * *

"So class, as you know, whenever Mrs. Porter isn't here, there had to be a sub, admin, or other teacher in the room with me, but as you notice, I'm the only one here. That's because today is the first day in my life as a substitute teacher," he announced, holding up his badge that said "Substitute Teacher" on it.

In all the classes that day, every student clapped and cheered at his announcement.

After teaching the lessons, he concluded by saying, "Now, Mrs. Porter would like you to do the next two lessons on your own this weekend. I know we always do them together, but time is running out. Yes, that means all six activities, two summary pages, and eight pages of practice."

No student in any of the periods dared to say a word. They sat up tall at the edge of their seats, shakily copying down the bullet points for their homework as Zachary wrote them down underneath the document camera. Since no one was mandated to wear masks anymore, Zachary saw their jaws drop in fear.

"If you get stuck, just search for it on YouTube. Hopefully, there will be tutorials for you. Mrs. Porter is on vacation, so she can't be reached by email. Um, this is due Monday, so I hope you do well. And oh, before I tell you about the ten Khan Academy assignments, there's something you should know."

The students listened eagerly, sweat pouring down some of their faces and hands gripping their wooden desks.

"Not only is today my first day as a substitute teacher, but it's also the first day I get to say, 'April Fools,' to students!"

All the students began laughing, impressed by the ingenuity of his delivery, exhaling in relief as the tenacious tension melted away. Since all the periods were great, he showed each of them his rope trick.

The following Monday was the big day. Zachary had to record his lesson for the assessor at his state's department of education. It was his final requirement for this semester. He had previously submitted four lesson plans for his class at Tributary University. Each lesson plan filled at least ten pages, requiring him to justify each component in terms of the UDL and SEL frameworks, educational technology, and strategies that drew on students' assets.

The video was more stressful because he needed three clips to annotate, hitting specific criteria without exceeding five minutes per clip. As soon as Zachary finished his lesson on vertex form of quadratic equations, he leaned against the podium and, ominously enough, almost physically collapsed, but he quickly recovered before anyone realized it.

"Oh, are you okay?" Mrs. Porter looked concerned after he told her about it once the class ended.

"Yeah," Zachary replied. "This means the world to me, and the state definitely stresses us teacher candidates out. I was just thankful it was over. I felt confident I got the clips I needed."

"Good! Now you can relax and enjoy the rest of the semester. You can finally teach without stressing about hitting every single point."

That night, after victoriously submitting everything to the assessor and letting out a huge sigh of relief, his phone rang from the school district.

"Hello?"

"Hello. This call is for … Zachary Corwin … This is a … one-day assignment … at … Canyon Mountain Middle School," said a robotic voice. It was an offer for a substitute teaching position for an eight-grade science teacher whom he observed a few times before. He gladly accepted it. He opened his computer, logged into his account, and pulled up the file that the teacher left. The sub plans explained that he would show a ten-minute YouTube video on genetics and CRISPR. The remaining forty minutes would be devoted to group work on their DNA research project.

That's simple enough, Zachary thought, but, as he did before every math lesson (and every time he taught at Royal Rangers), he would rehearse it, just to prevent stuttering as much as he could. Although half of the middle school knew Zachary, not everyone did. Some might still jump to conclusions that he was incompetent.

The eight o'clock school bell was about to ring the following morning. Echoing Mrs. Sanchez's approach, Zachary played music as the students entered. He chose "Sunflower" by Post Malone, since it had been popular lately.

"Oh, are you subbing for this class, Mr. Corwin?" asked one of the accelerated math students, eyes lighting up.

"Yes, I am." Zachary smiled and nodded.

"*Yes!*" he exclaimed, walking in and taking his seat.

"Hey, I watched your latest teaching update. It popped up in my For You Page," another student said as he entered.

The first period went well.

During second period, students kept chattering even after the bell rang.

"Atten—" Zachary started before stopping himself. He figured it would be difficult to refrain saying "Attention!" It almost slipped out since he was so used to saying it at Rangers when he needed to get the boys to stop talking, which made them snap to the position of attention and look at him quietly. But he knew he came as *Mr. Corwin* and not as *Commander Zachary*. Besides, most students wouldn't know how to perform drill commands properly, or what he'd expect after saying "Attention!"

Rarely did Zachary have to raise his voice, but when he did, he did so calmly and with a smile. Five years prior, in Royal Rangers, one boy asked why he never yelled. It simply wasn't in Zachary's nature, unless it was a life-or-death situation. He endeavored to quiet down the class of eighth-graders, most of whom were still enthralled by their conversations. A couple of the math students who had him as their student teacher were annoyed at their classmates, yelling out, "*Shhhh!*" After a minute, Zachary was able to gain control of the classroom and take the attendance.

Third period was prep, so he hung out in Mrs. Porter's classroom to help students as necessary.

Before the eighth and final period started, as Zachary was greeting all the students as they walked in, Abby came up, holding up her own copy of Zachary's novel. "Would you sign it sometime before the period ends?" she asked.

"I'd be honored to."

At the end of each period, Zachary did a trick that he prepared the night before. Three students picked three-digit numbers and wrote them in a notepad. A fourth student comes up and multiplies the three numbers. The product had been written on a piece of paper and stuffed in an envelope that he sealed the night before. The envelope was pointed out at the start of each period to remind students to behave if they wanted to see the trick.

Walking down the thoroughfare on his way home, a few eighth-grade girls on their e-bikes came up from behind him. "Mr. Corwin, I just bought your book!" one of them said as she rode by.

"Well, I hope you enjoy it," Zachary said with a grateful smile.

"I'm sure I will. I'll ask you to sign it once I get it. I'm excited to read it this summer. Have a good day, Mr. Corwin!" she said, dashing off with her friends down the street.

41

Peculiar Forlorn Heartache

The next few days were uneventful as far as substitute teaching jobs went. He simply volunteered at Canyon Mountain, helping out in all of Mrs. Porter's classes, and teaching math lessons to her students that Friday. On this day, April 8, 2022, Zachary brought his jugglebugs, which are cube-shaped beanbags that he juggled with. He stood outside Room Twenty-Two, juggling for passersby on their way to class, putting smiles on their faces.

"Mr. Corwin, you can juggle?" a few middle schoolers asked from down the hall, impressed.

"Yes, for over fifteen years now."

"That's sick," they said, smiling and giving him a thumbs-up as they walked into the classroom one door down.

Zachary felt grateful for being a person, now a substitute teacher, who could bring people happiness and understanding, not only for students, but all the faculty. Teachers, administrators, custodians, and the security team all had a good rapport with him, always happy to see him and his smile. He truly felt like he belonged and prayed that his career would be at that school once he got the teaching certificate.

The 2:45 bell rang. Zachary slowly walked through the front office to sign himself out. The office's Sony AM/FM radio they had since the 1990s was currently playing Avicii's "Wake Me Up."

"Well … uh, that's it," he lamentingly told the office lady. "No school for a week."

"That's right, spring break. Enjoy it!"

"Yeah." Zachary forced a smile and walked out.

As always, walking down the narrow avenue from Canyon Mountain right after school ended was no different than walking in the middle of a bike-a-thon, car parade, and the streets of Manhattan, *all* at once. Zachary shared the sidewalk with several clusters of students who promenaded in the same direction as him. To his right, seemingly hundreds of e-bikers zoomed past him at breakneck speed, weaving through a stop-and-go line of vehicles.

"Hey, Mr. Corwin!" "Have a good day, Mr. Corwin!" and "I'm subscribed to your channel!" were now constant calls from students, whether they were pedestrians, bikers, or passengers. After school, he would hear dozens of these calls. "Hi," he would reply with a wave and smile, adding, "Have a great day" or "Have a good weekend."

Several blocks later, a student ran up to him from behind. "Hi, Mr. Corwin. Are you walking this way?"

"Hey. Yes, I am."

"I just wanted to ask you some questions about autism and being autistic, if that's all right with you."

"Sure, always feel free to ask me anything about autism."

After getting his questions answered, the student thanked him and turned onto his cul-de-sac.

Zachary felt blessed to share insights with a student who genuinely wanted to learn more about autism and how to treat fellow students who were autistic.

Passing by a Subway along the thoroughfare, he heard someone call out, "Have a good spring break, Mr. Corwin!"

Zachary turned around to see a student, who had run to the front door to catch him on time, smiling and waving from the Subway. "Thanks. You too!" he called back, barely making out "Rescue Me" by OneRepublic over their ceiling speakers.

He continued to walk home, forgoing his usual smoothie at the juice bar at the nearby plaza, which was just off the thoroughfare. A half hour later, he was editing his latest teaching update, chronicling his adventures in student teaching and now substitute teaching. He tried to produce one every two or three weeks, but something vastly peculiar occurred while editing the segment about the upcoming spring break. Upon adding relatively sad music, he found himself reflecting on the past three months.

Unquestionably, his life stood in stark contrast to 2021 and earlier, where many people thought he was a nobody, or worse: a clown or alien life form, who deserves nothing but laughter, ridicule, and sheer bullying. Online and in person, he had been told not to have children; he had heard parents tell their child not to approach him or have anything to do with him. He was stared at, laughed at, cussed at, yelled at, and even followed by a vehicle, among other unsettling happenstances.

Now, that all seemed to change (for the most part). Suddenly, people, particularly students, accepted him as a kindhearted human being, saying hi to him whenever they saw him in or out of school, telling him that they subscribed and understand autism a bit more, letting him know that they had checked out his novel, and complimenting him on his juggling skills.

That always brightened his day. Furthermore, he finally got to share his knowledge in mathematics, teaching lessons and tutoring students to help them understand, which is what he always wanted to do since he was a young boy.

And now *all* of that is put on hold for ten days!

Overwhelmed by the sudden mixture of emotions and lonesome feelings, he discovered that someone or something turned the faucet on in his heart. No matter how much he tried, he couldn't stop it for one hour. He got incredibly close to calling Dr. Cornelius or Mrs. Porter, but was hesitant.

Is this normal or actually bad that I'm getting so distraught over this? he questioned.

Trying to fix it himself, the faucet continued to leak for one additional hour. He took to Facebook to unload his feelings, after which his mother called from work.

"Hey, Mom." Zachary rested his forehead in the palm of his hand, elbow pressed to his desk, feeling fatigued and dizzy from the emotions, thankful that he bypassed his smoothie, questioning if he would've held it down after feeling lonely and useless.

"Zachary," Mrs. Corwin said sympathetically, "remember when you graduated high school? You were happy that it was over. You celebrated with your friends at grad night."

"Yeah."

"Remember how you felt about a week, or a week and a half later?"

"No."

"You felt just as sad. Most of your friends moved across the country, or world, to attend their universities."

"I did?"

"Yes, you did. I remember it as if it were yesterday. And if you got through that, you'll get through this. Besides, it's just one little week."

After talking for a few additional minutes, Zachary decided it was best to go out on an evening walk.

"Hey, Zachary, where are *you* off to this evening?" Grandpa Corwin called out, watering his lawn and sporting his black-and-blue-striped suspenders. "And why do you have sunglasses on? It's just past sunset."

"Oh, um, I just … got to get some fresh air." Zachary came close to breaking down again, but recovered, pressing his lips tight.

"Ah." Grandpa Corwin discerned that something was upsetting him. "That's good. Whatever's going on right now, go walk it off. I'm praying for you."

Zachary couldn't say goodbye but simply waved and left. He kept his sunglasses on for a few blocks to obscure his red, emotional eyes. He didn't know what to do or where to go. He thought about going to Pastor Nguyen's church, but he knew that it'd be an exercise in futility. No one would be there this late on a Friday, anyway, especially since Rangers took their own spring break that week.

Walking through the nearby plaza, he saw two girls on their bicycles riding through the parking lot in his direction. "Oh, it's Mr. Corwin," one said to the other.

"Hi, Mr. Corwin!" both of them said and waved.

"Hi. Have a good spring break," he said, smiling and waving back, albeit very weakly, hiding emotions. A nearby restaurant was blasting Crowded House's "Don't Dream It's Over."

He decided to make his way to the church anyway. Motioning toward the doorknob, his hands started to shake, unsure of what he would say if a pastor was inside. After briefly rehearsing the words in his mind, endeavoring to be as concise as possible, he tried turning the doorknob, only to confirm his intuition that it was locked.

"Oh well," he said and continued his walk.

After half an hour, Zachary had begun to feel better, relieved by the fresh air and a couple of students saying hi to him. He breathed in deeply, catching the scent of nearby waxleaf privets. Looking up at the sky, he saw a distant airplane cruising at an altitude of eight thousand feet.

That's totally a Boeing 747. I'm ninety-five percent sure, he guessed, taking out his phone to check on his FlightAware app. *What'd I say? I called it!*

His mind tried to trouble him again, but he brushed it off. Not to be boastful, he always wished to share those moments with others. Unfortunately, he was totally alone for ninety-nine-point-nine-nine percent of these walks.

During the thousands of lonesome miles he walked over the decade, his brain constantly brought him things he wished to share with people, but couldn't because he was all by himself. Anytime he saw the moon rise above the horizon made him want to teach someone about how the lunar phases work. Walking under starry skies made him want to share tips on astronavigation. Taking diagonals across the street to save time made him want to explain why he did so, using right-triangle geometry. Watching an airplane in flight made him want to describe how planes fly and Bernoulli's principle.

And on and on and on…

After surviving Saturday, Sunday morning was another monster. While setting up for worship at the church, he began to break down right in front of the musicians and Pastor Nguyen.

"Time to go to the back room," Pastor Nguyen said, gently guiding him.

Zachary slumped onto the room's sofa. Pastor Nguyen took his seat on the adjacent chair. They sat there for ten silent seconds as the pastor patiently allowed Zachary to gather his thoughts. The room fell ethereally silent, only lit by the sun peering through the frosted windows.

"This stupid week is going to be a *long* week! It's going to feel like forever."

Pastor Nguyen drew a slow, deep breath before starting to respond. "Zachary," he said sympathetically, yet with firmness, "I love how you found something you enjoy doing—something that gets you out of bed in the mornings and gives you purpose—but if you think for one second that that's *all* who you are, then you got to stop and reconsider your values. Seriously, and I'm not meaning to say that harshly. That's not *just* who you are: a teacher. You're just as valuable here at this church—the worship team, the first response team, and Royal Rangers. You're equally as valuable to your family, your online community, your neighbors, you name it. You need to remember, your identity is not just 'Mr. Corwin, the teacher.'"

"I suppose you're right. I knew that deep down."

"Good," the pastor said as they both stood up and began walking back to the sanctuary. "I recommend taking a hike out in nature, away from the busyness of the city. That helps me clear my mind and refocus on God. You enjoy videoing airplanes and fire trucks. I enjoy taking pictures of the beauty of nature and sharing it on my Facebook page."

"Hey, what's happening?" The associate pastor walked up and greeted them, unbeknownst to him that Zachary was going through an emotional crisis.

"Oh, Zachary has a week off and is taking it hard," explained Pastor Nguyen.

"It's just, those students make me feel alive, you know?" Zachary elucidated, nearly choking up on his words. "Now I have one week without seeing wheels turning or lightbulbs going off. It's weirdly idiosyncratic that I'm getting *this* upset over it."

"Well, hey, whenever the Lord gives me a week off, I do the ABC prayer," the associate pastor explained, trying to console him. "I think of someone whose name starts with A and pray for them. Sometimes I even call them up to see how they're doing. You should try that. And hey, I do need help this week setting up for the Good Friday service, and I had no clue how I would accomplish that. Maybe that could give you something to do. I know it's not teaching at a school, but it's service for church."

After the service that morning, Zachary walked home, strolling through the nearby plaza.

This time next week, it will be less than twenty-four hours before returning to a school, either to sub or volunteer, he thought, trying to give himself motivation. It was the same exact thing he said in middle school, excited to visit the Montgomerys and feel a true sense of belonging. In 2008, after running the mile one Friday in P.E., his last period, he told himself that in one week, he would be standing at that same spot by the basketball courts, just one day before seeing the Montgomerys again instead of eight.

And just like that moment, half his life ago, Sunday, April 17 arrived, and he survived spring break. After serving at the church that morning, he accepted a job to substitute for a history class the following day at Canyon Mountain Middle School.

42

Thank God it's Monday!

"Hey, Zachary. Welcome back," the office lady greeted as Zachary signed himself in. The Sony AM/FM radio was currently playing "We Got the Beat" by the Go-Go's, which pepped up Zachary's morning even further.

"Good morning. Thank God it's Monday!"

"Great to see you back," said Mr. Flores, the custodian, after Zachary left the front office.

"Likewise. Thank God it's Monday!" he said, beaming ear-to-ear.

"Good morning, Zachary," Mrs. Porter said, running into him a minute later.

"Hey, thank God it's Monday!"

"What?"

"I'm just glad it's Monday, and I'm ready for another week."

"*I'm* not," Mrs. Porter groggily replied, turning around and walking away.

Zachary proceeded to Room Four, the history classroom where he was going to sub in. The morning bell rang, and students poured down the hallways of Canyon Mountain.

"Are you our sub?" one boy asked when he saw Zachary standing by the door to greet him and the other students. Ben Rector's "Living My Best Life" was being played on YouTube in the classroom.

"Yes, I am."

"Let's go! Are you going to do a magic trick for us?"

"Yes, um, sleight-of-hand. Not real magic. But yes, I plan to do a card trick if everyone gets their work done."

"I can't wait. Your cool tricks and the joy you bring to us are why you're everyone's favorite sub," the student said, smiling, walking in to take his seat.

"Hey, I think I remember you," said a student who overheard. "I think you juggled for Mr. Collingsworth's class, like five years ago, and you did all those tricks for us."

"Yep, that was me."

"I was there! You're pretty good at what you do," he said, giving a thumbs-up before turning around and sitting at his desk.

Zachary remained there, standing by the door, overwhelmed by the compliments. The words from both students were quite reaffirming to him.

During lunchtime, Zachary sat at one of the students' desks in Room Twenty-Two, in front of Mrs. Porter's desk. Only the two of them were in the large, empty classroom. Chatter and hollers by students at the lunch tables could be heard beyond the back wall.

"Okay, so what's up?" Mrs. Porter said neutrally.

"Um—" Zachary faltered, turning to glance at the open classroom door.

"Do you want me to close the door? Is it that distressing?"

"No, no. That's okay."

Zachary shyly divulged everything to Mrs. Porter, still unsure whether he was seeking advice or simply needed to talk to another professional in the education field.

"Wow, Zachary," Mrs. Porter said afterward. "You definitely have care for others and their education. I'd say, enjoy those feelings while they last, because once you reach my age, having taught for over fifteen years, you'll be counting down the days to vacations."

"Thank you, Mrs. Porter. Last Wednesday, I told all of this to Dr. Cornelius, one of my professors. He admired my compassion for students, staff, and education. I told him how student teaching and substitute teaching had been what was getting me out of bed in the mornings and giving me purpose in life. He beamed, saying, 'You found your passion!'"

"You had indeed."

"As a former high school history teacher himself, he said he could relate. Every summer, he had to say goodbye to his students. He was happy for them, but he would return to his empty desk in his empty classroom, sitting there depressed."

"That happens to me too, especially in my first few years of teaching. It happens to the best, most caring teachers. Those feelings prove how much you care about your work and about others."

"Well, these conversations reassured me a lot. Thank you."

"You're welcome. So, are you ready for your inquiry-based lesson tomorrow?"

"Yes, I am."

Zachary went up to the podium the next day and taught the introduction to completing the square to the first accelerated math class.

"So, we've just completed the square mathematically a few times, but now I want to show you how it works visually," he said halfway into his lesson. "Here, I have construction paper, on the back of which I glued magnets." He proceeded to stick them onto the board. "And, um, let's write the quadratic equation, uh, in standard form, and uh, Brandon? Can I please ask you to, uh, stop whispering? I can't concentrate on teaching the lesson."

"Sure, my bad, Mr. Corwin. Sorry."

Zachary nodded and looked down at the podium, hoping that Brandon didn't misconstrue him as being mad, which is why he redirected him as softly as possible. Glancing at Mrs. Porter from the corner of his eye, Zachary saw her give herself a silent fist pump. He continued his visualization on the whiteboard with construction paper, literally completing the square. As he worked through it, he explained why they divide the linear coefficient by two, square it, and add the product to both sides.

The lesson concluded with students getting in groups of three and writing down questions about what they learned, so that Zachary could answer them to the best of his ability. He came prepared, insofar as researching the centuries-long history of this specific math topic.

While reteaching the lesson during the second accelerated math class, it felt like it went smoother, which is typical, but in the middle of it, while the students were working quietly on a practice problem, he was put to the test. He noticed one of the boys, Aiden, whispering to a couple of students that were around his desk, holding up his workbook. He assumed he was asking for help or clarification, but after a few seconds, he realized they were chattering about something off-topic.

"Um, Aiden?" Zachary whispered loudly from the podium across the room.

Some of the students looked at Zachary. Others looked at Aiden. Others looked back and forth. Others continued working. Mrs. Porter sat still at her desk with arms crossed, wondering how this would play out.

"Please sit over there." Zachary pointed to a vacant seat by the back door.

"I'll return to my seat," Aiden quickly said, wide-eyed.

"No, please sit over there. You've been whispering to them off and on the past couple of weeks. I think you'd learn better over there."

"But—" Aiden started to protest.

"Right now," Zachary said, a hint of sternness in his voice.

"Yes, Mr. Corwin," Aiden said, walking over to his new seat in obedience.

The rest of the students remained silent. Mrs. Porter sat there, impressed that Zachary had called out a student without escalating the situation, finally showing a measure of assertiveness, a skill he still found difficult.

Later that day, just before SSR began, Zachary saw Aiden approaching, for he also had Mrs. Porter for SSR. By that time, Mrs. Porter had left, and Zachary had accepted a half-day substitute job.

"Hey, Aiden. I just want to say, I apologize for my tone earlier today, and—"

"Oh, don't worry about it, Mr. Corwin," Aiden said, apologetically, "I was being a distraction, and that was wrong. I'm sorry."

During SSR, students sometimes went up to Zachary or Mrs. Porter to ask math questions. On this day, Zachary was showing a student how to derive the Quadratic Formula from standard form on the whiteboard. Out of nowhere, halfway through the derivation, he heard, "Hi, this is Zachary Corwin." It was his own voice. Students started snickering.

"Whoa, that's a familiar voice," Zachary said, smirking. "Listen, as I've told some of you seven or eight times already, you could watch my YouTube videos *after* school, okay?"

"Sure, Mr. Corwin," the student said, chuckling as he closed YouTube.

Zachary continued the derivation, amused by the humorous prospect. Here he was, a small YouTuber in a classroom, with a couple of students blasting his videos. However, he would remain professional and ask students to turn it off until after school, if they'd still be interested in watching his videos.

The next couple of days rolled by. He stood by for a phone call from the district to fill in as a substitute somewhere. The only jobs that came up were ones he didn't feel ready for yet, like Physical Education at one of the elementary schools or high school Spanish. Thus, he ended up just volunteering at the middle school, helping Mr. Suzuki throughout Wednesday and Mrs. Jones throughout Thursday.

"We got through this week," said Officer Li, the school resource officer, beaming. "Happy Friday!"

"Well … um … uh, not me. I mean—" Zachary stumbled over his words, worried that the officer might think he was drunk, though he was confident she wouldn't since they ran into each other a few times already. "Fridays are my least favorite days. I look forward to Mondays, which are now my favorite days—the complete opposite of when I was a student."

Officer Li put on a grin, saying, "Oh, well, it's almost Monday!"

43

Fireflies of Gratitude

"I do declare, Zachary, you really made me feel old today," said Mr. Collingsworth. "How was your first day subbing at an elementary school?"

"Just amazing, and it was in our former classroom too."

"That's right. Room Fourteen is now a fifth-grade classroom."

"Just a full-circle moment, especially working in the same school as you, my former teacher. I enjoyed teaching the math lesson on order of operations. I used to go crazy with those when I was a student here, making up my own long-winded problems."

"No kidding! I remember writing on your math tests, 'Stop using Roman numerals!'"

"I remember." Zachary laughed. "And then in fifth grade, I tried figuring out math using Roman numerals. Also, today, I noticed nothing changed: Language Arts in the morning, Mathematics after recess, and either Social Studies or Science after lunch."

"Yessiree. Times haven't changed since you were a student."

"Coach Sullivan still teaches Physical Education; I ran into him. Mrs. Jackson is still the librarian, and some of the books I read are still being read by students today."

"So, besides teaching a math lesson, what else did you do today?"

"Well, at times, I handed out a worksheet or had them read silently for twenty minutes; at other times, I led them through reading a story, classic popcorn reading style."

"Did you show the students tricks or juggling?"

"Yeah. I always carry my rope trick, coin tricks, and at least one deck of cards in my pockets. I also brought my jugglebugs. I thought, after getting through each assignment, I'd show them a trick as an incentive. They totally enjoyed them all day."

"That's nice. And the students were nice?"

"Yes, uh, for the most part. Toward the end, they started getting giggly or conversational with each other."

"Meh, it is what it is. End of the day. School's almost out, you know?"

"Yes. And a couple of them asked me if I could be their sixth-grade teacher next year."

Mr. Collingsworth gave a light chuckle.

"Anyway, I have incredible news!" Zachary announced, eyes lit up.

"Tell me."

"Before I came today, I got an email from the state's department of education. I passed the first round of student teaching! One more to go."

"Congratulations, Zachary! And next semester will be your full-time student teaching, right?"

"Yeah. I'll be teaching two or three units. It's going to be more grueling, though: teaching a handful of lessons and so many more points to hit per lesson. I'll have to record three or four five-minute videos, *with annotations*, write a detailed reflection for each lesson providing evidence of UDL and SEL strategies, deliver assessments, provide graded samples from students, and more. I mean…*oh my gosh*!"

"My, you'll handle it! I know you will. I believe in you, I do!"

"I'm sure I will. I'm also confident that I'll surpass my required hours too. I only needed a hundred hours this semester, but I surpassed three hundred. Student teaching requires six hundred or so, total."

"You're a busy beaver. I'm sure that's not counting all the hours you've subbed."

As Zachary walked out of the school, a few of the students from the class he substituted for waved and called, "Bye, Mr. Corwin!" He overheard one of them tell her parent, "He did card tricks and juggled for us today," to which the parent responded, "Really? That's nice."

He was thankful for the opportunity to make students' days as well as to teach lessons. This carried on for the rest of May and early June, where there were more opportunities to sub than to volunteer at Canyon Mountain. In his district, there were thirty schools: twenty-two elementary schools, four middle schools, and four high schools. By June, he had subbed at eight different schools, gradually building rapport with students and faculty, leaving an impact in the community. Just as important, he learned in the process.

Throughout the month of May, students wrote letters of appreciation to their teachers. Much to his surprise and joy, Zachary received a dozen of them—some thanking him for all his help, others congratulating him on his social media success, or a few praising him as a substitute who actually taught the math instead of playing a boring video. But the letter that stood above the rest of them came from an accelerated math student named Jake.

It was the end of the period, and Zachary was subbing for Mrs. Porter again. Jake was the only student remaining, zipping up his backpack and swinging it over his right shoulder. "That was a radical lesson today, Mr. Corwin," he said as he walked over to him.

"Ha-ha! Yes, indeed. Well, you guys had to review radicals, like square roots, sooner or later, especially since you're using the Quadratic Formula more."

"I wanted to give you this, Mr. Corwin," Jake said, smiling. "It's just a little letter of gratitude."

"Thank you so much, Jake," he said, receiving the folded piece of printer paper. "I definitely appreciate it."

"You're welcome. Thank you for being who you are."

Zachary sat down at the teacher's desk and began reading the well-articulated letter. Words could not begin to express the jubilation, acceptance, worth, value, and inclusion that he felt upon reading the following:

> *Dear Mr. Corwin,*
>
> *I am truly honored to have been your student. You are not only an inspiration but also a genuinely remarkable person. As my middle school years come to a close in the next few weeks, I want to express how much of an amazing teacher you are. I have learned so much from you—not just academically, but in life as well. You have shown me that even the toughest challenges often have multiple solutions.*
>
> *It is rare to encounter someone as calm, composed, and patient as you. I hope one day I can have even a fraction of the patience and grace you show every day. Your guidance is deeply appreciated, and the way you help students understand math leaves a lasting impact, more than you might realize. On tests, you always take the time to explain concepts thoroughly, and the knowledge you share enriches the entire class.*
>
> *I also want to thank you for your patience with us middle schoolers. Every effort you make resonates with us, and your passion for teaching is truly inspiring. I am proud to say that Mr. Corwin was my teacher, and I hope you remember your first year at Canyon Mountain Middle School. It has clearly left a lasting mark. Teaching and helping others are clearly your gifts, and I believe your future will be even more successful. Know that everything you do makes a difference.*
>
> *Your student,*
> *Jake*

Over the months, he had read that thorough, heartfelt letter over and over again, especially when times got discouraging, like the time on June 1 when he subbed a science class at a high school on the other side of the district.

"Everything was going well," he recounted to Mrs. Porter during lunchtime. "By the end of the day, students were coming up to me asking, 'Are you the sub who juggles? The entire school is raving about it.' But before the last period—oh, man alive!—a student walked in asking me if I was the sub. After telling him I was, he said to me, 'Good luck controlling this class.'"

"Oh, geez." Mrs. Porter drooped, shaking her head.

"Yep, they were hollering, scrolling on their phones, and playing games on their Chromebooks all period long. One even belted out his singing. Another actually sprawled on top of a table when he entered the classroom, pretending to make a snow angel or whatever. I was doing more managing than anything, ensuring that they didn't burn the place down. I walked in circles a hundred times, telling them to be quiet and redirecting them to the worksheets and Gizmos activities they'd been assigned. They would say to me, unmeaningfully, 'Okay, I'm sorry, sir,' or, 'I got you,' as if they were going to obey. I mean, thank God it was a short day; all the periods were forty-five minutes."

"That school's the worst. Subs say that all the time. I've heard so many bad stories from there. If I were you, take a day off next time!"

Zachary appreciated the advice and understood where she was coming from, but he wasn't about to give up on any student, or any school for that matter, just because of one miserable forty-five-minute experience.

Due to his merciful and gracious nature, he always tried talking with the disrespectful students who had a poor attitude, pulling out his SEL strategies at times, but only once did he have to call a school counselor to escort a student, named Robby, out of class at Canyon Mountain. After he was gone, Zachary could then focus on Daniel and Alejandro, two other students who were lesser distractions.

That afternoon, as Zachary neared the exit of his favorite juice bar, he was greeted by three seventh-graders who were just arriving for an after-school smoothie.

"Mr. Corwin!" one of them, Luca, exclaimed, taking off his e-bike helmet. "Dab me up!"

"U-uh? What?"

"Here, I'll show you."

After learning something new, Zachary said, "Back in *my* day, we greeted each other with a little fist-bump routine, like this—" After teaching it to Luca, he pointed up at the juice bar's ceiling speakers, saying, "Hey, I know this song: 'Stitches,' by Shawn Mendes. Gosh, this takes me back to 2016."

"I'm sorry for how our class acted today," said Susie, her eyebrows furrowed in frustration. "Robby, Daniel, and Alejandro were *not* funny, thinking they could joke around like that, talk back to you, and disrespect you. You did *not* deserve that."

"Well, um, I thank you for your thoughtfulness. Everyone else was great in that class. It was just them three," Zachary replied, trying not to sound as frustrated as he was.

"Other than that, how was your day?" asked Luca.

"It was excellent. Honestly, I enjoyed it as always. Only two of the periods were a handful. Third period was when I had to call the office to have that student removed. It was the first time I ever had to do that as a sub, but I gave him a million chances, and he wasted every single one, back talk and all. He was also putting words in my mouth or twisting them. Eighth period was the class where half the students spent the entire time mumbling, while others were caught playing games or printing random pictures. I still don't know who it was that did that."

"Well, I'm still glad you were our sub," Susie said, reassuring him.

"It's humbling to hear that. Even last week, students came up to me, saying they were happy to hear that I was going to be their sub today."

The following week, the seventh-grade history teacher whom he subbed for that day handed Zachary a stack of apology notes from eighth period, including ones from Robby, Daniel, and Alejandro. It meant a lot to him to read what they all wrote, apologizing for how the class behaved, applauding his professionalism through it all, and saying how cool they thought it was to see his tricks and juggling at the end of the class.

While Zachary walked home that day, a student, who was playing basketball in his driveway with his friends, called out from across the street, "Sorry, Mr. Corwin, for how I behaved!"

"Yeah, I'm so sorry," said another.

"Thanks, Daniel and Alejandro," Zachary replied back. "I forgive you. Have a good afternoon."

"You too!"

Zachary felt blessed to have that moment, hearing the seventh-graders own up to their misbehavior and knowing there were no hard feelings.

Overall, having subbed in many classes at many schools, more students (from elementary school to high school) started calling out to Zachary, "Hi, Mr. Corwin!" from cars, e-bikes, parks, restaurants, and stores.

Humorously, during a neighborhood walk, he once had a short conversation with a couple of students who called out to him, though he never saw them. Instead, he just stared up at the voices coming through the dark mesh of the window screen as they talked. Another time, during a three-hour walk, he ran into the same two students four times.

All of a sudden, his cathartic neighborhood walks weren't plagued with fear of discrimination, but infused with kindness and acceptance.

44

Summer 2022: VBS & PR

"Hey, Mr. Corwin. Are you excited that summer vacation just began?" a middle schooler on his e-bike asked, stopping to have a conversation.

"Um, not really."

"Not really? Why?"

"Well, as a substitute teacher, I have nothing to do. The district said it's unlikely that I'd get any assignments this summer."

"Aw, that's not cool," the student said in sympathy.

"But I'll turn twenty-seven this summer," he said, smiling.

"Happy early birthday! And hey, I follow you on TikTok now!"

"Oh, thanks for the support. I just got it three or four weeks ago because students all across the district said, 'Get TikTok, get TikTok. It'll help you grow!'"

"Well, keep it up. Later!"

"Have a good evening."

As Zachary continued to walk, he saw a lawn sign in front of a house, advertising their church's VBS. "Perfect!" he said to himself with cheer. After rushing home, he looked up the various churches in his city and neighboring cities that were hosting VBSs, requesting to volunteer for twenty or thirty minutes, speaking his testimony as an autistic Christian and juggling for everyone.

After a week, he found himself walking down the same street as the house with the lawn sign. He had just been thinking about kindness. A "spontaneous thought," as he called them, hit him like a ton of bricks, which periodically happened throughout his life. He got on the camera and began speaking, "It takes a lot of people, work, and time to build a skyscraper or a bridge that won't collapse, but it hardly takes a millisecond to choose to be nice. With that perspective in mind, choosing kindness is therefore a piece of cake."

Having passed the lawn sign and realizing that no church had replied to his email yet, he included a call-to-action near the end of his video, asking people in his county to contact the churches on his behalf, knowing that many emails would probably carry more credibility than one random message from an outsider who may or may not be legitimate, despite working for the school district with positive feedback, earning the Gold Medal of Achievement in Royal Rangers, clearing multiple background checks, publishing a novel, and having thousands of followers on YouTube and Instagram.

Upon emailing all the churches again, a few of them replied, politely declining his free offer. He figured it was impossible anyway, since most were merely weeks away from their VBS. Only two churches accepted him: his old church and Pastor Nguyen's church. Although there wasn't time to speak, he did juggle for all the children during their lunch on one of the days. He planned to reach out a few months earlier the following year.

Neutral in his feelings, but with a twinge of frustration and sadness, he began rethinking about the state of his life. *I'm about to embark on a summer without going to schools or teaching at Royal Rangers*, he thought. *I sure as heck don't want to relive last summer. I feel better, socially, hearing many more people saying hi to me these days. But how can I get churches and schools to trust me enough to speak? Maybe a reason for being rejected is because they don't think I'm worthy or credible enough. Sure, I have over 5,000 subscribers on YouTube and 10,000 followers on Instagram now, but that's certainly not a billion. Besides, why isn't my novel selling every time I check? Why aren't news and radio programs doing stories about me or inviting me to speak? Wouldn't it be logical that if I got all over the news*, then *churches and schools would make time for me and take my calling seriously?*

At that moment, he desperately emailed dozens of news stations again. He implored others to do the same across social media.

"Fair warning: they never take unsolicited requests," a Facebook friend commented, inadvertently bringing him down.

"Wishing you the best of luck, but the news media is awful. They are too afraid of us autistics, not knowing how to deal with us in interviews," wrote a subscriber on YouTube.

After a week of sending emails, Zachary tried to be patient, but he felt like every gambit failed.

Abruptly, an incident nearly shattered his optimism as fast as it appeared. Since it was caught on body camera, he shared the footage as evidence of discrimination, adding his commentary afterward. He was walking through the parking lot of his local Target in mid-June. Several yards away, out on the avenue, a white sedan came cruising by. Groups of people moved in every direction, pushing shopping carts to and from the store, but only Zachary must have stood out like a sore thumb. Through his sunglasses, he saw the blond-haired passenger staring at him, his eyebrows furrowed in anger. Without warning, the man let out a demonic-like yell.

Zachary jolted as if he heard a real monster, seeing the man glaring at him before disappearing down the street. Just like that, it was over. His legs shook almost to the point of collapse. His heart felt like it had detached from the surrounding blood vessels, sinking into his stomach. He got on the camera a few blocks later, explaining how it happened within seconds. There was no time to defend himself or to prove to the gentleman that he was a human being with a heart, not some wild animal by the side of the road deserving such hatred. He elucidated that he was strong enough to push through it, making him fight harder for universal acceptance, but warned whoever watched that there was a limit. Not everyone was as strong as he was.

Although most people who commented were supportive, one old acquaintance was back with his rhetoric.

"Maybe if you stop looking and acting like such a weirdo, buy nice clothes, and work out at a gym, those normal people would feel scared of you and won't dare say anything!!! If you so much think you could be a real, successful school teacher just the way you are, then I'm sorry, but you're going to get bullied badly!!"

Shaking, Zachary noticed that it was the Omani who had trolled him over two years prior. "Oh, wow. You're back," he began to reply. "Are you telling me that the two videos I made for you in 2020 didn't make you understand once and for all that we're human beings, not weirdos, and that we have just as much purpose as you do? Haven't you watched all the other videos I've made since then? Can't you just read all the hundreds of comments I've received, thanking me for speaking out, saying that I've motivated them to keep going in life, or that I've helped them understand their friend or family member better? I'm sure those comments would make you eat your words. Please have a nice day, but accept us for who we are. You are insinuating that autistic people (which might become a majority one day) will never amount to anything. Listen, if I didn't care about you and everybody else, I wouldn't be wasting my time and energy replying to you. P.S. I am not joking, but I just thought about you a couple weeks ago, saying a prayer for you specifically, as well as other bullies of mine. I never forgot about all of you."

Twenty minutes later, the Omani replied, "Geez, I'm glad you still remember me, Zach. Two years? Good memory, weirdo. What I'm trying to beat you over the head with is that others will respect you based on your looks and actions, *not* for who you are! If you want to continue walking outside all stupidly, then don't be complaining about your constant harassment and bullying!"

"Oh, I now see where you're getting at," Zachary immediately replied. "Here's your problem. You, like most other people, are looking on the outward appearances of people, not the heart. Not all of us, myself included, could help how we look. I've worked out with personal trainers over the years. Doctors and nurses tried to figure out my underweight problem. There are so many variables that I'll spare, so I digress. Also, I cannot help how I sound. I had a speech delay and took speech therapy all throughout school, but I understand that I'm not perfect. How can your brain just not comprehend that? I'm not being mean to you; I'm simply trying to get you to have a paradigm shift. Some of us can't help how we look, walk, sound, or whatever. Would you call your own flesh-and-blood a weirdo if/when he or she gets a diagnosis? Listen, I'd respect you, whoever you are, by your heart and fruits, not your outward appearance, if I were to see you in person. I've already made a video responding to another mean comment, imploring neurotypicals as yourself to not judge a book by its cover. P.S. I can remember back to when I was 1 or 2 years old. I have the capability of remembering an incredible number of things, but I'm not going to talk about that here. I'm not here to gloat … ever."

After waiting an additional thirty minutes of hell, the Omani responded, "Wow, Zach. I'm glad you're starting to defend yourself for once. Clearly, I'm helping you become a better person, but appearance these days is everything! You keep missing my point! If you seriously want to be an influencer defending the weirdo community, and be taken seriously by people, then freaking invest in your appearance! Why do you think the news media continues to ignore you! Can't you use the social benefits and book royalties to buy some better-looking clothes, a forty-dollar haircut, sixty-dollar shoes, and fifty-dollar sunglasses??? Since you have a bad taste for fashion, ask some handsome teenager or college man to choose for you. And that attractive cover of your novel? It's a nice appearance, but I'm sure it wasn't you who could possibly have had the intelligence to design it. And hey, if you could go to college every day, then surely you could go to the gym. Stop using autism as an excuse!"

Zachary wasn't going to allow himself to walk away just yet. He wrote back, "How on this planet could you not have understood what I said. I *cannot* help how I look, due to personal reasons. And I shouldn't have to change my appearance, especially since nothing is wrong with it. There's nothing wrong with wearing a button-up shirt, a polo, a jacket, or what have you. Also, I wear a formal shirt whenever I teach, just to subliminally prove that I care about the work I do. My twenty-dollar sunglasses are just enough. No need to be extravagant. Besides, nobody ever complained how I looked before. Nobody. Furthermore, what makes you assume I get social benefits? I'm not getting any. Is that what you meant two years ago about wasting taxpayer dollars? Well, I appreciate all that you said and are supposedly doing. I both agree and disagree. As long as we go out dressed decently, that should be enough. Many people have said hi to me out in public; only in a few cases do people yell or cuss at me. Also, stop calling us "weirdo" because we are not weirdos. We are human beings. You just need to understand where I'm coming from. Either way, I will still treat you and everyone as a friend, regardless if you are one to me."

For the final time in his life, he received a reply from the man the next morning, scolding, "It's true that *nobody* cares about autistics. Want proof? How many times have you complained about ableism and nobody cares, except for your small weirdo community leaving you cliché comments? How many people under eighteen get bullied in schools, yet nobody cares? How many people got thrown out of their homes by their parents on their 18th birthday because they didn't want to deal with an autistic for the rest of their lives? Nobody cares!"

Zachary sat there in silence for a solid five minutes.

"*I* care!" he said to himself. "And I've done nothing but *prove* it. I've spent thousands of dollars and tens of thousands of hours to show it! And this man on the other side of the world is completely blind to that fact: a fact that I proved in my novel and on social media … And *nobody* knows that because I'm not on the news and I must have a low following."

He quickly opened his emails—nothing.

He checked all his notifications across social media—still nothing.

He wasn't getting as many comments anymore.

He then realized it had been three years since the unforgettable day he received the package containing his novel.

I put in so much time and energy leading up to it. I worked all summer to pay for it. I had so much high hopes once it was finally published. I spent months sharing my novel to new stations and autism organizations. In three years, I've left thousands of business cards for my book, wherever I went. I did every single thing that was recommended to me to promote my book. Every—single—freaking—little—tiny—thing!

"I'm dying here!" he said in an email to his publisher, after explaining all the heartache he had endured.

"Well, Zachary, sounds like you need to hire a publicist. Reach out to the PR firm I referenced below and tell them I sent you. Best of luck!"

"Publicist?" Zachary read it again. *Aren't those the people who concoct embellished stories? Publicity stunts?*

Upon doing some research, he realized how wrong his misconceptions had been. Although he highly respected *I Love Lucy*, it was because of that show that he shied away from publicity. Any time Lucy Ricardo mentioned publicity, there seemed to be a note of disdain in her voice.

The PR firm got back with Zachary the following day, saying that they were willing to work with him. He signed the contract and made the payment covering a four-week service period. The firm needed two weeks to get prepared and write a press release for his approval, based on the questionnaire he filled out.

Endeavoring to breathe within those two weeks, he texted his pastors. He prayed that this gamble wasn't a horrible investment. He described it as "driving along the edge of the world's sharpest and most precarious knife," adding that "just one tiny single wrong move could cause *everything* to come crumbling down."

In early July, he opened his emails and got three leads forwarded to him by his PR firm: one from a blogger, one from an online newspaper, and one from a radio station in Canada. For the next few weeks, he would get three or four leads a day, sometimes more. A few of them requested a copy of his novel to review. Zachary emailed some of them back, expressing interest in being interviewed, but they never followed up with their own inquiry. Other interviewers scheduled times for a video or phone call.

And then it happened. On his twenty-seventh birthday toward the end of that month, he had his very first official radio interview, which meant the world to him. It was a full twenty-minute dialogue. A week later, he had two radio interviews along the East Coast—one in the morning and one in the evening. A week after that, he was featured in a *Newsweek* article about autism that he helped write, followed by an Instagram live with a motivational influencer. This doesn't even count the dozens of blogs and social media posts where his story appeared worldwide.

Mr. Martinez, his former sixth-grade teacher at Washington Elementary, replied to his email, thanking him for sending his feature in *Newsweek*. "It brought me to tears," he admitted. "I'm so proud of everything you've accomplished."

* * *

"Hey, Mr. Corwin, can I get a fist bump?" said one student, Todd, who just graduated eighth grade at Canyon Mountain, riding up to him on his e-bike outside the juice bar. "Skywalking" by The Astronomers was heard playing softly through the ceiling speakers from inside.

"Sure," he replied, ready to give him one.

"*Snail!*" Todd punched through the air above Zachary's fist and immediately retracted it.

"Uh … You got me." Zachary had to quickly find something to say.

"I'm just kidding." Todd laughed, giving him a real fist bump after.

"Corwin," another student said, walking out of the juice bar with his buddy, "do you still remember my birthday?"

"Hmm, July 22?"

"Man!" He laughed in impressed disbelief. "I told you that six months ago."

"Happy belated birthday," Zachary said. "That was just a couple of weeks ago."

"What about mine? I told you, like, three months ago," said his buddy.

"Um—" Zachary felt like he was on the spot. The buddy had his helmet on, but focusing on the student's eyes and nose, his memory finally clicked in. Recognizing him from the day he subbed a history class, he pointed at him and said, "January 7!"

"Sheesh, Mr. Corwin. You're amazing."

"Well, unfortunately, I can't remember every single birthday you guys give me. Oftentimes, I get to make associations. For instance, Millard Fillmore, our thirteenth president, was born on January 7, in 1800, so once I recognized your face, I saw President Fillmore in my mind."

"That's sick," Todd said, smiling with wonder. "How was your day today?"

"It was incredible. I was filmed and interviewed for our local Spectrum News, which is going to run a featured story about me in two days."

All three boys marveled, their eyes lighting up. "What were they doing a story about, specifically?" one of them asked.

"About my novel, my life as an autistic, a commander at Royal Rangers, and being a social media influencer. The journalist came to my house to film the first part, and then we met at the local nature preserve. My Royal Rangers outpost would hike there before the pandemic all the time. Well anyway, a few of the boys whom I had mentored were also autistic. The journalist asked me if there was one boy in the program whom I made a special difference to. I immediately thought of one, named Lawrence, and contacted his mother. I haven't seen them since before COVID. Zoom just wasn't the same for him, and he didn't partake in virtual Royal Rangers. They since moved to a neighboring county. Anyway, the family was okay with it, and Lawrence and I were just interviewed and filmed hiking around the preserve. We planned to meet here in a few minutes to catch up on the past three years some more."

"You're gonna be famous one day, dude." The boy in the helmet shook his head, utterly astounded, turning to unlock his e-bike's chain.

After Zachary headed inside the juice bar to wait for Lawrence and his family, he felt proud of himself for finally getting the opportunity to reach and encourage more people. At that moment, the juice bar began playing "Born for This" by The Score.

As he waited, he reflected on the last image he saw: the boy unlocking the chain of his e-bike. He immediately had a flashback from seven years prior, when he walked past his local Albertsons during one of his neighborhood walks. He could still see it in his mind as clear as day.

"Hey, can you help us?" a group of boys yelled at the adults entering or leaving the grocery store. They looked to be sixth- or seventh-graders. "We can't unlock his chain," one of them explained.

Strolling down the walkway, Zachary noticed a woman about to enter the store. She smiled and apologized to the boys for being helpless in the situation.

Then a gentleman walked out, carrying two bags of groceries. He kept walking forward despite the boys yelling for help, but he looked back at them, smirked, and shook his head, probably assuming it was a prank. As a person who cared about people, Zachary's blood always boiled in rage to see such callousness from an adult who is supposed to be concerned about the safety and welfare of such younger age groups. Unfortunately, Zachary didn't think there was anything he could do.

Okay, if they ask me, I'll try to help, even though I probably can't. If they don't ask me, I'll keep walking, knowing that they have the intelligence to call their parents, Zachary thought. His stomach had already dropped upon seeing and hearing them, worried that they'd be mean to him. This fear stemmed from a few recent incidents, including the one from a year prior, in April 2014, when those middle schoolers held up traffic on their bikes, stared at him, and began cussing and insulting him due to his looks, which had instigated a soliloquy that night … *as always.* He constantly felt horrible since he was just a nice person who wanted everyone to succeed in life, yet people kept discriminating against him at first sight. It seemed like everyone accepted the neurotypical. Why not the neurodivergent, *too*?

Zachary slowed to a normal pace, since he always tended to walk faster than everyone else. Facing forward, he glanced through his sunglasses, seeing a couple of the boys stare up at him.

Aren't you going to ask me for help? Come on!

Suddenly, he heard whispering from them and swung around. *Huh?* he thought, wondering if he heard correctly.

"Can you help us!"

"Yeah, I can try," Zachary said, thankful to an extent. "What seems to be the trouble?"

"We can't unlock the lock to his bike. Do you have a pocketknife?"

Zachary walked up and grabbed ahold of the combination cable lock. "Listen, I don't believe a pocketknife will help. The lock and cable are designed to resist it. What's the combination?"

After the boys told him, he tried it, but lo and behold, it wouldn't work.

"I'm so sorry, but there's nothing I can do. There's a problem with the lock. Um, can't you call a family member?"

"Yeah, sure," the boy whose bike it belonged to said, wishing he didn't have to.

Zachary walked away, crushed that he couldn't help and prove to them that he fully cared, feeling off-kilter over what he thought he heard before he swung around. Since that day, he always wished he had said before leaving, "By the way, just out of curiosity, did I overhear one of you whispering, perhaps calling me, uh, Jack-donkey … but you didn't say donkey?"

Uncertain of the truth but assuming the probable, he had been haunted by their presumption ever since. What troubled him more was that he was wearing his Royal Rangers uniform at the time, which should've signaled everyone that he was competent, knowledgeable, and had achieved something that fewer than one percent of people managed to complete before turning eighteen: the Gold Medal of Achievement. Even the Eagle Scout was earned by fewer than five percent of Boy Scouts, according to the statistics.

He didn't deserve such treatment. *Nobody* does!

This was one of many fuels he absorbed, driving him to type endlessly on his novel.

Now, in 2022, his book was finally gaining media traction. He was more optimistic about a future free of such ableism and assumptions—not just for him, but for everyone else. He gripped the belief that someday, *all* neurotypicals will finally be nice and accepting.

Still, he had a lot more to do, and he devoted himself day and night for this noble cause. One Saturday in May 2022, he taught the First Aid Skills merit for six hours at the church. Afterward, he walked home. Waiting at a red light, he heard a man in his twenties fake a child's voice, saying, "Daddy? Daddy?" as if he were delirious or lost.

He looked over and saw an SUV in the turn lane. The driver paid attention to the light, but the passenger riding shotgun stared at Zachary. One second later, the green arrow came on. The SUV began speeding through the turn and onto the thoroughfare. That passenger never stopped staring at Zachary, nearly twisting his neck to maintain eye-contact with him as he and his friend rushed down the street.

"Oh look!" retorted a TikTok user, commenting on one of his videos that he made while wearing his uniform. "Big guy in his PJs. Let's go!"

What?! Zachary thought as his heart began accelerating. He couldn't understand it, especially since everyone with a brain would know how many years of hard work and dedication it required. He also took it as ableism, since it was, of course, one of his autism videos, explaining how he never allowed difficulty to stop him, even though it took him a longer time to procure the Gold Medal of Achievement.

In all candor, he wasn't going to lose his life over these people. He wished to change their mindset, yet with kindness, so as not to exhaust himself or get blue in the face. He'd get many comments on social media, imploring him to just ignore the rude people that come in life. He understood and agreed, but he needed to talk it out regardless, which is partly why he made such posts to begin with. Otherwise, it'd simply bottle up inside him until he exploded.

Here was the other reason, as he had already gone on the record to say: if he didn't post about these occurrences, then he'd be no different than a bully, being a bystander rather than an upstander, passively condoning their obnoxious hatred by not defending himself and the rest of the autistic community. The bullying would likely continue because no one was exposing it or taking a stand.

Still, he immensely thanked his supporters, letting them know how much they had cheered him up.

Over the years, ninety percent of people who saw Zachary in uniform complimented him. One day, a car slowed down and honked. Zachary looked over to see the driver smiling at him, giving him a thumbs-up for his accomplishments before driving off. He appreciated it, but felt guilt for taking negativity personally. Nevertheless, he couldn't ascertain how some people could be mean toward him, or anyone else in uniform, *especially* those who served in the military, risking their lives for their freedom. It was unfathomable.

One recent Saturday, boys from the Royal Rangers outpost were picking up trash down the neighborhood streets, each group being chaperoned by a commander. It was for the service project portion of one of the leadership merits. At one point, when traffic was heavier, Zachary noticed a driver smiling at him as if to say, "Good job for teaching these boys how to keep our communities clean." Moments after the driver left, one of the boys complained about another driver who gave them all a strange look, wondering what on earth these people in uniform were doing, cleaning up trash along the side of the road like that.

Five minutes later, one lady smiled, calling out from her kitchen window, "Are you guys working on a badge?"

"Yes," one of the boys replied with a grin.

* * *

"Hey, Zachary!" a couple of his Facebook friends would comment on his posts about getting in news stories. "Remember how you kept complaining about not getting on the news? Now look at you. Good things take time."

For three years, Zachary had endured heartache and relentless pressure. Now, he wished he'd known about PR from the start.

45

Nearly Beaten to Death

Canyon Mountain Middle School had their eighth-grade registration the following Friday, August 12. Eager to serve, Zachary volunteered to help. Students who remembered him from seventh grade called out saying hi, whether he was walking to the school or had just arrived. After checking in with Mrs. Porter, he was stationed in front of the cafeteria to help direct students.

The Weeknd's "Blinding Lights" pulsed through the nearby Bluetooth speaker as he got situated. Dazzling cirrocumulus clouds overhead painted a spectacular display across the bright blue sky.

"Hey, Mr. Corwin! Can I get a picture with you?" one student asked.

"Uh, sure, if you want. There've been several students who asked for one over the months."

"Thanks," she said as she took one on her phone. "You're one of my favorite YouTubers."

"Thank you for the support," Zachary said, smiling and feeling thankful for the acceptance.

That evening, as he ambled around the city, he noticed unusual commotion. As he drew closer, he saw the massive glass window outside Rite Aid completely shattered as if a car had barreled straight through it. Glass lay scattered all across the pavement. Groups of people stood outside to process the spectacle; one would think the apocalypse was happening. A police motorcyclist was standing by his unit, finishing up a report. Zachary noticed Truck 17 turning onto Thornwick Boulevard, heading back to the fire station.

Three people (two men and a woman) from the Rite Aid's district office were present, standing behind the yellow caution tape outside, conversing about the situation.

Zachary slowly walked up in disbelief. His hand was in his pocket, tempted to take out his camera and snap photos in case this became history. It was very unlikely, but just like in 2017, he was still intrigued with the idea of documenting events to prove he witnessed them.

All of a sudden, before he could make up his mind, one of the three aforementioned people turned to him and asked, "Hey, man. Are you from YouTube?"

Zachary froze.

The man, unprofessionally clad in a gray T-shirt, shorts, and flip-flops, spoke as quickly as an auctioneer, arms crossed and hat turned backward. "I'm the district manager. I asked you, are you from YouTube?"

"Huh?" Zachary felt intimidated, staring at the manager's face which showcased his stubble beard. *Why are you asking* me*? And in that tone? There are a dozen people standing out here*, he wished he had said. "Uh, yeah," he replied, realizing that he was wearing his hat with the YouTube logo on it. He could've said he just liked watching YouTube, which wouldn't be a lie, but he decided to explain, "I'm a YouTuber."

Abruptly, the district manager and the other two people began to laugh horrendously at the top of their lungs. The manager scrunched his eyes shut and laughed up toward the heavens, his arms still stubbornly crossed. The middle-aged woman, sporting her long blonde hair, couldn't help but cough between her bursts of laughter, squinting at him as if to say, "Who *is* this young fool?" The third person just gawked at him.

The freaking heck is going on? Zachary thought. *And he's supposed to be some responsible, professional manager? I bet his hair isn't even combed underneath that hat. Where's his necktie, which would prove that he cared about his career? At least a polo shirt with the Rite Aid logo or whatever? I'll at least give him credit for a well-kept mustache and short beard.* "Um, okay, I wasn't here to film a YouTube video, sir, but, if you don't mind—" Zachary pulled out his pocket-sized Canon camera, deciding to take a couple of pictures and see how they'd react.

"Oh, no!" yelled the manager with a childish smile and tone. "You can't take pictures of our scene."

Zachary's mouth hung open in astonishment at their babyish behavior, ignorance, and utter hatred for a human soul. *You can't do anything to me anyway. I'm in public, and I have the right to film and take pictures*, he shouted in his mind, but decided against escalating the situation, pocketing his camera.

"Okay. Again, I didn't mean to cause a stir just by walking up like everyone else," Zachary explained.

The manager stared at him, arms still crossed, scratching the back of his left leg with his right toenail, eyebrows furrowed, wearing an unneighborly smile.

"But, if you must know, I just surpassed 25,000 subscribers on YouTube as well as 75,000 followers on Instagram," Zachary continued, his heart racing. He hated throwing around his relatively big following like that, but he wasn't going to be treated like a nobody. He restrained himself from announcing his recent appearances in news media and the fact that he was a novelist. He presumed that these three characters would laugh at him more if he said he was autistic.

"Oh, we don't need that kind of publicity right now. Ha-ha-ha-ha!" The pretentious manager laughed, along with his two uncaring cronies.

Hearing that comment, he turned around and walked away, depressed. *What vitriol! Rite Aid must not care about their customers … Come on, Zachary, don't say that. A few people from the district office cannot reflect the entirety of the corporation. I'm just surprised that such a man chose not to wear a beater shirt, due to his professionalism … or the lack thereof. How absurd!*

Having already walked for over an hour, he turned around and headed back down the boulevard whence he came, pushing himself to make another loop around the city. He wasn't about to go home with *that* on his mind. Perhaps he could run into people who would, in turn, remind him that he had worth and value on this planet.

In the interim, he wondered what would happen if such people saw him on the news one day, realizing that he was honestly a kindhearted individual the whole time. They'd realize they shouldn't have been appallingly mean to him. However, he didn't want those three people exploited or lose their careers; just a private apology would suffice.

After nightfall, as he walked around Hemingway Beacon Library, which was adjacent to a park's playground, an e-bicyclist approached him from the shadows.

"Hey!" the bicyclist said.

"Yeah?" Zachary responded, barely making out the rider's face from the e-bike's bright headlight beam.

"You subbed for my class in fifth grade last year."

"Oh yes. I believe I recognize you now. Crystal Ridge Elementary, right?"

"Yeah! I had the greatest time at school that day. Thank you for being such a cool sub, man! Later!"

Zachary stood there for several seconds after the student rode off and disappeared into the night. He needed a moment to process it. He was genuinely amazed that he had been able to brighten many people's days, so much so that they cared enough to say hi to him, which was a stark contrast to most of his life.

Moments earlier, he had shuddered, recalling a harsh memory of being at that park two months before. Third-grade students from another elementary school ran up to him, saying how they remembered him for his card tricks and kindness. As they were talking with him, he noticed through his sunglasses that a nearby man turned to glance at him for a second, looking peculiarly at him, before turning back to his toddler on the spring rider. Then, out of nowhere, a woman came up to the three third-graders and dragged them away from Zachary. The woman, who was the mother of one of them, wouldn't even look at him.

And that was that.

Walking back home—no longer offended or physically shaken by that man and woman, nor by those three employees from Rite Aid's district office—he decided to stop at Circle K for the coffee he'd come to enjoy during the horrific, depressing summer of 2021.

"Hello, my friend!" said the manager, happy to see him again.

Phew, Zachary thought. *Thank God it wasn't the other employee of all nights.* "Hi, just here for cinnamon coffee," he said, smiling.

"Ah, I love our cinnamon coffee," replied the manager as he always said when Zachary brought it up.

As the coffee was being poured, Zachary got the mini creamer singles and sugar packs counted.

Just then, breaking the relative quietude of the convenience store, the front doors flung open.

"Hey, sir?" a young man in his early twenties said to the manager. "Mind if I use the air pump for my bike?"

"Oh, sure. Go ahead," replied the manager. "You just pay with the little bill acceptor that's next to it."

"Thanks!"

Zachary turned around for a second, catching a glimpse of him hurrying out, noticing only the young man's prominently thick black hair. After paying for his coffee and a little snack, he walked outside.

Looking up, he saw the young man on one knee, filling his bicycle tire with air. Another young man stood next to him, sporting a baseball hat that obscured his blond buzz cut, wearing a face mask. He leaned on his upright skateboard, an unbuttoned flannel hanging loosely over his T-shirt.

"Oh, great!" Zachary said under his breath. He noticed the skateboarder turned to look at him. That would've been okay if he wasn't staring longer than four seconds. "Too late to veer off in a different direction without looking like a crazy man."

Intimidated with tunnel vision, Zachary continued to walk dead ahead, sensing the man's continual gaze. Deep suspenseful stringed instruments playing an ostinato echoed in his mind, unnerving him. As he walked by, he noticed out of the corner of his eye that the man's head pivoted in sync with him, maintaining a fixed blank stare. While assuming the coast was clear, he heard a voice bordering a whisper, "NPC."

Turning around, Zachary asked, "What did you say?"

"Nothing."

"What?"

"*Nothing!*"

"Okay, sir. Have a good night."

After taking a few steps further, he heard again in a louder voice, "NPC."

Turning around a second time, Zachary repeated in a quandary, "NPC?"

"Yeah." He nodded twice, sounding like a gangster.

"Well, um, what is that?"

"I dunno," he said, flapping his arms once, playing ignorant.

"I don't either. Have a good night."

"Later!"

Okay, Zachary thought as he turned. *Just walk away.*

"Buzz off, man!" he heard the skateboarder holler from behind him.

Just walk away, Zachary, he told himself once he got to the sidewalk, adjacent to the night's busy traffic.

"Buzz off!"

Gripped by emotion and bitter anger, Zachary swung around. "Hey, *what did you say*?!"

Silence.

"What did you say?!"

The man began to roll slowly on his skateboard, staring expressionlessly at him. Having finished using the air pump, the bicyclist began to neatly coil the hose and put it back.

"Do you know I'm autistic, sir!" Zachary yelled back, keeping his distance.

The skateboarder pointed at him, turning and muttering something to the bicyclist who had just climbed onto his bike.

"I'm autistic!" Zachary began to defend himself for once. After years of abuse, he wasn't going to take it anymore, especially since he became a novelist, a much bigger social media influencer, and now a news media influencer. He shouldn't be treated like trash anymore.

No more 2021!

No more 2017!

No more 2014!

He was no longer going to be some zoo exhibit who always cowered in the face of discrimination.

Just then, the bicyclist turned to look at Zachary, giving him the most hideous smirk as if to say, "Aw, some man with the intelligence of a toddler, thinking he could succeed in life. What a lost cause."

Zachary didn't know what to do in that moment. It was one against two. He didn't want to concede to the ableists, making them feel like they had won as he had all his life.

I have to be practical here, he thought. *To my right is a dark abyss of the mall's parking lot. To my left is the corner to a main street with heavy traffic. Behind me is Thornwick Boulevard. And we're all silhouettes and shadows here, being almost nine o'clock at night. I've been walking for two hours now, so I'd immediately faint if I must run.*

He found himself taking one step backward onto the boulevard just in case, shouting in defense of autism at their two laughing faces. At that moment, he was met with the bright beams of a large pickup truck that had just sped out of the nearby parking lot. As Zachary leapt back onto the sidewalk seconds before being run down by the truck, a sight unfolded before him unlike anything he had ever seen.

A faint, haunting gust of cool air brushed him in the warmth of the summer night, but not in a refreshing way. He froze in horror as time stood still, seeing the skateboarder sprint toward him with his skateboard up over his shoulders, fiercely holding onto it with a death grip.

Trembling like a tremolo in a musical score, Zachary could hear imaginative violins screaming in high-pitched spiccato playing in a minor key. Before he could even think about what to do, a sudden ear-piercing voice tore across the entire premises like a sonic boom, stopping the skateboarder in his tracks.

"Hey! The devil you doing? Move it!" said a loud, deep voice.

Scared out of their wits, the skateboarder and bicyclist bolted in the opposite direction.

Zachary didn't waste any time trying to grasp what miracle just occurred. He spun around and crossed the boulevard, weaving around cars stopped at the red light, not looking back. At the most opportune moment of Zachary's life, a quick-thinking police officer, somewhere in the direction toward the main street, somehow happened to be watching through the darkness and jumped on his loudspeaker. He must've turned his head and had a clear line of sight past all the fuel dispensers.

How? Zachary began to think, grateful. *I wasn't being too loud, and they weren't jumping around being conspicuous enough to catch the officer's attention. Where did the officer even come from; I never saw his unit.*

Having crossed the boulevard, the ambiance felt calmer, but then he approached a couple of people standing in a parking lot, staring at him. From the darkness, the gentleman seemed to give him an odd smile, barely lit by the parking lot lighting. The younger woman next to him simply had a blank stare as Zachary's silhouette appeared out of nowhere.

"I was just getting some coffee. That was weird!" Zachary said, assuming that they witnessed the near beating.

The bystanders didn't say a word as they stepped out of the way for him to pass, staring at him as he walked away. Zachary noticed a few other people scattered across the parking lot, standing utterly still to stare at him.

Okay, now this is getting creepy, he said to himself.

Just then, turning to his right, he looked inside the Rite Aid that had lived across the street from the Circle K the entire time. The cocky, childish district manager was still there, smiling wryly at him with arms crossed.

Zachary continued to high-tail it out of there. Frightened to death, it was the most intimidating walk home in his entire life, even more scary than March 2021, when he had those encounters with those two bicyclists. He didn't have a choice but to go the long way around. After crossing the thoroughfare, several dark residential streets stretched ahead. At any moment, where surely no police car would happen to be nearby, the skateboarder and the bicyclist could leap out from the shadows and clobber him to death.

Making it home, coffee still in hand, he locked the door and collapsed in his room to catch his breath. He was too queasy to take a sip of his cinnamon coffee, shaken by the utter lack of acceptance he faced in the world for no apparent reason other than being autistic and trying to live life while encouraging others along the journey. Sitting at the foot of his bed, he realized that everything had been caught on his body camera. After washing his face, he took the footage, filmed his commentary, and pieced together a video. All the while, periodic screams—bloody murder—shattered the night outside his windows, rattling him to his core. He had no idea if there was a correlation or not.

What if those two young men were lurking in the darkness of the night? he thought as chills ran down his spine. *And they started attacking another pedestrian, thinking it was me?*

After completing his video, he restrained himself from publishing it right away. He knew it would be proper for his mother to find out in person, since she follows him on social media.

"What must I have done to be anathema to all these people this evening?" he questioned, pulling the covers over him with stress, pain, and sadness in his heart.

Upon arising late in the morning, he called his mother, who was at work, trying to get her to come home on a pretense, just for a few minutes. Alas, she was busy and couldn't spare any time until later. Zachary's anxiety surged. He couldn't wait any longer to expose what happened throughout his social media, determined to prove that the fight for universal acceptance was far from over.

Hanging up the phone, being told that he'd have to wait an hour for his mother's lunch break, he heard yelling and commotion outside. Rushing to his window, he saw a scene that almost made his heart physically stop. From beyond the front yard, riding on the street, rode the skateboarder, wearing the same vivid baseball cap, and the bicyclist with his thick black hair. The troublemakers, slightly younger than Zachary, were yelling something obscene to the neighborhood, but he couldn't make it out. All he knew was that terror had him in its grip. He felt permanently locked in his house, like during the pandemic curfews. He now knew they were prowling around his neighborhood. He was worried sick over the thought of what they might do to his mother when she came home, or to his grandfather the next time he watered the lawn.

What if I had been out just now taking one of my walks? he thought in horror.

An hour later, Mrs. Corwin unlocked the front door and stepped into the silent house, only to be shocked to find her father and son both waiting for her in the living room.

"What's going on?" she asked, somewhat concerned. "I thought you said you needed help with your phone, Zachary."

"Could you lock the door, Mom? *Now*!" Zachary was beside himself.

"Sure."

"Double lock, please."

"Absolutely. What's going on?"

"Zachary needed to have a word with both of us," Grandpa Corwin chimed in. "Obviously, something's really got him rattled."

Zachary confessed to them everything that had transpired the night before. In the middle of it, he saw his mother cup her mouth in tearful emotion, just as he had feared. He didn't want to play the victim. He insisted that he was fighting for what was right and could still face life head-on.

"Just walk away next time," they told him. "Just walk away."

Some of his friends and followers across social media told him the same thing in the comments after posting and sharing the video.

That night, he called Pastor Nguyen to explain everything.

"Wow!" the pastor said afterward. "You could speak on social media. You could speak on the news. You could speak at public venues. You could write books. But if you ever get approached like that again, just walk away."

"Yeah, tell me something new."

"They could've beaten you to where you wouldn't be able to teach again, if you know what I mean."

"Yes, I know what you mean."

"I seriously advise you to take some martial arts classes and get pepper spray."

"Pepper spray? Are you serious?"

"Yes, Zachary, I'm serious."

"Okay, well, see you in the morning for church."

Zachary wasn't about to walk to church by himself. The acoustic guitarist agreed to give him a ride. After poking his head out the front door and looking both ways, Zachary hurried down the front walkway to the guitarist's van.

Before going to the church, they agreed to go to a store to buy some pepper spray. Unfortunately, the only store they knew that carried some was the Rite Aid. It was immensely daunting for Zachary to return to the location that had wounded his feelings so deeply. Rite Aid's window had been completely boarded up. He shuddered, looking across the street to glimpse the gas station where his life could've ended. He quickly ran in and out, purchasing his first canister of pepper spray in his life, feeling a tad cowardly but acknowledging it was being proactive.

Playing the keys that morning, his brain showed him the skateboarder rolling in the back of the sanctuary, staring at him apathetically behind his face mask. Knowing that he was just seeing things, he refused to miss a beat and reconcentrated on his music.

Even though he now carries pepper spray in his pocket, he still arranged a ride home. During the rides there and back, he stayed hypervigilant, scanning everywhere for the skateboarder or bicyclist. He was prepared to duck should one of them appear out of nowhere, which he did several times out of sheer fright.

That afternoon, as he was in the kitchen washing dishes, he heard a random everyday noise from outside. Second nature now, he ducked, knowing that anyone on the street could see him through the kitchen window. Obviously, they had to be deliberately spying on him or trespassing for that to happen, but he couldn't be too careful, knowing that those scoundrels with ill intent were on the loose. He found himself doing that for the next few weeks with any sound from outside.

Moreover, he continued to get rides throughout the next year, especially when going to schools which prohibited pepper spray, since it was considered a weapon. Dropped half a block from a school was still unsettling. It only took just a short stretch of road for that skateboarder to appear out of nowhere, and Zachary knew that he couldn't outrun a skateboard.

Nevertheless, he refused to let this PTSD prohibit him from taking his cathartic neighborhood walks. After the incident with the two bicyclists in

March 2021, it took him two weeks before he got himself to walk outside again. Now, just three days after his harrowing experience, he was ready to face the community on one condition: he never allowed himself to loosen his tenacious grip on the pepper spray canister, which he tightly held in his jacket pocket.

At first, it seemed promising. As he neared the local park he had grown up visiting, laughter, or some sort of exclamations, suddenly reached his ears. From beyond the trees, two e-bicyclists appeared out of nowhere.

Zachary's heart pounded as he saw one of them having thick black hair, much like the bicyclist from that night. He was prepared to pull out the pepper spray if needed, his thumb resting on the actuator.

It was a standoff. Both of them stared at Zachary frozen in his tracks. He decided to walk forward but with caution. He looked intently at them, realizing that they looked younger than the two men from that night, more like high school students. He walked past them, wondering if they stopped just to politely let him go by first.

Continuing his walk, he decided to record a YouTube video, describing life with PTSD, yet never stopping in his mission. Circling around the outdoor mall, he heard a few young teenagers calling out in his direction from the Hometown Buffet. "Oh, my gosh! Are you Zachary Corwin, the substitute teacher?" one of them asked.

"My gosh! Yes, it is," exclaimed another. "Happy belated birthday, Mr. Corwin!"

"Thank you so much," Zachary said, spirits lifted, happy to hear a student nice enough to wish him a happy birthday, something which could only have been known from seeing his Instagram post or YouTube video. It was the third time since he turned twenty-seven that a student had said that. Walking closer to them, he made out "Shotgun" by George Ezra playing on the mall's sound system.

"I follow you on YouTube!" the first student exclaimed, sounding star-struck. "Can I get a picture with you?"

"Me too?" said the second, followed by a third who appeared.

"Sure, you can," he said, feeling validation and serenity surround him once again.

"What else have you been up to this summer?" one of them asked, putting away his phone after getting a photo.

"Just getting in a few news stories, writing articles, making several YouTube videos, and volunteering at Canyon Mountain. I helped out last Friday at the eighth-grade registration, and I'll be there next week to volunteer at the seventh-grade orientation."

Later, while walking down the nearby plaza, Zachary heard a skateboard slam on the pavement, a guy jumping on it, and the wheels starting to roll. His legs nearly gave way as liquid fire swirled in the blood around his chest. Looking up, he saw a man in his early forties with long sandy-brown hair skateboarding in his direction. After the guy rode past him, Zachary silently panted, but he continued to walk. He took the long way around home, finishing up the video he had started, explaining how his mind and body reacted to the sound of someone riding his skateboard.

Walking through his local park for the second time that day, a few students walked up to him from the playground, happy to see him again and asking him how his summer was going.

Even though two individuals had tried to ruin his life physically, mentally, socially, and psychologically, Zachary was reminded that many people still treated him like a human being, giving him a chance to succeed in life and find his purpose. He saw to it that he would never forget that.

46

Final Semester of Student Teaching

Dread hit Zachary like a freight train. His heart dropped like a sack of potatoes. As the semester began, he resigned himself to the fact that his prayers were not answered. Apparently, he and his fellow teacher candidates at Tributary University faced a rigorous battle to prove their worth and competence to the state without mercy.

Carrying out all the duties of being a full-time student teacher, in and of itself, was demanding enough. However, to make matters more arduous, they had to select five lessons in sequential order to plan out and teach. Each lesson plan required a thorough explanation of how it logically built on the previous one, how it made use of educational technology, if it differentiated instruction and why, how it engaged *all* students, how their learning was assessed formally and informally, how students self-assessed their understanding of the material, how they employed academic vocabulary, and how they transferred that knowledge to real-life scenarios. Many components of each lesson plan had to be backed up by UDL checkpoints, SEL strategies, and other pedagogical considerations.

While teaching the selected lessons, the candidates were additionally required to record each one and extract a handful of unedited clips that couldn't exceed five minutes each. Every clip had to be annotated with reasoning and evidence demonstrating that students were meeting standards, using academic language, gaining actionable feedback from the student teacher, and progressing through Bloom's Taxonomy, as well as showing how each lesson fits cohesively within the instructional sequence. To be allowed to send clips to the assessor, they had to collect permission slips from all the parents of the students in their selected class.

After teaching all five lessons, each candidate had to deliver a summative assessment, noting all the standards it was covering. After grading all the assessments, they needed to select a few to provide as student samples. Based on the results, they had to explain their reasoning for whether a lesson needed to be retaught or if students were ready to move on.

It all felt unbearably scrutinizing as if they were forced to justify every syllable—spoken and written. But if that wasn't laborious enough, they still had about five hours of classes a week to attend at the university, not to mention their own papers, additional lesson planning, and a monthly seminar they had to attend. In addition to that, four of the lessons (not part of the five lessons required for the state) had to be observed by a supervisor from the university.

Following Mrs. Porter's advice, Zachary chose the second accelerated math class. That way, he could teach it once, thereby feeling more confident the second time around. Almost always, the second lesson ran more perfectly than the first.

"Everything I must do for a teaching certificate is a ton of stress and hard work," he told the parents during Back-to-School Night, "but every time I'm in the classroom, in front of students, teaching a lesson or helping them out, it's *joy*! Over the past four weeks of teaching your children this year, I have been tremendously thankful for the acceptance and support I've received from them. They usually greet me as they enter the classroom, thank me when they leave, or strike up a brief conversation if they spot me across campus. As someone who grew up in Royal Rangers and was taught integrity, I strive to own up to my mistakes and apologize when necessary. Once, I apologized for messing up and stuttering, since they don't teach math the way *I* learned it, and one of the students said aloud, 'It's okay, Mr. Corwin. We know you're learning how to be a great teacher, and that you're a student like us.'"

"Aw," several parents responded with warm smiles.

Mrs. Porter and Zachary had ten minutes to speak with the parents of each period. After one of them, a lady walked up to Zachary and said, "I *knew* you were Mr. Corwin as soon as I first walked in. My son, Ryder, told me to look out for a young man, tall and thin with short brown hair, probably wearing a hat, and to say hi to him. I thought that was special because he never tells me to say hi to just anyone. He complimented you on your kindness and all your magic tricks."

"Thank you so much. Well, 'sleight-of-hand,' I always say. Not real magic. But yeah, Ryder is an exceptional math student, thoroughly understanding how to solve systems of linear equations using substitution or elimination."

"Ha-ha," she said, laughing and rolling her eyes. "All goes over my head. I barely passed basic arithmetic. Well, I have to get to the next class, but I just wanted to say thank you, *so much*, for all your kindness and the investment you show in our kids and their future. I could tell right away when I saw that student clap for you when you went up to speak."

"Thank *you* very much. It's my pleasure and my passion."

As Ryder's mother walked to the back of the classroom and out the door, Zachary noticed a group of cheerleaders who had lingered outside throughout his entire conversation, their eyes wide and mouths dropped as they stared at him. Venturing to find out what it was about, he walked over to them.

"Are you Zachary Corwin?" asked a seventh-grade cheerleader.

"Yes, I am," he replied with a smile.

"My gosh! I know you."

"Oh, um, was it from juggling or subbing at Washington Elementary?"

"No. YouTube. I've been subscribed to you on YouTube. I follow you on Insta and TikTok too."

Before he could respond, the one student from the math class who came that night, having overheard the cheerleader, asked him, "You're a YouTuber?"

"Yes, I am. I have been one since 2017."

Zachary continued sharing updates on his student-teaching adventures for the rest of the semester, alongside his autism awareness videos, planespotting, firebuffing, piano playing, and vintage home videos from a decade or two earlier.

Traipsing through the lunch table area one hot day in September, a seventh-grader ran up to Zachary, saying with a beaming smile, "I like your YouTube channel!"

"Thank you. I appreciate it."

"Yeah, I was watching your videos all night last night."

After the boy ran back to his table, another boy stopped him and asked a question he would never forget, sending him swiftly back to Room Twenty-Two.

"Um, Mrs. Porter?" he whispered shyly and startled. All the SSR students were quietly reading or working on assignments. Mrs. Porter was playing "Floridays" by Jimmy Buffett softly through her Bluetooth speaker.

"Yes?" she said, tunnel-visioned on her computer while she inputted grades.

"Remember a couple of times last spring, when a couple of students said they'd mistaken me for the mailman because of one of the light-blue button-downs I wore?"

"Yeah?"

"Well, I was just out, walking through the lunch table area, and one seventh-grader asked me, 'Hey, are you an eighth-grader here?'"

Mrs. Porter froze at her work. "You're kidding," she slowly said, aghast. "Well, I've told you before, a few teachers and admin told me, 'Your student teacher was walking by, and I was about to stop him, thinking he was one of our students.'"

"I surmise being tall and scrawny with a youthful appearance would make people mistake me as a high schooler. Fortunately, that doesn't always happen. Three years ago, when I looked even younger, I was meeting with the principal at Ironwood Peak High School to introduce myself as a former student and new author. I had to wait outside, so as I was looking at the historical pictures in the hallway, a School Resource Officer approached me, saying to my face, 'Can I help you with something?' I was taken off guard. 'No, I'm just waiting for the principal; I have a meeting with him. You can see my visitor sticker with the date here, Officer,' I said as I pointed it out to him. I know he was just doing his job, but almost mistaking me for a school intruder? Especially at my former high school that I went to? Well, at least he knew I was over eighteen … Or … Oh wait. What if he thought I was a student supposed to be in class? Oh, man," he moaned. "Thanks a lot," he added, half-jokingly.

"Well, Zachary, I want to inform you of something before I forget. Remember the after-school tutoring every Tuesdays and Thursdays?"

"Yes, and I've been excited to serve as a tutor."

"Well, there was some miscommunication with the district. You won't be getting paid after all."

"Oh, that's okay. It's my joy to help students anyway."

"Yeah, that's what Mr. Suzuki and Mrs. Jones tell me all the time. Okay. I just needed to let you know, though. You could count them toward your student-teaching hours, but I'm sure you'll surpass the minimum anyway."

Zachary smiled and nodded, turning to take his seat at the side table. Seated, he couldn't get himself to open his workbook to prepare for future lessons. His breathing became labored as an invisible cloud of fire surrounded him. Sweat began to pour as he gripped his black zip-front jacket with both hands, about to yank it off.

He paused. He looked around. All the students were minding their own business, working diligently.

"Aah! Put your vest back on! It's scary," one fifth-grade boy said at Royal Rangers one evening in 2018, covering his eyes with both hands.

"You're just now noticing?"

"You're *so* thin. Do you ever eat?" said another.

"Yes, I do, in fact." Zachary smiled on the outside but was frustrated on the inside. He had just taken off his awards vest so it wouldn't get in the way during a CPR demonstration, training the boys how they could save a life someday. Hearing those comments again as if it were yesterday, he once again struggled with the decision to take off his jacket. While debating, it felt as if it were two hundred degrees inside. Without wasting another second, he took it off for once in public and hoped that everyone wouldn't make a comment on how abnormally thin he appeared to be. Fortunately, no one seemed to mind or make fun of him; this acceptance had continued ever since.

After school, as the sea of students poured out of the campus gates like a deluge, Zachary headed into the library for tutoring. He put on his lanyard before returning to the front door, greeting students as they arrived and wishing everyone a good day. Throughout the semester, Zachary had gradually broken out of his shyness, boldly telling students to have a good day and letting them know he believed in them. It had gotten to the point that a few students beat him to it, wishing him a nice day first, which brought him joy. Since spring, he had been endeavoring to lead by example, ever so subtly, by picking up trash without making himself too noticeable, wondering if it'd encourage students to maintain a clean campus.

"Hey, Mr. Corwin," said Dr. Peterson, the school principal, with a broad grin. "I'm sorry to break it to you, but there has been a mistake up in the district office, and you won't be getting paid after all. You can go ahead and leave for the day."

"Mrs. Porter already told me that, and I'm totally fine with not being paid. I'd be happy to volunteer here and help these students every Tuesday and Thursday."

"You're so nice!" Dr. Peterson said, marveling and astonished at his willingness. Beaming ear-to-ear, she repeated, "You're so nice!"

"My joy, my passion," Zachary said with a closed-lipped smile before turning around and walking away to help students.

"Um, Mr. Corwin?" one of the accelerated math students asked a few moments later. "I'm stuck on how to help her. I want to know, how would *you* tutor this problem?"

Zachary happily helped, thankful for getting the chance. He did more supervising than tutoring, since there were a lot of student tutors who came from the accelerated math classes. To be part of the school's honors society, students not only had to maintain a high standard in their academic performance but also complete community service hours, which they could earn through tutoring.

The next morning, Zachary got up at 6 a.m. and spoke on a podcast for forty-five minutes, then headed over to Canyon Mountain for student teaching. This occurred a few times that semester, with Zachary getting up early for an interview on the news, a radio station, or a podcast, before heading off to school. He continued to receive invitations thanks to the PR campaign he had launched that summer.

Word got out in one of the accelerated math classes in late October that he was an Instagrammer. One student nonchalantly mentioned it during the final two minutes of class as students were packing up. Many students were surprised, since Zachary never explicitly mentioned his social media influence, preferring instead to let others tell them or let them discover him on their own.

"How many followers, Mr. Corwin? What's your Instagram handle?" asked Ryder.

"Uh, it's just my first and last name, same as YouTube and TikTok. I wasn't creative or anything. And, um, I'll let you look it up yourself and answer your own question about the follower count."

"Whoa!" Ryder exclaimed about ten seconds later. "He's got 102k!"

Amidst the murmuring, one student toward the back asked, "Was I just being taught by a celebrity."

"Well," Zachary quickly chimed in, "I'd never call myself a celebrity."

"Oh, so humble!" commented a student in the front, who had pulled out her phone to look him up.

Zachary wasn't fond of telling people all he had accomplished. Rather, he waited to let others speak for him when it came to those things. This was partly due to the principles by which he had been raised, yet some lessons came the hard way. In fifth grade, he kept telling a fourth-grader how good he was at handball. Hearing him yell, "All right, you don't have to brag!" at the top of his lungs was a turning point for Zachary. He had only said what he said because he wanted to have more friends. He was sick and tired of fellow students talking or playing together without him, always seeming to be looking at him as if he were unskilled or clumsy. He learned that he needed to prove his abilities and adopt patience and humility, rather than jumping on a soapbox to boast.

"Are you verified?" asked one of the students on the other side of the room.

"Um, no, but since I got all over the news and internet this past summer, I've been applying once a month to Instagram, but either they don't seem to get it, or all the media outlets I appeared on aren't considered newsworthy enough, including *Newsweek* of all magazines."

"Well, keep trying, Mr. Corwin. It'll happen one day. I believe in you," the student said, smiling.

"Thanks. I have been impersonated once on Facebook, so I'm not wanting the verification checkmark to be famous or anybody like that. I simply want a way to prove my credibility and that I know what I'm talking about. I also want to prevent impersonators from reaching out to people in my name for their own ulterior motives."

As the bell rang, students grabbed their backpacks and hurried to their next class.

"Have a great day … Have a great day … I know you'll do well … Have an amazing day," Zachary encouraged passersby as they walked.

"Hey, Zachary?" Mrs. Porter said, approaching him from behind. "I've noticed you always say the same thing every single day as students come in or pass by. 'Have a great day.' I'm not trying to be mean, but it sounds like you're reciting a script. As a teacher, you want to get to know your students and their interests. Instead of saying, 'Have a great day,' you could say, 'How was the soccer game you played in last night?' for instance."

"I tried doing that," he said in his defense. "I heard that Bobby had an extensive silver dollar collection. I've also been a numismatist all my life, so one morning, after he entered, we had a little conversation."

"See? That's what I'm talking about. I must've not heard, so I didn't know."

"But I agree in, um, maintaining a positive and safe learning environment."

"You see?!" Mrs. Porter snapped, pointing at him. "You just recited something you heard in your program at the university. Zachary, please take this as constructive criticism, okay? There's a difference between teaching and *being* a teacher. Being a teacher includes all the stuff that goes on behind the scenes: planning, grading, inputting grades, contacting parents, checking emails, making copies. Now, you're good at grading and making copies, but for the remainder of this semester, I want you to step it up with communications and computer work."

"Absolutely! I'm more than willing to do all that. *Believe* me."

"And I know you said you're not tech-savvy, but take the time *now* to learn. Make a Quizizz, a Kahoot, or an Edpuzzle. I'll also show you how to assign Khan Academy assignments."

"I really, really want to. And again, I'm willing to. But what I need to do for the state and my classes at the university is insanely overwhelming, especially on top of planning lessons."

"Well, you said you're almost done with—"

"I submitted it last night," he interrupted, giving a smile of relief. "I'm the first in my class. All my classmates marveled that I submitted a month early. I'll get my results by Thanksgiving."

"I'm so happy to hear that. Now you can concentrate on everything I'm telling you without worrying about hitting every objective bullet point. I noticed you going through the lesson exactly how the curriculum teaches it. Listen, the curriculum is not the Bible. It's nothing that you live by. In all my years of teaching math here, this is the fifth curriculum I've used, and, most likely, another will roll out within the next three or four years. I guarantee it."

"Yeah, I sort of figured that the teacher's edition was just providing guidelines to help us create our own lessons."

"For sure. Another part of being a teacher is having fun, bringing your own personality and experiences into lessons, and drawing on student assets."

"I know that. That's what the first semester of student teaching was about. Nathan, from last spring, played water polo, and if I would've planned some more, I would've modeled a quadratic equation using a toss of a water polo ball."

"And that would have been a good start."

"Well, thank you, Mrs. Porter, for the feedback. Judging by our conversation, I know you'll be very pleased with tomorrow's lesson. I'm very excited for it."

"I can't wait."

With thirty seconds left before the bell, a seventh-grader walked by Room Twenty-Two. "Hey, Mr. Corwin," he said with a cheerful smile, spotting him and Mrs. Porter, who were wrapping up their conversation at the doorway. "Are you going to be observing my English class again today?"

"Aw!" Mrs. Porter said, turning to Zachary with a smile.

"Sure," he said, before turning to Mrs. Porter to ask first if it was okay. "Unless there's anything else you need from me?"

"Nope. Go on ahead."

Sitting in Room Twenty-Three next door, Zachary was once again imbued by a wave of nostalgia, being in the same classroom he had been in half his life before, listening to the same English teacher he once had. Just then, halfway in the period, the teacher sent a student to sit outside. Twenty minutes later, the teacher called him back inside.

"I'm never going to college," the boy moaned. "I'll never be successful," he added as he slumped at his desk.

Zachary couldn't believe he was hearing that. A minute before the bell rang, the seventh-graders were leaning against the back wall, ready to leave school.

"Uh, hey," Zachary spoke above a whisper.

"Huh?" the demotivated boy responded, blinking back to reality.

"I just want to let you know," he said, pointing at him, "*you* can be successful if you choose to. It takes perseverance and hard work, believe me, but you *can* do it if you put your mind to it. Just know, *I* wouldn't be sitting here if I ever stopped believing in myself. Get it?"

Nearby seventh-graders who overheard watched in suspense, wondering what the boy's response would be. Not saying a word, the boy stifled a smirk. After a sigh of stress with minimal optimism, he gave Zachary a nod, still weighed down by the world surrounding him. Just then, the bell rang, and all the students ran out.

Zachary knew all too well that words were dead to people unless they chose to *act* on them. He certainly didn't expect a miraculous transformation of the boy just from hearing his encouragement, especially since he had just come up with it, inspired by the boy's self-loathing words. He did his part and left it at that, hoping that one day, the boy, or *anyone*, would talk to him about it so he could elaborate and answer any questions.

The moment he had been excitedly anticipating arrived the next day, during the accelerated math classes.

"All right, class," Zachary said after the first activity, "so we've been learning about function notation, for instance, 'f of x,' where f is the name of the function and x is our independent variable. Put in another way, f(x) is the output of the function when the input is x. Now, let's do the next activity to see what a function is and is not."

All the students turned the page to see two charts, A and B.

"For Function A, we see that we're given a name of someone as our input, and in the output column on the right, we see that person's birthday. So, let me propose, for the first input, we put 'Theodore Roosevelt,' so everyone, write that down. Now, if Theodore Roosevelt is the input, then October 27 is the output, because Roosevelt, our 26th president, was born on October 27, 1858. Now, as you write that down, can anyone determine why I chose Theodore Roosevelt?"

After a couple of moments and guesses, one student looked at the calendar and raised her hand. "Uh, because today is October 27?"

"Yes. So, for the next one, can somebody name any president that you know of?"

"Barack Obama," one student said.

"Okay, so when Obama is the input, August 4 would be the output. Hey, fun fact: I was here at this school, in Room Fifty-Four, watching his first inauguration live that morning in 2009."

"George Bush," another student chimed in.

"Which one?"

"Oh, um, the father?"

"Okay, so when George H. W. Bush is the input, June 12 will be the output. Okay, one more."

"Grover Cleveland?" said another.

"Which term?"

"Huh?"

"Kidding, it doesn't matter. Anyway, when Grover Cleveland is the input, March 18 will be the output."

"Did you just go memorize them all?" one student asked.

"Yeah, I sort of did," he said. "By high school."

"Do you have an, um, eidetic memory or something?"

"No, I neither have an eidetic nor the so-called photographic memory. Dates and numbers just come easier to me, and ironically, I always loved math and finding patterns."

All the students marveled at his capacity to remember dates.

"Okay, so let's look at Function B. Can anyone tell us what's different? Yes, Randall?"

"This time, the inputs are dates and the outputs are names."

"Right, so the first input is January 29. They chose Oprah Winfrey to be the output, but is that the only possible output?"

Several students shook their heads.

"No. Having memorized all the presidents, I could tell you that William McKinley could also be a feasible option, for he was born on January 29 in 1843."

A couple of students couldn't help but silently chuckle, clearly impressed.

"So, is this a function?"

"No," some students called out.

"Right, and why? … Yes, Susan?"

"Because, in order to be a function, for every input, there must only be one output."

"Absolutely! Is Function A a function?"

"Yes," the whole class said in agreement.

"So, let's just quickly fill out the rest of Function B anyway. If I were to choose, um, February 24, would that be a birthday of someone in here?"

One student's face lit up as she slowly raised her hand.

"Okay, so when February 24 is the input, then Camila could be the output. All right. What about, uh, July 22?"

A student in the middle of the classroom raised his hand, surprised.

"Okay, so when July 22 is the input, then Matthew could be the output. Um, April 28?"

Two students across the room raised their hands, and a few others chuckled.

"Okay, so when April 28 is the input, then either Javier or Max could be viable outputs. By the way, you two share the same birthday as James Monroe. *Okay*, last one: May 7?"

Every student's gaze shifted to the side of the room, the suspense almost tangible as another student raised her hand, prompting waves of giggles throughout the class.

"Okay, so when May 7 is the input, then Antonella could be an output. And you get the idea. The point is, every person only has one birthday, but there are millions of people around the world who were born on August 15, or November 17, or May 27, or August 1, or September 10, or August 4, or January 13—" As Zachary continued to rattle off seemingly random dates, he was in fact naming the birthdays of each student in the front row, one by one, in the exact order he passed their desks, from the left side of the classroom to the right—and those students realized that immediately. Unable to stop since he was on a roll, Zachary continued to recite the birthdays of the students sitting down the far-right column.

"That was a *very* impressive lesson," one student solemnly said afterward, wide-eyed.

"Thanks so much," Zachary replied, continuing to pass out the worksheet and the self-assessment rubric he created.

"Well, Zachary, I've got to hand it to you. Using their birthdays in the lesson made it very relatable, and I'm sure they'll never forget it," Mrs. Porter complimented after the second accelerated math class.

"Thank you, but I wish I hadn't gotten so tongue-tied in the second lesson," he admitted. "Other than that, I'll continue finding ways to draw on their interests in the lessons, since so many things can be modeled by functions, from allowance savings over time to a basketball player's points throughout a season. Also, the scores in a video game. I observed a student teacher from my class at the university teach a lesson in Dr. Thompson's science class at this school last spring. Her lesson had an Among Us theme to it, since she thought students loved that game. However, they complained, saying that Roblox is the latest craze. I wouldn't know, since I never had time for games after I started college. Minecraft, Fortnite, Among Us … and now Roblox? I can't keep up with this generation."

"Ha-ha. Well, I'm proud of you for keeping it in mind, and I look forward to your future lessons. You've been doing a better job finding worksheets and creating quizzes, not stressing over them or spending hours putting them together anymore. You're quieting the students who begin to chatter with more ease, especially the seventh-grade class. And you're also scanning the classroom more during your lessons and while they take their assessments."

"I'm definitely less worried than before when answering questions during their quizzes and tests. As you and other teachers know, I used to get very worried because I couldn't walk them through the solution during an exam."

"Right."

"And I used to feel bad when all I could say was, 'You're on the right track,' or 'Try to remember how we solved a similar problem in a previous lesson on this topic.'"

"Overall, *Mr. Corwin,* I've noticed that you're approaching this teaching role with increasing confidence each month. I can see why your supervisor struggles to find any feedback to give you, since your lessons are being taught exceptionally well. By the way, how many more does she have to observe?"

"She already observed three out of four. I invited her and my professor to watch my final lesson when that day comes. My professor used to work for the county's Department of Education; he's also the dean of the Education Department at the university."

"That'll be a big, exciting moment."

After school the following day, Zachary walked home through the crisp autumn air, carrying over sixty quizzes to grade. The four-page exams were from the two accelerated math periods. It took him a few hours to grade each of them by hand, but he enjoyed every minute of it. A sense of pride filled him as he saw that students had retained most of the strategies he taught them for solving functions. He was thankful to realize the concepts that most students missed, causing him to do a brief re-teach the following Monday. He grew fond of grading quizzes and tests as it served as his form of self-assessment, allowing him to gauge how well, or poorly, he had taught each standard.

"Mr. Corwin, who was our twenty-seventh president?" asked an eighth-grader, Ralph, who had heard about Zachary's impressive lesson.

Smiling, Zachary gave him the biography of William Howard Taft. Students have been giving him numbers between one and forty-six for weeks after that lesson, testing his memory. It completely took him back to his days as a middle schooler, when his peers would do the same exact thing throughout the same exact school. It felt as if no time had passed.

Suddenly, three girls rushed up to them. "What's your name and occupation?" one of them asked in a conspicuous rush, holding an invisible microphone up to Zachary inches from his mouth.

"Uh … um—" Zachary stuttered and needed to process it. Looking at the phone, held by another student as if filming, he responded, "Uh, I'm Zachary Corwin, a student teacher."

"Thanks!" the interviewer shouted and sprinted away with the other two, leaving Zachary baffled.

"Don't worry about it, Mr. Corwin," Ralph said, annoyed. "Probably one of those NPC tests."

"*What*?"

"Oh, uh—"

"Sorry, Ralph. Don't worry about it," Zachary said, ill at ease for being startled like that over those three letters.

"Don't apologize. I, uh, watched that video from August."

"I know. Again, I appreciate the encouraging comment you left on that video."

"It was terrible you went through that." Ralph pursed his lips and shook his head. "People used to make fun of me because I'm diabetic, but now I choose to ignore them." Wanting to change the subject so as not to make Zachary feel bad, he hastily asked him, "U-uh, I heard that you came here as a student. What was Canyon Mountain like back in the day?"

"Well, you know, I get that question often. For one, we would actually use the lockers. There were no Chromebooks, and we had a computer lab. Speaking about computers and such, we used those bulky CRT monitors. I remember back in the early 2000s, they were huge and boxlike; now, you guys have compact, lightweight laptops that easily fit in your backpacks. Also, almost everyone had flip phones. No apps or anything. We usually watched movies on those boxy TVs, typically from VHS tapes. My favorite books were *Hoot* by Carl Hiaasen and *Holes* by Louis Sachar; I loved both movie adaptations too. Many of the faculty who were here when I was a student are still working here today. Other than that, a fresh coat of paint, and a few new murals, everything else is pretty much the same. To my bitter frustration, just to add, I painted a mural outside the cafeteria in eighth grade; they told me it would be permanent, but it was painted over. Oh well."

47

The Final Days

Zachary stepped into the front office of Canyon Mountain just before the final math class of the day, the autumn afternoon sun streaming through the windows along the front façade. The office's Sony AM/FM radio was playing Percy Faith's "Deck the Halls." A Christmas tree, adorned with red and green and filling the air with its natural hallmark fragrance, stood in the corner next to the front door, bringing the festive spirit to all who entered the school.

He was on his way upstairs to make a few last-minute copies when he saw something that made him pause. Looking down the hall, underneath the office's fluorescent lights, he saw Dr. Cornelius from Tributary University, whom he had invited, signing in on the Raptor system. After all the lectures, guidance, passion, wisdom, and steady encouragement, the joy of seeing him there felt completely unparalleled. A silent flow of gratitude rose in his heart, since it was a profound honor to have him observe one of his lessons unfold, live and in person.

After making the copies, he returned to Room Twenty-Two. Dr. Cornelius had already taken his seat at the side table. After greeting him, he saw his supervisor walk through the door.

Perfect, he thought, thankfully.

He delivered the entire lesson on inverse functions, concluding with a Quizizz on their Chromebooks that he created. Once their self-assessment rubric was collected at the end, he called for everyone's undivided attention. The classroom settled into a deafening silence within four seconds.

"Class, I want to take a brief moment to tell you something. It has been a very wonderful experience being your student teacher these past few months. You have all been very patient with me, especially when I made some mistakes in the beginning, since I was learning *how* to teach effectively. Uh, well, what you just saw was my final lesson as your student teacher."

As he spoke the last sentence, a couple of the students straightened in their seats, staring at him in the eyes—some looking concerned, others sad, and still others confused.

"Ever since first grade, over twenty years ago, I dreamed of growing up to become a teacher someday. You guys have significantly been a part of my journey, giving me this opportunity in life to pursue my ultimate goal. I also want to take a moment to thank one of the greatest Mentor Teachers on earth—"

"Aw," Mrs. Porter said, unable to help herself.

Turning to his professor and supervisor, he continued, "as well as the faculty of Tributary University, who holds a strong commitment toward us teacher candidates, helping to train us to be the teachers we are today. With that said, thank you so much."

The world's quietest classroom erupted into thunderous applause, proud of Zachary and his unwavering dedication to their learning and to the education of future generations.

"Great job, Mr. Corwin!" whispered Mrs. Porter seconds later with a proud smile on her face. "Oh, and I loved how you waited until your *last lesson* to create your own educational game," she added, sarcastically.

"Oh well. I'm trying."

After the bell rang, students got up and walked out of the classroom, but not without saying something to the effect, "Congratulations, Mr. Corwin!" "Thank you, Mr. Corwin," or "Thanks for all your help."

"You deserve a gift, Mr. Corwin," said one of the students, beaming as he reached into his backpack to pull it out. "I hope you like Skittles!"

"Thank you, Bradley. I appreciate it."

"I hope you write about your journey," Sakura chimed in.

"A second book? Hey, you never know."

"I can't believe I'll never see you again," cried Miguel with fake tears.

"Well, I'm not leaving right away. My *final* final day is this Friday."

"You mean in two days from now?"

"Yes."

"Are you still going to sub and tutor us in math on Tuesdays and Thursdays?"

"Yes, I'll probably be subbing until June. I plan to help tutor here whenever I can."

"Sub for Ms. Ramirez, second period. We all hated the last sub. You're an amazing teacher, Mr. Corwin, because you bring magic into the classroom," Miguel complimented with a grin, patting Zachary on the shoulder before turning around and leaving.

"Bravo, Zachary! Great lesson," Dr. Cornelius said, shaking his hand. "I have to run, but let's talk about your lesson in my office when you get time."

"Okay, I look forward to it."

"Ready for our last little post-observation conference, Zachary?" asked the supervisor as she arrived at the door.

"Yes, I am," he said, taking a deep breath as they both exited the door and walked to the teacher's lounge.

"So many good things, Zachary. So many good things," the supervisor began. "As always, there's hardly anything I could say. I gave you one recommendation last time about color-coding, and I saw that you implemented that. I could tell it really helped the students. Choosing Think-Pair-Shares and Think-Alouds, which I see you do often, has also continued to be beneficial. In your informal assessments, when you asked them for a thumbs-up or thumbs-down, I saw a lot of thumbs-up, meaning they were understanding what you were teaching them."

After dissecting the lesson for the next five minutes, the supervisor wrapped up the conference, saying, "Your thank-you message to your students and to Mrs. Porter at the end was exceptionally well spoken. *Everyone* in that room could feel how heartfelt it was. I'm sure all the students appreciated it. You have a great career ahead of you."

Upon saying their goodbyes, Zachary headed downstairs to speak with the principal.

"Oh!" Dr. Peterson said, startled. "Hi, Zachary. Come on in. How long were you standing there by my door? I was deeply engrossed in answering this email and didn't notice you."

"About fifteen seconds. You seemed busy, and I didn't want to interrupt you," Zachary softly said, already nervous to be speaking with her. "Um, Dr. Peterson, I was wondering, now that my student teaching days are drawing to a close, how would you say I've been all these months, from your observation?"

"Well, I can't give you pedagogical feedback, since I haven't observed you teach a lesson, but overall, I can tell that you're a genuinely kind person, committed to supporting our students' learning, and have been very helpful across multiple math classes. Students and staff alike have said you're the best. I've heard nothing but good things about you, Zachary," she said, nodding her head with an affirming smile.

"Thank you so much. That's quite reassuring. Today was my final lesson as a student teacher, and Friday's my final day."

"Congratulations!"

"Uh ... one last thing, I know I asked you in the spring about volunteering to do my Autism Awareness assemblies. Can you still please keep me in mind? I plan to be subbing all winter and spring so that I'd have time to do these assemblies. After that, I'll possibly start my career next August, 2023. I'm not sure yet. It depends."

"Um, sure, I'll keep you in mind, Zachary. Thanks for all you do."

"No problem," Zachary said as he left, feeling confident that he'd get to lead assemblies at Canyon Mountain soon.

After leaving, he walked to his nearby Target and purchased a card for Mrs. Porter, later writing a thorough letter to express his deep thankfulness for all her help and the wisdom she imparted to him.

Over the next two days, Zachary received a dozen cards from the math students. One from the accelerated class revealed that she was nervous to be in such a challenging class, but seeing him there every morning with so much joy had made her feel better. A couple of other students gave him a Starbucks gift card or a chocolate bar to show their gratitude.

"You got me through the hardest part, which was starting," wrote one student.

"I'm sad to see a talented, educated student teacher leave. I hope you get a million YouTube subscribers one day!" wrote another.

Students have also commented on his latest teaching update on YouTube.

"You made a difference in my life. Good luck in your teaching career," commented one student.

"You will be greatly missed by all!" commented another.

* * *

The evening before his final day as a student teacher, Zachary arrived at Tributary University to talk with a few people in the Education Department.

"A huge congratulations on earning your teaching certificate!" said Mrs. Paxton. "As I told you before, I'd be very surprised if the state's assessor failed you. I guess you fully understand now that we weren't lying to you in the very beginning when we told you that this was a very rigorous program."

"Irrefutably!" Zachary panted.

"You should be so proud of yourself."

After the meeting with Mrs. Paxton was over, he went across the hall to have a mock interview with Dr. Morozov, one of his professors. At the end, Dr. Morozov said, "That was excellent. Just remember, bring in your own stories and experiences. Tell that panel how you would teach with your own personality. Otherwise, they'd go, 'Oh, great, he's just teaching word-for-word what the teacher's edition says.' I recommend having a friend ask you common questions the night before a job interview."

"Knowing myself, I'll probably rehearse it ten or twenty times over. It sounds like it'd be a lion's den—the final hurdle to overcome before my life is officially and permanently set."

"Don't stress over it. I'm sure you'll do well. Remember to add me and the other professors to your list of references. I can't wait to brag about you; there are so many things I could say. You did a phenomenal job in my class. Congratulations! You just completed and passed my course with an A."

"Thank you so much, Dr. Morozov!" he said, standing up and letting out a big sigh of relief, having officially completed the entire teacher certification program at that moment.

"By the way, did Dr. Cornelius tell you what he thought about your final lesson?"

"Not yet. I was going to knock on his office door this afternoon, but I heard he's not in today. I plan to visit him soon."

"He said it was the best lesson he had ever seen," Dr. Morozov said with a big smile.

"R-really?" Zachary said, unsure how to react.

"Yes. He couldn't stop telling everyone in this department. He said you had all the students completely silent for the entire duration of the period. He said they engaged well with the lesson and calmly played the Quizizz activity to practice what they learned afterward. He said it was the best lesson he had ever seen in the forty years he's been in education."

"Wow. I-I just need to process that. I can't wait to talk about it with him."

His final stop was down the hall to speak with one of the directors of the master's program. The director and one of the professors from the program came to his class one evening to pitch it to the teacher candidates. Zachary was sold to it and decided to pursue their three-semester route for a Master of Arts in Education, starting in January.

"Mr. Corwin, is this your last day?" one student asked him the next morning.

"As a student teacher, yeah," Zachary said, smiling, trying to hide his shivering from the blistering cold.

The student's friend, standing next to him, fell on his knees, pretending to cry.

"But I'm sure I'll be back to sub and tutor."

Walking near the lunch tables, he noticed that two seventh-grade students were following him. "Someone told me today's your last day. Is that true?" asked one of them.

"Yes, as bittersweet as it is. But I know I'll be back."

For the next seven hours, whenever students caught sight of Zachary, they would confirm with him that they heard correctly, unwilling to accept the news. During lunchtime and after school, he made the rounds, sharing the news with many teachers, administrators, and other faculty he had gotten to know. They all congratulated him on moving to the next chapter in his life.

"Corwin! What's up?" shouted Randall, one of the accelerated math students during lunch, waving him over with his friend.

"Hey, um, the sky?"

"What?"

"You asked me, 'What's up?' and I gave you a scientific answer: the sky."

"Ha-ha-ha! That's smart!" The two students burst into laughter. "I'll sure miss how you always made us students laugh."

Zachary was always thankful when he brought joy in people's lives, but in all candor, he had come up with that joke in response to the awkward phrases that would go over his head. However, he'd get frustrated every time students asked him that while riding their e-bikes at a million miles per hour, already gone before he could process what had just happened, irrationally fearing that he'd be thought of as incompetent or an easy target by them.

"So, Mr. Corwin," said the second boy, Bradley, the one who gave him the Skittles, "did you have a good experience as a student teacher overall?"

"Yes, I did, sort of. I strongly disliked all the work I had to do to prove to the state that I have what it takes, but I understand that they want us to be strong, competent teachers, which is why they held us to such high standards. But as I said months ago, whenever I was in front of you guys teaching a lesson or tutoring you in math, it was joy. One of the only experiences I'd probably still lose sleep over is that worksheet debacle."

"Oh, don't worry about it," said Randall.

"It's totally fine, Mr. Corwin," added Bradley.

Earlier in September, when Zachary would stress for a couple of hours, endeavoring to create the perfect worksheet from scratch, he inadvertently included a couple of questions that were above their math level, according to the Common Core standards. He assumed it would be okay since all they had to do was solve for one of the variables. The morning after assigning it as homework, he realized that most of the students had been emailing Mrs. Porter all night long and had arrived at school early to ask their former seventh-grade teachers in confusion. Being in Royal Rangers, Zachary owned up to it, apologized, and told them to burn it! He quickly said he was kidding and gave them permission to tear or crumple it up, which they all did slowly, putting on a deliberate little spectacle that he would never forget, yet all in good, forgiving spirits, each wearing a smirk.

"No hard feelings from *any* of us," promised Randall.

"Remember, we let you off easy since we knew you were in the learning process. Otherwise, it would have been a different story," Bradley said, winking.

"Hey, I gotta ask, can you do The Griddy, Mr. Corwin?" asked Randall with a grin.

"U-uh, the what?"

"The Griddy."

"I-I don't know what that is."

"It's a dance move," Bradley started to explain. "Here, let me take my backpack off and—" Before he was able to do so and demonstrate, the bell rang. "I'll show you later. Randall and I have an important presentation in our next period. Later, Mr. Corwin."

"Okay, I hope it goes well," said Zachary, relieved that he didn't have to talk his way out of doing a trendy dance meme in public. As he told Thomas when he was a boy, he was uncomfortable singing, dancing, and all that.

After the final bell rang for the day, he briefly visited a few more teachers before heading down the outdoor hallway to the school library. Suddenly, he heard, "Corwin!" Swinging around, he saw two eighth-graders sprinting toward him from the other side of the hallway at full speed.

"Mr. Corwin," they said, catching their breath. "Congratulations on completing your student teaching. Mind if we take a quick photo with you?"

"No, I don't mind. Go ahead."

Moments later, Mrs. Schlessinger, the librarian, expressed her deep sadness of not having him tutor the students regularly anymore on Tuesdays and Thursdays, but Zachary reassured her that he'll still try to come, even if he would sub somewhere else earlier in the day.

"Feel free to stay for the potluck, Zachary," Mrs. Schlessinger urged. "That's what all the teachers are in here for."

Looking around, he saw many teachers either conversing with one another or arranging their contributions on the long, narrow table. The Sony AM/FM radio, which was being borrowed from the office, was currently playing "Good King Wenceslas" by Roger Wagner Chorale.

"Uh, I'm good. I already ate lunch. Besides, I need to go home urgently to do a project."

"Okay, I was just offering. Enjoy your holiday break."

As soon as Zachary arrived home in record time, he rushed upstairs and slammed his bedroom door behind him. After tossing his books and notepad on his bed, he sat at his laptop. The images and sounds from that day alone clung to him like a vine around a tree. Tunnel-visioned with a mind made up, he opened a brand-new Word document. The first thing he typed was "Chapter 1" before saving the document to his computer, naming it "2nd Book."

48

Dream Come True

Checking his emails one afternoon in late January 2023, after subbing for an incredible sixth-grade class a few miles away, Zachary opened one that made him want to shout from the rooftops.

It read:

> *Dear Zachary Corwin.*
>
> *We found your information in a catalog of speakers for Willowbend Unified School District that you submitted a couple of years ago. We understand if this is last minute, but next week our school, Maplecliff Elementary, is hosting an Abilities Awareness Day, and we'd love to invite you to be a speaker! It'd be an all-day event. You would speak for ten minutes per class, for sixteen classes, third grade to sixth grade. Please reply as soon as possible if you feel up for this, and let us know how much you would charge for something like this.*
>
> *Thank you.*

Zachary felt overwhelmingly grateful, almost falling out of his chair. Having difficulty typing from excitement, he immediately replied to accept the invitation, concluding with, "Believe me, I'm willing to do these assemblies at *no* charge."

Outside the stately elementary school, towering underneath the warmth of the midday sun, the school counselor told Zachary, "Thank you so much again for coming and doing those amazing assemblies today."

"Especially at the last minute too," the principal chimed in. "I heard *so* many students and teachers talking about your message, your juggling, card tricks, science demo, and everything. It's always more impactful and memorable when you use visual analogies like that. Thank you for being a positive influence. You truly changed lives today."

"I feel so humbled to hear that," replied Zachary, nearly speechless. "It's certainly my pleasure. I just ask for one favor: could you please share my information with other schools you know, and with any other districts you have connections to as well?"

"Oh, absolutely!" said the counselor, the principal nodding alongside her. "I'll definitely put in a good word for you. Your story needs to be heard in every school."

"Thank you so much. I believe so too," Zachary said before leaving.

A light chuckle escaped Zachary's mouth at seven o'clock the next morning, right after he descended the staircase and was about to head to a subbing assignment. *Man*, he thought, *I feel like I just did a leg-day workout back when I had a personal trainer. Is this how my legs are going to feel after assemblies? Well, it's a price I'm always willing to pay.*

Still untrusting the neighborhood and being uncomfortable without pepper spray, he usually asked his grandfather or a friend if they could provide a ride to a school, even if the school was five or six blocks away. He had a driver's license since 2017, but he could never afford a car. Plus, he didn't want to be swindled by a used car dealer. On this cool winter day, he was back at Washington Elementary.

"Thank you for helping me!" said a third-grade boy with glasses and a cordial smile. The students were dispersed around the room, working independently on mathematics before lunchtime. The boy was practicing inequalities on the whiteboard and sought help from Zachary.

"You're more than welcome, Cameron," he replied, smiling inside and out, as delighted as Cameron was that he now understood it. "All right, *class, class!*"

"Yes, yes!"

"Please take a minute to finish your last problem, and get ready to go to lunch, but before lining up, would you like to see a card trick?"

"*Yes!*" they said in unison and began cleaning up faster.

After dropping off the students, Zachary walked over to the principal's office.

Knock, knock!

"Yes? Come in."

"Hi, Principal Miller."

"Hi," she said, taking off her glasses and giving a half smile.

"I'm not sure if you remember me, but in 2019, I introduced myself and told you that I published a novel about an autistic individual."

"Oh yes. I remember you. Mr. Collingsworth purchased one, and it's in our school's library."

"I know. After it arrived, I signed it, addressing it to Washington Elementary. I was truly thankful. Anyway, I also asked you if I could do a couple of volunteer assemblies about Autism Awareness, Acceptance, and Inclusion—free of charge. Then COVID happened. Anyway, since things are opening up, I'd like to reopen that request. May I please do some assemblies here anytime soon?"

"I'll definitely keep that in mind." Principal Miller put on a big smile. "When I'm ready, I'll email you a couple of dates and see if we could put something together."

"Thank you so much, Principal Miller. I definitely appreciate it. Have a nice day," Zachary said, walking out and feeling more optimistic about the future.

"Well, hey there!" Mr. Collingsworth said after running into him. "Who are you today?"

"Mr. Livingston."

"Ah, third grade."

"Yep. I told the students that I spent one whole year in third grade myself. Then they started laughing. I told them that you were my third-grade teacher, and some of your former students are in there."

"Did you tell them I was your best third-grade teacher?"

"Yeah, adding that it was because you were my *only* third-grade teacher."

Mr. Collingsworth laughed. "So, how are things now, having completed your student teaching and being a sub?"

"It's amazing! More students across town are saying, 'Hi, Mr. Corwin.' Many students were actually calling me, 'Best sub.' One group of fourth-graders on the other side of the city kept chanting, 'Best sub! Best sub!' at the end of the day … even from a distance, whenever they saw me. Students around this district literally begged me to come back. One teacher told me that her students were asking her to take a day off so I could sub for them again. Also—"

"Mr. Corwin! Oh my gosh!" a student interrupted, jogging over to him and Mr. Collingsworth. "You subbed for my class almost a year ago. Do you have any magic tricks on you?"

"Uh, some sleight-of-hand? Yeah, I have a card trick, but I could show you later, perhaps after I'm done talking with Mr. Collingsworth."

"Okay," the student said before running over to the handball courts.

"My word, Zachary! He was treating you like a rock star. Did you see his eyes light up? Sounds like you are an amazing sub and an amazing light to this generation."

"It's my honor, joy, and pleasure. I've subbed at twelve schools so far. Subbing has changed my life. It's giving me the opportunity to teach lessons in various subjects: math, science, social studies, music, and English. Once, I've subbed Elementary Music, and I got to play the patriotic songs I grew up with on piano, such as "Fifty Nifty United States" and Woody Guthrie's

'This Land Is Your Land.' Plus, they were singing along, which is always my joy. Just wanting to serve others, I accepted two half days a few times before, sometimes going to two different schools. It's like, this is my purpose. This is everything I ever wanted to do."

"I couldn't be prouder of you."

"Thank you. I'm also learning a plethora of new songs while subbing Elementary Music, such as 'One Nation' by Teresa Jennings and dozens of others from Plank Road Publishing."

"Well, you totally overcame a lot of challenges and are showing the world that being autistic shouldn't stop you."

"Exactly! And *that's* the message I will bring in my volunteer assemblies once given a word in edgewise. I've been asking principals *everywhere* I go. When I go to schools I haven't been to yet, I introduce myself to the principal and request to lead assemblies. Uh … I've honestly been thinking about taking this next academic year off, just to ensure that I get to every school in the county, which is my ultimate goal. I mean, I'll still sub on days I'm not leading assemblies."

"I do declare, that's a *massive* goal, and you know what? I support you on that endeavor. I hope you meet it because your message and story are powerful. So, are you getting sub jobs every day?"

"Almost every day, which I'm thankful for. On days I don't sub, I get to volunteer at Canyon Mountain. After I was done with student teaching, I asked Mrs. Porter, my former Mentor Teacher, if I could come back to help when work wasn't available. She said I absolutely could. The week before winter break, there were hardly any jobs available, so I just went to the middle school and volunteered all day in various Basic Skills classes."

"That's mighty kindly of you."

"That's exactly what some of the teachers said, marveling that I'd volunteer my time to help middle schoolers if I didn't have work. Speaking about that, one teacher I would help during my student teaching ran into me recently. She told me, 'After you left, many of my students were saying, "Where's Mr. Corwin?" "I miss Mr. Corwin," or "I want Mr. Corwin helping me with math again."'"

"Aw, how nice. That must've made all the difference in the world."

"It did. I was there subbing for the other accelerated math teacher. She teaches only seventh grade. She requested me to sub for two days, since I know how to teach systems of equations. In one period, one student asked me if I could teach the class every day. In another period, all the students asked me to be their accelerated math teacher next year when they're in eighth grade."

Mr. Collingsworth couldn't help but laugh with joy. "Are *all* students treating you like that?"

"Um, well no, unfortunately, but rather ninety-seven percent of them, I'd say."

"That's a very precise statistic there."

"Well, it's qualitative, not quantitative. In other words, I didn't actually collect data or anything, but it's how it feels to me. *Anyway*, one middle schooler called me a racist just for confiscating her phone that shouldn't have been out."

"And that was *her* problem. She knew the rules and tried to take advantage of you. Good for you for taking her phone."

"It was a bit hard for me. I never wanted students to think I'm horrible, mean, angry, or what have you. As always, I give a subtle courtesy reminder to the class whenever I noticed someone hiding their phone, but when she took it out again, that was an act of defiance, and I tried to explain as nice as I could why I had to take her phone. She said, 'That's racist!' because her family's from Mexico. I'm like, 'What? How?' That's *far* from the reason. I care about everyone's success in life; I don't care where on the planet they're from."

"So uncalled for. You mustn't take it to heart."

"I know. Then I have stories that make me question what is truly to be meant. I go on neighborhood walks all the time. One Saturday afternoon a few months ago, I was walking through Whisperpine Grove Heights, a mile away in the hilly parts of the city. About fifty yards from me was a cluster of e-bikers, looking like they were about to disperse. They looked like middle schoolers, but I couldn't definitively recognize any of them from that distance.

"Still being a shy person, I usually look down or away, always waiting for students to say hi first. On the flip side, I worry that if I don't say hi as I walk by, they might unreasonably assume that I don't care about them outside of school. If students see me facing them, even for a second, but I don't say hi, then they might think I'm ignoring them, which is why I look away."

"But why don't you just say hi first anyway? I say hi to my students all the time, even years later. Every caring teacher does."

"I know, but not only am I still shy, but what if I say hi to students I think I know, only to find out they're doppelgängers, subsequently wondering, 'Who was that man randomly saying hi to us children, or us teenagers?' Or what if I recognize correctly, say hi, but they're one of the students who hates me as a person, and I just didn't realize it when I subbed for them? Then I'd worry, asking myself, 'Why on earth would they hate me? Being autistic and awkward?'"

"Well, I think you're overdramatizing things."

"I *know* I am. I've always been good at that, unfortunately. Anyway, through my sunglasses, even though I was facing away, I saw one of those e-bikers look at me and point me out to a couple of them, but not like in an obvious way. A few of them turned to look at me, but didn't do anything. The teen who first saw me slowly backed up a few feet to get into the street, maintaining his gaze as if I were a threat or something.

"By now, we're like thirty yards away. He pointed at me once more, saying something to a friend. I don't know what. If it was all a misunderstanding on my part, wouldn't he had said hi to me? Next thing I know, he and one of his friends were flying down the hills on their Sur-Rons. I saw that same teenager looking back at me thrice. What am I supposed to think after that?"

"Well, I'd agree, Zachary. That just must've been an anomaly."

"Probably, especially since I didn't do anything wrong, but be a kindhearted, caring substitute teacher, and I'm *not* saying that boastfully."

"I know you're not. And what you said about yourself is true."

"Last August, if I may add real quick, I was walking by the Hometown Buffet, the place I saw you and met your family a couple of summers ago. Now, I walked through that outdoor mall all the time, ever since 2021. Since 2022, I ran into students a hundred times, all coming up to say hi. Sometimes they ask to see a card trick, let me know they watched one of my YouTube videos, or remind me of the day I subbed for their class. That *always* brightens my day like you wouldn't believe.

"But on that day in August, I saw a few students eating at a table in the outdoor dining area. As usual, while facing away, I prepared to be greeted with a 'Hi, Mr. Corwin,' though I never assume all students would know me. Again, it's one of the reasons why I don't say hi first. However, one of them didn't remain silent. Loud and clear, I suddenly heard, '*Oh*,' followed by a four-letter cuss word. I glanced at him through my sunglasses while facing straight ahead. He was looking away, mouth zipped shut, as the entire table went silent. The other four teens crowded around just stared at me, *expressionless*, as I walked past. I definitely recognized a couple of them from Canyon Mountain; they were about to be freshmen at the high school. I felt really torn because … what the heck did I do?"

Mr. Collingsworth looked down, taking a deep, sympathetic sigh. "It just comes with the territory, Zachary. Impertinence roams everywhere. Remember all the other ninety-seven percent of students, according to your statistic, who *do* accept you."

"I suppose. Well anyway, to change the melancholy subject, speaking tangentially about subbing in general, I believe I'm getting better at reading aloud to students."

"That's amazing. I'm happy to hear that."

"Yeah, remember almost twenty years ago? I hated reading. I'm still not fond of it, but in the sub plans sometimes, the teacher tells me to read a chapter or two to them. At first, I would pre-read it during a break, but now, I find that I'm improving."

"I'm so glad to hear that! Last thing I'd like to ask you, I'm not on social media much, but how's it coming along for you."

"I've actually been growing, thanks to the PR campaigns. I thought, maybe I'll research other PR firms, but they want $5,000 per month and a six-month commitment. *I don't have that much money!* So, I returned to the first PR firm and just began a three-month campaign. Thus far, I've gotten several leads; I'll be speaking for Scripps News soon. I've already spoken on Canadian and Caribbean radio programs. Oh, and in the United Kingdom too. I post many times a week on YouTube, Instagram, and TikTok. Yesterday, I posted a tribute montage of all my Boeing 747 videos, since Boeing announced that they just produced their final one. Last I checked, it was beginning to go viral on all three of those platforms I mentioned, especially Instagram, which is actually my highest following. I have amassed over 900,000 followers now, 40,000 subscribers on YouTube, and 25,000 on TikTok.

"Well, my goodness! I just might have to ask for your autograph one of these days. You just keep up that incredible work now, you hear?"

After Zachary concluded the conversation a moment later and returned to the classroom, he looked at the sub plans and ran out as fast as he could, furiously swinging the door open on the way out.

Oh, great, he thought. *I only went here for seven years of my life. How could I be three minutes behind?*

Being the first time substituting for Mr. Livingston, he didn't know where the students lined up after lunch. After recess, they went straight to Physical Education, so he just picked them up from there. Jogging through a sea of elementary school students who were conversing loudly in their lines, he looked around for his students, but couldn't find any of them. Suddenly, he heard, "Over here! Over here!"

Letting out a deep sigh of relief and laughing at himself, he walked over to the line of third-graders who stood roughly thirty yards away, all waving him over and jumping up and down. "Guys, I'm so sorry."

"Don't worry about it, Mr. Corwin. It's okay."

As he walked them back to the class, he felt a sense of serenity, knowing he was fulfilling his passion for being in the education field and subbing for students who understood and accepted him as a human being. He was quite impressed with this particular class as it was the best group of third-graders to date, quietly working and listening. As students re-entered the classroom, they silently nodded to the beat of "Cloud 9" by Itro and Tobu, one of Zachary's few go-to songs he would play at elementary schools as students entered. That, and "Dizzy" by Joakim Karud.

"Today was a ten out of ten," said one of them after school just as her mother arrived, thanking Zachary with two thumbs-up.

"I appreciate your compliment, Leslie. I try my best in everything. Have a good afternoon."

Since Leslie was the last student to be picked up by a parent, Zachary walked back to the classroom to gather his things and lock up, but not without a detour first. He paused at the spot on campus that offered a sweeping view of the field, the blacktop, the jungle gym, and the lunch tables. For a solid minute, he stood there, seeing in his mind fifteen to twenty years in the past. Although the jungle gym was completely replaced and the blacktop was repaved, the tall pine trees still stood over the same lunch tables, emanating the same scent. He began reflecting on Thomas out of nowhere, dimming his nostalgia a bit.

"Thinking back on your memories, Mr. Corwin?!" called out one of Mr. Livingston's third-graders by surprise, walking up from behind him with a big smile. He had been waiting for his after-school program to start and saw Zachary standing there.

"Yeah, José," Zachary replied, turning around and smiling with a deep breath. "You bet I am. As I've told your class, this was my elementary school, way back when."

***

"Left, left, left, right, left! Left, left, left, right, left!" called out the boys in unison on Friday evening.

"Column right, march!" commanded Jonah, the senior patrol leader and highest-ranking fifth grade boy in that age group.

"Left, left, left, right, left!" the third- through fifth-graders continued to shout, keeping perfect cadence as they turned the corner and continued marching down the street.

Honk! went an SUV.

Commander Zachary, having assumed the role of drill instructor during recreation, looked over to see one of the middle schoolers from Canyon

Mountain smile and wave at him from the passenger seat, eyes lighting up. He gave a closed-lipped smile and waved back.

"Column right, march!" Jonah cried out, leading the patrol through the parking lot, and stopping sharply before the church's side door. After all the boys came to a halt, standing at arm's length apart, Jonah commanded, "Left, face! Hand, salute!"

Zachary walked alongside them, followed by the lieutenant commander. Pivoting sharply, he gave them a full salute, which subsequently prompted the boys to put their hands down, resuming the position of attention.

"At your seats, there's a bearing card and a compass. Find your bearing and face that direction. Once you're confident, raise your hand, and we'll come check. Senior Patrol Leader Jonah is qualified to check you off as well, having already earned the Compass Merit last year. Remember, you must also account for magnetic declination. Let's go!"

At the end of the night, the associate pastor of the church walked up to Zachary. "Hey, bud!" he said. "I saw your Facebook post about leading assemblies at an elementary school. That's amazing!"

"Thank you. It was sure a blessing."

"I watched your YouTube video talking about it. That was cool," Jonah compliment, beginning to roll up the American flag to put it away.

"Thanks so much, Jonah," Zachary said. Turning back to the associate pastor, he went on to explain, "But I'd like prayer for many more opportunities. My hope is to do these in every school, public and private, in the county."

"You got it! That's a huge and noble goal."

"I just found out that there are 600 schools in this huge county, so it might take a few years. And that's just the public schools."

After the associate pastor walked away, one of the third-grade boys came and began rolling up the Christian flag. "I can't believe you were treated like that. It's so unfair!"

"Unfair, indeed, but it's part of living as an autistic in a broken world."

"Thank God, honestly, for that police officer. That guy could've killed you with that skateboard."

"That was quite a testimony, Commander Zachary," a fourth-grader who came to roll up the Royal Rangers flag chimed in. "Um … You look like everyone else. Sure, you may be tall. You may be thin. You could appear shy at times. You sometimes stutter. But you've accomplished so much. You're the best commander here, and I always enjoy seeing you. I cannot understand how people won't accept those who are autistic, but keep fighting the good fight, commander!"

"Thank you very much, Max. It means a lot to me to hear you say all that. Thank you for your acceptance and support."

"God's got you, which you know, so you've got this!" Max said, smiling, walking off to put the flag away.

"Commander Zachary, we're done with our clean-up duties," two boys said, coming up to him.

"Okay," he said, walking over to get the box of snacks. "So, military time or normal time?"

"Um, military time," said the first boy, following him with the second.

"Hmm, 1830 hours."

"6:30 p.m."

"Correct, pick a snack. Simon, military or normal time?"

"Normal."

"Okay, 2:35 p.m."

"1435 hours."

"Excellent."

"Hey, when are we going to march to the 'Hard Work' song again?" Simon asked as he was choosing a snack.

"Oh, the one from The U.S. Army Airborne? We could do that next week," Zachary assured.

"Cool. It's always fun."

"Commander Zachary?" One of the sixth-graders came up to him just after the two boys left with their snacks.

"Yes, Grant?"

"I watched your YouTube video about doing those Autism Awareness assemblies at that school. I really think that'd be an important message for *my* school too. I want to ask my principal to invite you, if that would be okay?"

"Absolutely. Here, let me write down my email, and tell your principal that I'm more than willing to do the assemblies *voluntarily*."

"Thanks! I'll do that. We're in Clearview Crystal Unified. I hope that's not too far for you."

"Just ten miles. That's not a problem. I'll go anywhere in this county for these assemblies."

49

The Sickening Insinuation

In the coolness of February's evening air, Zachary walked through the relative quietude of the outdoor mall, a pause from the rush of the ever-wakeful Thornwick Boulevard. He moved unhurriedly along the open-air promenade, listening to the light chatter of people window shopping or dining at outdoor tables. He sported his typical navy-blue slacks and baseball cap, now accentuated by a new black softshell jacket. The speakers lightly played "Mad World" by Tears for Fears.

In an instant, he heard someone shout, "Mr. Corwin!" Looking up, he saw eight students jogging or e-biking over to him.

"Mr. Corwin, remember us? You subbed for Mr. Taylor's sixth-grade class at Ulysses Elementary last month," one student named Emma said, which prompted nods from half the students.

"And you subbed for ours too, the other sixth grade class," said another named Bryce, and the rest nodded.

"Oh, the school down the boulevard. Yes, of course I remember you guys."

"Can you replace our teacher?" Bryce asked, his wishful thinking obvious.

"Mr. Corwin, do you remember my birthday?" asked Emma.

"Um—" Zachary said, having to look intently at her facial features before the date popped up in his mind. "July 5?"

"Oh my gosh!" she gasped, laughing.

"What about mine? I told you at lunchtime that day," asked César.

"Uh?" Zachary faltered, trying to remember, feeling like he was on the spot. "I know it's in October…Um, the ninth?"

"Crazy," he gasped, shaking his head as an employee from the nearby CVS Pharmacy walked out, passing by them.

"Mr. Corwin, I'm subscribed to your YouTube channel now," one of the students said, showing him on her phone.

"Wait! He's on YouTube?" questioned a boy named Caden. "What's his channel name?"

"'Zachary Corwin,'" Emma answered. "Yeah, he's on YouTube, Instagram, and TikTok."

A few students rushed to get their phones out.

"Can I get a photo with you, Mr. Corwin?" asked Emma. After getting one, she said, "Thanks. I'm such a big fan. I watch your videos every day."

"Thanks for your support. I hope my videos aren't getting too boring."

"No, they're not, actually. I enjoy all your videos about substitute teaching. I watched the one that had our classroom in it. I recognized the posters on the wall and thought it was super cool."

"Dude! Holy cow, we got a famous sub!" exclaimed Caden.

"How many followers does he have?" asked one of the other boys.

"975,000 on Insta."

"I posted a Boeing 747 tribute reel that went viral, garnering over 1.1 million views," Zachary explained. "It was the first time I got a million views on anything."

"Well, congratulations!" some of the sixth-graders said and clapped.

Zachary stood there, unsure of what to say as the students huddled over their phones, commenting aloud, while groups of people sauntered along the pathways, drifting in and out of the nearby shops and restaurants. One gentleman in his mid-thirties, wearing a black T-shirt, hat, and sunglasses, slumped onto a bench just beyond them in front of the CVS Pharmacy. Zachary couldn't help but notice how fast his fingers were typing.

"You've been on the news? Oh, my goodness. Look, he's on Google."

"Um, yeah, thanks to PR. Being on the news significantly boosted the SEO and, uh, the following," Zachary said, humbled for the apparent acceptance, though it felt weird to confirm their rhetorical questions. He refused to call himself "famous," so when Caden made his remark, he simply nodded with an awkward smile. Sure, he wasn't doing everything to be recognized, but rather make a difference in people's lives, educating the neurotypical and motivating the neurodivergent. However, it'd be a million times nicer and reassuring to be trusted and treated with respect by everyone in his city, county, or wherever he goes.

That does *not* mean being treated like a celebrity!

That does *not* mean forcing every single person to say hi to him, walking down the street, the outdoor mall, the nearby plaza, or a grocery aisle!

That *does* mean being respected and treated like a human being—something he had been denied a thousand times before. Whenever someone would have otherwise treated him with contempt, they would now recognize him and thank him for challenging their misguided notions about disabled people.

Just then, the gentleman wearing the black T-shirt stood up, held his phone to his ear, and started to walk away, but not without taking a glimpse back. Zachary heard him saying, "Some guy wearing a hat, talking to a group of kids. He's wearing blue pants and a black jacket."

Zachary nervously returned his focus to the eight sixth-graders, who were still talking about him in awe and unaware of the gentleman behind them. The gentleman crashed back down onto the bench and held up his phone, looking as if he were taking a picture of Zachary with the students.

Seriously, man? Zachary thought. Knowing full well what was transpiring, he put on a grin for the camera just to see what would happen. *I see you, you know.*

As the gentleman put his phone down, still looking straight ahead, he realized that Zachary had been smiling for the camera. "Oh, sorry, man!" the gentleman said, awkwardly grinning and giggling, knowing that he had been caught. The sixth-graders jerked their heads toward him, their faces twisted with disgust.

"I don't know who he is. I was making sure he wasn't some creep talking to all you young kids, ha-ha."

At those words, the students began defending Zachary. "Oh, no," Emma started, walking toward him. "He subbed for our class!"

"He's a famous YouTuber too," Bryce added, catching up with Emma.

The employee from CVS Pharmacy had returned at that moment. Having overheard everything, she said to the gentleman, "I know, sir. When I walked by moments ago and saw him talking to all these kids, I said to myself, 'Oh, this is not good,' but now it seems they all know him." Turning to Zachary, she said, "You're a YouTuber? How cool. What type of videos do you make?"

"A whole bunch of topics: Autism Awareness and substitute teaching, mainly, but I also post airplanes, helicopters, emergency vehicles, juggling—"

As he was answering, another student rose to his defense. Interrupting with a hint of irritation over the situation, he said, "Yeah, follow him. He's really good. He was my substitute teacher."

The gentleman chimed in, "I was just hanging out and making sure it was all good."

"Well … Um, thank you for your concern," Zachary said, forcing a smile. "We need to watch out for our youth." He genuinely meant it in his heart and mind, but was still shaken up that he had been mistaken for someone with ill intentions, even though clearly, it was a friendly conversation. The *students* went up to him first. The *students* talked with him. The *students* asked him questions. There were no signs of fear on any of the faces. Not even one of them. Anyone could've seen that.

"Yeah, of course," said the gentleman, accepting the gratitude.

"But he substituted for our classes," the students said to him, still defending Zachary.

"Oh, cool!"

"And he does card tricks and juggles," said another.

"Yeah, um—" Zachary said, smiling, walking closer just in case it got out of hand. "I do those as incentives for good behavior."

"I get it," the gentleman replied, still grinning.

"Thank you so much, Mr. Corwin, for that photo," Emma said, turning around to him.

"I'm gonna subscribe to you on YouTube right now," Caden hollered.

"Only if you want to."

"Oh, I do."

After saying goodbye to them, Zachary began to leave.

"Hey, continue being a good teacher, man. God bless you," the gentleman called out.

"God bless you too. Have a good weekend, all of you."

"You too!" they all replied to him.

Walking away, Zachary could still hear the students defending him to the gentleman. That, and Kelly Clarkson singing "Stronger" over the speakers. Even though he understood the gentleman's concern and that he left with apparent understanding from him (as well as from the employee from CVS Pharmacy), he nevertheless felt crushed over the insinuation.

How could he not recognize me or my kindheartedness at first sight? Zachary questioned that night at two in the morning. He was having an impossible time getting to sleep as a result, his frantic, reflective inner voice not knowing when to shut up. He kept thinking of the various ways it could've gone.

In the stillness of the night, AJR's "Way Less Sad" reverberated in his mind from a music playlist on YouTube. It was one of the songs he had listened to earlier that evening while working on his second book. Suddenly, the recalled lyrics began to speak to him in a relatable way.

How, despite nearly a million followers on social media, a novel out, and coverage in the news media around the world, including locally? I don't care if I have to sell all my stuff. I'm going to buy PR *and advertise like a storm until every neurotypical stops coming to their sick conclusions against us, based on first glance!*

After managing to fall asleep, *eventually*, he woke up that afternoon feeling sick, the memory instantly replaying against his will.

50

Sub by Day, Influencer by Night

"Zachary Corwin's in the house!" the elementary school principal at Roosevelt Elementary would excitedly yell out upon seeing him enter the office. This was one of the schools Zachary enjoyed subbing at. The principal appreciated his help and was always happy to see him. "Could I walk you to the classroom you'll be subbing in today?"

"Sure," said Zachary as he signed the payroll sheet.

"Sixth grade today. You ready?" the principal asked on the way, walking past a line of aromatic waxleaf privets, their nostalgic, honeylike fragrance drifting faintly through the morning air.

"Yes."

"How has the master's program been treating you?"

"Well, it's grueling, but I got a good grasp on it. We critiqued a curriculum in our content area. Mine is mathematics, of course. We're using the UbD framework (Understanding by Design). We write essential questions by unpacking the standards, create performance tasks, and more. We're learning big words such as ontology, epistemology, and axiology. In one class, we spent weeks studying various current issues in education, reading both sides of each argument, writing papers, and giving presentations about a couple of them."

"That all sounds like a headache to me. I can't imagine reliving that. My master's was in Educational Leadership, which prepared me for this position. After that, I'm like, 'I'm not going to pursue an Ed.D. Master's is enough.'"

After subbing an amazing day for sixth grade, he had one final thing to say a minute before the bell rang. "By the way, if you watch the local ABC station around 5:30 today, you'll most likely see me on there."

"What, really?" half the students said, marveling.

"Yes, I was in communication with a reporter this morning while you were at music. I was going to be interviewed inside this classroom via Zoom, but my phone wasn't having it."

Rushing home due to the time crunch, he got on his laptop and was interviewed in the nick of time.

"Mr. Corwin, you're famous!" an eighth-grader from Canyon Mountain said with a big smile the next day, walking home with his buddy. "I saw you on the news and was like, 'I know that guy!'"

Zachary had just arrived there after subbing across town, ready to donate an hour of his time to tutor the middle schoolers, being a Tuesday afternoon. "Oh, you got to watch that?"

"Yes. Totally surprised me."

"Yeah, the reporter texted me while subbing at Roosevelt Elementary. They told me that the CDC announced the prevalence of autism in eight-year-olds is now 1 in 36. They asked me to talk about being autistic and how early intervention helped me."

"Well, it was so cool seeing someone I know on there. Hey, before I go, do you remember my birthday?"

"September 8?"

The eighth-grader shook his head, maintaining a grin.

"September *10*," he said, just remembering and sounding confident.

"Yep! What about him?" he said, referring to his buddy.

"Um—" After Zachary stressed for a few seconds trying to remember, he said, "I-I apologize. I can't remember every single person's birthday."

"It's all right, Mr. Corwin," said the buddy. "It's July 24. I'll test you next time."

"Okay, that's right. I remember now. That's close to my birthday, and it's the same day President Martin van Buren died in 1862. I'll try to remember that association. Yes, test me next time."

After getting home from tutoring at the middle school, Zachary opened an email which read:

> *Hello Zachary.*
>
> *I'm the principal at Hollow Pine Elementary of Clearview Crystal Unified School District. Forwarded in this email is our school psychologist intern and PTA president. Grant, one of the boys whom you mentor at Royal Rangers, recently knocked on my office door. He told me about all the amazing things you do and how you promote Autism Awareness. He earnestly asked me to invite you to lead an assembly and mentioned that you're willing to volunteer for it. I know that April is Autism Awareness Month, and we'd love to schedule you for then.*

Just like the email from Maplecliff Elementary, Zachary was overjoyed to accept the opportunity. After exchanging a few emails, April 27 was set as the date for him to lead three assemblies for all the students.

* * *

As Zachary continued to work over the months, he found that some classes were easier to substitute in than others. In some cases, certain schools were easier than others. In secondary education, it depended on the period. Usually, the older the students, the easier it got due to maturity. Paradoxically, however, he sometimes subbed for third- and fourth-graders who were relatively perfect and for high schoolers who wouldn't listen for the life of him. A rare couple of classes didn't bother to notice his kindness, knowledge, or his willingness to brighten their days with sleight-of-hand tricks and juggling.

"Is he bribing us with magic tricks?" one student at a middle school across town retorted and laughed, bruising Zachary's heart. Maintaining professionalism, he proceeded to take the attendance.

Even though it was rare to encounter students who were real feeling bruisers, it was rarer to encounter adults in the school system who were condescending toward him, even passively.

"I'm subbing fifth grade today," Zachary firmly and confidently told the office manager one early morning.

"Oh, sure. Let me get the payroll sheet for you to sign. I'll also print out your roster and get you a computer and the key."

As the office manager was replying, Zachary subtly glanced back at the substitute teacher standing behind him in line, who had been staring at him strangely. He noticed her looking down, wide-eyed with a hesitant exhale. She was wondering to herself if he was a good fit to be a sub. Zachary simply stood there in his business-casual button-down, not saying a word, yet this woman judged him by his outward appearance and demeanor.

Trying not to let her wrong first impression ruin his day, he walked over to the classroom. He took the key and unlocked the door, but, as fate would have it, the key wouldn't work properly after lunch. Fifth-graders started going crazy, some running to the back door behind the building. Zachary followed and tried the back door without any luck. After that, the custodian came to the rescue.

As the students worked independently on a social studies assignment on their Chromebooks, Zachary calmly walked up to one of the students. Kneeling down to meet her at eye level, he whispered, "I have two questions for you. One, are you able to sing quietly in your mind?"

The student nodded, her gaze fixed, not saying a word.

"I apologize, but I noticed that your singing is distracting nearby students. My second question is this: out of curiosity, what was that song?"

"'You Belong With Me,' by Taylor Swift," she whispered.

"Ah, I *knew* it sounded familiar. Man, that takes me back to 2016. Anyway, you were singing great, but just sing in your mind until later, okay?"

The student smiled, replying, "Okay."

Having been scolded a few times as a child and teenager by well-meaning adults, Zachary didn't want students to misinterpret him if he ever had to use a strict tone. That's why he favored soft redirection, finding ways to compliment students whenever he could and letting them know there would soon be time to talk, sing, dance, or do whatever they liked (at recess, lunch, or after school).

"All right, class. You have about five minutes left … uh—" Looking up at the clock, he made some quick calculations. "Actually, five minutes and twenty-*three* seconds … but who's counting?"

"*You* are!" said one of the students, laughing.

Just then, the principal walked through the door, his emerald tie standing out prominently against his beige shirt. "Hey, Zachary, how has your day been?" he whispered.

"It's been fairly good," he whispered back. "Just mild redirecting throughout the day. These students like to talk. I'll put it that way."

"Ha-ha! This class has been known to be talkative all year, especially with substitute teachers, but you seem to have the magic touch. They haven't been as talkative when you're here, I noticed. Anyway, hey, I've been bragging about you to the other fifth-grade teachers. Did you bring your juggling stuff today?"

"Yes," Zachary replied, his eyes beginning to light up.

"I remember back to when you were a student at Washington Elementary. You were always great at juggling. I mentioned it to the other teachers, and they thought it'd be fun to bring the entire fifth grade together during Fun Friday, and you can show them juggling and card tricks."

"Wow, I'd love to do that. Thank you."

"I know it's not exactly the assembly you were asking me to consider, but I'm still working on that with our PTA."

After school that day, grateful for the opportunity to impress eighty fifth-graders, he stood about ten yards from the school fence, talking with one of the fifth-grade teachers, who complimented him on his talents.

"I'm just thankful I was able to pull off that card trick without a document cam," Zachary said, laughing.

Out of nowhere, a child's voice echoed in the air. "Thank you for subbing for my class last week, Mr. Corwin!"

Turning slightly, Zachary saw one of the third-graders walking briskly with her mother on the other side of the fence. "No problem," he called out in return. "Have a good afternoon."

"You too!" she hollered back.

"Aw! That's sweet," the fifth-grade teacher said, resuming the conversation.

Zachary, however, kept looking at the girl's mother through his sunglasses. The entire time the girl was talking with Zachary, who had obviously been cheerful to see him again, beaming ear-to-ear, her mother seemed to put on a different countenance. As she hurried along with her daughter, her face fell into a fixed icy stare at Zachary. Discombobulated, he couldn't help but think about that for months, as the image was burned into his mind against his will. As always, he tried hard to reason how he could've misconstrued it. He was easily taken back to the gentleman outside the CVS Pharmacy earlier that year, the manager of Albertsons in 2020, the father at the park in 2017, and so on.

* * *

April, the month for Autism Awareness and Acceptance, brought many opportunities for Zachary to promote his encouraging messages, social media, and novel. Thanks to his PR campaign, he was scheduled for several radio and podcast interviews around the world, as well as five television news interviews. Locally, having waited nearly six years, he was finally able to get into the school newspaper at the community college he attended. After being interviewed on campus, he walked into the library and found his novel on its shelf. He drew in a deep breath, proud of the sight.

At the top of the month, Zachary decided to get an earlier start that year, emailing a dozen churches to humbly request a day to speak and juggle at their VBS that summer.

April 27 finally arrived.

After getting off a Zoom meeting for a live news interview in Portland, he got ready and headed over to Hollow Pine Elementary for his three assemblies. After each assembly, the principal announced that the students would hold discussions with their teachers and write a paper on what they had learned.

Once it was all over, the psychologist intern approached Zachary and thanked him warmly. He mentioned that a mother of two autistic children at the school had been present. "That mother wanted me to pass along a big thank you from her," said the psychologist. "She wanted to tell you herself, but she was too overcome with tears after hearing your inspiring story."

"Thank you for relaying the message to me," said Zachary, grateful that his story seemed to be resonating with so many people there.

"You got to start charging for these assemblies!" said the principal, rushing up to him. "Well, we at least want to give you a gift to remember us by. It's a small jar with stickers, sunflower seeds, a wristband, and other tiny treasures. Also, here's a thank-you card."

"Thank you. I appreciate it. Would you be able to forward my information to all the other principals you know?"

"I'll definitely put in a good word for you. I overheard lots of students and teachers talking about what you did and said. I can't thank you enough. Thanks for coming."

As soon as Zachary got home, his legs started feeling the soreness again. Laughing it off, Zachary walked upstairs to check his emails. Already, there was another principal from that school district who had heard the wonderful praises about him. She expressed interest to set up a few assemblies for her school sometime in the future.

After replying to her email, he opened Frontline, the app where substitute teachers could accept jobs. He picked up an assignment for an eight-grade history class at Canyon Mountain.

"Mr. Corwin!" called a couple of eighth-graders in third period the next day, stepping into the classroom. "Windmills" by The Vamps played through the teacher's Bluetooth speaker, which was paired with Zachary's Chromebook that he borrowed that day.

"Good morning, Ricky and Luca."

"Mr. Corwin, congratulations on a million followers on Insta. You did it!" said Ricky, his eyes lighting up with excitement.

"And you finally got verified last month. That's sick, congrats," added Luca. "You're the first person I met who's actually verified on social media."

"Well, I'm just trying to help everyone on the planet, and I'm one eight-thousandths of the way there," Zachary replied, beaming. "Besides, to me, verification helps me look credible, trustworthy, and that I know what I'm talking about."

"Do you have merch?" Luca questioned.

"Um, well, you know, I never liked the idea of putting myself on products like that, worried that people would assume I'm just another arrogant 'kid' or … whatever. However, a representative from a website called Fourthwall reached out to me just a couple of days ago, coincidentally enough. I gave it a lot of thought, and I figured it'd be a good way to spread

Autism Acceptance. I plan to put my quotes on apparel, mugs, stickers (you name it). It could also direct people to my social media, where I spread such awareness, acceptance, and self-confidence."

"Make a YouTube video once your shop is up. I admire what you're doing for this world. You have my full support," Luca said with a closed-lipped smile.

"Speaking about what you do for the world, I watched that news story you were on the other week," Ricky noted.

"Me too." Luca nodded his head. "That was sick. I was like, 'That's my sub!'"

"Well, um, I suppose you'd say I'm a sub by day, influencer by night."

51

Ebbs and Flows

As May rolled in, life began to ride like a roller coaster with its ebbs and flows.

"It's the principal!" whispered one of the sixth-graders.

"Shh!" the student's aide whispered back. "You don't need to announce it."

Two seconds later, the principal opened the door and walked in, followed by a woman in a magenta dress. Zachary hadn't seen either of them before, being the first time subbing at this particular elementary school. Truth be told, he didn't even know which one was the principal.

"Hi," Zachary said softly, offering a little wave and a tentative smile. He returned to his math lesson, trying to steady himself under the weight of being watched by the senior administrator of the school and someone else whom he didn't recognize.

"So, Nathaniel," Zachary said, calling on him as he seemed to space out again, "what's our next few steps in calculating the standard deviation of a data set?"

"Uh!" he said, perking up. "Um, I believe we subtract every data point from the mean we just found, square the result each time, add them together, and divide by the number of data points?"

"Epic! That's *exactly* what we do next before our final step, which is taking the square root," Zachary said while writing it on the whiteboard, thankful that Nathaniel understood it and engaged with the material. By the time he finished writing, the principal and the woman with her had left, but not without smiling first. "*Phew!*" he said to himself, relieved.

"I enjoyed your math lesson," said the aide out at lunch. "Are you wanting to teach math when you get older?"

"Yes, I just got the teaching certificate in math this past January, and I'm going for my Master's in Education, currently," he informed. He had been walking back from the front office, trying to find out what was going on and if the principal was wanting to speak with him. So far, there were no answers.

While alone in the classroom, the phone rang.

"Hello?"

"Hi, this is the principal. Sorry, I was in a meeting. You don't have to worry. The new board president stopped by to check out some of our classrooms at random, and we chose your class as one of them."

"That was the board president?"

"Yes."

"Wow!" Zachary said, surprised, determining that she must've been the woman in the magenta dress.

"Anyway, I did want to speak to you afterward, and I suppose now's the best time. We were only inside for a minute, but I'm remarkably impressed with your math lesson."

"Oh," Zachary said, flabbergasted to hear that, especially coming from a principal, unsure of what to say. "Thank you. I just completed my student teaching at Canyon Mountain Middle School."

"I can tell," she asserted. "I was amazed that you got Nathaniel to talk. He rarely talks or participates in class. Really impressive, Mr. Corwin."

After the students left that day, Zachary, as always, finished filming his commentary on how the day had gone for his upcoming teaching update. He was about to leave the campus after dropping off his badge and the Chromebook he had borrowed, but the office manager stopped him.

"Zachary Corwin?"

"Yes?"

"I'm the office manager. The principal wanted me to ask you for your contact information. She told everyone in the office about your math lesson, getting a quiet student to speak, and the care that you show to our students."

Humbled to hear he was leaving such a legacy, he wrote his name, phone number, and district email down on a piece of paper. "Is the principal in, by any chance?"

"Right now, she's in an IEP meeting. Can I pass along a message for you?"

"No, that's fine. What about the assistant principal?"

"Oh, sure. He's right in there,." she said, pointing the way.

Zachary walked into his small office to introduce himself, thankful for the chance to share with him about his volunteer assemblies. To his surprise, he had already seen Zachary speak and was fully supportive of his proposal.

"I'll pass this request along to our principal," he assured him with a friendly smile. "Hey, thanks for being here, and outstanding job today!"

Zachary carpooled home with one of the teachers he knew from that school. He felt incredible about how the day had gone and the impact he left on students and faculty. He began feeling his sense of purpose again.

Upstairs in his room, he inserted his camera's SD card into his computer, opened YouTube Studio while waiting for the video files to copy over, and read some comments that totally loused up his entire day.

"Nobody cares what you believe."

"I hope your home burns down with you in it."

"Pour acid in a bucket and dump it all over yourself."

The hateful rhetoric that called for his death was written under three of his recent videos. Two were posted under Autism Awareness videos, and the middle one was posted under a firebuffing one. However, this guy's comments didn't compare to how vicious his buddy was.

"Yes, you're right. Autistics do look crazy. You look like an alien."

"You're not right in your head. Go back to your mother's womb, buster!"

"I sure hope you get drone-struck."

These three additional comments were posted by another user on his Autism Awareness videos and Shorts, yet they still didn't compare to the horrid barrage that he was about to be hit with next.

"Upload a video doing the Kurt Cobain. You can't have autism if you're dead!" screamed a third user.

Zachary sat there in lifeless terror, shaking like a leaf and regretting that he had drunk half of a Mocha Frappuccino. Doom overwhelmed him, and he forgot everything good that had happened that year. He looked at the date in the lower-right corner of the laptop's taskbar. He instantly realized that it was the six-year anniversary of receiving his associate's degree in mathematics at his college's commencement. He now questioned why he had labored over his education and in getting a novel published. There he was, also getting over the recent two-year anniversary of Thomas' suicide, unbeknownst to these trolls. Now, he's reading a comment begging for him to do the same, for no other reason than being autistic.

They were totally ignorant of all his accomplishments, like earning the Gold Medal of Achievement or publishing a novel, and the amazing things he could do, like juggling or playing piano. They were completely oblivious to the kindness in his heart and to the tens of thousands of people whom he had encouraged over the past decade.

Zachary didn't understand it.

It all started during recess, earlier that day, when a person who claimed to be a doctor from Germany commented on one of his Shorts about what it's like being autistic. "No one asked and no one cares" was all that this person wrote. Furthermore, using profanity, the user replied to comments that supported Zachary on that Short.

Zachary, of course, wasn't about to let anyone claim that no one cares about the disabled. Suppose this person runs into an autistic individual. What's he going to do? Bully them? Probably. And then that individual would commit suicide. He wasn't going to stand for that. Knowing he was called to change this sort of backward thinking and to get billions of people to accept one another, he decided to reply to this user, assuming it wouldn't elicit a response, much less an apology. He thought it might at least speak to other people who stumble across it.

A trait of being autistic, his response was quite lengthy. He spent the entirety of recess laboring over it: proofreading, correcting every autocorrect mistake, editing, and fixing all the typos his shaky fingers kept making on the phone. As always, he spoke professionally, telling the person that he or she also has purpose in life, but it's not to bully others, especially on the grounds of a disability, which people never asked to live with. He concluded with, "Have a great rest of your week," followed by a smiling-face emoji, teaching him or her how to show kindness, even in the face of adversity.

Within ten minutes, the user wrote back, "Man, I'm not reading all of that!"

Zachary felt hurt, especially after taking all that time to calmly show that autistics are human beings with hearts, pointing out that there were many people who cared and explaining why his uploads were so important in this century. *Oh well*, he thought and decided to walk away from the online conversation, but as he later found out, it was far from over.

Sitting there alone in his quiet room, a fourth user popped up and began trolling the daylights out of him too.

"These people are starting to be no different than pesky *gnats* who just won't go away … *no matter what!*" Zachary complained to himself, not out of indifference toward fellow human beings, but toward their attitude.

He couldn't bottle up his feelings any longer. Knowing he'd go insane if he didn't, he had to speak out. Over the next hour and a half, he labored over an impromptu video, trying to get his words right. He added proof that his novel had helped so many people so far, that he'd spoken on the news, and that a million people decided to follow his story on social media. If no one cares about autistics, how the heck did he rise up so high, against all odds? He spoke calmly yet emphatically, stressing the fact that he believed in everyone's purpose, including these bullies who just need to mature and find happiness in life.

Even though he was relieved to publish the video, he still felt a depressing sense of lonesomeness. Despite growing such a following on social media and appearing on various media outlets worldwide, his views and comments per video declined sharply throughout 2023, and he couldn't ascertain why. From late 2021 to late 2022, he'd get hundreds, if not thousands, of views per video, along with a couple of dozen comments. Now, he'd be lucky if five people left a comment, barely surpassing fifty views.

Within an hour, only two people rose up to his defense, encouraging him before heading over to the original trollish comments to give them a piece of their mind.

One additional hour dragged on like a sloth. Zachary couldn't concentrate.

Suddenly, the room began to brighten as the outside clouds began to dissipate. He clicked on his video, scrolled down, and read a new comment that nearly made him emotional, seeming to be a humble apology from one of them. Upon copying and pasting the comment on Google, however, he found that it was nearly word-for-word of Logan Paul's 2018 apology transcript.

"Well, all I can say is thank you," Zachary started. "Thanks for taking the time to modify Logan Paul's words to fit the situation. Giving you the benefit of the doubt, I will assume that you didn't know the right words to say and chose to use a prewritten speech. Regardless of your sincerity, I forgive you, of course. I would even take a bullet for you just to make you believe that disabled people are humans who deserve a chance, *and* that you have a great contribution to make in life, which isn't bullying or hurting others. Thanks for keeping the part where you apologized to those affected by mental health and suicide. As you heard in my video, that's what my lifelong friend did to himself two years ago, and I'm still not over it. I hope you have a better life, and I will pray for you and your buddies. I'm here if you ever need more information about Autism Spectrum Disorder."

Moments later, the user replied, "I felt sorry hearing about your friend, man. I hope you'll find peace someday. Have a good day."

Early the next morning, a quarter to seven, Zachary read a few additional comments of support. Despite apologies from half of the trolls, excluding the self-proclaimed German doctor who bashed him over his new video, he still felt lost and down. He knew that summer was coming up in a couple of weeks, and only two VBSs decided to take him up on his free offer to be a light to the children, whereas other churches said he wouldn't be a good fit, or implied that he was money-hungry using reverse psychology.

Despair and seclusion began to eclipse him like a skyscraper casting its ominous shadow on the street. He only had a couple of one-day opportunities that summer and nothing else.

No one to help.

No one to entertain.

Pure uselessness.

He decided to return to his local tutoring center, now having a bachelor's and a teaching certificate, but first, he had to get to work.

"Is there anything I can do to help?" Zachary asked a couple of teachers at lunchtime. For the second day in a row, he was subbing at a new school, this time for fourth grade. "My students have Physical Education after lunch for forty-five minutes, so I have nothing to do. I wasn't sure if there were students who might need help with math or science?"

"Hmm." One of the fourth-grade teachers thought, setting down her forkful of lasagna. "I don't particularly need any help. What about you, Gladys?"

"Neither do I," she replied, shaking her head and swallowing a Vienna sausage. "Wait, didn't the teacher have you hand out a few tests this morning? I'm sure she did. Would you mind grading them for her? I'm sure she'd be thankful."

"Sure, I can," Zachary said, heading back inside the classroom.

Halfway through, while reliving the memories of grading hundreds of papers as a student teacher, a knock on the door completely pierced the silence.

"Hey, Mr. Corwin?" Gladys said as a boy's head poked through the doorway. "I do have a student who needs help understanding fractions. Do you still have time to tutor?"

"Absolutely," he replied, capping the pen he was grading with. Gladys dropped the boy off and returned to her classroom.

The boy walked closer to Zachary, holding a worksheet in his right hand.

"Hey, do you know what type of airplane that is?" Zachary asked, instantly noticing the GeminiJets model held in the boy's left hand.

The boy shook his head.

"It's a Boeing 767 model in American Airlines' vintage Bare Metal livery. A classic. It's one of my favorite liveries, right after United's Battleship Gray."

"That's cool," he replied silently.

"So, let's start on that math worksheet you have there," he said as he grabbed an Expo marker, inviting the boy to sit in the front row.

Ten minutes thereafter, the door opened and two ladies walked in. Zachary didn't recognize who the first woman was, but to his astonishment, the second woman was the board president, this time elegantly dressed in a blue outfit that matched the clear summer skies.

Unable to find the right words, he defaulted to his usual "Hey."

"Man, you get around, don't you?" the board president said, since this school was on the opposite side of the district from the one he worked at the previous day.

"Yes, I do," he responded, nodding. "This is my twenty-third school I subbed at in the district."

"Wow, how long have you been a sub for?"

"Um—" he stuttered, buying time as he calculated in his mind. "Roughly fourteen months now."

"No wonder why you're a pro. The principal yesterday talked a lot about you. Have all the students been good to you?"

"Well … most of them. A week ago, for the first time, a student literally threw objects at me when my back was turned. Nothing big. Just crumpled Post-it notes, it felt like. I was subbing a math class at one of the middle schools. Most students seem to appreciate me over there, but it's certainly a different dynamic than the one where I student taught. While teaching my math lesson, I decided to use proximity to redirect the student who had been chattering as if I had no authority. Walking back a few moments later, I felt something hit the back of my neck. I turned around, and he just smirked at me, playing innocent, you know? Calm but firm, I let him know that I knew it was him and gave him a final warning. After that, he never bothered me again. One of the students sitting behind him marveled, saying to me, 'You're so calm.'"

"Anyone can sense that kind nature in you, indeed. How do you cope when those things happen, though?"

"Well, I understand if this sounds backward, but I start to get a boost of motivation and joy. I tell myself, 'I'm here for a purpose on these tough days. I belong here. This is my opportunity to be a light for these students.' I break out my SEL strategies and encourage them to make better choices. I find what they're good at, then edify them accordingly with sincere compliments and encouragement. Later, that teacher emailed me to apologize for the student throwing things at me.

"Some mornings, I get the class quieted down and give them a short pep talk. I tell them, 'Every day I enter a classroom, I view each student as "Star Students," and so I rely on you to perform as such. I shouldn't have to remind you how to behave because you know how to, and I know that. So be Star Students today.' And sometimes, they got the message, but I still had to guide them and give reminders throughout the day.

"One principal, a couple of weeks ago, told me during recess that I had been subbing for the toughest class in the school. Heck, one student from a different class showed pity for me that morning, and it was rough, but by the end of the day, those students were begging me to come back; one of them even pretended to cry. I told them, 'I'm proud of you. Whether you believe it or not, I'm proud of you. You guys did very good and had accomplished what you needed to accomplish. You see? I expected you to be Star Students. I *knew* you had the character in you, and today, you showed exemplary character. There was a little hiccup in the middle, but other than that, you were amazing!'

"Later, that teacher told me that her students were asking her to take a day off so I could sub for her again. I mean, as long as every day isn't a tough day, I've been able to handle it, once that mindset gets established."

"That's very beautiful. I wish all substitutes (and *all* teachers in general) could be like you. You're definitely setting the standard."

"It's Mr. Corwin, right?" asked the other woman, standing a few feet away.

"Yes."

"While you were having a conversation with President O'Sullivan just now, this student was explaining to me how much you've helped him understand fractions. Thank you for volunteering your time to do that."

"No problem. I love math and teaching, and it has always been my joy to help others understand … Oh, by the way, are you the principal here, I assume?"

"Yes, I am," she replied.

"I sort of put two and two together just now," he said, humiliated to admit his ignorance. "Um, I can tell you're busy now, but after school, could I swing by your office real quick?"

"Sure, you can. Is it urgent, though? Is it about a student?"

"No, not at all. I simply want to share a message that I bring to other schools in this county."

After getting a ride home that day, he grabbed his pepper spray and headed out for a walk. During the amble, he picked up an application from the tutoring center. Passing through the nearby plaza, he stepped into his local Staples to restock on stationery. Avicii's "SOS" was ringing out from the store's ceiling speakers.

While suffering decision paralysis over choosing the perfect brand of blue ink pens, an eerie sensation crept over him. A woman slowly passed by him like a noiseless phantom. Chills ran up his spine as he forced himself to continue looking down at the box of pens, pretending to read its fine print. A knot twisted in his stomach, but just like that, it was over. He quickly went over to check out.

After getting his favorite smoothie at the juice bar and walking toward his house, he noticed a middle-aged woman sitting with a small bag of groceries, presumably waiting for her ride. Zachary tried to pass by as normal as he could, but just as he expected, he heard her mutter, "Disgusting," clearly aiming her insult at him.

Man, what is it with this day?! Zachary questioned in his mind. *Or this season in my life? Really, just last week—*

"Mr. Corwin!" an eighth-grader called out from a large golf cart with six other students, unknowingly rescuing him from his depressing soliloquy that began to brew. Zachary smiled and waved back. As the driver continued down the parking lot, he overheard snippets of their excited chatter: "He's a YouTuber," "I follow him on Insta," "He knows magic," or "He subbed for my class."

Such a small "act of kindness," as he'd call them, completely lifted his mood and changed the course of his entire day. Suddenly, he began recalling "Revolution" by The Score, a song that he found and played earlier that day. He walked the rest of the way home with dignity. Come hell or high water, he was going to spark change in society.

Nevertheless, consumed with curiosity, he remained determined to find out what was going on with that woman inside Staples. While standing in the aisle, he had been facing her. Consequently, his body camera captured crystal-clear footage of what was unfolding. Leisurely walking by like a full-body apparition with long black hair, the woman glared at him, each step pronounced. He watched in terror as the woman's eyebrows were furrowed. She never stopped giving him the death stare.

And that was it.

Zachary sat there alone in his room, allowing his autistic brain to replay twenty years of similar moments.

A few months earlier, he walked into the office of a school he hadn't been to yet. The Irish office manager was softly singing "The Bonnie Banks o' Loch Lomond" as Zachary stepped in. Out of nowhere, while signing payroll, a rush of wind slammed against the back of his neck.

"He's a sub! It's grand," the office manager called out, placating the woman who stormed inside. Zachary swung around and saw the woman's back, already marching into the hallway.

He was about to launch into another full-blown soliloquy about being mistaken for a loitering intruder, though he decided to cut it off immediately. First, however, he quickly clipped the body camera footage of the other lady calling him "disgusting" for his little montage, proving that ableism still exists in the neighborhood.

52

Summer of Optimism

As summer vacation neared, Zachary felt better than he did a year prior. He had been hired as a math tutor and scheduled to work there three days a week, plus Sunday afternoons.

During the penultimate day of classes, he was out on recess duty at Washington Elementary, shaded by the tall pine trees beside the lunch tables. Being the last week, students were playing classic field day games or running through various inflatable obstacle courses. Some enjoyed popsicles, while others tossed water balloons at each other. All week, giant portable speakers set a fun vibe, getting everyone in a summer mood by playing songs such as The Beach Boys' "Kokomo," Ziv Moran's "Freedom Mile," and Sheryl Crow's "Soak up the Sun."

"Are you Mr. Corwin? Zachary Corwin?" asked a lady who approached him.

"Yes, I am."

"Wow, it's an honor to meet you in person. I attended the annual dinner that the school district hosted on Monday. Many students were present to receive various awards. Anyway, your name was suddenly brought up by a student that I was sitting next to during the meal. Once he mentioned your name, five or six other students from different schools were saying, 'Oh, he subbed for you too?' 'He's the coolest,' 'I learned a lot from him,' 'He does amazing card tricks,' 'He remembers birthdays very well,' and all. Anyway, it's my honor to thank you for all that you're doing in these students' lives and for the community."

As he listened to her, humbled beyond words, a couple of students standing nearby smiled at him, giving silent applause, as he had previously subbed for their classes.

After school, Zachary walked into Mr. Collingsworth's classroom to thank him for putting in a good word.

"Any time, Zachary! I'm thrilled you got the job. All my kids have been going to that tutoring center for a couple of years now. Maybe you'll get to tutor them this summer. We go on Tuesdays."

"That'd be wonderful. I'm working there on Tuesdays."

"How was today subbing second grade?"

"It was … um … loquacious … meaning they loved to talk. I'll put it that way. And sing, too. 'Baby Shark' is now stuck in my head. That, and the classic 'Did You Ever See a Lassie?' But we got everything done without incident."

"Meh, they're seven and eight. Remember being that age?"

"I remember *before* that age, and yes, I was quite talkative too. The thing is, I didn't understand the teacher's sub plan. After the bell rang this morning, I stood there at the door, just inside the classroom, watching hundreds of students rush to class, but none were coming into the room. The bell rang, and a few tardy students began sprinting, but no second-graders. Discombobulated and convinced I was in *The Twilight Zone*, I reread the top of the sub plans and instantly bolted out of there! Leaning against the classroom wall outside was a straight line of thirty second-graders, quietly waiting for me to show up.

"Last time that happened, I was subbing sixth grade at Ulysses Elementary. It was the first time I was there. The bell rang, and I didn't realize it was the start of the school; I was expecting a five-minute warning bell like every other school. Suddenly, the campus grew silent from my room. I glanced at the daily schedule chart on the wall and ran out of there. My class was the last one out on the blacktop, waiting to be picked up. They literally cheered when they saw me jogging toward them."

"Ha-ha!" Mr. Collingsworth couldn't help but laugh.

"And then at one point today, I told them, 'Don't laugh,' and I held up my arm. While stapling papers for the teacher, I accidentally stapled one onto my jacket's cuff. All the students began cracking up at that point. Oh, and I've been getting asked this a *lot* in elementary schools, but a few asked me, 'Who do you root for? Ronaldo or Messi?' I would never have heard of them if it weren't for students asking, since I don't watch any sports."

"Ah, at least watch the Superbowl. Anyway, how is your mission coming along, leading assemblies across the district?"

"Horrible!" Zachary said, taking a seat. "I mean, it's horrible in that I've only done a couple this spring, though I'm optimistic about next year. The principal at Ulysses Elementary told me that the PTA usually handles assemblies. I've invested all my time and energy trying to speak to principals. That's already daunting in and of itself, since I know how busy they are. After he told me that last month, I went home and emailed every PTA council in this county! All thirty of them for the thirty school districts. I also sent individual emails to all the private schools in this county I could find. Let's see how good *that'll* go," he added, feeling pessimistic.

"How many got back with you?"

"One! Just one in thirty councils. I delivered my story to them during their monthly Zoom meeting. However, someone from the county's Department of Education was in attendance, and we exchanged emails. She invited me over to the district's annual PTA vendor fair, which was last Saturday. They waived the fee for me and provided a spot. For six hours, I juggled, handed out my information, built connections, and said, 'I'm willing to come to your school for free, spreading Disability Awareness, Acceptance, and Inclusion.' One woman marveled and couldn't get over my willingness to come at my expense. A few people from across the county assured me that they'll be reaching out to me next year. Time will tell. There didn't seem to be many people, relative to a county with hundreds of schools, but I feel quite hopeful."

"Well, you've already accomplished a lot, you hear? Also, remember that word of mouth is just as powerful. Even though there weren't many people there, your information could still reach many schools, especially after doing more of these assemblies. Meanwhile, take some time to rest this summer, so that you can be rejuvenated to take on next year. Got any other plans this summer?"

"No, not much," he replied. "Just two VBSs who decided to let me speak."

"That's still excellent. My apologies again; I tried to get you to come to our church's VBS, but they require a six-month membership before anyone can volunteer with children and teenagers. They also require a background check and fingerprinting."

"I totally understand that. The churches I've attended are the same way. I have to do that every so often for Royal Rangers. I feel blessed, though, that the Baptist church in the neighboring city said yes, as well as the church I used to usher at. My current church isn't having one this year. Well anyway, I hope you have a good summer. I'll probably see you guys at the tutoring center."

"You bet. Anyway, last thing, is that second book of yours out soon? I'd like some good summer reading. Last I heard, you said you were up every night for three weeks straight, typing and typing until you were blurry-eyed!"

"Yeah. Well, nothing yet. I signed a contract with a publishing house, and they'll handle the rest. I'm having it traditionally published again in lieu of self-publishing. The latest publication date is December, but I don't think I can wait that long."

"Meh, with all the work you do, December will be here before you know it."

After returning the key and Chromebook in the office, Principal Miller stopped Zachary. Pointing at him with a big smile, she said, "Zachary, you subbed for my fifth-grade son's class over at Cunningham Elementary, and he said he had the best day ever! He came home that day, and the first thing he said was, 'Mom, my sub rewarded us with card tricks and juggling!' He said you became the favorite sub of his classmates too."

"Wow, thanks for letting me know. I'm grateful he had a good day. I'll never forget that day. I told them they were one of the best fifth-grade classes I've ever subbed for."

"Aw. You're welcome. I couldn't wait to tell you the next time I saw you. Have a terrific summer!"

"Thanks so much. You too."

Zachary walked away from the campus, vibing to Animal Island's "Gimme That Sunshine" playing through the speakers in the background.

Weeks rolled by. Tutoring at the center thrice a week, plus Sundays, proved to be a breakthrough, keeping Zachary busy and providing a valuable learning experience. He continued reviewing various math concepts while helping others and discovered different problem-solving strategies he could use in the future.

VBS week arrived at the Baptist church in the second week of July. That Thursday, Zachary led six twenty-minute sessions during the rotations portion, speaking to students from pre-K through sixth grade. He spoke about autism and inclusion, while performing all of his tricks. Being a Christian, he quoted biblical passages that encouraged him in life as an autistic, something he couldn't do in public schools, a boundary he understood and acknowledged.

After concluding his final session, he saw one of the children's pastors walk down the aisle toward him. The pastor began laughing silently at the spectacle, and Zachary shrugged with a smirk. A handful of students were surrounding Zachary, asking for his autograph.

"Well, thanks for coming," the children's pastor said a moment later.

"Thanks for accepting my request in that email," Zachary said, grabbing his bags and walking toward the foyer with the pastor.

"No worries. All day long, the kids wouldn't stop talking about it. It wasn't just the juggling and tricks, but your message too. It was empowering to them."

"I'm so thankful to hear that because the important thing in my heart is that they treat everyone with respect, even if they're disabled. And if they're disabled themselves, they have just as much purpose as the nondisabled. I simply do all the tricks to make it fun and easy for them to remember some of my main points."

"Well, we appreciate you. We hope to see you on a Sunday morning one of these days. And hey, I know you didn't ask for this, but we want to give you a little offering for this ministry of yours," the pastor solemnly said, handing Zachary an envelope with a check inside.

"I'm very appreciative of the donation. Thank you. As God is my witness, this will help spread Autism and Disability Awareness, Acceptance, and Inclusion."

"It's the least we could do."

"Before I forget, I'm curious, approximately how many people were here today?"

"You spoke to a total of about four hundred people, not including the volunteers, who also raved about you all day."

53

Caught in the Devil's Crosshairs

It was a hot summer day in mid-August. Cumulonimbus clouds began to peek over the distant hills, fifty miles away. Zachary, who had just gotten off work at the tutoring center, was about to undergo thermal sensory overload. Carrying his jacket and heading toward a frozen yogurt shop along the thoroughfare, three boys wearing e-bike helmets outside a pizzeria ran over to him, recognizing him from subbing their seventh-grade English class a few months before.

"Mr. Corwin!" they all shouted, sounding really excited. "Can we see a magic trick?"

"Sure," he said, putting down his laptop case and jacket. "I always carry at least one deck of cards on me."

"Yay!" they cheered.

The song, "Ways to Go," by Grouplove echoed from the pizzeria's open doors.

"So, pick a card, any card," Zachary said as he fanned out the deck but unexpectedly felt a haunting sensation. Just beyond the boys sat a woman with long blonde hair inside a red wagon. She was cradling a baby in her arms while a toddler sat opposite her, playing with his small toy dinosaur. Slowly, she took her sunglasses off and placed them on top of her hair.

As the boys deliberated over which card to choose, Zachary, facing the deck, kept a steady eye on the woman through the dark shades of his sunglasses. He noticed her scowling at him intently.

"That's it? Okay, remember it. Now tell me when to stop shuffling."

"Stop!"

"Okay, put it on top. Face-down." Zachary continued to glance back and forth between the boys and the woman. If passersby saw her, they'd assume she was the most lifelike statue in history. Not budging a nanometer, she maintained her menacing countenance, lips pursed for no apparent reason.

"Wait, what?" the boys exclaimed, mouths dropped.

"Where'd that red card come from?" one of them questioned.

"So was your card the seven of diamonds?"

"*What?!*" one cried out, putting his hands on his helmet in disbelief like the other two boys. "It was just blue!"

"I'll show you again real quick. Here, hold out your hand and take the card. Seven of diamonds, right? Now, place your other hand tightly over it." Continuing the latter half of his trick, he noticed that the woman's deadly glower remained fixed on him.

"I'm sorry. It must've not worked," Zachary said, sounding a bit down.

The boys drooped.

"Oh, wait! You have a red card in your hand. Is that the new card? Is that the ten of spades?"

The boy who held the red card turned it around and immediately covered his mouth with his left hand, taking a couple of steps backward. Eyes bulging, he held the ten of spades high with his right hand.

"No … *way!*" the other two boys said, emphasizing both words and began to chuckle. "Bruh!"

"Thank you for showing us," one of them said. "W trick, Mr. Corwin!"

"For real!" another chimed in.

"No problem. Have a great rest of your summer," Zachary said, noticing the woman slowly returning her sunglasses over her eyes.

"You too," they said.

"You're so cool," one added.

As Zachary walked away, he faced straight ahead, yet he glanced down at the woman through his sunglasses. The woman's head was turned away as if saying, "I refuse to even look at you as you pass by me," her lips still pursed.

Man, what's worse? Zachary thought, growing more agitated with each passing step down the thoroughfare, opting to skip frozen yogurt since his stomach wasn't hungry anymore. *That lady who never even met me in her life? Or that elderly gentlemen a couple weeks ago at the outdoor mall who kept cussing and cussing and cussing and cussing at me? And what'd* I *do?*

Zachary stormed into his room to check his emails. Since he found nothing of worth, he went through the rounds on social media, checking his notifications. His views and likes had sunk even further to rock bottom.

I don't get it, Zachary said to himself, frustrated. *Just a year ago, many people were commenting on my videos, asking deeper questions about being autistic, and I made videos in response. Where are they now? I mean, I'm not on social media to be famous or to have a high following to boast about. I'm not an actor, singer, dancer, or some celebrity of that kind. I don't post brain rot. I just want to encourage and motivate people, making a difference to eight billion individuals and the subsequent generations. There's a difference! I want to* eradicate *bullying and ableism. The heck is going on?!*

Zachary contemplated.

He wondered why things weren't going right in his autism advocacy, despite posting a couple of videos a week that he'd painstakingly create. Views and engagement were down, and he'd be lucky to sell even two books a month. He hadn't been able to afford PR since the three-month campaign ended.

Still contemplating, he thought, *If only I could get on national news like I dreamed.* (He had always desired to appear on ABC's *Good Morning America* and NBC's *TODAY*, not to mention *The New York Times*. Beyond that, he planned to try appearing on the British Broadcasting Corporation, the Australian Broadcasting Corporation, and the Canadian Broadcasting Corporation, among other major news outlets worldwide.) Continuing, he thought, *Then* all *the discrimination I received this month alone wouldn't have happened. Heck, why haven't those people from* TED *contacted me back? If I do a* TED Talk *and it goes viral on their platform, then so many people would be encouraged. Everyone on earth would treat every disabled person as a human and not a punching bag or garbage. Everyone in my own county would finally recognize me as an author who actually cares about people and their future. My social media would finally pick back up and grow bigger and bigger.*

In the interim, depressed, he could still hear the guy from the borough of Queens, New York City, going back and forth with him on TikTok recently.

"All your friends and family have deserted you, LOL," he commented, noticing Zachary's low number of views for someone with over 50,000 followers.

After a couple of exchanges, Zachary told him to Google his name, thereby proving he had spoken to millions of people around the world through his book and news media interviews. He reasoned that only a fraction of those people decided to look him up and give him a follow, but they must've not chosen to engage. All the man commented in return was, "Trust me. Millions of people don't know Zachary Corwin! This is rock bottom."

Zachary quickly changed the subject in his mind to avoid being hurt all over again. All the proof was right there on Google, yet this guy from Queens refused to look at the truth. He might as well refuse to believe 2+2=4, even if it were plastered on the billboards of Time Square or if Albert Einstein himself rose from the dead and said it to his face. No difference whatsoever.

He felt completely alone, staying up late at night making videos and posts, trying to figure out what to do. Around this time, he discovered several songs from both Øneheart and Antent. He began to feel attached to them, using them as background music for his Instagram stories, TikToks, and Shorts to convey his mood.

The next day, he relayed everything to his friend, Bill, over coffee, sitting outside his local Starbucks.

"The devil's trying to kill me," Zachary solemnly asserted, his voice still weak from feeling depressed over the entire situation. "It seems like I'm endeavoring to unearth and multiply the talents that God has entrusted me with, but it feels like the devil is forcing them to be buried not with sand, but with cement, and I'm laboring day and night (and midnight) to quarry those talents with which I can multiply and finally do my calling and purpose in life. I'm always telling God, 'I'm here! Please use me! *I'm* not the one burying my talents. The devil is.' … You know? I'll never quit. I'm *not* slowing down any time soon, but I'm feeling so drained by what my life is becoming."

"I completely hear you, Zachary. That sounds rough. So … those who followed you on all your platforms, do you know why they did?" asked Bill.

"Well, at first, I would post my piano playing videos from a chapel I used to attend, as well as planespotting videos. I made and uploaded some math tutorials, juggling videos, and early home videos that were digitized from those antiquated VHS-Cs. 2018 was when I significantly began posting Autism Awareness videos, and I kept doing so ever since. Later that summer, I'd take my photography of naturescapes and make slideshows that I'd upload as well. Since 2020, I'd post merit videos for Royal Rangers. Since 2021, I'd post firebuffing videos. Since 2022, I'd post videos telling funny stories to brighten people's days: Comedic Stories every Monday. On Fridays, I'd post some reaction videos that people requested, until it got too overwhelming with substitute teaching and the master's program. Oh, and I'd post videos updating everyone on how my education journey is going."

Bill stared at him for a solid five seconds. "Um … *Okay*, where should I begin? Tell me how the engagement was. Who would comment, and how long would it last?"

"I started getting comments from fellow piano players, especially those who loved the hymns as much as I do, but only for those videos. Only a couple of them stayed with me for a few months. Occasionally, a juggler would comment on my juggling videos. If I posted a home video of a place we went to, or if I posted a video of an event I attended, people would comment, saying that they went there too, but I never saw them again in my future videos. A couple of my math tutorials went a little viral. People thanked me; some said they subscribed to my channel, but that was the last I heard from them. For the first few years, it was hard to maintain consistent engagement, but after, *boom*. From 2021 to early 2023, especially, I started getting several comments per video."

"Did it matter what kind of video, or any video?"

"Well, fellow planespotters would only comment on such videos; others would comment on everything. Same thing with other subscribers, such as firebuffers and Royal Rangers. Of course, I subscribed to those who'd also upload videos; I'd watch, like, and comment on their videos too. It somewhat became a worldwide camaraderie. We'd later follow each other on Instagram and TikTok, where there are accounts with such interests. Not only them, but other communities would follow me, and I'd follow them, such as railfanners (A.K.A. trainspotters), cubers, fishermen, and artists. Many of them told me that they were autistic themselves, or have a family member who's autistic, because they had watched my Autism Awareness videos."

"So, many of them did leave a like and a comment on your Autism Awareness videos?"

"Yes, and they'd also congratulated me throughout my education journey too, supporting me in this endeavor."

"And now, most of them seemed to disappear? Do you have any hypotheses?"

"Yeah. Half of them stopped posting or began posting infrequently. They may have gotten too busy in life. A lot of them were still in middle or high school; their workload may have started taking a toll. The other half may have drifted away because I wasn't consistently posting content that interested them. For instance, it's rare for me to film a train. Additionally, I would post an aviation video or firebuffing catch once a week, so it was like every seven or eight videos, since I'd post every day."

Bill took a deep sigh. "All right, Zachary. I'm going to be brutally honest with you. You know that I've been YouTubing for five years myself. I don't have the following that you do; you have ten times as many subscribers as I do. The difference is, I have higher engagement. I get thousands of views, hundreds of likes, and dozens of comments each time. Why? Because I post one single niche on my channel."

"A niche?"

"Your channel's topic. You see, my topic is gaming, and I only post gaming content. Those who watch, comment, and subscribe are only gamers. They expect the next video to be a Minecraft video, a Fortnite video, or whatever, but it's always a game. If one out of every seven videos is about planespotting, one in seven about Autism, one in seven about math, and so on, then what would that be like for those who subscribed?"

"I guess I see your point."

"Look, you said that people thanked you for your math tutorials, right? And subscribed? They were expecting all your videos to be math tutorials. But then they see a video about an airplane pop up in their notifications? Or an episode about substitute teaching? I mean, those videos are entertaining and well put together. Anyone who watches them could tell that you had dedicated a *long* time to thoroughly put them together."

"And I have. Sometimes, I've spent hours on them, only to get under a hundred views," he said with a sigh of exhaustion. "I know I sound like some, young cocky person who only cares about a following and stardom. It's not that whatsoever."

"Far from it, I could tell. I know you better than that, and I know your heart."

"I suppose people assumed that I was just a music channel, Autism Awareness channel, aviation channel, juggling channel, wilderness survival channel, or whatever. I just wanted to share my interests, educate the world about being autistic, and encourage everyone. For years, I did everything by the book: keyword research, sharing across multiple platforms, hashtags, emails. You name it, and I tried it. Now it seems to all make sense."

"I don't know how to say this delicately, but I think you confused the algorithms, which is why all your social media accounts seem suppressed."

"You know? Come to think about it, my viral reel on Instagram was about the Boeing 747, not directly about Autism. It was posted just before a spike in followers."

"Perhaps it was shown to users who had an interest in aviation, especially since the Boeing 747 was trending that week. The keywords you used must've boosted it. Then, with more people watching, liking, and commenting, the algorithms pushed it out as if your niche was only aviation."

"Oh, my gosh," Zachary moaned, putting his head down on the table for a couple of seconds. "That explains *everything*. Oh, my gosh. What a paradigm shift." The gravity of the situation weighed on him. "It's too late. I've already posted thousands of videos and spent years building the following I do have."

"Listen," Bill said in an encouraging voice, "it might not be too late. I can tell that your main niche is Autism Awareness."

"Yes. From my heart, that's my primary focus. Bill, you know me to be very strong in my Christian faith. I never stopped praying, every day and every night, to finally make a big difference in this world. In this day and age of social media and incredible technology, what the freaking heck is precluding me from reaching eight billion people?! I thought it had finally begun once I found out what PR was a year ago and started to go viral a bit. All I want is to help the world be kinder and more accepting toward people. That's all."

"Well, why not make *that* your focus from now on: just posting Autism Awareness content and all your encouraging messages? That may significantly help the algorithms."

Zachary thought about it, overwhelmed by the hours he knew it would take to thoroughly plan this out. He stared out at the traffic, watching his life go by.

"You don't have to delete all of your other videos," Bill went on. "I heard that would be worse. You'd be suppressed for sure. Just focus on Autism Awareness content moving forward."

"Hmm," he said after a moment. "I think an idea is forming. I was wondering about all the people who followed me for music, and the people who followed me for aviation, and the people who followed me for firebuffing. And then I just stop posting such videos? Hey, you know? Those are special interests of mine, and that term is popular in the Autism community. Maybe I could just say, 'These are special interests that I have as an autistic person, and I'm not going to stop such hobbies as long as they still bring some happiness in my life. In fact, they help me escape from the stresses of the day, so I encourage all of you to find something that'll help you too.' I'll just lump everything together and post one of them each week, say, 'Special Interest Thursdays,' with that keyword in the title and description."

"Try that out," he replied, grinning.

"Yeah, that way I won't confuse the algorithms anymore. I could pick a couple of other days for Autism Awareness videos based on the type. Um, for instance, my general ones could be on Fridays, and one from a subseries, such as 'Dispelling Autism Myths,' could be on Tuesdays. And then I could still post 'Adventures in Substitute Teaching' on Saturdays, like I usually do, because I'm showing the world that I'm not giving up on my dream to become a teacher, even though I'm autistic. At the end of each video, I do give my common motivation anyway."

"There you go! And keep investing your time making YouTube Shorts from your long form Autism Awareness videos. I've noticed that some of them have been picking up views."

"I definitely will. And I suppose that a periodic home video wouldn't hurt. I usually upload them on anniversary dates. Well, Bill, I'm beginning to feel more optimistic than I was a few minutes ago. Now, I just have to do a little reformation when I get home and from here on out. Thank you so much."

"Anytime, Zach. I can see the joy coming back to you now."

Walking home down the thoroughfare, he passed by the pizzeria. Horrible feelings attacked him again. It was tough to stop dwelling over it and go to sleep the previous night. Upon awaking, that woman was still there in his mind, glaring at him as if he were about to attack or kidnap one of those boys, despite the obvious: those boys knew him well and talked to him *first.* He kept going over various scenarios. What would happen if she said something? What would happen if Zachary began talking to her? Then *that* led him down various paths, spiraling further down Hypothetical Lane.

A couple of weeks went by. So far, nothing improved on YouTube despite his reform, but he knew it would take time. Patience was unbearable, however.

Walking down the street alongside his former high school, excited for school to start back up the following week, he heard the rings of a bike bell from behind. He turned around and got out of the way for the gentleman. Glancing back, he noticed the man was grimacing.

I wonder how this *would turn out?* Zachary thought as he said, "Hey, have a good evening."

No response … as if he were a nobody. The man simply sped by him. Closely behind him were his two young sons pedaling their bikes.

"Hey," Zachary said, trying to bring some cheer to the atmosphere. "Have a good evening," he said, but the sons deliberately ignored him and faced forward the entire time.

Huh? he thought. *Did I not sub for their classes or something? Do they go to a private school?* By now, seeing way over ten thousand students a year, Zachary had run into doppelgängers. He realized that they only looked familiar, but were probably not students he subbed for. Otherwise, they would've said hi like all the other students who knew him. *Darn!* he dwelled. *If I had subbed for them and they had said hi, then that man would've realized I wasn't some inept idiot walking down the sidewalk. We may have had a conversation and left on better terms. He wouldn't have looked so arrogantly at me as if he owned the sidewalk. Not a single 'Thank you' for getting out of the way for him and wishing him a good evening? And those two boys seemed to follow his attitude: ignoring anyone who showed kindness.*

He reflected on what happened just a day prior at that same spot.

"Hi, Mr. Corwin!" a sixth-grader on his bike hollered from across the street. Following him were his parents.

Zachary smiled and waved back.

A few yards down the road, the mother called to her son, "Aw, it was your favorite substitute!" That totally brightened his evening, but twenty-four hours later, it felt like 2021 all over again.

By the time he got over it, several blocks away, he walked past a Subway nonchalantly. Looking in like any window shopper, lo and behold, that father and two sons were seated at a small table, enjoying a footlong. Getting stirred up emotionally again, he noticed a car that was stopped in front of the ice cream parlor next door with people inside. As soon as he passed by them, they began laughing out loud. He overheard one of the passengers say freakishly, "Bro, what the devil was that?"

Burning in pain, Zachary decided to call it quits and return home.

"What on earth is going on in society? What's the freaking problem with being autistic?" he said, alone in his room. "Is Murphy's Law the law of the land now? It's not just me, but every disabled individual! If *I'm* being treated like trash, then many other less-strong disabled people are too, and they'll either give up on their calling or commit suicide. I will *not* tolerate this. I will *not* be patient. It's time to reform society for the better!"

54

Unstoppable Determination Amid Chaos

Ten minutes of calming down and processing had passed. Zachary checked his emails, confirming to his dismay that the people from TED Talks hadn't responded yet. His publisher didn't update him on the status of his second book. He checked his social media notifications and saw nothing new. No comments and minimal views. Typical nowadays.

"To do this, I need to start with the youngest members of society: twelfth grade and younger," he said to himself with determination. "They're the leaders of tomorrow! They could learn now how to treat everyone with respect and say *no* to ableism. And, for some families out there, they could seriously teach their parents."

He decided to send an email to Dr. Peterson early, earnestly requesting to lead his volunteer assemblies at Canyon Mountain Middle School, trying for the third academic year in a row. He then sent an email to the principal at Ironwood Peak High School, with whom he had been in contact since 2019 regarding the matter. Next, he emailed the council president of his district's PTA, requesting again that his information be sent to every PTA president as a reminder. Finally, he emailed all the PTA councils in the county.

After he was done with all his emails, he logged into his bank account to check his balance. Sighing in hopelessness and despair, he thought, *I definitely don't have a budget for another month of PR.*

Returning to YouTube studio, he noticed the tab that said "Promotions." *Hmm*, he thought as he decided to explore. Advertising on social media was his last resort, which was what he did in the summer of 2019. Remembering how his past attempt didn't help him in the long run, he was hesitant.

He began to think anxiously as if under time pressure or duress.

Boom!

The three bicyclists and that passenger popped into his mind.

The woman in the red wagon reappeared with her pursed lips.

The cussing elderly gentleman reverberated in his thoughts.

The father at the park from 2017 came out of nowhere.

"That's racist!" yelled the student.

He could then see the skateboarder sprinting at him once again, about to beat the daylights out of him.

Finally, he heard a gunshot and envisioned Thomas crashing onto the floor, gun still in his hand.

In bitter rage, sad that there are people who currently treat others like utter garbage, Zachary went ahead and promoted a dozen of his recent Autism Awareness videos. He was willing to spend everything he had and sell everything he owned so that *everyone* would treat each other with respect, especially the adults who should know better. He headed over to Facebook and Instagram to boost some reels via Meta Ads, followed by TikTok's feature called "TikTok Promote."

He was unstoppable.

Within one month, only one email got back to him: the PTA council president. She shared his information to the PTA presidents of individual schools and invited him to be a speaker in their November meeting.

But that's a couple of months away, Zachary complained. *By then, wouldn't most schools have planned everything out?*

He had determined that he'd take this academic year off to lead assemblies amid substituting, hoping to start his career by August 2024. Unfortunately, if he couldn't get to all the schools this year, then he'd have to try again the following year, delaying his professional journey. This was something he was willing to do, thanks to the heart he had for spreading kindness and inclusion, thereby helping to end bullying, ableism, demotivation, and suicides.

He accepted it, praying that it wouldn't matter. Once the day came, the council president was moved to tears after hearing his story and seeing all his tricks, having an autistic son herself. Zachary nearly got emotional himself, thankful to God that his story was resonating and helpful. The room was packed, being held in the boardroom at the district headquarters.

"I strongly encourage everyone to take advantage of his free offer," the council president urged. "I will be emailing everyone his information and contact so that you can reach out and schedule assemblies."

PTA presidents from across the district complimented him as he returned to his seat.

"Could I have a word with you, Zachary?" one of the PTA presidents whispered. "Out there?"

"Sure."

In the main lobby, the president said, "I couldn't wait until after the meeting to speak with you. My name is Sophia, and I'm the PTA president for Canyon Mountain."

Zachary felt like he was about to shed tears.

"I love your message as it's so inspiring. You said in your speech that you want to speak to all students, but gathering them in the gymnasium might be inefficient."

"Uh, yeah, since it echoes, and students in the corners just talk to each other. Plus, my juggling, sleight-of-hand, and science demo require me to be hands free. It's rare that schools have something like a lavalier mic. I'm able to project my voice in multipurpose rooms, but I doubt I could do so in a large gym."

"Right. Well, I like what that high school principal suggested to you. Since everyone's required to take English every year from seventh to twelfth grade, just bring English classes together and do mini-assemblies until every student is reached."

"And I'm unequivocally willing to do that at all costs. Again, my record is sixteen assemblies in one day, followed by twelve, which I did last month in Clearview Crystal Unified."

"Well, I'd love to get you over to Canyon Mountain. I was thinking we could bring SSR classes together so you could do your assemblies. How does that sound?"

Zachary stood frozen, unable to speak as emotions surged.

"Are you all right, Zachary?"

"Uh, yeah," Zachary said quietly, holding back tears. "I've been trying desperately hard to speak at that middle school for four years now, not to mention the high school. Um, if I could be honest, Dr. Peterson, the principal, doesn't seem to care about my mission to make a difference and spread Disability Acceptance and Inclusion."

"What?"

"I have reason to believe it's true. I'm not saying it is, but I have proof to the contrary. In August, I emailed her *before* the school year began to ensure I'd be placed on the schedule. Set in stone. Surely, they can't have the school year completely planned out before it even starts, right? Besides, I've already asked her two academic years in a row. I waited a month, yet no reply. I walked by the school toward the end of their Back-to-School Night, waiting for the principal to come out. Once she did, I asked her from the sidewalk, 'Did you get my email?' She replied, 'It's been a long day, and I have a headache. I'll circle back to you tomorrow.' After waiting a bit, I just sent a second email. Instantly, she replied, and do you know what she said? 'I don't think we'll be able to incorporate your message this year.'"

"*What?*"

"I know! Like, it's only September. How on earth does she have the *entire* year planned? And to add insult to injury, all she said after that was 'Best of luck.' That's it! As if it's no big deal. I mean, I was called to make a difference in the lives of every single student in the county—motivating them to succeed, eradicate bullying, and promote inclusion. This is the third academic year I've humbly asked her. I replied back saying, 'Thanks for responding. If anything changes, feel free to reach out. Remember, I'm not charging one cent for this message, but it's from my heart.'"

"Well, I'll try to do whatever I can and speak to more people about it. I'll speak to the rest of our PTA and the other administrators at the school."

"Thank you so much! You may want to talk to the librarian, Mrs. Schlessinger. She has been on my side since the beginning of the year, after I started getting booked for assemblies. She's been working hard to bring English classes together in the library for my mini-assemblies. That might be a great venue."

"Okay, I will definitely keep you posted."

Zachary walked out that day feeling more optimistic than ever, believing wholeheartedly that he would meet his primary goal and speak to every school in the district by June 2024—*including* Canyon Mountain.

55

Unexpected Surprises

"It's Mr. Corwin!" sixth-graders at Washington Elementary whispered as they saw him walking toward their lines one morning. They drooped after he passed.

"Mr. Corwin, are you subbing for us today?" the fifth-graders asked in their lines.

"Good morning," he replied. "No, I'm subbing fourth grade today. Mr. Kowalski's class."

"Ugh," a quarter of the fifth-graders moaned.

Heading toward the fourth-grade lines, he realized that he forgot the line number.

"Mr. Corwin?" asked a couple of fourth-graders.

"Um, Mr. Kowalski's class?"

Suddenly, students in the middle and back of the line began cheering. One at the back raised both fists and jumped up and down.

"Good morning, but are you Mr. Kowalski's class?"

"Mr. Kowalski?!" a student in the adjacent line asked. "Over here!"

Zachary felt terrible. "Um, I'm so sorry!" Shifting to the other line, he saw the students who had just been celebrating start to slump since Zachary wasn't going to be their substitute after all. "So sorry, but have a great day … Good morning, Mr. Kowalski's class."

He waited a couple of moments as more students arrived. A trace of nostalgic pine scent surrounded the campus. Out of nowhere, he heard from behind him, "We got him!" Turning around, he saw one of the students running up to the line with his backpack on. Then he and his two buddies started jumping in a circle, like Ring-Around-The-Rosie.

"Looks like we have everyone. Let's go," he said with a smile, leading the class to the room. "Okay, I want to see two straight *parallel* lines—not scatterplot and definitely not perpendicular!" (He couldn't help but make a mathematical joke.)

"Are you going to show us magic tricks today?" one fourth-grade girl asked excitedly.

"Only if you're all good and listening, and if we get through everything."

Walking backwards, he asked, "So did you all have a good Thanksgiving break?"

Several students nodded and said yes.

"That's great," he said as he turned back around.

"Hey, Mr. Corwin?" one student said in a low voice, coming up to walk alongside him, though trudging along with a big, heavy backpack.

"Yes, Wendell?"

"I'm sorry you were almost beaten with a skateboard that night."

Zachary looked back at him, slowing down for a moment, but then remembered he was leading the class and picked up the pace again. "Oh, you must've watched that video," he said solemnly.

"I did. Are you all right?"

"Yes, I am."

"Thank God."

"That happened over a year ago. It was the most horrific experience in my entire life. I know many others suffered far worse, which is why I've been fighting hard to speak out in my county, on social media, and in news media. Anyway, I appreciate your concern. Since that night, there have actually been a handful of students who either told me they felt bad about it or commented on the video itself."

"Yeah, it was scary. I'm thankful you're okay, though."

"I appreciate that so much. Thank you."

"Hey, I bought your book too. I'd like you to autograph it whenever you can."

Overcome with gratitude to hear a fourth-grader say that, he replied, "Let me know when it comes. It'd be my honor to sign it."

Having arrived at the classroom, Zachary held the door open for the students and greeted them while they walked in. He chose Maximix's "Let's Enjoy" to provide the background music as they got situated.

"Chewbacca? Nice to meet you," he said, offering a handshake.

After shaking his hand, the boy took off his mask, smirked, and entered the classroom.

"Um, Dorothy? From *The Wizard of Oz*?"

The girl smiled and nodded, held up Toto, her stuffed-animal Cairn Terrier, and walked in the classroom.

"Is it costume day or something? All the teachers and some of the students are dressed in costumes," Zachary asked the remaining students as they hung up their backpacks, taking out their folders and books.

"It's Dress-as-Your-Favorite-Book-Character Day."

"Ah, that makes sense."

After taking attendance and getting everyone's attention, he said, "I want to say one thing real quick: this was my fourth-grade classroom nineteen years ago."

"Wow," the students said, marveling.

"Mr. Corwin, are you still tutoring at the center?" asked one of the girls at recess time right after being dropped off.

"No, not anymore. A couple of weeks ago, I walked in and formally resigned. They said tutors needed to report by 2:45, but that's impossible as a sub since I'm still working at that time. Also, they stopped opening the center on Sundays. They completely understood and apologized that it conflicted with my schedule, but it was fun (and a learning experience) while it lasted."

On his way back to the classroom, he noticed a few of the younger students huddled around a lunch table. Between hard, loud thuds, students cheered as if they were watching a championship match. "Hey, I'm surprised people still do bottle flipping," he said, wonderment etched across his face. "I remember when that craze was popular, like back around 2018."

"I was *born* in 2018," one of them said, astonished.

"Huh," he said to himself. "About two years after everyone was doing the dab."

An hour before school let out, the students quietly read their Accelerated Reader books. After nearly a perfect day subbing fourth grade, Zachary enjoyed the peace and quiet, unlike some of the classes he had recently subbed in. It was so quiet you could have heard a pin drop on the other side of campus. Abruptly, startling everyone, the loud fire alarm pierced through the silence.

"Fire alarm," Zachary said silently to himself, needing two seconds to process the information. Discombobulated, he assumed it was real, since Mr. Kowalski didn't mention anything about a drill in the sub plans. "All right. Everyone, form a line! Whose job is it to take the red backpack?"

For five minutes, they stood outside before being released back to their classrooms. Once everyone was seated in the classroom again, an awkward silence settled over the room as Zachary stood before them. "So—" he began, clearing his throat, "there was a fire drill you all knew about … and you didn't bother to tell the sub?!" he said, half-jokingly.

Several students began laughing, but did so apologetically.

Two minutes before school ended, students began packing up. One boy did The Griddy as he went out to retrieve his backpack, singing Ricky Desktop's "The Chicken Wing Beat."

"Thanks a lot," Zachary said sarcastically. "Now that tune is going to be stuck in my head. That, and 'The Banjo Beat' I heard constantly yesterday at another school."

"The power of meme songs," said the boy, winking.

"I suppose you're right. Do you know what *we* had in *my* generation that got stuck in our heads? A blond-haired boy who was called the Kazoo Kid. That and *KIDZ BOP*; I clearly remember the commercials for their first few albums back in early grade school. Now, there are what? Over eighty of them?"

A moment later, Wendell called Zachary over.

"Yes, Wendell?" he answered with a smile, but his expression quickly morphed into one of surprise.

Wendell pulled out Zachary's novel from his backpack, beaming from ear to ear. "Can you sign it now?"

Due to the shock, he didn't know how to respond. "Oh, you already have it with you. I thought you said you ordered it. Well, let me go ahead and sign it for you." He pulled out one of seven pens he always carried in his pocket. (He usually had a black and blue ink pen, a black and blue gel pen, a black and blue calligraphy pen, and a highlighter.)

After receiving his autographed copy, Wendell proudly ran up to his classmates to show them. After the bell rang a few seconds later, he went out to show all his friends around campus.

What an unexpected surprise, Zachary thought. He felt a strong sense of acceptance for the next several days as he revisited the conversation he had with Wendell that morning and the request to autograph his novel that afternoon. It made him question why he kept losing sleep over what others did or said. He determined that living with ableism his entire life had given him empathy, propelling him to be a voice for the voiceless and to confront such bullying, though fully aware that it'd be impossible to completely eradicate it from the face of the earth. However, he knew that he didn't have to endure more bullying to pursue his mission. He already had a lifetime supply of fuel. Moreover, if he was still being treated like a wild animal by the roadside by five percent of the population, then more work remained to be done. Though through it all, he had never forgotten his friends, family, and supporters around the world.

* * *

"Raise your hand if Mr. Corwin has ever subbed for you," said the principal at Granite Canyon Elementary, one of the schools in Zachary's district.

Half of the students in the multipurpose room raised their hands, excited to be there and hear him speak. Everyone inside was keeping warm from the outdoor fog on this late-February morning in 2024.

"Well, to most of you he needs no introduction, but my friend, Mr. Zachary Corwin, is here to give you a special and powerful message about disabilities and the importance of inclusion and being kind, while also providing some entertainment for us."

Zachary stood before two hundred students, ranging from third to sixth grade. He had just finished his first assembly, which was for pre-K through second grade.

What an unexpected surprise, he thought again, since he was only asked five days prior, but that was more than enough time for him to prepare. He was doubly excited because it was the first time he had done assemblies since the publication of his second book, which finally got released in mid-December. It mentioned every school in his district, which he got to tell the students and staff present.

The following day, he led an assembly at another elementary school on the other side of the district. Ever since speaking for the council PTA meeting in November, he had been invited by eight schools to speak. Beyond the district, he had invitations to speak at a dozen additional schools throughout the county. By June, he had spoken to students in twenty schools, with the largest assembly drawing six hundred attendees at one time.

After his second assembly at Granite Canyon Elementary, students, as usual, went up to him. Some asked how he did his sleight-of-hand tricks or how he made a cloud in a bottle. Others told him that their family member or friend is also autistic or has another diagnosis like ADHD.

"Could you give me tips on how to be successful in school and get into college?" one of the sixth-graders asked.

"Oh, absolutely," Zachary said, pleased to answer such a question, especially coming from an elementary school student. "When I was in seventh grade, I kept getting C's and D's, but in eighth grade, I decided to focus and listen to the teacher. I kept that mindset ever since, and between eighth grade and twelfth grade, I only got two B's. The rest were A's. Make sure you also ask questions to your teachers if you don't understand—before, during, or after class. That's what they're there for. Divide your time so you won't get bogged down, and keep up with your studies. That's my two cents worth. Hope it helps."

"It does," the boy said, grinning. "It does a lot! Thank you, Mr. Corwin."

That evening, he took one of his cathartic walks, going down Thornwick Boulevard, heading toward the outdoor mall.

Finally! he thought to himself with a deep breath of the cool, fresh air. He was quite thankful for the impact he had started to make, getting scheduled to speak at more schools.

Once his second book was released, he emailed everyone who had interviewed him during past PR campaigns. Some of them agreed to interview him again and help promote his second book. He also thought it would be easier since his social media had a much higher following. Unfortunately, it only lasted so long, and his own plan fell short. Based on what he earned as a substitute teacher, he decided he could budget for another month of PR, preparing for April: Autism Awareness and Acceptance Month.

Approaching him was a group of young men, about seven or eight of them. Zachary stepped off the sidewalk to show courtesy as they passed. As he was inches away from walking past them, out of nowhere, one of the guys lunged forward, raising his hands like claws and meowing like a cat.

"Have a good evening!" Zachary said with a smile, though he was confused. Stepping back onto the sidewalk and glancing at them, he saw another guy turn to look at him with a face that seemed to ask, "Who is this weird-looking lost cause walking all alone?"

Five seconds later, he could hear the group laughing among themselves.

Five seconds after that, he was hammered.

As usual, through this one tiny negative encounter, all remembrances of his family, friends, colleagues, and supporters vanished from his mind.

What an … unexpected surprise, ha-ha, Zachary said to himself, melancholically.

For the next hour, he walked aimlessly through the neighborhoods past the outdoor mall, questioning why he was still being treated like some creature, easily mocked as if it were no big deal. In those sixty minutes, as the skies became darker, he felt angry and distraught. He desired to punch every lamppost and street sign he passed, not caring if it made his knuckles bleed, but he forced himself not to with great strain.

I have two books out now. A million people decided to follow me on social media. I've volunteered my heart out, speaking to thousands of students, teaching them about disabilities and encouraging them to be kind *and* inclusive *toward one another. I've appeared in news media all around the world, not to mention podcasts and blogs, in ways too numerous to count. And over ten thousand students have enjoyed me as a sub.*

The freaking heck is going on? Why can't I get everyone, *even in my own city, to recognize that autistics are humans? How on earth do they not recognize me from the news or on social media? It's obvious. One million is merely one-quarter of the population of Los Angeles, one-eighth of New York City, one three-thirtieth of the population of the United States, and one eight-thousandth of the world's population. For everyone, including my hometown, I'll have to fight to get on all my local news stations* and *the national ones in New York City. I also need to get on the BBC in the UK and all the equivalent stations worldwide.*

Problem is, won't that cost me millions?

Wallowing in fear and anxiety for several, several blocks, he concluded that he'd have to sell everything he owns for a chance to be successful in this endeavor. Subbing was no longer profitable, but he wasn't about to ask for a dime for his assemblies. Monetization from both Meta and YouTube had been utterly negligible since his social media hadn't yet improved. There were incalculable paths to take in advertising, but as a novice and in a panic, he wasn't sure which one was the perfect choice, or if more than one existed. If that was the case, should he divide his budget evenly, or invest more in one and less in the other?

Heading home, he returned to the outdoor mall, feeling abysmally worthless beneath the stars and the glow of the mall's outdoor lighting. He was reminded of something he had noticed earlier that day while returning from his assemblies. He went to his favorite juice bar. As he waited for his smoothie, something in the trash can caught his eye. For years, he had left business cards everywhere (two for his books and a third one about his volunteer Autism Awareness speaking engagements). And there they were in the trash. Someone had folded them like useless napkins and thrown them in there. He pulled them from the trash in complete dismay, moving slowly in disbelief. He unfolded them and replaced them on the counter where he had originally left them, his mouth hanging open in sadness the entire time.

Now the pain was settling in, getting deeply offended that people showed utter disregard for Autism Awareness. Of course, he wasn't oblivious to that fact, but it was still shocking each time.

Is this 2024 or 2021? Or 2017? Or 2014? There is absolutely nothing I can do, is there? I'm chasing the wind. PR gets me on the news, but it rarely brings me an engaged following or book sales, so I cannot rely on a return on investment. The other PR firms will cost me between twenty and thirty thousand dollars, which I've been saving for. Whenever I advertise with Meta, Google, YouTube, and TikTok, I get many follows, likes, and comments from people, most of whom agree with me or thank me, but then I never see them again, unless I boost another video.

In a sudden flash, everything changed! It was as if the entire night sky opened like a curtain, shining with a brilliant, heavenly light. Without warning, Zachary's fears were completely washed away.

That's it! he thought, praying for his unexpected ethereal peace to remain as long as possible. *I had recently considered inquiring about becoming an adjunct professor in mathematics at Tributary University and at the junior college I attended. After all, I was told that with a master's degree, I could teach at that level! All I need now is patience until fall.*

Walking the remaining distance home that night, he maintained his peace and optimism, gripping them like a coin of pure gold. Once he was in his room, he knew he had to type out what had happened with those guys, sharing it with the world as he had in similar times past. Once he opened Instagram and pasted his writing to his story, he decided to include background music. Searching for something inspirational about perseverance, he was captivated by a chillhop track called "Keep Going" by Swørn. Since it was nine o'clock at night, he was worn out and chose to figure everything out in the morning.

To his unexpected surprise, when morning came, he found that his Instagram story had gone viral. Several dozen users reached out to him with messages of encouragement. He felt revived as he gained more support than he did when that skateboarder almost beat him in 2022 and when he had that encounter with the two bicyclists in 2021.

After processing everything, he was ready to organize his tasks.

First, he picked various YouTube videos, Instagram reels, Facebook reels, and TikTok videos to promote directly through the platforms' official tools.

I put in so much effort into these Autism Awareness videos. Since the algorithms seem to suppress me, despite all the SEO and keywords I've incorporated, then I'll simply advertise directly on their own platforms and force my videos to be seen—educating ableists that we're not aliens, raising awareness and acceptance among nondisabled people, and motivating disabled individuals and their families to keep going! I firmly believe last night wouldn't have happened if my videos hadn't been suppressed. Heck, for years nobody told me to stick to one niche; I just wanted one channel to share videos from my heart.

Next, he emailed Dr. Cornelius to request an urgent in-person meeting.

Finally, he decided to go along with a company from Boca Raton, Florida, that had reached out to him, purporting to produce audiobooks from his books. That Sunday after church, he had a consultation call with one of their employees. Feeling reassured of their credibility as a result, he signed the contract and paid the $359 upfront fee. It was a gamble with his PR and advertising budget, but they assured him it would boost his story. All he cared about was for disabled people to believe in their purpose in life and encourage neurotypicals to stop bullying.

After sending the payment, he returned to the boulevard and made a video at the site of his encounter, explaining exactly what had transpired.

After describing what this form of bullying does to the minds of autistic individuals, especially those who were less strong than he was, he offered a heartfelt thank-you to everyone who had sent him messages, playing a slideshow of screenshots he had taken, having previously edited out their names for privacy.

Since that moment in his life, that chillhop song, "Keep Going," became a favorite. He would play it whenever he needed a boost in perseverance and patience, remembering all the support he did have.

A few weeks of sleepless nights went by … *literally.* Zachary couldn't wait to speak with Dr. Cornelius. Once they finally found a time that worked for both of them, he asked him if he could help him secure a position there as an adjunct professor. Meanwhile, he had already applied to the junior college.

His master plan was to sacrifice a day or two of substitute teaching to teach math. He figured he could teach four or five evenings a week too. That way, he could continue subbing, conduct assemblies, gain invaluable classroom experience while awaiting a full-time career in secondary education, and significantly increase his income for advertising and PR. He believed that he would eventually reach a point where he'd no longer need to boost a video again and could instead focus solely on PR, working his way up to more expensive PR, speaking for national audiences in multiple English-speaking countries. Ultimately, he hoped he'd get to a point where PR would no longer be necessary—where news outlets, large and small, would consistently request interviews for the rest of his life.

Dr. Cornelius was ecstatic about the idea of Zachary working as an adjunct professor, saying he would help since he had connections.

* * *

In mid-May, Zachary was walking over to his local juice bar.

"Hey, Mr. Corwin!" a tenth-grader called out, wearing a varsity jacket for Ironwood Peak. He stood by the door, holding it open for Zachary.

"Jake? From Mrs. Porter's class?"

"Yeah," he confirmed as they walked in. Ben Rector's "Brand New" played on their ceiling speakers.

"How are you? How's math class?" Zachary asked.

"It's fun. I have a solid A. We're learning basic trig functions now."

"That's incredible. SOH-CAH-TOA, right?"

"Yep. What're you getting?"

"One of my favorites: the raspberry smoothie."

"Ah, okay. How's life?"

"It's good," Zachary said as Jake began to order two drinks. When he was done, Zachary continued, "I'm still subbing across the district and doing my volunteer assemblies."

"That's sick. Good for you."

"Are you ready to order?" asked the employee.

"Uh—" Zachary started.

"No, it's good," Jake interrupted. "I ordered the drink for you."

Zachary looked at him, unable to find the right words. "Oh, uh, you did?"

Jake nodded.

"Um, do you need me to, uh—" he stuttered, reaching for his wallet.

"No, I bought it for you. Don't worry about it."

Beaming with gratitude that a student bought a smoothie for him, he said, "Wow. You might not understand why I put it this way, but this is quite an … unexpected surprise. Thank you so much, Jake."

"Don't worry about it," he replied as they walked closer to the front, waiting for their smoothies. "Hey, some of us recently saw you at the high school, juggling in the library's meeting room."

"Oh yes, I was invited by the PTA to be this month's speaker. I thought that was you in the library. I was too busy concentrating on my words, juggling, and tricks, but I did notice lots of students peeking through the glass during my speech, as well as through the glass doors ahead that led to the hallway. I've worked desperately hard to be in all the schools, and the PTA knows that. Unfortunately, the principal missed it, but he already knows about my willingness to speak. In fact, in 2019, after publishing my novel, he asked me to speak, but then COVID happened. Now that the high school's PTA has heard me speak, they'll arrange for me to speak to all 2,200 students."

"That's epic! They better let you. You're like *famous* in this district."

"Time will tell. My former special education teacher was there, and she was in tears after my speech. Oh, and also, I spoke and juggled during Canyon Mountain's PTA meeting a couple of weeks before that. They seemed to reassure me that I could still do my mini-assemblies and make a difference in each of their lives, even though Dr. Peterson said no for … *whatever reason*."

"Ah, that sucks. I *so* hope you'll speak there too! My little brother now goes there. He's autistic as well, and he kept getting bullied and name-called badly. He finally mentioned it a month ago after keeping it to himself."

Zachary shuddered in anger but kept his composure, though his feelings were exacerbated by the sudden shriek of the blender firing up. He believed wholeheartedly that he may have been able to prevent it. *I wonder what on earth Dr. Peterson is thinking now*, he thought. *I hadn't heard from her within the past month. Hadn't she finally realized she needed to ask me to speak to* all *students in order to put an end to such bullying of autistic individuals, or any disability? Hadn't she realized that some neurotypical students still need to be educated?*

"Hey, I heard the news that your second book came out. Congratulations!" Jake said.

"Thanks." Zachary nodded, trying to uplift his own spirits so that Jake wouldn't think he was upset with him out of the blue.

"I remember you asking me permission if you could insert my letter of gratitude that I wrote for you a couple of years ago."

"Yes, I included it."

"Can't wait to read it, perhaps over summer."

Just then, the employee announced that the smoothies were ready.

"Well, later," Jake said with a smile, pulling out the keys to his truck from his jeans pocket.

"Wait. You're driving now?"

"Yeah. I got my license last month after I turned sixteen."

Speechless, Zachary stood there, marveling at how fast time had flown, having first met Jake when he was thirteen.

After Jake left, Zachary stayed inside to drink his smoothie. Seated at one of the tables, he couldn't get over the guilt he felt. He knew that many people supported him and accepted him as a human being. Why would he get angry over all the ableists? Then again, he wasn't the only disabled person who was being treated horribly by some.

I'm not trying to reinvent the wheel here, for crying out loud. I acknowledge that anti-bullying campaigns have existed for decades now, but we mustn't stop fighting harder. Every new generation needs to be raised with strong morals, learning about the different disabilities that bring diversity to the world. And I support other advocates out there too. I wish them the amount of success that they're looking for, depending on what they're comfortable with. Some people are satisfied with 100 followers, 1,000 followers, or 100,000 followers. For me, however, I'm not *stopping until eight billion people know that they have a purpose, disability or not, and that bullying is not part of it.*

After a moment of winding down from all his thoughts, he pulled out his phone to check his notifications. The first post that popped up on Instagram was from a national news media outlet. At first, Zachary saw a picture of a blond-haired boy in glasses with a big radiant smile. What he read underneath rattled him to the core, nearly dropping his phone on the ground: "This 10-year-old boy just committed suicide via asphyxiation for being bullied endlessly at school."

A gunshot reverberated in Zachary's mind, making him jolt in his seat as he was taken back to the day Thomas shot himself. He felt isolated and distant from the world around him. He began to mourn the boy, even though he had never known him. After all, he lived hundreds of miles away in a different state. The same thing happened when he found out that Naomi Judd's cause of death was also a self-inflicted gunshot wound, back in 2022.

He wondered if all the people around him, in the juice bar and outside it, knew what had happened. If they did, how many of them would care as much as he did? He wondered. He himself had been begged to commit suicide a year prior through those YouTube comments. With bullies thinking it's okay to push an innocent person toward suicide, it's no wonder why the world keeps hearing about it.

He began feeling angry again, not necessarily *at* the people who chose to take their own lives, but at the fact that it happened. It could have been prevented. He was also perturbed at the hypothetical notion that some people in the world were either callous about it or glorified it. This wasn't the first time Zachary had opened social media and seen a picture of a child, underneath which described their suicide.

What angered him most wasn't just that the person was a child; it was that bullying had contributed to it. He desired to pound the table in front of him, but he didn't want to be kicked out of the juice bar indefinitely. He knew this might have been prevented if someone like him had spoken at his school. If he had lived in that state, he would have definitely offered his free assemblies there too.

With a proactive mindset, knowing that child or teen suicide could strike anywhere, he felt more apprehensive than ever. Feeling discouraged again by the incredibly low amount of assembly requests so far, he sent Dr. Cornelius an email as soon as he got home. He asked if he, or someone in the county's Department of Education, could help him speak at every single school *no matter what.* He didn't tell him about the recent suicide, but that was what made him start to fight harder than ever—harder than he already was.

At this point in time, there were still several districts … *not just schools* … who never reached out to him yet. Only a couple of people from the vendor fair he participated in had contacted him. Members of his own district's school board told him they had passed his information along to all the other boards in the county, yet nothing came of it. There were still hundreds of public schools in his county alone, not counting the private schools. The couple of dozen schools he visited so far hardly made up five percent of all the schools in his county.

Meanwhile, he prayed earnestly for no more suicides as he fought to reach every school and prevent them before they could happen.

56

A Meeting with Dr. Vanderwyk

"Hi! You must be Zachary Corwin," a middle-aged woman said, clad in an amethyst dress.

"Yes, I am," he replied. "Dr. Vanderwyk?"

"Yes, sir. Step inside my office." After being seated in a small office room at the county's Department of Education, she straightened her black-rimmed reading glasses and asked, "So, how do you know my friend, Dr. Cornelius?"

"I took the credential program at Tributary University, and he was one of my professors. I also took their master's program over there. As of this month, I'm officially 'Zachary Corwin, M.Ed.'"

"Congratulations! You have to be so proud of yourself. Earning your master's is a major achievement in your education. It opens a lot of doors, especially in the teaching field."

"Thank you. Well, I have high respect for people like you and everyone else who had pursued their doctorate. The master's was grueling enough. I currently don't have any plans for an Ed.D. even though many friends of mine are already encouraging me."

"You'd definitely need to be passionate about research. You'd also need to weigh the pros and cons to decide if it's worth it. I've been working here for the county's Department of Education for thirty-five years now. I was definitely able to put what I learned in my doctoral program to good use. I have no regrets, but not everyone needs a doctorate. Are you planning to be a teacher your whole life, or do you eventually want to become a principal or join the school board?"

"A math teacher until they throw me out. I don't plan to retire until I'm forced to because it's all I ever wanted to be. I love math, breaking down concepts, and finding the ways math is applied in real life. That would definitely solve the perennial question, 'When are we going to use this in real life?'"

"Ha-ha, you have quite the passion. If every teacher shared the same sentiment, imagine the impact it'll have on students. Education would be transformed, and this world would be a better place. Well, a doctorate might not be needed in your case then, but I don't want to discourage you. You're only, what? Um?"

"Twenty-eight."

"Exactly. Things might change in the future. You still have your whole life ahead of you and a rewarding career, now with a master's. Do you know when you'll start?"

"Well, uh, it might be a few years. That's partly why I came in today. Meanwhile, I'm a substitute teacher."

"Amazing. How long had you been a sub for? And how many schools?"

"Three years now. I've subbed in almost thirty schools in my district, over fifteen thousand students so far."

"Wow, you're unquestionably passionate then. I used to sub, many moons ago, and I couldn't handle being in a different class every single day. Kudos to you. How has the reception been."

"Mostly positive."

"That's good."

"Most students are kind. A small fraction, however, seem to take advantage of me or are outright mean. Only *one* time in three years did I have to walk out, and it happened a couple of months ago. I was subbing sixth-graders who wouldn't listen to me for more than ten seconds at a time. *All* morning. At recess, one of them asked how my day was going, and I replied, 'You don't want to know.' I spent all of recess and lunch sitting at the teacher's desk, just depressed. I felt completely defeated. I had even written an entire math lesson on the whiteboard, but once I started, ninety percent of them didn't want to hear it. I promised to show them card tricks if we get through each assignment, which is part of my reward system, but it didn't matter, despite them begging to see one. I was like, 'That's not how it works.'"

"Aw, I feel so bad for you. How did you cope with that, or what was going through your mind?"

"It was hard. I felt totally devalued and disrespected. During recess and lunch, I was forcing myself to continue. I felt like I would be a 'quitter' and a hypocrite if I gave up on those students. I reminded myself of what motivated me in the past: 'I belong here today' and 'I'm called here to be a light in these lives.' That worked before, but that day was a different story. I kept thinking about my heroes in education: Ron Clark, Brad Cohen, and even Dr. Cornelius. Sure, they had difficult days too, but … *still.* I didn't want to walk out on them and get an admin to take over. Heck, I was subbing another difficult class at another school just a few months prior, also for sixth grade. The principal apologized to me and said she could take over for the final hour, but I told her that I'm willing to continue, and I did! Now, I'm all depressed, telling the office manager in a shaky voice that I can't continue after lunch. She understood and got the assistant principal to take over."

"Well, Zachary, you will have days like that. It comes with the territory. I'm amazed that you lasted as long as you did that day, but next time, don't be overstraining yourself like that. You need to remember to take care of yourself too. Even if you had stayed, it sounds like you wouldn't have been as effective as a substitute. Don't ever think of it as giving up; you needed a break for your well-being. Those students simply need more discipline in their lives."

"Thank you for the consolation. It was the Friday before President's Week. I would've brooded over it all week, but then a miracle happened the next day." Zachary held up seven fingers. "Seven!" he said as his countenance lit up. "That's the number of students who messaged me … *of their own volition.* They must've all found me on Instagram and apologized for how they and their class acted. They owned up to their behavior, apologized like mature students, wished me a good week off, hoped I would feel better, and said they wanted me to be their substitute teacher again. They acknowledged the effort I put into teaching them and said they enjoyed the card trick I showed them at the start. And get this: even the one student who was *absent* that day messaged me, apologizing for how her class acted and saying that I had every right to let the principal know."

"You are *kidding.*" Dr. Vanderwyk was amazed, her face flushed as tears threatened to spill from her eyes.

"I've received apology letters from students before, usually because their teachers made them. While I do believe those students were genuine too, this was perhaps one of the most reassuring and most validating moments in my three years working for the school district."

"I could imagine. Good heavens, that story nearly made me teary-eyed. There must be something about you that encourages students. Do you know what other faculty or parents say?"

"Many teachers and administrators, including principals, compliment me for being a 'good sub.' Last September, I ran into a group of students and parents who seemed to be on their way to a formal event. They said hi, and one of the mothers instantly knew who I was. She said, 'It is such a pleasure to meet you. I've been wanting to meet you for years now. You are such a gift and blessing to these kids, and the way you are with them is remarkable. I genuinely can't thank you enough."

"*Aw!* Well, I could speak to you for hours about this, but time is running short. I know you had another topic you wanted to discuss. So, tell me what brings you in today?"

Zachary explained everything to Dr. Vanderwyk over the next twenty minutes, emphatically describing his zeal to change every life in his county through his volunteer assemblies, letting her know that, to date, he had spoken to over eight thousand students.

She applauded his efforts, saying she would try her best to spread his information around.

He walked away, feeling less optimistic than before, but he remained hopeful.

A few days later, Zachary was invited to serve as the keynote speaker at a graduation for students with moderate and severe disabilities. After his twenty-minute message that was packed with all his tricks, dozens of people complimented him, saying it was the greatest keynote speech they had ever seen or heard. It was an acknowledgement that made him feel proud, knowing it had encouraged, motivated, and resonated with so many.

57

Money Pit

"Speak, oh wise one," said Pastor Nguyen one Sunday after church in late June, sounding a smidgen tired, his maroon necktie hanging loose, but eager to hear anything Zachary needed to say. Surrounding both of them were all the bandmates and a few trusted members of the church. Apart from them, no one else was present in the vast sanctuary. It was so bare that every spoken word reverberated through all the open space.

"Well, first, I want to thank you all for sticking around at the last minute. I hope you'll excuse me for being a bit vulnerable, but as a Christian, I feel I need to make a confession to all of you in whom I place a great deal of trust."

"Just take your time, and speak what's in your heart," said the electric guitarist.

Exhaling, Zachary said, "So, the school district sent out an email, asking subs with teaching certificates if they'd be interested in teaching a four-week course at one of the high schools. It's for credit recovery (for those who failed math last year). I applied to teach the algebra course, just to see what would happen. It'd be my first actual teaching job, albeit only for four weeks. I wasn't getting my hopes high or anything."

Zachary nervously heard his voice echo around the room, fearing that he was stuttering or beating around the bush, but he was grateful for their undivided attention. He continued, "They decided to interview me. I prepared by reviewing sample interview questions for teachers and donned my necktie. It was via Zoom, and the gentleman asked only a few questions, which was totally unexpected; I presumed it would be a full-blown interview. He thanked me and said they'd reach out once a decision is made."

"That sounds like an exciting opportunity," said the drummer. "Were you wanting us to pray for you to get the job, if the Lord wills?"

"No." Zachary, looking upset, shook his head. "Last night, they emailed me, saying I wasn't chosen."

"Ah," everyone moaned sympathetically, sinking in their seats.

"I was actually beginning to get excited, rehearsing my first lesson a few times. I don't know what is happening. Prayers seem to go unanswered."

"Zachary, I'm sorry to hear that, but remember, when one door closes, another will open," Pastor Nguyen said, consoling him.

"I just don't know what I'm going to do this summer, financially speaking. I mean, I'm not becoming a teacher for the money, but I realized that I can't survive anymore with what I make as a substitute teacher. June 30 will be my final paycheck from the school district, after which I won't receive another until September 30. I have no idea how I could possibly make my income last, due to all my monthly expenses. I'm sure the tutoring center won't hire me just for the summer.

"Moreover, I began considering to apply anywhere, even if it's a restaurant, coffee house, or whatever, but I don't know. I have a master's degree. That should count for something, right? Making coffee or whatnot? I don't have the mental bandwidth right now to learn a temporary trade, which probably wouldn't pay as much as subbing.

"You name it, and I've researched it over the past few months—passive income, semi-passive income, affiliate marketing, AI, or whatever mumbo-jumbo. I've watched countless hours of these guys, only to be slapped with, 'Oh, by the way, this is gonna cost you $2,000, or 3 payments of $1,000,'" Zachary said, shaking his head. "Others suggestions were free on YouTube. I've spent *hours* and *days* trying different things and lost some money as a result. I just don't know who to trust or which one I should invest in. My brain is just *scatterbrained* right now."

"Oh! … Huh?" Pastor Nguyen began to put two and two together. "Wait! Everything you just said, is *that* why, for the past month, you were trying to sell clothes, neckties, books, coins, stamps, clocks, flashlights, binoculars, cameras, and everything?"

"Yep," Zachary confirmed, nodding. "I was anticipating this summer for a little while. It was like 2018 all over again, doing whatever I could to raise the $3,600 for my novel."

"And once you had $3,600, that was ninety-five percent of all your money, right? And you spent all of it?"

"Yes," Zachary said, hearing gasps from some of his bandmates.

"I didn't know about that detail in your testimony," the violinist choked out.

"Hey, there was a need. I firmly believed that my novel could spread awareness and acceptance, and I still believe it will, once given a proper chance. If I was being discriminated in my neighborhood and online, then certainly there were people who needed to grow up and start believing that we disabled deserve a chance in life. I put in thousands of hours writing it, practically. Then all hell broke loose. I had to get republished, which was a slow, arduous trip through stress city. The media ignored me for three years until I found out what PR was. Same on social media; I've shared about my novel thousands of times. Rarely did anyone notice."

"Uh, Zachary," the acoustic guitarist chimed in, "Out of curiosity, how much would you have made this summer?"

"Based on my calculations, $4,000."

One of the singers inhaled sharply, widening her eyes in disbelief and sympathy. "That would've been $1,000 a week."

"And God knows, I sure could've used that for my mission in spreading Disability Acceptance and Inclusion."

"Yes, it's a noble mission—completely selfless—but you also have to remember to take care of yourself," the singer encouraged.

"I honestly stopped doing that in May 2021. '101% about everyone else and -1% about me,' I went on the record saying."

"Credit cards?" the electric guitarist interrupted.

"I already maxed out five of them."

"Aren't you still paying back student loans too?" asked Pastor Nguyen.

"Well, thank God, *literally*, I was just able to pause my monthly payments, temporarily. Forbearance, I believe it's called. There's no way … *just no way* … I could survive this summer if I had to pay them around $650 a month."

"Haven't you been saving all these years?" asked the bassist.

"Uh, well, that's sort of what I wanted to confess to you about. Listen, last month, a ten-year-old died by suicide, and the story made national headlines. If I was in that school district, I probably would've fought to do my assemblies before it happened, hoping it would've prevented it. That's why I don't charge for these assemblies. Even though I could never be in every school in the country, much less the world, I should still be able to reach everyone, right?"

Some of them nodded.

"Yes, I should, through my books and social media. Since I just found out I messed up the algorithms, I tried fixing it by promoting just my Autism Awareness videos. I posted Shorts, thinking, 'It just takes one to go viral.' When that didn't work fast enough, I spent everything on advertising—Google, YouTube, TikTok, and Meta. Before long, I spent nearly everything I had, and so far, it didn't work. My videos were getting engagement, but people weren't coming back. Some comments were trollish in nature, like, 'My brother and I aren't autistic, but we lined up toys as a kid. Calling this "autism" is laughable!' or, most commonly, 'Doesn't *everyone* do this?' I mean, the sheer ignorance. This is what I'm trying to dismantle through my advocacy videos, which I gladly volunteer making."

"Sheesh!" interjected the violinist, shaking her head. "It seems like a big trap. It's terrible."

"The PR campaign I had earlier this year was amazing. It landed me dozens of interviews for news, radio, and podcasts, but I hardly sold any books. I only got one or two comments on YouTube, saying they heard me on the radio, but that was it. No return on investment, financially, although I'm willing to spend millions of dollars and change billions of lives than to get money in return. Um, I guess I got carried away, if you know where I'm getting at."

Everyone in the sanctuary felt bad for him, but didn't yet know what to say.

Zachary continued, "So, I thought I'd continue to force my message out to everyone I could possibly reach, *without* shoving it down their throats at the same time. I told God that I'd sell everything I own if I have to, in order to make a difference, eradicate bullying, end suicides, et cetera. I prayed to Him hours on end, just like in 2021, although I wasn't prostrate on the ground again, fasting, or anointing myself with oil. I listed on eBay again, and, for the first time, I listed on Facebook Marketplace, but do you know what happened?"

Everyone shook their heads.

"Five minutes after listing my first item, I started chatting with a person who expressed interest in buying it. Then they said, 'For my safety, can I send you a 6-digit code.' After receiving the text on my phone, I got suspicious. While Googling about it, the person started getting agitated with me, asking whether I had received it. I found out he or she was trying to hack into my Google account or whatever. It was the first memory I got while trying to sell on Facebook Marketplace, endeavoring to make a difference in people's lives while stressing about economical burdens." Zachary shook his head.

"I'm sorry that happened to you," said the drummer. "You were wise to be cautious. But were you able to sell anything?"

"Yeah, I've sold eight or nine items so far, not just on Marketplace, but I also made an account on an app called Nextdoor, thinking I could sell on there too. It's convenient, since I meet buyers at a local park or the outdoor plaza, but once, I walked two miles just to sell a ten-dollar pair of binoculars. Again, I'll do anything.

"There was one incident, however. I was outside Staples, waiting for a guy. Ten minutes after our meet time, a Ford F-150 drove by. The driver looked at me and held up the peace sign with his fingers, yet was grimacing, which puzzled me. I figured he was the guy, so I waved back. Five minutes later, he slowly walked over, hands in his jeans pockets, seeming a bit angry, but I didn't want to assume; that may have been his normal expression. However, he just walked inside Staples after a brief glance and came out two minutes later, holding nothing. With his hands still in his pockets, he walked back to his car and left. I waited twenty more minutes and messaged the guy. According to Messenger, he saw it but didn't reply. I just walked away. To this day, I just don't know if that man was the guy or not, since there was no profile picture, but why would he stare at me from his truck and hold up the peace sign like that?"

"That was quite disturbing," said the singer.

"As for eBay," Zachary continued, "I started selling lots of coins and coin albums."

"Oh gosh," the pastor lamentingly said. "Your coin collection that you've spent your entire life building?"

"Mm-hmm," Zachary said, nodding. "Well, I decided to keep the Lincoln Cents, Jefferson Nickels, Roosevelt Dimes, and all the Washington Quarters. Everything else on the side, like my Franklin Halves, Ike and Presidential Dollars, old currency, Buffalo Nickels, Mercury Dimes—"

Everyone's eyes bugged out.

"I decided to sell them. It was painful, but I thought, 'Maybe I could recollect them later in life.' What helped me were Scripture verses that talked about treasures in Heaven instead of entropic treasures on earth, and how nothing is taken with us after this life anyway. I essentially invested most of my money in coins for over twenty years, so I was profiting a bit."

"And how much did you make from all of that?"

"Well, I only sold a third of them so far. Roughly $1,500. I would've made more if eBay stopped taking a ton out of it. I found out what Fiverr is, but I can't think of anything to offer that wouldn't put me in competition with hundreds of other users. Teachers Pay Teachers? I couldn't think of anything new or different. I did try a few eBay promos on Fiverr. While I was at it, I tried several book promos too. In total, I completely wasted around five-hundred dollars."

A couple of bandmates shook their heads, rubbing their hands across their faces. "I wish someone could've warned you," said the cellist. "I wished you hadn't done this alone."

"I learned a costly lesson. I went to various coin shops throughout May and they wouldn't take them. A philatelic shop wouldn't buy my old stamps since they were so common. I wouldn't have known anyway as I never became interested in stamps; a friend gave them to me. I also went to a bookstore to sell a couple hundred books, but after all that, they only bought twenty of them for fifteen dollars. Alas, Fiverr wasn't the only lesson that came at a great price." Zachary closed his eyes and shook his head, swinging forward to clutch the backrest of the pew in front of him, resting his head on the back of his hands for a couple of seconds.

All eyes widened as they straightened in their seats, concerned about what he would say next.

"Listen, I will never do this again! I thought, 'It just takes *one* scratcher.'"

Many began to press their hands to their faces in sympathy, some moaning softly.

"Let's say you got the grand prize, which is one in a gazillion," the electric guitarist pondered aloud, "after all the taxes are taken out, would you honestly gamble *all* of it with PR and ads."

Without any hesitation or giving it a second thought, Zachary straightened up, stared at him in his eyes, and asserted determinedly, "*Yes I will.*"

"Okay," he said quickly, looking to the side. "No further questions."

"*I* have a question, though," said the drummer. "How much money did you lose in the lottery?"

"U-Uh … *Ummm—*" Zachary knew there was no escape. "I won hundreds of dollars … but not without wasting a few thousand."

Some began to wail.

"Look, I'm *desperate*!" Zachary said in his defense. "The cheap ones had prizes of $20,000 to $30,000. That would be perfect for me to start the more expensive PR, which would finally help my books become bestsellers, boost my online presence, get me on national news, and make me a leading authority. And yes! I checked these firms out first. I communicated with them. I read their testimonials. They're legit.

"Listen, everyone, as I told God, I'd rather use this one short life, which is only a vapor, to make a difference to humanity than spend an eternity in Heaven without having done anything on Earth … and I'm literally stuck in quicksand. I can't get my content out there on social media, though I post every day, and I can't get in the news media without PR."

"Okay, I'm sure we all understand everything we need to," said Pastor Nguyen, taking charge of the conversation. "Zachary, maybe teaching this summer wasn't meant to be. What if you had gotten that job, but something awful would've happened?"

Bandmates started nodding their heads in agreement.

"Maybe those kids wouldn't have listened to you," the pastor continued. "They might fail their test at the end, and you'd get bad references from the school district as a result. The students might hurt you. They might get in a fight. You might try to intervene but end up getting fired. God saying no might be His way of protecting you from something you can't see."

Zachary exhaled, nodding as he tried to keep the faith. "I feel like everything that can go wrong in a person's life is going wrong in mine at the moment. *I know what to do, and I know what needs to be done!* I see the need out there. I hate being discriminated just for a disability. I hate seeing people commit suicide; I don't care how young or old they were, it shouldn't happen. I have the resources in my books and social media, but no one's seeing them!"

"Zachary," one of the singers said gently, her voice calm and reassuring, "I know this will be difficult to hear, especially since you're still young, but *everything* you described, that's life! Ten years ago, when my husband was furloughed without warning, neither of us could understand why. We prayed and searched for answers, but every job application was rejected. He even applied for positions that didn't interest him, but we needed to eat and have a roof over our heads."

A few eyes in the room began to well up as she was recounting the story, including Zachary's.

Almost tearfully, the singer continued, "We had to lean on our family and the church for support. It was the most painful storm we've ever faced, but we held onto our faith, trusting that God was working, even when we couldn't see it. Today, my husband has a job far better than the one he lost. Looking back, if he had stayed where he was, we wouldn't be where we are now. Let that be a lesson: what felt like a setback was, in reality, divine protection, guidance, and redirection in our lives."

"Zach," said the violinist, "this is just a thought, but had you considered private, independent tutoring? I think you'd be an excellent math tutor for my grandson. He's twelve."

Everyone began nodding.

"Uh … *yeah*," Zachary said, perking up. "For some reason, I used to think it was unlawful for me to work in the school district and tutor students on the side. I know that was against the policy at the tutoring center I used to work at. Ugh, I tend to process things more slowly and learn stuff the hard way. I guess that's quite a circuitous way of saying yes, I'm definitely willing to do that."

"Excellent! Let me talk with his parents, and I'll text you, okay?"

"Sure, thank you."

"And I'll see if I know anyone who needs tutoring too," a few other bandmates said.

"We'll be praying for you for sure, Zachary," said the pastor. "We truly appreciate you confessing this to us so that you're not walking through this alone."

"It feels so great to get this out of me. Truthfully, in the end, I know this is edifying me."

"It's because you're experiencing life and gaining wisdom as a result," the pastor confidently remarked.

"Absolutely. After facing what I had gone through in the summer of 2021, I felt equipped to tackle more storms of life, while being able to help others walk through theirs. It is quite timely we played that song today, 'Eye of the Storm,' by Ryan Stevenson."

After a lengthy prayer, Zachary walked home. He felt more hopeful, but he couldn't fight off all the burdens.

* * *

"Zachary!" Pastor Nguyen approached him as church ended the following Sunday. Handing him a white envelope, he explained, "We, as a church, are considering you qualified for some assistance, so this is a little $500 check to help get you through the summer."

Humbly receiving it, he said, "I don't know what to say. I wasn't asking for a handout, but I definitely appreciate this."

"Don't worry about it. We care about you, and we thank you for all the work you do for our church. You've faithfully served our worship ministry, Royal Rangers, the seniors at the chapel before COVID, the tech team, and everything else, all voluntarily too."

"Well, it was all from my heart. It's been giving me purpose and a sense of belonging in life. Thank you again for this; I promise I won't gamble it away."

"Ha-ha, I'm sure you won't. So, how's this past week been?"

"*Progress*! I'll put it that way. On Monday, I went to my old church, asking if their children, teens, or college students needed any tutoring. They gladly accepted my résumé and said that the various pastors would spread the word."

"That's excellent! I hope you get some clients from it."

"Please continue praying."

"You got it, Zachary. Also, I encourage you to pray the Lord's Prayer too; not just your own words."

"I've got that memorized since 2021, and on that note, those were quite befitting songs that we played today in the worship band: 'The Lord's Prayer (It's Yours)' by Matt Maher and 'Your Love Is Strong' by Jon Foreman."

"Absolutely."

"On Friday, I tutored for the first time at Hemingway Beacon Library, the one next to the park. It was for the violinist's grandson. That went very well. Yesterday, I worked here for two hours. The usher captain had me raking, dusting, sweeping, you name it. He handed me a hundred-dollar bill afterward, saying, 'It's so great seeing a person who wants to work for his money. Kids nowadays make millions while being lazy on the internet, but if something crashes big time in our world, so will their income. Without a college education, where do they think they'll go?'"

"Exactly," the pastor said, nodding. "Well, I'm thankful things are starting to improve for you."

"Amen," replied Zachary with a smile. "And hey, I posted my tutoring services on Nextdoor and a few local Facebook pages. Deep down, however, it just feels weird to be tutoring for the money. It's in my heart to help students. For over a decade, I was always willing to tutor, free of charge, as you know."

"But it's necessary with your situation, and you're still helping them."

"True. Anyway, someone already asked me to tutor her two high schoolers next Wednesday."

"There you go! Remember, it's one day at a time."

58

The Ableist in Uniform

"Hey, Zach! Need a ride?" a friend of his asked, pulling up beside him in his lustrous blue Ford Mustang.

"Hi, Charlie. Hmm, I was going to walk, but … okay. I'm heading to Hemingway Beacon Library to tutor math."

"The one next to the park? Sure, hop in!"

"Thank you," he said, closing the front passenger door and buckling up.

"No sweat. I saw you walking and thought I'd offer."

Five minutes later, just as Zachary hopped out of the Mustang, he glanced at his watch and saw that he was ten minutes early.

"Thanks again, Charlie!"

One second later, Zachary heard a very loud, "*Hey!*"

Looking up, he saw a student rushing up to him, coming from the playground forty yards away. The playground was packed with children and surrounded by parents. Two other students followed her. Zachary noticed that her voice caught the attention of one of the security guards, who swung around upon hearing it.

"Hi," Zachary replied with a wave. "Cunningham Elementary. It's Samantha, right?"

"Yep!"

"Yes, I remember you. Mr. Flores' fifth-grade class."

"Aren't you Mr. Corwin?" asked a woman, coming up from behind the children. "Hey, I remember you. You spoke for the PTA at Ironwood Peak High a few months ago. You are such an inspiration."

"Thank you, I appreciate it. It's been my goal to give that message to every student."

"We were just leaving, but I'm glad we had this opportunity to say hi. What're you doing here today?"

"I got into math tutoring this summer."

"Oh?"

"Yeah, so I'm meeting two new clients at the library over there."

"Well, I'll keep you in mind if I know anyone who needs tutoring."

"I greatly appreciate it. Thank you."

"Well, it's good to see you again," said the woman. "Good luck to you."

"*Bye!*" Samantha called, giving him a quick high-five.

Zachary turned around and headed toward the library, just beyond the playground. Halfway there, he passed the aforementioned security guard keeping watch over the park through mirrored shades. His hands rested on his hips. His black ball cap marked the private security agency he worked for. Zachary thought he was seeing his reflection, as the security guard was nearly as thin as he was, but not as tall.

Continuing along the serpentine, semi-crowded pathway, he reached the front of the library, where he arranged to meet his clients. A dozen people were scattered around, yet none acknowledged his presence, which told him his clients weren't there yet. Not knowing what they look like, he kept an eye out for a woman with two teens who looked to be in high school, one male and the other female.

At this point, he was five minutes early, so he decided to walk around the entire building, just in case they were there. Sauntering down the side of the library, weaving through a half dozen people and families, he quickly glanced back just in time to see the security guard march briskly around the corner.

Wait, Zachary thought a moment later as he continued forward, fear wrapping around him like a shroud. *Was that security guard* glowering *at me?*

Shrugging it off with a silent chuckle, knowing that he always assumed the worst, he continued circling the entire building, though he didn't dare look back. Still not seeing anyone who appeared to be his clients, he sat on the bench in front of the entrance, checking his messages and notifications on his phone. Many families walked in and out of the library, while several people lingered outside, talking with one another.

A moment later, a voice called out from behind him, "Excuse me, sir. Can I sit next to you for a minute?"

"Oh, sure," Zachary said, turning to see the security guard approaching him. "Absolutely."

"Thanks," he said as he sat down.

Seated underneath trees, Zachary assumed the guard needed shade from the sweltering July sun.

"How're you doing?"

"I'm doing good," he answered the guard who seemed to be wanting a cordial conversation. "I'm waiting for a couple of people to arrive. I'm a math tutor."

"Okay, so what's *your* name?" he asked, sounding as if he were sucking on a couple of Life Savers.

"Zachary."

"Zachary? Where are you from, Zachary?"

"From here—born and raised in this city."

"How old are you?" The guard seemed to be leaning closer to his face, talking just like the drunk whom Zachary tried to help at the county fair back in 2019.

"28. I'll be 29 in a few weeks."

"Okay. Do you have kids?"

Zachary began wondering where the guard was going with his line of questioning. Getting very creeped out, he calmly replied, "No."

After four seconds of silence, the guard reached the crux. In a deliberate, forceful voice, he said, "May I ask why you approached those kids over there?"

In that instant, everything clicked. Zachary knew exactly what was going on. Liquid fire pulsed around his quivering heart, echoing the terror of a person falsely accused of murder, with no one around to defend him. "U-uh … Oh, no, they recognized me from subbing for their class."

"So, you work at an elementary school?"

"For the district."

"The district? You're a *teacher*."

"Substitute teacher."

"*Substitute* teacher." After a few additional seconds of awkward silence, he asked, "So, you're just here, hanging out at the public library waiting to tutor someone? Is that what you said?"

"Yes … Yeah, she reached out to me on Nextdoor recently."

"Oh, okay. And how old is *she*?"

"Um … uh—" he stammered, feeling scrutinized as if he were a mouse in the crosshairs of a cat's vision. "Uh, the people I'm tutoring?"

"Mm-hmm."

"Well, um, the mother said eighth grade and tenth grade." Zachary wasn't about to divulge personal information, being a responsible school employee and math tutor. He didn't care if it was a security guard asking such questions.

"Okay. How often do you come here, and do you tutor inside the library?"

"Well, honestly, last Friday was the first time, but that was a different student. I'm just learning how to book a study room, which is better than outside, but today, I'll be tutoring at those tables over there."

"Okay, Zachary. Nice meeting you, man," he said, standing up and walking away.

"It's nice to meet you too. And what's *your* name?"

"My name is 'Security Guard.'"

"Okay," Zachary said, smirking inwardly. It was the final proof that the guard didn't believe a word he said. The obvious disdain in his voice only reinforced his certainty. Trying not to escalate the situation over the guard's ableist insinuation (and instead hoping to bring a bit of kindness to his drab life), he called, "Well, nice to meet you."

"Likewise. Take good care of yourself."

One minute passed. Zachary, shaking like a leaf on this hot summer afternoon, pulled out his phone to check his notifications. His clients were to arrive at any moment. Just then, a car pulled up in front of him. A boy hopped out with a few library books. They made eye-contact as he walked inside the library. Seconds later, the boy stepped out and glanced at him, giving a wave. Zachary gave a nod and a smile, ever so subtly, trying not to make it noticeable. The boy, whom he had subbed for in the past, got back in his mother's car, and they drove off.

Zachary was nervous to death, frightened to look over his shoulder. Suddenly, his phone in his hand began to vibrate. Having his blood pressure instantaneously raised as tall as the two-story library, he answered the phone. It was the mother saying they were stuck in traffic and would be five minutes late.

Oh swell! Zachary lamented as he hung up the phone, but he understood their situation.

Without warning, he heard the security guard walking up from behind him and asking, "Hey, I got one final question for you, man!"

"Yeah?"

"If you don't have kids, why would you be hanging out on a playground?" His tone was louder, more serious, and less friendly.

"Huh?"

"You were hanging out on the playground over there. Why would you be hanging out on a playground?"

That's a freaking lie! Zachary exclaimed in his mind, desiring to yell it in his face. Maintaining his composure and handling the predicament civilly, he explained, "I walked *by* the playground, not *through* it, sir. I went down the pathway because I was dropped off at the cross street over there. You saw that. Plus, I didn't know if the family arrived yet."

"Okay," he said, clearly unconvinced. "So, I'm gonna say this—that looked suspicious to me: a grown man to be hanging out on the playground."

"Oh—" Zachary tried to defend himself.

Cutting him off immediately, the guard continued his rampage of deceits, saying, "You looked suspicious to all the other people too, and they noticed it. So, in the future, if I were you, I wouldn't do that!"

Zachary stared at him, unable to believe the barrage of false accusations being hurled at him. *What're you talking about, sir? I've never stepped foot on the playground, and you know what? My bodycam will freaking prove it! What do you mean that other people saw it, especially when the 'it' never happened? Check the freaking security cameras that surround this library and park, you ableist!* As much as he wanted to say all that, he restrained himself from doing so. Instead, he said, "Okay. All right."

"I appreciate it, Zachary. Just know—*I see you.*" As the security guard strutted away with his chin held high, thinking of himself as some big hero, he glanced back over his shoulder. Though Zachary's head was facing back toward his phone, the guard, while still moving forward, fixed his gaze on him. The strangest look was etched on his face as if he assumed Zachary was a lying, childish, autistic clown who probably hadn't earned a high school diploma, much less a master's. He looked back ahead before disappearing like a phantom around the corner.

Moments later, Zachary looked up and saw a woman and her daughter.

"Hey," said the woman with a great big smile. "Are you Zachary?"

"Y-yeah," Zachary said, forcing a smile.

"Hi, nice to meet you. I'm Lucy. This is my daughter, Esperanza."

"Well, it's a pleasure to make your acquaintance."

Esperanza, expressionless, gave a subtle nod.

"Obviously, she's excited to learn math," Lucy said sarcastically. "So, where will you be tutoring at?"

"I was thinking about tutoring at those tables over there."

"Ah, perfect," Lucy said as they all walked over. Zachary's heart started to pound, but when he saw no sign of the guard anywhere, he felt momentary relief.

"Is this fine, Esperanza?" Zachary asked.

"Mm-hmm."

"So, I'll be back in an hour to pick her up and drop off my son," Lucy explained.

"Uh, okay," Zachary said, quickly smiling and nodding, but began to panic inside, not knowing beforehand that she was going to leave the premises.

After Lucy left, Zachary asked Esperanza which math she was studying in summer school, for she didn't come with any worksheets or textbooks. All she had was a brand-new notepad and a pencil.

"Just credit recovery."

"Okay, so my guess would be algebra?"

"Mm-hmm."

"Okay, so how about slope and graphing lines?" As Zachary began to write a problem in her notepad, he couldn't control his right hand from shaking. Trying hard to suppress it, he felt nervous that Esperanza would notice and wonder if there was something wrong with him. Fortunately, she didn't notice, and Zachary continued his tutoring session for the next hour."

"Um, is that Rodrigo?" Zachary asked Lucy once she returned with her son.

"Yes!" Lucy said, sounding surprised. "How do you know him?"

"From Canyon Mountain. I student taught there in 2022. Every time he'd walk past me, he said that he subscribed to my YouTube channel. I've subbed for one of his classes before too."

Lucy marveled, saying, "What a small world. Anyway, Esperanza and I will be inside the library. See you in an hour."

Zachary felt more reassured as he and Rodrigo walked to the table.

"Okay, so that went well," Zachary said an hour later. "If you'd like me to tutor you again in the future—"

"Yes! I want you to be my tutor," Rodrigo interrupted.

"I'm grateful to hear that and to be of help. So next time, we can practice more exponent laws."

"All right, thank you," Rodrigo said, offering to shake his hand.

After the handshake, they walked toward the entrance, where Lucy and Esperanza were exiting.

"Thank you, Zachary," said Lucy. "Hey, I'd like us to meet every week if that'd be okay with you. Esperanza said that she understands a lot more now."

No words could describe the feelings Zachary felt, grateful to hear how much he had helped both teens.

Parting ways, Zachary took the long way around. On film, he recounted the entire encounter with the security guard and explained what led up to it. By the time he was done, his camera battery was drained.

While filming off and on to sort out his thoughts, he noticed several high schoolers down the boulevard selling Fourth-of-July fireworks, all greeting him. Their Bluetooth speakers were blasting patriotic songs. As he was waving back, he suddenly froze, fearing that the security guard would jump out of nowhere, asking him why he would be waving at high schoolers.

It's just remarkable, Zachary said to himself, trying to understand why he was living this life. *Just yesterday, I was standing at the stoplight over there, waiting for the walk sign, when two students in two different cars, a minute apart, saw me and waved, their eyes lighting up. Why can't that security guard—or any other ableist who refuses to see me as a safe, trustworthy, competent human being with degrees, books, and a caring heart—just witness the thousands of times students said hi to me, on* and *off campus? What if that boy who returned his books said, 'Hey, Mr. Corwin,' while that guard was talking to me?*

Getting closer to his house, he walked through the local park he had grown up visiting.

How freaking stupid I am! he thought, kicking himself, seeing a handful of families. *Is that security guard here too? What about his brother, if he has one?* Intimidated by the less-than-one-percent chance, he walked briskly through the park and hightailed it out of there.

Abruptly, five minutes later, he heard a loud "Mr. Corwin!" echo through the neighborhood. Turning around, he saw an e-biker racing toward him from a few blocks away. After a short conversation about each other's plans for Independence Day, they departed. Three seconds later, Zachary heard, "Why were you talking to that teenage boy?" Startled to death, he realized that the voice, which sounded just like the guard's, was coming from his own mind.

He spent the next several hours painstakingly piecing together the clips, along with the footage from his body camera. Just as he had hoped, the footage proved that he was never on the playground. It also showed that he was clearly having an amicable conversation with a woman and three children. Obviously, he couldn't post their conversation, much less show the children's faces. However, although it was blurred, he did keep the ending so that viewers could hear them saying goodbye and could conclude that they had a great conversation, just like everyone else at the park that day.

That night, Zachary lay awake. He endeavored to fall asleep, but every time he shut his eyes, he was back at Hemingway Beacon Library. He was already feeling nauseated by the whole ordeal and skipped dinner as a result. This dragged on for hours in the darkness of his room. Peering out his window from his bed, he grew frustrated, seeing that the lamppost, which had been dark for months at this point, still hadn't been fixed by the city.

"This is *never* going to end, is it?!" Physically weak and exhausted, he summoned all his remaining strength to raise both arms and slam them down against his bed.

He woke up gasping for air as if he weren't breathing in his sleep, which increasingly got worse over the years, first noticing it in 2014. Doctors all said it was stress, which he suspected anyway, but who on earth could blame him after all the years of relentless insults, assumptions, and ableism, even though only a minority of people did those things?

As was tradition, Zachary walked over to Whisperpine Grove Heights to watch the annual fireworks show, but this time was different. Surrounded by a thousand people and being there completely by himself, he worried that one of them might be the security guard, off duty.

Twenty-four hours later, still offended by the guard's despicable vitriol, he took a second bite of his modest dinner, then instantly spat it out. He rushed downstairs to throw it into the refrigerator, saving it to warm up the following day.

For *three days*, he barely ate anything, replaying the encounter in his mind five hundred times against his will, due to his autistic brain. A rush of anger and pain flowed through his veins each time. By day four, he began reacquiring his appetite and strength, ready to work more efficiently, posting on social media, making new videos, discovering how to use OpusClips to make short-form content from his long-form videos, and advertising his tutoring services on Nextdoor and Facebook.

59

Surviving Summer 2024

Every single night, without fail, despite comfort from his friends and family, Zachary Corwin went to bed feeling utterly wretched. He kept saying lengthy prayers beforehand, which became laborious as he questioned why he was repeating the same words over and over *and over* again without them coming to fruition. It was different than his 2021 prayers, yet the ultimate outcome he was praying for remained the same: a person whom everyone respected and took seriously, allowing him to make a difference, whether at their school, church, library, podcast, radio program, television show, or news outlet.

Not striving to be a famous celebrity, he simply wanted the chance to change the world, getting everyone to accept each other, while being a math teacher simultaneously. He understood how impossible it was to get every human being kind and accepting, yet he remained ambitiously determined to see how far he could go.

Problem was, he wasn't getting anywhere. Financially, his social media advertising budget was too low to build an engaged following. His new videos, barring the one about the security guard, still garnered about twenty views each, unless he promoted them. The video about the guard, surprisingly, had amassed nearly 30,000 views with several comments supporting Zachary. Only one comment defended the security guard, failing to grasp the full story he had clearly laid out.

On the other hand, however, some of his Shorts and reels from OpusClips proved a breakthrough, increasing views and engagement. Unfortunately, book sales were still rare.

The following week, he noticed an older woman in a wheelchair trying to get onto the curb, but greatly struggled.

"May I help you?" Zachary said, jogging over.

"Much obliged, young man," the woman said with a smile of appreciation.

After assisting her, he looked up and saw the park and library on the other side of the street. His stomach twisted and tightened in knots. He approached cautiously and hesitantly. Slowly, while staying across the street, he scanned the area from behind a tree, being watchful for the thin man in uniform, wearing a black cap. A different security guard was circling the playground, while another stepped out of the library to make his rounds outside. As the guards kept patrolling, Zachary questioned whether his description was on their radar, terrified as if the first guard had spilled his lies to everyone in an attempt to demean him.

He could see it now: wanted posters with his face on them, despite being an innocent autistic individual.

Unaware if the security guard was inside the library or out, or if he was even working that day, he decided to wait there until he saw his tutoring clients arrive. While waiting, Zachary recalled his random act of kindness.

Why couldn't that security guard see what I did and know what a genuinely kind person I am, helping that disabled woman? … Wait, stop! I wasn't thinking that when I was helping her, and the Lord knows, I didn't help her to be seen or thanked. I knew it was the right thing to do.

By the end of July, he had five tutoring clients, meeting each of them in the library's study room upstairs. Only twice did he lay eyes on the security guard again, but he managed to dodge his sight both times.

"Hey, Zachary, one more thing," said Lucy on the first Wednesday of August. It was after the two-hour tutoring session with Esperanza and Rodrigo. "I watched that video of yours on YouTube, with that security guard here."

"Oh," Zachary said, his shoulders sagging, wishing she didn't have to watch it.

"That just wasn't right of him," she said, shaking her head with a hint of feeling creeped out.

"Oh well, it's okay."

"No, it's not okay. I sent that video to the police department because I'm sure that security guards are contracted by them. If not, they should know what to do about it. I'm sorry that happened to you."

"Well, uh—" Zachary was thankful, but he didn't know how to respond in the moment. "I appreciate it. I felt tremendously offended by him because he assumed that I was lying about being a substitute teacher. He lied to me and about me. And he viewed me as some ped … uh … pe … I can't even say it. It shudders me."

"You don't have to."

"I was like, 'Come on! I volunteered working with children since I was in high school. I volunteered as a commander in Royal Rangers for eleven years. I've been a substitute teacher for the school district for three. I've passed so many background checks, fingerprinting, safety trainings, abuse awareness and prevention trainings, and mandated reporter trainings that I lost count.' I mean, I'm not callous. I understand that he was, in theory, looking out for children. I'm not against that. But why did he single *me* out for no reason? If I was walking up to children in the playground, then sure, put me in handcuffs. Take me to prison. But I was not. My bodycam and the park's security cameras had proven that he was a liar."

"He sure was! My blood boiled when that Barney Fife of a security guard wouldn't even give you his first name. I thought they were required to by law."

"Well, I think only police officers are required to identify themselves with their name and badge number, but I could be wrong. Still, that day, I was one of hundreds of people here, having a friendly, cordial conversation with not just three children, but an adult! We were all smiling, looking like great friends talking with each other. The girl grinned as she said bye, giving me a high-five. None of them looked fearful. Like, why would all four of them be standing and smiling if I was some creep like he thought? Wouldn't they be sprinting to him? Or to a police officer?"

Lucy shook her head, saying, "It doesn't make any sense. That's why I think something was off with that fellow. I honestly question if he was a real security guard."

"Another thing I thought of, in retrospect, was this: when I was tutoring Rodrigo later that day, a guy came up to us, asking me if I was a registered voter. So, let me get this straight. *I'm* questioned for walking around the building, talking to no one, but that gentleman was able to go up to random people without any problem? Also, I'm not trying to be mean whatsoever, but the park and library are filled with homeless people too. My heart goes out for them, don't get me wrong, but why on earth would that security guard single me out like that?"

"It's horrible. I'll let you know if or when the police get back to me."

"Thanks. I'm eager to find out myself. Hopefully, they'll respond. Please keep me posted."

"Definitely. Have a nice day."

"Last question, Mr. Corwin," asked Rodrigo, before getting into the car. "Do you have rizz?"

"Uh … the … *what*?"

"*Rizz*!" he repeated, grinning. "Bruh! You know."

"Oh, *stop*," Lucy called out with embarrassed laughter.

"U-Um, I don't know what that means, so I shouldn't answer either way," he responded, fearing there was some ulterior meaning to it.

"It's this new TikTok vernacular, Zachary," Lucy explained. "Every kid these days is saying it. You'll hear it every day once school starts back up."

"Ha-ha, thanks for the warning."

Feeling up for it, Zachary decided to walk for a few miles before returning home. Ambling along the hills of Whisperpine Grove Heights an hour later, Zachary heard a few middle school boys laughing among themselves, bouncing words like "Skibidi" and "Cringe" back and forth. Looking up, he was struck by the brilliant beams of their e-bikes' headlights, the sky now astronomical twilight.

"Mr. Cor-win!" shouted the blond-haired boy.

Phew, Zachary thought, relieved that he was running into students who knew him, since being greeted by anyone those days was too few and far between, making him wonder if he was literally, supernaturally invisible to society.

Finishing his sentence, the blond-haired boy hollered, "Suck my—"

"*G-Good evening*, Mr. Corwin!" one of the other boys interrupted, clearly sounding appalled at his friend. Quickly, he asked, "H-How was your day?"

"Um, s-swell … And yours?" Zachary shakily responded to him, hearing the other two boys snicker as they continued down the road.

"It was great. Have a good night, okay?"

Zachary continued traipsing up the hill, each step feeling heavier than the last. Darkness finished blanketing the neighborhood, suffocating him beneath the August-night cloud cover. Deep-tone wind chimes sang in the light nocturnal breeze, but instead of soothing him, he felt even more sick.

Trudging the rest of the journey home, feeling devalued in the world, he angrily yelled at God in his heart, questioning what on earth was happening.

Unexpectedly, a couple of e-bikes swerved around the corner, their headlights shining brighter. They were the two indifferent students from moments ago. Seeing Zachary as they raced past him, they began giggling. He could hear them taunting, "Mr. Corwin … Mr. Corwin," in a slow, ghostly drawl, until they reached the corner and disappeared in the darkness.

And this wasn't the first time students did that to him.

What the heck do people on this planet want *from me?! After everything I accomplished, the degrees I hold, the books I published, the videos I posted, the social media following I built, the Gold Medal of Achievement I earned, the interviews I was a part of, the skills of piano and juggling that I had labored to get better at, the tens of thousands of dollars I spent trying to educate and encourage billions of people worldwide, the debt I incurred repeatedly this summer as a result, the thousands of students I've brought joy to as a sub, the thousands of students I encouraged through my* volunteer *assemblies! The heck do these people want from me?!*

Doesn't the small percentage of mean students know all I've done in this community and in this world? Don't they realize I'm just trying *to help them (and eight billion others) believe in themselves, succeed in life, accept and include disabled people in society, and be* kind *to one another? Don't they understand that I don't have to be a teacher, but because I care about them and the future of this world, I choose to stoop low, teach, and encourage them, even though my degrees could earn me well-paying careers? Do they assume I did* everything *for myself—the Gold Medal, my degrees, piano, juggling, et cetera? Give me a freaking break!*

What about that petulant security guard? What about that driver who pointed his camera at me one morning while he sped by? What about that young man who said, 'Hey, Hey, H-hey, Hey,' at the crosswalk last week as we walked past each other, trying to trip me up? What about that student's grandfather at the school musical last spring who saw the 'M.Ed.' after my name on my jacket and rolled his eyes? What about every other adult *the past several years, young and old, who just gawks at me? What's preventing them from recognizing me as the person who's done so much to help the world so far?*

It's because I can't afford any more substantial advertising, much less PR. If my videos go viral in lieu of all the brain rot, if I make it into every local and national news outlet, and if I make it into every school (public and private), then for sure, on a personal level, I should never face discrimination again.

Beyond that, in the grand scheme, I shouldn't have to worry about seeing others discriminated against, baselessly predicated on a disability, because kindness would prevail over all the lingering malice on this planet. I shouldn't have to read about another child committing suicide again, or anyone for that matter, because they'd feel included in life, thanks to nondisabled people accepting them as human beings.

These darn ableists (the security guard, the father in 2017, and hundreds more) literally have no clue they're glorifying suicidal ideation because, according to them, it must be acceptable to treat people as their punching bags. The only difference is that most people aren't as strong as I am, and they might take their own lives. Had they ever thought of that?

Oh … yes. I'm sure some have. I'm not assuming everyone. 'Do you think they don't care?' I could hear people pushing back against me. No, I never said that at all. I do believe many people care.

Walking the rest of the way home was arduous, but he survived the trek.

Akin to *every single night* since June, after a couple of soliloquies and repeated prayers, he rested his head on his pillow, feeling as if his heart might stop at any moment. His breathing increasingly got difficult with all the stress. Shakily, his hands curled into fists, craving a punching bag.

The stress and tension he felt from his failed efforts pressed on him like dental floss wrapped a hundred times around his heart; then ghostly hands would tightly grip the two ends and begin pulling and releasing the dental floss like a pulse, attempting to eventually slice his heart to shreds.

He'd use that same imagery in 2021 to describe his feelings in his emotion-ridden posts that worried many friends.

A few weeks later proved no easier. Walking down a road in his neighborhood, a train of six e-bikers raced past him. One of the boys in the middle turned back and recognized him.

"Mr. Corwin," he said, somewhat dazed, "why'd you snitch on—"

Being a distance away, his voice became muffled, and Zachary couldn't make out the name. Combined with the auditory sensory overload of the e-bikes and chatter, his brain began spinning in circles.

"What?" he asked from across the street, ready to account for his decision, but suddenly, before the boy could answer, another e-biker blazed past him from behind and screeched to a halt, sliding to a stop right beside the boy.

Zachary watched in confusion as the e-biker quickly said something to the boy, never looking at Zachary even once. Next thing he saw, both of them were hurtling toward their buddies at a hundred miles per hour.

"What? Wait!" Zachary called out, but it was too late.

That encounter kept him up for weeks. If it was because he wrote a name down for the teacher to discipline, then that was his responsibility as a substitute teacher. If it was a misunderstanding, he needed to make sure it was resolved as soon as possible. Another thing that hurt him was the fact that he recognized a couple of those students, including the one who asked him why he snitched.

I don't get it, he said. *These were the same students who'd always say hi to me a year ago whenever they saw me at school or out in the neighborhood, usually rushing up to me. One even stopped on his e-bike and told me that I was a good sub; another would always ask me to show him a card trick. Now, they don't seem to care? Worse, some began looking creeped out whenever they saw me. What the heck is going on? What'd I do wrong?*

Traversing the thoroughfare half an hour later, his darn three-pound brain conjured the idea to stop by a Jack in the Box. After getting his lunch to go, he decided to take the shortcut home. Fifty yards up ahead, a girl came into view, looking to be in tenth or eleventh grade, walking in the same direction as him.

He never assumed that every child or teenager he encounters has had him as a substitute before. Heck, some might be homeschooled or attend a private school. However, when he would glance over and see students he recognized not acknowledging him, despite momentary eye-contact, he would feel perturbed. It was worse when their eyes bulged out or when they began whispering to a friend beside them before rushing away. This started becoming more and more frequent.

This was his form of self-assessment as a substitute teacher. If students were not saying hi to him, or even giving him weird looks or gestures, then he'd grade himself with an F … F *minus*!

I failed, somehow, he would lament in his mind. *After all I've done, seriously? The tricks and juggling to make boring school days vanish. The kindness I show every student, telling them to have a good day and holding the door open for them. The help I've given them so that they could understand the math (or* any *assignment) which has been my priority.*

The teen girl turned around nonchalantly, then faced forward again, but a second later, she jerked her head back around and fixed her gaze on Zachary. Facing away, Zachary kept an eye on the situation, looking through his sunglasses. The girl continued walking forward for ten feet, all while maintaining a creeped-out stare, her mouth closed and eyes widened.

What? Are you freaking serious? Zachary moaned to himself, complaining about how life was treating him … again! *Obviously, she must recognize me as being a substitute teacher, but why the heck is she giving me that look, like a few other students since 2022 every now and then?*

The girl began giving beckoning signals as if communicating with someone. Out of nowhere, another teen girl popped out from parked cars. Still fifty yards apart, as each of them kept walking forward in a straight line, both girls kept an eye on him, looking creeped out as if they wished he wouldn't see them. The first girl looked like she wanted to hide. The second girl hid behind a car, before peeking out to see if Zachary noticed.

He did, through his sunglasses, but to them, it looked like he kept facing down or away while he walked. He had reached the point of no return in the parking lot. He could either take his last opportunity to turn left and take the long way around, or continue forward and run into them. Curious as he was to know what the heck this was all about, he decided it'd be wiser to turn left. He did so without missing a step.

Once he got home, he threw his hamburger into the refrigerator to warm up later, no longer hungry.

Is there some conspiracy going on against me that I don't know about?! What on earth must have I done that was so wrong, when I've tried to be nothing but kindhearted and selfless? I even ceased from caring about myself and gave up finances to motivate others. I'm stressing myself literally *to death, feeling physical pain in my heart as I struggle to breathe. How haven't I died from a hundred heart attacks by now … this year alone?*

Slouching in his chair, trying to recall the thousands of people who truly cared about him as a human, including the hundreds of students who *would* greet or compliment him, an email popped up.

"Oh, good," he said to himself, half thankful and half sad. "Just sold the Buffalo Nickel collection for $300."

Walking up to his closet to get the Dansco album, he couldn't help but notice how bare his shelf was. Only a fifth of his collection remained, yet he would do anything to fulfill his life's mission. Glancing at what was left, he recited the Scripture verses in his heart that he had shared with Pastor Nguyen. Remaining was his core collection. "Only in an emergency," he whispered. "Only in an emergency."

Slowly, he turned around, forcing himself to walk forward. A suspenseful drum rhythm pounded inside his mind.

All of a sudden, the two teen girls from earlier that day jumped in his thoughts.

Taking a couple of steps forward, creaking the floorboard beneath him, he heard, "Mr. Corwin, why'd you snitch?"

In a flash, the blond-haired e-biker from Whisperpine Grove Heights, came into remembrance.

A few steps later, the stern-faced security guard began hurling his false accusations at him again.

Abruptly, "What the freak was that thing?" was heard, followed by the memory of another passenger from the previous week, who yelled gibberish at him as the pickup stormed down the thoroughfare.

"NPC," said the skateboarder before charging at him.

"Ha-ha-ha-ha!" the cocky district manager of Rite Aid said, laughing.

"What's *wrong* with you?" yelled the manager of Albertsons.

Out of nowhere, years of harsh ableism intruded into Zachary's thoughts like a hurricane.

Bang! A gunshot rang out, obliterating all his thoughts. In a vision, he saw his best friend Thomas collapse to the floor, hearing his handgun slam onto the ground with an ear-shattering crash.

Without a second heartbeat, Zachary pursed his lips in lifeless anger, tossed the Buffalo Nickels album onto his bed, and rushed to the closet. He pulled out his core collection he had spent decades building and prepared to take pictures for eBay. Subsequently, he took pictures of the vintage books he desired to keep, posting them for sale on Nextdoor and Facebook Marketplace.

After posting all the listings of items he never wanted to sell, he went for an evening walk to get some fresh air and clear his mind, praying it wouldn't be loused up again.

60

Zachary's Momentary Lifesavers

Walking past a Starbucks, a boy rushed out the door to stop him. "Mr. Corwin?" he asked.

"Yeah?" Zachary turned around, seeing the boy and hearing the classic "Fly Like an Eagle" by Steve Miller Band, coming from inside the Starbucks.

"You subbed for my class last year, sixth grade at Ulysses Elementary."

"Oh yes. I recognize you," he said with a weak smile.

"You know, it's funny. I still follow you on TikTok, and the other day, one of your videos showed up on my For You Page."

"Oh, really?" Zachary asked, smiling genuinely for the first time in a while.

"Yes, I was with my cousins, and I told them, 'That's my substitute teacher, no cap!'"

"Well, uh, thank you for letting me know." Zachary didn't know what to say, but wanted to express his gratitude.

"You're welcome. You always make my day. I thought I'd let you know that. Well, bye." The boy waved with a closed-lipped smile before re-entering Starbucks.

Two minutes later, Zachary stood at a red light along the thoroughfare. Another middle schooler was walking toward him down the sidewalk. Passing Zachary, he said with a reassuring smile, "You're a pretty good sub!"

"Thanks so much. You don't know how much that means to me."

61

Recovering His Worth

"Hey! Hey!" A concerned-looking man walked briskly toward Zachary.

"Yeah?" Zachary said, putting on a smile, though worry lingered beneath it.

"Do you know where you're going?"

"Uh, yes. Room 214. I've been subbing a tenth-grade English class all day."

Looking down at the man's shirt, Zachary noticed the school's emblem embroidered above the words "Campus Safety." *Great, here we go again,* Zachary thought, exhaling sharply. *You have* got *to be joking!*

"All right, so are you new to this school?"

"Uh … I'm relatively new."

"*Relatively new*," the man repeated slowly with a grin. In Zachary's mind, the man was either thinking it was a clever way to put it or sizing him up as inept.

"I mean, I've only subbed here four or five times, but I'm not brand-new either. I know my way around."

"All right. Take it easy."

"Have a nice day," he said, wondering if he should've told him that he was a student there at Ironwood Peak for four years, but it happened so fast that he couldn't process it in time. The auditory sensory overload was getting to him anyway, hearing multiple students talking and laughing, and listening to the campus' portable Bluetooth speakers blasting "What Makes you Beautiful" by One Direction.

Walking away, relieved that he wasn't paraded to the office with hands behind his back, he dwelled, *Swell! My first day back at work since the academic year began, and this happens. I surmise I'm still shaking off the PTSD from that other security guard. Now this one. I'd understand if he didn't recognize me and just wanted to help, but why'd he approach me like that so quickly? Why'd he stop me, calling out, 'Hey! Hey!' from like twenty or thirty feet away? Why me? I saw a* couple *of substitutes all morning going from point A to point B, just like me, and* they *weren't stopped by campus safety. Even now at lunchtime! We're all wearing lanyards with badges too. Heck, during the break, a couple of students came up to say hi to me, excited to see me again. Where was he then? That would prove I'm not an intruder disguised as a sub with a fake badge.*

In the long term, this memory loitered in his mind for the next several months, but as soon as it was over, he tried to distract himself … which didn't take long.

"Mr. Corwin!" a few students exclaimed, running up to him. "Remember us from Canyon Mountain Middle School?"

"Yes, I do."

At that moment, the song through the speakers switched to "Good Time" by Owl City, featuring Carly Rae Jepsen, which took Zachary back to when he was a high schooler at that school, since it came out right after his junior year.

"Corwin!" Four more students came up from the other side, wearing varsity jackets.

"Remember my birthday?" one of them asked.

"Uh, September 10, right?"

"What the heck? I told you three years ago," the student responded, rubbing his forehead underneath his spiky hair.

"What about mine?" asked another with surfer hair, a binder and composition notebook held in his left hand at his side.

"June 18, I believe. And your brother, July 6?"

The student laughed in astonishment as two other students came up from behind.

"And mine?"

"Uh—" Zachary felt tensed as he struggled to recognize the student, but then it clicked once he recognized his curtained hairstyle. "Um … Oh *Xavier.* January 2. My gosh, I hardly recognized you. And, uh, Henry?"

"Mm-hmm!" he confirmed with a nod and a closed-lipped smile.

"My goodness. What a difference a few years makes."

"How's life?" "How was your summer?" "Subbing for another year?" "Remember substituting my seventh-grade history class a couple of years ago?" were some of the incessant questions Zachary got asked.

"Got a card trick on you?" one requested.

"Yeah," Zachary replied.

"Oh, watch him cook!"

By now, he was surrounded by twenty high schoolers who were all eager to see him again. As he pulled out one of his decks, fearing that campus safety was breathing down his neck, Henry said, "Mr. Corwin, please! Can you say, 'Just give me my money!' Just like that."

Half the students roared in laughter. "Bruh, shut up!" a couple of them told Henry, playfully.

"Do you know what that means anyway?" Xavier asked Zachary.

"No," he answered as he was taking the cards out of the box. "And I don't know if I want to find out, ha-ha, but I bet it's some TikTok meme."

"Imagine being that student—" one student started.

"Okay, pick a card," Zachary interrupted, now ready to show them his first one. After baffling them with a couple of card tricks, the bell rang. Students began heading to class as the brand-new song, "Way Back," by Henrik, played through the speakers.

"You're the GOAT, Mr. Corwin," a few of them complimented before departing. "Take the W."

One student stayed behind. "Mr. Corwin, I read your second book. It was very good!" he said.

"Hey, thank you so much," Zachary replied, feeling eternally grateful that a student appreciated his book. "The one about my experiences in student teaching and subbing?"

"Yeah. It was so cool to read about the schools you named, schools I actually attended, mentioned in a book sold around the world. It gave me a little sense of pride."

As Zachary was heading to Room 214, he passed by the infamous dogwood tree near the hangout spot he frequented as a student, now taller with a broad, spreading canopy. After a subtle glance, recalling what it symbolized to him way back when, he continued forward and didn't look back.

For the remainder of the day, the dark clouds from summer were being pried off of Zachary as he gained confidence, realizing that several students still accepted him for who he was. This fact was solidified the following Monday when he was back at Canyon Mountain. Every period, students came in enthusiastic to see him again. During his prep period, walking to the office building, he passed many classrooms with open doors, hearing gasps or whispers, "It's Mr. Corwin!" from inside. Throughout nutrition and lunch, he overheard some groups of students pointing him out as their substitute from elementary school.

"High-five, Mr. Corwin?" one student asked.

"Sure," Zachary said, stretching his hand as high as he could reach.

"Ah, that's too high." The student grinned as his buddies snickered. "Like ten-feet high."

"Just jump for it, man," Zachary encouraged.

"All right," he said determinedly, but as he did, Zachary jumped in tandem, a joke he pulled hundreds of times as a substitute.

"All right, how about a real high-five?" Zachary offered.

"Thanks, Mr. Corwin."

"Mr. Corwin, how tall are you?"

"*Every* student, *every* day, asks me that without fail, even if I lead assemblies in a different district. I'm six-foot-four-and-a-half … and don't you forget that half," he replied facetiously.

After school, walking down the narrow hallway of the office building, Zachary overheard a couple of administrators conversing over pizza and talking about an upcoming DUI checkpoint along the thoroughfare. *Bam!* He was instantly taken back to summer 2021, that wretched summer. There had been a DUI checkpoint, and police vehicles were everywhere. A couple of employees at a nearby restaurant had stood outside to witness the scene. Zachary noticed that one of the employees was glowering at him until he was out of sight, as if he were going to turn on them and start attacking. Her arms had been folded, yet she seemed ready to fight back if she had to. The harsh memory resurfaced because he happened to have walked by at the most inopportune time of the administrators' conversation.

Returning the key, badge, and Chromebook, the office lady, who remembered him from being a student, asked, "Oh, so how was your day, Zachary?"

"Horrible!"

"Huh?" she asked, wondering if she had heard correctly.

"Just kidding."

"Ha-ha! You got me good. My heart's still racing."

"I say that all the time, pause for a second, and then reveal it was a joke. I had one of the most amazing, validating days as a substitute teacher."

"Aw, I'm so happy to hear that."

"And it was for my former history teacher, as you know. That happened a couple of times at the high school where I subbed for my former teachers. Full circle. Hey, I once subbed for my classmate in the master's program last year too. He teaches English, and I just had to accept the job."

"That's amazing. Full circle, indeed. Oh, and thank you for calling me to confirm that the student switched periods."

"No problem. His name wasn't on the roster yet, and judging by his demeanor, I couldn't ascertain whether he was giving me a hard time. You know, as a sub, I had to take hundreds of phone calls and make dozens of them myself. Just as I'm getting better at reading aloud, I believe I'm getting better at taking and making calls. I've always hated phone calls. I still do, to some extent, due to sensory overload, since I prefer written or face-to-face communication, but I'm gaining a lot of confidence."

"Wow, Zachary, you've come such a long way. I hope to see you get a job here and soon."

"Thank you. I'd love that, but only once I reach every school in my volunteer assemblies. Last night, I was invited back to an elementary school in the Willowbend Unified School District. I did assemblies there last February, and a few of the students remembered me. Anyway, last night was their Back-to-School Night. They asked me to give two presentations to the parents. In both of them, I noticed a few mothers covering their mouths or wiping their eyes. A couple of them came up afterward to thank me, explaining that their child is autistic and that my message had given them hope."

"Your story is, in fact, inspiring, and Autism Awareness is so needed. I can't understand why Dr. Peterson hasn't made time for you yet."

Abruptly, a sense of frustration and hurt rushed through his veins. All he could say was, "The PTA and I are working on it."

"Oh, I could tell you're still upset over it. I am too. But you must remember all the thousands you've made a difference to, not to mention the millions on social media and on the news."

Zachary tried to keep a stiff upper lip. "Yeah," he whispered, nodding. "Well, I've received similar comments on social media. One father recently thanked me for giving him hope for his six-year-old. Also, I recently got a big package from a school I led assemblies at. It contained thank-you cards from students thanking me, including drawings they did of me juggling."

"Aw, that's sweet. Well, just be patient. It'll come."

Life in the community appeared to improve from then until December. By then, more students in the district, on campus, or across town, were acknowledging him, saying hello or asking to see a card trick. He was tutoring over a dozen students with glowing testimonials.

Unfortunately, Royal Rangers didn't follow suit. With a massive loss of commanders, the outpost had to merge age groups. From September through December, time dragged slowly for him at his outpost, taking a toll.

"It's just depressing, Pastor Nguyen," Zachary confessed upstairs in the office one chilly, windy night. "I'm literally sitting there doing nothing as the senior commander leads. All I'm doing is leading the games during recreation. I'm no longer leading the drill commands and pledges. I'm no longer contributing during the Bible lessons. So far, the other commanders had been teaching the merits, and I'm just … *there*."

"That sounds rough, I know."

"Yeah. I sub all day, going from 6:30 or 7:00 a.m. I tutor most afternoons too. On Fridays, I tutor math for two hours. Then I rush home, put on my uniform, get my stuff, and come here. I hardly have time to get a bite to eat, literally. I mean, I love what I do, and I'm greatly indebted to the Royal Rangers program, but if I'm doing nothing for about eighty minutes, then why the heck am I there?"

Pastor Nguyen listened intently, letting him speak his heart over the backdrop of the night's howling wind.

"Pastor, honestly, I've sat there with splitting headaches before, having worked all day and then not doing anything. If I were fully involved for the entire time, like I have been for the past decade, I wouldn't be getting headaches. In all candor, I came home after those nights barely surviving the drive, feeling as if death were imminent. It felt like my eyes would literally shoot out of their sockets and my head would explode."

"Well, Zachary, I do appreciate your honesty, vulnerability, and trust over the past hour as we've talked. I'm definitely going to be there in support of you. Give me five minutes to send a quick email, and then I'll be downstairs."

"Thanks, Pastor Nguyen. I never thought this day would come. I'm so thankful you could be there by my side."

Zachary slowly descended the carpeted staircase and stepped into the sanctuary, where the boys and commanders were setting up for the night. "Joy," by North Point Kids, featuring Lauren Lee, was currently playing over the church's sound system. It was the last night before the Christmas party the following week.

"Boy, it's really blowing hard out there!" one third-grader shouted as he entered from the side door, just arriving with his older brother. Both he and his brother were wearing thick checkered jackets and black faux fur trapper hats.

"Commander Zachary," greeted the senior commander with a big smile as always, though melancholy was etched across his countenance. "I'll let you give your little speech after the pledges and announcements. One commander couldn't make it, so he'll be on speaker phone. I told him what you were going to say."

"Thanks," Zachary said softly, giving a little smile.

Once Zachary stood before his entire outpost and Pastor Nguyen, the sanctuary fell silent, so silent that everyone could hear the leaves rustling in the wind outside.

"Everyone," he started, "I thank you for being here and taking a minute to listen to me. This is my twenty-fifth year in Royal Rangers, year twelve as a commander. I never thought I'd admit this, but burnout is real. As a substitute teacher, private math tutor, worship musician, and commander, it just got too overwhelming for me. Let me tell you, this decision took me *months*, but tonight, I'm announcing that I'll be taking a sabbatical as your commander."

The atmosphere in the room grew quieter than silence itself. Boys from kindergarten to twelfth grade stared at Zachary. The jaws of some of the boys dropped in disbelief. Others had a sad expression on their faces.

"This isn't a resignation, and it's nothing that anyone did. I just need time to process everything. But from my heart, I didn't want to just disappear from your lives without telling you guys. I made sure I took this courtesy to let you know in person and to say goodbye for now."

Pastor Nguyen took over from there, explaining how it's normal for people to take sabbaticals. After a group prayer, one of the high schoolers walked up to Zachary, shook his hand, and solemnly told him he would be missed.

Turning around, Zachary saw a line of three boys.

"Thank you for everything you taught me," said an eighth-grader, shaking his hand.

"Thank you, Commander Zachary," said a second-grader and a fifth-grader, each shaking his hand.

He departed that night shrouded in gloom but was grateful for the full heart, knowing how much those boys and commanders had appreciated his service all those years.

A week later, he decided to do his Christmas shopping at the local Target. A Mannheim Steamroller playlist filled the store for the patrons. While he was making his purchase, the woman who had checked out before him lingered behind.

"Are you Mr. Zachary Corwin?" asked the woman, who had stopped him as he wheeled the cart out of the checkout lane.

"Yes, I am," he replied with a smile.

"You've subbed in my sixth-grade daughter's class a few times last year. Alejandra at Harrison Magnet School."

"Oh yes. I remember her and subbing at the school."

"Well, when she saw you up there in front of her class and heard you tell your story, it really encouraged her. She is also autistic, and she came home saying, 'If he could do it, *I* can do it,' so I'm very thankful for you, from the bottom of my heart."

"No problem whatsoever. It means the world to me to hear that."

Walking home, Zachary was counting all the recent blessings he had received. He was prepared for a pleasant two weeks off, prioritizing his tasks and getting a lot of things done. By this time, he had built a PR budget and was about to enter another campaign starting in January. He was feeling very optimistic about his life. Up ahead, two young gentlemen were approaching on their e-bikes. After a quick glance, Zachary realized he didn't recognize them. After they passed, in the background, he heard one of them chuckle and say, "Bro, did you see that thing?"

62

Why Does it Matter?

Standing at the corner of the thoroughfare and Thornwick Boulevard, Zachary waited for the walk signal to light up, breathing in the frosty air in the moments before sunset. Before his turn came, the green arrow lit up for a few moments. A high school student hollered out at him from the first sedan that turned onto the thoroughfare. "Happy New Year, Mr. Corwin! I bought your book!" she yelled out.

Zachary smiled and waved, unable to process in time for a formal reply, just like the times when other students zoom past him on their e-bikes, shouting, "Corwin! What's up?" By the time Zachary registered what happened, the students were halfway down the block.

As tradition, he took a leisurely lap around the outdoor mall. While vibing to a relatively new song, "Home," by Good Neighbours, he was stopped by an unfamiliar voice.

"Whoa, Zachary. How are you?"

"Uh, hi. I'm fine. How are *you*?" he said with a smile, not remembering who he was.

Fortunately, the mysterious young man identified himself. "It's Christopher, from Washington Elementary, Canyon Mountain Middle, and Ironwood Peak High."

"My gosh, I remember you."

Christopher and Zachary were eager to catch up; they spent the next few minutes talking with each other. Upon walking away toward the CVS Pharmacy, Zachary almost got emotional. Timely, "In Between" by Wilderado happened to be bouncing off the outdoor walls of the mall's edifices, stirring his state of flux. *Here was a person who used to tease me a lot,* he thought to himself, *but now he's treating me as if we had always been best friends?*

Inside the CVS Pharmacy, a few firemen from a local fire station walked past him, each carrying a few groceries. It happened so fast that Zachary couldn't thank them for their service, something he always does whenever he comes across law enforcement, firefighters, and military personnel.

Twenty minutes passed by. "Thank you for your service," he said with a smile as he ran into one of them. Shyness usually made him reticent, but after years of pushing beyond his comfort zone, he felt more confident.

However, the young fireman, looking like he had just been hired, did something unexpected. He stared at Zachary and smirked, a snicker escaping under his breath.

After five seconds of awkward staring, Zachary broke the silence. "Uh, well, have a great day."

They both turned around and walked away, awkwardly. The fireman didn't say a word. As if fate was watching over the situation, the ceiling speakers began playing "Rude" by Magic!, whisking Zachary back to 2014. A couple of moments later, while standing in the checkout lane, he turned and saw the same fireman standing beside another, both staring at him from afar with strange smiles on their faces.

What? Zachary thought, confused. *Did that fireman think I was faking my gratitude … or that I'm some kind of prankster?*

After checking out and heading toward the entrance, his phone vibrated. After tending to some social media comments, he noticed one of the firemen walking toward him with a bag of groceries, having just checked out. He placed his phone back in its case and stepped aside out of courtesy, but having done so, the fireman still said in a monotone voice, "Coming through, bud," as if Zachary were childishly blocking his way.

"Thank you for your service," he politely said.

"Thanks," the fireman replied in a low voice, seeming to be ungrateful, not once meeting Zachary's eyes.

He was utterly discombobulated that two, possibly three, firemen had suddenly thought of him as insane without taking the time to get to know him. He turned and saw a second fireman carrying his bags of groceries, following the first. "Thank you for your service," he told him, now having to force a smile to mask his hurt.

"Aw, for sure, man," he said with a big, warm smile of gratitude. "Thank you for your support."

Okay, that's reassuring, Zachary thought as soon as the fireman passed by him, yet his stomach started talking back to him.

After the encounter (which eventually kept him up for months), he walked for hours around the neighborhoods until it was too dark to film. He stressed and labored over getting his words right and concise. By the time he got home, his battery was drained.

"Okay, I have *high* respect for firemen—their strength and resilience, their *incredible* wealth of knowledge and skill, and risking their lives to save people—but I had a problem with a couple of them today, based on everything I recounted," Zachary said in the middle of his video. "It was the first time in my life I thanked someone for their service and was met with such ungratefulness in return. I'd understand if they just got a call, but they didn't. I'd understand if they were tired, but they didn't seem tired, judging by them smirking at me, giving me strange looks, and even dismissiveness. Now, how is an autistic like me supposed to interpret that?

"As an autistic, it's easy to misconstrue people. Lately, in my life, I've learned to take a step back and process before jumping to conclusions. After I was done shopping today and pulled out my phone, I saw a comment that read, 'ur stupid,' but then I expanded it and the user continued, 'just joking, ur clever.' I almost got fired up inside, especially after dealing with that first fireman, but I'm thankful I paused to read the entire comment before even considering how I would've responded. *Gentle*, of course, yet firm.

"Other times, I carefully reasoned through why certain things happened the way they did before assuming the worst. For instance, a couple of years ago, I was standing at an intersection, waiting to cross the street. One passenger a few lanes over, who was around my age, looked at me with a blank expression before rolling up his window. My autistic brain thought, 'Seriously? You think I'm going to come over, reach in, and rob you guys?' I tried to reason that I was probably wrong. It might have been too cold.

"While that questionable experience was mostly reconciled in my mind, an incident a few days ago didn't resolve so easily. I was walking down a neighborhood street, and I heard, 'Hey … Hey … Hey.' I turned around and saw this young man in a black Ford F-150 point his phone at me and take my picture. Then he stormed off. I mean, how do I reconcile *that*? A similar incident occurred ten years ago too.

"But just to add real quick, not everyone in my city is an ableist. Between takes, as I'm walking around filming this, I was approaching a father and his young son down the street. I turned off the camera and stepped out of the way for them as a courtesy, as I usually do, just like those firemen. And do you know what the father said? 'Thank you,' he told me. *That's* what the world needs: more courtesy, kindness, compliments, and acknowledgements."

Zachary continued to incorporate that message while spreading Autism Awareness, Acceptance, and Inclusion worldwide. A few weeks after all this, he spent the entire day, from morning to night, being interviewed four times thanks to his latest PR campaign: a television news segment for an NBC News affiliate, two podcasts, and a program on NPR radio.

Why Does it Matter?

During his interview with NPR radio, the host asked him an important question that made him pause and reflect for a second. He was eager to answer it for the world to understand, yet it caught him slightly off guard, since he wasn't quite sure how to do so concisely.

"Why does it matter, Zachary, what other people think of you?"

"Um … That's a great question. I guess it's because I'm a person whom people can trust. Whenever I get teased, negative comments, or cussed at, it hurts me because they are assuming I'm incompetent or have nothing to contribute to society. I *know* I've been placed on this planet to teach and encourage others, whether that be math, disability awareness, or what have you. And then I worked hard to improve my skills in juggling, piano playing, sleight of hand, video making, and other creative pursuits.

"I feel called to bring hope and joy into people's lives, and therefore, I believe I should have equal opportunity to do so. If these were people who'd hold my fate in their hands, then I could be sure they wouldn't give it to me, judging me on my outward appearance or speech impediment. It'd tell me that they don't trust me or believe me. Listen, I want everyone to succeed in life. I believe in their purpose, but it seems they wouldn't believe me if I told them. They might assume I'm just pretending to be on their side, offering false compliments, so to speak.

"Since high school, over a decade ago, I have desired to fulfill all the passions I just listed, but only Royal Rangers truly gave me that chance. Of course, there were other events, every now and again, that used my skills. Still, there were hundreds of hours each month that I spent at home alone, doing nothing of great value and desiring to be used in my calling, and that was *after* all my schoolwork. I went to apply at a tutoring center, but they said I'm underqualified. I kept asking different ministries at my church, but they essentially told me no. I'm not saying all of that was discrimination, but still, whenever people from the outside were mean to me, I just felt pitiful about it. And in the worst-case scenario, they might tell their family or neighbors to stay away from me, even though I've never done anything wrong. Something like that actually happened to me at my local Target years ago.

"Again, I'm a person whom people could trust, and it's not just me, but *all* disabled people should get an equal chance, but they're not. *That's* why I'm advocating."

63

Special Subbing Days Amid Obstacles

It was a misty, foggy morning at Jefferson Elementary, which was a mere fifteen-minute walk from Zachary's house. Each step felt like a squirt of water in the face.

"Guys, we've got Mr. Corwin as our sub today!" a fifth-grade boy excitedly told his classmates, having just heard it from his teacher. "Big W for us!"

Zachary was in the middle of reviewing the sub plans. Joyous over their acceptance, he walked over to let the students in. "Well, only *part* of the day," he revealed. "I'm a 'Roving Staff' today, so they're sending me to eleven classrooms throughout the day."

"Ugh," many students moaned.

"Well, hey, at least we got you this morning," said the fifth-grade boy.

"Yep, for the first forty-five minutes. I learned a few new tricks since subbing for your classes last year: one with cards, one with a pen, and one with a cube, similar to a Rubik's cube."

All the students began cheering as they walked in and took their seats, listening to Avicii's "Levels," which Zachary chose to play for that day as students entered.

"But we've got to get through some math first, then grammar."

"Hey, Mr. Corwin. Can you put me in your next YouTube video?" one of the boys asked a minute later, setting his folder and Chromebook on his desk.

"Same!" said a girl who overheard.

"Well, sorry, I'm not allowed to put students on social media or mention names or anything personal like that," Zachary explained.

"Why? I give you my permission," the boy insisted.

"That's actually what several students had said in the past—"

"Did someone say you couldn't put us on YouTube?" the girl interrupted.

"No, but it was common sense to me. I've even digitally removed names, personal information, and students who accidentally appeared in the background before."

Moments later, during independent math time, one of the fifth-graders whispered to Zachary, "Can you mew?"

"Uh, what?" he whispered back.

"*Mew.*"

"Do you want me to be quiet?"

"Never mind." The student chuckled and got back to work.

Mute? I've already been quiet for twenty minutes, he thought as he walked away, having misheard what the boy said.

"How was your day so far?" a sixth-grader later asked while the class was working on an Edpuzzle about ancient Egypt.

"Wild. You guys are my fifth class today. I'm subbing eleven classes for twenty to forty-five minutes each, but I've been enjoying every minute of it. It's keeping me on my toes. Also, I was on live television news in Virginia this morning, being interviewed about Autism Spectrum Disorder and my story being autistic. I had to get up at 5:30 for it."

"Wow, that's incredible. Can I ever watch it?"

"Well, I usually get a copy of my interviews and upload it to YouTube."

Unexpectedly, a loud sound crept into the room, breaking the silence. All eyes shifted to a student in the middle of the room.

"I didn't do it!" Zachary called out to interject a little humor.

"Sorry, I didn't know my Chromebook's volume was up that high, and I thought my headphones were plugged in all the way," the student apologized, embarrassed.

"That's okay. It happens," Zachary reassured him as he continued his rounds. Out of nowhere, a thought intruded upon his mind again. *Fine, most of my morning went well*, he thought, *but I just can't forget that man in the gray pickup this morning.*

While having morning parking lot duty, he beckoned a vehicle to move forward, just following protocol. The gentleman in the driver's seat simply disobeyed and sat there, staring at him. The passenger door opened. His son slowly got out, swung his backpack over his shoulder, and began to walk toward the front gate. *Okay, sir*, he thought. *That's fine.*

But as the pickup passed, the driver hollered, "Hey, it doesn't make sense to come all the way over to you, especially since the gate behind you is locked."

"What?!" Zachary called back, not making out everything he said. "What?" he repeated just before the driver floored it. "I'm just a sub here, following orders!" he shouted, knowing there was no way the driver could've heard.

Having lunch duty, Zachary was stationed out in the field. The sun shone over a bright blue sky, which was populated with cumulus clouds above the horizon. One of the fifth-graders playing soccer ran up to him and said with a grin, "Hey, I read your novel. It was very good!"

"Thank you. That means a lot."

"You're welcome," he replied, giving a thumbs-up. "See ya!"

An hour later, he was in his penultimate class of the day. The third-graders were taking a math test about multiplication. Zachary sat down at the teacher's desk, having just made his rounds for ten minutes and was about to relax. The instant he got seated, a third-grader's hand shot straight up. Sighing but smirking inside, Zachary got up and walked to him.

"I'm done. What do I do now?" he whispered.

"Uh … *Oh*, let me get something." Zachary walked over to get a piece of paper from his folder. "Here you go," he said in a low voice. "It's a calculus exam. Just use a separate piece of paper, number the problems, and watch out for the implicit differentiation and integration by parts." Taking a few steps back, he saw the boy's eyes bug out as he pressed his hand on his forehead. "Are you serious right now?" the boy softly said in a high-pitched voice.

Seconds later, Zachary grabbed the mock calculus exam he created as a joke for early finishers, and said, "I'm joking. You could just read silently, go on Epic, or on Typing Club."

"Phew," the boy panted and laughed. "Bet!"

Five minutes later, Zachary took a deep breath. He endeavored to give the class instructions, but nothing was coming out. Trying again, he choked out, "I do apologize for breaking the complete dead silence—"

Immediately, the students looked up at him, surprised.

Nervous to have done so, he continued, "It's a minute before your last recess, so let's get ready for that. Thank you all for being such a wonderful class. I'll be sure to let your teacher know how well you've behaved."

"Thank you, Mr. Corwin," a few of the students said.

A minute later, all the students were outside running around, screaming, and playing, except for one. "Mr. Corwin?" she asked as Zachary was gathering his things to head to his last class of the day.

"Yes, Michelle?"

"My brother is in middle school, and he's subscribed to your channel. I heard you wrote a couple of books and are speaking about autism."

"Yes, I have," he replied, smiling.

"I think that's very brave of you, helping everyone be friends to each other, even if they're different."

Zachary, humbled by her words, didn't know what to say. He smiled, nodded, and said, "Thank you. I do the best I can, and I know it's the right thing to do."

"I shared your videos to my cousin over in Wyoming. He's also autistic, and I thought they could encourage him. Thank you for standing up for what's right. You're like Dr. Martin Luther King Jr. Because of him, I have a best friend. She's from Africa, and she's in the other third-grade class. We wouldn't have become best friends if it hadn't been for him. Because of you, I know many autistic people will have best friends too."

For the next fifteen minutes, the student gave up her last recess to keep the conversation going. Zachary felt honored by the opportunity, grateful that there were students of all ages who truly understood his mission and appreciated it.

The walk home gave him space to reflect on the many positives that had unfolded throughout the day. It had been one of the most meaningful days of subbing, marked by genuine acceptance and the impact he made in students' lives. In a moment, it was abruptly interrupted by a zombie-like yell. Zachary whipped around like a flash of lightning and caught a glimpse of a man in his twenties riding his bicycle a quarter block away. He rode along the cross street and randomly decided to yell at him, just like the passenger in the white sedan in June 2022 and a couple of other times in his life. Just like that, it was over, and Zachary knew it. He knew that in his heart, yet his stomach still twisted and his legs threatened to give out on him. He trusted the neighborhood more those days, confident that he'd be safe without pepper spray as long as he stayed in crowded areas instead of neighborhoods.

There's still more work for me to do, he concluded, deciding to keep boosting his social media videos through ads, even if it meant spending his entire monthly wages.

After getting settled in his room, he checked his emails.

> *Hello Mr. Corwin,*
>
> *My name is Jackson. I've asked for your email and the principal at Cunningham Elementary sent it to me. A couple of months ago, you did an assembly at the school. My sixth-grade son, Fischer, was there, and he is also autistic. He was moved to tears because, for the first time, he came across someone who genuinely understood what it's like to live as an autistic every day.*

Zachary nearly got emotional, barely holding it in, profoundly thankful that his message resonated to yet another student.

Continuing, Jackson wrote:

> *My wife and I would like to know if you would be willing to meet with us some day. Fischer has many questions to ask. We could grab coffee, and perhaps you could also share some advice to help him with the transition from elementary to middle school. If you're open to it, we think you could be a really helpful resource for him.*

Zachary replied, saying that he was more than willing to meet and answer Fischer's questions, which took place the following Saturday.

After he finished checking all of his other emails, he opened up Instagram and saw that he had received a comment. As he read it, he had to look twice. He felt as if someone was pressing down on his chest.

"Can change on a dime." That short simple comment appeared on a reel he had posted, featuring clips from dozens of his interviews on news programs, radio shows, and podcasts, where he had encouraged the world by saying that autistic people are not limited and that everyone has a purpose. And all this user, Patricia, could say was, "Can change on a dime."

"I'm offended!" Zachary couldn't help but say. *Am I not trustworthy in your eyes, after everything I've done? And after I proved it by showing clips from all these interviews across multiple states and countries? Do you honestly assume that just because I'm autistic, I could suddenly turn and become an evil person at any time? This is the problem: neurotypical people like Patricia assuming that we have nothing to contribute to society.*

Before he knew it, he was launched in a full-blown soliloquy. He clicked on the profile and discovered that she lived in the adjacent city. Looking at the pictures, he didn't recognize her, but he did notice that she posted family-friendly content, like sunsets and reel-estate. As he usually does for trolls with a public, family-friendly profile, he followed Patricia, trying to prove what kindness truly is, spreading positivity. After following her, he liked and commented on a few of her posts, praising the stunning naturescapes she had captured around the city.

* * *

The following Sunday, after morning rehearsal at the church, the acoustic guitarist noticed Zachary staring oddly at the piano keys. "Anything wrong?" he asked.

"Oh, it's just the Gbsus4 chord. I mean, it's kind of simple, but arpeggiating it is a nightmare. My fingers feel like they must twist like a pretzel just to pull it off, then quickly land the next chord on the right beat. This isn't the easiest key to play in."

"Ah, those sus chords! They're pretty sussy, aren't they?"

Zachary chuckled. "Uh, that's exactly what all the students would say. Very cringe, no cap," he said, imitating the students. He winked and rubbed his forehead in lighthearted annoyance.

"Golly, I could tell you've been around them too long."

"Yeah, those are the phrases I got comfortable repeating. I would get overly worried about ulterior double entendres that I was unaware of if I repeated any, but then I heard other teachers using their jargon too."

"Ha-ha! Anyway, are you feeling down? I could tell something was up during this morning's practice. Is it finances again?"

"Oh, uh, no," Zachary stuttered, snapping upright in his seat. "Um, kind of, uh, no … yeah. Boy, this is embarrassing on my part."

"Take your time," the guitarist said, taking a seat on a chair.

"U-um, I got an email on Friday after school. Apparently, Tributary University dropped its math and science majors, so it'll be very competitive for me to be an adjunct professor there. The only math course they offer is College Algebra, and they already have enough professors."

"I'm so sorry to hear that."

"It's such a serious setback to my plan. I mean, I love math and teaching, as you know. I was really excited and looking forward to it; they said I'd probably be hired too. But I was also counting on the increase in income for, well, you know, um, PR and advertising. I haven't told this to anyone, but one night recently, I was walking through the outdoor mall, feeling horrible, when suddenly it felt like the night sky opened up and shone brightly. Now it feels like a black hole again, almost as if I'm crossing the event horizon." He buried his head in the palm of his hand for a second. "And so I emailed my former community college, asking for an update on my application. They replied with a screenshot of their fine print. Circled in red, they kindly reminded me that applicants should not email regarding the status of their application. I just don't know what to do because I'm not optimistic about them anymore. It seems like the sky is falling … like an *avalanche*. I was told that, with a master's degree, I could be a professor."

"Well, keep trying. A door will open someday, and it will open to the perfect job for you. You mustn't take any rejection to heart."

"Oh, I know. I'm definitely not stopping. Also, that reminds me of a comment I got on YouTube. This man suggested that I find a different purpose in life if I can't handle rejection. I replied to him saying, 'There are two main types of rejection: one, being rejected for a lack of qualifications or they hired someone else, and two, being rejected based on prejudice. In life, there will be the first type of rejection, and I'll be understanding when that comes, but for the second type of rejection, although it exists, I'm not going to stand for it and be silent on the issue.' He commented on an

Autism Awareness video I posted about being harassed in the neighborhood, not a video about careers or whatnot, but I told him I appreciated the comment so that I could clarify my point."

"Well, anything *positive* going on recently?"

"Uh, yeah. I got a text last night from the mother of one of my tutoring clients. She said her son passed his final. It's the third time he's taking Algebra 1 at his high school, so this was his last chance. Both of them are incredibly appreciative for me, which made me feel amazing. I usually see that mother recommending me whenever she comes across posts from people looking for a tutor."

"That's so wonderful, Zachary. Great job. See? You're definitely helping students"

"Indeed, and I know that in my heart. In fact, another client, a middle schooler, commented on that aforementioned video, cheering me up by saying how much I've helped him in math and in understanding Autism more through my videos. Anyway, I was planning on offering my tutoring services even after becoming an adjunct professor, if I had the time. As I've been tutoring students, I began feeling joy inside. I'm like, 'This is precisely what I've been wanting to do all these years. Now, I'm finally getting the opportunity.'"

"Excellent. How much are you charging, out of curiosity?"

"Um, well, I leave it up to each family and what they are comfortable with."

The guitarist gasped, his mouth hanging open in stunned disbelief.

"Well, a lot of people told me to charge fifty dollars, but I really want students to succeed. If families cannot afford that, I don't want my fee to stand in the way. My average has been between twenty and fifty dollars per session."

"Zachary, I wouldn't take any *less* than fifty dollars per hour. Are they all from your school district?"

"No. Some came from other school districts, and others came from private schools."

"Well, if they could afford private school, for sure they could afford fifty dollars per hour, but I understand your heart; that's incredibly nice of you. Just pray about it, okay?"

"Sure, but it still feels a little funny charging for services that I always wanted to do, even for free."

"Yeah, but they're paying you for your time, expertise, and passion. Plus, you sort of need the extra cash, right? If people pay you, then obviously you're of great significance to them. Had tutoring been profitable for you?"

"Oh yes, definitely. It increased my budget so that I'm not spending my entire income like before, unsure of which avenues would actually work," he said, masking his gloom, knowing that thousands he had already spent on social media advertising hadn't worked well yet.

"Do you ever follow and support other advocates on social media?"

"All the time. I find hundreds of them. I like, comment, and follow them, sometimes sharing or reposting them. I'm definitely not trying to do this alone, and I'm definitely *not* in competition with any of them. They're usually very appreciative and follow me back. A couple of them actually stay and support my future posts. However, some of those people disappear after a week or a month."

"Well, keep going. Focus on the blessings in your life, and trust in God. Recall the lyrics to the song we all played today, 'Honey in the Rock.'"

"And have patience," he added with a wry smile, knowing it was true, even though it was tough to accept. "I absolutely loved playing that song on the keyboard with you guys today, by the way."

"I actually got to hear Brandon Lake and Brooke Ligertwood singing it in concert."

"That's incredible you got to see them in person. Anyway, another plus is that I'm receiving an award soon."

"*Really?* For what?"

"It's for an annual reception for the school district and the entire PTA council. The PTA president from Ironwood Peak High School nominated me for one of the awards because of all my efforts: leading volunteer assemblies and being a dependable, sought-after substitute teacher. It'll take place in May."

"Great. How many assemblies did you do this year?"

"Just nine, and only a third of them were in my district. Makes me so frustrated. If the community college doesn't hire me, then I have a plan B. I just applied to three schools to be a math teacher."

The guitarist's eyes lit up in astonishment.

"But they're in other districts. I thought that if I have to start now, I'll begin with a private or charter school. I didn't want to apply just yet because I'm trying to do my assemblies in every school, but financially, I cannot go any longer. I need enough money to survive, and apparently, I need to spend the rest on PR and advertisements."

"Well, I can't tell you what to do or think, but I wouldn't spend all your money on ads and such. I know your heart, and your mission is noble, but still. What are the results of your ads so far?"

"Sort of the same: increased engagement per post with mostly positive feedback, but I rarely see the same users again. Less than five percent were trolls, but that comes with the territory. One guy on YouTube said, 'Man, I wouldn't be paying or wasting money on this.' I'm like, huh? Obviously, ableism exists in the world, and my videos spread awareness by dismantling the stereotypes of autism. When people understand, they're more likely to accept us in society. Furthermore, suicides, especially among children and teens, should significantly decline because everyone would treat each other with respect and include one another. If my videos, which I create and share *freely*, won't pick up and take off, it'll take a million times longer for this world to have such peaceful acceptance, which is why I force them through the algorithms using ads."

"I hear you. Well, if you continue to post on social media, it should pick up, sometime."

"I said the same thing for years, posting endlessly with SEO and sharing it all around, but it hadn't work. It always felt like I was ignored or censored for trying to make a positive change, getting people to understand us disabled individuals and accept us in society. It's 2025, yet I'm still discriminated against by ableists in my neighborhood and occasionally on social media. But I get what you're saying. I've stepped back from many things that weren't profitable. I haven't bought a lottery ticket or scratcher in months. I decided to hold off on purchasing another month of transit shelter ads. Literally *no* book sales whatsoever; I'm only selling a couple of books a month.

"Also, last year, I gave a $359 down payment for audiobooks, but they ended up being AI voiceovers. I told the guy from Boca Raton that I wasn't interested, but he insisted that I stay. It dragged on for five or six months, and I still hadn't heard back. Then he ghosted me for two months. Finally, I reported the fraudulent company to the BBB and the FTC. I posted all over social media to warn others, and a few people commented that they'd been scammed by the same guy too. The company blocked me and my friends on Facebook just for submitting a review on their page. I also gave a one-star rating and review on Trustpilot.

"It's so lifelessly depressing. I mean, it's only $359, but it's the principle of the matter. Still, I could seriously use that money for good. I must've sent them a hundred emails, telling them to refund me. Alas, the BBB and FTC haven't done anything … yet. Apparently, they have a sister company in St. Petersburg, Florida, writing résumés for people, using the same phone number, so I reported them too."

"Well, please remember all the positive things in your life instead of dwelling over the negatives," the guitarist encouraged. "Try to lay some of your burdens down, like that song we played today, and give it to God. We all go through ebbs and flows."

Zachary nodded. "My grandfather always sang that song, ever since I was a boy. It's just incessantly stressful, especially since my progress seems to be sinusoidal instead of exponentially increasing."

Strolling home that afternoon, he spotted a gentleman in a T-shirt who wore his baseball cap backward, standing just outside the local Subway. Seeing Zachary walking toward him thirty feet away, he briskly opened the door and fiercely whispered to his son, beckoning him to come over that instant. Waiting for his son, he glanced sharply at Zachary for a second, who was now mere inches away. Passing by, Zachary caught a familiar middle school boy approaching his father out of the corner of his eye. His glance through the sunglasses was so subtle that neither the father nor the son realized that they've been caught, so to speak. After Zachary was about twenty feet away, the father got down at his son's level, points at him, and sternly asks in a loud whisper, "*Who* is *that guy?!*"

"That's Mr. Corwin," the son replied in a low voice. "He's a substitute teacher—"

Unbeknownst to them, their voices were still picked up by Zachary's ears, despite the distance. He had no clue how it ended, which is why, a city block later, he felt hammered. In his mind, he envisioned swinging around, saying, "Yes, that's me. Did you say Mr. Corwin? Oh, hi, Harrison." From there, it was fifty-fifty how it could've unfolded. The father may have become furious. After all, he seemed to consider him as a creep, giving all his secretive behavior.

"Hi, Mr. Cor—" Harrison may have started, eliciting his father to say, "Who the heck are you, and how do you know my son's name, you bum?" Regardless, Zachary could've informed him, "I subbed for Harrison's class at Cunningham Elementary in fifth grade as well as at Canyon Mountain a couple of months ago. I actually student taught his older brother, Harvey, in Mrs. Porter's class back in 2022. Oh, by the way, wasn't Harvey born on March 7? And Harrison, it's September 3, right?"

As always, a few scenarios ran through Zachary's mind, resurfacing intermittently for the next year. What bothered him most was simply not knowing. Why did the father act so agitated and secretive? Why was he even concerned about him at first sight? Why couldn't he simply ask him himself like a normal person would? Did he have a problem with a strange-looking autistic individual teaching all the children in his district? Was he insinuating the same things the security guard at the park did, just based on outward appearance?

Once he got home, he checked his notifications and emails again.

"I read the first line of your book," one Instagram user commented. "ChatGPT could do better, you fraud. Womp, womp!"

Aghast, he spent the next several minutes deliberating, *Do I really want to respond? Is it even worth it? What would I even say that would change his heart? There's literally nothing I could say, other than adding fuel to the fire. 'Don't feed the trolls,' people always tell me. I know that not everyone will appreciate or make sense of my writing, but at least be nice to everyone and yourself.*

Taking a deep breath, he decided to move forward and read the other comments. After all, that user only discovered him because the reel was promoted. All the other comments were positive. One woman thanked him for helping her see things differently, glad that she and Zachary both didn't give up on achieving their dreams.

That's what it's all about, Zachary thought, feeling glad.

After checking his social media notifications, he went to check his emails. He saw one from the community college. His heart skipped a beat. He paused for a few moments, allowing his snack to digest and settle before opening it. He always assumed the worst—*rejection*—which was accurate half the time. He learned the hard way years ago not to be eating anything when opening such fifty-fifty chances, and in his case, it was usually ten-ninety (ninety-percent chance people rejected him, when he knew he was qualified). Of course, deep down, he knew some places had competition, so he couldn't take it personally.

He took a deep breath and opened the email, but his stomach immediately dropped. Muscling through it, he began to read, "Zachary Corwin, thank you for your interest in working at our college—"

Here it comes, he lamented.

"Unfortunately—"

I knew it, he thought, regretting that he ate his little snack.

"Unfortunately, your Master's in Education and teaching certificate from the state won't cut it. We require a master's degree or higher in the following areas: pure math, applied math, or statistics. Obviously, a doctorate is generally regarded more highly than a master's, and even then, it's competitive. I'd advise pursuing a master's in either of those fields while serving as a teaching assistant. Doing so might possibly put you in a good standing."

He felt utterly hopeless, begging God for help, even though he never stopped praying for it. By this time, he had sold his entire coin collection for a total of thousands of dollars, and most of the proceeds went toward PR and advertising, just hoping one of his videos would take off, or that his books would finally sell and make a difference.

Didn't work yet!

Once it finally happens, in theory, he should be set for life. Any subsequent video would be shown to many, educating about autism or encouraging people to never give up in life. Since there had evidently been many adults who discriminated against him at first sight, then clearly, his message still needed to be heard by everyone. After that, he could focus on PR until he never has to pay for PR again, since news outlets would automatically reach out to him. Finally, he could enjoy life as both a respected math teacher in secondary education and an influencer to billions of people.

Where is everyone in my county anyway? he questioned. *Why have I been to only nine schools this year when, in theory, hundreds of them heard about me? Why haven't churches, libraries, or other places asked me to speak? Where the heck is TED Talks?*

Closing out of that email, he noticed another one had arrived. Upon reading it, joy overwhelmed him, temporarily freeing him from the prison chains of his depressing troubles and giving him optimism that the future is brighter than it seemed.

"Hello Zachary Corwin—"

"Hooray, a 'Hello' this time," Zachary said to himself. "Okay, *that's* promising."

> *I have many friends who are teachers across the county, including the district in which you work, and your name has come up dozens of times within the past several months. Before I go any further, I want to tell you that my daughter is autistic and is in fifth grade. One of her best friends attends a school where you led assemblies at, in Willowbend Unified. The friend told me that you greatly helped her understand autism, empowering her to be a better friend to my daughter. She told me, 'I will always be her friend.' As a mother, I could not have hoped for a more remarkable result from an assembly.*

Zachary panted from sheer joy, struggling to believe what he was reading.

Continuing:

> *That said, I'm the PTA president of a school, also in Willowbend, and we would be eternally grateful to have you come and speak. That is, if you're still booking assemblies. Lastly, I understand that you don't even charge for these assemblies? We respect that decision as it is a testament to your selfless heart, but we'll be glad to give you a small honorarium for your time anyway: a $200 Visa card. In the future, if you ever decide to monetize your assemblies, don't be intimidated to charge up to a thousand dollars.*

Zachary once again felt humbled by an email, yet guilty for taking things personally. Still, he wasn't going to stand by while people treated him or others poorly, online or in person.

Early the next morning, Zachary unlocked Room 25 of Warner Elementary. Small groups of students stood sporadically along the row of classrooms, conversing with one another.

"Are you our sub today?" one sixth-grader asked, catching the attention of a distant sixth-grader.

"Yes," Zachary replied with a smile, opening the door, about to head in.

The distant sixth-grader gasped. In an excited whisper, cupping a hand around his mouth, he called out to the first sixth-grader, "Spencer! *Spencer!* You got the best sub."

"What?" questioned Spencer.

"You guys got the best sub," he answered, still whispering and edging over in a low crouch. "He does card tricks and juggling. You're gonna love him."

"*Oh!* He's the guy who subbed on the only day I was absent. My classmates told me all about him, and I heard about him the past couple of years. *Finally*, I got him as a sub."

When Zachary arrived at the teacher's desk, he found the two-page sub plans, which was dwarfed by the skyscraper of papers, packets, and books, organized by paperclips and oversized rubber bands. Everything was stacked neatly in the order of the day's lessons, from the morning warm-up to the final activity. He always admired it when teachers were this organized.

After starting to play his song choice, which was "Windfall" by TheFatRat, he opened the door to let students in, who walked to their desks bopping to the music.

At recess time, the students ran out, hollering, "How'd he do that trick?"

At least it wasn't like other schools, Zachary thought, relieved. *Those students literally screamed and sprinted out the door.*

"Hey, Mr. Corwin," said Chase. "Thanks for the help."

"No problem, Chase. Using 'special' as an insult isn't kind. It's derogatory. That's why I stepped in when I heard that. I've heard students say 'special,' 'that's SPED,' or 'that's … R-word,' whether or not they were talking with, or about, autistics or other disabled people."

"It used to bother me, but not much anymore. Anyway, I got two questions for you. I'm subscribed to you, and I know that you write and speak about autism, so, what's your number-one challenge with autism? And what's your number-one accomplishment."

"Oh, boy … You're putting me on the spot. It's hard to choose one. Number-one challenge? I'd just say it's the social factor of being autistic. I was teased a lot. I made friends, but I was super shy to spend time with them unless they came to me first. Number-one accomplishment? Hmm, publishing books? Gold Medal of Achievement through Royal Rangers? That's what I would say."

"Okay, thanks." The student smiled and ran out to recess.

Heading toward the office to make copies, Zachary heard one of the sixth-graders call out to his friends from other classes, "That's my sub! He's goated, no cap!" Looking over at him, Zachary saw the student pointing, his eyes lighting up. He waved in return. A teacher, walking in the opposite direction, smiled at him. Without stopping, she said, "The whole school is raving about you. They all want you to be their sub."

On the way back from making copies, a student handed him a folded piece of paper. "This is for you; it's from the class," the student said.

"Thank you." Opening it up, he read, "Thanks for being the best substitute ever!" Surrounding the message, all the students signed their names. "Thank you *so* much," Zachary repeated. He always appreciated notes from students, but a couple of times, he received notes like this, signed by the entire class of their own volition.

Closer to the classroom, eight students rushed up to him, begging to see a card trick.

"Let him cook!" shouted one student as Zachary pulled out a deck of cards.

"Okay, someone, name a card," Zachary prompted.

"Three of clovers," said one student.

"Three of *clubs*?" Zachary corrected with a smile. "All right, so there's one card that's flipped down. Take it out; turn it over."

"What the sigma?!" the student said, astonished. The other students began hollering. Nervously, Zachary looked up and saw a few aides glancing over at them. The last time that happened, he had been surrounded by thirty students all pressing against him, and each other, to catch a glimpse of the card trick. Ultimately, a couple of aides had to break it up. Fortunately, that was not necessary on this day.

"That was cool, Mr. Corwin. Not gonna lie," said another student, smiling.

"Oh, he's flexing!" Another student ran away, giggling.

Being a sub for a few years, Zachary knew what that new idiom meant, but he didn't know what to make of that. *Did he like my trick, or did he think it was dumb?* he questioned. Not giving it another thought, he successfully carried out the rest of the day.

"Mr. Corwin, normally, you direct traffic over there," said one of the fifth-graders after school, pointing to where he should be stationed at.

"Oh, thanks. I've never done parking lot duty at this school before."

Zachary alternately held vehicles back while letting e-bikers and pedestrians pass, and vice versa. While vehicles were coming in the parking lot, students began to pile up on their e-bikes in front of Zachary.

"Thank you, Mr. Corwin," said Spencer, who was first in the growing line of bicycles.

"No problem, Spencer. It was a pleasure to sub for your class."

"I'm just so happy I got to have the coolest sub in the district today."

"That definitely means a lot ... like you wouldn't know," Zachary said as he made the switch.

"All right, have a good day!" he said as he rode off, turning onto the street. As the train of thirty e-bikers and pedestrians were pouring out of the school's premises, several of them thanked Zachary, wishing him a good afternoon.

Ten minutes later, a couple of blocks away, Zachary heard someone running behind him. Dismissing it as a student rushing home for something, he continued walking, but suddenly, the student called out, "Mr. Corwin!"

Turning around, he saw one of the fourth-graders whom he hadn't officially met yet. "Yeah?"

"Mr. Corwin," he repeated, jogging the rest of the way to him, his heavy backpack bouncing against his shoulders. "Phew," he panted, completely out of breath. Zachary was worried something was wrong and was prepared to help in whatever was needed.

"I just ... want to let you know ... I think ... it's really cool ... that you're a sub ... and do tricks ... all at the same time," he choked out between breaths.

Zachary let out a sigh of relief, knowing that there wasn't an emergency, and thanked him for the compliment.

"All right, bye!" The student gave a quick wave as he turned around, hurrying back toward the school. "You're the GOAT!" he was heard yelling back.

As Zachary turned around himself, trying to process everything that had just happened, a student in the passenger seat of a car waved and said hello to him. He returned home feeling more positive, accepted, and included than ever.

64

A Tireless Advocate

Cirrostratus clouds hung overhead at a middle school across town.

"Hey, welcome back!" said the office manager.

"It's great to be back," Zachary replied, smiling. "Subbing seventh-grade math today."

"Math? Right up your alley, buddy," said the campus safety officer who was leaning against the back wall.

On the way to the classroom, Zachary noticed a student turn and look at him. Expecting the usual hello from this particular student, he instead gave him an uncharacteristic grin before turning and walking away. Zachary stopped and stood there for a couple of seconds, taken aback. *What happened?* he questioned.

When the morning bell rang, students began pouring into the classroom.

"I think this guy subbed for me like two years ago," a student in first period remarked to her friend at her table.

"What's that?" Zachary, who heard, asked as he was turning down the music he chose for that day, which was "Try" by P!nk.

"I think you subbed for my class in fifth grade," she responded, chuckling.

"Oh yes. I remember you. You were in Mrs. Perez's class, weren't you?"

The student's countenance instantly flipped to a mix of shock and being freaked out.

"Carla. Right?"

"Oh my gosh! How does he remember my name?! You're a creep!" she flippantly remarked.

"What did you say?" Zachary managed to ask after a two-second pause, wondering if he heard correctly, visibly perplexed.

"Uh—" the student looked around and pointed at a random student sitting at another table. "She called you a creep!"

Zachary looked at the girl at the other table, knowing that the fault had been redirected onto her. The girl looked completely taken aback, worry etched on her face. She shook her head at him as if saying, "What? I'd never say that." Zachary, still stunned for being treated like that, signaled to the innocent student that she wasn't in trouble.

The bell rang at that moment. Speechless, Zachary turned away, his mouth slightly open. He shook his head and walked to the whiteboard. "Good morning, class. I'm Mr. Corwin," he began, his voice sounding weak as if recovering from the flu.

A short break followed the first two periods. Walking out, a student spotted Zachary. Shouting and pointing, she said, "Hey! The YouTuber!" Other students ran up to him, asking to see a card trick.

"Whoa, what is that?" nearby students questioned, pointing upward. "There's a rainbow around the sun."

"It's caused by cirrostratus clouds: very thin, high-altitude clouds made partly of hexagonal ice crystals. Light from the sun goes through the crystals, slows down, *refracts* (which means bending), and that's why we're seeing a solar halo." Zachary couldn't help but explain. "Rain's likely to occur within twenty-four hours, though not guaranteed."

"How do you know that?" one student asked, amazed.

"I taught the Weather Merit at Royal Rangers a couple of times. If teaching and medicine wouldn't work out, I was going to become a meteorologist."

"Oh, Zachary," said the office manager a moment later, running into him. "I understand that you have prep next period, but would you mind covering an eighth-grade math class?"

"No, I wouldn't mind at all."

"Perfect! The sub plans and math packets are in there; everything's all ready to go."

Twenty-five minutes later, Zachary was standing before a class of eighth-graders, asking them rhetorically, "Are any of you guys even listening to me?"

"No!" one student, Stevie, had the audacity to say while he was mewing.

Employing a little humor to see what would happen, Zachary responded, "Well, if you weren't listening to me, how could you have answered my question?"

"*Ohhhh!*" the student next to him hollered in his ear. "You got *owned*!"

Speaking at Stevie's expense, another student started, "Imagine being that one guy—"

"Hey! That's enough," Zachary said firmly, putting an end to the teasing, feeling like it was partly his fault to begin with. He sagged while ninety percent of the students kept shouting at each other in conversation, despite knowing who he was and what he had accomplished in his life. *So these are the students who only respect me outside the classroom, but once I'm their sub, they treat me like I'm invisible?* he thought, struggling to decide whether or not to muscle through the practice problems. He scanned the classroom and saw only ten percent of the eyes on him, eager to continue, pencils in hand.

But come on, I've got to be practical!

Hiding the emotions of worthlessness and dejection, Zachary resigned to his fate and pleaded with them to listen for just thirty final seconds.

"Bet!" a few students said as the room fell silent.

"You know, for twenty minutes, I've tried hard to help you understand how to find the volume of three-dimensional shapes. Your teacher said in the plans to do ten practice problems, and we're barely halfway in the second … *after twenty minutes*. That is egregious. I have a teaching certificate in math. I am a math tutor on the side. Nothing would satisfy me more than seeing *all* of you succeed. But, you know, I tried my best to help, and obviously, most of you don't want my help. Just know, if you're not taking the time *now* to learn, you're really going to struggle once the exams come, and your grade *will* reflect what kind of student you are. That said, for like the first time in years, I give up—"

"Aww!" a couple of students said, feeling bad for him.

"*Not* on any person in this room, but I'm simply giving up trying to teach you guys, since I've realized it's an exercise in futility, teaching in a vacuum and literally wasting my breath and energy. For those of you who actually want to learn this, continue working independently, and raise your hand if you have any questions."

Zachary moped back to the desk and slumped onto the chair, beginning to write a lengthy note to the teacher. Just like that, the room that had been completely quiet for him erupted back into chaos.

Crash! After a sudden thud that nearly caused some extra seismic activity, most of the students began laughing at the top of their lungs, including the student who caused it. A boy had deliberately fallen out of his seat and onto the floor.

Shaking his head, Zachary asked himself, *Am I subbing* eighth *grade … or preschool?*

For the remainder of the period, a few assiduous eighth-graders raised their hands, requesting for his help.

Halfway into fourth period, back with the seventh-graders who had been exceptional for him, Zachary suddenly received a text, email, and Instagram message at the same time. While the students worked on independent practice, he pulled out his phone and read, "Hi, Zachary, I know this is super short notice, but would you be willing to speak on ABC again today? It'd have to be within an hour. The CDC just reported that the prevalence of autism in eight-year-olds in the U.S. is now approximately 1 in 31."

His heart dropped right then and there. He desired to contribute to the breaking news story but wondered how it would all work. Out of nowhere, he got the idea to do the interview during his lunch break, using the borrowed laptop.

Fortunately, it worked this time!

"He's a tireless advocate," the reporter said toward the end of the news segment, which aired at 5:30 that afternoon.

Hmm! Zachary pondered. *'A tireless advocate,' she said. Ha-ha! That's* exactly *who I am! I'm going to go with that, just like when that Facebook user called me 'Ambitious' back in 2019. I'm definitely the embodiment of both. I think I'll use that. 'Tireless advocate.' Nice!*

"Did I see you on the news?" several congregants asked after church the following Sunday morning.

"Yes," he replied with a smile, shaking inside. He was tense, not because of the recognition, but because he was in the same sanctuary as Kaitlin and Pastor Andrés. It was their first time back in a couple of years since their move. At that moment, Kaitlin was catching up with her friends near the front of the sanctuary.

Once again, let's find out if she truly hates me for being autistic, Zachary said to himself, knowing that he never did anything wrong to deserve all she did. *I hope I'm overreacting, though.* He pulled out his phone and began browsing, standing a few feet away from the left doorway of the sanctuary.

Not looking up at her, he sensed Kaitlin walking down the left aisle toward him. His heart began racing.

For no apparent reason, Kaitlin quickly backed up, passed the front pew while dodging groups of congregants, and briskly began to walk down the right aisle.

Continuing to look down at his phone, pretending to check notifications, Zachary slowly began walking toward the right doorway. In his peripheral vision, he saw Kaitlin halt, then walk even faster across the front, down the left aisle, and dart out the door.

I just can't believe it! Zachary thought afterward. *What the freaking heck did I do?*

Five minutes later, he wanted to share with one more friend about the blessing of being interviewed on ABC at the last moment. The only problem was that his friend was in the middle of a conversation with Pastor Andrés and Kaitlin. For five minutes, he waited behind his friend next to the parking lot, pretending to check his notifications again.

"Chuck," Zachary instantly said once the conversation was over.

Kaitlin immediately barreled out of there, rushing the long way around her family Volkswagen to get to the front passenger door. She did this instead of simply walking in front of the vehicle like an ordinary person would.

That does it! "Have a nice day, Kaitlin!" Zachary said with a smile, just to spread some kindness and positivity, but Kaitlin looked down, refusing to answer. *It's not my prerogative. It's God's. But I sure hope she's not in children's or teen ministries with such animosity toward a protective class of people. If she still worked here, I would at this time let the pastors know everything, but thank God she doesn't. I pray she'll become a better and stronger Christian someday.*

"Hey, how's the job hunt coming along, Zach?" asked Chuck, an older gentleman with a short white mutton chop beard.

"Still nothing. I'm probably going to end up subbing yet another year. Fortunately, that'll provide time for more assemblies, since it'd be almost impossible to lead any if I'm a full-time teacher. Unfortunately, I'll be in financial ruin, since, for the time being, I need to advertise if I'm going to encourage everyone on the planet."

"Well, I'm still praying. Sometimes, especially at private schools, they don't hire until October or November because enrollment numbers aren't finalized yet. That's what happened to me. They didn't hire me until January, in fact, eons ago. Also, they might have many applicants, but only one or two positions, being smaller schools than public schools."

"Yeah, they probably have a higher standard too."

* * *

For Zachary Corwin, summer 2025 was not a living hell financially like summer 2024. It was a living hell *socially* like summer 2024 and almost like the horrid summer 2021. As in parts of 2024, he noticed students he recognized giving him strange looks or simply turning their heads away, not even acknowledging him as they went by. He could not understand what the heck was happening.

Of course, it was mostly *adults* who thought of him as some alien.

The first major incident occurred two days before his thirtieth birthday. Walking by the pizzeria along the thoroughfare, he noticed five young men huddled around a small table, some shirtless and others in T-shirts. Through his sunglasses, he noticed one of them giving him a weird grin, whispering to the other four to glance over. Abruptly, all five guys immediately dropped their heads, three scrambling on their phones and two shoving food in their mouths.

As Zachary walked by, he saw one of the eaters smirking, pretending to chew quickly, obviously exaggerating. Speaking in a low voice while holding his fork and refusing to look at him, the man murmured, "Yum, yum, yum, yum, yum."

It was *strange*!

Ever since that day, Zachary wished he had turned around to let them know that he understood what they were doing. He also knew inside his heart that this wasn't random. He discerned it.

After a week of feeling pain and dyspneic over it, he finally got it off his chest by uploading a video about it to social media. After all, he'd be a hypocrite if he didn't, having told millions not to bottle things up inside. In this video, after years of hinting at it, he was more direct in his warning: people who are not as strong as him *will* commit literal suicide if these pathetic, vulgar, darn-stupid acts of discrimination continue!

That night, he was browsing on Nextdoor. Suddenly, he saw a post that sent shivers down his spine. It wasn't the neighbor's post itself, but it was a person who commented on it. Lo and behold, it was Patricia from Instagram, the one who had little trust in autistics, assuming that they'd "change on a dime." Same profile picture and everything. In lieu of stewing over it any longer than he had, he decided to make a second video about her original comment from Instagram the next day.

A week later, he was taking his typical walk through the outdoor mall, listening to Nelly Furtado's "I'm Like a Bird," teleporting him back to the early 2000s in early grade school. Out of nowhere, while wondering if he should fly away to some other place, a group of students called out to him, asking how his summer had been and if he learned any new tricks.

Finally, a break in the storm clouds! he said, half-optimistically. As he was showing them, more students from around the mall gathered to watch. Some asked him if he remembered them or their birthdays.

Even though ninety-nine percent of this encounter was positive, some middle-aged gentleman with a long, flowing beard had to louse it up.

"Magic tricks? How much you chargin'? Ha-ha-ha-ha!" he scoffed without missing a step.

"For free!" Zachary called out annoyed, but the gentleman kept walking, paying no attention to what he said. *Can't you let me explain, sir? I'm a substitute teacher, and I've been great at the job. Just ask all these many students surrounding me! I'm autistic and the author of two books about it. I've been featured in hundreds of news outlets, radio shows, podcasts, magazines, blogs, and websites over the years. I happen to be a social media influencer who talks about autism and encourages neurotypical ableists like you to grow up and be kind, not just to us, but also to be kind to themselves too!* Alas, as always, Zachary's autistic mind dwelled on that one percent for a long time thereafter, wishing he had conveyed that message to him, but in gentler terms. Sometimes, he felt guilty for getting so riled up in his thoughts, grateful he hadn't actually said all the things he had wanted to say out loud.

Once he got home, feeling irritated, he worried that he had misconstrued a dogwalker. A block away from his house, a dogwalker spotted him from twenty yards away, having looked over his shoulder. For no apparent reason, he stopped and faced Zachary until he passed by. After he was several yards away, the dogwalker continued and turned the corner.

The heck? Zachary thought, instantly reminded of walking down the same sidewalk when that silver Ford F-150 followed him in 2021.

Within twenty-four hours, he received two rejection letters from schools he had applied to. Both schools thanked him for applying, but with so many applicants, they chose someone else.

Darn it! he thought, *and with the school year starting in a few weeks, could the other four schools have already rejected me without telling me? If that's the case, how on earth could I afford the PR and advertising in the budget that I need in order to get everyone* kind *to one another?!*

He didn't care if he went into debt. He hardly had anything left to sell, especially after selling his entire coin collection following decades of the hobby. With money he earned as a sub, as well as a tutor, he began setting up advertisements across social media. He also labored over several videos and dozens of Shorts. This time, he experimented with various new tactics, such as stock footage, captions for viewers to read, and asking questions, all to boost engagement, which seemed to work by the end of summer.

"After all, I'm a 'tireless advocate,'" he said to himself with a smile of determination. "Not even the devil himself will stop him."

One week into August, frustrated as he mulled over the fact that many people seemed to hate him at first sight (both in person and on social media), even though he had shown nothing but kindness and respect, he decided to email Dr. Peterson at Canyon Mountain. He was already discouraged that he hadn't done his volunteer assemblies over there yet, even though the PTA had given him hope. He had patiently waited the entire 2024-2025 academic year for the opportunity, but nothing came from it. He also wondered what the heck happened with all the other schools who obviously knew him. The only reason he has been without a well-paying career was because of his heart to change his entire community beforehand.

And now look, he lamented. *The city is still littered with ableism and arrogance, here and there, although I* am *appreciative for the thousands of kind people I come across. I just wonder why I get so perturbed over a measly five or so percent of the human population. But hey, if I don't, I probably wouldn't have the push to keep spreading awareness and acceptance, right? Still, I don't know how much longer I could live with this garbage.*

After sending the email, he read a news article that popped up on Google. Earlier that day, a sixty-year-old in California buried himself in sand and shot himself.

Zachary slammed his fist onto his laptop's palm rest on impulse and broke down right then and there, feeling entirely alone and helpless. He vowed that he'd sell all his stuff to get *all* news media, social media, schools, and churches to finally pay attention and listen to him.

He did everything—*everything.*

He wrote the books. He created and posted the videos. He liked, commented, and followed several other advocates. He painstakingly spent the hours emailing schools, churches, and news media on his own.

The double hockey-sticks is going on?! It's all in the hands of the algorithms, which always failed me, even when I did hours of keyword research for SEO. But I'm not *stopping, even if I must continue working and uploading day and night. After all, as I've proven for several years, I* am *a tireless advocate!*

65

The Painful Email

The sun rose over the hills, shining across the warm, crystal-clear August skies. Zachary got up at seven o'clock on this Sunday morning and got ready to serve at church. Before leaving, he checked his notifications and emails.

"Oh, he's high as f—Uh … what did I almost read?" Zachary read a comment on his Instagram reel, still blurry-eyed. He moped as he began feeling his heart beating without placing his hand over his chest. He was already fired up in his mind, thinking about a response. First, he thought about what his mind wanted to say, but then, his heart edited out the anger parts.

He thought about it and decided to respond firmly but politely, entreating the user to begin understanding and trusting autistics, who deserve a life as much as he does, concluding with, "Have a nice day" and a smiling emoji. He never heard from the user again.

Throughout 2025, he seemed to withstand trollish comments better than before, deciding to walk away from them and let others reply if they choose to. Rarely did he have to delete the comment, and once, he deleted his own. One night, ten users hammered him simply for commenting on a fellow advocate's reel.

"It's just not worth it," he said before deleting his own comment, automatically deleting the vulgar replies. That split-second choice brought instantaneous relief. It was as if a thousand-pound weight had been lifted from his shoulders. Before he did so, however, he checked the pages of everyone who had replied. Only three had public family-friendly pages. He followed and left encouraging comments, just to prove that autistics can have a heart. He also wanted to show what true kindness is, hoping they'd realize how wrong and ableist they were. After all that, one of them sent him a private message, apologizing for how wrong they had been and applauding his efforts.

See? It was worth it, Zachary thought, feeling grateful. *Even if it's ten percent or even one percent, it's still progress.*

In a blink of an eye, decision paralysis struck again as queasiness ran up and down his digestive system.

That was quick! he thought as he saw that Dr. Peterson had responded. For a miserable two minutes, his cursor hovered over the unopened email, knowing he had to leave for church in five minutes.

Click!

On impulse, Zachary couldn't help it, but he instantly felt like he was going to lose his breakfast ... even though he hadn't eaten anything since dinner the night before. That showed how fearful he was of rejection, even though he knew what he stood for was right. (Not only had *he* said that, but thousands of others told him how vital his presentation on Autism and Disability Awareness, Acceptance, and Inclusion was to society.) He had been rejected more often than not, so much so that his optimism had sunk to the depths of the Mariana Trench. The optimism was still there, but toward rock bottom, sinking lower than pessimism. Thus, before he even sent the email, he jumped to the conclusion that Dr. Peterson would reject him.

Feeling like he'd pass out, he began reading.

"Hi, Zachary. I hope your summer is going well—"

"Still a ten-ninety chance. Move on," Zachary said aloud.

Forcing himself to glance below that first paragraph, he continued to read.

"My stance on this public speaking request remains the same. I am unable to organize an assembly for you or set up any speaking engagements with classes, SSR periods, or otherwise—"

Zachary couldn't believe what he was reading, especially since this was the fifth academic year he had been politely asking. He might as well have been asked to vacate the planet, since his message of kindness, acceptance, and disability inclusion was apparently unimportant to society.

How hypocritical that Canyon Mountain has posters in the office about mental health, he thought. *One even has the suicide hotline number on it. I took pictures of them in case I needed to prove it. But they don't care about a person like me—a person who has a track record of making a difference to others—to volunteer his time to talk about these important matters?!*

He finished the rest of the email, then immediately slammed his fist against the desk in front of his laptop, sending a loud thud echoing through the entire house.

"*Ugh!* God, not again," he lamented, flinching. Looking down, he saw dead skin and blood trickling from the base of his little finger. His right hand had rapidly raked along the edge of the laptop as it came crashing down, scraping off flesh with it.

Clasping his hands in prayer, he said, "Oh God! *Please!* I care about helping others so much. Please help. As I've prayed a thousand times since

2020, I'll pray it again: help me to help the helpless when I feel helpless to help them. Please reverse this. Please get me these assemblies. I've only done so few of them this year, and I don't get it. And where's Washington Elementary? Where's Ironwood Peak High School? Where's all the other schools in this district? Where's all the private schools? I don't care how You do it, but *just do it … Immediately*! Depression is rampant among students, as You know. Ableism is real. I even witnessed students making fun of autistics. There were many child suicides and teen suicides within the past two years *alone*." His face twisted in anguish, not wanting to think about it.

Continuing, he prayed, "O God! Finally start using me to the fullest. I've had what it takes for years, yet here I am, still waiting, hardly doing anything, not taken seriously, and harassed by people for being autistic. I've sold almost everything I own and spent tens of thousands of dollars, ninety-or-so percent of it being a waste. I literally stayed up many nights writing books or making videos, fighting fatigue. God! Haven't I shown that nothing's going to stop me? Why don't You start using me, a broken person, to help a broken world?! This is the life You've given me and put breath in—so *Use It!*"

His head then sunk in his hands, crushed by the weight of rejection and society's discrimination, knowing that all tribulation would impeccably vanish once he finally began living his full purpose: a math teacher, speaker, and a worldwide influencer. On a personal level, all he wanted was a chance. He didn't want money, mansions, fancy cars, fame, or glory. He merely wanted a chance to make a difference in *every* person's life, be respected by others in society, be a valued math teacher and tutor whom *all* students would listen to, and to have an equal chance to bless others through music, juggling, and more.

"Whoa! Speaking of music!" he exclaimed aloud and rushed to church.

Thank God it was a Sunday. Although he felt better handling negative comments, as far as his feelings were concerned, he still chose to open up his notifications while being surrounded by friends, such as at church. That way, after processing the comments, he didn't feel alone. Conversing and spending a little time with those who cared about him helped him forget the trollish comments.

Once church ended at eleven thirty, several bandmates instantly walked over to Zachary, looking concerned. "Are you okay today?" asked the drummer.

"Oh, yeah. I just have quite a headache right now," he admitted, rubbing his forehead.

"Could you tell us what's going on?" asked the bassist.

Zachary explained how Dr. Peterson refused to allow him to make a difference for *every* student—telling everyone that *they have a purpose*, spreading Disability Awareness, promoting acceptance and inclusion, and ending bullying. "I mean, I admit that I can't guarantee that for every person, but still."

"What audacity! And this person has a doctorate degree?" the singer said, her face contorted in shock.

"This is preposterous," added the cellist.

"You're not overacting?" the bassist questioned, wanting to confirm.

"No. I have all the proof. I have the emails from this year and previous years. I'm so hurt right now. I emailed her again *before* the school year began, knowing the entire year couldn't possibly have been planned out yet. The entire PTA was on board with me since 2023. I was relying on them to actually do something, perhaps overriding Dr. Peterson's purview somehow. Same with the PTA at Ironwood Peak High. I was so optimistic, but now, I feel hopeless."

"We can't overstep someone's purview," said the drummer, "but the superintendent can. She's not above whoever the superintendent is."

"That was my final resort, emailing him again like I did a couple of years ago. The board president emailed me back, saying that the superintendent is a fan of my work, but I haven't heard anything since. Please pray that I'd find people with connections."

"Absolutely," the three bandmates reassured him in agreement.

"Try to reflect on that brand-new song we all played today: 'Left It In the River' by Jamie MacDonald," the harmonica player suggested. "Listen to it again, and pay attention to the lyrics. You got to start releasing all your burdens that have been weighing down on you. You've been looking almost like a different person since you joined this worship team over three years ago."

"I loved doing that song. I will listen to it again. Anyway, I mean, to Dr. Peterson's credit, the rest of the email said this," Zachary continued, opening up the email on his phone. "'One possible way for you to secure an opportunity would be to wait until club rush is finalized, which won't be until September. Then, determine whether any of the established clubs would be an appropriate fit for your presentation. If a student or staff member chooses to start a club centered on topics aligned with your message, you could reach out to the staff advisor overseeing that club, asking him or her whether they'd be interested in having you speak to their members. The decision would rest with them. If they agree to collaborate with you, please inform me because I will need to review everything you'll say and approve it before proceeding.'"

"*What?!*" exclaimed the drummer, while the other two bandmates stared at Zachary, shaking their heads.

"I know. I was like, 'Yeah, right. Big deal. I'm *not* called to speak to only 5 or 10 students at a school, but rather the *entire* student body.' I told her that I had brought people to tears, including students. I told her that I had received emails and direct messages from people thanking me, saying my assembly was the first thing their child excitedly talked about when picked up from school that day. Sometimes, parents left comments on the school's Instagram posts about my assemblies, saying similar things. Moreover, the schools plead with all other schools on their social media to invite me over too."

"What about your books and all your news interviews?" asked the bassist. "Doesn't the principal know about them? I'm restraining myself from cussing in a church sanctuary, but why the freaking heck would she need to review what you would say as if you're a liar and would spew hate, or if your ideas are too radical or whatever?—"

"Exactly!" the singer interrupted in a quandary. "Does this person not trust you? Does she not realize that you've already spoken to *thousands* of people and received high praise?"

"Yeah, that's where I was getting at," the bassist said. "Zachary, if you were just getting started with assemblies, or if this was your first school, I'd understand if principals need to review it, but you already have *years'* worth of testimonials from across this entire county, not just the district. You've already spoken to PTAs and to the entire PTA council. What the heck?"

"Indeed," Zachary responded. "I've spoken to over 12,000 students so far. My goal is all … what? Half a million? It's not just this middle school, but where's all the other schools in this county, public and private? 12,000 is such a low percentage in comparison."

"If it's of any consolation, 12,000 is still a lot," the drummer reassured him. "You've done more than most people, especially since you yourself are autistic. You struggle often, yet you have the fortitude to write books, make hundreds of videos, do over a dozen assemblies in one day, and be a highly respected, sought-after substitute teacher."

"And I told her all that," said Zachary, rubbing his forehead. "If I must do one or two dozen mini-assemblies at the middle school, I will. That's much better than the gymnasium, where it echoes and most students tune out … All right, heck! I'm not trying to gloat whatsoever, but I would tutor students on my lunch break. I would tutor after school a couple of days a week for free. If I didn't get a sub assignment, I would just volunteer there to help students just because I cared about everyone there. I mentioned that school by name many times in my second book. Heck, I actually quoted that principal many times, accolading her. Furthermore, I'm an employee of the school district, and I've truly mattered in the lives of *thousands* of students as a substitute teacher. I mean, why would she continue to say no to me, especially in a generation with more disabled people, ableism, depression, and lack of motivation. This is just *so* enigmatic!"

"No one says you're gloating, Zachary," the singer reassured him.

Zachary sighed and thought for a moment. Continuing, he said, "Listen, I've gotten to know Dr. Peterson since 2022. She is a *highly-qualified* principal, in my opinion, but she doesn't seem to understand the impact my assembly *will* make to the *entire* school. I guess I'm also taking it hard because this was the middle school I went to. It's where I did my student teaching at. Still, I feel silenced as if an enemy is blocking a life-changing message from being heard. I'm sick and tired of trying to piece this puzzle together and somehow get assemblies at that school and every other school, at all costs, especially since there's a need out there."

"And your message *does* change lives, Zachary. How long has she been a principal there?" asked the bassist.

"Uh, since 2020 or 2021."

"They'll cycle her out very soon. Mark my words." The bassist nodded with a reassuring smile. "Principals don't really stay long at one school."

"Hopefully, the next one will have enough sense to have you speak," said the singer. "It's such an important message. Many people in this church still talk about the time you spoke that one Sunday a couple of years back. I remember it … and, uh, I often read your heartfelt Facebook posts … I sometimes watch your videos on YouTube … uh—"

The drummer placed his hand on the singer's shoulder to comfort her as she began sniffling.

"And I admire your heart … I-It's just … beautiful," she said, taking the handkerchief the harmonica player offered and wiping her tears.

"And I drove you to that banquet you were invited to speak and juggle at," said the drummer, his hand still placed on the singer's shoulder. "I remember that octogenarian commenting how he had listened to hundreds of keynote speakers within the past sixty years, and that yours, by far, was the best he had ever seen."

"Thanks for the reminder," Zachary responded with a faint smile, though he was still morose. "I remember that too … but, uh, it's just beyond me why schools spend a fortune on other speakers when, *hey*, I'm right here, for *years*, offering to do them for free, *with* the kind of entertainment that helps the message *stick*. And *with* a vast number of testimonials, *with proof*."

"Yes, it's rare to see a motivational speaker who juggles or does magic or whatnot," said the bassist.

"In fact, in case I was never clear, *that's* exactly why I chose to volunteer all these years, despite needing the income," Zachary went on to explain. "My message is far more important than assigning a price to it. Principals and PTA members told me to consider charging for assemblies, even upwards of a thousand dollars if I decide to travel. I feared that if I were to put a price tag on them, even one cent or nickel, they'd assume I'm a charlatan and say, 'That's too much,' or, 'You must not be doing this from your whole heart; you just want the money.' Again, my mission is *every* school in the county. However, I'm *not* saying that those who charge for their assemblies have ulterior motives, but still."

"Essentially, you're forcing them to show their true colors," said the bassist. "If they turn you down, they can't just say, 'Oh, it was out of our budget.' This definitely sounds like the enemy doing this."

"I can't think of an alternate, logical reason," the electric guitarist said in agreement. "It seems conclusive. Somehow, they think you're ineffective, and they refuse to believe in all those testimonials."

"I'm just not sure," Zachary said, looking down, feeling weary. "It just seems like everything fell on deaf ears. I've been getting my name out there for *years*, including through word of mouth. They *have* to know me by now. They *must*. They had *years* to invite me to their schools. I mean, I'd understand if a school is all booked for one year, but after two or three?"

"It's like, 'Come on! Give me a break!'" The bassist finished the sentence for him.

Zachary nodded.

"Well, let us all pray for you and this situation, but know this, Zachary, you always have our support. *Do not* give up on the fight!" said the drummer. "And we know you won't."

66

Scaling Mount Everest

Trudging up the stairs felt like a steep hill. Zachary was bringing up a bottle of cold water from the refrigerator, preparing to call it a night.

What a Sunday, he thought as he collapsed onto his bed.

Rubbing his forehead because of the unrelenting headache, he couldn't help but think about the walk home from church. He decided to buy his favorite smoothie at the nearby plaza. His recollection was still vivid, and he could still hear Avicii's "The Nights," which was currently stuck in his head. As soon as he exited the juice bar, two e-bikers, one behind the other, came riding past him in the parking lot.

"Zachary Corwin!" the middle-school boy in front said.

Huh? Zachary thought, waving as he usually did and saying hi. *What?* His quandary came from the snarky manner in which the boy said it, not to mention his wry grin, which didn't appear to be one of kindness. In a flash, the student was gone. The middle school boy trailing him rode by a few seconds later. Popping a wheelie on his Sur-Ron, the second boy glanced at Zachary, who had waved and said hi, but he ignored the salutation, speeding off with his friend. *Wait … I subbed for his class before. I recognize him. He used to get excited to see me throughout last year, asking me if I still remember his birthday. December 7. I know. I remember. What the heck happened? Where did I fail as a sub?*

In anguish, walking toward the stoplight a hundred yards away, without taking a sip of his smoothie, he questioned the current state of his life. *I guess it'll never end, will it? Come to think about it, I've noticed that same student, the one born on December 7, speeding down the street on his e-bike lately, looking as if he's begging me not to turn and see him as he rides by. You know, I've been noticing that a hundred times these past few months. I've seen students begin to loudly whisper as they see me coming down the sidewalk or walkway, but as I pass by, they're as silent as a mouse and didn't bother to say hi. What the freaking heck is happening? Am I invisible? Is there a false conspiracy against me? I've done nothing wrong. On the contrary, I've been a number-one supporter of everyone, helping them succeed in their academics and motivating them to continue this life!*

Zachary banged the crosswalk button, causing his already bruised knuckle to feel more sore.

A moment later, an e-biker rode up from behind and stopped beside him. Turning, Zachary gave a subtle, neighborly smile and wave, but the e-biker, who looked like he was about to start high school, just stared at him expressionlessly and gave a tiny nod. Within a second, Zachary turned back to face the pedestrian signal on the other side, realizing he didn't recognize the student anyway, though he was sometimes bad with faces, especially when helmets were involved. The last thing he wanted was for it to be the other way around, with students assuming *he* was the one ignoring them. He had always been a shy person anyway because he was autistic. That's partly why he wore sunglasses and faced away, waiting for *them* to be the ones who called out to him. Moreover, suppose he walked by a group of students who attended a private school. Waving first might cause them to wonder, "Uh, why'd that man just wave at us?"

Without warning, just as he began feeling the pulsating dental floss tearing his heart to shreds again, Zachary heard someone say from behind him, "Yo, are you a teacher?"

"Yeah. Well, a substitute," he said, turning around to the e-biker.

"*Really?!*" the e-biker asked, leaning in for a fist bump. "What's good?"

"Are you going to Ironwood Peak High next year?" Zachary asked as he returned the fist bump.

"Yeah."

"I went there as a student all four years."

"That's nice. I like your book."

"Oh, *thank* you … *so* much. I appreciate it," Zachary said gratefully as the walk sign lit up.

"All right. Have a good day."

"You too."

As the student rode down the crosswalk, Zachary took a drink of his smoothie for the first time since encountering the two middle schoolers moments earlier. He had been wondering if his appetite would ever come back that afternoon, but fortunately, it did, once he received that validation.

Swell, Zachary thought. *One act of kindness from a single person, and suddenly all pain fades away. Then you feel guilty for getting upset over five percent of the population. Look, I don't want anyone to feel indebted to me as if they feel obligated to give me special friendship or invite me to parties. Being autistic and someone who had struggled in social gatherings, I'm not seeking that anyway. If I'm asked to speak, juggle, play piano, tutor, or whatever, then that's a different story. As long as I'm* involved, *I won't be bored to death, suffering literal physical headaches. I want to offer my encouragement to society and have an equal opportunity in life to succeed. All I'm asking in return is simple acknowledgement (not strange stares, being cussed at, or running into such sardonic behavior). That's all. At least everyone else would be strengthened to continue their lives with more acceptance, optimism, and hope.*

And come to think about it, a couple of weeks ago, there was also that middle schooler who circled back on his e-bike to ask me if I was Mr. Corwin, requesting to take a picture with me.

Remembering that moment with the e-biker at the corner became a catalyst for many others from that summer alone, one after the other, helping him to sleep better than he otherwise would have that night.

* * *

"Class, may I have your attention for a second?" Zachary said, standing before a room of thirty fifth-graders at Washington Elementary. He had just turned down the song he chose to play after lunchtime: "Ordinary," by Alex Warren, which came out earlier that year.

All the students sat up straight at their desks.

"I want to let you know that not only I, but a ton of us teachers are starting to go berserk. Listen, we've all been hearing the same thing from you six or seven times an hour, for the last six or seven weeks, and we'll probably keep hearing it for the next six or seven months, but anyone who says it in my presence again will drop and give me six or seven pushups. You hear me?"

Zachary, of course, couldn't say all that without students beginning to giggle and snicker.

"I'm like, come on!" he said, breaking character and laughing. (It was hard enough to keep a straight face saying all of that.) "Now I'm noticing those pesky two numbers everywhere: 6:07 p.m. 67% left on my phone's battery, 67 degrees Fahrenheit, and my printer at home requires the HP 67 ink cartridges … *So*, no more 'skibidi' or 'rizz' or 'Ohio' or whatever?"

"No," a few students said. "That was so 2024!"

"Um, you're kidding. 2024 was just last year."

"Yeah. That's a *long* time ago," a student responded as if his opinion was fact.

"Huh? After recess, when I said the AJR song, 'Burn the House Down,' takes me back to 2022, you sounded as if 2022 was an eternity ago. I did my student teaching in that year. Oh well. Anyway, please get out your storybook: *Hatchet*, by Gary Paulsen. We'll popcorn read one paragraph at a time until we finish all of chapter twelve."

All the students rummaged through their desks, pulling out their own copy. One student returned from the restroom, singing the ending of AJR's "World's Smallest Violin," causing some students to laugh and sing along.

"Hey! … Waterfall," Zachary prompted, breaking up the disruption.

"*Shhhh!*" the students said, quieting down.

"I'm sorry, guys. That's a marble." He got up and removed one marble from the marble jar and placed it back inside the jar next to it. It was a strategy some teachers employed to reinforce good behavior and subtly remind students to practice self-discipline. Once they earn every marble, a movie day or a party was their incentive. Other teachers throughout the district gave table points on the whiteboard. If teachers didn't have anything, Zachary would pick one of the strategies he learned as a substitute teacher and use it. "Max, please take a seat quietly. That's not how we re-enter the classroom … Oh, thanks a lot. Now that song is stuck in my head."

Some students snickered.

"All right, who wants to start first?" Zachary asked and waited several seconds. "Well, don't all raise your hands at once … Okay, Daisy. Start us off."

After Daisy read, Amy read.

Then Alexia. Then Kim. Then Keisha and so on.

"Okay, so we're halfway through the chapter, and the girls had read perfectly … All right, fellas. *Your* turn."

A few of the boys raised their hands, getting the message. Robert read next, followed by Omar, followed by Gael, and so on.

Toward the end of the school day, after the fifth-graders were packed up and ready to leave, Zachary did a juggling performance for them, thanking them for being a decent class.

"Guys, we got the best sub!" a student exclaimed as his face lit up.

"You never had him as a sub before?" one of the girls asked, surprised.

"You should juggle for the entire school," said one of the boys after Zachary finished his juggling finale.

Frozen, Zachary looked at him and explained, "Maybe one of these days, Liam. I do lead volunteer assemblies across the county, and I have a powerful juggling analogy, among other important stuff. I've been asking Principal Miller to lead assemblies here for years."

A minute later, in walked Principal Miller, checking in for the last moments of school.

"Can he lead an assembly here?" Liam instantly called over.

Principal Miller smiled and replied, "We're talking about setting one up."

Oh, that's *reassuring!* Zachary thought, trying to remain optimistic.

A moment later, the bell rang, and students began pouring out the door. One student came up to him, saying, "Mr. Corwin, I was that person on Instagram who commented, 'I wish he could be my sub. Just for one day.'"

"Oh yes. I remember that. Well, I hope the day went well for you."

"It did. Thank you for teaching me and for choosing me as a volunteer for that card trick. Bye."

"No problem."

As the students walked off to their after-school program or to the front gate, a woman approached Zachary. "Hey, you're Mr. Corwin, right?" she asked.

"Yes."

"I'm Mrs. Williams, one of the fourth-grade teachers here. One of my colleagues, Mr. Kowalski, whom you subbed for many times, told me, 'Request Mr. Corwin to be your sub. He's great.' If you don't mind, could you give me your phone number and email for when I need a sub?"

"Sure."

After Mrs. Williams left, a gentleman walked by, saying, "Well, well, Mr. Corwin. How'd you do surviving fifth grade?"

"Superb, Mr. Collingsworth."

"That's great to hear. Are you still doing private tutoring on the side? How's that going?"

"Yes. Since it's October, it's finally picking back up. I've received a lot of thank-you messages from parents. Most of the time, the students actually say thank you too. Before Christmas break or summer vacation, I've received thank-you cards and treats from the students and their families."

"Aw, that's nice."

"However, I think the most rewarding moment in my tutoring life came when I received a text from the mother of an eleventh-grader. He was taking Algebra 1 for the third time. His mother said that he passed both finals, thereby passing the class. She said it was all because of me and that she couldn't thank me enough."

"That's *outstanding*, Zachary! I'm proud of you."

"Thanks. And just last night, a tenth-grader from a different school district, taking Algebra 2, pointed at me and told her mother, 'He saved my life tonight, helping me understand piecewise functions.' Then the student gave me five dollars of her own money as a tip."

"Just amazing. Well, I've got to run, but take good care of yourself, you hear?"

After he left, a group of students walked by with the supervisor from their after-school program.

"Hey, Mr. Corwin!" a few of them near the back of the line called out and waved.

"Hey, I found your YouTube channel and subscribed," one of them said, causing other students to marvel, unaware of who Zachary was. "I was searching 'Washington Elementary' just for the heck of it, and you popped up."

"Thank you for your support, Timmy," Zachary replied, smiling.

Everyone stopped walking as the supervisor began checking who was present and who wasn't.

"I found your YouTube channel too," said one of the fourth-graders.

"Oh, thank you."

Transforming his warm smile into a smirk, he added in a very-low voice, "and I reported your channel."

Zachary's expression fell. "What?" he questioned.

"Shut up, Marcus," Timmy whispered into the school bully's ear.

Not listening to him, Marcus blame-shifted to another student. "He said he reported your channel!"

Taken aback, Josiah, the wrongfully-accused student, froze. Jaw dropped, horror washed over his face. *How childish can you be, Marcus?* he thought. "Mr. Corwin, I'd *never* do that!" he said.

"Yes, yes, I know," he said, calmly reassuring him, diffusing his stress. Looking back at Marcus, he said, "I believe I heard *you* saying that."

"No, *I* didn't say that," Marcus denied, playing innocent and walking away.

"What'd you say then?"

Marcus smirked, staring straight into his eyes, and walked away nonchalantly.

"Hey, I'm talking to you."

Marcus ignored him and kept walking.

"Hey!" Zachary yelled, taking a few steps toward him.

The supervisor looked up from her clipboard and shouted at Marcus to come over, stopping him in his tracks.

"I'm cooked!" Marcus whispered under his breath, eyes wide with fear of discipline. "U-uh—" he stammered in front of the supervisor, looking toward his upper right, trying to figure out what to concoct as an answer.

At that moment, Zachary walked up to the supervisor, and said, "You know, I'm willing to forget it. Have a nice day, Marcus."

"But what happened?" asked the supervisor, stopping Zachary from returning to the classroom.

"Um … He just said something against me. But it was to *me*, not a student, so don't worry about it. It's okay."

After walking back inside the classroom, he overheard the other students explaining to the supervisor what Marcus said. Feeling rather depressed, Zachary reminded himself of what he said years ago: "If people aren't fond of what I post on social media, that's fine as long as they're not mean about it. That's their right. I *never* told anyone they must subscribe … *ever*. I just pray they've already accepted themselves and treat everyone with respect." He also had to remind himself that he must stay professional as a substitute teacher and that his social-media life shouldn't stand in the way.

A couple of months went by, bringing more positives than negatives. On his way back from a Christmas party at a church he was invited to, he walked through the parking lot heading toward the outdoor mall. Walking past a parked car, he caught sight of a passenger staring in his direction. He glanced over a few times, each glance lasting only a split second, yet the lady kept her eye on him.

The lady remained expressionless, a hint of vigilance in her eyes as if Zachary might suddenly swing around, lunge, and smash into the windshield.

Trying to write it off as a misinterpretation, Zachary kept recalling similar moments over the past few months when he had seen that expression on people sitting in their cars, not that he was spying on them, but something he couldn't help but notice as he casually walked by.

Unhurriedly, he strolled through the mall's walkway, serenaded by the classic Christmas songs sung by legendary artists, such as Andy Williams, Bing Crosby, Perry Como, Burl Ives, and Gene Autry.

The automatic doors opened as he passed the CVS Pharmacy, and out came a family. A few yards down the walkway, a voice whispered behind him, "Hey, he's the person who goes to our school. He does magic tricks and is on Instagram." It was a third-grader, sounding starstruck. Zachary gave a subtle smile as he kept walking forward, thankful that his ears had the blessing to hear it.

At the last minute, he decided to walk inside the Chick-fil-A for dinner. After ordering the Original Chick-fil-A sandwich to go, complete with their signature dipping sauce, he stood by and waited, enjoying listening to one of his many favorite Christmas songs over the ceiling speakers, "Celebrate the Child," arranged by Jay Rouse.

"It's Zachary!" a boy called out.

Turning, Zachary saw Mr. Collingsworth and his youngest son, Jerome, waving at him, a few booths down. "Hey," he greeted them and walked over. "Boy, it's very crowded in here tonight."

"You better have a seat," Mr. Collingsworth said, scooting over. "You're going to be waiting at least five minutes."

"I haven't seen you at the tutoring center, Zachary," said Jerome. "I'll never forget you tutoring me a couple of times."

"I know. I had to resign almost two years ago."

"My dad told me. A few students kept asking where you went."

"You were quite famous over there," Mr. Collingsworth said, winking.

"'The tutor who did card tricks,' they'd say," Jerome added. "Do you have any cards on you?"

"As a matter of fact, yes. I always carry three or four decks on me nowadays," he explained, causing Jerome to laugh. "All right. Pick a card, any card."

By this point, Chick-fil-A was playing "When Love Came Down," by Point of Grace.

After a few tricks, Jerome thanked him. "I just remembered, I saw you on TV a couple of times."

"Oh yes, they were interviewing me on the news about autism, and I got to tell my story."

"That's cool, and you still pop up on YouTube."

"Well, I'm still posting consistently."

"You're amazing, by the way, like, you're really, really cool," Jerome said, shaking his head and marveling.

"I appreciate it. Thank you." Zachary thought for a second, not wanting the attention to be solely on him, per se. Immediately, he added, "Uh, I always try my best, you know? And as I start out in my YouTube videos nowadays, I say something to the effect, 'I'm autistic. Autism is a neurodevelopmental condition that I never asked for, but I'm making the best of it, and I'm encouraging everyone along the journey.' I'm like, if *I* can do it, so can you, disability or not. Inside everyone are passions, and I'm simply encouraging people to find those passions and never give up on them."

Once he got home half an hour later, he transferred all the pictures of the Christmas party from his SD card onto his computer. About a third of the way through his chicken sandwich, he began looking through them, but he paused at the photo that a gentleman took for him. He was sitting on a rustic bench in front of a snowy backdrop, beside a few Christmas trees.

"Huh," he said aloud and began to contemplate. The bench was long enough for two, maybe three people. Although he knew twenty or so people at the event, there were still a couple hundred he didn't know. His mind began to remind him how lonesome he had felt throughout his life. Here he was, smiling on a bench at a party, looking totally happy, yet with no one beside him.

It reminded him of Vincent van Gogh's painting *Bedroom in Arles*, evoking the same feelings of solitude and lonesomeness.

It reminded him that, despite being photogenic, he seldom appeared in photos on the Facebook page of his high school youth group. Even then, he was usually by himself.

It reminded him of the night he realized he possessed only one of many items around his room, yet his two windows shattered the streak of seclusion, offering him hope.

The following night, he was approaching the pizzeria along the thoroughfare, just after dusk. Around an outdoor table stood a group of young men, all scrolling on their phones and conversing with one another, bopping to Linkin Park's "Burn It Down" that one of them was playing off of YouTube.

As soon as Zachary came into view, all four of them immediately pivoted 180 degrees, turning from facing the street to facing the pizzeria. *You've* got *to be kidding!* he lamented. *Wait! Aren't these the same guys from July, right before my birthday?*

As he walked past, their backs were completely turned toward him as if he had been shunned. A couple of steps later, he subtly glanced back to see if he was just imagining it, but upon doing so, he noticed one of them doing the same, checking to see if he was gone yet. He continued to walk, vanishing in the shadows.

The rest of the way home was uneventful, precluding even a single break from the internal chaos. Slowly, he climbed up the stairs in physical pain, grasping onto the banister. Fighting a headache and mild dyspnea, which was becoming more and more frequent, he questioned why he kept pushing himself. He felt utterly debilitated from the lack of relative acceptance, purpose, and inclusion in life, knowing full well that life would never be perfect anyway. Still, he believed it could be better. He could still be a forceful, transformative advocate without enduring such unprovoked hatred.

He quickly checked all his social media accounts. Although his reels and Shorts were picking up views, he still wasn't growing much overall. His main videos on YouTube, for instance, stayed below a hundred views, despite posting at least twice a week and hiring professional thumbnail designers on Fiverr.

Why didn't I just start an autism-only channel? Why wasn't it made super crystal clear to my autistic brain? Then again, I wouldn't have gotten the momentary support from people across all kinds of niches. It's too late now.

Many people, I've noticed, whether well-intentioned or bad, are motivated by the number of likes, views, and comments. I get it. Otherwise, most of them quit. I understand why. Yet I just never gave up these past eight years on YouTube, despite rarely getting sustained engagement in that way. I just kept going, motivated by the belief that one day, it'll happen, and I could supersede the brain-rotting channels out there and spread imperative messages, together with fellow advocates.

The lack of assemblies, the lack of news media inquiries, and the continuation of ableism in the neighborhood drained him. It had reached the point where comedy videos that used to cheer him up on YouTube weren't as cheery anymore. He tried holding it in, but realized he'd be a hypocrite if he did. After a couple of days of misery, as this loomed over him like pesky houseflies, he decided to post about it publicly across social media, allowing him a chance to process and get his feelings out.

For Nextdoor, he started out by saying:

> *Neighbors, please know that it comes with great fear and trembling to post this, but if I don't, I'm passively responsible for the bullying that goes on in this community and the world. If you read until the end, I give my top summary on how people could help and feel belonging, but I'm just one person. I'm sure every one of us has a unique way to encourage others.*

After describing what happened, he wrote:

> *Incidents like this fuel my fight against ableism, even though it's exhausting and heartbreaking, especially since I've spent years advocating, teaching over 13,000 students in my volunteer assemblies thus far, publishing books, reaching millions online, and appearing on TV, radio, and print media worldwide. Despite all that, in my own neighborhood, people still treat me as if I'm some alien. People sometimes give me weird stares, whether I'm at a store, a restaurant, or wherever. These experiences remind me that what I do matters, and it's not just for me, but for thousands of others who need acceptance, inclusion, and hope.*
>
> *If you're disabled like me, keep going! You have a purpose, and your joy matters. If you're a supporter of this, thank you. Keep teaching and advocating for acceptance, especially to young people who don't yet understand. Ask your schools, churches, and community venues to prioritize disability inclusion and allow advocates like me to speak, teach, and inspire. If you have connections, please tell them that I've been willing to lead assemblies for free.*
>
> *And if you've ever treated someone like I was treated that night, know that you have the power to change too. Your purpose isn't to*

> *harm others, and there's a place for you in this world where your actions can bring joy instead of pain.*

It took him nearly two hours to type all of his thoughts and feelings, trying to choose the right words while endeavoring to be both thorough and concise.

Apparently, half of his posts performed better on Nextdoor than on any other platform, and for this post in particular, he received an outpouring of support with mostly positive comments, including a couple of encouraging direct messages. A few people thanked him, saying that they learned something or that they were encouraged.

Suddenly, the storm clouds of life were dissipating. Zachary was grateful he still got to help others, even when traversing low valleys.

A couple of days later, a user on Nextdoor sent him a direct message:

> *Hi, Zachary.*
>
> *I'm Megan, and I'm currently the president of Ironwood Peak High School's PTA.*
>
> *First, know that you are an incredible person, advocate, speaker, author, tutor, and substitute teacher. It's amazing how much you have accomplished. My son and daughter both had you as a sub, and they always came home saying wonderful things about you.*
>
> *Second, it deeply saddened me to hear what those young men did the other night and in July. I agree with you that your assemblies should be a universal priority, as they not only teach about autism and disabilities, but kindness and inclusion. I cannot fathom how a middle-school principal said no to you. Would you mind sending me an email? Please include the story of what happened the other night and everything you say and do during assemblies. I will send it to our superintendent for him to read.*

Without hesitation, Zachary spent the next hour typing and piecing together an emphatic email that would reach the eyes of the superintendent. *If this works, this will be an answer to prayer*, he thought as soon as he clicked Send.

67

Mixed Reception

"How were the past two weeks, Mr. Corwin?" an e-biker in ninth grade asked him on the last Friday of winter break.

"Hectically busy," he said with a sigh, but also with a smile. "How was yours?"

"It was good. Got this new Sur-Ron for Christmas," he announced, looking at it proudly.

"Nice … Please be safe riding those things."

"Sorry for interrupting your vlog," the other ninth-grader apologized, taking his AirPods out of his ears. Even from a distance, Zachary could hear "Where the Sky Hangs" by Passion Pit playing loudly through them.

"Oh, never worry about that. Always feel free to interrupt me, and that goes with *anyone.* I don't own the city or whatnot. The worst that could happen is I'd start all over, which wouldn't be a problem for me."

"All right."

"But that's what I've been doing the past couple of weeks: producing *dozens* of videos and reels for Autism Awareness. I never thought it'd take this long. I even worked from evening to dawn, no joke, within the past two weeks. I also started a 30-day challenge yesterday for the first time in over eight years of having a channel. We'll see how that goes. I was subbing Elementary Music at Cunningham the day before winter break, and one of the sixth-graders recommended it to me, adding, 'It might help get you to 100,000.'"

"That's sick. What's the challenge about?" one of them asked.

"Well, on a personal level, I decided to film and upload every day. I'm not going to produce and schedule them ahead of time, though I'm not going to stress myself with all the fancy editing I normally do. It's also going to be a challenge for the viewers because I intend to encourage and motivate them to live fulfilling lives. Some of the topics I'm going to talk about include these: the impact of saying hello, acts of kindness, having patience, humility, self-advocacy, overcoming stage fright, tips for success, tips for writing and book marketing, and stuff like that."

"That sounds exciting. I hope it goes well for you," the other one said.

"Thanks. Well, have a nice day."

"You too."

"Oh, by the way," Zachary called out, turning around a few seconds later, "happy belated birthday? It was, what? Four days ago, wasn't it?"

"Jeez! How do you remember that?!" the boy asked, marveling as he rode away and popped wheelies.

Forty-eight hours later, Pastor Nguyen delivered the benediction, and Zachary turned off the keyboard.

"*Ow!*" Zachary quietly gasped, standing up in pain.

"Are you all right, Zach?" one of his bandmates asked.

"Yeah, um … I'm fine," he replied, laughing it off to himself. He limped a few feet away, trying not to look conspicuous. He caught his breath before attempting to bend down to pick up the keyboard's black dust cover. After leaning over an inch, he froze in pain and immediately placed his right hand over his lower back.

"Can I help you, Zach?" The bandmate placed his guitar on the stand and rushed over to him.

"U-Uh, I got it," Zachary said after falling on his knees.

"C'mon. Let me help you with that." He picked up the dust cover.

"Do you need help getting back up?" the singer asked as she and the drummer came over.

"Uh … Ow! I guess I can't do this on my own," he admitted, panting and squeezing his eyes shut.

The drummer and singer helped him stand back up, but he declined to sit back down on the bench.

"What's going on, Zachary?" asked the drummer.

"Just my lower back. Standing up from a seated position is a pain … uh, *literally*. It comes and goes, and I have a good theory about why. I'm sure it's because I'm sitting for hours on end sometimes. I try to catch myself when I'm slouching, but I'm absentminded most of the time."

"What are you doing that takes hours?" asked the singer.

"Day and night, I've been putting videos together, namely my Autism Awareness videos and my substitute teaching series. I'm now at the start of my first 30-day challenge too. I've also been immersed in a new writing project, typing nearly nonstop for half a week now."

"And you're staring at that bright computer screen for hours?" The singer looked at him concerned.

Zachary shut his eyes as they involuntarily watered, too sensitive even to think about it.

"Don't you think you should get things checked out by a doctor?" the guitarist suggested.

Shaking his head, Zachary replied, "I just don't have time for that, especially since it's nothing, I'm sure. Just like the past few times, it'll go away within a few days. I always tolerate these sorts of things. I kept making videos during this two-week vacation since I had time and didn't want to burn myself out in a few months. I'm still praying they'll finally kick off, though I'm never going to stop anyway until my death. I need to pursue this writing project too. Ableists need to read it and become better human beings, disabled people need to read it and become motivated, and nondisabled people who accept us need to read it and become strengthened in their advocacy and inclusion."

"If you say so, but—" The bandmates tried reasoning with him for another minute, but it was no use, since Zachary Corwin, the tireless advocate, had already made up his mind, witnessing every day the need to continue his work at all costs.

Carefully stepping down from the stage, Zachary was greeted by one of his older friends with Spina Bifida. "Hey, Zachary," she said, wheeling herself over to him in her wheelchair. "I want to let you know, we gave your novel to our son, who is late-diagnosed autistic, and he told us, 'When I'm reading this, it's like I'm reading about myself. It makes so much sense; it's my entire life written out.' We ordered your second book for him. Thank you."

"Thank *you* for letting me know. It makes me feel great to hear that. That was one of my goals in writing the novel."

* * *

The next four weeks passed by rather quickly. At the end of the month, he picked up a five-day assignment, subbing for a co-teacher at the middle-school side of a combined campus, a confluence of middle and high school. For every period, he helped students with their math while the main teacher led, though he took over during SSR.

"*Look! It's Zachary Corwin! Oh, my God!*" one fourteen-year-old yelled at the top of his lungs on Monday morning, pointing at him and drawing the attention of a few passersby as they headed to their classes. It was an unnatural, cynical greeting as though the student believed Zachary was pretending to be some celebrity rather than the kind-hearted and helpful individual he truly was. Dumbfounded, he watched the student laugh his way into the classroom. He wondered what he had done to deserve such uncalled-for mockery after everything he had done for the school, the community, and the world.

"All right, your ticket to the magic show is to complete this small worksheet," said the main teacher toward the end of each period that day, amazed to find out that Zachary knew sleight-of-hand. Each day that week, he performed tricks as a brain break in the middle of every class.

On Friday morning, circumstances left him with no choice but to take an Uber. The driver, a gentleman with a long white beard wearing an old-fashioned walrus hat, was on speakerphone the entire time, which Zachary didn't mind. He was too preoccupied scheduling his daily uploads on his phone. (He'd post two or three Shorts, TikToks, and Facebook reels a day, and sometimes an Instagram reel.) He also enjoyed the old-time music the driver played lightly on the radio. During the long Uber ride, he listened to the classics, such as The Four Aces' "Harvest Moon," Guy Lombardo's "Boo Hoo," The Monotones "Book of Love," "Boogie Woogie Bugle Boy," "My Boyfriend's Back," "Has Anybody Seen My Gal?" and "Rock and Roll Is Here to Stay," all of which Zachary was able to recognize. It was as if he were transported back in time to the generation he once wished to live in.

"Oh, are you driving someone?" asked the friend right before they turned into the school's parking lot?

"Yeah, I've got a kid going to high school here on the east side."

Zachary widened his eyes in sheer wonderment, wondering if he was dreaming. "Perfect," he said sarcastically to himself under his breath.

"Not a big deal," the driver continued. "He's getting dropped off in like 30 seconds."

Zachary sat there, unknowing what to do or say as the driver hung up the phone.

"Well, I hope you have a great day at school," said the driver.

With his heart beating hard, Zachary replied, "Uh, thanks."

"School's great. You have something that keeps you busy and makes you smarter. Do you play any sports?"

"Um … No."

"Meh, get into something, even if it's pickleball. You guys got that at your school?"

"Hmm, not that I'm aware of," he said, glancing at the football field outside the window. "But we do have a lot of football."

A second later, the Uber driver stopped. "All right, Zachary. There you go, brother."

"Thanks so much. Have a good day," Zachary said and high-tailed it out of there. He honestly was not offended that his youthful appearance could mistake him for a high schooler, as long as he was not prevented from doing his job. However, he didn't know how to correct the Uber driver on the spot. *Would he even believe me?* he asked himself. *Or would I need to take a few minutes to gather the proof?*

The incident reminded him of the week before, when he spoke at a school eighty miles away via Google Meet. That evening, he told his story for twenty minutes to faculty and parents, followed by an additional twenty minutes for Q&A. The counselor asked what his age was. He surprised everyone when he said thirty, since most of them had guessed early twenties at first sight. Nevertheless, they appreciated his speech and applauded him afterward.

It also took him back to the days he used to gamble on the lottery, buying hundreds of scratch-offs and draw-game tickets. Many clerks at various convenience stores would question his age and require to see some form of identification. One took a look at him and yelled, "Wait! How old are you?!" only to be proven wrong a minute later upon examining Zachary's driver's license.

"Can Mr. Corwin be here every day?" one of the seventh-graders asked his main teacher later that day at the middle school side.

"Aw!" the teacher said. "Mr. Corwin, did you hear that?"

"Hear what?"

"Mitchell asked if you could sub in here every day," she repeated as Mitchell turned around, beaming from ear-to-ear.

"I feel honored that you appreciate me as a sub, Mitchell. Thank you." Zachary smiled.

After the bell rang, the main teacher left as the SSR students poured in. Zachary randomly chose "Never Alone," by Felix Jaehn and Mesto, to be the song.

Taking charge once SSR began, Zachary said, "Okay, as you all know, you can read or work on assignments. As always, if you have any math or science questions, please raise your hand. I'm happy to help."

As Zachary made the rounds ten minutes later, he heard a student say, "What time is it?"

"Ah, that's a quarter!" Zachary said, swinging around and pointing at him.

"What?"

"That's a quarter. Any time a student asks what the time is, they owe me a quarter."

Dead silence.

"I'm *kidding*, Dylan," he revealed with a grin.

As Dylan chuckled and got back to work, Zachary walked around a couple more table groups. All of a sudden, he saw something that made him freeze mid-step, his eyes lighting up in sheer surprise.

The student sensed him standing there, turned around, and held up the book he pulled out of his backpack. "I'm halfway through your second one, Mr. Corwin," he said with a big smile. "I'm enjoying it."

"Thanks. It makes me happy to hear that, and … *wait!* You're Fischer, right?"

"Yes, the one who was moved by your assembly last year, um, and my dad reached out to you. I'm so happy you're my sub today. I wished I had been here all week, but, um, I had the flu."

"I totally remember you. It's nice to see you again. Also, yes, something must be going around. I had the flu a couple of weeks ago."

"Sorry to hear that. Glad you're better, though. Um, anything new or exciting?"

"I'm completing a 30-day challenge on social media today. I managed to get through every day, even though I was so exhausted, suffering fatigue and headaches for four of them because of the flu, but viewers wouldn't have been able to tell unless I said something, which I probably will in tomorrow's reflection video."

After SSR, all the students left for lunch, except for one.

"Again, I've really been enjoying your second book," Fischer complimented. "You're a person whom a lot of autistic people look up to, including me. You overcame many challenges, and it's motivating. Continue to never give up."

"Thanks, Fischer. It's very humbling and reassuring to hear that, especially coming from a student. I try my best and hope to encourage everyone."

"You're welcome, Mr. Corwin. How'd, uh, that 30-day challenge go for you, out of curiosity?"

"Um, well, I'm happy that I was able to accomplish the goal and speak out what was in my mind and heart. However, I was disappointed by the lack of views. Only one surpassed a hundred views. However, I did get a ton of positive comments on YouTube and TikTok, and some on Facebook and LinkedIn, including new people. Nextdoor was the best, as usual these days, with dozens of likes and comments. I only got two negative comments; both came from Nextdoor. First, I got an email saying that I received a comment. I could only read the first part before it cut off. It started out as, 'It's funny how Nextdoor—' I clicked on it to continue reading, but for some strange reason; Nextdoor had deleted my post, even though it didn't say anything wrong. It was just to spread encouragement."

"Sorry that happened."

"A couple of days later, one of my neighbors commented, 'Get a real life,' and that was it. Short and direct. And the post was about intrinsic versus extrinsic motivation. In my reply to him, I pointed out everything that I had done with my life, such as my books, news interviews, social media, and volunteer assemblies, explaining how it made a difference in people's lives."

"Like *my* life."

"Yes. One person came to my defense, asking him if he got up on the wrong side of the bed that morning or if he was having a rough day. And do you think the man apologized? No. He simply deleted his comment. Oh well. It comes with the territory, but my hope is for all ableists to eventually understand. I don't hate the man."

"I feel that. I know your heart. Uh, by the way, um, I'm also curious, is there a third book coming in the future?"

Zachary stared at Fischer, trying to keep a straight face. "Well, it just so happens … Now, I haven't gone public about it yet, but I'm halfway done with my third one. It's my new writing project that has been keeping me up late at night."

"Incredible! I can't wait to read it when it comes out."

"I hope you enjoy it if you buy a copy. It's another fictional piece, based on my life as an autistic and getting into education, while fighting discrimination at the same time, exposing how real it still is. The idea came to me in December, and I tried dismissing it for days, to be honest, but I couldn't stop thinking about it—during my walks, while subbing, getting work done at home, or trying to get to sleep at night. It was like an uncontrollable urge.

"On New Year's Eve, I began typing the first sentence of chapter one, and I hardly took a break since. I type all day and half the night. Even when I'm subbing, as students work quietly or during breaks, I'm usually typing out more storylines and emailing them to myself. Then, I paste everything into the Word Doc once I get the time after coming home from tutoring and editing that day's video for the teaching update on YouTube. Now that the 30-day challenge is nearly complete, I'll have even more time. So far, I have over 80,000 words. I never thought this book would get that long, and I'm getting a bit nervous."

"Don't worry about the length, whether it's 150 pages or 500 pages."

"That's reassuring to hear that. My second book is huge, and I never want to intimidate readers, but everything I put is important, I believe. As an autistic, I also tend to put in a lot of details so that people wouldn't misinterpret me."

"I'm the same way. Well, um, it was nice talking with you. I have to get my lunch."

Ten minutes later, Zachary stepped out of the classroom and began walking around the campus. Upon taking a deep breath, he said to himself, "I surely love the aroma of waxleaf privets."

Coming from the bookshelf speaker in the quad, the song, "Stargazing" by Myles Smith, drifted through the air and into everyone's ears.

One of the middle schoolers approached him, remembering him from a month before. "Can you please sub for that English class again? The last sub was horrible!"

"Sure, Dominic. Sorry to hear that," he replied as a couple more students came up to him, asking to see a trick. "All right, you're going to stop at the ten of diamonds."

"He has aura!" one of them exclaimed after the trick, as she and her friend couldn't believe how Zachary knew the card.

"Bro is tuff!" commented Dominic with a grin.

"*Okay*, back to the benches, blacktop, or field," a campus safety officer told the middle schoolers.

"Are you serious right now?" one of them said in a high-pitched voice as she left, giggling.

Turning to Zachary, the officer said, "Sorry if they bothered you. I wasn't sure if you were heading to the office or back to the classroom."

"Oh, it was no bother," he explained. "You could ask nearly every school in this district, but I almost always volunteer during lunch, recess, nutrition, or whenever. I offer tricks, like card tricks and coin tricks, and I'm also an extra set of eyes to help supervise."

"Hey, I've heard of you!" the officer said, his eyes lighting up. "Several people at the local middle and high schools talk about you. The sub who does magic."

"Well, sleight-of-hand. I simply walk around the campus, helping to supervise, and wait for students to come up and ask me to show them a trick. I don't go to them first. It always brings me joy, though, when they come up asking to see one."

"And that's totally fine. Thank you for all that you do."

Crossing the quad, he vibed to "Someday We Will Dream About Today" by The Sways, coming from the speaker. He took out his phone and pretended to scroll on it. In reality, he filmed himself picking up a piece of litter and throwing it in the trash, ensuring no students were visible in the video. This was for his daily video, challenging viewers to pick up trash and keep the world clean, something he always did since high school if there was time.

Re-entering the classroom, he suddenly felt his phone vibrating in its case on his belt. It was Megan, the PTA president at the high school, inviting him to be a speaker for February's PTA meeting a week and a half later. After getting off the phone, agreeing to be the speaker, he prayed that it would work this time.

Returning his badge and key, he said to the office manager at the front desk, "I'm returning these. It was a great day. Thank you."

The office manager just sat there, a soft smile on her face, looking down at her fingernails.

"*Have* a nice *day*," he said, a bit more forcefully.

The manager continued to admire her fingernails, and Zachary stormed out of there.

It took him forty-five minutes to walk home from the middle school, being a distance away. Queasy, he mulled over how he had been treated. The manager's expression made it clear to him: "I'm ignoring you." It was the same look the bullies in elementary school had given him, some singing Britney Spears songs or other contemporary pop songs from back in the day, just to drown out Zachary's cries.

He felt dejected. This wasn't some childhood bully. This was a childish adult working in administration. He wished he would've said something to her, since there were no students around, though it wouldn't have been profane. It would have started with, "I *said*, 'Have a good day,'" which might have sparked a conversation about treating others like human beings with respect. Or, it might have escalated to a heated argument. He knew that she was competent at her job, undoubtedly, and didn't feel the need to report it; there was simply something between them. It was nothing to be fired over, and that was the last thing he'd want.

People may rightly wonder why he got perturbed with the office manager subtly ignoring him like that. It began earlier that morning. After signing in on the payroll sheet, he left the office and began walking down the indoor hallway toward the classroom. He was the only person in there. Instantly, he stopped to admire the artwork taped to the walls. Thinking it would make a good B-roll clip, he started filming for a few seconds. As he turned off the camera and slipped it back into his jacket pocket, he froze, barely catching a conversation from beyond the office door left slightly ajar.

The indoor hallway, like an echo chamber, carried the faint words to his ears: "The kids all love him. He does magic tricks—"

Zachary leaned closer, aware that one of the administrators was talking about him. He listened intently, hoping to get an extra boost of strength for the day.

"But, you know, he—" the administrator continued, her voice falling silent before it cut off completely.

And that was it.

Unable to know how the conversation began or ended, what its purpose was, and who had been involved, Zachary traipsed the rest of the way to the classroom, weighed down by the sense that administrators may have degraded him for some ableist reason.

(That day wasn't the first run-in with the aforementioned office manager. He was simply testing to see if he had jumped to the wrong conclusion the last time he subbed there. After getting things settled in the classroom, he returned to the office to request a laptop, but he had to wait for the manager's phone call to end first. Hanging up the phone, the office manager swung her head and raised her eyebrows, waiting without a smile. Upon hearing that he needed a laptop, she got up, exhaled loudly, pursed her lips, walked into the other room to get one, handed it to him, and slumped back into her chair, wearing a glum expression.)

After the long trudge home that day, his appetite returned for his favorite smoothie. However, he almost turned around and walked out. Seated sporadically throughout the juice bar were small groups of students, either studying together or scrolling on their phones. For the twentieth time in a few months, he walked into a crowd of students, most of whom he recognized, yet they didn't care to notice. They neither said hi nor asked him to see a trick. On the contrary, some outright looked as if they were frightened, either nudging or whispering to those next to them, prompting other students to glance over with bewildered expressions.

In all candor, he had the common sense to let the students initiate a conversation or request to see a trick. Nevertheless, being autistic, his curiosity constantly nagged at him. He questioned if he was misinterpreting things, yet some experiences were unreconcilable. If students didn't want to say hi or see a trick, that was fine. But when it seemed that they were genuinely scared of him, for who knows what, his stomach dropped. He felt invisible or like an outcast, forever shunned.

If he was going to be their substitute teacher, or possibly their math teacher in the future, he had to ensure that he was someone they could trust. However, he couldn't fathom why this was happening, especially in 2026, since he had spent years proving his care and competency.

Having had enough of this, Zachary stepped out of his comfort zone and began saying hi whenever eye contact was made.

The students usually reciprocated his kindness with merely a wave or a half-smile. Others expressed how truly thankful they were that Zachary would wish them a good day.

Whenever students said hi first, he began telling them, "Hey, thanks for saying hi," to get the subliminal message across not to ignore people they know, and that even if they don't know someone, it doesn't hurt to spread kindness once in a while.

One day, he smiled and gave five dollars to a homeless man. In return, the man thanked him, adding, "Not a lot of people say hi, though we must also remember the little blessings we get in life." That moment stuck out for Zachary, causing him to fight harder to spread kindness through waving, smiling, and saying hi, not just holding the door open for people or letting others go first as he walked around the city (a habit he had carried since he was a boy). It certainly goes a long way!

He had acknowledged that encountering some students who would never appreciate his heart was inevitable and just part of the territory. However, it troubled him beyond measure when, all of a sudden, several students seemed to adopt that unfriendly attitude, especially those who used to always enjoy running into him, saying hi, requesting to see a trick, talking about his social media or books, or asking about autism.

Sad that he had committed to buying the smoothie, he sat in the corner until the drink was made, feeling completely unknown in a juice bar with fifty people in it. As if on cue, their ceiling speakers began playing "Broken" by Lovelytheband. He scanned the juice bar, wondering if any of the adults there happened to have watched the news on the days he was interviewed. *Did any of them subscribe to* Newsweek*?* he questioned in his mind. *Had anyone read one of the local magazines I was featured in?*

With everything that was going on, plus all the things that had happened at the middle school earlier that day, he understandably questioned, "What on earth am I doing wrong here? It's all upside down. The more I had put myself out there—encouraging people through assemblies, social media, and news coverage—the more I seemed to be viewed as a creep, alien, or some invisible creature? What *am* I doing here? Had I gotten my entire calling wrong? Was I meant to be a teacher, author, influencer, and advocate? This just doesn't make *any* sense at all!"

After four minutes of isolation and sifting through depressing thoughts, he walked out without yet taking a sip of his smoothie. Not one person said hi to him. As Zachary walked out, a bearded man in his sixties kept his eye on him expressionlessly.

Ten seconds, man? Zachary complained in his thoughts. *You stared at me the entire ten seconds I spent walking through the juice bar and out the door? If you recognized me from somewhere or had a question about who I am or how I look, why don't you ask me a question like a normal person would?*

Even though he had been mulling over these frequent incidents, and his interpretations thereof, he was completely in his right mind and fully aware of his surroundings. He had not been hallucinating these occurrences, and he was able to maintain all his jobs and responsibilities with a coherent, rational mind.

Suddenly, a high school junior called out from the bench outside, "Hey, Corwin! Do you remember my birthday?"

Turning around, he instantly replied, "March 16."

Bouncing and almost falling out of his seat, he exclaimed, "*How* the f— I mean … the heck? That was like four years ago and you still remember?"

"Uh, yeah," he replied, nodding.

"That's *crazy*! Do you have a photographic memory or something?"

"No, but I've always been accused of having one. If I did, though, everything would be infinitely easier."

"No kidding."

"I'd probably have every birthday memorized within seconds, unless I'm misunderstanding how a photographic memory actually works."

"For sure. Well, to me, you're like a savant anyway. So, how've you been?"

"Well, probably not 'savant.' Anyway, I'm still subbing."

"That's dope. Are you trying to be an actual teacher someday?"

"Yeah, uh, eventually."

"Well, I hope that works out for you," he said with a reassuring smile. "Anyway, Corwin, I have to be somewhere in a couple minutes. Catch you later."

"Thank you, Robby. Have a great afternoon." As he took a sip of his smoothie, he was struck by the dramatic shift in Robby's disposition, for he was the same defiant, mouthy seventh-grader whom Zachary had to call for an escort back in 2022.

Walking further down the nearby plaza, he determined that nothing was going to stop him, and that he was going to continue the fight, come hell or high water, despite what people assumed at first sight. As P!nk's "Just Like Fire" was playing through the plaza's own sound system, two middle-school girls on their e-bikes stopped to have a conversation. "Hi, Mr. Corwin! When are you going to sub at Canyon Mountain again?"

"Well, first of all, thank you for saying hi."

In the middle of their conversation, which only lasted a minute, a Tesla Model 3 came to a sharp halt and sat there. Glancing through his sunglasses, Zachary saw the young man and woman inside the vehicle stare at them, mouths hanging open. They sat there until the conversation was over, thirty seconds later. The couple's look of concern was burned into Zachary's mind. *What was the problem?* Zachary asked justifiably, given the circumstances. *Did you seriously make the same assumption as that ableist security guard did at the park, just for me talking with students in a public setting? Wouldn't you have seen those girls running or heard them screaming if I was that type of evil person? What's the problem with me living on* your *planet? I don't hate you, and I pray for you like I do for everyone, but you seriously have got to be more trusting of disabled people at first sight!*

Trying hard to find some feasible reason to continue his calling in life, he ran into a high school teacher.

"Hey, you're the person who subbed for me in December," she said. "Chemistry."

"Oh yes. I remember."

"I want to let you know that all the students enjoyed having you. And one of those periods was usually my noisiest class. I always worry when they have a sub. I thought I'd let you know because that really speaks *volumes* on how you are as a sub, so thank you."

"It means *so much* to hear that … like, you wouldn't believe."

68

The Moment of Anticipation

The big morning arrived.

Zachary rehearsed his thirty-minute speech a few times. He was a natural by now, but he got extra nervous that morning. He received a text from Megan right after waking up. Heart pounding with gratitude, he read that the superintendent had a last-minute cancellation, freeing him to attend the PTA meeting at the high school. It was indeed an answer to prayer, but this meant he had to get every word correct and concise in order to make the best impression.

In other words, *he couldn't stutter*.

He planned to do everything he normally does while leading assemblies, adding an introduction beforehand and an emphatic call to action afterward. It would mean so much for him to win the superintendent's favor, especially if it meant the superintendent would require *all* schools to invite him to volunteer his assemblies.

Not only was he speaking before the PTA and superintendent, but the principal of the school, the one who had invited him to speak to the students in 2019, was also in attendance. Additionally, his former special education teacher was there, struggling to hold back tears as she listened to her former student. As he spoke, the room fell completely silent. The superintendent and principal had their eyes fixed on him, hanging on his every word.

At the end of his speech, he concluded, "Through kindness and self-acceptance, many students might acquire the motivation not only to be good citizens at home, school, and in their community, but also to choose life and pursue their aspirations. Their grades, academic learning, and social-and-emotional growth would also improve, which I know the principals and the school board care about. However, people can teach all they want; our words are dead unless they choose to act on them. If students aren't motivated in life, it's a waste of breath. I believe my assemblies *will* help put an end to bullying and promote inclusion in schools and in the rest of society."

After all the applause, Megan walked up and stood beside him. In tears and with a hint of struggle, standing before everyone, she expressed how eternally grateful she was for Zachary and pleaded with the principal and superintendent to take his mission seriously.

As soon as the PTA meeting adjourned, the superintendent walked up to Zachary, shook his hand, and reassured him that he would do something about it.

69

From Now Until Heaven

"Come on. You must be patient," Zachary told himself.

A couple of weeks had gone by. He remained hopeful that he would get in all the schools before June 2026, *including* Canyon Mountain. Nevertheless, *zero* of the many private schools in his city had ever contacted him. One Saturday, he painstakingly searched up every private school in his area and sent them each an email, attaching files of his many testimonials and notifying them that April—Autism Awareness and Acceptance Month—is coming up in a couple of months. After two hours of stressful work, one of the schools replied, "Thanks for reaching out, but we aren't interested."

What? Zachary questioned in his mind. *You're not interested in the importance of Disability Acceptance and Inclusion for your students?!*

For the millionth time in the past few years, he ran his hand through his hair in anguish and frustration, squeezing tightly and releasing it a few times over, watching several hairs flutter to his desk. It meant so much to him to change every human being in his city and county, even though he knew many schools had already adopted acceptance and kindness initiatives. He had spent well over a hundred thousand dollars trying to spread his message to eight billion people, yet he was still rejected in his own city, not out of being hated necessarily, but simply because he was not taken seriously.

Are they freaking blind to the fact that ableism and suicide is still rampant today? he questioned.

The following Sunday, he wasn't needed to play piano at Pastor Nguyen's church, so he decided to pay a visit to his former church where he had once served as an usher. During the walk there, he passed by many houses whose fences were ornamented with star jasmine. Approaching an alley, a white SUV quickly appeared, about to pull out of the alley. Seeing Zachary on the sidewalk, the driver slowed down, coasting.

Oh, great, Zachary lamented as he always did in these situations. It seemed that every time he approached an alley or intersection, the quiet streets suddenly filled with vehicles. Having the courtesy not to take up people's time, even for a few seconds, he would pretend to be preoccupied and walk away from the corner. Then, he would return and cross once the traffic died down slightly or completely. It was better if there were more pedestrians crossing at the same time, though. *You first*, he'd tell them in his mind.

Being in a hurry to church, he felt extra stressed but decided to slow down anyway so that the driver could pull out of the alley. However, the driver slowed down himself.

Zachary grunted and sped up, but as soon as he did so, the driver picked up speed.

Both came to a screeching halt.

Shaking his head, Zachary resorted to jogging past the car. After all, he did have the right of way as a pedestrian. A moment later, the SUV driver stormed out of the alley, then slowed down once he got alongside Zachary, matching his speed for five seconds. Intimidated, Zachary couldn't help but glance over, clutching his pepper spray in his pocket just in case. To his disgust, he saw the driver doing something awkward toward him. With an extended right arm, the driver slowly yet animatedly waved his hand as if saying goodbye. Zachary didn't know what to make of the creepy gesture, but he knew it was derisive.

What happened at the church nearly made it worse. Apparently, the church combined both services for a special Sunday, so Zachary arrived as everyone was leaving. Walking into the sanctuary, he scanned the room to see if anyone he knew was there, for it was always great to say hi to old friends. A couple of minutes later, he walked behind the back row of pews.

In a flash, the senior pastor and worship leader came into focus straight ahead, and he began heading in their direction. Standing in the middle was a man who was keeping his eye on him. Zachary didn't know what to make of it, but fortunately, that was the moment the pastor noticed him. With a loud friendly voice, the pastor said, "Zachary Corwin!"

"Hey!" he called back. As he walked past the man staring at him, he glanced at his jacket which said "Security" on it.

After a brief, cordial conversation with the pastor and worship leader, Zachary walked out of the sanctuary filled with trepidation, not just because of the driver, but also because of the security guard. He felt singled out as a potential threat by him, despite having a *long* history with the church and being one of fifteen hundred people there.

The church was hosting a family event in their courtyard that day, just outside the foyer. As Zachary stepped outside and began heading toward the street, Jelly Roll's "Run It" blasted out amid the sounds of children screaming and playing. Out of nowhere, a sixth-grade boy called out to him. "Hello, sir! … Hi!"

"Hi, uh, thanks for saying hi," Zachary stammered as he turned around, needing to take a second to process the spontaneous greeting.

"You had subbed for my music class at Cunningham Elementary a few times."

"Yes, I remember you. It's always a pleasure to sub, especially for Elementary Music."

"Well, can I tell you something?"

"Absolutely."

"I've seen you on YouTube. I watched that video of yours, the one where you said, 'It's not weird to be autistic or disabled. It doesn't mean you're a lost cause. Everyone is unique, and you still have purpose just the way you are.'"

"Oh yes. That was one of my recent ones."

"Well, I watched the entire video … and, uh, it actually made me tear up a bit."

Zachary stood there speechless, unsure of what to say. "I'm thankful that it spoke to you."

The boy continued, "I also saw you on the news many times. I'm so glad you never gave up on your dreams. Look at you now. You're a star!"

Grateful beyond words, Zachary knelt down to meet him at eye-level. "And that's what *anyone* could achieve if they don't give up on *their* dreams."

* * *

A week later, another private school informed him that they won't accept outside speakers.

Do they even understand? Zachary felt queasy before calming down and reasoning through it. *At least they thanked me for reaching out and were sort of kind about it.*

Determined, he posted on Nextdoor, exhorting neighbors with connections to other schools to help him by contacting them on his behalf. He once again resolved to be unstoppable and often listened to the song "Unstoppable" by The Score to give him a boost, among other motivating songs.

"I'll be honest. When I read that you wanted to lead assemblies voluntarily and at your expense, I got suspicious, but then I looked you up on Google and found out what you're all about," commented one neighbor on Nextdoor an hour later. "Thank you so much for what you're doing for our children and teenagers. Keep up this noble mission!"

Dozens of other neighbors thanked him, saying they were impressed by what he had done so far in the county, reassuring him that they would try to help.

Unfortunately, a few people still trolled him on social media, including one librarian on X named Tracy. She commented on a few of Zachary's posts, asking him questions about living as an autistic person and a content creator. A couple of nights later, he opened up X and read a reply from Tracy: "Sigh. Still didn't answer my questions. Also, one of your words in your response to me was ungrammatical in that context. Blocked! Good riddance!"

All that, just for answering exactly how he should have, based on every word Tracy used in each of her slightly ambiguous questions.

* * *

Zachary woke up nearly gasping for air as though he had stopped breathing in the middle of the night. He started out with several shallow breaths before graduating to relatively deeper breaths just to procure enough oxygen. His head felt dizzy and his chest sore the entire time, as if he ran ten miles nonstop. He was unsure if the pain was his heart or all the muscles surrounding it. He rolled over and went back to sleep, and the cycle repeated a few times until daybreak. After waking up for the day, it took him fifteen or twenty exhausting minutes before he could force himself out of bed.

This was daily life for him, and it got increasingly worse over the years. It was especially tense on days when he didn't have a place to work or volunteer, such as most Saturdays or during vacations. This was in spite of always having things to get done at home, like putting videos together or writing his book, but on these days, he was extra lethargic, despite sleeping off and on for ten hours or more.

He wrote it off as stress, heartache, feeling underused, and loneliness, since he had been fighting to have a voice in society. Moreover, the number of inappetent days was also increasing; he tried eating, but nearly lost it after a few bites. The closer and closer he got without success and complete acceptance, the worse his body reacted.

What have I ever done? he often wondered, sometimes at one or two in the morning. *How is it that I have fought a hundred thousand times more than most people and* still *haven't gotten to where I'm supposed to be, while those who fought a hundred thousand times less became successful? I'm* not *competing against them unless they promote evil things, but why am* I *like this? Why is* everything *going wrong with me?*

He told himself he didn't have time to go to a physician, knowing they'd probably tell him it's stress, urging him to slow down, but he *couldn't* slow down with all the unacceptance, ableism, brokenness, crimes, and suicides in the world. After all, he had heard that bullying was still going on, even in his own school district. A PTA member from an elementary school messaged him on Instagram about it, asking if he'd be willing to talk one-on-one with an autistic seventh-grader who was being pushed around … at *Canyon Mountain Middle School* of all places, despite having asked for years to lead assemblies there to prevent this from even happening.

He continued to fight, pushing himself to work all day long as a substitute teacher five days a week, then spending two or four hours tutoring almost every day, including weekends. At least he loved education and mathematics, but the lack of sufficient funds was killing him, especially after wasting tens of thousands on worthless fluff and scams. He found himself spending nearly his entire monthly income just trying to make a difference with his voice, yet it seemed most people weren't listening for an assortment of reasons. He once again considered applying for a full-time teaching position, since financially, he couldn't survive like this.

He still persevered, refusing to take no for an answer.

However, he was crushed.

If I become a full-fledged math teacher, he thought, *I cannot do my assemblies since I'd be working during school hours. Still, I can't keep going like this anymore without greater* PR and *a much higher investment in advertising. And if there's* one thing *I have categorically refused to do, it's charging even one cent for my assemblies, and I'm going to* keep *it that way, even at the expense of my livelihood!*

From here, until the day I get to Heaven—whether that day is soon or a hundred years from now—I will *not stop* fighting *until everyone in this entire world respects one another … or close to it. I will* not *stop fighting for equity and universal acceptance among us disabled people. And if it also means one more year of financial hell just to lead assemblies in* every *school, so be it! As I've already gone on the record saying, without apology: God first, eight billion people second, me last!*

70

The Glorious Assembly

"Are you nervous?"

"Oh, no. Definitely not," Zachary said with a chuckle as he watched many students pour inside the room. "My record is between five or six hundred students at one time. Plus, I've given this presentation a hundred times."

"You're a natural at this," replied the school counselor. "You got this!"

After quieting all the students down, the counselor introduced Zachary. "Today, I have an incredibly special guest who will amaze you and is sure to inspire you," she started. Putting on her reading glasses, she read from his common bio, "Zachary Corwin had been diagnosed with Autism Spectrum Disorder. Because of that, life had been filled with adventure and struggle. Not allowing Autism to stop him, he became an author of three books and is telling the world what it is like being disabled, how people could be friends with them, and how everyone has a purpose despite a disability. Zachary had appeared on television news, radio, podcasts, and magazines around the world. Today, over a million people follow his story on social media, encouraging others to embrace the gifts they have to share with the world, and that anybody can do whatever they set their heart and mind to do, disability or not. Please welcome Zachary Corwin."

"Thank you very much," Zachary said with a wide smile as all the students cheered and applauded. The school principal and some of the teachers sat in the back. "Good morning, everyone. It's a pleasure to be here. First, I want to thank the PTA for inviting me here today.

"For the next twenty or so minutes, I will hopefully be an encouragement to you guys, as well as an entertainer with the things I brought today," he said, gesturing toward the table where he placed his bag, a water bottle, decks of cards, and papers. "And if I get to say everything in a timely manner, I can open this secret envelope, on which says, 'DO NOT OPEN UNTIL APRIL 2, 2026.' Below says, 'Sealed since March 19, 2026,' so for two weeks, I had this sealed with something special inside, so if you want me to open it at the end, I expect you guys to be good listeners.'"

Students nodded as the entire room was quiet enough to hear a pin drop.

"Real quick, any 'magic' that you might see won't be real magic. They're just sleight-of-hand—*illusions*—but I use them to illustrate my points.

"So my story begins over twenty years ago, when I received a diagnosis of autism. Autism Spectrum Disorder is a neurodevelopmental disability. It's a neurotype, so it's all about how our minds work. It affects our social interactions, how we communicate with one another, how we learn, and how we behave.

"Within the past twenty years, I have observed and come to terms with both the pros on one hand," he said, holding up his left hand, palm open, "and the cons on the other," he added, raising his right. Shifting from open palms to a thumbs-down on one hand and a thumbs-up on the other, he explained, "So the ups and the downs. The good and the bad. The positives and the negatives.

"Some of the negatives include these: one, it's hard to concentrate, so reading, doing homework, studying, test taking, and trying to go to sleep at night have all been a struggle. Therefore, it usually took me longer to get work done than most of my peers in school. I was almost always the last person to finish an exam. It usually takes me one or two hours just to fall asleep after going to bed for the night … like *every single* night. And that's because it's hard to shut my mind off when it's supposed to. Music, television or radio shows, or movies I've watched keep blasting in my head. Oftentimes, I think about or dwell on things that happened ten, fifteen, or twenty years ago. Other times, I wonder what's going to happen next week.

"You also might be noticing, I'm trying my best to enunciate every syllable that I'm speaking. That's because when I was three years old, I was diagnosed with a speech delay, so I had to attend speech therapy from elementary school through high school, which helped out a lot.

"Then there's the social factor, which is a big one for many of us. I have many videos on YouTube that just focus on social challenges alone. Whenever I'm interviewed for news, radio, podcasts, or magazines, that's usually what the host and I discuss, at least in part." Holding up his novel, he continued, "And I don't think it's a coincidence that the longest chapter in my novel deals with social interactions.

"This one is bifurcated. On one hand," he explained, holding up his left hand for a few brief seconds, "we are typically very shy. I had made hundreds of friends by the time I graduated high school, but it was always hard for me to put my foot forward and ask any of them if I could spend time with them. I usually waited for them to come to me. I can't speak for all of us, but I, for one, am not antisocial. I always desired to socialize. In social situations, I'd find myself pressed against the wall, my eyes spinning one way and my head spinning the other. I saw all my peers inviting themselves into conversations without any problem, but I thought if I did the same, they'd yell at me for intruding.

"I came up with a card-trick analogy that I'll start now and conclude later." He grabbed one of his decks of cards with his left hand. "As we grow up in school, we all begin to make friends," he elaborated, beginning to pile a few playing cards in his right hand. "And then we make more friends. In middle school, we make a lot of friends, and by high school, we have a ton of friends." He held up the deck in his right hand to represent the many friends. "And friends are good—especially strong, supportive friendships—but what might it look like for those of us who are autistic? Stay tuned for that," he said, placing the deck back onto the table.

"Then I had my share of being teased for being autistic, and that started in kindergarten. When I was in kindergarten, a couple of my classmates began to yell at me one day, and they said, 'Go away, Zachary! You're *not* our friend! You're *not* playing with us!' I had neighbors, who were my age, who would literally vote me out of their presence a couple of times. In the latter half of elementary school, I continued to make more friends, but there were still some students who poked fun at me. I was name-called a lot, and at one point, a student chucked a handball at my face just to get me to go away."

Upon revealing the last detail, Zachary saw the jaws of several students across the room drop in shock, disgusted that someone would do that to him.

"By the time I reached middle school, the prevalence of bullying dropped, and friendships continued to increase. And that lasted the next six years until high school graduation. Still, it was hard for me to socialize. I will say, however, that by eleventh grade, I started talking to my friends more, and you know what? They wouldn't have known unless I went up to them and told them.

"I will say, within the past decade since graduating high school, I still faced bullying. I've been stared at, cussed at, gone near ran for my life, followed by a vehicle, almost beaten with a skateboard, begged to not have children, and even begged to take my life.

"So, you could imagine that the level of shyness brings loneliness, and the prevalence of bullying for something I never asked for brings hurt, but nevertheless, I continued to develop the skills with which to entertain people and ultimately make a difference in people's lives." Walking toward the table, he continued, "In third grade, I picked up piano playing, and in fifth grade, I picked up juggling." Pulling out three of his jugglebugs, he began to perform. "So I became a juggler."

"*Wow!*" all the students exclaimed in awe, marveling.

"Again, within the past twenty years, I have observed the pros on one hand." He juggled two in his left hand. Tossing both of them to his right, he continued, "And the cons on the other hand." Performing a slightly advanced trick with three, he revealed, "But I view autism as a different lens through which to view the world.

"So here is my juggling analogy," he introduced, juggling the cascade. "Juggling represents passion. Passion is what you want to do in life. It's what's going to bring you joy. And whatever your passions are, never give up on them. Or at least, don't knock it until you've tried it. And if a mistake happens along the way, big or small, which happens to *all* of us, and something drops—" He dropped a jugglebug on purpose. "Then what do you do? Should you run and hide under the covers? Should you give up?"

"No," some students whispered, while others shook their heads.

"Right. You bend down, pick it back up, and keep going," he said, literally picking up the jugglebug and beginning to perform advanced tricks with three. "And from there, you can do more and more amazing things … And that's my juggling analogy for you."

Zachary took a little bow while the students began applauding.

"Now, you just saw three. Do you want to see four?"

"Yes!" the students shouted excitedly.

Picking up a fourth jugglebug, Zachary held them all out in front of them. "All right, you saw four. Back to three." He threw the fourth one back on the table and started walking away. "*Kidding!*" he said, swinging around and picking the fourth one back up.

After laughing at his joke, the students began cheering as Zachary juggled four. "Okay, so before I pull out the bigger things to juggle, I ask for a couple more minutes of your time.

"Here is my Be-Number-One Encouragement that I came up with in late 2021. I encourage everyone here to be number one. Now, being number one shouldn't be viewed as a competition (where everyone's competing for first place and there's only one winner). No, being number one should be viewed as a *rank*, which anyone can build up to and achieve, and here's how you could achieve it, under my definition.

"Being number one means that you know what you want to do in life; you know what's going to bring you joy. Yet even in the face of adversity—such as a disability, illness, bullying, or what have you—you choose to never give up on what you want to do and who you want to be in life. But we also must adopt patience and learn to go *through* things rather than around them. I found that the outcome is much greater when you take your time than when you rush through it.

"At the same time, you set standards *not* based on other people, but rather based on yourself and what you could handle. What I mean by that is this: it's okay to look at other people and be influenced by them, but don't try to be them. Be yourself. Don't try to be someone you're not. If I was driven by jealousy, I would not be standing here today; that's for sure. Just be yourself, because the truth is, we're all unique just the way we are, and we all have unique skill sets and different levels of mastery per skill.

"What's a skill set? A skill set is the collection of all skills a person could learn and develop over the course of a lifetime. Some of us may be good at math, cooking, and singing, but not yet at science, reading, or skateboarding, whereas others may be good at science, reading, and skateboarding, but not yet at history, baseball, or camping. And again, that's what makes each of us unique.

"I believe that, disability or not, anybody can do whatever they set their heart and mind to do—*as long as* it's practical. And behind the disability, we have a heart and a mind.

"I never allowed autism to cause me to give up in life. By the time I graduated high school, I had earned a medal that is equivalent in rank to Eagle Scout. I later earned a couple of math degrees, a teaching certificate in mathematics, and a Master's in Education. Therefore, I more or less told myself that I'm unstoppable when it comes to pursuing my passions and aspirations. In fact, that's the theme of my second book." He held it up for everyone to see. "This book chronicles my journey through student teaching and my adventures as a substitute teacher, all while navigating the challenges and embracing the strengths of being autistic."

"Now, I understand that some people can see the things I've done, or the achievements of others, and say something that I contend is a negative mindset to have." He picked up one of the playing cards from the table, and continued, "On this card, in big red letters on the Post-it note, I wrote the words, 'I CAN'T,' but this is how quickly it is to choose to go from a negative mindset to a positive mindset. You can go from saying 'I can't' to—" He shook the card. "'I *can*.' And now, in big green letters, the Post-it note says, 'I CAN.'"

While all the students gasped at the trick, he expounded, "Now, I admit that results may not happen overnight, but what *is* as quick as lightning is your choice to persevere, be kind to yourself and other people, and to say, 'I can!'"

Pulling out his three juggling clubs from the bag, he told them, "Now, I've talked a lot about the hardships of being autistic. Here are some of the positives. Can someone pick a number between one and nine?"

"Three!" one boy in the back called out.

"Great. And another?"

"Nine," a girl in the front row said.

"Okay." He began to juggle the clubs while saying, "103 times 109 is 11,227. Can someone call out a number between forty and sixty?"

"Fifty-seven!"

"All right. 5,057 squared is 25,573,249."

Students gasped in wonderment.

"Okay, let's segue from mathematics to United States history," Zachary said, continuing to juggle the clubs. "Can someone pick a number between one and forty-seven?"

"Fourteen."

"All right, our fourteenth president was Franklin Pierce. He was born on November 23, 1804. He died on October 8, 1869. And he served from March 4, 1853, to March 4, 1857." Catching the final club, he let out a big sigh of relief as the students burst into applause.

"Now, before the juggling finale—"

"There's still a finale after that?" some students murmured among themselves, already impressed by what he had done.

"I ask, yet again, for a few more minutes of your time." Picking up the water bottle from the table, he explained, "This is an empty plastic water bottle. It's transparent. You can see through it. Now let's say this water bottle represents a person who is disabled, impairing him or her from being able to talk like everyone else, or walk like everyone else, or act like everyone else. And what I want people to understand is that nobody asks for that.

"Nobody asks to be autistic. Nobody asks to have Tourette's Syndrome. Nobody asks to have Down Syndrome, or Cerebral Palsy, or Muscular Dystrophy, or Spina Bifida, or be confined to a wheelchair. *Nobody asks for a disability*—whether physical or developmental, whether they were born with it or it was acquired sometime in their life. *Nobody* asks to be disabled. Therefore, I contend it's unfair when other people take this one attribute of a person and poke fun at them as a result.

"And when people are made fun of, especially for something they never asked for, they have a choice. Unfortunately, many may choose to hold it in, and I was a master at that growing up. Once that happens, they might start to feel twisted and tied up in knots." Zachary twisted the water bottle down the middle, making an obnoxious crumpling noise. Some of the students perked up where they were sitting.

Holding up the bottle while covering the middle with his hand, he continued his science-demo analogy. "On the outside, it looks like a normal transparent water bottle, but if only you could see them on the inside," he said, rotating his wrist to reveal the twisted portion of the bottle, "you would see the hurt, pain, and loneliness. And if they don't do anything about it, but keep bottling everything up inside, then *this* is what might happen."

Zachary released the pressure, thereby making a cloud in the bottle.

"And now, all of a sudden, you have either a translucent or opaque cloud. You can no longer see through it clearly or at all. What people might do is twist themselves once again," he said, twisting the bottle again and holding it up. "As you can see, it goes away for a while, but do you know what?" He released the pressure again, forming another cloud. "It's just going to come back. And what I encourage people to do is to release the cloud in the bottle. Here's how it looks like in real life: you find someone whom you could trust. This could be a parent or another family member, teacher, counselor, principal, or another administrator. *Anyone* whom you trust. And *talk* it out. Don't bottle things up inside, thereby releasing the cloud in the bottle." Zachary unscrewed the water bottle cap, releasing the cloud visibly into the room for a brief few seconds before disappearing.

"Whoa!" the students exclaimed.

"Remember the stack of cards that represented all the friends you have?" Zachary asked, holding part of a deck in his right hand.

"*Yeah*," said the students in unison.

"So, on the outside, it looked like I had a lot of friends," he said, pointing out the apparent thickness of the stack. "And I did … but their friendships were rather superficial. Many of them were like, 'Hi, Zachary. How is your day going? How was the weekend? How was the test? Okay, see you later.' And that was it for the most part. I rarely hung out with any of my friends outside of school—after school, during weekends, during the breaks, *during summer vacation*—but there came moments in my life, especially in high school, when I desired to spend time with friends, wondering, 'Who could I call? Who could I reach out to on Facebook? Who would *actually* be my friend outside of school?'"

Shaking his right hand back and forth, the deck still in it, he went on, "I just got so frustrated, desiring to spend time with friends but battling shyness and nervousness, that suddenly—" he said as he tossed everything over to his left hand, "it felt like they all vanished, and the only person there with me was the joker, trying to bring me down.

"Where did all my friends go?" he asked as the students' jaws dropped in awe, having watched Zachary apparently vanish the deck into thin air, leaving only the joker.

"The point of this illusion is to show what loneliness is like, and when you feel like you're all alone. Again, in eleventh grade, I began to talk things out and to communicate with my friends, which helped a bit, but like I said before, they wouldn't have known unless I told them. Once you do that, you'd realize that your friends were there the entire time."

Students voiced their amazement as they witnessed Zachary return to the table, grab the deck of cards, and place it atop the joker card.

"In conclusion, here is something you all could do. I want you to imagine yourselves as one big team—your class, your grade-level, the entire school. Team is spelled T-E-A-M. I understand that this may sound cliché, but it's true. *Together* Everyone Achieves More is what TEAM stands for. Team members look out for each other and reflect a diversity of backgrounds.

"So if you see someone sitting alone or someone being teased, or if you discern in your heart that they are shy, then I invite you to go up to them and be a friend to them. Find out what they like, and find out what they don't like. That comes by *talking* with them; have *conversation* with them. Introduce them to your friends, invite them to spend time with you guys, and help them feel included in life.

"At the same time, you don't have to overdo it. For instance, some of us wouldn't like going to the movies or listening to a concert, but we'd be perfectly content playing a board game or a video game at home, or going out for a bike ride, but you wouldn't know unless you *talk* with them first.

"I'm a proponent of Disability Inclusion, which goes a *long* way for us all. I could testify to that.

"Well, thank you so much for being a wonderful audience. As promised, I have a couple of juggling finales." He proceeded to juggle a basketball, a club, and a jugglebug simultaneously. After, he juggled three basketballs. "Hmm. Am I forgetting something?"

"Uhhh—" students said, pointing at the envelope.

"Oh yes," he said with a smirk. "So, I need three volunteers … Oh, gosh! It's always hard to choose when there are so many hands raised."

Zachary chose three students to come up and write a random three-digit number into a notepad. Afterward, a fourth student came up and multiplied the three numbers that were in the notepad.

"And so the product is 148,562,592." He wrote it on the whiteboard. "And you can verify that, right?"

"Mm-hmm." The student with the calculator nodded.

"All right, thank you very much! Okay, see you all later."

Silence with a few awkward chuckles pervaded the room.

"Kidding! Now, I had this envelope sealed for two weeks now," he said, walking over to retrieve it.

"No way!" dozens of students began to say.

"So, let's open it."

"*Noooo.*" More students began to join in as he opened the letter and pulled out the folded piece of paper.

"It reads, 'On April 2, 2026, three students will each choose a 3-digit number whose product is—'" He slowly opened the paper further, building the suspense. Everyone, including the faculty in the room, held their breath.

"148,562,592!"

All the students roared with applause, some leaping to their feet, jaws dropping and hands resting upon their heads.

Once the students quieted down fifteen seconds later, Zachary told them, "Okay, so they allotted five minutes for Q&A. You can ask me anything, *except* 'How did I do those tricks?'"

After Zachary answered over a dozen questions, the principal came up and said, "Now wasn't that just an incredible assembly?"

Students applauded one final time, but after they quieted down, everyone noticed the principal standing frozen like a statue, staring into the crowd. Five seconds dragged on before a few students sympathetically said, "Awww! It's okay."

The principal sniffled, pulled out a handkerchief, and blew her nose. Regaining her composure, she instructed, "The next time you're in English class, you're going to discuss what you've learned from Mr. Corwin. Then, you're going to write a half-page reflection paper about it and how you could help others feel included. You may now look to your teacher for dismissal. Thank you."

As some students poured out of the room, others went up to thank Zachary and compliment him. Some introduced themselves as being disabled, or having a sibling who is disabled. Others complimented him for his tricks, hoping to get a clue about how he did some of them. A couple of the teachers thanked him as well, one of whom almost got emotional.

A few minutes later, it was just Zachary, the counselor, and the principal. "The students really enjoyed it, especially the juggling," said the counselor, turning down the Bluetooth speaker, which had been playing "Days I Will Remember" by Tyrone Wells as students exited. "Did you hear that applause?"

"Ha-ha, yes," Zachary replied. "But I've led some assemblies at elementary schools where they were literally screaming."

"Aw, how cute."

"Zachary!" the principal called out, coming up to him in tears.

He turned toward her and solemnly stared at her in the eyes.

"I am so truly sorry … I just … apologize. I don't know what to say."

"It's okay, Dr. Peterson. I forgive you," Zachary said, fighting tears himself.

"I realized how wrong I was in my judgment. I should've let you do these assemblies a few years ago when you first asked me. I can see that your presentation had left an impact on all students … including me. I've overheard them reflecting on the things you've said as they were leaving. As God is my witness, I will definitely spread the word to every school I know."

"I really, really appreciate that, Dr. Peterson. If you also have connections to schools in other districts and private schools, please let them know I'm willing to leave an everlasting impact there too. And at *no* charge."

"Absolutely. Do you have other assemblies lined up soon?"

"I do, in fact. On Thursday, I'm *finally* doing them at Washington Elementary, and in a couple of weeks, I'll spend four days leading several mini-assemblies at Ironwood Peak High School. Throughout May and early June, I'm scheduled to speak at all the other elementary, middle, and high schools in this district that I haven't already been to.

"For the private schools, I have been emailing them once a month, and most hadn't yet replied, but I refuse to assume that they're ignoring me. However, I had received replies from a couple of them recently, saying they were all booked for the year but were highly interested in reaching out next year, so I'm remaining hopeful."

In tears, Dr. Peterson said, "I'm so happy for you. I'm sorry again. Your message could've helped many people, including us adults, years ago, yet I deliberately chose not to make time for you. I'll forever regret it."

"Well, please don't worry about it. At least I have the opportunity now to do these assemblies, and those past students from years ago will receive the message at the high school in a couple of weeks."

"Oh," the counselor interrupted, "your next group is coming in two minutes."

"*Right*," Zachary quickly said, eager and ready to do the next assembly. "One down. Eleven more to go. I'm very thankful for this room; it's just spacious enough to hold a few classes at a time."

"And much better than the gymnasium," added the counselor. "I'm grateful that we could make it work for you, Zachary."

"It works perfectly, since each period is sixty minutes, and I could do two assemblies per period, being able to reach all 1,100 students in one day."

* * *

Zachary Corwin continued to be a well-respected substitute teacher and math tutor throughout the 2026-2027 academic year. On days he wasn't subbing, he led his volunteer assemblies across the county at schools—public and private—that finally accepted his free offer, changing over a hundred thousand lives.

By spring 2027, it was time to apply for a teaching position, satisfied with the number of schools he had visited across the county by then, though he was far from meeting his ultimate goal, which was to appear in every single school.

He knew he could still reach everyone in his county and beyond, now since TED Talks reached out to him at last. His talk on the red circle went viral across social media, encouraging and motivating millions of people and increasing his online visibility. Consequently, he never had to pay for social media advertising again, since he began receiving the views he felt he should've received years earlier, had he not disrupted the algorithms.

Furthermore, all three of his books were selling by the millions instead of by the dozens. He could now allocate his wealth to PR until he no longer had to pay for PR again.

In August 2027, he began his career as a math teacher, finally fulfilling a dream he had cherished since childhood. It was at a school in his district that served both middle and high school students, allowing him to teach everything from seventh-grade math through Calculus.

Though few and far between, he still faced discrimination from people who hadn't yet understood that autistic people are still human beings, but he personally handled it much better than before, knowing that he had more support, acceptance, and inclusion. He said a prayer for them and calmly continued raising awareness about autism and other disabilities, despite what a small minority thought.

As a math teacher, tutor, author, social media influencer, and tireless advocate on news and radio, he made the impact he had always hoped to make—teaching, encouraging, and motivating hundreds of millions of people for generations to come.

Stepping once more into his classroom before school one morning, years down the line, Zachary stood in gratitude, fully aware of the many odds he had overcome to get to where he was, never caving into the pressures of society and crushing the false stereotypes of autism to smithereens. He got "Thunder" by Imagine Dragons queued up for when students arrive.

With a ring on his finger, he straightened the picture frame on the wall, which displayed a photo of his new family, happily married with two children.

He never departed from his axiom: It was never about the accolades, but about the lives he changed.

About the Author

Matthew Kenslow was diagnosed with Autism Spectrum Disorder at around six years old. As a result, his journey in life has been marked by challenges, adventure, and growth. Not allowing autism to stop him, he became an author and a social media influencer, and he's now telling the world what it is truly like to be autistic.

Matthew has appeared on television, radio, magazines, and podcasts worldwide, including features in *Newsweek*, Spectrum News, ABC7 Los Angeles, WGN, NTD, and many more. Through his assemblies, he teaches children and teenagers how they can be friends to those who are disabled, and how everyone has a purpose in life.

Today, over a million people follow his story on social media, where he explains what life is like as an autistic person, encourages everyone to embrace their strengths, and shares his belief that anyone can do whatever they set their heart and mind to do, disability or not.

If you enjoyed this book, *The Tireless Advocate*, it would be really appreciated if you would leave a review and share it with others.

Follow Matthew Kenslow on social media, where he frequently posts on platforms including Instagram, YouTube, TikTok, Facebook, X, and LinkedIn, under his name.

To support his mission, check out his website, matthewkenslow.com, where he sells products featuring his quotes on apparel, tumblers, mugs, and more.

www.ingramcontent.com/pod-product-compliance
Lightning Source LLC
LaVergne TN
LVHW090258210926
848480LV00001B/63